**DO NOT REMOVE
CARDS FROM POCKET**

MAGAZINES FOR YOUNG PEOPLE

SECOND EDITION

Magazines for Young People

Formerly Magazines for School Libraries

BILL KATZ LINDA STERNBERG KATZ

R. R. BOWKER
New Providence, New Jersey

Published by R. R. Bowker Company, a division of Reed Publishing (U.S.A.) Inc.
Copyright © 1991 by William A. Katz
All rights reserved
Printed and bound in the United States of America

International Standard Book Number 0-8352-3009-0
International Standard Serial Number 0000-1368

Computer composition by Vance Weaver Composition

Cover design by Judith Kazdym Leeds © 1991

ISBN 0 - 8352 - 3024 - 4

9 780835 230247

CONTENTS

Contents

■■■■■ PROFESSIONAL EDUCATION AND LIBRARY JOURNALS ■■■■■

The graphic appeal and shorter format of magazines make them one of the most attractive and least daunting materials to be found in a school media center, and a helpful tool in encouraging young and reluctant readers. While the attractions, for example, of a new biography on Thomas Jefferson will not be immediately apparent to most young-sters, the latest issue of a tennis or film or science journal is sure to inspire interest—and keep students coming back for more. A greater number of publishers are also catering to the school-age market and producing journals specifically geared toward children, even preschoolers. Statistics based upon *Ulrich's International Periodicals Directory* reveal that the number of periodicals for children has increased approximately 34 percent in the last decade and over ninefold since 1940.

Of course, many adult magazines are also appropriate for a younger audience. So how is one to select not only the best periodicals, but those most likely to appeal to and be read by children from the 70,000-or-so serials currently in circulation?

In *Magazines for Young People*, we hope to offer librarians, teachers, and layper-sons a reliable, critical reference for the selection and acquisition of periodicals for children and young adults. Another purpose of the book, of course, is to suggest to younger people the vast number of magazines available for their personal enjoyment.

In this second edition of the guide, we have carefully selected and evaluated approximately 1,000 titles, the majority of which are suitable for young adults. While it follows the pattern established in *Magazines for School Libraries*, and, to a lesser extent, the sixth edition of *Magazines for Libraries*, a few changes and enhancements have been instituted.

Titles are arranged alphabetically by subject within three newly created sections: (1) Children's Magazines, suitable for youngsters 4 to 14 years of age, or those in elementary and/or junior high or middle school; (2) Young Adult Magazines, suitable for those from 14 to 18 (and older) or those in high school or the latter years of junior high or middle school; (3) Professional Education and Library Journals, which are subdivided for teachers and administrators and other educators, and then for librarians (both public and school) serving a younger audience. Ranging from the fantasy land of *The Amazing Spider-Man* to the more esoteric sphere of applied linguistics, coverage is broad yet balanced.

Subject headings were selected to fit the needs of a young audience, although they generally conform to those used in the standard guides, indexes, and bibliographies. Whether the topic be Africa, Computers, or Craft and Recreational Projects, an estab-lished expert in the field reviews the content and purpose of each periodical and points out individual strengths and weaknesses. A special effort was made in this edition to carefully indicate precisely why a particular title is suitable, say, for a 14 year old or a younger child.

For each section and subject, consultants have also highlighted "First choices," or the major titles a library should consider for a particular age group and/or subject area. These are listed more or less in order of preference. The number is kept small in order to assist the library with a limited budget.

The selection of best and better is hardly fixed. Much depends upon the individual school or public library, as well as individual needs. So "First choices" is only a suggested guide that the user may employ or not, depending upon need.

Following "First choices" in the Young Adult section, there often appears another listing, "Suitable for children." This designates, by age, the titles in that particular young adult grouping that may be of use to some, although hardly all, younger people. Again, choices are made by editorial advisers and consultants. These "Suitable for children" titles may be listed in the Children's section under the relevant subject—usually with a cross-reference to the main annotation in the Young Adult section.

Consultants

The specialist responsible for the initial title selection and evaluative annotations for each subject is identified at the head of that section. Full title, affiliation, and address information for all the consultants follows this Preface. While the introductory material for each subject is written by the editor, the words of the consultant are often incorporated.

General Editorial Advisers

This edition of *Magazines for Young People* has also benefited from the advice of a board of experienced editorial advisers. These eight professionals represent a broad group of interested professionals who were instrumental in devising the final form of this new edition, including such basic changes and additions as the subdivision by age group and the expanded section on abstracting and indexing journals. They are also responsible for a number of the written annotations. The names, affiliations, and addresses of the eight advisers are listed on page ii.

Editorial Advisers/Professional Journals

While the general advisers were helpful in suggesting titles for the professional section, particular thanks goes to three people who not only made the major selections in this area, but wrote the majority of the annotations. They are:

Education: Sy Sargent, Associate Professor, College of Education and Human Services, University of Wisconsin-Oshkosh, Oshkosh, WI 54901.

Library: Barbara Via, Head of Reference Services, Thomas E. Dewey Graduate Library of Public Affairs and Policy, University Libraries, State University of New York at Albany, Albany, NY 12222.

Paula A. Baxter, Head, Art and Architecture Collection, The New York Public Library, New York, NY 10018.

Many people were involved in the preparation of this guide, especially the subject consultants, whose critical insights and hands-on experience represent the real strength and value of this book. I am most grateful also to our general editorial advisers for their vision, creative suggestions, and support throughout the revision process. This book would not have been possible without the dedication and assistance of Nancy Bucenec, Production Editor, and the thoughtful guidance of Marion Sader, Publisher. My warmest appreciation and thanks to one and all.

ADAMS, LIESE.
Head, Public Services, Porter Public Library, 27333 Center Ridge Rd., Westlake, OH 44145

BATT, FRED.
Associate University Librarian for Public Services, California State University, Sacramento, CA 95819

BAXTER, PAULA A.
Art and Architecture Collection, The New York Public Library, New York, NY 10018

BOWDOIN, SALLY.
The Harry D. Gidenose Library, Brooklyn College, CUNY, Brooklyn, NY 11210

BRAUCH, PATRICIA.
Head of Reference, Brooklyn College Library, CUNY, Brooklyn, NY 11210

BRAUN, ROBIN.
Director, Stohlman Library, St. Elizabeth's Hospital, 736 Cambridge St., Brighton, MA 02135

BURNS, GRANT.
Reference Librarian, University of Michigan-Flint Library, Flint, MI 48502

CHAPMAN, KAREN.
Assistant Commerce Librarian, Commerce Library, University of Illinois, 101 Library, 1408 W. Gregory Dr., Urbana, IL 61801

CROFT, VICKI F.
Veterinary Medical Pharmacy Library, 170 Wegner Hall, Washington State University, Pullman, WA 99164

DALE, DORIS CRUGER.
Professor, Department of Curriculum and Instruction, Southern Illinois University, Carbondale, IL 62901

DELONG, DOUGLAS A.
Acquisitions Librarian, Miller Library, Illinois State University, Normal, IL 61761

DOWELL, CONNIE V.
Head, Reference Department, Library, University of California, Santa Barbara, CA 93106

ELLIS, ALLEN.
Assistant Professor of Library Services, W. Frank Steely Library, Northern Kentucky University, Highland Heights, KY 41076

ENGLAND, CLAIRE.
Associate Professor, University of Toronto Faculty of Library and Information Science, 140 St. George St., Toronto, Ont. M5S 1A1, Canada

FULLER, DAVID R.
Consulting Geologist, 9813 Murden Cove Dr., Bainbridge Island, WA 98110

GAMBRELL, CAROL.
Reader Services Librarian, Suffolk Community College, Selden, NY 11784

GARGAN, WILLIAM M.
The Harry D. Gidenose Library, Brooklyn College, CUNY, Brooklyn, NY 11210

GOMEZ, JONI.
Sterling C. Evans Library, Texas A&M University, College Station, TX 77843

GUERENA, SALVADOR.
Head, Collection Tloque Nahauque, University of California Library, Santa Barbara, CA 93106

HARWOOD, JUDITH ANN.
Undergraduate Librarian, Morris Library, Southern Illinois University, Carbondale, IL 62901

HAUPTMAN, ROBERT
Assistant Professor, Learning Resources Services, St. Cloud State University, St. Cloud, MN 56301

HAVLIK, ROBERT J.
University Engineering Librarian, University of Notre Dame, Notre Dame, IN 46556

HEER, LYNN.
Stac Library Center, University of Florida, 307 West Hall, Gainesville, FL 32611

HOFFMAN, FRANK.
School of Library Science, Sam Houston State University, Huntsville, TX 77341

HOSTETLER, JERRY.
Assistant Director, Learning Resources Service, Southern Illinois University at Carbondale, Carbondale, IL 62901-6510

HUANG, SAMUEL T.
Reference Librarian, The University Libraries, Northern Illinois University, DeKalb, IL 60115

JACOBS, GLORIA.
Head of Technical Services, Chelmsford Public Library, Boston Rd., Chelmsford, MA 01824

JAUNZEMS, DAGMAR.
Production Manager, Clark Art Institute, Art and Architecture Thesaurus, Williamstown, MA 01267

JERKICH, LOUIS J.
Head Reference Librarian, County Library, 110 East Park St., Chardon, OH 44024

KAGAN, ALFRED.
Reference Bibliographer, Homer Babbidge Library, University of Connecticut, P.O. Box U-5GP, Storrs, CT 06268

KELLOUGH, JANE L.
Sterling C. Evans Library, Texas A&M University, College Station, TX 77843

KOPP, JAMES J.
Systems Librarian, Washington State University, Pullman, WA 99164

KOPP, SUE.
Reference Librarian, Education Library, Washington State University, Pullman, WA 99164

KUPFERBERG, NATALIE.
Science Reference Librarian, Brooklyn College Library, CUNY, Brooklyn, NY 11210

LACKS, BERNICE K.
California State University Library, Fresno, CA 93740

LAGANA, GRETCHEN.
Special Collections, The University of Illinois at Chicago, P.O. Box 8198, Chicago, IL 60680

LAGUARDIA, CHERYL M.
Assistant Head, Reference, for Data Services & Bibliographic Instruction, University of California, Santa Barbara, CA 93106

LEICH, HAROLD M.
Area Specialist (Russia/Soviet Union), European Division, Library of Congress, Washington, DC 20540

LENOX, GARY J.
Library Director, University of Wisconsin Center-Rock County, 2909 Kellogg Ave., Janesville, WI 53545

LIND, JUDITH Y.
Director, Roseland Free Public Library, 20 Roseland Ave., Roseland, NJ 07068

LUCHSINGER, ARLENE E.
Assistant Director for Branch Libraries, University of Georgia Libraries, Athens, GA 30602

MAROTTI, FRANK JR.
Bibliographic Instruction Coordinator, Newton Gresham Library, Sam Houston State University, Huntsville, TX 77340

MCKINLEY, MARGARET.
Head, Serials Dept., University Research Library, University of California, Los Angeles, CA 90024

MAXSON, WAYNE.
Reference Supervisor, Frostburg State University Library, Frostburg, MD 21532

MENDELSOHN, HENRY NEIL.
Bibliographer and Reference Librarian for Social Work and Criminal Justice, Graduate Library for Public Affairs and Policy, University at Albany, State University of New York, Albany, NY 12222

NASE, LOIS M.
Assistant Engineering Librarian, Engineering Library, Princeton University, Princeton, NJ 08544

NORDEN, MARGARET
806 N. Howard St., Unit 417, Alexandria, VA 22304

OHLES, JUDITH K.
Assistant Reference and Instruction Librarian, Purdue University Libraries, West Lafayette, IN 47907

PASTER, AMY L.
Assistant Librarian, Pennsylvania State University, E205 Pattee Library, University Park, PA 16802

PERSON, ROLAND C.
Assistant Undergraduate Librarian, Morris Library, Southern Illinois University, Carbondale, IL 62901

PHILLIPS, PHOEBE F.
Head, Monographic Cataloging, Robert Manning Strozier Library, Florida State University, Tallahassee, FL 32306

PROKOP, MARY K.
Public Relations/Reference Librarian, Chatham-Effingham-Liberty Regional Library, 2002 Bull St., Savannah, GA 31499

RAPHAEL, HONORA.
Music Librarian, Walter M. Geboth Music Library, Brooklyn College, CUNY, Brooklyn, NY 11210

RAYMOND, TERRI M.
Children's Services Coordinator, Norfolk Public Library, 301 E. City Hall Ave., Norfolk, VA 23510

REGAN, LEE.
10811 Cedar Ave., No. 6, Fairfax, VA 22030

ROEHLING, STEVE.
Assistant Head, Reference Dept., Charleston County Library, 404 King St., Charleston SC 29403

ROSENFELD, MARY AUGUSTA.
Administrative Librarian, Smithsonian Institution Libraries, Washington, DC 20560

SAPP, GREGG.
Head of Access Services, The Libraries, Montana State University, Boseman, MT 59717

SARGENT, SY.
Associate Professor, College of Education and Human Services, University of Wisconsin-Oshkosh, Oshkosh, WI 54901

SCHLIPF, FREDERICK A.
Executive Director, The Urban Free Library, 201 South Race St., Urbana, IL 61801

SECKELSON, LINDA.
Library Director, American Craft Council Library, 45 W. 45th St., New York, NY 10036

SIMMONS, LINDA L.
Assistant INFONET Coordinator, Oregon Health Sciences, University Library, P.O. Box 573, Portland, OR 97201

SWAIN, RICHARD H.
Cleveland State University Libraries, 1860 E. 22nd St., Cleveland, OH 44115

TAYLOR, DEONNA L.
Shearson Lehman Hutton, World Financial Center, 200 Vesey St., New York, NY 10285

TSANG, DANIEL C.
Social Sciences Librarian, Main Library, University of California, P.O. Box 19557, Irving, CA 92713

VAN DESTREEK, DAVID.
Library Director, Pennsylvania State University Library, York Campus, York, PA 17403

VIA, BARBARA.
Head of Reference Services, Thomas E. Dewey Graduate Library of Public Affairs and Policy, University Libraries, State University of New York at Albany, Albany, New York 12222

WELLE, JACOB.
Assistant Librarian, Allentown College of St. Francis de Sales, Center Valley, PA 18034

WELLS, ELLEN B.
Chief, Special Collections Branch, Smithsonian Institution Libraries, Washington, DC 20560

WHITE, LIBBY K.
Reference Librarian, Schenectady County Public Library, 99 Clinton St., Schenectady, NY 12305-2083

WHITEHEAD, OLIVE F.
Retired Librarian, 4615 Spruce St., Philadelphia, PA 19139

YORK, HENRY E.
Social Sciences and History Librarian, Cleveland State University, Cleveland, OH 44115

YOUNG, WILLIAM F.
Reference Department, University Library, University at Albany, State University of New York, 1400 Washington Ave., Albany, NY 12222

INTRODUCTION

Anyone working with young people realizes the importance of magazines. Not all young persons are avid book readers, but almost every student at least glances at a magazine. By now it is a truism that students' papers and talks are based, for the most part, on standard periodical articles. For entertainment, aesthetic delight, and information of both a general and an esoteric nature, there is nothing like magazines. No one realizes this more than the young person, either in or out of school.

The librarian, the teacher, and the parent must choose not only the best magazines but those that children and young adults *wish* to read. In the preparation of this work, particular stress has been placed on the latter consideration. At the same time, the proper weight has been given to traditional reasons for magazine selection.

Quality is a main criterion of any selection process. Nevertheless, one has to realize that quality is relative to the audience and subject matter. One may, for example, dismiss a magazine about rock music as being of poor quality when compared to one about opera, but this is to confuse content with questions of excellence. One must compare quality honestly within the context of the intended audience and the subject matter. That has been done here, from magazines about agriculture and automobiles to those concerned with television and travel.

Audience

Age levels and grade levels are at best only approximations. Certain magazines are obviously for young children or for teachers, but the vast majority defy categorization. Students or adults have as many reading interests at as many reading and intellectual levels as there are individual magazines. This is particularly true in late junior high school through high school. Thus, many magazines ostensibly aimed at adults have received a high school designation because they are accessible to students at that level and present either information relevant to the curriculum or material of general interest.

There is no satisfactory definition of *children's* when it modifies magazine. The problem is that a child of 10 years may be perfectly capable of reading a young adult title while a teenager may have difficulty with a magazine for 10 year olds. Rather than attempt to solve that problem, what is offered here is the middle ground that defines *children* generally as those from ages 4 to 14 years.

In terms of grades, it depends on which system the particular area is employing: It may be preschool (generally under five years of age), elementary (from six to eleven years of age), middle school, junior high, and so on. Given this confusion on who is at what grade level, throughout the book the emphasis is on age ranges rather than grades. An exception is made in the Classroom Publications subsection of the Children's Magazines section, where the publishers have clearly designated a grade level for each of their magazines. Ages 14 to 18 are considered here as young adults.

Selection Policy

The selection of each title was subjected to three levels of review: (1) The view of the consultant who wrote the annotation and made the initial choice; (2) the editorial adviser who modified, added, and otherwise checked the title for suitability; (3) the editors. All followed a well-defined approach to the selection of magazines, newspapers, and indexes.

The first consideration is the audience. Here, the primary audience is the student, a reader with many of the same interests, values, and needs as adults. At the same time, due weight is given to differences in age, experience, reading ability, education, and curricular requirements.

An effort is made not to insult the intelligence of either the student or the teacher by listing inferior titles. That does not mean that light reading has been excluded, but such selections are balanced with magazines that suggest new frontiers of thought, new challenges, and new educational experiences.

For librarians, teachers, and administrators, the same criteria are followed. Emphasis is placed on what the professional person needs by way of educational assistance, especially to keep up with the changing aspects of the various disciplines. The basic teaching journals and magazines in the subject areas found in the majority of elementary, junior high, and high schools are listed.

Aside from focusing on the audience and judging the subject matter, there are some objective methods of evaluation, of determining whether or not a magazine is of value to a particular library in a particular community. These same criteria, by the way, may be used by the librarian who is trying to choose between two or more titles of equal value.

1. *What is indexed.* Stress is upon the major general indexes (which are annotated in the beginning of the guide, preceding the Children's Magazines section). Here, of course, the major indexes are *Readers' Guide to Periodical Literature* and *Magazine Index*, as well as *Magazine Article Summaries*. Consideration is given to both the printed form and the CD-ROM version. The major subject indexes, primarily from the H.W. Wilson Company, are considered. All of the titles in R.R. Bowker's *Children's Magazine Guide* are annotated. Basic professional magazines for teachers and librarians are also frequently indexed in *Education Index* and *Current Index to Journals in Education*. No librarian, teacher, or, for that matter, parent will buy or not buy a magazine because it is or is not indexed. Nor should they, particularly as newer titles sometimes take several years to find their way into an index. Also, a community may have special interests that may not be reflected in the basic indexing services. To that end, other indexes are included (and annotated), but again, only those likely to be of most value to the audience to which this guide is addressed.

2. *What is found acceptable by other experts.* Rarely does a month go by in which a list of periodicals—usually for a particular grade or subject interest—is not published in one journal or another. Such listings have been reviewed by the editor and accepted in part, rejected, or used simply to confirm earlier choices. The alert school librarian or media specialist should read a few popular titles, as well as the professional journals, since such listings are also published there from time to time. These are of special value either as reminders of new titles or as notification of magazines that may suddenly become of interest because of a new subject in the curriculum.

3. *What is purchased by school libraries of various sizes.* We are grateful to a number of librarians for assisting us by sharing their basic list of periodicals—particular thanks to Charles McCambridge (one of the editorial advisers) for sharing his list with the

consultants. A word of caution, however: One must consider the hazards of using the studies and selection policies of other libraries, since their final choices must be individual, reflecting the special needs of the persons being served.

4. *Price*. Price must be considered, particularly when designating the essential titles. Prices have tended to level off a bit during the past two years, but periodicals remain expensive, and where there is a choice between one magazine at $25 a year and another at $50, and both are of the same general quality, the vote should go to the former. The price range of similar periodicals should be checked regularly, and unless there is a substantial difference between them, the nod should go to the one that is more reasonably priced.

5. *The intrinsic quality of the individual title*. This is, of course, a major consideration. Articles, features, and stories should be written by qualified authors, and normally the author should be identified in terms of his or her background. The subject matter should be current, accurate, and biased only insofar as the magazine stresses a particular viewpoint. The writing should be acceptable for the grade level that it is intended to reach; the magazine should never "write down" to its audience. The material must be appropriate for the designated readership. If the magazine is for the average high school student, it should be neither too difficult nor too easy. The type of article published should appeal to the intended reader. If the magazine is billed as a popular one, it should be truly "popular" without being insulting. If it claims to be a learned journal, it should be that in more than name; it should contain truly exploratory and original research.

6. *The relation of the magazine to the subject covered*. First and foremost, an effort has been made to include magazines offering an overview of the topic and magazines concentrating on a particular area of the topic that interests a majority of the audience.

7. *Point of view*. This is a prime consideration, particularly in magazines covering current events and controversial subjects. Within the annotation, an effort has been made to indicate the political or other bias of the magazine. This seems especially important when dealing with general magazines, which often disguise, knowingly or not, the philosophical convictions of the editor and most of the writers. Needless to say, every major point of view is represented in this guide.

8. *Format*. While content should be the major consideration, it almost always follows (some little magazines excepted) that the format signals the quality of the content. The cover should be attractive without being ostentatious. One should quickly be able to locate articles, features, departments, and so forth in a good table of contents. If there are illustrations, they should be appropriate, and they should be of good quality. Aside from picture magazines such as *Life*, there should be a good balance between illustrations and copy. All too often, the popular magazine stresses the picture at the expense of the editorial matter, and there is little of real value in the issue. There should be no more than a few editorial or typographical errors. (It may be unreasonable these days to expect a completely "clean" issue, but at least an effort should be visible.) Finally, the magazine should be of a manageable size, not so small that it will disappear on the magazine rack or so large that it won't fit anywhere. The paper, binding, and the like should be sturdy enough to withstand more than one reader's use. And one can at least hope that the ink will not come off on one's clothing or hands.

9. *Advertising*. Most periodicals, other than journals that are financed by a grant or an institution, have advertising. One should ask whether it is appropriate and not offensive and whether there is too much of it. When there are more advertisements than copy (often ads are of as much interest to many readers as is the editorial material, but this is the

exception rather than the rule. Too much advertising (more than 50 percent in any issue) is a signal to try another title.

10. *The relationship between the magazine and the curriculum.* This consideration is kept in mind throughout. Not all the magazines are directly related to course work, but where a choice had to be made between two equally good titles, we have favored the one more likely to be of value to the subject being studied in school.

11. *Will the magazine be read?* There is no guarantee that even the best magazine, measured by the preceding ten points, will be popular. Here instinct, experience, and luck must play a part. Librarians and teachers who truly know the audience should be able to choose, from the 1,000 titles, the 13, 130, or 260 that will actually be read and not serve merely to decorate the library. But popularity should not be the only guide. There are some magazines, particularly back files, which may not be used heavily but are consistently valuable sources of reference, not only for today but for years to come; these must be purchased as well. Still, in ordering for the average school library, a major consideration is the desires and needs of the audience, both potential and actual.

Recommendations about Selection

It seems to the editors that there are several other factors that the teacher or librarian should consider in making selections. Some cautions are negative. (1) Don't select a magazine only because it is indexed. Many magazines that are not indexed, at least in popular Wilson indexes, can still be valuable. (2) Don't buy only for people who use the library now. One reason many people stay out of the library is that they have not found any magazines of interest to them. Add to the collection those titles that can increase usership. (3) Don't purchase a publication simply because it is well known. The magazine may be marvelous, but if an audience for it does not exist in your school, it is a waste of money. (4) Don't buy only what is currently well known. Try a few out-of-the-way, different magazines that view the world from an unusual perspective. As one person put it, a good librarian should follow the dictum "When in Rome, do as the Greeks do." (5) Don't seek to acquire "total balance" in the collection. It will probably end up in a state of inertia. Strike out for magazines that will be of concern to the readers. While every effort should be made to offer various points of view, there is no law that six horse magazines, for example, must be balanced against six automobiles titles, particularly if the library is 3,000 miles from the nearest ranch.

There are also positive considerations. (1) Listen to the requests of people who use the library, whether they be students or teachers or administrators. Encourage them to ask for magazines not in the library. (2) Try to find out why those who don't use the library's magazine collection are reluctant to do so. It may well be that the material is too difficult, that it simply does not include areas of their interest, or that it does not serve the curriculum. (3) Include more than curriculum-oriented materials. In this guide, for example, one finds a section on comics. Of course, not all comic books are appropriate, but some are—particularly for slow or reluctant readers—and enough are cited here to allow an intelligent choice. (4) Check the local newsstands and drugstores to see what magazines are new, which sell well, and which are sold out within a day or two. Conversely, check to see which ones are rarely purchased. (5) Be adventuresome, imaginative, and ambitious for the readers. Go out and buy new magazines that have yet to be indexed, evaluated, or judged. Let the readers determine whether or not they should be added to the collection. (6) Read as much as possible in the literature about magazines and their selection.

Samples

Now and then the librarian may wish to examine a magazine before entering a subscription. There are two approaches, one obvious and the other not so obvious. The first is to seek out the title in a larger library nearby or, if it is a new magazine, to look for it on a newsstand. The second is to request a sample copy from the publisher. When it is known that the publisher will supply a sample copy, that information is noted in this guide in the bibliographic data preceding the annotation. Since not all publishers answered that query from the editor, ask the publisher for a sample when in doubt.

The request for a sample copy should be made on library stationery, with a brief note that the periodical is to be considered for permanent addition to the library's collection. Most publishers will grant the request, although in this day of computers and distribution centers far from the editorial rooms of the magazines, there is no guarantee that a sample will be in the next mail.

Reviews

Ongoing reviews of current magazines, many of which are suitable for the audience of this book, are found in the editor's column in *Library Journal*. Now in its twentieth year, the column is an effort to evaluate six or ten magazines in each issue.

VOYA is a well-known source not only of excellent book reviews for young people but also for suggestions about magazines. The annotations are as thoughtful as they are current. *School Library Journal* frequently runs special feature articles about new magazines, as do *American Libraries* and *Wilson Library Bulletin*. See, too, the quarterly *Serials Review* and *Serials Librarian*, which frequently contain specialized bibliographies of general-interest magazines for adults and young people. Both journals are also useful for keeping up with the latest in everything, from the best vendors, to cataloging, to methods of storage.

Comprehensive Guides

Current information about price, frequency, and the like can be found in the annual *Ulrich's International Periodicals Directory* (R. R. Bowker). This is not a selective guide. It is a straightforward listing of over 70,000 periodicals from around the world.

The abbreviated names of companies that offer microform versions of particular titles and those vendors that provide online services are included in the bibliographic information in this book, when applicable. Further information about individual titles, as well as other periodicals offered by the microform and reprint companies, can be had by writing them at the addresses given on page xxii, under Microform and Reprint Companies.

> **Title**. Date Founded. °Frequency. °Price. Editor.
> Publisher and Address. Illustrations. Index. Advertising.
> Circulation. °Sample. Refereed. °Date Volume Ends.
> °Microform. °Reprint. [°Indexed. °Book Reviews.
> °Audience.]
>   Annotation.

The periodicals in this book are listed alphabetically, by title, under the subjects given in the Contents. All subject classifications used, as well as variations in wording of subject headings and as many additional subject cross-references as the editor expected would be useful, are listed. The reader should refer to the Index of Titles and Sections when a title is not found under the first subject consulted.

The bibliographic data in the entries contain the items shown in the box above. Items preceded by an asterisk are fully explained in the paragraphs below.

The Abbreviations section lists the general abbreviations found in the bibliographic information and the acronyms used for the microform companies, online vendors and databases, and abstracts and indexes.

Frequency and Price

The frequency is given immediately after the founding date, and the symbols used are explained in the General Abbreviations section. The price quoted is the annual subscription rate given by the publisher, usually as of 1990. Prices are relative and, of course, subject to change—probably upward. Furthermore, the fluctuation of the dollar makes the prices of foreign magazines even more relative.

The phrase "Controlled Circ." is found after some titles. This means the magazine has a controlled circulation and is sent free to certain individuals whom the advertisers are trying to reach. Such a magazine is financed solely by advertisements, and the controlled circulation indicates the publisher has targeted a certain audience or audiences for the advertisers. "Others" means those who are outside of that select audience and must pay for the title. Often the publisher is willing to send the magazine free to libraries, but in any case an inquiry should be made.

Sample

Publishers were asked whether or not they would send a free copy of the magazine to a library if requested. Those who replied favorably are indicated by the single word "Sample." The request should be made by the head of the library, or by the head of the serials department, and written on official stationery. The indication that publishers are willing to send samples to institutions does not mean they are necessarily interested in sending them to individual subscribers.

Date Volume Ends

Several librarians indicated it would be helpful to know when a publisher ends a volume—obviously for purposes of binding. The information provided is from the publisher.

Microform and Reprint

Companies providing microform runs of magazines are indicated, and information concerning the publisher of some reprints is noted. The librarian should consult *Guide to Microforms in Print* and *Ulrich's International Periodicals Directory* for additional information.

Indexed

Information as to where titles are indexed or abstracted is given in brackets. Indicated here are only the *major* subject indexes in which the periodicals are indexed. Major must be emphasized. Not all indexing for each title is included. Indexes and abstracts that are employed are annotated in the Abstracts and Indexes section, which begins this book.

The term "index" in the bibliographic description indicates that the publisher has an index to the periodical.

Book Reviews

Information given refers to the approximate number of reviews that appear in a typical issue of the periodical, the average length, and whether or not they are signed. This information, when applicable, can be found in brackets.

Audience

There are two basic audiences, also given in brackets. The first consists of children and/or young people. The second audience is the professional—teacher, administrator, librarian. The needs of this audience are considered in the final part of the guide.

Magazines suitable for children are found in the Children's Magazines section. However, for many of the subject areas in the Young Adult section there are magazines listed that may be suitable for both the young adult and child. These are indicated (1) in the Children's section as a cross-reference to the Young Adult section; and (2) at the head of the various Young Adult subsections by the designation "Suitable for children." See the Preface for more information on this.

The audience for magazines is indicated by age groups (4 to 18 years inclusive); for example, 4–8 years, 10–12 years, and so on. The audience for young adults (14–18 years, plus) makes up, by far, the greater portion of this guide.

In the final section all of the titles are intended for use by professionals. The letters "Pr" indicate this, and the age ranges these magazines are primarily to be used with is also given. For example, Pr/Ages 8–12 would indicate that the professional would use this title working with the 8 to 12 age group.

ABBREVIATIONS

GENERAL ABBREVIATIONS

a.   annual
aud.   audience
bi-m.   Every two months
bi-w.   Every two weeks
d.   Daily
fortn.   Fortnightly
irreg.   Irregular
m.   Monthly
n.s.   New Series

q.   Quarterly
s-a.   Twice annually
s-m.   Twice monthly
s-w.   Twice weekly
3/yr.   Three per year
w.   Weekly
Controlled Circ.   Controlled circulation, i.e., free to certain groups

ONLINE VENDORS AND DATABASES

BRS Information Technologies   1200 Rte. 7, Latham, NY 12110

CompuServe, Inc.   Box 20212, 5000 Arlington Centre Blvd., Columbus, OH 43220

DIALOG Information Services, Inc.   3460 Hillview Avenue, Palo Alto, CA 94304

Dow Jones News/Retrieval   Down Jones & Co., Inc., Box 300, Princeton, NJ 08543-0300

Information Access Co.   11 Davis Dr., Belmont, CA 94002

LRI (Legal Resource Index)   *see* Information Access Co.

Lexis   *see* Mead Data Central, Inc.

Mead Data Central, Inc.   Box 933, Dayton, OH 45401

Medis   *see* Mead Data Central, Inc.

Newsearch   *see* Information Access Co.

NewsNet   subsidiary of Independent Publications, Inc., 945 Haverford Rd., Bryn Mawr, PA 19010

Nexis   *see* Mead Data Central, Inc.

Orbit — Pergamon Orbit Infoline, Inc.   800 Westpark Dr., Suite 400, McLean, VA 22102

RLIN — The Research Libraries Group, Inc.   Jordan Quadrangle, Stanford, CA 94305

STN   Chemical Abstracts Service, American Chemical Society, 2540 Olemtangy River Rd., Columbus, OH 43210

VU/TEXT Information Sevices, Inc.   1211 Chestnut St., Philadelphia, PA 19107

WILSONLINE — H. W. Wilson Co.   950 University Ave., Bronx, NY 10452

ABSTRACTS AND INDEXES

API   Alternative Press Index
ASTI   Applied Science and Technology Index
AbrRG   Abridged Readers' Guide
Acs   Access
ArtI   Art Index
BI   Business Index
BioAg   Biological and Agricultural Index
BioG   Biography and Genealogy Master Index
BioI   Biography Index
BoRv   Book Review Digest
BoRvI   Book Review Index
BusI   Business Periodicals Index
CIJE   Current Index to Journals in Education
CMG*   Children's Magazine Guide
CMI   Canadian Magazine Index
CanEdI   Canadian Education Index
CanI   Canadian Periodical Index
ChBkRvI   Children's Book Review Index

ChildDevAb   Child Development Abstracts and Bibliography
ChildLitAb   Children's Literature Index
ECER   Exceptional Child Education Resources
EdI   Education Index
GSI   General Science Index
HAPI   Hispanic American Periodicals Index
HumI   Humanities Index
IFP   Index to Free Periodicals
INeg   Index to Periodicals by and about Blacks
MI   Magazine Index
MRD   Media Review Digest
MagA   Magazine Article Summaries
NatN   National Newspaper Index
Nyt   New York Times Index
PAIS   PAIS Bulletin
PerA   Periodical Abstracts on Disc
RG   Readers' Guide to Periodical Literature
ResEduc   Resources in Education
SocSc   Social Sciences Index

*For those magazines indexed in R. R. Bowker's *Children's Magazine Guide*, see the list at the end of this section.

MICROFORM AND REPRINT COMPANIES

AMS   AMS Press, Inc., 56 E. 13th St., New York, NY 10003
B&H   Bell & Howell, Microphoto Division, Old Mansfield Rd., Wooster, OH 44691
CPC   Clearwater Publishing Co., Room 400, 1995 Broadway, New York, NY 10023
ERIC   Eric Document Reproduction Service, P.O. Box 190, Arlington, VA 22210
GLB   Gaylord Brothers Inc., P.O. Box 4901, Syracuse, NY 13221
IA   Information Access Corp., 404 Sixth Avenue, Menlo Park, CA 94025
ISI   Institute for Scientific Information, University Science Center, 3501 Market St., Philadelphia, PA 19104
JAI   Johnson Associates, Inc., P.O. Box 1017, 321 Greenwich Ave., Greenwich, CT 06830

KTO   Kraus Microform, One Water St., White Plains, NY 10601
Kraus   Kraus Reprint and Periodicals, Route 100, Millwood, NY 10546
MCA   Microfilming Corporation of America, 21 Harristown Rd., Glen Rock, NJ 07452
MCE   Professional Data Services (Formerly Microcard Editions, Inc.), c/o Congressional Information Services, 4520 East-West Hwy., Suite 800, Bethesda, MD 20814
MIM   Microforms International Marketing Corp., Fairview Park, Elmsford, NY 10523
MML   Micromedia, Ltd., 144 Front St. W., Toronto, Ont. M5J 1G2, Canada
PMC   Princeton Microfilm Corp., P.O. Box 235, Princeton, NJ 08550

Pub   Publisher

RP   Research Publications, 12 Lunar Dr., Woodbridge, CT 06525

SHSW   State Historical Society of Wisconsin, 816 State St., Madison, WI 53706

UMI   University Microfilms International, 300 N. Zeeb Rd., Ann Arbor, MI 48106

W   World Microfilms Publications, Ltd., 62 Queen's Grove, London, England

MAGAZINES INDEXED IN R. R. BOWKER'S CHILDREN'S MAGAZINE GUIDE

 The Book Report
Boys' Life
Calliope
Career World
Chickadee
Child Life
Children's Digest
Cobblestone
3-2-1 Contact
Cricket
Current Events
Current Health 1
Current Science
Dolphin Log
Emergency Librarian
Faces
The Good Apple News-
    paper
Highlights for Children
Hopscotch

The Horn Book Maga-
    zine
Humpty Dumpty's Mag-
    azine
Instructor
International Wildlife
Jack and Jill
Junior Scholastic
Kid City
Ladybug
Learning
National Geographic
    Magazine
National Geographic
    World
National Wildlife
Odyssey
Owl Magazine
Children's Playmate
    Magazine

Plays
Ranger Rick
Scholastic Choices
Scholastic Science
    World
School Library Journal
Scienceland
Sesame Street Maga-
    zine
Sports Illustrated for
    Kids
SuperScience Blue
SuperScience Red
Teaching K-8
Technology & Learning
U*S*Kids
Wee Wisdom
Zillions
Zoobooks

Note: The symbol is used throughout this book to highlight these magazines.

ABSTRACTS AND INDEXES

There are definite first choices for elementary, junior high, and high school in the area of abstracts and indexes. Beyond a basic half dozen, much depends on the budget. For example, if funds allow it is advisable to have at least one indexing service on CD-ROM. Most indexes, including Wilson, are now in this form. They also are online, and this is noted. Few libraries will offer online services, although they are a distinct possibility where funds permit.

The primary choices, the "Basic Indexes," are listed and annotated first. The second part, "Beyond Basics," offers other possibilities. Finally, indexes for the teacher and librarian are considered under the "Professional" heading.

It should be stressed that the designations "Basic Indexes," "Beyond Basics," and "Professional" are relative. All of the services might be used, at one time or another, by young adults (if not children), and certainly by teachers, administrators, and other adults.

Basic Indexes: Children

1. Children's Magazine Guide
2. Readers' Guide to Periodical Literature
3. Abridged Readers' Guide to Periodical Literature

Basic Indexes: Young Adults (in order of preference)

1. Readers' Guide to Periodical Literature; *and/or* Magazine Index *or* Magazine Article Summaries
2. Abridged Readers' Guide to Periodical Literature (if above not purchased)
3. General Science Index
4. Social Sciences Index
5. Humanities Index
6. Book Review Digest

BASIC INDEXES

1 **Abridged Readers' Guide to Periodical Literature.** 1935. 9/yr. $60. H. W. Wilson Co., 950 University Ave., Bronx, NY 10452. Online: WILSONLINE. [*Aud*: Ages 6–18.]

The only advantage of this cutdown version of the larger index is that the library is likely to have most of the magazines indexed. This will eliminate frustration on the part of children and young adults, but it does not solve the problem of failure to have articles in certain desired subject areas. The junior version of *Readers' Guide to Periodical Literature*, this index includes only 60 titles. Most libraries should take the senior title, which is the best-known author-subject index to general periodicals.

2   Book Review Digest. 1905. 10/yr. Service basis. H. W. Wilson Co., 950 University Ave., Bronx, NY 10452. Online: WILSONLINE. [*Aud*: Ages 14–18.]

This is the reference to which most high school students turn for background information on current books or classics. It nicely augments such standard reference works as *Masterplots*. Defects in this index are that it (1) covers only 80 periodicals and (2) insists on four reviews for fiction and two reviews for nonfiction before there is an entry, thus effectively eliminating many first books. On the positive side, (1) there are brief excerpts from the reviews that indicate the tone of acceptance or rejection, and give a good idea of content, and (2) there is an excellent subject index as well as an author-title index.

3   Children's Magazine Guide. 1948. 10/yr. $33. Judith M. Balsamo. R. R. Bowker, 121 Chanlon Rd., New Providence, NJ 07974. Subs. to: P.O. Box 7247-8599, Philadelphia, PA 19170. [*Aud*: Ages 6–14.]

The basic index to children's magazines, this is a subject approach to over 35 titles. In addition, a dozen professional journals are indexed. The subject headings are numerous and follow the vocabulary and interests of readers from 6 to 14 years of age, although a few titles may be for even younger children. The 30 pages are in two sections, the first for children's magazines and the second for professional works. In addition, there are several features, including a quiz on how to use the index. A first purchase for all libraries, school and public.

4   General Science Index. 1978. 10/yr. Service basis. H. W. Wilson Co., 950 University Ave., Bronx, NY 10452. Online: WILSONLINE. [*Aud*: Ages 10–18.]

One of the major indexes for high schools, this indexes 108 general science periodicals. It is a spin-off of the more thorough *Applied Science and Technology Index* and *Biological and Agricultural Index*, and follows the subject pattern established by Wilson in other indexes. As usual, there is an author listing of citations to book reviews in a separate section. All the sciences are included. Larger libraries will find that most titles indexed here are indexed in the two other services.

5   Humanities Index. 1974. q. Service basis. Elizabeth Pingree. H. W. Wilson Co., 950 University Ave., Bronx, NY 10452. Online: WILSONLINE. CD-ROM: Pub. [*Aud*: Ages 10–18.]

A basic index for high schools, this covers almost 300 titles. Subject fields indexed include archaeology and classical studies, folklore, history, language and literature, performing arts, philosophy, religion and theology, and related topics. The main body of the index consists of author and subject entries interfiled. Citations to book reviews follow the main body of the index. There is a bound annual cumulation. The titles indexed are those found in large public libraries, but major titles are found in medium to large high school libraries.

6   Magazine Article Summaries. w. $289. EBSCO Industries. Subs. to: P.O. Box 11318, Birmingham, AL 35202. Online: BRS. [*Aud*: Ages 10–18.]

Here over 300 general titles are indexed and abstracted, including about 70 that are not in *Readers' Guide to Periodical Literature*. This index has several advantages: It is weekly, it has a bimonthly subject index, and the abstracts are easy to read. The problem is that the indexing is more selective than in *Readers' Guide* and the abstracts are rather short. Still, if the library can afford a third index (after *Readers' Guide* and *Magazine Index*) this would be a good choice either in print or in CD-ROM (1984 to date, monthly, $1,600; quarterly, $800;

annually, $400). Beginning in 1990, at an added cost, some of the magazines became available in full text for searching on CD-ROM. This is a tremendous advantage, particularly for schools with a limited magazine collection.

7   **Magazine Index.** 1977. m. $2,350. Magazine Index, 11 Davis Dr., Belmont, CA 94002. Online: BRS, Dialog, Mead Data Central. [*Aud*: Ages 10–18.]

One of the primary rivals to *Readers' Guide*, this is found in many high school, junior high, and public libraries. The publisher provides an enclosed fiche reader with a rapid searching mechanism for this index on microfiche. Authors, titles, subjects, and product names are arranged in a single alphabet. About 400 popular U.S. magazines are indexed, including children's, special-interest, news-stand, sports, auto, literary, and some academic periodicals. The monthly fiches are cumulated for five years. Earlier years are cumulated in a separate index to be read on a separate, manually operated fiche reader. Supplementary paper indexes, "Hot Topics" and "Product Evaluations," are issued monthly in loose-leaf form.

Note: The CD-ROM version takes several forms, although the most popular is *Infotrac* (1980 to date, monthly, $5,150). A less expensive version is *Magazine Index Select* (1985 to date, monthly, $2,600), and there are other versions as well.

8   **Readers' Guide to Periodical Literature.** 1900. s-m. $120. Jean Marra. H. W. Wilson Co., 950 University Ave., Bronx, NY 10452. Online: WILSONLINE. CD-ROM: Pub. [*Aud*: Ages 6–18.]

The best known and most popular of the American periodical indexes, *Readers' Guide* indexes nearly 204 periodicals. It may be the only index to which high school students are introduced and may be the only one with which college students are familiar. This means that periodicals indexed in this guide are much more heavily used than others not indexed, contributing to uneven usage of the periodicals collection in many libraries. Instruction of readers in the use of other indexes appropriate to an individual library could be an important factor in preserving its periodicals collection. *Readers' Guide* has quarterly and annual cumulations. It is easy to use, with author and subject entries interfiled in one alphabet. An author index of citations to book reviews follows the main body of the index. Indexing may be current within four months. *Readers' Guide* will continue to be popular and heavily used in all but the most specialized libraries.

Beginning in 1986, *Readers' Guide Abstracts* became available. It is issued every six weeks in eight cumulations. Each volume year includes two full years of abstracts. A print version with about 25,000 abstracts is issued monthly for $250. *Note*: The abstracts also are available as part of the WILSONLINE service and on CD-ROM ($1,995).

9   **Social Sciences Index.** 1974. q. Service basis. H. W. Wilson Co., 950 University Ave., Bronx, NY 10452. Online: WILSONLINE. CD-ROM: Pub. [*Aud*: Ages 10–18.]

The third of the subject indexes that should be in most high school and public libraries, this is a multidisciplinary index, without abstracts, covering major journals from most social and behavioral sciences. It also covers social welfare journals. There is an index to reviews of social science books.

■■■■■■■■■■■■■■■■■■■■■■■■■ **BEYOND BASICS** ■■■■■■■■■■■■■■■■■

These are services that should be found in larger high school and public libraries. Few libraries can afford them all, but some are worth considering when they support the school's programs and/or the community needs of teenagers.

10   **Access: the supplementary index to periodicals.** 1975. 3/yr. $125. John G. Burke and Ned Kehde. Access, P.O. Box 1492, Evanston, IL 60204-1492. [*Aud*: Ages 14–18.]

    Access's stated purpose is to complement existing periodical indexes. National general-interest publications are indexed until *Readers' Guide* begins indexing them, at which point *Access* deletes them. *Access* indexes about 150 titles, including regional and city magazines and many popular newsstand periodicals. The third issue of *Access* each year is an annual hardbound cumulation. Indexing not yet in printed form is available in the Burke Electronic Information Services Diskette, which is sent to all subscribers. Since *Access* supplements *Readers' Guide*, it is an important tool for public and academic libraries.

11   **Alternative Press Index.** 1969. q. $125 (Individuals, $30). Ed. bd. Alternative Press Center, Inc., P.O. Box 33109, Baltimore, MD 21218. Circ: 1,000. [*Aud*: Ages 14–18.]

    API has established itself as the leading index to periodicals of liberal and radical political persuasions. It indexes over 200 journals and newspapers, for most of which access to indexing is otherwise difficult or impossible. The indexing is by subject. The majority of the periodicals covered are published in the United States, but the index does include a number of foreign journals, particularly those from the United Kingdom. The range of subjects covered is as broad, in its way, as that of the *Readers' Guide to Periodical Literature*, but the political slant of the typical citation is clearly left—well left of center. With *API*, and with at least a fair sampling of the journals it covers, a library does a better job of helping its users find out about real "alternatives."

12   **Applied Science and Technology Index** (Formerly: *Industrial Arts Index*). 1913. m. Service basis. Joyce Howard. H. W. Wilson Co., 950 University Ave., Bronx, NY 10452. Online: WILSONLINE. CD-ROM: Pub. [*Aud*: Ages 14–18.]

    Applied Science and Technology Index indexes English-language periodicals covering all areas of the applied sciences and engineering. The main body of the index lists journal citations under alphabetized subject headings. A separate section lists citations to book reviews for the field. Over 300 periodicals are selected for indexing. The selection of periodicals for review is based on subscriber vote. Periodicals included are a mix of trade and basic society publications. *Applied Science and Technology Index* is published monthly with an annual cumulation. As with the other Wilson indexes, *Applied Science and Technology Index* is available online through WILSONLINE, as well as on CD-ROM through Wilson.

13   **Art Index.** 1929. q. Service basis. H. W. Wilson Co., 950 University Ave., Bronx, NY 10452. Online: WILSONLINE. CD-ROM: Pub. [*Aud*: Ages 14–18.]

    Still the most basic index for art. Indexing over 200 journals as well as a number of yearbooks and museum bulletins, it covers archaeology, architecture, art history, city planning, crafts, film, design arts, museology, photography, and related fields. The emphasis is on English-language periodicals (especially American), but major foreign publications are included. Access is by subject and author.

14 **Biography and Genealogy Master Index.** 1975. 5 yr. cum. $795. (a. supplements $235). Barbara McNeil. Gale Research Co., Book Tower, Detroit, MI 48226. Online: DIALOG. [*Aud*: Ages 14–18.]

The basic set has over 3 million citations to biographical material in 350 biography sources. The supplements average about 400,000 citations to about 100 editions and volumes. While this is not an index to biography in periodicals, it is included here because it is used closely with *Biography Index*.

15 **Biography Index: a quarterly index to biographical material in books and magazines.** 1946. q. $85. H. W. Wilson Co., 950 University Ave., Bronx, NY 10452. Online: WILSONLINE. CD-ROM: Pub. [*Aud*: Ages 14–18.]

This is a guide to biographical material appearing in 2,600 periodicals analyzed in other Wilson indexes, selected additional periodicals, current books of individual and collected biographies, and incidental biographical material in nonbiographical books. Each issue has a list of analyzed books that includes obituaries, letter collections, diaries, memoirs, and bibliographies. The main section is alphabetically arranged by names of biographees, most of whom are American. There is also a list arranged by profession or occupation, as well as an annual bound cumulation and a triennial cumulation. Other biographical reference works such as *Current Biography* and *Contemporary Authors* are themselves compilations of biographies and are not indexes to biographical sources.

16 **Biological and Agricultural Index.** 1964. m. (exc. Aug). Service basis. Syed M. Shah. H. W. Wilson Co., 950 University Ave., Bronx, NY 10452. Vol. ends: July. Online: WILSONLINE. CD-ROM: Pub. [*Aud*: Ages 14–18.]

Biological and Agricultural Index provides indexing to more than 200 English-language periodicals in the biological and agricultural sciences. Included are agricultural economics, animal husbandry, cytology, ecology, forestry, horticulture, nutrition, soil science, and veterinary medicine, as well as botany, zoology, entomology, genetics, and marine biology. Periodicals indexed are selected by a committee of librarians. A controlled list of subject headings is used, and many cross-references are provided. An index to book reviews is included as a separate section in each issue. Monthly issues cumulate quarterly, and an annual hardbound issue covers the entire August-through-July period. Like the other indexes from H. W. Wilson, *Biological and Agricultural Index* is sold on a service basis, with subscription price based on the number of indexed titles received by the library. A good, easy-to-use, basic index.

17 **Book Review Index.** 1965. bi-m. $170. Gale Research Co., Book Tower, Detroit, MI 48226. Online: DIALOG. [*Aud*: Ages 14–18.]

This is an author/title index to all book reviews appearing in some 450 periodicals. Casting a much broader net than *Book Review Digest*, this index does lack excerpts from the reviews as well as a subject index. The reviews cited are in abbreviated form and should be read carefully. The order of searching is to turn to *Book Review Digest* first. Lacking a citation there, move to *Book Review Index*.

18   **Business Index.** 1979. m. Price varies (approx. $1,800). Information Access Corp., 11 Davis Dr., Belmont, CA 94002. Online: BRS, DIALOG, Mead Data Central. CD-ROM: Pub. [*Aud*: Ages 14–18.]

This is on the familiar microform reader, and monthly additions are provided via a microform reel which is loaded into the machine. The result is that the user may search five years of about 800 periodicals by subject at one place, that is, there is no need to look through various volumes as with the Wilson indexes. (A similar format/approach is used for the company's now-famous *Magazine Index*.) Another version of the same index is offered as part of the company's CD-ROM Infotrac. While the subject is the primary approach, the single alphabet index allows entry by author and sometimes by title. Special features include graded book reviews, as well as a selective index to some business newspapers, including *The Wall Street Journal*. There are brief descriptive abstracts for most of the citations. This is by and large the best of the business indexes for the layperson, both in terms of coverage and ease of use. Only the price makes it prohibitive for many libraries.

19   **Business Periodicals Index.** 1958. m. + q. and a. cumulations. Service basis. Walter Webb. H. W. Wilson Co., 950 University Ave., Bronx, NY 10452. Online: WILSONLINE. CD-ROM: Pub. [*Aud*: Ages 14–18.]

This subject index to over 300 business periodicals remains a "core" index for all types of libraries due to its unique subject headings, which have been honed over years of experience. Although *BPI* covers fewer than half of the titles found in the *Business Index*, it remains a valuable tool that facilitates quick retrieval of hard-to-find topics with headings such as "New Products-Failure." Articles on important businesspeople can sometimes be found under individual names, and there is a handy list of citations to recent book reviews in the back of each volume. Overall, a particularly useful index for school and public libraries.

20   **Canadian Magazine Index.** 1985. m. (cumulates). Price varies. Luci Lemieux. Micromedia, 158 Pearl St., Toronto, Ont. M5H 1L3, Canada. [*Aud*: Ages 14–18.]

CMI began indexing American magazines of most interest to Canadians and found in most libraries. It now indexes 18 of these magazines along with 350 Canadian periodicals chosen to reflect their availability in libraries and to provide regional and topical coverage for people with popular, special, and academic tastes in their pursuit of national news and information. It notes new nonfiction Canadian books; has form entries for drama, short stories, reviews of books, and the performing and visual arts; and isolates obituary material within its subject and name access points. Many public and school libraries will want to carry *CMI*.

21   **Canadian Periodical Index/Index de périodiques Canadiens.** 1938. m. (cumulates). $200 Can. (varies). Ed. bd. InfoGlobe, 444 Front St. W., Toronto, Ont. M5V 2S9, Canada. Circ: 1,725. Vol. ends: No. 12. CD-ROM: Pub. [*Aud*: Ages 14–18.]

Partially in response to its direct competitor, *Canadian Magazine Index, CPI* has undergone significant changes and enlargement. This is a bilingual reference tool. It gives access by form (book and drama reviews, poetry, and short stories) in addition to major access by author, subject, and corporate names to a wide variety of French- and English-language journals. The journals have significant national or regional Canadian content.

22 **Hispanic American Periodicals Index (HAPI).** 1970. a. $240. Barbara G. Valk. UCLA Latin Amer. Center Publns., 405 Hilgard Ave., Univ. of California, Los Angeles, CA 90024. [*Aud*: Ages 14–18.]

HAPI indexes close to 250 journals in the social sciences and humanities whose scope regularly encompasses Latin American subjects. The hard sciences and technology are excluded. It also indexes some of the leading journals covering the U.S. Latino experience. The index provides separate author and subject sections, with the use of cross-references to assist in locating the right terms. Book reviews, which are all cited in a separate section, are retrieved by book author name. Since the journals indexed are worldwide, many of the bibliographic references will not be in English. Often they are in Spanish or in other Western European languages. The index is presently composed of annual volumes from 1976 through the present.

23 **Index to Periodical Articles by and about Blacks.** 1960. a. $90. G. K. Hall & Co., 70 Lincoln St., Boston, MA 02111. [*Aud*: Ages 14–18.]

The last edition of this useful tool indexed 37 Afro-American periodicals. All such periodicals, along with other publications that contain a large number of articles concerning blacks, are considered for inclusion. The index features interfiled author and subject entries. Creative works and reviews can be accessed by title under their respective subject headings. A heading called "First Facts" lists entries concerning events "that break patterns of race and sex discrimination." This index, though issued annually, is not current, but runs several years behind. Thus, it must be used for retrospective searching. Presently, articles from 1950–1985 have been indexed.

24 **National Newspaper Index.** 1979. m. Price varies. Information Access Corp., 11 Davis Dr., Belmont, CA 94002. Online: BRS, DIALOG. CD-ROM: Pub. [*Aud*: Ages 14–18.]

Distributed monthly on microfilm to be read on ROM equipment. Each monthly issue is a cumulation of all articles indexed since 1979. It provides subject access to the *Christian Science Monitor*, *New York Times*, *Wall Street Journal*, *Los Angeles Times*, and *Washington Post*. Coverage for the latter two is from 1982 on. This index covers only the news articles, excluding weather charts, horoscopes, and so forth. Also can be searched online as "Newssearch" database, which is updated daily, and on CD-ROM.

25 **New York Times Index.** 1913. s-m. $565. University Microfilms, 300 N. Zeeb Rd., Ann Arbor, MI 48106. Microform: UMI. Online: DIALOG. [*Aud*: Ages 14–18.]

Published by the New York Times Company and distributed by UMI, the index is based on the final late city edition but covers the Sunday regional edition as well. It has a subject arrangement that includes geographic, organizational, and personal names. The indexing could be improved, for example, an article on the FBI's Library Awareness Program was found under "United States—Espionage" but not under "FBI" or "Libraries." There also is a time lag of several months before the indexes are available. The subscription price includes an annual hardbound cumulation. Abstracts are included for significant articles, and articles of unusual interest are highlighted. Back files are available on microfiche. Available online, it is also found as part of numerous CD-ROM databases, such as *National Newspaper Index*, but not in such detail.

26 **PAIS Bulletin** (Formerly: *Public Affairs Information Service. Bulletin*). 1915. m. $295. Lawrence J. Woods. Public Affairs Information Service, Inc., 11 W. 40th St., New York, NY 10018. Index. Online: BRS, DIALOG. [*Aud*: Ages 14–18.]

This index has a strong reputation as a major resource for accessing social science literature, including political science, sociology, economics, demography, social work, and business. Within these disciplines the focus is on factual and statistical information pertaining to public policy issues. Books, pamphlets, government publications, and reports from public and private agencies are all included. *PAIS Bulletin* is a subject index; the annual cumulations contain the author indexes. Each issue also has a useful listing of material indexed, which is valuable for identifying and obtaining many of the citations.

27 **Periodical Abstracts on Disc.** 1988. m. $1,750. University Microfilms, 300 N. Zeeb Rd., Ann Arbor, MI 48106. [*Aud*: Ages 10–18.]

Here one finds slightly over 450 general periodicals indexed and abstracted. The service is available only on CD-ROM. It is worth considering because of the broad coverage and the excellent abstracts. (Full text is available on *General Periodicals on Disc*. 1990 to date. m. Inquire for price.)
See also *Resource One/On Disc*.

28 **Resource One/On Disc.** 1988. m. $795. University Microfilms, 300 N. Zeeb Rd., Ann Arbor, MI 48106. [*Aud*: Ages 10–18.]

This indexes about 130 periodicals. The service is available only on CD-ROM, not in print. It is tailored for small libraries and for junior high and high school students in particular. All but 18 of the titles (as of 1990) are found in *Readers' Guide*, but this has the decided advantage of offering abstracts for each and every entry.

PROFESSIONAL

In addition to the preceding services, *all of which may be used by professionals*, these are the indexes and abstracting services used primarily by teachers, librarians, and administrators. Some may be helpful to students. Here, as throughout this volume, indexes for professionals are indicated by age level. The "Pr" before the age level indicates that these services are for the professional to use with the appropriate ages given. This does not preclude using an index in high school that is primarily for elementary grade teachers, but at least the audience guidelines give direction to the librarian who may wish to purchase the service. Public librarians may want the indexes, too, for specialists as well as for the general public.

29 **Canadian Education Index/Répertoire Canadien sur l'éducation.** 1965. 3/yr. (cumulates). $184 Can. Maureen Davis. Canadian Education Assn., 252 Bloor St. W., Suite 8-200, Toronto, Ont. M5S 1V5, Canada. Circ: 350. Vol. ends: No. 3. [*Aud*: Pr/Ages 6–18.]

CEI is an author and subject index to a discipline-oriented but comprehensive list of Canadian educational periodicals, reports, and monographs. A very large number of the periodicals come from associations and boards of education and are not indexed elsewhere. Certainly the broad range of small and mainstream magazines is not brought together as conveniently elsewhere for an audience that sets a priority on education and education-related information.

30 **Child Development Abstracts and Bibliography.** 1927. 3/yr. $43.50. Hoben Thomas. Univ. of Chicago Press, 5801 Ellis Ave., Chicago, IL 60637. Circ: 5,800. Sample. [*Aud*: Pr/Ages 6–18.]

The official publication of the Society for Research in Child Development. It abstracts both books and periodical articles that consider any aspect of child development and related areas. The list of items analyzed makes this a useful buying guide as well.

31 **Children's Book Review Index.** 1976. a. $82. Gary Tarbert and Barbara Beach. Gale Research Co., Book Tower, Detroit, MI 48226. [*Aud*: Pr/Ages 6–14.]

This is a spin-off of the company's *Book Review Index*. It does little more than lift children's books from that index and offer them as a separate work. Reviews appearing in both the children's and adult publications are arranged in a single alphabet by author. Each volume has a title index. There is a useful 20-year cumulation (1965–1984) for $350.

32 **Children's Literature Index.** 1973. q. £11. C.H. Ray. Intl. Federation of Lib. Assns., Children's Libs. Section, Tan-y-capel, Bont Dolgadfan, Llanbrynmair, Powys SY19 7BB, Wales. Circ: 500. Online: MIM. [*Aud*: Pr/Ages 6–14.]

Published by the Children's Libraries Section of the International Federation of Library Associations, this more than 30-page service includes 20- to 75-word abstracts. Over 400 abstracts give access to articles in British, U.S., Russian, Australian, and other journals. Entries are arranged under subject headings within the fields of children's fiction and nonfiction, psychological and educational criteria, illustration, book selection, awards and prizes, children's book publication in various countries, and authors and illustrators. Each entry gives appropriate bibliographical references (with addresses of the abstracted journals) and a short descriptive annotation. The March issue each year contains indexes.

33 **Current Index to Journals in Education.** 1969. m. $207 (s-a. cumulations, $198). Oryx Press, 2214 N. Central Ave., Phoenix, AZ 85004-1483. Online: BRS, DIALOG, Orbit. CD-ROM: Various pubs. [*Aud*: Pr/Ages 6–18.]

Though published by a private firm, *CIJE* is a product of the U.S. Department of Education's ERIC system. It provides virtually complete indexing of a list of about 800 education periodicals, and selective indexing of important education-related articles in other periodicals. Entries can be accessed by author, by title, and by the issue of the journal they appeared in. In addition to the usual bibliographic information provided by indexes, the entries provide short abstracts of the articles they describe. *CIJE* does not index all the periodicals covered by *Education Index*, but because of the abstracts and because it does index the greater number of periodicals, *CIJE* should be the first choice if a choice must be made.

34 **Education Index.** 1929. 10/yr. (Sept–June). Service basis. Mary Louise Hewitt. H.W. Wilson Co., 950 University Ave., Bronx, NY 10452. Online: WILSONLINE. CD-ROM: Pub. [*Aud*: Pr/Ages 6–18.]

Education Index provides thorough indexing of about 350 education periodicals, using the subject-and-author approach that many users will know from *Readers' Guide to Periodical Literature* and other Wilson Company indexes. The subject headings, adapted to the special terminology of education, are not always the same as those in the *Readers' Guide*.

ERIC. *See* **Current Index to Journals in Education** and **Resources in Education.**

35   Exceptional Child Education Resources. 1969. q. $75. Council for Exceptional Children, 1920 Association Dr., Reston, VA 22091. Circ: 800. Online: BRS. [*Aud*: Pr/Ages 6–18.]

ECER selectively indexes and abstracts material dealing with the education of the handicapped. More than 200 journals are scanned regularly, and abstracts of books, dissertations, conference papers, government documents, and other items are included along with those of periodical articles. Each issue is indexed by author, title, and subject. Some of the entries are also available through the ERIC system, but this well-put-together service is nevertheless a must for academic libraries serving programs in special education.

36   Index to Free Periodicals. 1976. s-a. Pierian Press, P.O. Box 1808, Ann Arbor, MI 48106. [*Aud*: Pr/Ages 6–18.]

With about 50 periodicals being scanned twice a year, the index is arranged by subject plus some title and author headings. The unique aspect of this index is that every periodical scanned is free, or controlled circulation. At any rate, they come at no charge to libraries and cover a vast variety of topics.

37   Library Literature. 1933. bi-m. + a. cumulation. Service basis. H. W. Wilson Co., 950 University Ave., Bronx, NY 10452. Online: WILSONLINE. [*Aud*: Pr/Ages 6–18.]

Library Literature is an international index to library and information science, with a strong emphasis on U.S. librarianship. It is the basic index for practitioners and students of library science in the United States. The majority of titles indexed are in English. In addition to coverage of over 200 periodicals, the index includes references to monographs, pamphlets, theses, and some audiovisuals. Book review citations are provided in a separate section after the main author/subject index. The format is the same as that of all other Wilson indexes, with the expected high level of accuracy.

38   Media Review Digest. 1970. a. $200. Pierian Press, P.O. Box 1808, Ann Arbor, MI 48106. [*Aud*: Pr/Ages 6–18.]

The publisher scans a wide variety of periodicals—about 200—for reviews of anything classifiable as "media." Arrangement is by form of medium, and there are numerous indexes that allow one to easily find what is needed. There usually is an indication of whether the review is positive or negative. Here, "review" is interpreted in its broadest sense, so that much of the material may be no more than a note about the medium. Nevertheless, this remains the one fixed point for finding such material. The index covers films, filmstrips, videotapes, slides, transparencies, globes, charts, and other nonprint media.

39   Resources in Education. 1966. m. $51 (s-a. indexes, $20/yr.). Subs. to: Supt. of Doc., U.S. Govt. Printing Office, Washington, DC 20402. Circ: 5,000. Online: BRS, DIALOG, Orbit. CD-ROM: Various pubs. [*Aud*: Pr/Ages 6–18.]

A product of the U.S. Department of Education's ERIC system, *RIE* makes available indexing and abstracts of miscellaneous education documents, most of them not available through normal publishing channels. Most of the documents themselves are available for purchase, in microfiche and sometimes in paper copy, from the ERIC Documents Reproduction Service, or they can be used in microfiche at libraries that are in the U.S. Depository Library system. More than 15,000 documents are indexed each year. Among them are dissertations; policy papers produced by local, state, and federal government education agencies; reports of research done under government contract; research studies done by universities; and so on. Along with its companion ERIC publication *Current Index to Journals in Education* and *Education Index*, *RIE* is one of the three education indexes that are basic for libraries.

CHILDREN'S MAGAZINES

[Terri M. Raymond]

The earliest children's magazines were *St. Nicholas* and *Wee Wisdom*, with *Boys' Life* following close behind. Today the trend in children's magazines is to publish nonfiction, with science magazines being the most abundant.

Publications in this section are geared primarily for children ages 2–14. For convenience, the audience is designated here by the age of the reader—for example, ages 4–12. In some cases "not recommended" titles are annotated. This is not the usual practice, but the thought is that such information will be of help to parents as well as to librarians.

Children's magazines are more important than ever if only because there are now more children. The number of children 13 and younger is expected to rise to 50 million in 1995, from 45 million in 1990.

The number of children's magazines has not increased over the past few years. There is little that can be done to encourage publishers in this area, but at least one will find here the basic titles from which teachers, librarians, and parents can choose.

First choices   Primary choice depends on the age group for which the magazine is being selected. Beyond that, the basic general titles found in most public and school libraries include *Boys' Life*, *Chickadee*, *Cobblestone*, *Cricket*, *Kid City*, and *Sesame Street*.

Circulation   The circulation of a given magazine is by no means the best way to evaluate its worth, but at least it is some indication of popularity. Among the children's titles (subject and general), the leaders claim circulations of:

9,000	Stone Soup
12,000	Creative Kids
16,000	Scienceland
23,000	Plays
42,000	Cobblestone
97,600	Odyssey
100,000	Chickadee
110,000	Owl
120,000	Cricket
130,000	Child Life
140,000	Zillions (Formerly: *Penny Power*)
175,000	Wee Wisdom
260,000	Kid City
290,000	Children's Playmate
300,000	Children's Digest
370,000	Turtle
450,000	Your Big Backyard
500,000	Jack and Jill

500,000	Muppet
600,000	Barbie
600,000	Humpty Dumpty's Magazine
700,472	Ranger Rick
1,200,000	Sesame Street Magazine
1,300,000	National Geographic World
2,650,000	Boys' Life
2,800,000	Highlights for Children

40   **Acorn.** 1978. q. $11. Susan Pagnucci. Bur Oak Press, 8717 Mockingbird Rd. S., Platteville, WI 53818. Illus. Circ: 1,500. [*Aud*: Ages 4–10.]

Features: This is an attractive activities magazine with large drawings and photographs and easy-to-follow instructions. Parts of it can be used by the youngster, while other sections are for the parent or teacher to read to the child or help the child with a project. Issues are centered around a single theme, from bears to foreign countries. *Length:* 50 pages. *Journalistic Quality:* Cleverly and imaginatively edited with an obvious appreciation for reader interests. The simple art projects, from flannel figures to story puppets, make it particularly valuable. It deserves a much wider circulation and is a good addition to school and public libraries.

41   **Barbie.** 1984. q. $7. Karen Harrison. Welsh Publg. Group, Inc., 300 Madison Ave., New York, NY 10017. Illus. Adv. Circ: 600,000. Sample. Vol. ends: Nov. [*Bk. rev*: 3, 30 words. *Aud*: Ages 4–12.]

Features: The magazine is composed of fashion spreads, hairstyle and beauty ideas, articles on crafts and fitness, and Barbie stories. Regular features include "Love from Barbie" (a readers' greeting from Barbie), "Your Page" (readers' letters and illustrations), "What's Happening" (tidbits and photos of TV, rock, and movie stars), and "Tricks and Teasers" (puzzles and word games). *Length:* 32 pages. *Journalistic Quality:* Visually effective—printed on glossy paper in full color. The content is a bit contrived but upbeat. This magazine is sure to be popular with preteen girls. Keep in mind that it is loaded with advertisements.

42   **Boys' Life.** 1911. m. $15.60. William B. McMorris. Boy Scouts of America, 1325 Walnut
 Hill Lane, P.O. Box 152079, Irving, TX 75015-2079. Illus. Adv. Circ: 2,650,000. Sample. Vol. ends: Dec. Online: DIALOG. [*Indexed*: CMG. *Bk. rev*: 8, 80 words, signed. *Aud*: Ages 8–17.]

Features: This magazine is published for Cub Scouts, Boy Scouts, and Explorers. The tenets of self-reliance, clean living, good citizenship, and discipline are stressed through the regular features, which consist of comics, jokes, articles, and fiction. Topics range from magic and hobby news to sports and hero stories. Regular features are abundant: "Magic," "Readers' Page," "Think and Grin" (jokes and cartoons), "Hitchin' Rack" (letters to the editor), "The Pedro Patrol," "Peewee Harris," and "The Tracy Twins" (Scout comics). *Length:* 66 pages. *Journalistic Quality:* A well-written, thoughtfully conceived magazine. Photography and artwork are excellent. Illustrated in black and white and full color.

43 **Buried Treasure.** 1988. m. $15. Virginia Spencer. The Learning Exchange, 25935 Detroit Rd., Suite 331, Westlake, OH 44145. Illus. Sample. [*Aud:* Ages 8–12.]

Features: One October issue featured Halloween in Ireland, Scotland, and France. Numerous games, puzzles, and question-and-answer features are offered. According to the editor, "the contributors are educators, artists and children's counselors from the Northeast Ohio area." *Length:* 8 pages. *Journalistic Quality:* The material appears in typescript with a few line drawings. While it would not win prizes for appearance, it does offer the child a view of the primary holidays and events for each month.

Calliope. *See under* HISTORY.

Career World—Real World. *See under* YOUNG ADULT/OCCUPATIONS AND CAREERS.

44 **Chickadee.** 1979. 10/yr. $19. Catherine Ripley. Young Naturalist Foundation, 56 The
[CMG] Esplanade, Toronto, Ont. M5E 1A7, Canada. Illus. Circ: 100,000. Sample. Vol. ends: Dec. [*Indexed:* CMG. *Aud:* Ages 4–9.]

Features: Chickadee is crammed full of good things that will "interest children in their environment and the world around them"—the publisher's goal. A typical issue offers "Who Is in the March Today" (a story about muskrats), a hunt for hidden creatures in the march, and a "Which is not the same?" page. Each issue features a poster depicting an animal, "Daisy Dreamer" (cartoon strip), and "Hoot" (letters and pictures from readers). Answers to puzzles and questions are in each issue. *Length:* 32 pages. *Journalistic Quality:* This magazine is graphically pleasing, with excellent photography. The lettering throughout is large, colorful, and eye-catching. The headings are bold and contrasting and are complemented by attractive borders. This high-caliber publication is from the publisher of *Owl* (see Environment, Conservation, and Outdoor Recreation section), and is intended for the age level preceding *Owl*'s. Highly recommended.

Coulicou is a similar title published in French for French-speaking Canadian children. It is available from the publisher for $20 (Canadian) a year: Les Editions Heritage, 300 Avenue Arran, St. Lambert, Que. J4R 1K5, Canada.

45 **Children's Magic Window.** 1987. bi-m. $16.98. Finders Publg., 3718 Macalaster Dr. N.E., Minneapolis, MN 55421. Illus. Adv. Circ: 100,000. Sample. Vol. ends: Nov. [*Bk. rev:* 5, 30 words. *Aud:* Ages 6–13.]

Features: A digest-sized magazine, *Children's Magic Window* has a wide variety of articles and stories (wagon trains, sports figures, birds, comic book characters). Departments include "The Wishing Well" (new toys and games on the market), "Natural Wonders" (photo-story), "Things People Do," "Kids Like You," "Fun Facts," "That's Entertainment" (reviews of videos, books, and movies), and many others. Jokes and riddles, a coloring page, and a hidden-activity page are included in each issue. *Length:* 96 pages. *Journalistic Quality:* The stories and articles are diverse, well written, and brief. The graphics are varied as well. Black-and-white and color photos are used. The artwork and covers are pleasing. The small format (5″ × 7½″) of the magazine may be a minor flaw—issues could easily get lost in magazine stands.

Choices. *See under* YOUNG ADULT/HOME ECONOMICS.

Classical Calliope. *See* **Calliope** *under* HISTORY.

46   **Cobblestone.** 1980. m. $22.95. Carolyn P. Yoder. Cobblestone Publg., Inc., 30 Grove St., Peterborough, NH 03458. Illus. Circ: 42,000. Sample. Vol. ends: Dec. [*Indexed*: CMG. *Bk. rev*: 5, 50 words. *Aud*: Ages 8–14.]

Features: This is a one-theme-per-issue publication. Topics have included "Lighthouses," "The Constitution," "Jazz," the "U.S. Mint," and "Harriet Tubman." Each issue examines a part of America's past with skillfully conceived articles, photographs, songs, cartoons, poems, puzzles, recipes, biographies, maps, and contests. "Dear Ebenezer" is a letter-to-the-editor feature, and "Crazy Capers" is a regular cartoon. *Length:* 48 pages. *Journalistic Quality:* This small-format magazine is well organized. The writing is lucid and appealing. Black-and-white photographs and illustrations are of exceptional quality and the cover art is superb. A finely crafted magazine with an original approach to history. A winner.

Consumer Reports. *See under* YOUNG ADULT/CONSUMER EDUCATION.

47   **Creative Kids** (Formerly: *Chart Your Course*). 1980. 8/yr. $24. Fay L. Gold. GCT, Inc., P.O. Box 6448, 350 Weinacker Ave., Mobile, AL 36660-0448. Illus. Circ: 12,000. Vol. ends: May. [*Bk. rev*: 3, 160 words, signed. *Aud*: Ages 6–14.]

Features: This magazine is the "first magazine by and for gifted, creative and talented children," according to the publisher. Stories, poems, art, and music are submitted by children, parents, and teachers. Fun activites—such as mazes, scrambled words, and hidden words—are also included. "Snap the Shutter" is a two-page spread of photos taken by children. "Viewed and Reviewed" (books) is another regular feature. *Length:* 32 pages. *Journalistic Quality:* The magazine is printed on stock paper and is graphically pleasing.

48   **Cricket.** 1973. m. $29.97. Marianne Carus. Carus Corp., 315 Fifth St., Peru, IL 61354. Illus. Circ: 120,000. Vol. ends: Aug. [*Indexed*: CMG. *Aud*: Ages 6–12.]

Features: Children's literature, poems, stories, articles, songs, crafts, and jokes are the focus of *Cricket*. Regular features include "Letterbox" (letters from children to the *Cricket* characters); "Ugly Bird's Crossword Puzzle"; "Cricket and Ladybug" (cartoon); "Cricket League" (a story, art, or poetry contest); and "Old Cricket Says" (letters from the editor on any subject—tornados, archaeology, etc.). *Length:* 80 pages. *Journalistic Quality:* A high-quality, tasteful publication. Contributors are internationally known authors (Eleanor Estes, Lloyd Alexander, Jean Fritz) and illustrators (David McPhail, Tomie de Paola, Steven Gammell). Each issue is done in black and white and one other color. *Cricket* exposes children to a variety of writing styles and artwork in children's books. It helps to promote international understanding through stories from other countries. Highly recommended.

Current Biography. *See under* YOUNG ADULT/GENERAL INTEREST.

Current Consumer & Lifestudies. *See under* YOUNG ADULT/GENERAL INTEREST.

The Electric Company. *See* Kid City.

Flying. *See under* YOUNG ADULT/AVIATION AND SPACE SCIENCE.

Foxfire. *See under* YOUNG ADULT/GENERAL INTEREST.

Happy Times. *See under* RELIGION.

49   **Hidden Pictures Magazine.** 1989. bi-m. $17.70. Jan Keen. Highlights for Children, Inc., 2300 W. Fifth Ave., P.O. Box 269, Columbus, OH 43272-0002. Illus. Sample. Vol. ends: Dec. [*Aud*: Ages 5–12.]

Features: A new magazine by the people who publish *Highlights for Children*. Its pages contain much the same material—imaginative activities, including (literally) hidden pictures. The puzzles, riddles, games, and creative reading develop language skills as well as the ability to think and reason. *Length:* 32 pages. *Journalistic Quality:* One of the better of the children's group, this boasts numerous illustrations that are carefully done and well balanced.

50   **Highlights for Children.** 1946. 11/yr. $19.95. Kent L. Brown, Jr. Highlights for
 Children, Inc., 2300 W. Fifth Ave., P.O. Box 269, Columbus, OH 43272-0002. Illus. Circ: 2,800,000. Sample. Vol. ends: Dec. [*Indexed*: CMG. *Aud*: Ages 2–12.]

Features: The subtitle "Fun with a Purpose" gives some indication of the focus of *Highlights*—basic skills, creativity, and ideals for living. Issues contain poems, stories, puzzles, jokes, riddles, rebus stories, things to make, hidden pictures, matching, and find the picture. "Goofus and Gallant," a cartoon concerned with manners, is a regular. *Length:* 42 pages. *Journalistic Quality: Highlights* has colored illustrations on newsprint paper. The artwork reflects realistic pictures, softly textured. Pictures are racially and sexually balanced. A large variety of activities is offered—there is something for everyone.

51   **Hopscotch.** 1989. bi-m. $13.50. Donald P. Evans. Hopscotch, P.O. Box 10, Saratoga
 Springs, NY 12866. Illus. Circ: 4,000. [*Indexed*: CMG. *Aud*: Ages 6–12.]

Features: Subtitled "The Magazine for Young Girls." The 45 nicely illustrated pages are edited for 6- to 12-year-olds, "with youngsters 8, 9, and 10 the specific target age." A typical issue may open with a short story or feature, often with a social or historical slant; move on to a biographical sketch; offer a game or two, then narrative poems and puzzles; and conclude with a suggestion for a particular holiday or event. There are features specifically labeled science, pets, and so forth, and even short book reviews. Other features are "Cooking," "Poetry," "Puzzle," and "Potsy's Post Office." Some numbers focus on a single topic, such as the February/March 1990 issue on China. *Length:* 45 pages. *Journalistic Quality:* Most of the 1,000 or so word pieces are signed, as are the numerous photographs and line drawings. The young girl's point of view is stressed. The average reader is challenged rather than pampered. The writing is objective. No religious or political point of view is apparent. All in all a superior general magazine for the target audience.

52   **Kid City** (Formerly: *Electric Company*). 1974. m. $13.97. Maureen Hunter-Bone.
 Children's Television Workshop, One Lincoln Plaza, New York, NY 10023. Illus. Adv. Circ: 260,000. Sample. Vol. ends: Dec/Jan. [*Indexed*: CMG. *Bk. rev*: 3, 20 words. *Aud*: Ages 6–10.]

Features: Each issue is centered around a theme (e.g., ranches and cowboy life, the dark). A step up from *Sesame Street*, this magazine contains comic stories, true and strange facts, pencil activities, mathematics activities, crosswords, jokes, a make-your-own-cartoon page, and mazes. Children will be thoroughly entertained while learning mathematical and reading skills. *Length:* 32 pages. *Journalistic Quality:* This tightly constructed publication includes diversity in its writing as well as its artwork. The stories and articles are well organized. The activities are thoughtfully prepared and graphically adventurous.

53 **Kid Life and Times.** 1987. q. $11.95. William Hulmes. Kid Life, P.O. Box D, Bellport, NY 11713. Illus. Sample. [*Aud*: Ages 6–12.]

Features: Education is as important here as entertainment. There are good features and stories to encourage the young reader to use imaginative abilities and reading skills. There are the usual stories, although some of these are from the youngsters themselves. Various contests liven things up, including art and writing. *Length:* 36 pages. *Journalistic Quality:* An above-average magazine, this can be recommended for most children.

54 **Kidstuff.** 1981. m. $24. Sheila Debs. Guidelines Press, 1307 S. Killian Dr., Lake Park, FL 33403. Illus. [*Aud*: Ages 3–6.]

Features: These are activities for the teacher/parent who is helping the preschool child. Still, the various songs, puzzles, and the like can be enjoyed by the child directly. This title falls between a magazine for and a magazine about children. *Length:* 20 pages. *Journalistic Quality:* It functions primarily as an idea source for everything from bulletin boards to games. The quality of such directions is high and all is easy to understand.

55 **Ladybug.** 1990. m. $29.97. Carus Corp., 315 Fifth St., Peru, IL 61354. Illus. Vol. ends:
[CMG] Aug. [*Indexed*: CMG. *Aud*: Ages 2–7.]

Features: This is an edition of the successful and famous *Cricket*, by the same publisher, for a younger target audience. It is directed to ages 2 to 7 and their parents and contains numerous learning activities with a particular focus on reading and understanding. The fun of puzzle solving and an appreciation of the joys of reading are emphasized. Bright illustrations make up most of each issue. *Length:* 40 pages. *Journalistic Quality:* Skillfully edited and written, this follows the same high-quality standards as *Cricket*. It is by far the best magazine of its type for this age group. Highly recommended for parents and, of course, for all libraries serving youngsters.

56 **Lollipops.** 1986. 5/yr. $16.95. Jerry Aten. Good Apple, Inc., 1204 Buchana, Carthage, IL 62321. Illus. Circ: 15,000. [*Aud*: Ages 3–5.]

Features: This is a colorful magazine with numerous illustrations. The idea is to educate the child through simple activities offered for use by the teacher and the child, as well as the parent. Games, for example, teach the basics of grammar, and simple poems and songs reinforce the lesson. There are particularly good puzzles and riddles. A separate bibliography provides additional readings for the adult. *Length:* 25 pages. *Journalistic Quality:* Most of the magazine is to be read to the child. The stories are of such a quality that they will fascinate children and, equally important, rarely bore the adult.

Mad. *See under* YOUNG ADULT/GENERAL INTEREST.

57 **Market Street.** 1980. q. $2.95. Market Street, P.O. Box 33478, San Diego, CA 92103. Illus. [*Aud*: Ages 6–13.]

Features: Each issue is built around a particular theme, normally dealing with the economics of daily living from the point of view of the child or teenager. There are puzzles, good illustrations, stories, and the like. *Length:* 25 pages. *Journalistic Quality:* While suitable for older grades, most of the focus is on the elementary-level interests. A teacher guide is available. While some of this may appear a bit too fundamental, when one considers the age group, it is at least passable. More sophisticated children may wish to skip it.

58   **Mickey Mouse.** 1988. q. $7. Pat Berry. Welsh Publg. Group, Inc., 300 Madison Ave., New York, NY 10017. Illus. Adv. Sample. Vol. ends: Fall. [*Bk. rev*: 3, 35 words. *Aud*: Ages 4–8.]

Features: Famous Disney characters abound—all of Mickey's friends are included in this glossy publication from the Welsh Publishing Group, Inc. Regulars are "Message from Mickey," "Mickey Mail," "Goofy's Giggles" (jokes), "Minnie's Diary" (information on current TV stars), a poster, and "Family Timer" (things to do for family fun). *Length:* 40 pages. *Journalistic Quality:* The writing is adequate. A fast-paced, gimmicky publication—much of it is advertisements. Not much to it—not recommended.

59   **Muppet.** 1982. q. $7.50. Jim Lewis. Welsh Publg. Group, Inc., 300 Madison Ave., New York, NY 10017. Illus. Adv. Circ: 500,000. Sample. Vol. ends: Fall. [*Bk. rev*: 10, 60 words, signed. *Aud*: Ages 7–13.]

Features: The publisher states that this is a *"People magazine* for kids." Indeed, it features celebrity interviews, articles on rock and TV stars, and photographs of favorites from the entertainment industry. Regular departments are "The Muppet Mailbag," "Muppet Round Ups" (record reviews), "Coming Attractions" (movies, TV, and home video reviews), a Fraggle Rock and other Muppet characters cartoon, a Miss Piggy's advice column, and a Muppet centerfold. *Length:* 36 pages. *Journalistic Quality:* Humorous, upbeat writing style and pleasing graphics are characteristics of this glossy publication. Pure entertainment—likely to be popular with this age group.

National Geographic. *See under* YOUNG ADULT/GEOGRAPHY.

60   **News in a Nutshell.** 1989. 10/yr. $15. Judy Brown. News in a Nutshell, 35 Hilton Ave., Toronto, Ont. M5R 3E5, Canada. Illus. [*Aud*: Ages 10–13.]

Features: In-depth features and short articles cover Canadian news events and personalities. There is a nod to U.S. and international news. In addition there are short, illustrated pieces on everything from plants and animals to music. There is a one-page focus on cities and a fun page. *Length:* 8 pages. *Journalistic Quality:* This is well written and nicely illustrated with line drawings. The factual data are presented carefully, and difficult words and special terms are nicely defined. Particularly useful for Canadians, in and out of school.

61   **Our Kids.** 1988. m. $15.07. Jolene Davis. Our Kids, P.O. Box 40486, San Antonio, TX 78229. Illus. Adv. Circ: 30,000. Sample. [*Aud*: Ages 7–15.]

Features: This magazine offers events of interest to youngsters and their families in San Antonio and Houston (each city has its own magazine, but the two are basically the same except for place-of-event news). It might be dismissed as too parochial, but there is more. Each issue has numerous stories and features that will appeal to youngsters in any part of the country, for example, a piece on collecting, another on computers; games, puzzles, crafts; and so forth. *Length:* 46 pages. *Journalistic Quality:* There are numerous illustrations and the newsprint format is quite pleasing. Some of the features are for parents—for example, items on home child care, health news, educational features. The result is a magazine for both children and parents. Much of the circulation is controlled, hence free. Ask for a sample.

Penny Power. *See* **Zillions.**

62 **Sesame Street Magazine.** 1971. 10/yr. $14.97. Marge Kennedy. Children's Television Workshop, One Lincoln Plaza, New York, NY 10023. Illus. Adv. Circ: 1,200,000. Vol. ends: Dec. [*Indexed*: CMG. *Aud*: Ages 2–6.]

Features: Early learning concepts are featured via stories, poems, and activities with Bert, Ernie, and other familiar Sesame Street characters. The magazine follows the format of the popular television program—each issue is sponsored by a letter and a number. Issues are thematic and invite participation. Children will learn decision-making, listening, and directional skills without knowing it. There are drawing and cut-out pages and a photographic story of a family doing "typical" family things (buying new shoes, going to a restaurant). The "Parents' Guide" in the back of the magazine includes recipes, a health page, and tips on child rearing. *Length:* 48 pages. *Journalistic Quality:* The illustrations are colorful and simple. Pictures of entire objects are displayed, which is important for this age group. The information in the 16-page parent guide is accurate and informative.

63 **Snoopy.** 1987. q. $7.80. Louisa Campbell. Welsh Publg. Group, Inc., 300 Madison Ave., New York, NY 10017. Illus. Adv. Vol. ends: Fall. [*Bk. rev*: 5, 50 words. *Aud*: Ages 4–8.]

Features: The newest publication from the Welsh Publishing Group, Inc., *Snoopy* is composed of articles, stories, mazes, matching puzzles, recipes, and posters starring the famous Peanuts Gang. Every issue contains "A Snoopy Story" (rebus), "A Few Words from Linus," a "Please Read to Me" story, "Sally's Silly Riddles," "Lucy's Advice Column," and a 15-page parent section, which reviews books and provides tips on child care, pediatric health-care issues, and more. *Length:* 40 pages. *Journalistic Quality:* The graphics of this glossy magazine are stunning—clear, colorful artwork and good action photography. The quality of the writing is adequate. The subtitle states it is for preschoolers, but some of the articles and the humor would be lost on a preschooler. Sure to be popular with the young ones.

64 **Stone Soup.** 1973. 5/yr. $22. Gerry Mandel. Children's Art Foundation, P.O. Box 83, Santa Cruz, CA 95063. Illus. Circ: 9,000. Vol. ends: May. [*Bk. rev*: 2, 200 words, signed. *Aud*: Ages 6–13.]

Features: Stone Soup is a magazine by and for children. The average age of the authors is eleven; of the artists, six. Stories, poems, book reviews, and art are included. Photos of the artists and writers are a nice inclusion. Stories vary in length from one to four pages. SOme of the work in *Stone Soup* comes directly from the Children's Art Foundation School. This publication gives children from the United States and Canada an avenue for creative thought. *Length:* 48 pages. *Journalistic Quality:* The covers are in full color, with approximately 25 half-tone pictures. Stories and poems are appealing. *Stone Soup* is a forum for budding artists and authors. A quality publication.

65 **Surprises.** 1985. bi-m. $12.95. Jeanne Palmer. Surprises, P.O. Box 236, Chanhassen, MN 55317. Illus. Adv. Circ: 51,000. Sample. [*Aud*: Ages 6–12.]

Features: Subtitled "Activities for Today's Kids and Parents," this offers puzzles and games as well as easy-to-follow instructional projects. In the latter category, for example, one finds "clowning around," which shows the child how to make a clown's mask or bake a cake. Most material, though, is geared to teach the child spelling, reading, and mathematics—but always in a painless fashion. The people who think up the one- or two-page games and puzzles are to be commended as much for imagination as for an understanding of children. Most of the instuctions can be handled by a second or third grader. Those in lower grades will need a bit of help from a parent or teacher to get them started. *Length:* 50 pages. *Journalistic Quality:* The material is presented in a colorful format with passable drawings and diagrams. Advertising is at a minimum and more for the magazine itself than for an occasional book or encyclopedia.

66   **Tapori.** 1974. m. $7. Fanchette Clement-Fanelli. Fourth World Movement, 172 First Ave., New York, NY 10009. Illus. Circ: 2,000. [*Aud:* Ages 6–12.]

Features: A newsletter that is directed to younger children, this celebrates the delights of one world. Particular emphasis is put on the United Nations and the rights of the child. *Length:* 6 pages. *Journalistic Quality:* The mimeographed, hand-written letters and illustrations are imaginative enough to appeal to both children who can read and those who still require an adult's help. Incidentally, except for the insistence on peace, there is no political ax to grind.

67   **Think, Inc.** 1987. m. $15. Tamra Keller. Think, Inc., P.O. Box 5275, Arvada, CO 80005. Illus. Sample. [*Aud:* Ages 8–12.]

Features: Intended for children ages 8–12, this is a newsletter edited by an editorial consultant for a national textbook publisher. Between illustrations and simplified yet never insulting text, it is a good combination for the more imaginative child. There are numerous articles and quizzes that live up to the publication's title. Each number centers on a single topic, from junk food to solar energy and crystals. While the issues are in tune with the curriculum, they are neither academic nor stuffy. Quite the contrary. The children who use the newsletter delight in its fresh approach. In addition to the easy-to-read pieces, there is a section in each number that describes a career. *Length:* 6 to 12 pages. *Journalistic Quality:* The publication is accompanied by a useful guide for parents that suggests parallel learning activities. The overall quality is exceptionally high, both in terms of format and content.

68   **3-2-1 Contact.** 1979. 10/yr. $15.97. Jonathan Rosenbloom. Children's Television Work-
   shop, One Lincoln Plaza, New York, NY 10023. Illus. Adv. Circ: 400,000. Vol. ends: Dec. [*Indexed:* CMG. *Aud:* Ages 8–14.]

Features: Articles, puzzles, projects, and experiments cover a variety of topics. Features are a Peanuts cartoon, "Tomorrow's News Today" (brief science news stories), "Any Questions?" (answers to questions children pose), "The Bloodhound Gang" (a serialized mystery story), "Factoids, Extra" (an untypical maze), "Reviews of Software," and a word search with a twist. The short articles give just enough information to explain the subject but also entice youngsters to want to know more. *Length:* 40 pages. *Journalistic Quality:* Good photography and artwork combined with clear writing on interesting topics make *3-2-1 Contact* a success. Not standard fare, this title makes science fun.

69   **Wee Wisdom.** 1893. 10/yr. $8. Judy Gehrlein. Unity School of Christianity, Unity Village, MO 64065. Illus. Circ: 175,000. Sample. Vol. ends: Aug/Sept. Microform: UMI. [*Indexed:* CMG. *Aud:* Ages 6–12.]

Features: A nondenominational magazine, *Wee Wisdom* is the oldest children's magazine in continuous publication in the United States. Features include "Action Corner with Pete and Polly," "Dear Wee Wisdom," "Dear Readers," "Good Words Booster CLub," and "What's the Good Word?" Every issue contains stories, poems, crafts, hidden pictures, mazes, dot-to-dot puzzles, a color and fill-in-the-blank comic strip, and a calendar for the month. *Length:* 48 pages.

Journalistic Quality: Full-color cover with muted soft illustrations is characteristic. Available in Braille.

70   **Young Generation.** 1974. m. $13.80. Winston Lam. EPB Pubs. Pte., Ltd., 162 Bukit Merah Central, Singapore 0315. Illus. Adv. Circ: 80,000. Sample. [*Aud:* Ages 7–13.]

Features: This is a carefully illustrated children's magazine for Asian Americans, and for just about anyone else who enjoys unusual jokes, games, quizzes, stories, and so forth. Much of the material is in cartoon fashion with just the right dash of foolishness to appeal to children. The illustrations are fast-moving, fun, and well done. About three quarters of every issue is in English with the remainder in Chinese. *Length:* 40 pages. *Journalistic Quality:* Culturally it has appeal for any child. There may be an essay on the police; "How Many Learned to Fly," a fairy story about the Queen Bee; and a good folk yarn about Bigfoot. There are some obvious Chinese slants, such as a report on a Chinese school, but essentially it speaks to a universal audience.

71   **Zillions** (Formerly: *Penny Power*). 1980. bi-m. $13.95. Charlotte Baecher. Consumers
 Union of United States, Inc., 256 Washington St., Mount Vernon, NY 10553. Illus. Circ: 140,000. Sample. Vol. ends: June/July. [*Indexed*: CMG. *Aud*: Ages 8–14.]

Features: The goal of this *Consumer Reports* publication is to teach children to make informed decisions about money matters and to become smart consumers. (*Note*: According to the publisher this "is a transformation of *Penny Power*. . . . The penny we said had power 10 years ago is virtually obsolete.") Regular features abound: "I've Got a Question" (advice column), "Ad Madness" (spoof on advertising), "Commercial Break," "Loose Change," "Pick of the Flicks" (children's reviews of VCR movies), "Pen Power" (letters to the editor), "PPB Squad," and articles on movies, music, television shows, clothing, food, allowances, toys, home video games, and snack foods. The items tested and rated can be anything from headphones to peanut butter. It is a power-packed magazine. *Length:* 40 pages. *Journalistic Quality:* The layout is pleasing. The pace is varied and the artwork superb. The humorous, upbeat writing style is sure to grab and hold children's attention. An entertaining, one-of-a-kind publication.

SUBJECT MAGAZINES

There are few subject magazines primarily for children, that is, ages 4 to 14 years. Conversely, many of the magazines for young adults—ages 12 years and over—may be used, if only in part, in the school library and/or by the teacher in elementary and junior high or middle school. With this in mind the sections below are made up of two basic entries: (1) The annotated magazine itself; and (2) cross-references to young adult titles that can be found in the next section of this guide.

In view of the scarcity of children's subject magazines, there are no recommended titles, although in some areas this is evident depending on the age level and interest level of the title. Also, one may turn to the parallel young adult section to find (1) recommendations, some of which are suitable for children; and (2) a general introduction to the subject matter, which may be useful.

■ AMERICANS: BLACKS, INDIANS, LATINOS

Chispa. *See under* Science.

Claudia. *See under* YOUNG ADULT/LATIN AMERICA, LATINO (U.S.).

72   **Daybreak Star: the herb of understanding** (Formerly: *The Indian Reader*). 1975. m. $24 (Individuals, $16). Gail Stevens, Kathryn Oneite, and Sharon Mathers. United Indians of All Tribes Foundation, P.O. Box 99100, Seattle, WA 98199. Illus. Vol. ends: May. [*Aud:* Ages 9–14.]

Features: The best, if not the only, Native American magazine for students from the fourth to the eighth grade. Its pages are written and edited by students and adults. For the past two years, each issue has covered a different geographical area. The magazine also includes games and puzzles, and ends with review questions on the articles. *Daybreak* aims to integrate the curriculum areas of mathematics, science, literature, and creative writing. *Length:* 24 pages. *Journalistic Quality:* Student writers describe climate, housing, food, and clothing. There is always a legend from the area and charming drawings. Although based in Seattle, it has a national circulation. Highly recommended.

Ebony. *See under* YOUNG ADULT/AFRO-AMERICAN.

Hombre de Mundo. *See under* YOUNG ADULT/LATIN AMERICA, LATINO (U.S.).

Spice! *See under* YOUNG ADULT/AFRO-AMERICAN.

73   **Turtle Quarterly.** 1979. q. $10. Tim Johnson. Native American Center for the Living Arts, Inc., 25 Rainbow Mall, Niagara Falls, NY 14303. Illus. Adv. Circ: 3,000. Sample. Vol. ends: No. 4. [*Bk. rev:* Occasional, 200–300 words, signed. *Aud:* Ages 8–18.]

Features: An attractive, glossy magazine with a focus on the arts, crafts, and culture of the American Indian, primarily those of New York State. *Length:* 45 pages. *Journalistic Quality:* Especially good in the area of education. The authors and photographers are professors and Native Americans. This is an important title for teachers and those who wish to understand the roots of Native American society and government.

■ ARTS

See also: MUSIC AND DANCE

74   **African Arts.** 1967. q. $22. John F. Povey. African Studies Center, Univ. of California, Los Angeles, CA 90024-1310. Illus. Adv. Index. Circ: 5,000. Vol. ends: Aug. Microform: UMI. Reprint: UMI. [*Indexed:* ArtI. *Bk. rev:* 3, 200–700 words, signed. *Aud:* Ages 8–18.]

Features: African arts have exercised a strong influence on Western artists since the turn of the century. This is evident in each issue of this excellent overview. The 100 or so beautifully illustrated pages are complemented by six to eight articles ranging from current artists to anthropological findings. The quality of the reproductions and the writing is exceptional. The average high school student will enjoy the magazine. *Length:* 100 pages. *Journalistic Quality:* If the text is difficult, which it rarely is, one can turn to the superior art reproductions. Even the advertisements have a given appeal. Ranging over a wide period of time, and covering all of the arts from sculpture and beads to textiles and paintings, this is a basic journal for almost all high school collections, and may be considered by some in upper elementary grades.

75   **Carnegie Magazine.** 1927. bi-m. $12. Robert J. Gangewere. Carnegie Inst., 4400 Forbes Ave., Pittsburgh, PA 15213. Illus. Adv. Index. Circ: 13,000. Vol. ends: No. 6. Online: DIALOG. [*Aud:* Ages 10–18.]

Features: Here is an art magazine that can be read, if only in part, by those from 10 to 12 years and up. It is the only museum publication in continual circulation that speaks to a wide range of people and ages. The magazine opens with brief one-page discussions of art, literature, music, and science and then offers more thorough articles on a variety of topics, from plant collecting, dinosaur replicas, and the work of Thomas Eakins to the letters of George Bernard Shaw written to actress Mary Hamilton. *Length:* 40 pages. *Journalistic Quality:* Format and illustrations, especially those in color, resemble general-interest magazines such as *Time*, *Discovery*, and *Science News*. Its purpose is to "collect, preserve, interpret and exhibit objects from natural history and our cultural heritage" and in that spirit, it nicely succeeds.

Plays. *See under* YOUNG ADULT/THEATER.

■ AUTOMOBILES

Given that 16 years of age is the minimum age for driving in many states (it is older in others), there is no automobile magazine suitable for children. Conversely, there is great interest in the subject among youngsters. Librarians may wish to have some of the basic titles. The most suitable for junior high/middle school, ages 12–18 (and annotated in the Young Adult/Automobile section), are:

Auto Racing Digest
Car Craft
Cycle
Cycle Guide
Dirt Bike
Hot Rod
Motor Trend
Road & Track

■ COMICS

There are a number of comic books that may be suitable for younger children, and these are listed and annotated in the Young Adult/Comics section.
Comics younger children will enjoy include:

	Ages	Grades
Casper the Friendly Ghost	5–10	K–5
Walt Disney's Comics and Stories	5–18	K–12
Alf	5–18	K–12
Archie	6–14	1–9
Superboy	6–14	1–9
Teenage Mutant Ninja Turtles Adventures	6–14	1–9
G.I. Joe: A Real American Hero	7–14	2–9
The Real Ghostbusters titles	7–16	2–10
Superman titles	10–18	5–12

Spider-Man titles	10–18	5–12
Wonder Woman	10–18	5–12
Justice League titles	10–18	5–12
Avengers titles	10–18	5–12
Classics Illustrated	12–18	6–12
Teenage Mutant Ninja Turtles	12–18	6–12
Batman titles	12–18	6–12
The 'Nam	12–18	6–12

■ **COMPUTERS**

There are no computer magazines per se for children, although some young adult titles, depending on the child's computer experience, are suitable for consideration (and annotated in the Young Adult/Computers section). For ages 12–18, these include:

Ahoy!	InCider
Analog Computing	Info
Compute	Nibble
Family and Home Office Computing	Rainbow

■ **CURRENT EVENTS**

There are no large circulation general news-and-opinion or current-events magazines directed to young adults or adults that are suitable for children. Most require at least a senior high school reading and comprehension level, and the three leaders (*Time*, *Newsweek*, and *U.S. News and World Report*) suggest the average reader will have a minimum of two years of college.

Given this situation, the average school library will have the three major titles as much for the librarians and teachers as for the few children who may find a useful article in one of them via the major indexes.

For listings of titles, see Classroom Publications: General Current Events, in this section, as well as listings in the Young Adult/News and Opinion section.

■ **ENVIRONMENT, CONSERVATION, AND OUTDOOR RECREATION**

Adirondack Life. *See under* YOUNG ADULT/ENVIRONMENT, CONSERVATION, AND OUTDOOR RECREATION.

Audubon. *See under* YOUNG ADULT/BIRDS.

Chickadee. *See in this section under* GENERAL MAGAZINES.

The Conservationist. *See under* YOUNG ADULT/ENVIRONMENT, CONSERVATION, AND OUTDOOR RECREATION.

Farmer's Digest. *See under* YOUNG ADULT/AGRICULTURE.

Field & Stream. *See under* YOUNG ADULT/FISHING AND HUNTING.

Fishing Facts. *See under* YOUNG ADULT/FISHING AND HUNTING.

Horse & Rider. *See under* YOUNG ADULT/HORSES.

Horseman. *See under* YOUNG ADULT/HORSES.

76 **International Wildlife.** 1971. bi-m. $16. Bob Strohm. Natl. Wildlife Federation, 8925
 Leesburg Pike, Vienna, VA 22184. Illus. Circ: 340,000. Microform: UMI. [*Indexed*: CMG,
MI, RG. *Aud*: Ages 10–18.]

Features: With the firmly stated editorial creed "to create and encourage an
awareness among the people of the world of the need for wise use and proper
management of those resources of the Earth upon which our lives and welfare
depend: the soil, the air, the water, the forests, the minerals, the plant life, and the
wildlife," this is one of the best magazines for this audience. *Length:* 50 pages.
Journalistic Quality: With beautiful color illustrations and clear use of language,
it presents the aspects of nature that exist all around us but are seldom noticed by
the average person. It is international in scope and the photography is excellent.
A very good item for the browsing area, it is well worth the modest cost of the
subscription.

Mother Earth News. *See under* YOUNG ADULT/ALTERNATIVES.

The National Future Farmer. *See under* YOUNG ADULT/AGRICULTURE.

77 **National Wildlife.** 1962. bi-m. $16. Bob Strohm. Natl. Wildlife Federation, 8925
Leesburg Pike, Vienna, VA 22184. Illus. Adv. Circ: 850,000. Vol. ends: Oct/Nov.
Microform: B&H, UMI. [*Indexed*: CMG, RG. *Aud*: Ages 10–18.]

Features: One of the best-known and best general magazines devoted to the
protection of the environment. The pages contain mainly color illustrations with
only a few black-and-white. Sharing an editorial creed with *International Wildlife*, this magazine covers a variety of topics ranging from toxic wastes to bears,
to wasps, to marmots, to building forest service roads. *Length:* 58 pages. *Journalistic Quality:* The editorial leadership has passed from John Louis Strohm, who
established the tone and range of the publication, to Bob Strohm, who seems to
be intent on continuing the good quality.

Outdoor Life. *See under* YOUNG ADULT/FISHING AND HUNTING.

78 **Owl Magazine.** 1976. 10/yr. $19. Debora Pearson. Young Naturalist Foundation, 56
The Esplanade, Suite 304, Toronto, Ont. M5E 1A7, Canada. Illus. Circ: 110,000. Sample.
Vol. ends: Dec. [*Indexed*: CMG. *Aud*: Ages 6–14.]

Features: The goal of *Owl* is to interest children in their environment and the
world around them. Articles, stories, jokes, crossword puzzles, and experiments
are standard fare. Regular features include "Dr. Zed's Experiments," a poster,
"Might Mites" (comic strip about three children who can shrink), "Hoot Club
News" (contest information), and "Whatsit" (a photo identification puzzle).
Length: 31 pages. *Journalistic Quality:* Fluently written articles and stories that
are informative but enjoyable are the rule. The artwork is especially appealing—
colorful headings and excellent photographs make for a nicely structured magazine.

Hibou is the French-language version of this magazine for French-speaking
Canadian children. It is available from the publisher, Les Editions Heritage, 300
Ave. Arran, Saint Lambert, P.Q., J4K 1K5, Canada. The cost is $20 Canadian a
year.

79 Ranger Rick. 1967. m. $15. Gerald Bishop. Natl. Wildlife Federation, 8925 Leesburg

Pike, Vienna, VA 22184. Illus. Circ: 700,472. Sample. Vol. ends: Dec. Microform: B&H,
UMI. [*Indexed*: CMG. *Aud*: Ages 6–12.]

Features: Plants and animals around the world are the primary focus of this
nature magazine. Stories, articles, puzzles, and games on trees, conservation
issues, and animals are featured. Some regulars include "Dear Ranger Rick"
(letters to the editor), "Adventures of Wise Old Owl," and "Whooo Knows?"
(letters to Wise Old Owl). Subscribers receive a membership card to the Ranger
Rick Nature Club, a sticker, and a poster. *Length:* 47 pages. *Journalistic Quality:*
Excellent photos combined with science facts presented in a fun way make for a
high-quality product.

Sierra. *See under* YOUNG ADULT/ENVIRONMENT, CONSERVATION, AND OUTDOOR REC-
REATION.

Wilderness. *See under* YOUNG ADULT/ENVIRONMENT, CONSERVATION, AND OUT-
DOOR RECREATION.

■ FAN MAGAZINES

Almost all of the fan magazines—that is, those dedicated to celebrating the lives, loves,
and cares of movie and television stars—are suitable for younger children as well as
young adults. It depends more on the maturity of the individual than on any arbitrary
age/grade bracket. Those that may be particularly suitable for some children are listed
below, but others, almost as good for the age bracket, will be found in the Young
Adult/Fan Magazines section.

Big Bopper	Ages 10–18
16 Magazine	Ages 12–18
Splice	Ages 11–14
Super Teen	Ages 11–14
Teen Beat	Ages 11–14
Teen Generation	Ages 11–14
Tiger Beat	Ages 11–14
Wow	Ages 12–18

■ FOREIGN LANGUAGE

The majority of foreign-language publications are graded by ability in the language rather
than by chronological age. There are three foreign-language publications that are suitable
for children who speak Spanish, French, or others as a first language and English as a
second language. Among these (annotated in the Young Adult section), the following are
suitable for children:

Amigo	Ages 9–12
Amisol	Ages 6–9
Bonjour	Ages 6–8

See the Young Adult/Foreign Language section for listings of titles.

■ **GAMES AND HOBBIES**

In addition to the titles listed here, almost all publications in the Young Adult/Hobbies section are suitable for children who have enough interest and reading ability in the particular subject area described. See also the Young Adult/Models section for titles that may be useful for children, at least when assisted by adults, or at the junior high level.

Coins. *See under* YOUNG ADULT/HOBBIES.

Computer Entertainer. *See under* YOUNG ADULT/GAMES.

Crafts 'n Things. *See under* YOUNG ADULT/CRAFT AND RECREATIONAL PROJECTS.

80 Dragon. 1976. m. $30. Roger Moore. TSR, Inc., Publg., P.O. Box 756, Lake Geneva, WI 53147. Illus. Adv. Circ: 120,000. Sample. [*Aud:* Ages 8–18.]

Features: The sole purpose of this illustrated magazine is to show the reader different approaches to Dungeons and Dragons, a game that is very popular among young people. Various strategies of play are suggested. There are interviews with winners and numerous features that point out new equipment and new approaches to the contest. *Length:* 40 pages. *Journalistic Quality:* While some of this information is suitable for elementary grades, *Dragon* is primarily of interest at the high school level.

81 Frisbee Disc World (Formerly: *Frisbee World*). 1976. bi-m. $5. Dan Roddick. Intl. Frisbee Disc Assn., P.O. Box 970, San Gabriel, CA 91778. Illus. Circ: 12,000. [*Aud:* Ages 8–18.]

Features: This periodical has the usual features and articles plus interviews with Frisbee buffs. There is some coverage of local events, and each issue has a listing of regional and local chapters of the sponsoring association. *Length:* 25 pages. *Journalistic Quality:* Although Frisbee in the 1990s is not as popular as it was in the 1970s, it is still very much around. This magazine is a good one for fans.

Games. *See under* YOUNG ADULT/GAMES.

82 Pack-O-Fun. 1975. q. $4.95. Marie Petersen. Pack-O-Fun, Inc., 14 Main St., Park Ridge, IL 60068. Illus. Vol. ends: Fall. [*Aud:* Ages 5–13.]

Features: Some features included are "Craft Recipe," "Kids in the Kitchen," "Pen Pals" (two-page feature), "Idea Exchange," and "News from You." Primarily, this magazine contains ideas for quick gifts to make for holidays and seasonal events, party crafts and games (all made from common household objects—paper plates, spools, gum wrappers, plastic bottles), word puzzles, and experiments. *Length:* 46 pages. *Journalistic Quality:* Primarily black-and-white illustrations with some color. The instructions are clearly written, and a large variety of crafts is presented.

Popular Mechanics. *See under* YOUNG ADULT/CRAFT AND RECREATIONAL PROJECTS.

Popular Photography. *See under* YOUNG ADULT/PHOTOGRAPHY.

Workbench. *See under* YOUNG ADULT/CRAFT AND RECREATIONAL PROJECTS.

■ **GEOGRAPHY AND TRAVEL**

Canada and the World. *See under* YOUNG ADULT/CANADA.

83   **China Pictorial.** 1951. m. $15. Qian Hao. China Pictorial, Huayuancun, Beijing, China. Illus. Adv. Index. Circ: 1,000,000. Microform: B&H, MIM. [*Aud*: Ages 10–18.]

   Features: There are brief articles, but one can appreciate the picture given of modern China without reading them. The text is simple enough that those with a beginning understanding of reading will have little difficulty with most of the words. The oversize magazine focuses on the scenery of China, the life of the people, and works of art. A propaganda tool, its main purpose is to show the good life in China. *Length:* 35 pages. *Journalistic Quality:* Thanks to numerous pictures and a minimum of text, this colorful journal is ideal for elementary grades as well as high school classes. Although produced by the government of China, it offers a useful introduction to the country.

Discovery. *See under* YOUNG ADULT/GEOGRAPHY.

84   **Equinox.** 1982. 6/yr. $22. Bart T. Robinson. Telemedia Publg. Subs. to: 7 Queen Victoria Rd., Camden East, Ont. KOK 1JO, Canada. Illus. Adv. Circ: 166,500. Sample. Vol. ends: No. 6. Microform: MML. [*Indexed*: CMI, CanI. *Aud*: Ages 12–18.]

   Features: With hyperbole and élan, this magazine with its five or six well-illustrated feature articles identifies itself as a magazine of Canadian discovery with "journeys to the stars, the depths of the oceans, the roof of the world and the heart of the animal wilderness and beyond the boundless vistas of imagination!" Content is not restricted to Canada. Articles may cover highly photogenic animals like pandas and gorillas or scenic spots like the Guilin caves in China and the Costa Rica rain forest, which Canadians, among others, helped to purchase and so preserve. The regular departments review some science, and "Habitat" is a chronicle of environmental change. *Equinox* styles itself, a trifle inaccurately, as Canada's answer to the *National Geographic. Length:* 42 pages. *Journalistic Quality:* It is never dull in presentation and is never off the popular mark with its coverage. Desirable in junior and senior high school libraries and generally recommended for public libraries.

85   **Focus.** 1950. q. $12. Janet Crane. Amer. Geographical Soc., 156 Fifth Ave., Suite 600, New York, NY 10010. Illus. Index. Vol. ends: Fall. Microform: UMI. Reprint: Kraus. [*Indexed*: RG. *Aud*: Ages 12–18.]

   Features: To enable one to study the world methodically is the purpose of this outstanding magazine, prepared by professional geographers with young adults and some younger children in mind. *Length:* 36 pages. *Journalistic Quality:* Departments include "Weatherwatch" and a travel department called "Destinations." Four or five articles in each issue, each with several large pictures and maps, attempt to "put the knowledge and experience of geographers, and those with affinities to geography, in a readily available format." This is a good source of geographical information.

Murzilka. *See under* YOUNG ADULT/USSR AND EASTERN EUROPE.

National Geographic. *See under* YOUNG ADULT/GEOGRAPHY.

86 **National Geographic World.** 1975. m. $12.95. Pat Robbins. Natl. Geographic Soc., 17th and M Sts. N.W., Washington, DC 20036. Illus. Index. Circ: 1,300,000. Sample. Vol. ends: Dec. Microform: UMI. [*Indexed*: CMG, MI, RG. *Aud*: Ages 8–13.]

Features: This general-interest magazine gives brief coverage of a wide variety of topics—nature, art, geography, underwater exploration, and space. Every issue contains "Kids Did It" (a brief paragraph on unique accomplishments of children around the world), a photo identification activity, a glossy poster, and "Why in the World" (answers to questions children ask, e.g., How can earthworms see underground?). *Length:* 31 pages. *Journalistic Quality:* The writing is upbeat and will captivate youngsters. The high-quality photos that have been the backbone of the adult magazine appear here too. The drawn artwork is also colorful and appealing. Winner of numerous honors, *National Geographic World* is top of the line. Highly recommended.

Soviet Life. *See under* YOUNG ADULT/USSR AND EASTERN EUROPE.

■ **HEALTH**

87 **Child Life.** 1921. 8/yr. $13.95. Steve Charles. Children's Better Health Inst., Benjamin Franklin Literary and Medical Soc., Inc., 1100 Waterway Blvd., P.O. Box 567, Indianapolis, IN 46206. Illus. Adv. Circ: 130,000. Sample. Vol. ends: Dec. Microform: B&H, UMI. [*Indexed*: CMG. *Aud*: Ages 7–9.]

Features: A small format encompasses health-related articles and stories. Also included are art activities, hidden pictures, jokes, poems, recipes, dot-to-dots, and word finds. "Fitness 500" (health superheroes) is a regular cartoon. "Ask Dr. Cory" (a medical advice column) and "You Pictured It" (readers' drawings) are also regulars. *Length:* 46 pages. *Journalistic Quality:* Simply told stories, lively, interesting articles, and a varied format combine to make each issue appealing. Publisher erroneously claims it is the oldest children's magazine in America.

88 **Children's Digest.** 1950. 8/yr. $13.95. Elizabeth Rinck. Children's Better Health Inst., Benjamin Franklin Literary and Medical Soc., Inc., 1100 Waterway Blvd., P.O. Box 567, Indianapolis, IN 46206. Illus. Adv. Circ: 300,000. Sample. Vol. ends: Dec. [*Indexed*: CMG. *Bk. rev*: 2, 170 words, signed. *Aud*: Ages 8–10.]

Features: Mazes, cartoons, crafts, poems, hidden pictures, word puzzles, dot-to-dots, recipes, jokes, and riddles appear in this magazine. Features consist of "Page of Poetry," "Jokes and Riddles," "Mirthworms" (a comic strip), "Ask Dr. Cory" (a two-page advice column), "Book Beat" (book reviews), "What Do You Think?" (readers' opinions), and "Tim Tyme" (a comic strip). The articles cover health, sports, nutrition, and exercise. *Length:* 46 pages. *Journalistic Quality:* Illustration and writing are adequate. The word "Children's" in the title may be a put-off to children in this age bracket. Recommended only if additional material on this subject is needed.

89 **Children's Playmate Magazine.** 1929. 8/yr. $13.95. Elizabeth Rinck. Children's Better Health Inst., Benjamin Franklin Literary and Medical Soc., Inc., 1100 Waterway Blvd., P.O. Box 567, Indianapolis, IN 46206. Illus. Adv. Circ: 290,000. Vol. ends: Mar. [*Indexed*: CMG. *Aud*: Ages 5–7.]

Features: The elements of this magazine include stories, poems, articles, hidden pictures, recipes, matching, word puzzles, book reviews, jokes, and riddles. "Lines That Rhyme" is a page of poems sent in by children on health, exercise, good food, and safety. "Ask Dr. Cory" (questions and answers on health-related issues) is also a feature, as is a two-page cartoon called "Jet and Rocket Spac eAge Pals." *Length:* 48 pages. *Journalistic Quality:* Cartoon-style illustrations predominate. The graphics are adequate. The writing is patronizing, and some of the dialogue unrealistic. Not recommended.

Current Health I. *See in this section under* CLASSROOM PUBLICATIONS: SUBJECT.

90

Humpty Dumpty's Magazine. 1952. 8/yr. $13.95. Christina French Clark. Children's Better Health Inst., Benjamin Franklin Literary and Medical Soc., Inc., 1100 Waterway Blvd., P.O. Box 567, Indianapolis, IN 46206. Illus. Adv. Circ: 600,000. Sample. Vol. ends: Dec. Microform: B&H, UMI. [*Indexed:* CMG. *Aud:* Ages 4–6.]

Features: Supposedly a health, nutrition, and safety magazine, this title seems to have more of a general-interest focus. Included in each issue are hidden pictures, a rebus story, connect the dots, stories, poems, and activities. "Humpty at Home" (a black-and-white comic strip), "You Draw the Pictures" (artwork sent in by readers, reduced to a very small size), and "Ask Dr. Cory" (questions and answers on health from parents) are regulars. *Length:* 47 pages. *Journalistic Quality:* The vocabulary words for the easy-to-read stories are a bit difficult for this age group in some cases, and the graphics and layout are somewhat dull. Not recommended.

91

Jack and Jill. 1938. 8/yr. $13.95. Steve Charles. Children's Better Health Inst., Benjamin Franklin Literary and Medical Soc., Inc., 1100 Waterway Blvd., P.O. Box 567, Indianapolis, IN 46206. Illus. Adv. Circ: 500,000. Sample. Vol. ends: Dec. Microform: UMI. [*Indexed:* CMG. *Aud:* Ages 6–8.]

Features: The articles in *Jack and Jill* encourage children to practice good health habits. Most of the articles and stories relate to health, hygiene, exercise, nutrition, or safety, but general articles are included as well. Word games, recipes, poems, jokes, and puzzles are typical. "Mirthworms" (a cartoon), a "Peanuts" cartoon, "Did You Know?" (questions and answers on health), and "Ask Dr. Cory" are in each issue. *Length:* 47 pages. *Journalistic Quality:* This is one of eight magazines published by the institute—a lot of overlapping in age ranges seems to exist (i.e., 6–8 years, 7–9 years). The writing is not particularly engaging; some of the print is very small. The artwork is adequate. Not recommended.

92

Stork. 1984. 8/yr. $11.95. Deborah E. Black. Children's Better Health Inst., Benjamin Franklin Literary and Medical Soc., Inc., 1100 Waterway Blvd., P.O. Box 567, Indianapolis, IN 46206. Illus. Adv. Sample. Vol. ends: Dec. [*Aud:* Ages 1–3.]

Features: The newest publication from the Children's Better Health Institute contains stories, poetry, and craft activities (pinwheels, masks). "Mirthworm" (comic strip) and "Ask Dr. Cory" (a question-and-answer forum for parents) are regular features. Typical activities are "Which One Is Different?," "Peek-a-Boo," and "What's Wrong with This Picture?" A nice feature on the last page is the "Baby of the Month" photo. *Length:* 47 pages. *Journalistic Quality:* The illustrations lack vitality, the writing is flat, and the activities are not really age-appropriate. Not recommended.

93   **Turtle.** 1979. 8/yr. $11.95. Beth Wood Thomas. Children's Better Health Inst., Benjamin Franklin Literary and Medical Soc., Inc., 1100 Waterway Blvd., P.O. Box 567, Indianapolis, IN 46206. Illus. Adv. Circ: 370,000. Sample. Vol. ends: Dec. [*Aud:* Ages 2–5.]

      Features: Incorporated in every issue are poems, stories, pencil activities (alphabet, numbers, shapes), puzzles, hidden pictures, dot-to-dots, bedtime stories, and rebus rhymes. Regulars are "Cousin Cooter," "Our Own Pictures" (several pages of small-size pictures sent in by readers), "Ask Dr. Cory" (questions and answers of a pediatric nature), and one page devoted to parents and teachers. *Length:* 47 pages. *Journalistic Quality:* The illustrations are small and uninteresting. Most of the activities are not particularly engaging. Misses the mark. Not recommended.

■ **HISTORY**

      American Heritage. *See under* Young Adult/History.

      American History Illustrated. *See under* Young Adult/History.

94   **The Beaver.** 1920. 6/yr. $19. Christopher Dafoe. Hudson's Bay Co., Hudson's Bay House, 450 Portage Ave., Winnipeg, Man. R3C OEY, Canada. Illus. Adv. Circ: 29,200. Sample. Microform: MML. [*Indexed:* CanI. *Bk. rev:* 3, 500–700 words, signed. *Aud:* Ages 8–14.]

      Features: A popular magazine for both younger children and teenagers, this can be recommended for all school and public libraries. *The Beaver* expands on its title by explaining that while the magazine explores Canada's history, it is not exclusively the Northern and Northwestern history that was historically the primary focus of the Governor and Company of Adventurers Trading into Hudson's Bay. Naturally, articles on this distinctively Canadian company often appear, but this is not a company/trade journal, and such articles are an important contribution to understanding the development of commerce and the settlement and expansion westward in Canada. *Length:* 40 pages. *Journalistic Quality:* With a long-standing reputation for excellent illustrations and readable presentation, this magazine offers a variety of articles on indigenous crafts and industry, art and literature, social custom and history, on the North and its peoples.

95   **Calliope: world history for young people** (Formerly: *Classical Calliope*). 1990.

5/yr. $17.95. Rosalie F. Baker and Charles F. Baker III. Cobblestone Publg., Inc., 30 Grove St., Peterborough, NH 03458. [*Indexed:* CMG. *Aud:* Ages 9–15.]

      Features: From the publishers of *Cobblestone: The History Magazine for Young People* and *Faces: The Magazine about People*, a new expanded *Calliope* offers quality resources for enriching the world history curriculum. Designed to help young readers understand how historical events intertwine and interrelate, each issue probes a theme in depth. The inaugural issue examines the motivations of explorers of the mysterious East, with star billing given to the ancient Egyptian mariners, Alexander the Great, Marco Polo, Christopher Columbus, and the fabled Prester John. Thematically related word games and crossword puzzles of different levels of difficulty mix delight with instruction. This magazine is highly visual, with useful maps and stimulating photographs. Regular columns include "Fun with Words," "Time Line Facts," and "The Muse's Corner," the last presenting a topic problematic for past as well as present civilizations. Insight into the differences between Western and Eastern cultures, in ancient and medieval times and today, can in the editors' words "set the stage for better relations between these two parts of the world." Issues are promised on epic heroes, major naval and land battles, and "travel" in time from Byzantium to Constantinople to present-day Istanbul. *Length:* 50 pages. *Journalistic Quality:* A fine resource to initiate young minds into the excitement inherent in the remembrance of things past. Written for youngsters, but will also intrigue teachers. Curriculum planners will find much of value

Cobblestone. *See in this section under* GENERAL MAGAZINES.

Early American Life. *See under* YOUNG ADULT/HISTORY.

96 **The Goldfinch.** 1980. q. $10. Carolyn Hardesty. State Historical Soc. of Iowa, 402 Iowa Ave., Iowa City, IA 52240. Illus. Sample. [*Aud:* Ages 9–13.]

Features: This is a nicely illustrated magazine that is carefully edited for children and teenagers. The historical material is crafted via the usual short features and articles, as well as through games, puzzles, contests, and so forth. While the focus is on Iowa, there is material that gives a broader picture of the United States and the Middle West. *Length:* 32 pages. *Journalistic Quality:* This is a carefully edited magazine and one of the best available at the local/regional level.

97 **The Green Mountaineer.** 1981. 3/yr. $5. Vermont Historical Soc., 109 State St., Montpelier, VT 06602. Illus. Circ: 4,000. [*Aud:* Ages 8–11.]

Features: The content is from Vermont and New England history and each issue is built around a theme. The illustrated pages of this magazine are a delight to the young eye. There is judicious use of line drawings, photographs, and other black-and-white illustrations, which are found on almost every page. The text, including quite marvelous letters to the editor, moves from a colorful description of a skyscraper to "footpaths in the wilderness." Many stories are followed by a list of the more difficult words, with definitions. The games, puzzles, and craft projects follow the theme of the issue. *Length:* 18 pages. *Journalistic Quality:* Recommended for school and public libraries in any part of the country. The material is universal in its appeal.

98 **Roots** (Formerly: *Gopher Historian*). 1972. 3/yr. $5. Mary Nord. Minnesota Historical Soc., 240 Summit Ave., St. Paul, MN 55102. Circ: 4,500. Sample. [*Aud:* Ages 10–14.]

Features: This is quite typical of several local historical society publications for children—this one ideal for ages 10 to 14. The scope is limited to Minnesota historical events and regional and national personalities who had an influence on Minnesota history. There are excellent illustrations, and the short articles are written for the young person with an interest in the subject. *Length:* 42 pages. *Journalistic Quality:* Material is factual, and never cute. While of limited interest to those outside of the state, it serves here as an example of what may be available. Librarians should consult with their city, county, and state historical societies for information on such magazines, not to mention brochures, exhibits, and other pertinent activities.

■ **LANGUAGE ARTS**

Analog Science Fiction/Science Fact. *See under* YOUNG ADULT/FICTION.

99 **Bear Essential News for Kids.** 1979. m. Free. James Williams. Bear Essential News for Kids, 2406 S. 24th St., Phoenix, AZ 85034. Illus. Adv. Circ: 450,000. Sample. [*Aud:* Ages 5–12.]

Features: This free publication is for children and parents interested in creative writing. Most of the material consists of contributors' writing. There are other features and illustrations, but it is pretty slim going in terms of education. *Length:* 30 pages. *Journalistic Quality:* It is assumed that readers will purchase the numerous advertised items and services directed to parents and children. Because it is free, it is worth considering.

100 **Chart Your Course!** 1980. 8/yr. $20. Fay L. Gold. G/C/T Publg. Co., Inc., P.O. Box 6448, Mobile, AL 36660. Illus. Circ: 10,000. Sample. Vol. ends: May. [*Aud:* Ages 8–14.]

Features: The publisher claims that this is "the world's first magazine by and for gifted, creative and talented children." The content depends on submissions by young contributors, but each issue usually includes articles, prose, poetry, reviews, essays, puzzles, games, art photos, and comics. Regular features are "Write Away, Right Away!" (a list of pen pals) and "Letters to the Editor." *Length:* 40 pages. *Journalistic Quality:* This unique magazine is printed on heavy stock paper, and the illustrations are done primarily in one or two colors. The attractive layout offers variety and invites children to look, read, and do. A great forum for budding authors, illustrators, and photographers.

101 **Children's Album.** 1984. bi-m. Free. Kathy Madsen. EGW Publg., 1320 Galaxy Way, Concord, CA 94520. Illus. Adv. Circ: 20,000. Sample. [*Aud:* Ages 8–13.]

Features: A free publication that stresses the creative writing skills of children in the elementary grades. (It is sent at no charge to schools and libraries, although for individuals the subscription is $12 a year.) In addition to the emphasis on writing, there is an interest in teaching the joys of working with crafts and art. *Length:* 34 pages. *Journalistic Quality:* Numerous illustrations and how-to-do-it projects are intelligent and well within the grasp of the average reader. The magazine is well edited.

102 **Free Spirit: news & views on growing up.** 1987. 5/yr. $10. Judy Galbraith. Free Spirit, 123 N. Third St., Minneapolis, MN 55401. Illus. Adv. Circ: 3,000. [*Aud:* Ages 11–18.]

Features: The primary feature of this magazine is the voices of the readers, who are encouraged to provide problems, solutions, and discussions. *Length:* 8–12 pages. *Journalistic Quality:* This is edited for above-average teenagers and will appeal primarily to them and their parents. The subject matter—from how to pass tests to how to understand others—is nicely handled, and most of the advice seems sound enough. *Note:* About one-third of the circulation is free, that is, the editor is selling the audience as much as the content in a controlled circulation magazine. Librarians should request a free subscription.

Merlyn's Pen. *See under* YOUNG ADULT/JOURNALISM AND WRITING.

103 **Prism.** 1985. bi-m. $19.95. T. C. Coyne. Prism, P.O. Box 030464, Fort Lauderdale, FL 33303. Illus. Adv. Sample. [*Aud:* Ages 10–18.]

Features: Young people seeking a place to publish or trying to find pen pals or both will turn to *Prism*. The issues are made up entirely of contributions from young readers. The poetry, prose, and essays vary in quality, yet all reflect a magnificent optimism about life, the country, and the future. *Length:* 50 pages.

Journalistic Quality: The self-confidence of these young authors may be typical of the "gifted and talented," for whom the magazine is edited. The middle-class, sunny focus is often on a single topic such as love or the Constitution. The magazine may inspire young writers to send in samples of their work. One could do worse.

Quill & Scroll. *See under* Young Adult/Journalism and Writing.

Read. *See in this section under* Classroom Publications: Subject.

Scholastic Action. *See in this section under* Classroom Publications: Subject.

Seedlings Series. *See* Short Story International.

104 **Shoe Tree: the literary magazine by and for children.** 1985. q. $15. Joyce McDonald. Natl. Assn. for Young Writers, P.O. Box 452, Belvidere, NJ 07823. Illus. Sample. [*Aud:* Ages 8–14.]

Features: The National Association for Young Writers (NAYW) has a lofty aspiration: "Helping Children Write to the Top." At a time when the National Assessment of Educational Progress has found the writing skills of children dismally lacking (of 17-year-olds, 76 percent could not write an imaginative description and 80 percent could not write a persuasive letter; scores were more abysmal for younger groups), it is imperative to find ways to reward youngsters' efforts to excel in creative verbal expression. *Shoe Tree* is named for the ancient legendary oak tree of Belvidere, in whose shade folk paused to put on shoes before entering church—and to exchange stories with rarely seen neighbors. The magazine features creative writing, artwork, and book reviews by children from five to fourteen. In the column "Author to Author," an adult talks to young writers as peers; "Branching Out" gives "Exercises for Creative Growth" (suitable for independent or directed use). *Length:* Varies. *Journalistic Quality:* The quality of the creative efforts is high, and any youthful writer/artist can be proud to be showcased here. Teachers and librarians will value this to spark the imaginations of the talented in their classrooms and libraries.

105 **Short Story International: Seedlings Series.** 1981. q. $15. Sylvia Tankel. Intl. Cultural Exchange, 6 Sheffield Rd., Great Neck, NY 11020. Illus. Sample. Vol. ends: Dec. [*Aud:* Ages 10–12.]

Features: Tales from other lands are reprinted in this quarterly. It comes in a paperback format, but is sent through the mail second class. Each issue contains six to eight short adventure stories from around the world. Issues reviewed contained stories from the United States, China, India, the USSR, Japan, Canada, and Tanzania, to name a few. *Length:* 64 pages. *Journalistic Quality:* Vivid descriptions are found in most of the stories. A staff artist provides at least one black-and-white illustration per writing. This magazine would probably be best used in a classroom or school library, or a public library where a demand for short stories exists.

Stone Soup. *See in this section under* General Magazines.

Teen Power. *See under* Young Adult/Journalism and Writing.

Writing. *See under* Young Adult/Classroom Publications.

■ **MUSIC AND DANCE**

American Square Dance. *See under* YOUNG ADULT/MUSIC AND DANCE—DANCE.

106 **Blast!** 1987. Every 3 weeks. $42.50. Brian Ashley. Ashley Communications, Inc., 19431 Business Center Dr., Northridge, CA 91324. Illus. Adv. [*Aud:* Ages 8–12.]

Features: The timeworn formula includes trivia quizzes, reader letters, and ample color photos of top teenybopper stars. Nevertheless, the feature profiles and interviews are generally more substantial and informative than the fare served up by competitors. *Length:* 20 pages. *Journalistic Quality:* This is a fanzine (see the Fan Magazine section for more of the same) directed to younger readers. It also has appeal for teenagers.

107 **Circus: the rock & roll magazine** (Formerly: *Circus Weekly*). 1969. m. $22. Gerald Rothberg. Circus Enterprises Corp., 3 W. 18th St., New York, NY 10011. Illus. Adv. Circ: 363,926. Microform: UMI. [*Aud:* Ages 8–18.]

Features: Among fan magazines this is one of the most popular, and perfectly suited for anyone from age eight up. Even those who lack reading skills can enjoy the pictures. This youthful version of *Rolling Stone* melds elements of fanzine and music-trade publications. Topics relevant to teenagers are included, such as sports, drugs, and the mass media; however, the meal ticket remains rock, with a pronounced heavy-metal bias. *Length:* 45 pages. *Journalistic Quality:* The review section covers film videos (6–9, 200 words) and record albums (12–15, 200 words). The lean, straightforward text is complemented by a highly attractive format—glossy paper stock and profuse illustrations, many in color.

108 **Clavier's Piano Explorer.** 1980. 1/yr. $6. Ann Rohner. Accent Publg. Co., 200 Northfield Rd., Northfield, IL 60093. Illus. Sample. [*Aud:* Ages 7–14.]

Features: This magazine/newsletter attempts to encourage the beginning pianist. In addition to standard material about the joys of the piano, as well as how it is mastered, there is material from composer biographies to puzzles and musical instrument studies. *Length:* 16 pages. *Journalistic Quality:* There is good to excellent artwork, as well as some original work from young readers. Normally this is distributed free to students by piano teachers, but the cost is so low that libraries may wish to consider it. Send for a sample.

Dance Magazine. *See under* YOUNG ADULT/MUSIC AND DANCE—DANCE.

Guitar Player. *See under* YOUNG ADULT/MUSIC AND DANCE—MUSIC.

109 **On Key: the magazine for young pianists.** 1982. m. $15. Joan Bujacich. JDL Publns., 33 S. Fullerton Ave., Montclair, NJ 07042. Subs. to: P.O. Box 1213, Montclair, NJ 07042. Illus. Sample. [*Aud:* Ages 6–14.]

Features: The title tells almost all. This magazine, for students from about 6 to 14 years of age, covers music appreciation—from the classical to the popular— more than music teaching. There are articles and regular features that give advice on playing the piano, including both original and well-known scores. *Length:* 20 to 30 pages. *Journalistic Quality:* The overall intent is to involve the young reader with the glamor and joys of the instrument and its performers. It works well.

110 **Prima Ballerina.** 1989. bi-m. $9.95. Kathryn Wheeler. Prima Publg., P.O. Box 77265, Atlanta, GA 30357. Illus. Adv. Circ: 50,000 (controlled). [*Aud:* Ages 6–14.]

Features: One of the few dance magazines for children, this concentrates on ballet but does have limited coverage of jazz and tap dancing. There are full-color illustrations on almost every page. Most are pleasing shots of ballet dancers from Kyra Nichols to Cynthia Gregory. The large-type, simple but journalistically acceptable prose covers such topics as "Being Marie in the NYCB Nutcracker" (4 pages); "The Nutcracker Kids" (4 pages, primarily illustration); "The Rockettes Holiday Kick-off" (1 page); "The Elegant Mr. Astaire" (1 page); "Dancing Feats" (3 illustrated pages); and "A Dancing Hairstyle" (2 illustrated pages). *Length:* 30 pages. *Journalistic Quality:* The drawback for parents may be the advertisements, which plug books, competitions, dolls, and, of course, dancing schools. Still, the advertising is necessary to keep the price of the periodical within reach, and in these days the ads will probably interest the children as much as the features do. *Note:* This is a controlled circulation magazine that goes to dance studios and students. It should be free to libraries. Sample.

Rolling Stone. *See under* YOUNG ADULT/MUSIC AND DANCE—MUSIC.

111 **Song Hits.** 1942. 6/yr. $10. Mary Jane Canetti. Charlton Publns., Inc., Charlton Bldg., Derby, CT 006413. Illus. Adv. Circ: 75,000. Vol. ends: Dec. [*Aud:* Ages 10–18.]

Features: This is a popular look at the mainstream song hits on MTV and related stations. Full details are given about the performers, and the tone is suitable for younger children as well as teens. *Length:* 45 pages. *Journalistic Quality:* This title tends to reflect the pop music mainstream to a greater extent—with respect to its features and reviews (recordings and concerts)—than do other publications in the field.

■ NEWSPAPERS

Local newspapers should be included in the average library for children, at least those in junior high. The typical classroom publication often fulfills the role of the "national" newspaper for this age group. If a paper other than the local one is to be on hand, it should be the *New York Times* and/or the *Washington Post*.

For title listings, see the Young Adult/Newspapers section.

■ PETS

Cat Fancy. *See under* YOUNG ADULT/PETS.

Dog Fancy. *See under* YOUNG ADULT/PETS.

112 **Kind News.** 1983. 9/yr. $20. Humane Soc., P.O. Box 362, East Haddam, CT 06423. Illus. Circ: 120,000. Sample. [*Aud:* Ages 6–12.]

Features: This comes in two editions. The junior edition and the senior edition have much the same material, but the latter has more depth. It is published by the National Association for the Advancement of Humane Education, and the idea is to stress kindness to animals, both domestic and wild. Particular attention is given to the type of animals the younger child is likely to encounter. *Length:* 4

to 10 pages. *Journalistic Quality:* This is carefully edited and the writing is good and well within the grasp of its audience.

113   **Pets Magazine.** 1983. bi-m. $15. Marie Hubbs. Moorshead Publns., Ltd., 1300 Don Mills Rd., North York, Toronto, Ont. M3B 3M8, Canada. Illus. Adv. Circ: 67,300. Vol. ends: No. 12. [*Aud:* Ages 8–18.]

Features: Pets Magazine is an attractive, colorful magazine that will appeal to responsible pet owners/animal lovers of all types and almost any age. It seems quite suitable for younger as well as older children and teenagers. Each issue contains informative articles written by veterinarians on pet health and nutrition, as well as other useful articles concerning animal care and behavior training. Recent issues have included articles on such topics as pets as presents; finding your lost pet; managing skin diseases in pets; winter hazards; and the biting, aggressive dog. *Length:* 40 pages. *Journalistic Quality:* The overall medical/scientific quality of this magazine is high, since the editorial director is a practicing veterinarian. *Pets Magazine* is highly recommended for libraries seeking an attractive, authoritative magazine devoted entirely to pet health, nutrition, and welfare.

Tropical Fish Hobbyist. *See under* YOUNG ADULTS/PETS.

■ **RELIGION**

There are school papers for almost every religious group and denomination in America. Most of these are passed out in the religious schools. What follows are a few typical titles, no better or worse than hundreds of others but given here to illustrate what is available. See *Ulrich's International Periodical Directory* for a listing of many of these titles.

114   **La Bande a Quenoeil.** 1980. 10/yr. $20. Bernard Mercier. La Bande a Quenoeil, 1000 Sainte-Anne-de-Beaupre, P.Q. GOA 3CO, Canada. Illus. Sample. [*Aud:* Ages 8–15.]

Features: This is a colorfully illustrated French-language magazine for children that places particular emphasis on information rather than entertainment. The numerous features and stories will delight the average reader. A typical issue ranges from art and biology to music and the natural sciences, in separate sections. *Length:* 30 pages. *Journalistic Quality:* Non-Catholics can skip the part on moral and religious education, although generally this is informative as it is predicated on the fact that the reader is of the faith. The magazine might serve, too, as a beginner's introduction to French, at almost any level from age 10 to 18. Individual issues may be gathered together to form a type of encyclopedia, although this is not really recommended. The single numbers may be enjoyed for themselves.

115   **Happy Times.** 1964. m. $7. Earl H. Gaulke. Concordia Publg. House, 3558 S. Jefferson Ave., St. Louis, MO 63118. Illus. Circ: 49,000. [*Aud:* Ages 4–8.]

Features: A religious magazine/paper published by the Lutheran Church, Missouri Synod, Board of Parish Services. It has a good selection of features, fiction, and articles that should appeal to many younger children. *Length:* 64 pages. *Journalistic Quality:* The religious message is there, but done with care and attention to the interests and needs of the readers. The activities sections are particularly useful.

116 **Keeping Posted.** 1955. 7/yr. $6.25. Aron Hirt-Manheimer. Union of Amer. Hebrew Congregations, 838 Fifth Ave., New York, NY 10021. Illus. Circ: 23,000. Vol. ends: Apr. [*Aud:* Ages 10–14.]

Features: Each issue explores a theme such as Jewish mysticism, the "Shtetl" (a village culture of eastern Europe), the new Jewish woman, Jews in sports, drug use, and Holocaust survivors. Articles are by experts who can write in an informative, popular style. Often interviews with individuals who participated in the events being analyzed are featured. *Length:* 20 pages. *Journalistic Quality:* Stunning black-and-white photographs and artwork are the hallmark of this publication. Although sponsored by the Reformed, or liberal, branch of Judaism, denominational bias seems lacking. An excellent resource.

117 **Pockets.** 1981. 11/yr. $12.95. Board of Discipleship, 1908 Grand Ave., P.O. Box 189, Nashville, TN 37202. Illus. Circ: 80,000. Sample. [*Aud:* Ages 6–12.]

Features: A Christian general magazine, this features stories, puzzles, articles, recipes, and numerous other attractive items in its pages. There are colored line drawings and some photographs on almost every page. While the stories are inspirational, they are well written and free of any overt Christian message. The Bible is represented, but is hardly a major theme. *Length:* 32 pages. *Journalistic Quality:* All and all quite a good entry for children. A sample should be requested.

118 **Shofar.** 1984. m. $14.95. Gerald Grayson. Shofar, 43 Northcote Dr., Melville, NY 11747. Illus. Adv. Circ: 12,500. [*Aud:* Ages 8–13.]

Features: This is a religious magazine for Jewish children. The features deal with Jewish identity and celebrate prominent Jews from Barbara Streisand and George Burns to artists, politicians, and so forth. There is much about current events and related matters. In addition, one finds poems, puzzles, games, and just about anything else to hold the child's attention. *Length:* 48 pages. *Journalistic Quality:* This is a nicely written, carefully edited religious magazine with wide appeal for its target audience. It includes family educational programs as well as material for religious lessons.

119 **Story Friends.** 1905. w. $10. Mennonite Publg. House, 616 Walnut Ave., Scottdale, PA 15683. Illus. Circ: 11,000. Sample. [*Aud:* Ages 4–9.]

Features: This title is typical of many Sunday school papers for youngsters. The pages are nicely illustrated and include poems, puzzles, games, and skillful short prose pieces. *Length:* 4 pages. *Journalistic Quality:* Each issue carries a moral message suitable for the age group. It can be read aloud by the child or read to younger children by an adult.

Wee Wisdom. *See in this section under* General Magazines.

Youth Update. *See under* Young Adult/Religion.

■ SCIENCE

120 **The American Weather Observer.** 1984. m. $12 (Nonmembers, $18). Steven D. Steinke. The American Weather Observer, 401 Whitney Blvd., Belvidere, IL 61008. Illus. Adv. Index. Circ: 1,500. Vol. ends: Dec. [*Aud:* Ages 12–18.]

Features: This monthly newspaper includes observational data by month, significant weather events as reported by members, weather folklore, and weather happenings nationwide. The February issue presents the previous year in review and the membership directory of the Association of American Weather Observers (AAWO). Suitable for young adults and the general public. *Length:* 20 pages. *Journalistic Quality:* Published by AAWO, this tabloid is written for and about the amateur observer. Its purpose is to enhance communication among and education of weather enthusiasts, amateur or professional. Articles, chapter news, and columns are written by staff and AAWO members.

121 Animal Kingdom. 1898. bi-m. $10.95. Eugene Walter. New York Zoological Soc., Zoological Park, Bronx, NY 10460. Illus. Adv. Index. Circ: 153,600. Vol. ends: Dec. Microform: B&H. [*Bk. rev:* 1, 450 words, signed. *Aud:* Ages 12–18.]

Features: There is hardly a child or young adult who would not enjoy and profit from this magazine. Everything from apes to zebras is covered in this colorfully illustrated, easy-to-read journal. *Animal Kingdom* is edited for animal lovers rather than animal experts, but the articles are well researched and authoritative and treat exotic and remote species as well as the more common zoo inhabitants. BOoks, television shows, and the like are reviewed. *Length:* 30 pages. *Journalistic Quality:* This is as well written and as neatly edited as any magazine of its type. A must for all public and high school libraries.

Archeology. *See under* YOUNG ADULT/ANTHROPOLOGY AND ARCHAEOLOGY.

122 Chispa: la forma mas divertida de aprender. 1981. m. $25. Julieta Montelongo. Innovacion y Communicacion, S.A. de C.V., Tlacopac No. 6 (Apartado Postal 19-456), Mexico, D.F. C.P. 01040, Mexico. Illus. Index. Vol. ends: Dec. [*Aud:* Ages 8–12.]

Features: A Spanish-language science magazine for children in grades three to six. There are six to nine articles and reports per issue with a focus on topics related to astronomy, physics, biology, botany, and anatomy. Features include a children's corner (letters to the editor), an activities section for science experiments, craft ideas, science problems and solutions, puzzles, and games. The January issue contains a calendar for the upcoming year. *Length:* 30 pages. *Journalistic Quality:* It is similar to *Owl Magazine* and *Highlights for Children,* in that the one- to two-page articles contain brief but interesting facts, with color illustrations. *Chispa* is an entertaining and educational magazine recommended for elementary school and public libraries.

Current Science. *See in this section under* CLASSROOM PUBLICATIONS: SUBJECT.

123 Discover. 1980. m. $27. Paul Hoffman. Family Media, Inc., 3 Park Ave., New York, NY 10016. Illus. Adv. Circ: 925,000. Vol. ends: Dec. Microform: B&H, UMI. Online: VU/TEXT. Reprint: UMI. [*Indexed:* GSI, MI, RG. *Aud:* Ages 12–18.]

Features: Edited for laypeople and young adults, this serves as a colorful, well-illustrated introduction to current science for the 12 and 13 year old as well. Topics range from the mundane to the world shaking and there is little in the current news that is not covered in each issue. *Length:* 80 pages. *Journalistic Quality:* The challenge of presenting lively, informative articles on current developments in all the sciences and health sciences is successfully met by *Discover* magazine. Students can use it for term papers.

124   **Dolphin Log.** 1981. bi-m. $20 (Membership). Pamela Stacey. Cousteau Soc., Inc., 8440
[CMG]   Santa Monica Blvd., Los Angeles, CA 90069. Illus. Vol. ends: Dec. [*Indexed*: CMG. *Aud*:
Ages 7–15.]

     Features: Dolphin Log is devoted to the earth's global water system. The
editors state that their philosophy is "to delight, instruct and instill an environmental ethic and understanding of the interconnectedness of living organisms,
including people." They do this by featuring articles, water-related stories,
experiments, and such in the magazine. There is a letter to the editor ("You and
Yours") feature and several other regulars: "News from Calypso," "Creature
Feature," "Nature News" (tidbit articles), and "Discover" (an experiment of
some sort). *Length:* 16 pages. *Journalistic Quality:* The underwater photography shots are excellent. The writing is factual in nature. This is a brief, well-done
specialty magazine. Recommended where an interest in this subject exists.

125   **Faces.** 1984. 9/yr. $21.95. Carolyn P. Yoder. Cobblestone Publg., Inc., 30 Grove St.,
[CMG]   Peterborough, NH 03458. Illus. Vol. ends: Dec. [*Indexed*: CMG. *Aud*: Ages 8–14.]

     Features: Every issue contains approximately eight articles, word puzzles,
recipes, stories, projects, games, puzzles, and legends. Issues are theme centered.
Topics have included "Masks," "Rivers," "Early Humans," "Stargazing,"
"Birthdays," "Deserts," and "Money." Firsthand accounts of adventures and
expeditions to far-off lands are a trademark. The notion of taking the common
and expanding outward is *Faces'* best feature. *Length:* 37 pages. *Journalistic
Quality:* The 7-×-9-inch covers are striking. The feature authors are archaeolo-
gists, museum curators, historians, and professors of anthropology. It is published
in conjunction with the American Museum of Natural History in New York City.
One piece of fiction is included in each issue. *Faces* successfully combines
information and fun. This publication challenges children to perceive human
societies and cultures in a new way. Past issues are available for purchase. An
outstanding publication.

126   **Griffith Observer.** 1937. m. $10. E. C. Krupp. Griffith Observatory, 2800 E. Observa-
tory Rd., Los Angeles, CA 90027. Illus. Index. Circ: 3,000. Sample. Vol. ends: Dec.
Reprint: Pub. [*Bk. rev*: Occasional, 100 words. *Aud*: Ages 12–18.]

     Features: The *Griffith Observer* is a small, delightful, monthly intended for a
general audience. Its purpose is to present astronomy and its related studies in
such a light that an enduring interest in the physical sciences is generated in its
readers. There are one to three feature articles per issue, one of which often
pertains to the history of astronomy. In additon, each issue has simplified sky
maps of both the evening and the predawn sky, plus a calendar of objects to
observe in the coming month. *Length:* 24 pages. *Journalistic Quality:* Most
issues are well illustrated with black-and-white photographs, but occasionally a
color issue has been produced. Although the educational approach and its readability make this magazine suitable for general readers from advanced junior high
students up, most school and public libraries will want to use it as an adjunct to a
subscription to *Odyssey.*

127   **Odyssey.** 1979. m. $16. Nancy Mack. Kalmbach Publg. Co., 21027 Crossroads Circle,
[CMG]   Waukesha, WI 53187-1612. Illus. Adv. Circ: 97,600. Sample. Vol. ends: Dec. [*Indexed*:
CMG. *Bk. rev*: 4, 125 words, signed. *Aud*: Ages 8–14.]

     Features: Regular features of this space science publication include "Find It
1-2-3" (finding constellations), "The Starry Sky," "What's Up?," "Telescope
Targets," "Cadet Classifieds" (announcements for clubs, newsletters, pen pals,

trading cards), "Books in Focus" (reviews of space science books), and "Future Forum" (readers' opinions on space-related topics). Articles and stories focus on planets, stargazing instruments, technology, constellations, and so on. *Length:* 39 pages. *Journalistic Quality:* Some of the photos in the magazine are blurry. Overall the graphics lack punch. However, the interesting topics and informative writing offset this. *Odyssey* is an intriguing magazine. Highly recommended.

Scholastic DynaMath. *See in this section under* CLASSROOM PUBLICATIONS: SUBJECT.

Scholastic Math. *See in this section under* CLASSROOM PUBLICATIONS: SUBJECT.

Scholastic Science World. *See under* YOUNG ADULT/CLASSROOM PUBLICATIONS.

Science Challenge. *See* **Biology Bulletin Monthly** *under* YOUNG ADULT/CLASSROOM PUBLICATIONS.

128 **Scienceland.** 1976. 8/yr. $15.95. Albert H. Matano. Scienceland, Inc., 501 Fifth Ave., New York, NY 10017-6165. Illus. Circ: 16,000. Vol. ends: May. [*Indexed*: CMG. *Aud*: Ages 5–8.]

Features: The goal of *Scienceland*, state the editors, is "to nurture scientific thinking." This interactive science/nature publication for young children encourages them to respect and appreciate nature. Issues are theme centered. Each article has at least one question, sometimes more, for the child to contemplate, which stimulates thinking, imagination, and dialogue. One regular feature is "Can You Tell?" Photos of parts of plants or animals close up are provided for the child to identify. Answers to puzzles and questions are given in the issue. *Length:* 26 pages. *Journalistic Quality:* Short, well-written text accompanies large, colorful photographs of plants and animals. The magazine contains the right kind and the right amount of text for this age group.

Sea Frontiers. *See under* YOUNG ADULT/SCIENCE.

Smithsonian. *See under* YOUNG ADULT/GENERAL INTEREST.

SuperScience. *See in this section under* CLASSROOM PUBLICATIONS: SUBJECT.

129 **Weatherwise.** 1948. bi-m. $38 (Individuals, $23). Patrick Hughes. Heldref Publns., 4000 Albemarle St. N.W., Washington, DC 20016. Illus. Adv. Index. Vol. ends: Dec. Microform: UMI. [*Indexed*: MI, RG. *Aud*: Ages 12–18.]

Features: A popular weather periodical, this is written mainly for the amateur weather observer and is highly suitable for young adults. Meteorology, climate, and weather topics are presented in an understandable style. Regular features include "Using Your Computer" and "Weather Talk," anecdotal tales regarding the weather. Another regular section is "Weather Watch," containing a review of the previous two months' weather; a synopsis of U.S., Canadian, and Alaskan weather; unusual weather phenomena; and information on major weather events. *Length:* 35 pages. *Journalistic Quality:* This is well written, although most of the information is in the form of statistical data, which takes a bit of time to decipher. Still, the figures are clear enough and easy to understand. Nicely illustrated, too.

130 **Your Big Backyard.** 1979. m. $10. Gretchen Traas Spencer. Natl. Wildlife Federation, 8925 Leesburg Pike, Vienna, VA 22184-001. Illus. Circ: 450,000. Vol. ends: Dec. [*Aud*: Ages 3–5.]

Features: Types of activities included in this participatory science magazine are a "Read-to-Me" story, a gardening or cooking activity (to be done with adult help), photo stories on animals and plants, and puzzles and matching activity pages. A nice touch for this age group is a space on the inside cover for children to write their names. *Length:* 19 pages. *Journalistic Quality:* The language and length of text are age appropriate. The superb photographs and artwork are clear, colorful, and appealing.

131 **Zoobooks.** 1980. 10/yr. $15.95. Linda C. Wood. Wildlife Education, Ltd., 3590 Kettner
 Blvd., San Diego, CA 92101. Illus. Index. Circ: 350,000. [*Indexed:* CMG. *Aud:* Ages 6–14.]

Features: The basic editorial policy is simplicity itself. In each issue the focus is placed on a particular, popular animal. It is the one you are most likely to see at a zoo, or, in some cases, the backyard. Easy-to-understand information is presented on everything from the anatomy of the animal to its natural habitat. The delight of this well-edited magazine is the emphasis on full-color illustrations. There is concentration, too, on related matters from simple crafts to the care of pets. *Length:* 20 pages. *Journalistic Quality:* Useful in libraries and at home because of the universal appeal of the subject matter and the excellent editorial copy and the fine illustrations.

■ **SOCIAL SCIENCES**

Junior Scholastic. *See in this section under* CLASSROOM PUBLICATIONS: SUBJECT.

132 **Scouting: a family magazine.** 1913. 6/yr. $3. Walter B. Babson. Boy Scouts of America, 1325 Walnut Hill Lane, P.O. Box 152079, Irving, TX 75015. Illus. Adv. Circ: 1,000,000. [*Indexed:* MI. *Aud:* Ages 8–18.]

Features: For those adults who work with Scouts of all ages, this magazine provides a myriad of troop activities. Some articles report on programs carried out by volunteers; others are activities designed by Scouting professionals. Occasionally, there is an article on an issue pertaining to young people that is not directly related to Scouting. *Length:* 45 pages. *Journalistic Quality:* Even though Scouting is the thrust of this magazine, there is much in these pages to be used by any adult working with youth. A nicely designed magazine with interesting and colorful photographs. Recommended.

■ **SPORTS**

Amateur Baseball News. *See under* YOUNG ADULT/SPORTS.

Boys' Life. *See in this section under* GENERAL MAGAZINES.

Football Digest. *See under* YOUNG ADULT/SPORTS.

133 **Game Player's Sports for Kids.** 1989. bi-m. $12.95. Signal Research, Inc., 300-A S. Westgate Dr., Greensboro, NC 27407. Illus. Adv. Circ: 100,000. [*Aud:* Ages 7–14.]

Features: The features that make this a bit different from other sport magazines for the age group include (1) information on specific sports figures, often in sports (such as soccer) that are not well known to youngsters; (2) related information, which may include geographical and historical data on a particular area or country that is closely related to a given sport; and (3) interviews with leading sports figures. *Length:* 45 pages. *Journalistic Quality:* Well-written articles and features, and within the understanding of the age group. The emphasis on related activities and background gives it an added dimension.

134 **Info AAA** (Formerly: *AAU News; Amateur Athlete*). 1920. bi-m. $8 Members ($12 Nonmembers). Chip Powers. Amateur Athletic Union of the United States of America, P.O. Box 68207, Indianapolis, IN 46268. Circ: 6,500. Sample. Vol. ends: Nov/Dec. [*Aud:* Ages 10–18.]

Features: Competition results in the Junior Olympics Games are extensively reported as well as other Amateur Athletic Union activities. Special projects are highlighted and each issue features a volunteer profile. *Length:* 50 pages. *Journalistic Quality:* Edited for the amateur athlete of almost any age, and suitable for ages ten and up, this is a basic item in many school libraries. Teen sports enthusiasts and participants will appreciate this magazine published by the national organization governing amateur competition in the United States. Schools and communities with strong athletic programs will find it a helpful title.

Inside Sports. *See under* YOUNG ADULT/SPORTS.

International Gymnast Magazine. *See under* YOUNG ADULT/SPORTS.

135 **Kid Sports.** 1990. bi-m. $9. K Sports, 1101 Wison Blvd., 18th Fl., Arlington, VA 22091. Illus. Adv. Circ: 100,000. [*Aud:* Ages 6–14.]

Features: Following in the footsteps of the successful *Sports Illustrated for Kids*, this magazine is subtitled "The official sports magazine for kids." The features stress advice from numerous sports stars. In one issue, for example, a player explains the fine art of base stealing. There are features on how to play and succeed at various types of sports as well as news about events and personalities. *Length:* 45 pages. *Journalistic Quality:* The photographs, layout, and design are excellent and the magazine will have wide appeal for many children. It is not as large as its rivals, but the writing style is equal to anything now about.

136 **Racing for Kids.** 1989. m. $18. Racing, P.O. Box 500, Concord, NC 28026. Illus. Adv. Circ: 20,000. [*Aud:* Ages 10–14.]

Features: All the emphasis here is on racing cars, for both the amateur and the professional. There are particular features on drag racing and various types of cars on and off the track, and on personalities who are closely connected with the sport. Highlights of races are found in each issue. *Length:* 42 pages. *Journalistic Quality:* The subject is not one with wide appeal for younger children, but those over ten will find the material of some interest. It is well written, although a bit on the "gee-whiz" side. The stock-car information is nicely presented.

Skiing. *See under* YOUNG ADULT/SPORTS.

Soccer Digest. *See under* YOUNG ADULT/SPORTS.

Sports Illustrated. *See under* YOUNG ADULT/SPORTS.

137   **Sports Illustrated for Kids.** 1988. m. $17.95. Jason McManus. Time Inc. Magazine Co., Time & Life Bldg., Rockefeller Center, New York, NY 10020-1393. Illus. Adv. Circ: 800,000. [*Indexed:* CMG. *Aud:* Ages 8–13.]

Features: Using the same formula that made *Sports Illustrated* such a success, the publisher serves it up again with illustrations, stories, hero worship, and so forth. This title is, however, much more compact. The junior model has stories about famous athletes mixed in with yarns about the kids down the block who excel in sports. A wide variety of sports are covered, from archery to the favored football and baseball. *Length:* 84 pages. *Journalistic Quality:* The style is simple and the aim is to entice the child by using children and teenage sports idols as centerpieces in each number. All sports are covered from boxing and karate to football and tennis. Room is left for the girl player, and there are the usual departments that introduce youngsters to the world of the consumer. Actually, older readers will prefer the original; and while this is snappy and good reading, it is not quite up to its older cousin.

This magazine is such a success that there is rumor that the idea is being copied by other publishers. As of this writing, for example, Times Mirror promises a junior edition of *Field & Stream.*

Surfer Magazine. *See under* YOUNG ADULT/SPORTS.

Swimming World and Junior Swimmer. *See under* YOUNG ADULT/SPORTS.

World Tennis. *See under* YOUNG ADULT/SPORTS.

YABA World. *See under* YOUNG ADULT/SPORTS.

CLASSROOM PUBLICATIONS

There are several publishers of the current events classroom paper or magazine. Scholastic is the largest with over 40 publications, most of which are directed to students from kindergarten through high school. These are intended for group purchase, and usually at least 10 subscriptions are required at the rates given here. Individuals may subscribe, too; but this rarely is the case.

As the magazines are employed in the class, few school or public libraries take out individual subscriptions. At the same time there are a handful that are well indexed and of a wide enough scope to be considered by at least some libraries.

The class papers are of two basic types. One is for the beginning reader from grades 1 to 6, and this is limited normally to simple vocabulary, 8 to 10 pages on newsprint, numerous illustrations, and exercises to improve reading skills. (These are listed in the first part of this section.)

A second type is used in subject areas, normally for grades 7 to 12, from art classes to the social sciences. The subject magazines are liberally illustrated and have professional layouts that make them a match for any general magazine on the newsstand or in the library. Many are for improving reading skills.

Note, too, that unlike the audience designation in the rest of this guide, here the designation is by grade, not age. The compilers employ this audience method primarily because it is the one favored by the publishers and each of the classroom magazines is so labeled.

Actually, few students from grades 10 to 12 are that involved with this type of magazine, primarily because it tends to be associated with "forced" reading and with younger children. The exception, as noted, is for the student with reading problems.

Most of the classroom publications have so-called teacher's editions that supply necessary background, and not, incidentally, answers to questions, puzzles, and problems. These are at an extra cost, although where 10 or more copies are taken they have been sent free.

Prices here are for the multiple (10 or more a year) subscription. The single subscription is about two-thirds more; but these are so infrequent (according to the publishers) that the multiple cost is given. And while there is a charge for the teacher's edition, in most cases this is free when 10 or more copies of a given title are ordered. For example: *Scholastic Scope* is $9.50 each for less than 10 and $5.95 each for more than 10 with a teacher's edition ($20) free with more than 10.

The frequency is based upon issues during the school year, i.e., normally about 10 months with monthly or biweekly issues, except during holidays.

All of the publishers listed here are reliable and their publications are tested in thousands of schools. The one drawback with at least a few of the magazines is that they may contain advertising that can be at odds with the message of the editorial material.

Samples are available, but not always.

The major publishers listed here—with addresses that are not repeated in the bibliographic data for the magazines—include:

Curriculum Innovations, 3500 Western Ave., Highland Park, IL 60035

Field Publications, 245 Long Hill Rd., Middletown, CT 06457

Scholastic Magazines, Inc., 730 Broadway, New York, NY 10003. Subs. to: P.O. Box 644, Lyndhurst, NJ 07071

•••••••••••••• **Classroom Publications: General Current Events** ••••••••••••••

The two largest classroom publishers are Scholastic and Field. By now their 8-page-or-so newspapers are so well known as to demand little or no description. Someone, someday, should launch a serious study of how these papers (with circulations of from 1.5 million to 3 million) influence American education. But that is hardly the purpose here. They are briefly categorized by grades, i.e., those grades established by the publishers them-selves. As noted, all have teacher's editions and all are available in most schools. Few librarians bother, although this is not the case with the more elaborate subject classroom magazines that are considered in the next section.

Scholastic News Series

All of these titles are prefaced by the standard "Scholastic News" (for example, *Scholastic News: News Ranger*). None carries advertising. Most are 8 pages on news-print. Except for the kindergarten publication and the first- and second-grade papers (each 32 issues), all are 26 issues a school year. Teacher's editions are available.

Kindergarten

Let's Find Out. $4.50. A colorfully illustrated four pages, which presupposes the reader is just beginning. Most of the material is to be read to the child. There usually is a yearly theme around which the issues are built. Classroom posters augment the issues twice each year.

Grade 1

News Pilot. $2.15. This follows the same general pattern, with emphasis on health and safety and the holidays.

Grade 2

News Ranger. $2.15. Vocabulary now becomes important and many of the stories are constructed around mastery of new words as well as phonetics and reading ability scales.

Grade 3

News Trial. $2.40. Fiction is now important as are other subjects tied to the curriculum for this age group, for example, geography, science, current events, and so on.

Grade 4

News Explorer. $2.40. By the fourth grade the emphasis is more on current events and personalities in the news. There is a focus, too, on poetry and fiction.

Grade 5

News Citizen. $2.65. Again, an emphasis on world news with particular attention to different nations and their place in the scheme of things.

Grade 6

Newstime. $2.65. For the first time there is a real effort made to cover the news in some depth and problems are considered with pro-and-con discussions.

Field Publications

All are prefaced with "Weekly Reader," for example, *Weekly Reader Edition 2*. With the exception of the nursery school edition, all have 27 issues a year, and most are 8 pages in length without advertising. The price for each is $3.25.

Nursery School

Pre-K Edition. 24/yr. Simple pictures and few words to support the typical nursery school program.

Kindergarten

Edition K. Full-color pages with loads of pictures and a beginning effort at reading skills.

Grade 1

Edition 1. Here beginning reading skills are fostered with large visuals and a limited vocabulary.

Grade 2

Edition 2. Where children are involved with the news, then the news is covered. Illustrations.

Grade 3

Edition 3. Here there is more attention to the news, although, again, much of it is child related.

Grade 4

Edition 4. Maps begin to appear, along with illustrations of national and international interest.

Grade 5

Edition 5. The news is expanded and the reading level made more difficult, although still well within the range of average students.

Grade 6

Senior Edition. A shift to major international news and more of an editorial policy that concentrates on other countries and personalities outside of the United States.

Summer editions (6 issues, all $3) are:

Kindergarten through first grade

Summer Edition A. Most emphasis is on colorful illustrations, puzzles, and jokes.

Grades 2–3

Summer Edition B. Primarily games, jokes, puzzles, and a dash of news related to children.

Grades 4–6

Summer Edition C. The emphasis is on the delights of summer.

■ **CURRENT EVENTS**

138 **Current Events.** 1902. 26/yr. $7.90. Field Publns. Illus. [*Indexed*: CMG. *Aud*: Ages 6–8.]

This is one of the country's oldest classroom publications, and familiar to almost everyone. The eight-page newspaper literally brings the news of the world to its audience. Events are current and the reporting is the same as found in adult newspapers, but at the reading level of its primary audience. There are vocabulary and comprehension features. Overall, a good newspaper that caters to the best in the student.

•••••••••••••••••••• **Classroom Publications: Subject** ••••••••••••••••••••

139 **Current Health I.** 1977. 9/yr. $5.95 (Minimum 15 subs. to one address). Laura Ruekberg. Curriculum Innovations. Illus. Index. Sample. Vol. ends: May. [*Indexed*: CMG, RG. *Aud*: Gr. 4–7.]

Intended primarily for use by students in grades 4 through 7, this "one-of-a-kind" periodical provides health education with current health information. The major areas covered in each issue are nutrition, disease, drugs, first aid and safety, your healthy environment, fitness and exercise, your personal health, and psychology. The first article is a feature that is introduced on the full-color cover. On the lighter side, there are riddles, word games, and puzzles. The writing style is simple and lively, and two-color illustrations supplement the text. Each issue includes a free teacher's guide. A second version of this is *Current Health II*, for junior and senior high school students. This follows the same pattern. Note: *The Human Sexuality Supplement* is available with this subscription for an additional $2 a year.

140 **Current Science.** 1927. 18/yr. $6. Vincent Marteka. Field Publns. Illus. Index. Circ: 373,465. Sample. Vol. ends: May. [*Indexed*: CMG. *Aud*: Gr. 5–8.]

Regular features of this magazine include reports of the most current scientific developments in health, physical science, earth science, and life science. The precise and simple style makes it potentially appealing for lower-level reading high school students although it is intended primarily for grades 6 through 10. Each issue begins with a long feature story; recent articles address AIDS, sun-powered cars, and snowflakes. The overall reporting is supplemented with news briefs of national and international interest. Color and black-and-white photographs and graphics enhance and further elucidate the content. Teacher's guide is available.

141 **Junior Scholastic.** 1937. 18/yr. $5.95. Lee Baier. Scholastic. Adv. Circ: 700,000. Sample. Vol. ends: May. Microform: UMI. [*Indexed*: CMG. *Aud*: Gr. 6–8.]

A well-established classroom magazine for younger teens, with a focus on social studies. Compact articles about subjects of interest such as change in

China, child abuse, and U.S. history ("Lucretia Mott, Abolitionist") are presented in a simple, explicit style. News briefs provide the balanced current perspective. Maps, graphics, and photographs supplement copy, providing a variety of approaches to the content of each issue. Teacher's guide is available.

142 **Know Your World Extra.** 1971. 18/yr. $7. Field Publns. Illus. Circ: 185,000. [*Aud*: Gr. 6–10.]

This is for the student who is having reading problems, and finds the vocabulary level for his or her grade level difficult. The reading levels are for the first to third grades, and the 12- to 16-page biweekly features numerous illustrations that help the reader comprehend the stories. The topics in the news are current and the material is well presented.

143 **Read.** 1951. 18/yr. $6.25. Edwin A. Hoey. Field Publns. Illus. Index. Sample. Vol. ends: May. Microform: UMI. [*Aud*: Gr. 6–9.]

This brief 32-page newsprint title is promoted as "The Magazine for Reading and English." In spite of this suggested classroom utilization, it would also be a worthwhile addition to a young adult public library collection. With content having potential appeal for both junior high and high school readers, its seventh-grade reading level would make it quite suitable for lower-level high school students. Entries are short and introduce a variety of literature including drama, nonfiction, and the short story. Reinforcement exercises may accompany some of the entries or appear in subsequent editions. Games and puzzles as well as student contributions of poetry are regular features. Teacher's guide is available.

144 **Scholastic Action.** 1977. 14/yr. $5.95. Scholastic. Illus. Circ: 210,000. [*Aud*: Gr. 7–9.]

The 32 pages are edited for students with reading problems, and in this respect it works out rather well. The stories are of interest to the age group, but the style and the vocabulary are for somewhat lower grades, i.e., about fourth to seventh grades. It is nicely illustrated and there are no advertisements.

145 **Scholastic Choices** (Incorporating *Co-Ed*). 1956. 8/yr. $5.50. Karen Glenn. Scholastic.
[CMG] Illus. Circ: 250,000. [*Indexed*: CMG. *Aud*: Gr. 7–12.]

This is a basic home economics title, at least in the classroom publishing area. The focus is on how to make the best of life via a type of *Consumer Report* approach. Reasonably good articles on everything from health and food to clothing and how to purchase this or that are found in each issue. There are less acceptable pieces on how to develop as a human being.

146 **Scholastic DynaMath.** 1981. 9/yr. $5.95. Scholastic. Illus. Circ: 210,000. [*Aud*: Gr. 5–6.]

A basic, easy to follow 16-page mathematics magazine that can be used by the grades indicated as well as by slower students in higher grades. Math is used in a practical way and problems are built around daily living, from sports and shopping to television. The 16 pages do not carry advertising.

147 **Scholastic Math.** 1980. 14/yr. $5.95. Scholastic. Illus. Circ: 200,000. [*Aud*: Gr. 7–9.]

The familiar 16-page format, with good illustrations and editorial material, serves to back up math teachers in grades seven through nine. The math is built around the usual interests of the student, from shopping to sports. Similar in scope and appearance to the junior edition, *Scholastic DynaMath*.

148 **SuperScience.** 1989. 8/yr. $4.95–$5.75. Scholastic. Illus. [*Indexed*: CMG. *Aud*: Gr. 1–3
(CMG) (Red ed.); Gr. 4–6 (Blue ed.).]

Two relatively new entries. The first, *SuperScience Red*, is a 16-page science
magazine for grades 1–3 that follows the normal Scholastic pattern. The focus is
on what the publisher calls "hands on" projects such as "Make Bert Jump," which
calls for a paper cup and a penny to be used to explain eye movement. Full color
is used throughout, as are line drawings and photographs. The makeup is quite
appealing and the copy is written for the specific needs of the grade levels the
magazine reaches.

SuperScience Blue, for older children, runs to 32 pages, but follows the same
general format. The focus is on specific scientific situations in each of the issues.
For example, in the numbers examined the material centered about the eyes in
the red edition and in the blue edition on tornadoes and wind power. A teacher's
edition, as usual, can be had with each of the magazines.

149 **U*S*Kids.** 1987. 11/yr. $18.95. Terry Borton. Field Publns. Illus. Circ: 20,000. [*Indexed*:
(CMG) CMG. *Aud*: Gr. 1–5.]

A 40-page look at what kids are most excited about, for example, in one issue
animal eyes, games, puzzles, friends, the family, a pet show, and chocolate. Each
page has large type, numerous color illustrations and an extremely pleasing
format. Much of it, in fact, resembles a better-than-average advanced picture
book. It is sure to win the hearts and the minds of the readers it targets. It is one of
the better such magazines and is equally as suitable for the class, for the home,
and for the library.

YOUNG ADULT MAGAZINES

■ **AFRICA** [Alfred Kagan]

See also: AFRO-AMERICAN; GENERAL INTEREST

African affairs are a major concern to the world at large and to the United States, and at least one African magazine should be included in the Young Adult section. While none are edited exclusively for young people, several adult titles are acceptable. Most of these deal with politics and the daily life-styles of the people. They cover numerous study areas from foreign affairs to geography. The titles here deal solely with Africa and its people. The journals truly comprise an interdisciplinary group that deserves careful attention by librarians and teachers. It seems hardly necessary to add that these titles are particularly important in libraries serving a black population.

First choices   (1) *New African*; (2) *Africa Report*; (3) *African Arts*.
Suitable for children   Ages 12–18: *African Arts*.

150   **Africa Today.** 1954. q. $48 (Individuals, $15). George W. Shepard, Jr. and Tilden J. Lemelle. Africa Today Assocs., Grad. School of Intl. Studies, Univ. of Denver, Denver, CO 80208. Adv. Index. Circ: 2,000. Sample. Refereed. Vol. ends: Oct/Dec. Microform: B&H, UMI. [*Indexed*: PAIS. *Bk. rev*: 7–15, 200–2,000 words, signed. *Aud*: Ages 14–18.]

While this is a scholarly overview of modern Africa, much of the material is within the grasp of the advanced high school student. Each issue has five to six articles built around a current political, economic, or social theme. Most of the material is by American experts, although Africans are well represented. About half of each issue is devoted to major book reviews, fiction and nonfiction, which will be of more interest to teachers and librarians than to students. One section includes news of U.S. events, meetings, announcements, and so forth. Although the articles are written for adults and academics, there is no reason this should not be found in larger high school collections, particularly as the coverage is so current and so objective.

African Arts. *See under* CHILDREN/ARTS.

151   **African Concord: the premier Pan-African weekly.** 1984. w. $125 (Individuals, $100). Fidel Odum. Concord Press of Nigeria, Ltd. Subs. to: Medialink Intl., Inc., 191 Atlantic Ave., Brooklyn, NY 11201. Illus. Adv. Circ: 90,000. [*Bk. rev*: 1–2, 250 words, signed. *Aud*: Ages 14–18.]

From time to time satire is needed in viewing world affairs, as amply displayed in this London-based publication from the people who bring the world the Nigerian daily newspaper, *National Concord*. An antiestablishment bias is evident in most of the news stories and features. There is excellent, broad coverage of politics, business, and the economy in Africa. Other sections of the world are considered. The result is a weekly summary that is witty, easy to read, and relatively complete. It will appeal to many high school students looking for something a bit different.

152   African Report. 1957. bi-m. $31 (Individuals, $24). Margaret A. Novicki. African-American Inst., 833 United Nations Plaza, New York, NY 10017. Illus. Adv. Index. Circ: 14,000. Vol. ends: Nov/Dec. Microform: B&H, UMI. Reprint: UMI. [*Indexed*: HumI, PAIS, SocSc. *Bk. rev*: 1, 600–1,100 words, signed. *Aud*: Ages 14–18.]

This journal calls itself "America's leading magazine on Africa" and offers an overview of current affairs on the African continent. Each issue contains 15 to 18 articles and interviews, and an "update" section of news items by country. Sponsored by the nonpartisan African-American Institute, the journal is free of bias, although it has a definite point of view—that Africa must be left to its own internal affairs but given all possible economic and social assistance. Writers are from Africa and from American universities. Thanks to the wide coverage, this is an ideal magazine for larger high school collections. The prose style, which is primarily directed to college-educated adults, may be a problem.

153   New African (Formerly: *New African Development; African Development*). 1966. m. $70. Alan Rake. IC Publns., Ltd., 122 E 42nd St., Rm. 1121, New York, NY 10168. Illus. Adv. Circ: 47,106. Microform: UMI. [*Aud*: Ages 14–18.]

A news magazine with the *Time/Newsweek* format, this has appeal for high school students because of its familiar, glossy appearance and its popular coverage of African affairs and personalities. There is a gossip column, sports news, and articles dealing with everything from music to films. Of all of the African titles this may be the most acceptable for high schools, although the price is a bit high. The 60 to 80 or so pages offer an overview that generally is free of bias. Coverage often is extended to Third World nations outside of Africa. See, too, *African Concord* for a somewhat similar format and style.

■ **AFRO-AMERICAN**   [Frank Marotti, Jr.]

There are no magazines specifically for children or young people in this area. Most of the general adult titles are suitable, however, and particularly the more popular, easy-to-read periodicals such as *Ebony*. Every collection, public and school, should have at least some of these titles. Where there is a major black community, it stands to reason that these and others may be considered necessary.

First choices   (1) *Ebony*; (2) *American Visions*; (3) *Spice!*
Suitable for children   Ages 12–18: *Ebony*; *Spice!*

154   American Visions: the magazine of Afro-American culture. 1986. bi-m. $18. Gary A. Puckrein. The Visions Foundation, Frederick Douglass House, Capitol Hill, Smithsonian Institution, Washington, DC 20560. Illus. Adv. Index. Vol. ends: Dec. [*Bk. rev*: 3, 500–700 words, signed. *Aud*: Ages 14–18.]

This journal covers the aspects of Afro-American culture of value to the typical young person. The articles inform readers not only of black accomplishments in the past, but of current activities and needs as well. Subjects include the arts, film, music, biography, history, celebrations, language, family life, and national issues of concern to the black community. Through bibliographies, a national calendar of events, and regular columns featuring archives, cultural centers, or museums around the country, readers are encouraged to go beyond reading the magazine. Illustrations are superb, as are the book review essays. *American Visions* will enlighten and entertain everyone. This title is a must.

155 **Blacfax.** 1982. q. $8. R. Edward Lee. Blacfax, 214 W. 138th St., New York, NY 10030. Illus. Adv. Circ: 1,200. Sample. Vol. ends: Summer. [*Aud*: Ages 14–18.]

A 19-page compendium, this publication presents little-known information about Afro-American culture and history. A typical issue contains a list of birthdays of prominent blacks, profiles of individuals such as Paul Robeson and Sojourner Truth, and personal reflections and memoirs. The arts are also covered, including, for example, a discussion of gospel music and showcased poetry. Minimal illustration is used to accent copy, which is computer-generated. This is a useful and enlightening source for social and retrospective perspectives.

156 **Black Collegian: the national magazine of black college students.** 1970. q. $10. Kuumba Kazi-Ferrouillet. Black Collegiate Services, Inc., 1240 S. Broad St., New Orleans, LA 70125. Illus. Adv. Circ: 205,000. Vol. ends: Mar/Apr. Microform: B&H, UMI. [*Indexed*: INeg. *Bk. rev*: 5, 25–500 words, signed. *Aud*: Ages 14–18.]

In addition to information on employment opportunities, there are current data on scholarships, internships, grants, and foreign exchange programs. Despite its practical bent, the *Black Collegian* does not neglect social or cultural questions. Interviews, feature articles, and regular columns (most notably on black art) remind students that there is more to life than a good job. Film, record, and book reviews, plus photo spreads dealing with subjects like travel, fashion, cars, and sports, heighten the magazine's appeal. Although this veritable paper placement office focuses on college blacks, high school students and the general public could well be inspired to pursue higher education after examining its contents.

157 **Black Enterprise: black America's guidebook for success.** 1970. m. $12.95. Earl G. Graves. Earl G. Graves Publg. Co., Inc., 130 Fifth Ave., New York, NY 10011. Illus. Adv. Circ: 242,000. Sample. Vol. ends: July. Microform: B&H, UMI. Reprint: UMI. [*Indexed*: BusI, INeg, PAIS, RG. *Bk. rev*: 1–3, 25–500 words, signed. *Aud*: Ages 14–18.]

This magazine offers practical advice to students who simply have a dream. Readers are kept well informed of the sociopolitical conditions that exercise powerful influence on the climate for black business/career opportunities. Succinct departments supplement the well-written, illuminating feature articles in an organizational framework enhanced by excellent graphics. The yearly careers issue is outstanding. Nonblacks can gain insights into black perceptions of key events and economic conditions.

158 **Callaloo: a journal of Afro-American and African arts and letters.** 1976. q. $34 (Individuals, $16). Charles H. Rowell. Johns Hopkins Univ. Press, Journals Publg. Div., 701 W. 40th St., Suite 275, Baltimore, MD 21211. Illus. Adv. Circ: 1,000. Sample. Vol. ends: Fall (No. 4). [*Bk. rev*: 3, 1,000–3,000 words, signed. *Aud*: Ages 14–18.]

What began as a literary magazine providing an independent outlet for the creative expression of southern blacks has been expanded into a journal that publishes works by and about African, Caribbean, and Latin American authors as well. The black experience is explored through criticism, drama, essays, fiction, and poetry. Cultural studies, folklore, interviews, and visual art add variety to the literary core. Special issues provide in-depth analyses of celebrated black writers. *Callaloo's* physical format is especially attractive. This is a first-rate publication that excites the imagination by its emotional, intellectual, and visual appeal.

159   **The Crisis.** 1910. m. (bi-m. June/July & Aug/Sept.). $8. Fred Beauford. Crisis Publg. Co., 4805 Mt. Hope Dr., Baltimore, MD 21215. Illus. Adv. Index. Circ: 328,500. Vol. ends: Dec. Microform: B&H, UMI. Reprint: Kraus. [*Indexed*: CIJE, INeg. *Bk. rev*: 1, 1,200–1,600 words, signed. *Aud*: Ages 14–18.]

Founded by W.E.B. Du Bois, this journal has been forced by new developments to change over the years. Its purpose is to stimulate debate over matters important to the Afro-American community. Each issue is devoted to a single major topic on which feature articles convey the views of various writers. Recent issues have dealt with black poverty, black leaders, presidential candidates, the black family, sports, and career options. In the spirit of Du Bois, the periodical regularly offers theater, dance, book, and music reviews. News from the NAACP, including "battles" in progress, rounds out the contents. This is not a "flashy" publication, but it challenges the intellect with readable prose and well-stated arguments.

160   **Ebony.** 1945. m. $16. Lerone Bennett, Jr. Johnson Publg. Co., Inc., 820 S. Michigan Ave., Chicago, IL 60605. Illus. Adv. Circ: 1,753,373. Vol. ends: Oct. Microform: B&H, MIM, UMI. Reprint: UMI. [*Indexed*: INeg, MI, RG. *Aud*: Ages 10–18.]

Often referred to as the black *Life*, this tremendously successful publication skillfully employs photojournalism to chronicle Afro-American achievements of the past and present. Emphasis here is on the positive aspects of the black experience. Racial harmony is promoted by featuring popular personalities and topics that demonstrate the common interests Americans share, rather than their differences. Afro-American history, current social issues, entertainment, personalities, business, health, sports, fashion, food, and self-improvement receive regular attention. Positive role models abound. Each May, *Ebony* selects the "100 Most Influential Black Americans." The August issue is devoted entirely to the examination of one aspect of black life. The list of prominent individuals of all races who have appeared within its covers over the years is impressive. This magazine fosters pride at the same time that it informs and entertains.

Essence. *See under* WOMEN.

161   **Jet.** 1951. w. $36. Robert Johnson. Johnson Publg. Co., Inc., 820 S. Michigan Ave., Chicago, IL 60605. Illus. Adv. Circ: 850,000. Vol. ends: Oct. Microform: B&H, UMI. Reprint: UMI. [*Indexed*: INeg, MI, RG. *Aud*: Ages 14–18.]

Along with its cousin *Ebony* (by the same publisher), this offers easy reading for students, particular as the material is popular and heavily illustrated. It is a required item in any library serving a black young adult population. The vest-pocket magazine encapsulates news, entertainment, personalities, and issues of interest to blacks. Typically, an in-depth cover story is accompanied by about 20 short features dealing with education, justice, religion, sports, gossip, labor, business, and politics. Pages may disappear, as most issues spotlight a swimsuit-attired "Photo-Beauty of the Week." A quick perusal of *Jet* will educate and amuse young people who desire a succinct overview of Afro-American life.

162   **Sage: a scholarly journal on black women.** 1984. 2/yr. $25 (Individuals, $15). Patricia Bell-Scott and Beverly Guy-Sheftall. Sage Women's Educational Press, Inc., P.O. Box 42741, Atlanta, GA 30311-9741. Illus. Adv. Circ: 1,000. Sample. Vol. ends: Fall. [*Bk. rev*: 2–3, 1,000–2,000 words, signed. *Aud*: Ages 14–18.]

The subtitle points out that this is scholarly, but it is well within the reading skills and interests of advanced high school students (though not recommended for those who have problems with reading). This interdisciplinary journal discusses, promotes, and deals with international black womanhood. Each number focuses on a theme. Information may be conveyed in the form of art; photographic essays; interviews; book, exhibit, or film reviews; research reports; bibliographies; reader commentaries; documents; essays; or announcements. Its interdisciplinary approach, varied format, and ground-breaking studies broaden its appeal to those who might not otherwise be interested in a feminist journal.

163   **Southern Changes.** 1978. bi-m. $30 (Individuals, $25). Allen Tullos. Southern Regional Council, Inc., 60 Walton St. N.W., Atlanta, GA 30303-2199. Illus. Circ: 7,000. Sample. Vol. ends: Dec. Microform: UMI. Reprint: UMI. [*Bk. rev*: 1–3, 500–5,000 words, signed. *Aud*: Ages 14–18.]

One of several periodicals suitable for high school collections, this is an excellent source of historical and current information about the civil rights movement. Its publishing organization is composed of leaders in education, religion, business, labor, and the professions who are interested in improving race relations in the South. An interracial team addresses questions concerning social, economic, and political justice, urging individuals and policymakers to adopt measures that will foster equality in the region. National news related to the South is covered, as well as women's rights, the environment, schools, culture, labor, agriculture, economic development, and urban affairs. Most of these stories are investigative in nature. Many articles impact specifically on blacks. The articles are well written, and photographs frequently accompany them. Many contributors are veterans of the desegregation efforts of earlier years.

164   **Southern Exposure.** 1973. q. $20 (Individuals, $16). Eric Bates. Inst. for Southern Studies, P.O. Box 531, Durham, NC 27702. Illus. Adv. Index. Circ: 3,000. Sample. Vol. ends: No. 4. Microform: UMI. Reprint: UMI. [*Indexed*: Acs. *Aud*: Ages 14–18.]

A lively, imaginative periodical suitable for high schools, this is edited by young people and sponsored by an organization that grew out of the civil rights movement. Authors encourage grass-roots movements and intercultural understanding. Regional issues relating specifically to blacks receive ample coverage, plus news about farmers, labor, women, gays/lesbians, and other interest groups. Topics include history, culture, politics, education, economics, the environment, local news, and national trends that impact on the South. Investigative pieces, photographic studies, and statistical features are definite strengths.

165   **Spice!** 1986. 10/yr. $15.99. Chris Botta. Go-Stylish Publg. Co., 475 Park Ave. S., New York, NY 10016. Illus. Adv. [*Aud*: Ages 12–18.]

Promoted by its publishers as the "Total Magazine for Black Teens," this title attempts to cover the gamut of teen interests: music, celebrities, fashion, beauty, food, health. Its cover and content layout suggest that it is a teen fanzine, but it offers much more than celebrity coverage. In newsprint and glossy color photographs, each issue is prefaced with a letter from the editor that usually addresses some aspect of civil rights or race relations, attempting to instill a sense of ethnic pride and self-awareness within the readership. A regular feature is "Black Achievement," which profiles an outstanding African American; Debi Thomas, U.S. figure skater, and Madame C. J. Walker, a pioneer in the black hair care industry, have been portrayed. Nonfiction articles are well written and especially informative—an article on sunglasses contains explicit description of the different types. Other articles address adolescent relationships, such as interracial dating, and sociopolitical affairs such as apartheid. Girls may find the magazine more appealing than will boys but a unisex approach is obvious—for example, male models are featured in fashion sections and subjects of celebrity interviews are favorites of black male teens. This magazine is recommended for libraries serving black youth.

■ **AGRICULTURE**   [Arlene E. Luchsinger]

The agriculture and farming magazines in this section will appeal primarily to high school students, although one or two have reading material of interest to younger readers. Most offer practical approaches to farming and related areas, as well as innovative methods of agriculture. Choice is limited to periodicals that are broader in coverage, taking in more than a single area of agriculture.

First choices   (1) *Farm Journal*; (2) *Successful Farming*; (3) *Farmer's Digest*.

Suitable for children   Ages 11–18: *Farmer's Digest*; *The National Future Farmer*.

166   **Agricultural Research.** 1953. 10/yr. $11. Lloyd E. McLaughlin. U.S. Dept. of Agriculture, Agricultural Research Service. Subs. to: Supt. of Docs., U.S. Govt. Printing Office, Washington, DC 20402. Illus. Circ: 36,000. Vol. ends: Dec. Microform: UMI. Reprint: UMI. [*Aud*: Ages 14–18.]

This is one of the few research journals that are useful in a high school or public library. Brief contributions by government scientists highlight the diversity of current research projects of the U.S. Department of Agriculture. Written for the layperson, the signed articles discuss issues of interest to today's farmers. The use of computers in diet studies, soil and water relationships, control of insects and other pests, and the treatment of childhood nutritional deficiencies are subjects of recent research articles. Although no bibliographies accompany the articles, high school students will find this magazine helpful in identifying topics for term papers.

167   **Enthusiast.** 1939. q. Free. Carol Stewart-Kirkby. Guelph Agriculture Centre, P.O. Box 1030, Guelph, Ont. N1H 6N1, Canada. Illus. Circ: 25,000. [*Aud*: Ages 14–18.]

This 16-page, illustrated publication is a 4-H and Junior Farmers' look at Canadian agriculture. It provides educational information relating to organizational and individual leadership development, according to the editor. The short articles cover such items as food and nutrition, classroom 4-H clubs, raising money, and so forth. While primarily for Canadian high school students, it is quite appropriate for young adults in the United States. Besides, it is free and has been around a long time. Recommended.

168   **Farm Journal.** 1877. 14/yr. $12. Earl Ainsworth. Farm Journal, 230 W. Washington Sq., Philadelphia, PA 19105. Illus. Adv. Circ: 838,000. Vol. ends: Dec. Microform: UMI. Reprint: UMI. [*Indexed*: BusI, RG. *Aud*: Ages 14–18.]

This leading publication for farmers is an essential purchase for libraries serving young adults interested in agriculture. It presents well-written, authoritative information on livestock, poultry, and crop production. Articles cover agricultural economic outlook and price forecasts, legislation and government programs affecting farmers, farm credit, foreign investors in agriculture, labor and marketing problems, human relations issues in farm operations, and food preparation.

169 **Farmer's Digest.** 1937. 10/yr. $11. H. Lee Schwanz. Farmer's Digest, Inc., P.O. Box 363, Brookfield, WI 53005. Illus. Adv. Index. Circ: 25,000. Sample. Vol. ends: Apr. Microform: UMI. Reprint: UMI. [*Aud*: Ages 11–18.]

Young adults with any interest in the practical side of farming will be delighted with this tried-and-true magazine. As a general-interest publication, it selects and reprints current agricultural and farm-related information from more than 200 farm and technical publications, as well as U.S. Department of Agriculture and university sources. This magazine will provide junior high and high school students with ideas for writing term papers or reports.

170 **The National Future Farmer.** 1952. bi-m. $3. Wilson W. Carnes. Natl. Future Farmer Org., P.O. Box 15160, Alexandria, VA 22309. Illus. Adv. Circ: 410,860. Refereed. [*Aud*: Ages 11–18.]

The title suggests the audience, and the magazine, while primarily for teenagers, can be enjoyed by younger readers. This is the membership publication of Future Farmers of America, a youth organization of teens involved in farming, and it provides interesting insights into farming in America. The "News in Brief" column contains information and announcements of general interest. Coverage of regional and national conventions is augmented by "Chapter Scoop," a forum for activity on the local chapter level. Quite a few articles explore pertinent issues and concerns, including farm management, marketing, technology, and the creative accomplishments of members.

171 **New Farm: magazine of regenerative agriculture.** 1979. 7/yr. $15. George De-Vault. Regenerative Agriculture Assn., 222 Main St., Emmaus, PA 18049. Illus. Adv. Circ: 40,000. Sample. Vol. ends: Nov/Dec. Microform: UMI. Reprint: UMI. [*Aud*: Ages 14–18.]

This magazine offers numerous new approaches to farming. Directed toward those who are interested in agriculture without the use of chemicals, each issue contains articles that encourage the use of organic farming techniques. Subjects include soil fertility, tillage methods, weed and pest control, crop rotation, cover-crop cultivation, and erosion control.

172 **Progressive Farmer.** 1886. 3/m. Feb–May; s-m. Jan., Oct., & Nov.; m. June–Sept. & Dec. $12. C. G. Scruggs. Progressive Farmer, P.O. Box 2581, Birmingham, AL 35202. Illus. Adv. Circ: 650,000. Sample. Vol. ends: Dec. Microform: UMI. Reprint: UMI. [*Aud*: Ages 14–18.]

Note the circulation, and it is easy to see that this is a popular magazine among youth as well as adults. It is inexpensive and addresses the problems and concerns of farm families, particularly those of the South and Southwest. This is published in 18 regional editions, with articles covering farm production and management, personal finances (including retirement income, budgeting, and even bankruptcy), purchase and maintenance of machinery, and livestock and crop production. A regular section, "Country Place," includes decorating tips, house plans, recipes, and gardening ideas. Separately published sections on peanuts, pork, tobacco, wheat, corn, soybeans, and cotton have news articles on herbicides, new crop varieties, crop production, and foreign trade of these individual commodities.

173 **Successful Farming.** 1902. 14/yr. $12. Loren Kruse. Meredith Corp., 1716 Locust St., Des Moines, IA 50336. Illus. Adv. Circ: 575,700. Vol. ends: Dec. Microform: UMI. [*Indexed*: RG. *Aud*: Ages 14–18.]

Fourteen regional editions of this successful magazine provide management guidance for farmers and their families, including teenagers. Articles offer practical help in making decisions that affect the profitability of the farm business and the welfare of the farm family. All phases of farming, including livestock, crops and soil, machinery, buildings, economics, and management, are subjects for discussion and advice. There are monthly reports on government policies, programs, and finances. A feature on machinery buying compares available hay balers, chemical sprayers, or tractors. The use of chemicals for pest and weed control as well as the cost of chemicals and chemical safety are featured in an annual special issue. "All Around the Farm" provides an opportunity for farmers to share ideas.

■ ALTERNATIVES [Gretchen Lagana]

See also: CIVIL LIBERTIES; NEWS AND OPINION

"Alternatives" means anything that is not in the mainstream of the culture. Many of the topics covered by the alternative press do become popular—for example, the environment, concern for endangered animal populations, food products, and so forth. Also, alternative magazines offer a type of editorial material often favored by younger people because it challenges the accepted way of doing things. The political bias may be either left or right, but never center.

First choices (1) *Utne Reader*; (2) *Whole Earth Review*; (3) *Mother Earth News*.
Suitable for children Ages 12–18: *Mother Earth News*.

174 **Amicus Journal** (Formerly: *Amicus*). 1979. q. $10 Members ($8 Nonmembers). Peter Borrelli. Natl. Resources Defense Council, Inc., 40 W. 20th St., New York, NY 10011. Illus. Index. Circ: 68,000. Sample. Microform: B&H. [*Indexed*: API, PAIS. *Bk. rev*: 2, 500–1,000 words, signed. *Aud*: Ages 14–18.]

An environmental magazine, this challenges the young reader. It is underwritten by the Natural Resources Defense Council (NRDC), a not-for-profit membership organization dedicated to protecting endangered natural resources and the quality of the human environment. *Amicus Journal* reflects NRDC's involvement in the areas of energy policy and nuclear safety, toxic substances, air and water pollution, urban transportation, natural resources and conservation, and the international environment. In addition to in-depth articles, it includes commentary, editorials, book reviews, and poetry.

175 **Communities: journal of cooperation.** 1973. q. $22 (Individuals, $18). Charles E. Betterton. Community Publns. Cooperative (Stelle), 105 Sun St., Stelle, IL 60919. Illus. Adv. Circ: 3,000. Microform: UMI. [*Indexed*: API. *Bk. rev*: 1–2, 200 words. *Aud*: Ages 14–18.]

Some 100,000 intentional communities exist throughout the world, ranging in size from the tiny village to the space-age city. *Communities*, which is published by the Stelle Foundation, an organization of individuals interested in networking with intentional communities worldwide, offers information on all aspects of communities and cooperative living. Each issue contains a reader service that connects people looking for communities with communities looking for people. This magazine will be of interest to young adults seeking information on the development of a more cooperative society.

176 **EastWest: the journal of natural health and living** (Formerly: *East West Journal*). 1971. m. $18. Mark Mayell. Kushi Foundation, Inc., P.O. Box 6769, Syracuse, NY 13217. Illus. Adv. Circ: 80,000. Vol. ends: Dec. Microform: B&H, MIM, UMI. Reprint: UMI. [*Indexed*: API. *Aud*: Ages 14–18.]

Topics covered in this handsome and popular alternative health monthly will appeal to young people interested in natural life-styles, holistic health, whole foods, organic gardening and agriculture, science, spirituality, and the arts. Special departments offer practical information on travel, classes, workshops, and special events.

177 **Mother Earth News.** 1970. bi-m. $18. Bruce Woods. Mother Earth News, Inc., 80 Fifth Ave., New York, NY 10011. Illus. Adv. Circ: 700,000. Sample. Microform: B&H, UMI. [*Indexed*: Acs, RG. *Aud*: Ages 12–18.]

Of all the alternative magazines, this has the widest appeal for young readers and high school students. The scope is wide enough to include almost every interest, and the presentation is objective and factual. This is one of the oldest and most successful of the alternative life-style magazines promoting self-reliance, and although it has inspired many imitations, the original remains among the best. *Mother Earth News* attempts to keep the reader abreast of the latest do-it-yourself-for-less news and deals with a wide range of topics, including food, health, housing, energy, and the environment. Articles are well written, and the instructions that accompany workshop projects are clear. There are numerous photographs, charts, diagrams, and references accompanying both articles and projects.

178 **Science for the People.** 1968. bi-m. $24 (Individuals, $15). Seth Shulman. Science Resource Center, Inc., 897 Main St., Cambridge, MA 02139. Illus. Adv. Vol. ends: Dec. Microform: UMI. Reprint: UMI. [*Indexed*: API. *Bk. rev*: 1, 1,200 words, signed. *Aud*: Ages 14–18.]

Published by the Science Resource Center, Inc., a not-for-profit corporation, *Science for the People* bills itself as the only national magazine devoted to the political significance of science and technology. Now more than 20 years old, it has grown from a mimeographed newsletter (to keep chapters of Scientists and Engineers for Social and Political Action mutually informed) to a handsome, professionally produced periodical that offers a progressive view of science and technology. International, national, and grass-roots topics are regularly covered. Articles, authored for the most part by teachers, activists, and professional writers, are clearly written for the young adult interested in the political analysis of science and technology.

179 **Utne Reader: the best of the alternative press.** 1984. bi-m. $24. Eric Utne. Lens Publg. Co., Inc., 2732 W. 43rd St., Minneapolis, MN 55410. Illus. Adv. Circ: 75,000. Microform: UMI. [*Indexed*: API. *Bk. rev*: 30, 50–300 words, signed. *Aud*: Ages 14–18.]

This broad overview of what is going on in the alternative press is excellent for the young adult collection. Some describe the *Utne Reader* as the Swiss army knife of New Age counterculture for those too busy to read magazines. Each issue revolves around a theme, with articles excerpted from alternatives to illustrate aspects of that theme. Recent topics have included psychotherapy, corporate crime, channels, the new sobriety, alternative travel, and the need for meaningful ritual. Reviews of alternatives (and of specific issues of alternatives) appear throughout the magazine in departments, columns, and various news notes. Order information is always listed. The graphics are excellent. Stranded on a desert island with only one alternative to read? Let it be *Utne Reader*!

180   **Whole Earth Review** (Combining *Whole Earth Software Review* and *CoEvolution Quarterly*). 1974. q. $20. Kevin Kelly. Point Foundation, 27 Gate Five Rd., Sausalito, CA 94965. Illus. Adv. Index. Circ: 50,000. Microform: UMI. Online: DIALOG. [*Indexed*: API, Acs, HumI, MI. *Bk. rev*: 30, 50 words, signed. *Aud*: Ages 14–18.]

This extremely popular magazine amoung young people (and adults) offers ways of doing things that are not found in other magazines. It promotes "access to tools and ideas" through articles arranged around a set of common themes (the most recent have dealt with cultural geography and robots), departments, and reviews. Health, land use, communications, politics, households, and crafts are regularly covered. The short book reviews and various lists of information sources that appear throughout each issue, the high standards of writing and editing, the engaging style and wealth of information, as well as the handsome format, make *Whole Earth Review* a valuable resource for a wide audience.

181   **Workbook.** 1974. q. $25 (Individuals, $12). Julie Jacoby. Southwest Research and Information Center, P.O. Box 4524, Albuquerque, NM 97106. Illus. Sample. [*Indexed*: API, PAIS. *Bk. rev*: Various number and length, signed. *Aud*: Ages 14–18.]

This is another version of the *Whole Earth Review* for the same audience, but with a twist—to provide "sources of information about environmental, social and consumer problems." Each issue opens with a primary topic and then moves to "Sources of Information" subdivided into agriculture, women, youth, and aging. Under each topic are descriptive and evaluative 150- to 300-word reviews of books, periodicals, reports, and pamphlets that offer alternative solutions to pressing social problems. The 40 to 50 pages suggest lesser known, certainly lesser reviewed, items—material of value to laypersons and acquisitions librarians. Librarians will be pleased to note that full bibliographic information is given for each item, as are addresses for organizations and publishers.

■ **ANTHROPOLOGY AND ARCHAEOLOGY**

See also: SCIENCE

Neither anthropology nor archaeology is normally studied as a separate subject in elementary or high school, but both are important parts of other cultural and science courses. Therefore, the titles given in this section have a role to play in any medium- to large-size public or school library collection. It should be noted that archaeology generally is considered a subdivision of anthropology, which seeks to give a comprehensive understanding of mankind's culture.

First choices   (1) *Archaeology*; (2) *Current Anthropology*.
Suitable for children   Ages 12–18: *Archaeology*.

182   **Archaeology: a magazine dealing with the antiquity of the world.** 1948. bi-m. $20. Peter Young. Archaeological Inst. of America, 15 Park Row, New York, NY 10007.

Illus. Adv. Index. Circ: 90,000. Vol. ends: Nov/Dec. Microform: SZ, UMI. Reprint: SZ. [*Indexed*: ArtI. *Bk. rev*: 3–7, 300–600 words. *Aud*: Ages 12–18.]

A thoroughly popular, easy-to-read journal, this can be appreciated by both older children and high school students. It is noteworthy for its sparkling style and the excellent illustrations accompanying each of the five to six major articles. The language is free of jargon and the writers intentionally aim their copy at the educated layperson, including the interested high school student. Coverage is worldwide and includes all time periods. There are excellent features on photography, museum shows, current books and films, travel, and related matters.

183 **Current Anthropology.** 1960. 5/yr. $105. Adam Kuper. Univ. of Chicago, 5720 S. Woodlawn Ave., Chicago, IL 60637. Illus. Index. Circ: 5,300. Microform: JAI, UMI. Reprint: JAI. [*Aud*: Ages 14–18.]

One of the few general anthropology journals for the young adult, this is an excellent choice where there is an intense interest in the field of anthropology. It is not, though, for the casual reader. Its usefulness is evident from the illustrations, the critical comments accompanying each article, and the numerous reports of ongoing activities in the field. The writing is technical, but smoothed over in such a way that a high school student can understand it with careful reading.

184 **Ethnology.** 1962. q. $30. Arthur Tuden. Univ. of Pittsburgh, Dept. of Anthropology, Pittsburgh, PA 15260. Illus. Index. Circ: 2,800. Refereed. [*Aud*: Ages 14–18.]

Cultural anthropology is not normally a major part of a high school course, but there is much material here relating to wider concerns. It attracts some of the best people in the field, and while they may not all write with the verve of a trained journalist, at least they usually offer original ideas. The five to eight articles usually report on activities in the field, although "think pieces" are not that unusual. The magazine's potential audience is wide in that the articles are concerned with all aspects of human culture from religion and mythology to comparative art.

185 **Expedition: the magazine of archaeology/anthropology.** 1958. 3/yr. $15. M. Voigt. Univ. Museum of the Univ. of Pennsylvania, 33rd & Spruce St., Philadelphia, PA 19104. Illus. Index. Circ: 6,000. Sample. Vol. ends: Summer. Microform: JAI, UMI. [*Indexed*: ArtI. *Aud*: Ages 14–18.]

This joins *Archaeology* as one of the few titles in the field of interest to a young adult. The scope is international; the related field of anthropology is covered with skill and verve; and there are superior color illustrations for almost all of the articles and numerous features. Finally, the material is authoritative and presented in an easy-to-understand fashion. The success of the journal is due in no small way to the expert handling by the University Museum.

186 **Plains Anthropologist.** 1954. q. $15. Joseph A. Tiffany. Univ. of Iowa, Iowa City, IA 52242. Illus. Index. Circ: 850. Microform: UMI. [*Bk. rev*: 4–5, 250–750 words, signed. *Aud*: Ages 14–18.]

An anthropology journal with wide appeal for younger people, this emphasizes studies of the prehistoric and Native American occupants of the ecological niche. It also includes studies of the Hutterites and other European settlers. The authorship is primarily professional, but footnotes and jargon are minimized so that the journal is fully intelligible to a young reader. Archaeological site reports are mingled with more general papers on such topics as buffalo migrations and the computer analysis of artifacts. Archaeology dominates, but there are ethnographic and historical studies among the seven to ten articles in each issue. These are adequately illustrated with photographs, maps, charts, and diagrams. A good choice for public and high school libraries.

187 **Popular Archaeology.** 1972. bi-m. $16.75. William Jack Hranicky. Popular Archaeology, P.O. Box 11256, Alexandria, VA 22312. Illus. Adv. Circ: 7,700. Sample. Microform: UMI. [*Aud*: Ages 14–18.]

This joins *Archaeology* as a journal directed to the young adult and layperson. It is the weak member of the two, although having said that it has much to recommend it, particularly to young people. The format is poor, and the illustrations, such as they are, tend to be flawed. The articles, features, and news items bring the average issue to only 15 to 25 pages, or less, so the subscription price is about right for quantity. The writing, however, is much above average, the reports are current, and the general approach is such that it will have wide appeal. Try a sample, especially in high schools. Public libraries would do better with *Archaeology*.

■ **ART AND ARCHITECTURE**   [Art: Dagmar Jaunzems. Architecture: Steve Roehling]

In one sense, almost any illustrated art magazine will be of benefit to younger children as well as more sophisticated teenagers. The graphics alone will inspire, as will, of course, the numerous reproductions of famous works of art. This is much the case for the architectural journals annotated in this section. The choice has been limited to titles that can be understood by the interested young reader. Many are quite within the reading range and experience of high school students.

First choices   (1) *Art in America*; (2) *ARTnews*; (3) *Architectural Record*; (4) *Artist's Magazine*.

Suitable for children   Ages 10–18: *Carnegie Magazine*.

188 **American Artist.** 1937. m. $24. M. Stephen Doherty. Billboard Publns., Inc., 1515 Broadway, New York, NY 10036. Subs. to: One Color Court, Marion, OH 43305. Illus. Adv. Index. Circ: 160,000. Vol. ends: Dec. Microform: B&H, UMI. [*Indexed*: ArtI. *Bk. rev*: 2–3, 500 words, signed. *Aud*: Ages 14–18.]

Edited for traditional, basic art and artists, this is an ideal magazine for young people beginning in art. It appeals primarily to amateur artists and students working in traditional modes—though professionals have been known to peruse it. Articles range from interviews with artists to discussions of problems with animal portraits. It is nicely rounded out by notices of upcoming competitions and gallery shows, tips on technique, and notes on the art market and new supplies. The March issue contains a very useful directory of art schools and workshops. This easily readable and amply illustrated journal should be in every high school and public library.

189 **Antiques & Collecting Hobbies: devoted to the preservation of the antique arts** (Formerly: *Hobbies*). 1931. m. $18.50. Frances L. Graham. Lightner Publg. Corp., 1006 S. Michigan Ave., Chicago, IL 60605. Illus. Adv. Circ: 16,000. Microform: UMI. [*Indexed*: BoRvI, MI, RG. *Aud*: Ages 14–18.]

The "granddaddy" of magazines for collectors has a new name that more accurately describes its mission. It features several departments that appear regularly: "Music Memorabilia," "Dolls," "Museum News," "Postcards," "Classics in China," "Numismatics," "Philately," "American Historical Glass," and "The Bookshelf," among others. Display and classified advertisements constitute about one-half of each issue. This is a good general title for public libraries and many high school libraries.

190   Architectural Record. 1891. m. $42.50. Mildred F. Schmertz. McGraw-Hill Information Systems Co., 1221 Ave. of the Americas, New York, NY 10020. Illus. Adv. Index. Circ: 77,000. Vol. ends: Dec. Microform: UMI. [*Indexed*: ArtI, MI, RG. *Aud*: Ages 14–18.]

Written primarily for architects, this is not easy reading even for senior high school students. At the same time, the numerous illustrations and the importance of the title give it a first place in any collection serving young adults involved with the subject. Emphasis is on projects in the United States, but major foreign projects are also covered. There are three or four feature articles in each issue, along with a feature section on a particular theme. Two additional issues are included with the annual subscription: one on houses, in mid-April, and another on interior design, in mid-September. Advertisements abound and they are informative.

Art and Man. *See in this section under* CLASSROOM PUBLICATIONS.

191   Art in America. 1913. m. $39.95. Elizabeth C. Baker. Brant Publns., 980 Madison Ave., New York, NY 10021. Subs. to: 542 Pacific Ave., Marion OH 43302. Illus. Adv. Circ: 50,000. Microform: B&H, MIM, UMI. [*Indexed*: ArtI, RG. *Bk. rev*: 2–3, 1,000 words, signed. *Aud*: Ages 14–18.]

Provides excellent coverage of contemporary international art with an appeal to a broad audience. Of the five to six lengthy articles featured, about half spring from current exhibitions, which serve as a basis for an evaluation of the artist, style, school, and movement. A fairly lengthy section is given to short, illustrated exhibition reviews (primarily in the United States). Many excellent color reproductions and photographs enhance the appeal of this glossy, well-put-together journal. It should be a core item in most libraries.

192   Artist's Magazine. 1984. m. $24. Michael Ward. F&W Publns., 1507 Dana Ave., Cincinnati, OH 54207. Subs. to: P.O. Box 1999, Marion, OH 43305. Illus. Adv. Circ: 173,358. Vol. ends: Dec. [*Aud*: Ages 14–18.]

This is perhaps the only magazine that is truly designed for the amateur artist. *American Artist* is its more sophisticated relative. Each issue of this "how-to" journal contains three to four articles written by artists describing their work and technique. Special sections give advice (e.g., on how to set up a studio) or provide a basic lesson (e.g., on watercolor). Other departments deal with technical problems, the art marketplace, and supplies. Excellent color illustrations, photographs, and step-by-step instructions abound. The text is clear and kept to a minimum. The December issue contains an annual index.

193   ARTnews. 1902. 10/yr. $32.95. Milton Esterow. ARTnews Assocs., 48 W. 38th St., New York, NY 10018. Subs. to: P.O. Box 969, Farmingdale, NY 11737. Illus. Adv. Circ: 75,000. Vol. ends: Dec. Microform: B&H, MIM, UMI. Reprint: UMI. [*Indexed*: ArtI, RG. *Bk. rev*: 3–4, 300–500 words, signed. *Aud*: Ages 14–18.]

As the title implies, this journal provides news on current events in the art world and it will be of interest to older teenagers who are interested in art. The fairly short six to seven feature articles range from interviews with artists, art historians, and dealers to a discussion of the restoration problems of Leonardo da Vinci's *Last Supper*. A large part of the magazine is devoted to news about personalities, galleries, exhibitions, auctions, and places to visit. The expanded exhibition review section (approximately 35 pages) gives about 50 percent coverage to U.S. galleries and the other 50 percent to the international scene. Excellent color illustrations as well as photographs of people and places complement the very readable journalistic copy. One of the best journals for keeping up with trends and changes in the world of art.

194   Canadian Art. 1984. q. $20. Jocelyn Laurence. Maclean Hunter, Ltd., and Key Pubs. Co., Ltd., 70 The Esplanade, Toronto, Ont. M5E 1R2, Canada. Subs. to: 777 Bay St., 8th Fl., Toronto, Ont. M5W 1A7, Canada. Illus. Adv. Circ: 20,000. Vol. ends: Winter (Dec.). [*Indexed*: CanI. *Bk. rev*: 1–3, 500 words, signed. *Aud*: Ages 14–18.]

Canada's basic popular journal covering contemporary Canadian art. Inuit and Indian work as well as film and dance are also briefly touched on. It is Canada's *Art in America* but without the international coverage. Articles discuss the work of artists—often focusing on current exhibitions. Artists, curators, and art consultants are interviewed; exhibitions are reviewed. News of major happenings on the Canadian art scene.

Carnegie Magazine. *See under* CHILDREN/ARTS.

195   Communication Arts. 1959. 8/yr. $47. Patrick S. Coyne. Communication Arts, 410 Sherman Ave., Palo Alto, CA 94303. Illus. Adv. Index. Circ: 55,000. Sample. Vol. ends: Jan/Feb. [*Bk. rev*: 1–2, 300–400 words, signed. *Aud*: Ages 14–18.]

Half of this title's annual eight issues serve as juried showcases for leading work in advertising, illustration, photography, and general graphic design. Remaining issues also serve as designer showcases, with special attention to the use of computers for all types of graphic design and production, and to the work of individual freelancers and small companies. The magazine's own lively design and high-quality production values make it an excellent vehicle for the purpose, and a necessary addition to graphic arts and photography collections.

196   Fine Homebuilding. 1980. bi-m. $26. Mark Feirer. The Taunton Press, P.O. Box 355, Newtown, CT 06470. Illus. Adv. Index. Circ: 205,000. [*Bk. rev*: 25, brief, signed. *Aud*: Ages 14–18.]

A deservedly popular magazine on fine custom home design and construction. Since most architectural periodical literature is devoted to public buildings, this title fills a niche in the literature and fills it very well. Practical information about construction and new products and techniques is presented along with inspiring articles on home design and projects. Articles on architecturally significant houses and on renovation are occasionally included. The photographs and text are first-rate.

197   Fine Print: the review for the arts of the book. 1975. q. $58 (Individuals, $49). Sandra D. Kirshenbaum. Fine Print, P.O. Box 3394, San Francisco, CA 94119. Illus. Adv. Circ: 3,000. Vol. ends: No. 4. [*Indexed*: BoRvI. *Bk. rev*: 3–8, 600 words, signed. *Aud*: Ages 14–18.]

This journal is the authoritative domestic chronicle of the world of fine bookmaking and its related arts of typography and bookbinding in the United States and abroad. Not surprisingly, it is also a very handsome purveyor of fine-press news and reviews, discussions of particular typefaces, and essays on the challenge of book design. Its coverage includes broadsides, pamphlets, and other outputs of the private-press world, as well as books. Separate inserts, which serve as examples of fine printing, are a regular if potentially problematic feature. This title is a must for graphic arts and printing collections, and an important addition to coverage of literature and history.

198 **FMR.** 1984. bi-m. $66. Ed. bd. Franc Maria Ricci Editore, S.p.A., Via Durini 19, Milan, Italy. Subs. to: 220 E. 65th St., New York, NY 10021. Illus. Adv. Circ: 115,000. Vol. ends: Nov/Dec. [*Aud*: Ages 14–18.]

While hardly an essential item for teenagers, this does offer inspiration in the unusual and rich pictures as well as the literate text. The "most beautiful magazine in the world" is edited for "affluent and educated readers with cosmopolitan tastes," but it is also a visual feast for anyone to browse through—brilliant, full-page color illustrations far outnumber the pages of text. Only renowned experts with a flare for language are chosen to write the articles. It is obvious that no expense is spared.

199 **International Review of African American Art** (Formerly: *Black Art*). 1976. q. $20. Samella Lewis. Museum of African Amer. Art, 3000 Biscayne Blvd., No. 505, Miami, FL 33137. Illus. Adv. Circ: 7,000. Vol. ends: No. 4. Online: WILSONLINE. [*Indexed*: ArtI. *Aud*: Ages 14–18.]

A beautifully illustrated magazine devoted to the African American artist. Each issue is dominated by a theme and provides interviews with artists and biographical information within the text of the articles. Contributors range from Maya Angelou to Mae Tate and subjects include such noted artists as Malaika Favorite and Georgia Alice Speller.

200 **Metropolitan Museum of Art. Bulletin.** 1942. q. $18. Joan Holt. Metropolitan Museum of Art, Fifth Ave. and 82nd St., New York, NY 10028. Illus. Index. Sample. Vol. ends: No. 4. Microform: UMI. Online: BRS, DIALOG, WILSONLINE. Reprint: UMI. [*Indexed*: ArtI. *Aud*: Ages 14–18.]

This premier bulletin from one of the world's great museums contains nothing superfluous. Each bulletin focuses on a single subject written by museum staff and resident experts. The style is straighforward and informative; color and black-and-white reproductions are superb.

201 **Museum of Fine Arts, Houston. Bulletin.** 1970/71. 3/yr. $4. Celeste Marie Adams. Museum of Fine Arts, Houston, 1001 Bissonnet St., Houston, TX 77005. Illus. Circ: 10,000. Sample. Vol. ends: May. Online: DIALOG. [*Aud*: Ages 14–18.]

A bulletin from a major museum with full-page color illustrations dominating the text. While the museum boasts a collection as expansive as that of any metropolitan museum, the strength of its bulletin lies in issues covering regional and special collections and minority-produced art.

202 **Ornament.** 1974. q. $25. Robert K. Liu. Ornament, Inc., 1221 LaCienega, Los Angeles, CA 90035. Illus. Adv. Circ: 6,000. Vol. ends: Summer. [*Indexed*: ArtI. *Bk. rev*: 3–6, 100–300 words, signed. *Aud*: Ages 14–18.]

Ornament is about the art of personal adornment in ethnic, contemporary, and ancient manifestations. Not limited to jewelry, it treats textiles, beadwork, leather, headgear, any and all types of body decoration. Each issue offers a balanced presentation of articles on individual artists, ethnic ornament, and history; exhibition reviews and a column on the history, forms, and uses of beads are regular features. *Ornament* is elegant and lavish.

203   **Philadelphia Museum of Art. Bulletin.** 1903. q. $18. George H. Marcus. Philadelphia Museum of Art, P.O. Box 7646, Philadelphia, PA 19101-7646. Illus. Circ: 8,000. Vol. ends: No. 4. Online: BRS, DIALOG, WILSONLINE. [*Indexed*: ArtI. *Aud*: Ages 14–18.]

Fine color plates highlight the slim volumes of the Philadelphia Museum *Bulletin*. Issues are devoted exclusively to exhibitions and collections in the museum. There is generally one in-depth article per issue, usually by a member of the museum staff. Since the *Bulletin* often presents articles on upcoming exhibitions, an issue will become a catalog with a full listing of exhibition items closing the article.

204   **Progressive Architecture.** 1920. m. $36. John Morris Dixon. Penton Publg., 600 Summer St., P.O. Box 1361, Stamford, CT 06984. Illus. Adv. Circ: 75,055. Vol. ends: Dec. Microform: UMI. Online: DIALOG. [*Indexed*: ArtI. *Bk. rev*: 3, 200 words, signed. *Aud*: Ages 14–18.]

One of the most important architectural magazines. It is directed toward those in the architectural profession, but because of its overall excellence in documenting and presenting information about the latest in the field, it can be appreciated by the young adult as well. The scope is international with about six feature articles per issue. Coverage of building design and technology is very strong, as is new-product information and other news of interest to the practicing architect. Photographs are usually in color; architectural line drawings are plentiful and well done.

■ **ASIA AND ASIAN AMERICANS**   [Asia: Richard H. Swain. Asian Americans: Daniel C. Tsang]

Here are magazines concerned with Asia proper (China, India, Japan, etc.) and Asian Americans. There should be titles from each of these areas in most public and school libraries. The primary trouble spot is China, where one must consider propaganda, particularly in the popular titles. Aside from politics, however, they are easy to read and quite entertaining. A common thread among the Asian-American titles is rejection of the notion of Asians as sojourners or as exotic "Orientals." Instead, they confront the problems and issues of an Asian living in the United States.

   First choices   (1) *China Pictorial*; (2) *Rice*; (3) *Asian Week*.
   Suitable for children   Ages 7–13: *Young Generation*. Ages 10–18: *China Pictorial*.

205   **Asian Week: an English language journal for the Asian American community.** 1979. w. $17. Patrick Andersen. John Fang, Pan Asia Venture Capital Corp., 809 Sacramento St., San Francisco, CA 94108. Illus. Adv. Sample. Vol. ends: No. 51. Microform: SHSW. [*Aud*: Ages 14–18.]

This weekly tabloid in newsprint, though based in San Francisco, has a Los Angeles bureau and covers national news. As such, it is the only Asian-American English-language weekly that circulates nationally. The news items are written primarily for adults, but teenagers will find them of value. The paper is wide in its coverage and appeals to the interests of almost every member of the Asian community. A good choice for high school and public libraries.

206   **Asiaweek.** 1975. w. $75. Michael O'Neill. Asiaweek, Ltd., Fifth Fl., Crawford House, 23 Tong Chang St., Quarry Bay, Hong Kong. Illus. Adv. Circ: 70,000. Sample. [*Aud*: Ages 14–18.]

A weekly newsmagazine providing photojournalistic coverge of all aspects of contemporary Asian culture and society. Since the layout and editorial policy seem quite similar to those of *Time* and *Newsweek*, the audience for *Asiaweek* will include young adults who are familiar with these two newsmagazines and feel at ease with their editorial styles. This is the easiest and most entertaining way to keep abreast of current affairs in Asia. *Asiaweek* should be seriously considered by any librarian wishing to provide current information on Asia.

207   **Beijing Review** (Formerly: *Peking Review*). 1958. w. $24. Wang Xi. China Books & Periodicals, 2929 24th St., San Francisco, CA 94110. Illus. Adv. Index. Circ: 100,000. Vol. ends: No. 52. Microform: B&H, MIM. [*Indexed*: SocSc. *Bk. rev*: 2–4, 100 words. *Aud*: Ages 14–18.]

Although this magazine contains propaganda, it is easy to read and is a good choice for political/social science classes. It is the most widely circulated official English-language publication of China. The presentation of events in China from the Chinese government's viewpoint makes this periodical a must in any Chinese periodical collection. Full-text translations of official documents and laws provide the researcher with invaluable information on government policy. Discussions of the official Chinese stance on international situations provide insight into China's position on world affairs. Excerpts of press editorials and commentaries are frequently featured.

China Pictorial. *See under* CHILDREN/GEOGRAPHY AND TRAVEL.

208   **Illustrated Weekly of India: the features magazine.** 1880. w. Rs. 520. K. C. Khanna. Bennett and Cole & Co., Ltd., Times of India Bldg., Dr. Dadabhai Naoroji Rd., Bombay 400001, India. Subs. to: M/s Kalpana, 42-75 Main St., Flushing, NY 11355. Illus. Adv. Sample. [*Aud*: Ages 14–18.]

While not easy reading, this magazine does combine the graphics and the style of the more familiar *Time* and *Newsweek*. It will be of some interest to young adults because this mass circulation magazine includes photojournalism, commentary, entertainment, and English-language fiction and poetry in its large-format weekly issues. The editorial style is somewhat conservative, if overoptimistic, and its popular orientation makes it suitable for high school and public libraries with an interest in India.

209   **India Today: the complete newsmagazine.** 1975. bi-w. $39. Aroon Purie. Living Media India, f-14/15 Connaught Pl., New Delhi 110001, India. Illus. Adv. Sample. Vol. ends: Dec. [*Bk. rev*: 2–4, 500–1,000 words, signed. *Aud*: Ages 14–18.]

Almost identical to *Time* in format, this biweekly magazine takes a liberal, democratic stand on most issues. More serious than the *Illustrated Weekly of India*, *India Today* is perhaps the best single choice for a public or school library to provide an Indian perspective on current Indian and international culture and events.

210   **Japan Quarterly.** 1954. q. $20. Aoki Toshio. Asahi Shimbum Publg. Co., 5-3-2 Tsukiji, Chuo-ku, Tokyo 104, Japan. Subs. to: Japan Publisher's Trading Co., Ltd., P.O. Box 5030,

Tokyo Intl., Tokyo, Japan. Illus. Adv. Sample. Vol. ends: Dec. Microform: UMI. [*Indexed*: PAIS, SocSc. *Bk. rev*: 2–6, 500–1,500 words, signed. *Aud*: Ages 14–18.]

Published by Japan's largest daily newspaper, this journal is meant to present English-speaking readers with the best side of Japanese culture and current events. The articles are well written and informative, and special features include a chronology of events and a guest column entitled "How Others See Us." Other useful features include translations of Japanese literary works and the "Recent Publications on Japan," a list of current books and magazine and newspaper articles.

211 **Rice: the premier Asian-American/Pacific Rim magazine.** 1987. m. $22. Chin S. Wang. Rice, 878 Market St., San Francisco, CA 94102. Illus. Adv. Sample. [*Aud*: Ages 14–18.]

Despite its name, *Rice* is a serious, if glossy, magazine that covers important issues in the Asian-American community. Though obviously aimed at the yuppie Asian Pacific, it has managed to run a cover story portraying black and gay Vietnamese Americans, for example, while continuing to cover familiar topics such as Asians in Silicon Valley.

212 **Southeast Asia Chronicle** (Formerly: *(Indochina Chronicle)*). 1971. irreg. $2.50/issue. Ed. bd. Southeast Asia Resource Center, P.O. Box 4000-D, Berkeley, CA 94704. Illus. Adv. Circ: 4,000. Sample. [*Bk. rev*: 2–6, 250–1,000 words. *Aud*: Ages 14–18.]

Each issue is devoted to a topic related to current social and political events in Southeast Asia and could be used as background reading for advanced high school courses on Southeast Asia. The articles are well written and supported with ample documentation and photographs. This is an excellent way to find out about subjects not covered in other journals.

Young Generation. *See under* Children/General Magazines.

■ **ASTRONOMY** [Louis J. Jerkich]

While the majority of astronomy journals are technical, a surprising number are directed to the amateur and the young adult. The latter have easy-to-follow, accurate texts. Most, too, boast good-to-excellent illustrations. A distinguishing feature of many journals intended for the general public or a school audience is the presence of a sky almanac and star charts.

First choices (1) *Astronomy*; (2) *Sky & Telescope*; (3) *Weatherwise*.

Suitable for children Ages 8–14: *Odyssey*. Ages 12–18: *American Weather Observer*; *Griffith Observer*; *Weatherwise*.

American Weather Observer. *See under* Children/Science.

213 **Astronomy.** 1973. m. $24. Richard Berry. Kalmbach Publg. Co., P.O. Box 1612, Waukesha, WI 53187. Illus. Adv. Index. Circ: 167,000. Sample. Vol. ends: Dec. (No. 12).

Microform: B&H, UMI. Reprint: B&H, UMI. [*Indexed:* RG. *Bk. rev:* 3, 1,000–1,500 words, signed. *Aud:* Ages 14–18.]

The first title in this section is by and large the best for school and public libraries. *Astronomy* has long billed itself as the "world's most beautiful astronomy magazine" and the truth of this billing may in part explain why it has the highest circulation by far of all publications in this field. It is certainly one of the leaders in promoting astronomy among laypersons. Regular departments covering news stories and hobby information are still present, and the expanded monthly sky almanac is now both easier to locate (at the center of the magazine) and more visually attractive to the naked-eye and telescopic observers it serves. The sky map and other diagrams have been revamped with more color and more clarity of detail. The attractive layout and the informative, well-written feature articles combine with its breadth of scope, readability, and educational value to make this a highly recommended purchase for the reading rooms of public and high school libraries. Kalmbach Publishing also produces *Deep Sky* and *Telescope Making* for those with a more serious interest in observation, as well as *Odyssey* for younger readers.

214   **Deep Sky** (Formerly: *Deep Sky Monthly*). 1983. q. $12. David J. Eicher. Kalmbach Publg. Co., P.O. Box 1612, Waukesha, WI 53187. Illus. Adv. Circ: 13,500. Sample. Vol. ends: Winter (No. 4). [*Bk. rev:* 1–3, 900–1,500 words, signed. *Aud:* Ages 14–18.]

The school that has astronomy courses and a telescope will put this journal high on the list of must titles. It is ideal for the younger reader with imagination. This title is for amateur astronomers who want to delve more deeply into telescopic observation of the night sky but have exhausted the suggestions in *Astronomy* or *Sky & Telescope*. It is the only popular magazine devoted specifically to the techniques and results of deep-sky observation and astrophotography. Each issue contains three major articles focused on galaxies, nebulae, star clusters, unusual stars, or observational and photographic techniques. Regular features include sections on double stars, variable stars, and observation with a small telescope; the section on scanning the literature contains reviews of recently published research in professional journals with relevance for deep-sky observers.

Griffith Observer. *See under* CHILDREN/SCIENCE.

215   **Mercury: the journal of the Astronomical Society of the Pacific.** 1972. bi-m. $29.50 (includes *Sky Calendar* and membership). Andrew Fraknoi. Astronomical Soc. of the Pacific, 390 Ashton Ave., San Francisco, CA 94112. Illus. Adv. Index. Circ: 7,000. Sample. Refereed. Vol. ends: No. 6. Microform: B&H, UMI. Reprint: Pub. [*Aud:* Ages 14–18.]

Mercury is the nontechnical journal received with basic membership in the Astronomical Society of the Pacific. The intended audiences are amateur astronomers (including young people), science educators, and interested general readers. The articles and features are informative, highly readable, and illustrated with black-and-white photographs. There is an emphasis on reviewing recent developments in astronomy and on the connections between astronomy and other research fields. This society has a strong interest in education and the dissemination of information to the public. In that light, its "Astronomical Resources" section in each issue is particularly useful because it provides a briefly annotated reading list of both introductory and advanced books and articles dealing with specific aspects of the field, as well as annual annotated lists of new astronomy books received in the previous year. The Abrams Planetarium's *Sky Calendar* (see below in this section) is sent free to recipients of *Mercury*.

Odyssey. *See under* CHILDREN/SCIENCE.

216   **Sky & Telescope.** 1941. m. $21.95. Leif J. Robinson. Sky Publg. Corp., P.O. Box 9111, Belmont, MA 02178. Illus. Adv. Index. Circ: 100,000. Sample. Vol. ends: June & Dec. Microform: IA, UMI. Reprint: Pub, UMI. [*Indexed*: MI, RG. *Bk. rev*: 4–5, 350–1,000 words, signed. *Aud*: Ages 14–18.]

Along with *Astronomy*, this is a basic journal for school and public libraries serving young people. It has long had the respect of professional astronomers as well as of amateurs. For the most part, its feature articles tend to be slightly more technical in language and presentation than those of its chief competitor, *Astronomy*, and it also has about 10 percent more advertising. Nevertheless, serious amateurs and professionals looking for an overview of developments in the field of astronomy will find this a valuable resource. In addition to the long feature articles, regular departments provide readers with news about recent research and events in the field; there are several pages of star maps and descriptions of astronomical objects to observe in the coming month. There is also something in each issue for the amateur telescope maker to enjoy. Most libraries will want to have both this title and *Astronomy*, but at least one of the two should be in the collection.

217   **Sky Calendar.** 1968. m. $6. Robert C. Victor. Abrams Planetarium, Michigan State Univ., East Lansing, MI 48824. Illus. Circ: 16,000. Sample. [*Aud*: Ages 14–18.]

Intended for skywatching laypersons, teachers, and students, the *Sky Calendar* is composed of separate monthly pages mailed at quarterly intervals. It offers high value at a bargain price. Each month's sheet has on one side a map of the evening sky depicting the principal constellations, some prominent star clusters, nebulae and galaxies, and the mid-month positions of observable planets. The other side of the monthly sheet has the "sky calendar," which in diagrams and brief text points out the highlights of each day's major astronomical events and the noteworthy positions of the moon and planets against the starry background. Because this guide is quite easy to read and use, it is an excellent teaching tool for the classroom, planetarium, or astronomy club, and librarians may even want to post the calendar on a bulletin board. It is worth noting that *Sky & Telescope* uses frames from the calendar in its planet pages, and that the Astronomical Society of the Pacific distributes the *Sky Calendar* to all its members.

218   **Telescope Making.** 1978. q. $12. Richard Berry. Kalmbach Publg. Co., P.O. Box 1612, Waukesha, WI 53187. Illus. Adv. Circ: 3,500. Sample. Vol. ends: No. 4. Reprint: Pub. [*Aud*: Ages 14–18.]

This is the "magazine *for*, *by*, and *about* telescope makers." In their quest to see more of the heavens, many amateur astronomers have designed and built their own telescopes, and this quarterly is their forum. Some 50 to 60 pages of informal articles per issue report on detailed telescope designs, the testing of optical systems, replicas of famous telescopes, major gatherings of telescope makers, and how to build observatories or transport telescopes and equipment. There are many illustrations and diagrams to complement the text. Of special value in each issue is the classified product directory providing names and addresses of commercial sources for the components needed by telescope makers.

Weatherwise. *See under* CHILDREN/SCIENCE.

■ **AUTOMOBILES**   [Lynn Heer]

In school libraries there is no more popular section than the one devoted to automobiles, and while the titles are directed to young adults and older drivers, at least two or three may be part of the collection in the lower grades. The American fascination with the automobile is reflected in all of the titles listed here. All can be recommended. Choice really depends on the specific interests of the readers—from a love of hot rods to a love affair with foreign cars. In some cases multiple subscriptions may be wanted to allow for much wear and for later binding. Note, too, that the basic titles all are indexed in *Readers' Guide* and in *Magazine Index* as well as related services. Therefore, it is relatively easy for the student to locate information on a used car or a potential hot rod.

First choices   (1) *Car and Driver*; (2) *Road & Track*; (3) Motor Trend; (4) *Hot Rod*.
Suitable for children   Ages 12–18: *Auto Racing Digest*; *Car Craft*; *Cycle*; *Dirt Bike*; *Hot Rod*; *Motor Trend*; *Road & Track*.

219   **Auto Racing Digest.** 1973. bi-m. $9.95. Michael Herbert. Century Publg. Co., 990 Grove St., Evanston, IL 60201. Illus. Adv. Microform: UMI. [*Aud*: Ages 12–18.]

This is a colorful, well-illustrated report on all types of auto racing throughout the world. It is one of the best of the magazines covering auto racing, and its articles are written for the racing enthusiast interested in everything from stock cars to Formula One Grand Prix events. In addition to a thorough report on each important race, there are articles and features on the drivers, the various types of vehicles, and racetrack conditions. *Auto Racing Digest* has action photos, statistics, and something of interest in every issue for anyone interested in auto racing. It is similar to *Autoweek*, an older and well-respected auto racing weekly.

220   **Autotech Magazine.** 1988. m. $21.75. C. Van Tune. LFP Inc., 9171 Wilshire Blvd., Suite 300, Beverly Hills, CA 90210. Illus. Adv. Sample. [*Aud*: Ages 14–18.]

Any teenager who drives for fun, frolic, and fashion will delight in reports of road tests that unequivocally state which convertible is best. Employing an easy-to-follow grading system, the editors "examine them closely not for acceleration, braking or slalom expertise, but for the things people buy convertibles for: Top down enjoyment." All price ranges are given. The 100 or so pages, liberally illustrated with color photographs, include three or four technical articles (tires, compression ratios, car leaks, superchargers, etc.) or features. The primary audience is the person involved with cars for speed and status, not just transportation, but even the most conventional driver will enjoy the snappy reports.

221   **Autoweek.** 1958. w. $23. Matt DeLorenzo. Competition Press/Crain Communications, 1400 Woodbridge Ave., Detroit, MI 48207. Illus. Adv. Circ: 161,111. [*Aud*: Ages 14–18.]

A weekly devoted exclusively to auto racing of all types throughout the world. The lengthy articles focus on the auto industry, sports sedans, performance, and sports cars. This is a must for all auto racing fans because of its extensive coverage of the international Grand Prix Formula One and stock car races. A calendar of events lists the important upcoming races. A classified section is included in each issue. This is similar in format to *Auto Racing Digest*.

222   **Car and Driver** (Formerly: *Sports Car Illustrated*). 1955. m. $14.98. David E. Davis, Jr. Diamandis Communications, Inc., 1633 Broadway, New York, NY 10009. Circ: 900,000. [*Indexed*: MI, RG. *Aud*: Ages 12–18.]

Thanks to enthusiastic, objective reports as well as excellent and frequent illustrations, this is a favorite among teenagers and is suitable for some younger readers. It covers domestic, foreign, and sports cars. Each issue contains several in-depth "road test" articles describing that particular auto's history, lineage, and performance. Detailed specifications are given for the engine, drivetrain, dimensions and capacities, interior comfort, suspension type, brakes, steering, wheels, and tires. Test results include acceleration, braking, handling, fuel economy, and interior sound level. Several articles in each issue focus on racing and automotive engineering topics.

223   **Car Craft.** 1953. m. $17.94. Jim McGowan. Petersen Publg. Co., 8490 Sunset Blvd., Los Angeles, CA 90069. Illus. Adv. Circ: 407,726. Microform: UMI. [*Aud*: Ages 14–18.]

Similar to *Hot Rod* in scope and format, this title is one of the standards of the genre. Feature articles describe how to modify cars to obtain more power and speed and how to improve their high-speed handling. The beautifully illustrated articles cover everything from street rods to classics. A calendar of events covers the major races along with race results. Like *Hot Rod*, it is certain to be popular in any public or high school library.

224   **Consumer Reports (Automobile Buying Guide).** 1936. m. $18. Irwin Landau. Consumers Union of the United States, 256 Washington St., Mt. Vernon, NY 10553. Illus. Circ: 3,850,000. [*Aud*: Ages 14–18.]

Although not considered an automotive magazine, *Consumer Reports* evaluates one or more autos or category of autos in each monthly issue. In each annual "Buying Guide" there is a frequency-of-repair survey compilation from subscribers detailing their experiences with their vehicles in actual daily use. This is a valuable piece of information for a potential purchaser of either a new or a used auto. For several years the April issue has been devoted primarily to automobile evaluations, because the auto is such an important consumer purchase.

225   **Cycle.** 1952. m. $13.98. Phil Shilling. Diamandis Communications, Inc., 1633 Broadway, New York, NY 10009. Illus. Adv. Circ: 32,398. Microform: B&H, MIM, UMI. [*Indexed*: MI, RG. *Aud*: Ages 12–18.]

This is one of the basic magazines to consult for cycle and cycling accessories and tools evaluations. Several very detailed road tests are included in each issue with both color and black-and-white photographs of the cycle tested. Also covered in the tests are specifications on all aspects of the engines, transmissions, and performance. In addition, there are technical articles on various cycle mechanical parts. Racing events are also covered in each issue. Recommended for all libraries.

226   **Dirt Bike.** 1971. m. $14.98. Rick Sieman. Hi-Torque Publns., Inc., 10600 Sepulveda Blvd., Mission Hills, CA 91345. Subs. to: P.O. Box 9502, Mission Hills, CA 91345. Illus. Adv. Circ: 176,062. Vol. ends: Dec. [*Aud*: Ages 12–18.]

This is the authoritative title of the off-road sports world. Starting with its spectacular cover, *Dirt Bike* is packed with black-and-white and color action photos. There are sections on technical maintenance, skills, racing events, product evaluations, and so on. An ongoing series is "Places to Ride," a series that will eventually cover all 50 states. Regular columns are "From the Saddle" (human interest) and "Mister Knowit-all" (questions from readers). *Dirt Bike* has a responsible attitude. Bikers are cautioned against trying the stunts in the action photos; these are only for the experienced and professionals. There are reminders about appropriate equipment for safety, and a concern for environmental and ecological matters.

227 **Four Wheeler Magazine: world's leading four wheel drive magazine.**1962. m. $14.87. Rich Johnson. Penthouse Intl., 1965 Broadway, New York, NY 10023. Illus. Adv. Circ: 222,835. [*Aud*: Ages 14–18.]

One of the best of the magazines devoted to the highly popular four-wheel drive vehicles. Each issue contains several feature articles covering racing and hunting using the four-wheel drive vehicle. Numerous technical articles and departments in each issue provide the latest information on the mechanical repair and maintenance considerations of owning and operating these vehicles. The primary emphasis of the magazine is on keeping these vehicles in top condition and on improving their performance.

228 **Hot Rod.** 1948. m. $17.94. Jeff Smith. Petersen Publg. Co., 8490 Sunset Blvd., Los Angeles, CA 90069. Illus. Adv. Circ: 794,996. [*Indexed*: MI, RG. *Aud*: Ages 12–18.]

One of the more popular automobile magazines in junior high and high school. This is the high-performance-oriented magazine that has spawned legions of imitators. *Hot Rod* is written for readers who want speed, high performance, and outstanding appearance from their autos. The articles are a mixture of "how-I-did-it" with color photos and technical articles describing how various automotive parts/systems function and how it is possible to modify them for speed and performance improvements. This title remains one of the best of the automotive magazines in terms of quality and reader appeal. It is a definite choice for all public and school libraries.

229 **Kart Sport.** 1982. m. $20. Joe Xavier. Kart Sport, 5570 Ashbarn Rd., Baltimore, MD 21227. Illus. Adv. [*Aud*: Ages 14–18.]

The kart is a cut-down version of an automobile and is raced both on tracks and off-road. This is a popular type of auto racing that continues to grow in popularity. The articles are short and easy to read for both the veteran kart-racing fan and the newcomer. The issues have lots of photos and ads.

230 **Motor Magazine.** 1903. m. $16. Wade Hoyt. Hearst Corp., 645 Stewart Ave., Garden City, NY 11530. Illus. Adv. Circ: 125,500. Microform: UMI. [*Aud*: Ages 14–18.]

A basic title in the field, this is primarily for the automotive mechanic or student. Each issue covers the latest in maintenance and repair techniques for automobiles and trucks. The articles are technical, although well within the understanding of a high school student mechanic. Features cover new products, labor, legislation, the automotive service business, and other items of interest to professional mechanics, shop owners, and managers. The emphasis is on the repair and service aspects of the industry. This is an appropriate title for the vocational-technical school library or special automotive collection.

231 **Motor Trend.** 1949. m. $19.94. Mike Anson. Petersen Publg. Co., 8490 Sunset Blvd., Los Angeles, CA 90069. Illus. Adv. Circ: 745,363. Microform: UMI. [*Indexed*: MI, RG. *Aud*: Ages 14–18.]

This is one of the best of the general-interest auto magazines. It covers all types of autos sold in the United States along with product evaluations. Feature articles describe the details of new models and provide projections of automotive industry trends from the viewpoint primarily of the general public/consumer. Several extensive road tests are described in each issue, offering detailed performance data along with several pictures of each car tested. Owner surveys and long-term tests are found in many issues. This title is also known for its prized "Car of the Year" award. This is a top-notch auto magazine of interest to a wide audience. Recommended for school and public libraries.

232 **Popular Hot Rodding Magazine.** 1962. m. $16.94. Pete Pesterre. Argus Pubs. Corp., P.O. Box 49659, Los Angeles, CA 90049. Illus. Adv. Circ: 243,722. [*Aud*: Ages 14–18.]

This standard title has been around for a long time. It differs from *Hot Rod* by emphasizing racing events. It does overlap with that title in its coverage of parts, accessories, repair, new products, and customizing. The magazine is attractively illustrated and easy to read. The do-it-yourself articles and features are well written and of value to both adults and high school students interested in auto mechanics either as hobby or profession. Articles cover automotive engineering made simple, project cars, drag races, and hot rods.

233 **Road & Track.** 1947. m. $19.94. Tom Bryant. Diamandis Communications, Inc., 1499 Monrovia Ave., Newport Beach, CA 92663. Illus. Adv. Circ: 700,000. Microform: UMI. [*Aud*: Ages 14–18.]

This is one of the best of the general-interest auto magazines. It is a venerable standard for the auto enthusiast and emphasizes sports/performance automobiles, most of which are quite expensive. Its evaluations are on the opposite end of the spectrum from what one finds in *Consumer Reports*. The road tests in each issue give extensive details on comfort as well as the performance and mechanical specifications of the engine, drivetrain, and suspension. Each issue contains articles on various sports/performance autos and auto racing events. Recommended for all public and high school libraries.

■ **AVIATION AND SPACE SCIENCE** [Robert J. Havlik]

See also: ASTRONOMY

Magazines found here are for the aviation buff and for the young adult interested in the thrills of space flight and exploration. An extensive literature has developed in both areas, and the titles may move from the glossy newsstand item to the highly technical scientific journal. Choice is not always easy. The magazines selected are those that are indexed and are most likely to appeal to the high school reader. Most of these are characterized by relatively easy-to-follow articles and usually numerous illustrations. Where a narrow selection is necessary, one should follow the first choices listed below. If more interest (and money) is evident, then any magazine in this section will be suitable for the average high school or public library.

First choices (1) *Flying*; (2) *Air & Space/Smithsonian*; (3) *Aviation Week and Space Technology*.

Suitable for children   Ages 10–18: *Flying.*

234   **Aero: the aircraft owners magazine.** 1968. m. $24. Mary F. Stlitch. Fancy Publns., Inc., P.O. Box 6050, Mission Viejo, CA 92690. Illus. Adv. Circ: 89,000. Vol. ends: Dec. [*Bk. rev*: 1–2. *Aud*: Ages 14–18.]

     The objective of this magazine is to assist aircraft owners in buying, selling, maintaining, and operating private airplanes. Obviously, it will be the rare student who owns a plane, but the discussion of the subject will be of great interest to any young person involved with flight. It supplies useful tips on how to continue to fly safely; how to get the best buys on services, products, and fuel; how to be aware of the latest regulations and airport/airway changes; and how to keep maintenance costs down.

235   **Aerospace Historian.** 1954. q. $25. F. Clifton Berry, Jr. Air Force Historical Foundation, Sunflower Univ. Press, 1531 Yuma, P.O. Box 1009, Manhattan, KS 66502-4228. Illus. Adv. Circ: 4,500. Refereed. Vol. ends: Dec. Microform: UMI. Reprint: UMI. [*Bk. rev*: 10–15, 200–750 words, signed. *Aud*: Ages 14–18.]

     While there is a flood of magazines devoted to the history of military aviation, none has the authority of this journal. It is sponsored by the Air Force Historical Foundation, and its basic goal is to publish articles on the preservation and perpetuation of the history and traditions of American aviation with emphasis on the U.S. Air Force. It has many excellent articles ranging from balloon operations to automatic rocket launch processing and includes stories of foreign aircraft against which Americans have fought. The articles are written by aerospace historians and military professionals, and all are important statements on the history of American aviation.

236   **Air & Space/Smithsonian** (Formerly: *Air and Space*). 1987. bi-m. $18. George C. Larson. Smithsonian Institution, Natl. Air and Space Museum, 370 L'Enfant Promenade S.W., Washington, DC 20024-2518. Illus. Adv. Circ: 350,000. Vol. ends: No. 6. Microform: UMI. Reprint: UMI. [*Bk. rev*: 4–5, 800–1,000 words. *Aud*: Ages 14–18.]

     Any younger reader who has been to the Smithsonian will enjoy this excellent journal. Of course it appeals too to others who simply have an interest in air and space flight. The goal of the National Air and Space Museum (NASM) in Washington, D.C., is to show where U.S. aerospace technology has excelled and where other countries have made significant contributions. In addition, it houses the world's most outstanding collection of historic airplanes and rockets. The articles are based on NASM exhibits and research done in the NASM library. Each issue covers a broad range of topics from aviation history to the latest scientific and cultural advances in space science. The book reviews vary in length and general interest and frequently include reviews of new movies that have general aeronautics or space themes. This well-written and colorful periodical will be one of the few read from cover to cover in a public or school library.

237   **Air Progress.** 1941. m. $26.50. Michael O'Leary. Challenge Publns., Inc., 7950 Deering Ave., Canoga Park, CA 91304. Illus. Adv. Vol. ends: Dec. Microform: UMI. Reprint: UMI. [*Indexed*: ASTI, MI. *Bk. rev*: 1–2. *Aud*: Ages 14–18.]

     Teenage readers will thoroughly enjoy this glossy journal. It covers, in a narrative style, a broad range of piston aircraft types. A special feature is the "Annual Guide to New Avionics." *Air Progress* is one of the oldest general aviation magazines, and the publisher has produced several spin-off publications. *Air Progress Military Airpower* deals with today's warplanes and the men who fly and build them. *Air Classics* magazine covers famous airplanes, pilots, and historical air battles. *Warbirds International* reports on all the latest restorations. *Air Combat* deals with aerial combat intelligence. *Unlimited: The Magazine of High-Performance Air Racing* is even more specialized. Journals such as these are heaven for the aviation buff and are interesting for their archival value. Unfortunately, they are largely unindexed, and the articles are hard to retrieve once the issues are out of print.

238 **Aviation Week and Space Technology** (Continuation of *Aviation Week*; incorporating *Space Technology*). 1916. w. $58. Donald E. Fink. McGraw-Hill, Inc., 1221 Ave. of the Americas, New York, NY 10020. Illus. Adv. Circ: 139,045. Vol. ends: No. 26. Microform: UMI. Online: DIALOG. Reprint: UMI. [*Indexed*: ASTI, MI, RG. *Aud*: Ages 14–18.]

This weekly news and feature magazine is familiar to anyone who is interested in aeronautics or space flight. It has been revamped to enhance its role as the preeminent information source for the global aerospace/defense industry and includes a new section called "Aerospace Business." Although there is now a greater emphasis on space technology to meet the growing needs of the industry, this title will continue its feature sections "Air Transport," "Business Flying," and "Airlines." The illustrations are colorful, exciting, and applicable to the features; data are accurate. The journal continues to have one of the highest subscription renewal rates in the country and is frequently cited all over the world as an authoritative source of information on all matters of aerospace/defense-related high-technology activities. If a school or public library can afford to subscribe to only one magazine in the field, this should be it.

239 **Flying: world's most widely read aviation magazine.** 1927. m. $18.98. Richard L. Collins. Diamandis Communications, Inc., 1633 Broadway, New York, NY 10009. Illus. Adv. Index. Circ: 339,692. Vol. ends: Dec. Microform: UMI. Online: DIALOG. Reprint: UMI. [*Indexed*: MI, RG. *Bk. rev*: 1–2, signed. *Aud*: Ages 10–18.]

This widely read magazine is favored in many public libraries and schools because of its scope and the relatively easy reading matter, which is augmented by numerous illustrations. There are several features, such as "Pilot Reports," that will set the reader dreaming of purchasing a plane. Feature articles, using many beautiful color photographs illustrating the experience of flying, make this an upbeat journal that will stimulate the enjoyment of flight for all.

240 **Plane and Pilot: the magazine for active piston-engine pilots** (Incorporating *Airways*). 1965. m. $16.95. Steve Werner. Werner Publg. Corp., 16000 Ventura Blvd., Suite 800, Encino, CA 91436-2782. Illus. Adv. Circ: 75,000. Vol. ends: Dec. Microform: UMI. Reprint: UMI. [*Bk. rev*: 1–2. *Aud*: Ages 14–18.]

Students interested in the joys of learning how to fly will thoroughly enjoy this magazine. Even those without a desire to fly will find the illustrations and brief articles of value. It contains feature articles on new aircraft, events of interest, and news items. A special "Careers in Aviation" issue makes this a cut above the rest for younger people. Not only do articles review current and future jobs in the industry, but a guide to universities, schools, and flight facilities will help answer many questions high school students may have regarding a future in aviation.

241 **Space World.** 1963. 12/yr. $30 ($18, if under 22 or over 64). Leonard David. Palmer Publns., Inc., 318 Main St., Amherst, WI 54406. Illus. Adv. Index. Circ: 18,500. Vol. ends:

No. 12. Microform: B&H, UMI. Reprint: UMI. [*Indexed*: MI, RG. *Bk. rev*: 1–2, signed. *Aud*: Ages 14–18.]

Space World is published in cooperation with the National Space Society, founded by the late Dr. Wernher von Braun and recently merged with the L-t Society. *Space World* publishes nontechnical articles on U.S. and foreign space activities, including assessment of Soviet programs, space tourism, and planetary programs. In addition to feature articles by freelance authors and a special section called "Space Advocate," which is an up-to-date review of the society's activities and policies, there are several department sections such as "Readers' Forum," "Washington Orbit," "Careers," and "Milestones." The "Reviews" department features one or two signed reviews on recent space-oriented books of a more popular nature. The journal will be of most interest to high school readers who are aware of the effect that an increased knowledge of space has on their lives.

242 **Spaceflight: the international magazine of space and astronautics.** 1956. m. £35. G. V. Groves British Interplanetary Soc., Ltd., 27/29 S. Lambeth Rd., London SW8 1SZ, England. Illus. Adv. Index. Circ: 5,000. Vol. ends: No. 12. Microform: UMI. [*Bk. rev*: 6–10, 200–300 words. *Aud*: Ages 14–18.]

Difficult concepts are made relatively easy in this journal directed to young adults and adults. Its goal is to report on a wide range of astronautical topics of interest. In addition to "Society News and Correspondence," regular sections include "Soviet Science," "Up-Date-USA," "European Rendezvous," "Space at JPL," and "Book Reviews," which are short descriptions of new books, videos, and slide sets. The feature articles are short, well-illustrated papers on such topics of current interest as secondhand spacecraft, supplying power to lunar stations, space for rent, and the threat of space debris to future space exploration.

■ **BIRDS** [Olive F. Whitehead]

See also: ENVIRONMENT, CONSERVATION, AND OUTDOOR RECREATION

Magazines in this section are for children and young adults who are bird-watchers, or have an interest in birds. If there is a local bird club, both public and school libraries ought to receive a few publications for assistance in the identification of birds. All of the magazines nicely supplement courses about birds.

First choices (1) *Audubon*; (2) *American Birds*.
Suitable for children Ages 4–9: *Chickadee*. Ages 10–18: *Audubon*.

243 **American Birds: a bimonthly journal devoted to the birds of the Americas** (Incorporating *Audubon Field Notes*). 1947. 5/yr. $27.50. Susan Roney Orennan. Natl. Audubon Soc., 950 Third Ave., New York, NY 10022. Illus. Adv. Index. Circ: 14,500. Refereed. Vol. ends: Nov/Dec. Microform: UMI. [*Indexed*: BioAg. *Bk. rev*: 2–5, 300–1,000 words, signed. *Aud*: Ages 14–18.]

Thanks to excellent illustrations and a wide coverage of the subject, this is an ideal bird magazine for teenagers. Major areas of interest are the changing distribution, population, migration, rare occurrence, ecology, and behavior of the birds of North and South America, including Middle America and the West Indies. Each issue except the Christmas bird count publishes ten or more articles on field identification, new records, changes in distribution, and migration. Four issues have a long section entitled "Changing Seasons," which lists bird sightings by geographical regions. These sections denote the time of year and activity—Autumn Migration, Winter Season, Spring Migration, and Nesting Season. In the July issue "The Christmas Bird Count," made during the preceding December, is published.

244   **Audubon** (Formerly: *Bird-Lore*). 1899. bi-m. $20 (Membership). Les Line. Natl. Audubon Soc., 950 Third Ave., New York, NY 10022. Illus. Adv. Circ: 434,987. Vol. ends: Nov. Microform: B&H, MIM, UMI. [*Indexed*: RG. *Aud*: Ages 10–18.]

The basic bird magazine, this may be enjoyed by children (if only for the excellent pictures) and by all young adults. *Audubon* has broadened its coverage into all fields of biology: botany, entomology, ichthyology, ornithology, zoology, and so forth. Articles on the preservation and conservation of natural resources appear in almost every issue. As the voice for an organization with an aggressive policy against pollution and for protection of natural resources, *Audubon* will appeal to readers sharing these concerns.

245   **Bird Watcher's Digest.** 1978. bi-m. $15. Mary Beacom Bowers. William H. Thompson, P.O. Box 110, Marietta, OH 45750. Illus. Adv. Index. Circ: 58,000. Vol. ends: July/Aug. Microform: B&H. [*Bk. rev*: 8–12, 30–100 words. *Aud*: Ages 14–18.]

This attractive magazine publishes articles written for it and a few reprinted from other sources. All aspects of observation and identification of bird life throughout the world are described by amateur and professional ornithologists. An interesting section publishes replies to queries from readers about bird behavior or appearance that is unusual for the species. Poetry, humor, cartoons, and color photographs enhance the appeal of the magazine.

Chickadee. *See under* CHILDREN/GENERAL MAGAZINES.

246   **Journal of Field Ornithology** (Formerly: *Bird-Banding*). 1930. q. $35 (Individuals, $18). Jerome A. Jackson. Assn. of Field Ornithologists. Subs. to: Ornithological Socs. of North America, P.O. Box 21618, Columbus, OH 43221-0618. Illus. Index. Circ: 1,800. Refereed. Vol. ends: Autumn (No. 4). Microform: UMI. [*Bk. rev*: 4–12, 100–300 words, signed. *Aud*: Ages 14–18.]

Each issue contains original articles reporting on studies of birds in their natural habitats. In addition to bird banding, population counts on individual species, migration, ecology, behavior, songs and vocalization, and wildlife management are studied. Beginning in 1989, the North American breeding bird surveys are published as an annual supplement. Articles include a Spanish translation of the title and abstract, and the journal includes a Spanish table of contents in addition to its English one. Contributors are from throughout the world, but especially from North, South, and Central America.

247   **The Living Bird Quarterly** (Formerly: *Living Bird*). 1982. q. $25 (Membership). Jill Crane. Cornell Lab. of Ornithology, 159 Sapsucker Woods, Ithaca, NY 14850. Illus. Adv. Circ: 14,000. Vol. ends: Autumn. [*Aud*: Ages 14–18.]

This attractive magazine from the Laboratory of Ornithology at Cornell University presents readable articles on all aspects of bird life. Environmental concerns including conservation of habitats, acid rain, and destruction of tropical rain forests are covered regularly. "Bird Notes" reviews current research and activities related to ornithology. The articles are written to appeal to the general reader. Such a magazine with its many colorful illustrations should be available in public libraries and in school libraries where there are active bird clubs.

■ **BOATS**   [David Van deStreek]

See also: SPORTS

While few high school students can afford a large boat, almost any young adult can either dream or find the funds to purchase (or rent) a small boat. Appeal is naturally wider in communities near the water, but even inland the boat magazine has a large circulation. The titles selected are all suitable for teenagers, although many of them, such as *Boating*, are geared for adults with large budgets.

First choices   (1) *Motor Boating & Sailing*; (2) *Small Boat Journal*.

248   **Boating.** 1956. m. $21.94 G. Doug Schryver. Diamandis Communications, Inc., 1633 Broadway, New York, NY 10009. Illus. Adv. Index. Circ: 191,934. Sample. Vol. ends: Dec. Microform: UMI. Online: DIALOG. [*Indexed*: Acs, MI. *Aud*: Ages 14–18.]

The most popular of all boating periodicals—if circulation can be used as the measure—this magazine is written for the boating interest group that favors high-performing sports boats and motor yachts. Most of these boats are well beyond the reach of young adults, but there is no harm in dreaming or in studying the possibilities for the future. Feature articles are general, regularly addressing issues of naval electronics, seamanship, and sport fishing, in addition to the standard fare of boat tests. Articles are well written and informative, often with a technical orientation. The magazine is highly polished, with slick pages and extensive color and graphics. Advertising is abundant and seems to dominate the almost 300-page publication. It can be either a distraction or a source of consumer information, depending on the reader. As the magazine is increasinlgy oriented toward more exotic and expensive boats, libraries subscribing should consider balancing this with *Small Boat Journal*.

249   **Canoe: North America's resource for canoeing & kayaking.** 1973. bi-m. $15. David Harrison. Canoe America Assocs., P.O. Box 3146, Kirkland, WA 98083. Illus. Adv. Circ: 60,275. Sample. Vol. ends: Dec. Microform: UMI. [*Bk. rev*: 2–3, 350–500 words, signed. *Aud*: Ages 14–18.]

The magazine of choice for canoeists and kayakers, this is crammed with information useful for either sport. Aimed at both beginners and experts, it regularly features columns addressing technical and practical aspects such as paddling techniques, equipment, and health. The heart of the magazine, however, is the large number of trips described, varying from day outings to international packaged tours. These narratives often feature finely styled prose and also contain very important trip-preparation information and resource contacts. Other special features are directories of paddling schools and outfitters, and water tests of new canoes and kayaks. The year-end issue is an annual buyer's guide for equipment and accessories. The magazine is endorsed by the American Canoe Association.

250   **Fathom: surface ship & submarine safety review.** 1969. q. $13. W. G. Welge. Supt. of Docs., U.S. Govt. Printing Office, Washington, DC 20402. Illus. Vol. ends: Spring. [*Aud*: Ages 14–18.]

A popularly written publication from the Naval Safety Center. This is somewhat technical, but much of the material will appeal to young adults who have access to boats or are interested in the sport. The signed articles by U.S. Navy personnel address equipment, training, and behavioral aspects of boating safety. The articles are often motivational in tone and emphasize preparedness.

251   **Motor Boating & Sailing.** 1907. m. $15.97. Peter Janssen. Hearst Magazines, 224 W. 57th St., New York, NY 10019. Illus. Adv. Circ: 142,000. Sample. Vol. ends: June & Dec. Microform: UMI. [*Indexed*: MI, RG. *Aud*: Ages 14–18.]

One of the oldest and most widely circulated boating magazines, this might be the one to purchase if school or public libraries need only one general-purpose periodical. It has all the production qualities of a successful publication—glossy pages, lots of color, and stylish graphics. Covering both sail and powered craft, it blends basics with technical material and can appeal to the casual or the well-seasoned boater. The writing is sound and authoritative, with feature articles pertaining to virtually every aspect of boating. The price of success, however, is a magazine that is literally heavy with advertising; with issues commonly numbering from 200 to 300 pages, there are relatively few pages that are untouched by an advertisement.

252   **Sail.** 1970. m. $21.75. Patience Wales. Cahners Publg. Co., 275 Washington St., Newton, MA 02158-1630. Illus. Adv. Circ: 175,212. Sample. Vol. ends: Dec. Microform: UMI. [*Indexed*: MI. *Bk. rev*: 3, 300–600 words, signed. *Aud*: Ages 14–18.]

One of the highest circulation boating periodicals, this has all the qualities that establish and maintain popularity with a wide range of readers. Limited to sail craft, it emphasizes the pleasure aspect of sailing, while still providing a balance of practical information. Features are often written in a first-person narrative style, emphasizing the basics without becoming overly technical. These are directed to the full range of sailors from beginners to die-hard enthusiasts. Each issue is thick and contains a lot of advertising, but this is integrated well with the feature parts of the magazine, and tends not to be offensive or distracting. A very complete magazine that should be one of the cornerstones of any boating collection.

253   **Small Boat Journal.** 1979. bi-m. $17.95. Richard Lebovitz. Billian Publg. Co., 2100 Powers Ferry Rd., Atlanta, GA 30339. Illus. Adv. Circ: 58,000. Sample. [*Bk. rev*: 3, 500–750 words, signed. *Aud*: Ages 14–18.]

Intended for those whose tastes, ambitions, or budgets are modest (i.e., younger readers), this magazine covers all types of boats under 30 feet in length, whether powered by oar, sail, or motor. It is literally packed with interesting and usable information, oriented toward equipment, seamanship, boat design, and customizing. It also contains a good amount of product assessment and evaluation. Like the boats that it features, the magazine has a compact quality, with regular columns containing more lines per inch than most boating periodicals. The graphics are very good, though color photography is used sparingly. Numerous excellent line drawings are employed to illustrate and highlight textual material. With its target audience being the largest group of boat owners, the publication fills a very useful niche, and should have broad appeal to those who prefer unpretentiousness both in their boats and in their magazines.

254   **WoodenBoat: the magazine for wooden boat owners, builders, and designers.** 1974. bi-m. $19.95. Jonathan A. Wilson. WoodenBoat Publns., P.O. Box 78, Brooklin, ME 04616. Illus. Adv. Index. Circ: 103,180. Sample. [*Bk. rev*: 1–2, 750–1,000 words, signed. *Aud*: Ages 14–18.]

Dedicated to the art, the craft, and the people involved with wooden-hulled boats, this magazine, like the vessels that it venerates, is a finely crafted periodical. If offers easy-to-follow directions for the care and the construction of wooden boats. While the building may be a trifle advanced for most young readers, the emphasis on upkeep is well within their understanding. Also, the numerous, illustrated articles on the lore of the boat will be appreciated by any age group.

■ BOOK REVIEWS

See also: Professional Education and Library Journals/Library and Book Review Journals/Media and Media Reviews

There are no general book reviews suitable in their entirety for younger readers. On the other hand, many of the subject magazines do carry limited book reviews, as well as notes on video, recordings, and so forth. Those with such features are noted in all of the sections.

First choice   (1) *New York Times Book Review.*

255   **Bestsellers.** 1989. q. $45. Donna Olendorf. Gale Research, Inc., Dept. 77748, Detroit, MI 48277-8748. Illus. [*Aud:* Ages 14–18.]

This title offers 85 pages of basically favorable comment on 25 to 30 current popular writers. The three-page profiles open with a plug for the author, a typical 150–300 word excerpt from the best-seller being considered, and well-chosen comments from five or six typical reviews. Add less than world-shaking views of the writer, and one has the formula worked out by *People Magazine* pretty well in hand. Among those with their best pen forward are Tom Wolfe, Erich Segal, Elmore Leonard, Judith Krantz, Donald Trump, Lee Iacocca, and other talk-show types. A few heavies are aboard—Don DeLillo, Gabriel Garcia Marquez, and Paul Kennedy. The editor/publisher can boast, along with Danielle Steel, "a strong sense of responsibility for my readers." So, while totally predictable, the new publication should be welcomed by all libraries where reading is fun.

256   **Books/100 Reviews** (Formerly: *West Coast Review of Books*). 1974. bi-m. $8.94. D. David Dreis. Rapport Publg. Co., Inc., 5265 Fountain, Upper Terrace, Los Angeles, CA 90029. Adv. Circ: 80,000. [*Indexed:* BoRvI, ChBkRvI. *Aud:* Ages 14–18.]

A lively reviewing tool that balances examination of new trade titles with retrospective looks at older publications, this has some appeal for young adults seeking more than what is found in the *New York Times.* Published in Los Angeles, this magazine seems to be imbued with some of that city's fast-paced entertainment ethic. Issues offer about five feature articles, and regional literary activities receive the most attention. Some sections actually excerpt portions from important new works. Although *Books/100 Reviews* is an excellent choice for western libraries, it also contains enough substance to belong in medium- to large-size collections nationwide.

257   **The Los Angeles Times Book Review.** w. Inquire. Jack Miles. Los Angeles Times, Times Mirror Sq., Los Angeles, CA 90035. Illus. Adv. Index. Circ: 1,358,420. Vol. ends: Dec. Microform: UMI. [*Bk. rev:* 12–25, 600 words, signed. *Aud:* Ages 14–18.]

This is Los Angeles's answer to the *New York Times Book Review.* It is shorter than its East Coast counterpart, but employs the same general newspaper review tabloid format and features. Basically, each issue has about 12 one- to two-page reviews and several small sections containing multiple book notes on a related topic. Befitting its city of origin, the reviews often focus on drama, television, and other entertainment industry publications. Subscription information is disappointingly unclear. Recommended for those western and other large libraries where the *Los Angeles Times* is an essential fixture.

258 **The New York Times Book Review.** 1890. w. $22. Harvey Shapiro. The New York Times, 229 W. 43rd St., New York, NY 10036. Illus. Adv. Index. Circ: 1,560,000. Vol. ends: Dec. Microform: Pub. [*Indexed*: BoRv. *Bk. rev*: 50, 50–3,000 words, signed. *Aud*: Ages 14–18.]

The *New York Times* remains one of the most authoritative newspapers in circulation; this influential 50- to 60-page review magazine, published with the Sunday *Times*, appeals to a large audience with an appropriately wide range of interests. This includes young adults, at least those interested enough in reading to consider book reviews. It is not, though, for your average teenager, if only because the reviews are primarily of adult books. A historically distinguishing feature of the *NYTBR* is its ability to offer expertly written, highly readable commentary on current books. Reviews vary in each issue from lengthy essays on scholarly monographs to brief descriptions of paperback fiction. There are regular departments, for example, the "In Short" summaries of new novels and nonfiction, punctuated by small graphics and boxed abstracts, as well as occasional special sections on science-technology titles or children's books. The magazine also profiles best-sellers through lists that should be considered reliable guides for public library acquisitions. This is the one newspaper book review that is essential for school and public libraries.

■ **BUSINESS, ECONOMICS, AND LABOR**

[Business: Karen Chapman. Economics: Deonna L. Taylor. Labor: Carol Gambrell]

All of the magazines in this section support the curriculum in high school or the needs of young adults who turn to the public library. The popular titles, from *Money* to *Nation's Business*, are well known to adults. They are informative, often biased, and usually as involved with politics and the state of the nation and world as with business, economics, or labor per se. It is hard to imagine high school students reading them for amusement, but many are necessary to support course work.

First choices (1) *Nation's Business*; (2) *Challenge*; (3) *The Economist*; (4) *Money*.

259 **Advertising Age: Crain's international newspaper of marketing.** 1930. w. $76. Rance E. Crain. Crain Communications, Inc., 220 E. 42nd St., New York, NY 10017-5806. Illus. Adv. Index. Circ: 93,823. Sample. Vol. ends: Dec. Microform: B&H, IA, MIM, UMI. Online: Nexis. [*Indexed*: BI, BusI. *Aud*: Ages 14–18.]

Still the leader among advertising magazines, this broad-based title covers all major advertising news, trends, and developments, and all major types of advertising from incentives to broadcasting to direct marketing. There are frequent profiles of winning campaigns, in-depth special reports on such techniques as test marketing, and histories of major companies. Besides longer feature articles, each issue contains people news, international news, print-media news, direct marketing news, editorials, help-wanted ads, and several regular columnists. Considering the wealth of information and relatively low price of each issue, this title is a bargain. Highly recommended for public and high school libraries with interest in advertising and related areas of business.

260   **AFL-CIO News.** 1956. bi-w. $10. Rex Hardesty. AFL-CIO, 815 16th St. N.W., Washington, DC 20006. Illus. Circ: 75,000. Vol. ends: Dec. Microform: UMI. Online: DIALOG. Reprint: UMI. [*Bk. rev*: Occasional, signed. *Aud*: Ages 14–18.]

Young adults looking for the labor point of view should turn here first, followed by the more objective *Monthly Labor Review*. This official newspaper of the AFL-CIO covers major labor stories, labor legislation, and union activities. In it can be found stories about efforts to privatize the post office, recent wage settlements, the cause of a building collapse, and how a congressman voted on a recent bill. Occasionally, the *American Federationist* appears as an insert with an in-depth article on a topic such as the trade crisis or presidential candidates. The stories are professional and reportorial, but can be rather staid. Because of the ALF-CIO's importance, this is a useful source for current awareness and research on organized labor's viewpoint on a wide range of current issues.

261   **Business Week.** 1929. w. $39.95. Stephen B. Shepard. McGraw-Hill, Inc., 1221 Ave. of the Americas, New York, NY 10020. Illus. Adv. Index. Circ: 864,683. Microform: UMI. Online: DIALOG, Mead Data Central. Reprint: UMI. [*Indexed*: BusI, PAIS. *Bk. rev*: 1, 1,000 words, signed. *Aud*: Ages 14–18.]

While much more colorful than in past years, this is still not up to the wider coverage found in *U.S. News & World Report* (see News and Opinion section). Still, it has a certain appeal for young adults who are deeply involved with business as a probable career. Articles report on current business activities and events that have an impact on the U.S. economy. The articles are usually quite short, except for the cover story, which is an in-depth feature. *Business Week* is attractive and easy to read and is recommended for public and high school libraries.

262   **Challenge: the magazine of economic affairs.** 1952. bi-m. $42 (Individuals, $32). Richard Bartel. M.E. Sharpe, Inc., 80 Business Park Dr., Armonk, NY 10504. Illus. Adv. Index. Circ: 5,000. Refereed. Vol. ends: Nov/Dec. Microform: UMI. [*Indexed*: BI, BusI, PAIS. *Bk. rev*: 1–3, several pages, signed. *Aud*: Ages 14–18.]

Although they write for the layperson (and advanced high school students), the contributors to this magazine tend to be eminent scholars or economists from industry and government. The writing is clear, nontechnical, and objective. Topic coverage is broad, with articles usually discussing high-impact current issues such as the regulation of financial markets, the trade deficit, the debt crisis, and electoral cycles. Diversity of viewpoints is encouraged. Each issue contains five or six articles, interviews with nationally known figures, and in-depth book reviews. A unique feature is a listing of further readings on each topic.

263   **Dollars & Sense (Somerville).** 1974. m. $36 (Individuals, $19.50). Patricia Horn. Economic Affairs Bureau, Inc., One Summer St., Somerville, MA 02143. Illus. Circ: 8,500. Sample. [*Indexed*: API, PAIS. *Aud*: Ages 14–18.]

Dollars & Sense analyzes economic issues from a democratic left perspective for adults and young adults. Topics include labor, working women, welfare, and health care, as well as trends in trade and employment. Jargon-free language, accessible layout, and clear charts and illustrations appeal to the general reader. Written by journalists under an editorial collective that includes reputable Ph.D.'s in economics, the articles are generally well researched. This fills a gap between hard-to-read scholarly journals in economics and the popular newsmagazines, offering an alternative both in political slant and in focus on bread-and-butter issues of general concern.

264 **The Economist.** 1843. w. $98. Rupert Pennant Rea. Economist Newspaper, Ltd., 10 Rockefeller Plaza, 10th Fl., New York, NY 10020. Illus. Adv. Index. Circ: 169,598. Microform: UMI. Online: Mead Data Central, VU/TEXT. Reprint: UMI. [*Indexed*: BusI, PAIS. *Bk. rev*: 3–4, 500–750 words. *Aud*: Ages 14–18.]

British in origin, *The Economist* reports world news and current events, with sections for business and financial news. Many consider this not only a business magazine, which it is, but a world version of *Time/Newsweek*. It not only reports in a lively way on activities in England, where it is published, but has a large section on the United States as well as coverage of Europe and third-world countries. It supposes an educated audience, but an advanced high school student should be able to make sense out of most of the analysis.

265 **Forbes.** 1917. bi-w. $48. James W. Michaels. Forbes, Inc., 60 Fifth Ave., New York, NY 10011. Illus. Adv. Index. Circ: 735,000. Vol. ends: Dec. Microform: B&H, MIM, UMI. Online: DIALOG, Mead Data Central. Reprint: UMI. [*Indexed*: BusI. *Aud*: Ages 14–18.]

Forbes is a general business magazine that celebrates capitalism. The short articles report on company activities, industry developments, and economic trends. Investment tips are also given. The magazine extols the joys of the free enterprise system. One of its familiar special issues contains the "Forbes 400," a list of the 400 richest people in America. On the whole, it provides some of the best coverage of business news available, making it a recommended purchase for public libraries.

266 **Fortune.** 1930. bi-w. $47.97. Marshall Loeb. Time, Inc., Time & Life Bldg., Rockefeller Center, New York, NY 10020-1393. Illus. Adv. Circ: 724,822. Vol. ends: June. Microform: B&H, MIM, UMI. Online: VU/TEXT. Reprint: UMI. [*Indexed*: BusI, PAIS. *Bk. rev*: 1, 1,500 words, signed. *Aud*: Ages 14–18.]

Fortune is a general business magazine that reports on companies and industries, developments, and trends. Its articles tend to be longer than those in other magazines of this type, and frequent use of sidebars allows the reader to learn more about corollary issues. *Fortune*, which recently won the National Magazine Award for general excellence, is an interesting, attractive magazine that is highly recommended for public libraries.

267 **ILO Information.** 1965. 5/yr. Free. Jan Vitek (U.S. editor: Susan Epstein). Intl. Labour Office, Washington Branch, 1828 L St. N.W., Suite 801, Washington, DC 20036. Illus. Circ: 40,000. Sample. Vol. ends: Dec. [*Aud*: Ages 14–18.]

The International Labour Office (ILO) works to advance social justice by providing expert advice and technical assistance to 150 individual countries and by setting international labor standards. *ILO Information* is an unofficial report of these activities and concerns. Since ILO's activities are so wide ranging, this eight-page publication also becomes a record of problems, solutions, and events of concern to the world's workers.

268 **Modern Office Technology.** 1983. m. Controlled circ. (Others, $40). Lura K. Romei. Penton Publg., 1100 Superior Ave., Cleveland, OH 44114. Illus. Adv. Circ: 160,000. Vol. ends: Dec. Microform: B&H, UMI. Online: DIALOG. Reprint: UMI. [*Indexed*: BI, BusI. *Aud*: Ages 14–18.]

Containing topical and timely articles aimed at personnel in the modern office, this journal covers a wide variety of subjects: electronic communications, computer networks, facsimile transmission systems, as well as records management via the personal computer. Additional articles deal with personnel and economic issues. Of special interest is the section on business products, which includes a picture and a short description of new products.

269   **Money.** 1972. m. $33.95. Frank Lalli. Time, Inc., Time & Life Bldg., 1271 Ave. of the Americas, New York, NY 10020. Subs. to: P.O. Box 54429, Boulder, CO 80322. Illus. Adv. Index. Circ: 1,900,000. Vol. ends: Dec. Microform: B&H, UMI. [*Indexed*: BoRvI, BusI, RG. *Bk. rev*: 1, 700–1,000 words, signed. *Aud*: Ages 14–18.]

While the most popular of the business/economics magazines, this is not the type of title most teenagers will read. It should be in public and school libraries, however, because it reflects interests of adults who are involved with money at every social level. Every issue has a special report—consisting of four or five feature articles—on some aspect of consumer spending or finances. There are six to ten additional pieces on various aspects of spending and investments for the middle-income American. *Money* is written in a popular style for the reader with little technical knowledge of economics, investments, or consumer behavior. Advice and commentary are relatively conservative. As in *Time*, trends and events are brought down to a personal level by interviews with ordinary folks who are in the mainstream of these trends. Issues of *Money* always seem to be among the most worn and tattered of the current periodicals in any library. Recommended for general collections in public, academic, and high school libraries.

270   **Monthly Labor Review.** 1915. m. $16. Henry Lowenstern. Bureau of Labor Statistics, U.S. Dept. of Labor, Washington, DC 20212. Subs. to: Supt. of Docs., U.S. Govt. Printing Office, Washington, DC 20402. Illus. Index. Circ: 14,000. Vol. ends: Dec. Microform: UMI. [*Indexed*: BusI, PAIS, RG. *Bk. rev*: 1–2, 500–1,000 words, signed. *Aud*: Ages 14–18.]

This is a basic source of statistics and information about what is currently happening in the field of labor in the United States. Half of each issue is devoted to a monthly updating of statistics grouped under six main topics: the labor force, compensation and collective bargaining, prices, productivity, injury and illness, and international comparisons. Within these topics, data can be found on such things as the cost of living, wage rates, and hours of labor. Most of the statistics are for the United States as a whole and are not broken down geographically.

271   **Nation's Business.** 1912. m. $22. Robert T. Gray. U.S. Chamber of Commerce, 1615 H St. N.W., Washington, DC 20062. Illus. Adv. Index. Circ: 9,000,000. Vol. ends: Dec. Microform: B&H, UMI. Online: DIALOG. Reprint: UMI. [*Indexed*: BusI, RG. *Aud*: Ages 14–18.]

Nation's Business is a business magazine that can be read and understood by the general reader, including senior high school students. Articles report on current business activities and topics such as product quality, entrepreneurship, going public, and so forth. Companies and business persons are profiled. Since this publication lacks the detail (and jargon) of the leading general business magazines such as *Business Week* or *Fortune*, it is appropriate for public and school libraries.

272   **The Office: magazine of information systems and management.** 1935. m. $40. William R. Schulhof. Office Publns., Inc., 1600 Summer St., Stamford, CT 06904. Illus. Adv. Circ: 165,000. Vol. ends: Dec. Microform: B&H, UMI. Reprint: UMI. [*Indexed*: BI, BusI. *Bk. rev*: 5–8, 50–100 words. *Aud*: Ages 14–18.]

This monthly magazine covers a wide variety of subjects. Topics include information technology, database management systems, and word processing, as well as specific subjects such as electronic typewriters, telephone equipment, and copying machines. Other articles are directed toward the office manager and deal with such matters as employee relations and effective use of human resources.

■ CANADA [Claire England]

Canadians realize that the bestselling magazines in their country are products— newsmagazines and a magazine digest—from the United States. The magazines that are big sellers in Canada, defined as those with circulations over 75,000, are newsmagazine in format or particularized in audience. The national newsmagazine is *Maclean's*, which claims that, one way or another, 2.5 million people read it each week. Its successful format has been re-created, or particularized, into regional newsmagazines. Regionalism works well in Canadian publishing. One particular audience is genre specific, with women's magazines generally being successful. Another audience is found in the readership for outdoors, nature, or life-style magazines.

The publications listed are a sample from the Canadian periodicals normally available in libraries. In spite of some salutary and many not-so-salutary influences in the serial trade in Canada, it is heartening to realize that such a wide and diversified offering of significantly Canadian periodicals is available.

First choices (1) *Maclean's*; (2) *Harrowsmith*; (3) *Saturday Night*; (4) *Canadian Consumer*.

Suitable for children Ages 10–18: *The Beaver*; *Canada and the World*. Ages 12–18: *Equinox*; *Maclean's*.

273 **Arctic.** 1947. q. $50 (Individuals, $35). Ona Stonkus. Arctic Inst. of North America, Univ. of Calgary, 2500 University Dr. N.W., Calgary, Alta. T2N 1N4, Canada. Illus. Index. Circ: 2,600. Sample. Refereed. Vol. ends: No. 4 (Dec.). Microform: UMI. [*Indexed*: CanI. *Bk. rev*: 6–8, 500–1,000 words, signed. *Aud*: Ages 14–18.]

Although this features advanced studies, much of the material is edited in such a way as to be within the grasp of a senior high school student. The Arctic Institute of North America has both an American and a Canadian corporation. The latter is responsible for this scholarly journal with its original research articles and well-turned-out presentation. The Natural Sciences and Engineering Research Council and the Social Sciences and Humanities Research Council of Canada support this journal with its multidisciplinary focus and attempt to appeal not only to specialists but also to more general readers. It mixes short profiles of people with longer articles on any theme of northern scholarship, including medicine, the fine arts and humanities, education, and the social sciences.

The Beaver. *See under* CHILDREN/HISTORY.

274 **Canada and the World** (Formerly: *World Affairs*). 1934. 9/yr. $16 Can. Rupert J. Taylor and Linda E. Taylor. R/L Taylor Consultants Publg., P.O. Box 7004, Oakville, Ont. L6J 6L5, Canada. Illus. Index. Circ: 29,000. Sample. Vol. ends: No. 9 (May). Microform: MML, UMI. [*Indexed*: CMI, CanI. *Aud*: Ages 10–18.]

Edited for younger readers as well as high school students, this features three or four "long" articles (1,500 words or two pages) in each issue, reviewing current information about a country, world area, or topical subject (space, prison system, homosexuality). Shorter news briefs of articles also appear and are usually loosely organized around a theme such as the postindustrial society, religion, the third world, or women. Projects for teachers to use are suggested, and the magazine is very much geared to an educational market. Almost upper elementary school in its style, presentation, and approach, it is a magazine well used by students in high school and in undergraduate courses.

275 **Canadian Business.** 1928. m. $40. Wayne Gooding. CBMedia, 70 The Esplanade, Toronto, Ont. M5E 1R2, Canada. Illus. Adv. Circ: 90,000. Sample. Vol. ends: Dec. (No. 12). Microform: B&H, MML, UMI. Online: DIALOG. [*Indexed*: BusI, CMI, CanI, PAIS. *Aud*: Ages 14–18.]

Several publications focus on general trade and commerce in Canada, including a daily Toronto-based newspaper, the *Financial Post*, and a weekly Montreal-based newspaper, the *Financial Times*. The newspapers are for those who always want a finger on the pulse of commerce, while *Canadian Business* serves a slightly less anxious audience. *CB* is the most widely read general business newsmagazine in Canada. It has photo essays and capsule news on commerce and industry. In its five or so feature articles, it reports on such diversified topics as office romances and pay equity; it can examine a particular industry or do a special survey, like the one on AIDS, in various relationships to the business world. Shorter articles are found in the regular columns about entrepreneurs, business critics, and management. Although a trade and special-interest journal, *CB* can have something for everyone and should be found in public libraries and high school libraries with an interest in the subject.

276 **Canadian Consumer/Le consummateur canadien.** 1963. 12/yr. $33. Paul Reynolds. Consumers' Assn. of Canada, P.O. Box 9300, Ottawa, Ont. K1B 5C4, Canada. Illus. Adv. Index. Circ: 156,300. Sample. Vol. ends: Dec. [*Indexed*: CanI. *Aud*: Ages 14–18.]

Young adults looking for tips on what to buy will turn first to this basic Canadian title. (Americans, of course, will use *Consumer Reports* and related magazines.) The Consumers' Association of Canada is a nonprofit organization that examines and recommends products for the domestic market. Readers are often asked for their responses to products and service industries. The short articles are intended to stimulate debate, and the tests and tabular summations of research on products are designed to help family purchasing and point to needed legislation or investigation. An annual buying guide adds to the usefulness of this magazine. Different products, conditions, laws, and standards can be in force north of the border, and libraries serving patrons wanting consumer information would be remiss if they overlooked this home-grown magazine.

277 **Canadian Dimension.** 1963. 8/yr. $30 (Individuals, $22). Ed. bd. Dimension Publg., Suite 801, 44 Princess St., Winnipeg, Man. R3B 1K2, Canada. Illus. Adv. Circ: 5,000. Sample. Vol. ends: No. 8. Microform: MML, UMI. [*Indexed*: CMI, CanI. *Bk. rev*: 1–3, 500–600 words. *Aud*: Ages 14–18.]

This magazine announces itself as socialist in orientation, claiming to be "undogmatic, unprincipled, well-researched, combining sophistication and practical experience with a rank and file perspective." It "prints stories others won't," is "nationwide, regionally balanced" and gives a voice to "politic commitment, independence, honesty." The rhetoric accurately describes this provocative, zestful, often graphically strident magazine that can put a discussion of defense policy or labor issues alongside a poem, a short piece of fiction, and the reviews of films or books from the popular and alternative cultures. While not affiliated with any political party, it has a left-of-center orientation and the sometimes sharply critical look at various aspects of Canadian life does add another, and necessary, dimension to the more standardized journalistic reporting of national newsmagazines. Senior high school libraries could consider the title, and public libraries should have it on their shelves.

278   **The Canadian Forum.** 1920. 10/yr. $35. Can. (Individuals, $23 Can.). John Hutcheson. Canadian Forum, 70 The Esplanade, Toronto, Ont. M5E 1R2, Canada. Illus. Adv. Circ: 5,500. Vol. ends: Dec. Microform: MML, UMI. [*Indexed*: API, CanI. *Bk. rev*: 1–3, 500–1,000 words, signed. *Aud*: Ages 14–18.]

The *Forum* has long been the established, critical commentary for Canadian political, cultural, and artistic life. For Canadians, it claims to illuminate the national identity; investigate the past, present, and future; and provoke political discussion. With justification, it labels its thrust intellectual and its mandate progressive. There are thematic issues, examining, for example, the identity and particular cultural problems of Quebec. In the regular issues, foreign affairs and national trends are probed. There are always informed opinions; analyses of literature and the performing arts; award-winning short fiction and poetry; and incisive book, film, and theater reviews. Important for its public affairs and literary coverage, the *Forum* is a standard choice for involved senior high school and public libraries.

279   **Canadian Geographic** (Formerly: *Canadian Geographic Journal*). 1930. 6/yr. $26.75. Ross W. Smith. Royal Canadian Geographical Soc., 488 Wilbrod St., Ottawa, Ont. K1N 6M8, Canada. Illus. Adv. Index. Circ: 153,000. Sample. Vol. ends: No. 6. Microform: MML, Pub. [*Indexed*: CMI, CanI, SocSc. *Bk. rev*: 10–12, 350–500 words, signed. *Aud*: Ages 14–18.]

Any young Canadian familiar with *National Geographic* will turn to this magazine for much the same coverage, but limited to Canada. The text and photographs make it ideal for most young adults. The aim of the Royal Canadian Geographical Society is to make Canada better known to Canadians and to the world, and to increase the awareness of the significance of geography in Canadian life, well-being, culture, and development. Geography is seen in its broadest sense, and this truly excellent journalistic magazine with its informative articles and good photography surveys people and places, resources and environment, wildlife and wilderness, heritage, and evolution in the context of the beauty of Canada. Its leaning toward geography as an academic discipline is only particularly evident in its departments on geography, place names, and the type of books reviewed. Certainly a magazine that is useful for high school and public libraries because of its general appeal.

280   **Canadian Heritage** (Formerly: *Heritage Canada*). 1973. 9/yr. $22. Judy Lord. Heritage Canada Foundation, Canadian Heritage, P.O. Box 1358, Station B, Ottawa, Ont. K1P 5R4, Canada. Illus. Adv. Index. Circ: 30,000. Sample. Vol. ends: No. 4. Microform: MML. [*Indexed*: CMI, CanI. *Bk. rev*: 1–3, 250 words. *Aud*: Ages 14–18.]

Young adults who enjoy the more familiar *American Heritage* will turn to this magazine also. Six or so feature articles, with plentiful and good photographs, tackle the preservation of Canada's past. This magazine celebrates the character of a city street and the charm of a country byway, combining science with architecture and history with practical preservation know-how in its claim as the voice of a broad-based national heritage movement. The newsmagazine format places items discussing the national heritage policy alongside items on people and crafts, castles and corners.

281   The Canadian Historical Review. 1920. q. $44 Can. (Individuals, $26.50 Can.). H. V. Nelles and Colin Howell. Univ. of Toronto Press, Journals Dept., 5201 Dufferin St., Downsview, Ont. M3H 5T8, Canada. Illus. Adv. Index. Circ: 2,580. Sample. Refereed. Vol. ends: No. 4. Microform: JAI, MIM, MML, UMI. Reprint: UMI. [*Indexed*: CMI, CanI, HumI. *Bk. rev*: 1–30, 500–800 words. *Aud*: Ages 14–18.]

For generations this journal has covered the spectrum of Canada's history with sometimes lively and always authoritative articles. Opinion, point-of-view, or survey pieces discuss historiography, the historian's role in different contexts, and the broader problems of copyright and research methods. The good reviews and extensive bibliography of recent historical publications are important contributions to the well-researched articles. The *Review* is a good choice for high school and should be found in many public libraries as well.

282   City & Country Home (Formerly: *Home Decor Canada*; *Canadian Home Decor*). 1982. 10/yr. $40. Barbara Jean Neal. Maclean Hunter, Ltd., 777 Bay St., Toronto, Ont. M5W 1A7, Canada. Illus. Adv. Circ: 88,000. Sample. Vol. ends: Dec. [*Indexed*: CMI. *Bk. rev*: 0–1, 200 words. *Aud*: Ages 14–18.]

The Canadian equivalent of the magazines that stand around *House Beautiful*, this is of limited interest to most young adults. At the same time it does afford a view of the home that some will enjoy. The sections on shopping, art and antiques, travel, fashion, cuisine, and gardens not so subtly reveal that this magazine is aimed at an affluent audience of essentially urban people who are buying into a life-style while becoming informed about architecture, interior design, and the history and innovations in homes and landscapes. In this home-decor journal, Canada's heritage architecture is often featured along with ways to preserve and renovate it. A general discussion of arts and letters appears beside the glossy coverage of food and fashion.

Equinox. *See under* Children/Geography and Travel.

283   Harrowsmith. 1974. 6/yr. $16. Mike Webster. Telemedia Publg. Subs. to: 7 Queen Victoria Rd., Camden East, Ont. K0K 1J0, Canada. Illus. Adv. Index. Circ: 153,985. Sample. Vol. ends: No. 6. Microform: MML, UMI. [*Indexed*: CMI, CanI. *Bk. rev*: 0–2, 250–500 words, signed. *Aud*: Ages 14–18.]

Harrowsmith is about country life as it is often viewed and sometimes lived by people who have careers in the city and houses in rural pockets or semirural dormitory towns for large metropolitan areas. The magazine talks about a life-style that is comforting in a homey, country-folk way. *Harrowsmith* is sophisticated in its appreciation of crafts and its articles on organic gardening and how to lure butterflies and beneficial insects to the garden. Many libraries, particularly public and school libraries, would find this magazine, which has a sizable following, worthwhile. The focus on a quiet, comfortable, and simplified life is a specific theme with a perennially popular appeal.

284   Maclean's. 1905. w. $60.50. Kevin Doyle. Maclean Hunter, Ltd., 777 Bay St., Toronto, Ont. M5W 1A7, Canada. Illus. Adv. Circ: 640,000. Sample. Microform: MIM. Online: Nexis. [*Indexed*: CMI, CanI, MI. *Bk. rev*: 1–2, 500 words, signed. *Aud*: Ages 12–18.]

Most Canadian teenagers will be familiar with this highly popular general magazine. It is found in most homes, and should be in school and public libraries.

Like *Time* or *Newsweek* in format, *Maclean's* is Canada's bestselling weekly newsmagazine. Although it is international in scope, it views world events and trends from the Canadian perspective. It has regular sections on politics, business, entertainment, sports, leisure, science and technology, health, and people. It has opinion (and opinionated) columns and reviews of current art, theater, and literature.

285   **Nature Canada.** 1972. q. $28 Can. Barbara Stevenson. Canadian Nature Federation, 453 Sussex Dr., Ottawa, Ont. K1N 624, Canada. Illus. Adv. Circ: 18,500. Sample. Vol. ends: Fall (No. 4). Microform: MML, UMI. [*Indexed*: CMI, CanI. *Bk. rev*: 5, 500 words, signed. *Aud*: Ages 14–18.]

The Canadian Nature Federation, which publishes this magazine, developed out of the Canadian Audubon Society. The aim of the federation is to promote awareness, understanding, and enjoyment of the country's wildlife and wilderness areas. People are a factor in the natural ecosystems, and human existence must be guided by ecological principles. To this end, education is a part of the well-illustrated, well-written outdoor recreation and wildlife stories that can be about anything in the natural world from monarch butterflies to beluga whales, from forest management to species conservation. This magazine is useful in public and high school libraries.

286   **Performing Arts Magazine** (Formerly: *Performing Arts in Canada*). 1961. q. $12 Can. Emslie Dick. Canadian Stage & Arts Publns., 52 Avenue Rd., P.O. Box 517, Station F, Toronto, Ont. M4Y 1T4, Canada. Illus. Adv. Circ: 80,550. Sample. Vol. ends: Winter (No. 4). Microform: MML, UMI. [*Indexed*: CMI. *Bk. rev*: 0–5, 350 words, signed. *Aud*: Ages 14–18.]

News and views about the theater, dance, opera, ballet, and film in large and small cities across Canada are recorded in this magazine. *Performing Arts* explains that it has behind-the-scenes stories; profiles on companies, troupes, and performers; discussions of trends; all the current news; and other arts-related information not available elsewhere. Since these claims are justified, and this is almost a professional performer's reading as well as the general public's entrée to on-stage arts, the magazine deserves a place in many public and school libraries.

287   **Saturday Night.** 1887. m. $35.50. Robert Fulford. Saturday Night, 511 King St. W., Suite 100, Torotno, Ont. M5V 2Z4, Canada. Illus. Adv. Circ: 136,000. Sample. Vol. ends: Dec. Microform: B&H, MML, UMI. [*Indexed*: CMI, CanI, MI, PAIS. *Bk. rev*: 1–2, 750–1,000 words, signed. *Aud*: Ages 14–18.]

This highly popular magazine is found in most school and public libraries in Canada. Most of the text will be relatively easy to follow for senior high school readers. This general-interest magazine features Canadian newsmakers at home and abroad. It claims that its reporting goes beyond the explanation of events into who makes events happen, how they happen, and how they affect Canada. The five or six long articles on people and affairs in politics, labor, religion, science, and economics are combined with comments on books, art, music, and society. As a magazine of comment and opinion it is more popular and "newsy" in orientation and audience appeal than *The Canadian Forum* (see above in this section) but not quite as timely, broad, or "quick-scan" as *Maclean's* (see above in this section).

288   **ThisMag** (Formerly: *This Magazine*; *This Magazine Is about Schools*). 1966. 8/yr. $21 Can. (Individuals, $18.50 Can.). Lorraine Filyer. Red Maple Foundation, 70 The Esplanade, Toronto, Ont. M5E 1R2, Canada. Illus. Adv. Index. Circ: 7,500. Vol. ends: No. 8. Microform: MML, UMI. [*Indexed*: API, CMI, CanI. *Aud*: Ages 14–18.]

    ThisMag began with education, and later, for a brief time, was subtitled "Education, Culture, Politics." Now long grown beyond its original somewhat high school approach and restricted target audience of persons interested primarily in education, it has become a "left of center" general-interest magazine about politics, labor, culture, and international affairs. It also has fiction and poetry. It advertises that it challenges the mainstream with lively journalism attacking the status quo where it lives—on the fence. Each issue has an investigative reporting article along with one or two other articles on topical subjects. It can be read by high school students and should be available to patrons in many public libraries.

■ **CIVIL LIBERTIES**   [Lee Regan]

      See also: NEWS AND OPINION

As monitors of the information gateways, librarians have a special responsibility to design and promote various alternative strategies (e.g., through catalogs and special lists, instruction, vendor relations, vertical files) to provide access to greater varieties of information. To ignore whole categories of information by elevating considerations of style and format to the neglect of content—the kind of prejudice for media gloss that librarians often criticize—is just another form of institutional censorship, which we suffer at grave intellectual risk. The selections and evaluations in this section are properly only suggestions for consideration. Librarians and students are not only welcome to conduct further research, they are invited and challenged! By discovering, comparing, using, supporting, and publicizing these and other similar periodicals, we continue to exercise social commitment to their aims—as informers and participants in public decision making, as dissenters and protestors against limitations and violations of right, and as watchguards of liberty.

    First choices   (1) *Center Magazine*; (2) *Index on Censorship*.

289   **Center Magazine: a publication of the Center for the Study of Democratic Institutions.** 1963. bi-m. $30 (Membership). Paul McDonald. Center for the Study of Democratic Institutions, P.O. Box 4068, Santa Barbara, CA 93140. Illus. Index. Circ: 18,000. Vol. ends: No. 6. Microform: B&H, UMI. Online: WILSONLINE. [*Indexed*: MI, RG, SocSci. *Bk. rev*: Occasional, 400–500 words, signed. *Aud*: Ages 14–18.]

    A standard civil liberties title, this is a basic choice for most school and public libraries. Note, too, that it is well indexed. There are four or five articles per issue on a range of topics, for example, affirmative action, the arms race, ethics in journalism, and science and politics. Some recent articles have been reprints of previously published discussions. Of special interest, a three-year project called "Liberty and Equality in American Constitutional Life" presents contemporary perspectives on constitutional amendments.

    Dollars & Sense. *See under* BUSINESS, ECONOMICS, AND LABOR.

290   **Free Inquiry.** 1980/1981. q. $22.50. Paul Kurtz. Council for Democratic and Secular Humanism, P.O. Box 5, Buffalo, NY 14215. Illus. Index. Circ: 25,000. Vol. ends: No. 4. Microform: UMI. [*Indexed*: PAIS. *Bk. rev*: 1–2, 700–1,500 words, signed. *Aud*: Ages 14–18.]

Well written and edited, this humanistic approach can be appreciated and understood by most high school students. The publication's aims are to promote traditions of democracy, secular humanism, and principles of intellectual freedom; to disseminate humanistic ideals; and to objectively examine biblical scholarship and religion. Its stated humanist principles and values include the belief that "democracy is the best guarantee of protecting human rights from authoritarian elites and repressive majorities"; the separation of church and state; and the right to privacy and freedom of individuals "to express their sexual preferences, to exercise reproductive freedom . . . and to die with dignity." Articles focus on religious beliefs and institutions, as well as humanistic philosophy and thinkers, historically and internationally.

291   **Freedom: investigative reporting in the public interest** (Formerly: *Freedom Magazine*). 1968. m. $18. Thomas G. Whittle. Church of Scientology, Western United States, 6331 Hollywood Blvd., Suite 1200, Los Angeles, CA 90028. Illus. Circ: 100,000. [*Aud*: Ages 14–18.]

Basic problems, many of which are in the news from day to day, are considered here. Most of the material is suitable for the young adult, and little of the subject matter is without interest. The magazine has a glossy look and subject matter that should attract the reader's attention. As indicated in the subtitle, the subject scope is unlimited (for example, Agent Orange victims, drug abuse, the economy), but the operating themes are "honesty" and mental "freedom." A recent issue contained an interview with a Hollywood actress ("surviving without drugs") and three articles on the abuses and problems of drug therapy in treating hyperactive children. There is also a two-page feature, "Human Rights Advocate of the Month."

292   **Human Rights: official publication of the ABA Section on Individual Rights and Responsibilities.** 1969. 3/yr. $18 (Nonmembers). Anthony Monahan. Amer. Bar Assn. Press, 750 N. Lake Shore Dr., Chicago, IL 60611. Illus. Adv. Vol. ends: No. 3. Online: LRI, WILSONLINE. [*Indexed*: SocSc. *Aud*: Ages 14–18.]

Human Rights is the official publication of the American Bar Association's Section on Individual Rights and Responsibilities. It presents current legal developments in an engaging style and a format that is accessible to all readers. Committees of the ABA Section on Individual Rights provide accurate examples of the magazine's content: access to civil justice, drug-law reform, the death penalty, First Amendment rights, health and environmental rights, immigration and nationality law, international human rights, minority rights, and rights of the underrepresented (including the elderly, gays, women). Each issue has seven to ten short feature articles, plus many additional news items or reports on current events, actions by legal groups, issues, and persons. Occasionally, a single theme is addressed by several articles. Topics have included AIDS, censorship, housing bias, and sex discrimination.

293   **Index on Censorship.** 1972. 10/yr. $32.50. Andrew Graham-Yooll. Writers and Scholars Intl., Ltd. (London), c/o Fund for Free Expression, 485 Fifth Ave., New York, NY

10017. Illus. Adv. Index. Circ: 5,000. Vol. ends: Dec. [*Indexed*: API, PAIS. *Aud*: Ages 14–18.]

Aside from its primary editorial drive, this serves multiple purposes in high schools. It covers all aspects of freedom of expression, including artists, free speech, press censorship, and cases of dissident writers and publishers. It is global in scope, with occasional articles on the United States (e.g., American publisher Grove Press on censorship of novels). Six to ten articles per issue often include poems and excerpts from banned authors' works, plus a five-page "Index/Index" giving a short, country-by-country record of trends and news. Patrons of the magazine include such notables as Joseph Brodsky and Iris Murdoch. It is especially appropriate for English and journalism studies and to supplement readings in contemporary international area studies.

294   Political Pix. 1988. 50/yr. $39. Jerice Bergstrom. Political Pix, P.O. Box 804-C, Norwich, VT 05055. Illus. Circ: 10,000. Vol. ends: No. 50. [*Aud*: Ages 14–18.]

Advertisements remind us of Boss Tweed's complaint against Thomas Nast and quote from Emerson, "caricatures are often the truest history of the times." Six pages of current political cartoons from across the country "speak" volumes (without text). Guaranteed to bring smiles, raise eyebrows, and spread opinions.

295   Reason: free minds & free markets. 1968. 11/yr. $24. Virginia I. Postrel. Reason Foundation, 2716 Ocean Park Blvd., Suite 1062, Santa Monica, CA 90405. Illus. Adv. Circ: 38,000. Vol. ends: No. 11. Microform: UMI. [*Indexed*: PAIS. *Bk. rev*: 4–5, 500–1,000 words, signed. *Aud*: Ages 14–18.]

Four or five feature articles plus columns, editorials, and book and media reviews cover the broadest range of general-interest topics, mostly domestic with some international (especially on foreign aid and military) coverage. The perspective is that of a very popularized libertarianism—more debunking and stylish than economic or philosophical. This is an "outreach" kind of magazine that will find readers in most libraries.

■ COMICS   [Allen Ellis]

The scene is familiar in American popular culture: the child in a drugstore, supermarket, or newsstand, intently poring over the latest issues of comic books, with the proprietor promptly admonishing, "Don't read the funny books! Whaddaya think this is—a library?" Of course the irony of this scenario never escaped the child—libraries do not have comic books. Yet the scene is a remnant mainly of the 1940s–1960s. Today, we are told, children do not read much of anything. The intended audience for most comic books is much older, and comic books are not so readily found in accessible locations, but more often in (and sometimes *only* in) specialized comics shops. Finally, comic books are increasingly found in libraries, as many librarians and other educators recognize their power as tools for teaching or encouraging reading and reasoning, or worthy of research as social indicators, or even as—dare it be said—a legitimate art form. Reviews of comics and related publications appear semiregularly in *Booklist* and are even to some extent making their way into such forums as *Time* and *Newsweek*.

Comic books were spawned in the 1930s, enjoyed what is now nostalgically regarded as a golden age in the 1940s, were crippled by censorship in the 1950s, struggled to be innovative while inoffensive (except for their "underground" cousins) in the 1960s, barely survived the 1970s, and faced their most turbulent decade in the 1980s. Indeed, anyone who has not kept up with comics would find themselves in a somewhat familiar yet decidedly different world. The following comments are general in nature, and true at the time of their writing, yet very little remains constant in the volatile world of today's comics.

First and foremost, disregard the notion that comic books are children's literature. Most are designed for reading by young adults, and comparatively few are suitable for children. Very few of them are "comic," and the overall tone of today's comics tends to be rather grim. Since so many people have preconceived notions of what comic books *should* be, they are often targets of attack by censorship groups and sensation-seeking journalists. Genre variety, while not completely gone, has largely been edged out, with the superhero replacing the cowboy/girl, the soldier, the funny animal, and the jungle king/queen. The common superhero is not the costumed Boy Scout of old, but is often a tormented, angst-ridden antihero whose methods are often as questionable as the bad guy's. Death is a strong selling point, and it can visit upon any but the most merchandising-profitable character, good or bad.

Comic creators—the writers, artists, letterers, colorists, editors, and so forth—are no longer nameless entities, but can have a more loyal following than the characters they interpret. They enjoy more freedom today than the medium has ever been allowed, and the results are varied as they attempt to define the limits of the medium. This may mean an overreliance on sex or violence, particularly for the lazier creators, yet while there is considerable garbage, there is also genuine treasure to be found. The self-policing Comics Code Authority, established in the 1950s, is still around, and those comics submitted to the code for approval still bear the seal, though it is less prominent on the covers, reflecting the relaxing of standards once rigidly enforced.

As it has been for years, the market is led by two publishers, Marvel Comics and DC Comics, Inc., yet there are dozens of other publishers in existence. Unfortunately, the small press titles tend to be where the most innovative material appears. These "independent" publishers, as they are called for want of a better term, find it hard to compete with the "big two" and because of their smaller press runs their product tends to be more expensive. To keep costs down, color is often sacrificed, and the Ted Turner mentality that if it is not in color it is not as good runs rampant throughout comics buyers. These smaller publishers also suffer erratic publication schedules, so several months (even years) may separate issues, a particular problem with continued stories. Particularly for this latter reason, some of the best comics, such as Eclipse's *Zot* and Dark Horse's *Concrete*, are not listed below.

There is also great experimentation in the ways comics are presented. Comics vary in form and price, from the standard comic book–format at 75¢–$3 to hardcover "graphic novels" at $20 or more, with various grades of paper or production techniques influencing the cost. Probably better than television, the comics industry makes excellent use of the limited series form, and much of comics' best work ends up in the mini-series format—often to the distress of potential subscribers, since such titles are seldom offered for subscription. Critically and commercially acclaimed examples include Frank Miller's *Batman: The Dark Knight Returns* and Alan Moore's *Watchmen*. Such series usually end up in trade paperback or even hardcover editions, as might other reprints or new material. We are currently in a golden age of reprints of prime comic book and comic strip art, with *The DC Archives Series*, *Marvel Masterworks*, Fantagraphics' *Complete E.C. Segar Popeye*, and Kitchen Sink's reprints of Milton Caniff's *Steve Canyon* as a few examples.

Besides the erratic publication schedules and limited-series problems noted above, subscribers face an array of other concerns. Changes in editors or creative teams are common, and can produce a book radically different from the one originally subscribed to. Story continuation from one issue to another is the norm, and a recent trend particularly irritating to subscribers is the "crossover epic," wherein a story line may be continued in different titles. The summer months bring special annual editions that may start, end, or carry on a story line begun in the regular title, and changes from monthly to biweekly publication are becoming common for some titles during the summer. Despite the subscription information cited below with each title, publishers often offer special subscription rates, found advertised in the books themselves. There are also several subscription services available through which subscribers can, on a monthly basis, select the titles they want based on printed descriptions of individual issues, sometimes at a considerable discount from the cover price. Such subscription services advertise in comics themselves or in the various publications about comics, about which see later in this section.

The following titles were selected mainly on the basis of their popularity, recognizability, and the probability of their being around for several years, as well as their intended audience. The suggested beginning audience level is, of course, subjective. Comics can be enjoyed by all ages.

First choices   There are none. Select according to the interests of the readers.

296   **ALF.** 1988. m. $12. Welsh Publg. Group, Inc., 300 Madison Ave., New York, NY 10017. Illus. Adv. [*Aud*: Ages 5–13.]

Like *Heathcliff*, *Count Duckula*, *Camp Candy*, and others, *ALF* is a remnant of Marvel's "Star Line" comics for younger readers. It continues the adventures of the Alien Life Form from the once-popular NBC prime-time and animated Saturday-morning television programs. ALF is a stranded alien from the blown-up world, Melmac, living in suburban America with the Tanner family, who try to keep his existence a secret. ALF is loud, obnoxious, sarcastic, and selfish, and loves cats. For snacks. These elements, particularly the latter, are toned down for the comics version, but the horrible puns and clever wordplay of the television shows are intact. The title pokes fun at various elements of American popular life (including Marvel Comics characters), producing a series accessible to but not limited to younger readers.

297   **The Amazing Spider-Man.** 1963. **Spectacular Spider-Man.** 1976. **Web of Spider-Man.** 1985. **Marvel Tales.** 1964. All m. $12 (each). Marvel Comics, 387 Park Ave. S., New York, NY 10016. Illus. Adv. [*Aud*: Ages 10–18.]

Since Peter Parker was bitten by the radioactive spider that gave him his super powers, he has been the most steadily popular of Marvel's characters. Revolutionary at his inception, as a normal person with normal problems, Spider-Man was a stereotypical high school nerd who combined his scientific knowledge with his accidental powers to fight crime, realizing that "with great power comes great responsibility." Marvel has allowed him to grow, and he is now married and the author of a bestselling photography book. Lest it seem that he has become *too* successful and happy, he manages to have more than his share of personal problems, which he tries to balance with his web-shooting, crime-fighting career. The story lines in *Amazing*, *Spectacular*, and *Web* may intertwine, and a fourth title devoted to the character was slated to begin in the summer of 1990. *Marvel Tales* is a reprint book of previously published Spider-Man stories, with regular backup stories of new, often humorous material.

298   **Archie.** 1942. 10/yr. $10. Archie Comic Publns., Inc., 325 Fayette Ave., Mamaroneck, NY 10543. Illus. Adv. [*Aud*: Ages 6–18.]

Archie is still, of course, the perennial teenager—still flanked by his pal, the gluttonous and lazy Jughead; his rival, the egotistical Reggie; and his girlfriends, the blonde and every-pining Betty and the rich and spoiled brunette Veronica, whom Archie hopelessly continues to pursue; and the faculty at Riverdale High. The Archie line of comics includes over a dozen regular titles. Though serious issues such as the environment and animal rights are occasionally given treatment, the stories are generally simple and humorous, designed for readers younger than the characters portrayed.

299   **The Avengers.** 1963. **Avengers West Coast.** 1985. Both m. $12 (each). Marvel Comics, 387 Park Ave. S., New York, NY 10016. Illus. Adv. [*Aud*: Ages 10–18.]

Besides the Fantastic Four and the various mutant teams (X-Men, etc.) The Avengers are Marvel's answer to the traditional "heroes from various series gather to oppose catastrophic menace" theme. The Avengers' lineup is constantly changing, as characters come and go and switch back and forth between the main New York and West Coast teams. One can usually count on such Marvel standards as Captain America, Iron Man, and Thor being involved. The menaces are usually of a cosmic nature, and when they are not battling such menaces, stories are devoted to the organizational mechanics of the teams, as well as interpersonal relationships.

300   **Batman.** 1940. **Detective Comics.** 1937. Both m. $12 (each). **Legends of the Dark Knight.** 1989. m. $18. DC Comics, Inc., 666 Fifth Ave., New York, NY 10103. Illus. Adv. [*Aud*: Ages 12–18.]

For over 50 years Batman has been one of the most popular "non-super superheroes"—indeed, his reliance on only his natural talents (the inherited fortune helps) is part of his appeal. Bruce Wayne's vigilantism is based on having witnessed his parents' murders and vowing vengeance on the criminal element. To this aim, he has dedicated his life to the development of his mind and body. The stories tend to be dark, grim, and very violent, and readers debate over Batman's sanity in his crusade. A new version of the sidekick, Robin, has recently been introduced, and his presence will probably lighten the proceedings somewhat. Despite his popularity with children, current Batman comics are not well suited for the average pre–junior high student. Stories may be serialized between the *Batman/Detective* titles. Stories in *Legends* operate outside the regular continuity, for a more mature audience, with every five issues devoted to a new story and creative team.

301   **Casper the Friendly Ghost.** 1958. m. $12. Harvey Comics Entertainment, Inc., 100 Wilshire Blvd., Suite 500, Santa Monica, CA 90401. Illus. Adv. [*Aud*: Ages 5–12.]

As with all the Harvey line, including books featuring Richie Rich and Hot Stuff, the Little Devil, this is an excellent title for the beginning young reader. Though there are undoubtedly certain factions that would stress the dangerous occult nature of ghosts and devils, not to mention the capitalistic brainwashing potential of "the poor little rich boy" (Richie Rich), these comics should be regarded as harmless, often charming little fantasy adventures.

302 **Classics Illustrated.** 1990. s-m. $3.75 each (no subs.). Berkley Publg. Group, 200 Madison Ave., New York, NY 10016. Illus. Adv. [*Aud*: Ages 12–18.]

Much publicity has been given to the return of *Classics Illustrated*, the forerunner of which was notorious for use as a substitute for reading the original work in school assignments. A joint venture by First Publishing (one of the more successful of the "independent" comics publishers) and the Berkley Publishing Group, *Classics Illustrated* promises a more sophisticated package than its predecessor, illustrated by the best artists available, in a square-bound high-quality format and designed to inspire interest in the original works. The first four titles were Poe's "The Raven and Other Poems," illustrated by Gahan Wilson; Dickens's "Great Expectations," illustrated by Rick Geary; Carroll's "Through the Looking Glass," illustrated by Kyle Baker; and Melville's "Moby Dick," illustrated by Bill Sienkiewicz. The publishers plan two titles each month and to keep back issues in print. Endorsed by Literacy Volunteers of America, Inc.

303 **G.I. Joe: a real American hero.** 1982. m. $12. Jim Buckley. Welsh Publg. Group, Inc., 300 Madison Ave., New York, NY 10017. Illus. Adv. [*Aud*: Ages 7–18.]

Despite the title, there is no single "Joe," but rather a team of antiterrorist specialists, men and women, and real Reagan/Bush–era American heroes they are, as the highly ordnanced G.I. Joe Team clashes regularly with the equally heavily armed Cobra Team, which is bent on world domination. Basically, this title features one side making the other go kablooey and the other side recipro-cating, with regular characters dying often enough to make it—for want of a better term—interesting. Still, the title has been consistently popular, chiefly with preadolescent boys, and like the similarly flavored *Transformers*, is based on a line of toys by Hasbro and a concomitant animated television series.

304 **The Green Hornet.** 1989. m. $18. Now Comics, 332 S. Michigan Ave., Suite 1750, Chicago, IL 60604. Illus. Adv. [*Aud*: Ages 12–18.]

The Green Hornet began on the radio in the 1930s, created by George W. Trendle, who also created the Lone Ranger (the Hornet was the son of the Ranger's nephew). Publisher Britt Reid, the Green Hornet, and his oriental valet, Kato, posed as criminals and fought crime outside the law through radio, motion picture serials, comic books, and television. The Now Comics series began by outlining the character's crime-fighting career, presenting it as a legacy of the Reid family by tying in the radio and television versions, and introducing a modern Green Hornet and a new Kato, a daughter of the original and a martial arts/technical expert, along with an arsenal of high-tech weapons, including their car, the Black Beauty. The series, if it remains as it began, is quite violent, and, while new, is proving to be quite popular for a non–DC/Marvel superhero title.

305 **Justice League America.** 1987. **Justice League Europe.** 1989. Both m. $12. DC Comics, Inc., 666 Fifth Ave., New York, NY 10103. Illus. Adv. [*Aud*: Ages 10–18.]

DC Comics originated the hero team concept in 1940 with the Justice Society of America, followed by the Justice League of America in the 1960s. When the DC Universe was revamped in the mid–late 1980s, the Justice League Interna-tional (JLI) was formed as global protection against all the things that can happen when superheroes are around. While the JLI has U.N.–sanctioned embassies around the world, the two major divisions are Justice League America and Justice League Europe. Noble as all this sounds, the JLI is perhaps the most inept superhero group ever, and these are essentially humor titles, depending on your concept of humor. These heroes squabble, trade insults, make horrendous jokes, fall down a lot, and, basically, do not get (or deserve) respect. The members are mostly DC's newest characters, or ones without their own titles. Old-timers like Batman are usually around, mainly to grit their teeth and propel the groups into action. Two of DC's bestselling titles, though the novelty may wear off.

306 **The 'Nam.** 1986. m. $18. Marvel Comics, 387 Park Ave. S., New York, NY 10016. Illus. Adv. [*Aud*: Ages 12–18.]

The 'Nam endeavors to tell the story of U.S. participation in the Vietnamese conflict as those times were experienced by the common people, both in Vietnam and at home. It is an ambitious project, told in real time, so in essence it is designed to be a 12-year maxi-series. Characters come and go as they are killed, reassigned, shipped home, and so forth. *The 'Nam* is a code-approved book, but while areas like violence and language are toned down to accommodate the sensitive, the writer, Doug Murray (a Vietnam veteran, and soon slated to temporarily leave the title), attempts to present an objective, factual representation of events. The letters page is frequently interesting as other vets write in with their views, and younger readers express their appreciation for the book's helping them to understand the war and the times—perhaps its best recommendation. For a more realistic (i.e., *not* code-approved) depiction of the war, however, Apple Comics publishes *Vietnam Journal*.

307 **The New Titans.** 1984. m. $21. DC Comics, Inc., 666 Fifth Ave., New York, NY 10103. Illus. Adv. [*Aud*: Ages 12–18.]

Originally conceived as "The Teen Titans," a team of kid sidekicks working out of the shadows of their mentors, the New Titans are no longer junior versions of established heroes, but largely well-conceived individuals in their own right. One of the hallmarks of this series is characterization. The characters have problems, and not just teenage whining about parents not understanding, but larger concerns such as growing up in general, dealing with adult feelings and problems, proving one's worth, and finding acceptance. It is not all soap opera either, as there is more than an adequate share of action, which tends to be more interesting because the team is not as powerful as those found in most comics. The leader of the New Titans is Nightwing, formerly the boy/teen wonder Robin, having grown up and away from Batman. This title also features some of the strongest (in terms of character) and most well-rounded (in terms of character) female characters in mainstream comics.

308 **The Punisher.** 1987. m. $12. **Punisher War Journal.** 1988. m. $18. Marvel Comics, 387 Park Ave. S., New York, NY 10016. Illus. Adv. [*Aud*: Ages 13–18.]

Frank Castle's wife and children were rubbed out when they stumbled on a gangland kiling, and Castle, swearing vengeance, set out to methodically eliminate the criminals. As The Punisher, he keeps himself on the cutting edge, if you will, of weapons technology (a special "Arsenal" feature appears in *PWJ*, providing details on the latest in personal combat equipment), assisted by Microchip, a stereotypical computer wizard who tries to act as Castle's conscience (though The Punisher never listens, much to the delight of his fans). Rivaling Marvel's *Wolverine* among the most popular and violent of code-approved comic books, it is all very cathartic, since The Punisher blows away drug dealers, terrorists, murderers, and the like—particularly those who escape justice on legal technicalities—who are portrayed as richly deserving their punishment. Still, Marvel keeps The Punisher out of its superhero pantheon, since he is, after all, a criminal, albeit a useful one.

309 **The Real Ghostbusters.** 1988. **Slimer!** 1989. Both m. $18 (each). Now Comics, 332 S. Michigan Ave., Suite 1750, Chicago, IL 60604. Illus. Adv. [*Aud:* Ages 7–14.]

Based not so much on the very successful films but rather the popular animated television series and Kenner toy line, the *Real* Ghostbusters (as opposed to an earlier group with the same name and, presumably, less able attorneys) continue their battle against hostile paranormal phenomena. The titles make light of ghosts, witches, demonic possession, and the like, concepts that some real-life groups and individuals take quite seriously, but it should in no way be taken as an endorsement of belief in the occult—it is all science-fiction-versus-the-supernatural fun. *Slimer!* concentrates on the adventures of the team's whiny, gluttonous, mucous mascot (based on the "green ghost" in the movies, and a charming character indeed).

310 **Superman.** 1987. **Action Comics.** 1938. **Adventures of Superman.** 1939. All m. $9 each. **Superboy.** 1989. $12. DC Comics, Inc., 666 Fifth Ave., New York, NY 10103. Illus. Adv. [*Aud:* Ages 10–18.]

An American icon, Superman should need no introduction, yet DC thought so when his much made-over makeover in 1986 sought to bring the Man of Tomorrow up to date. The changes included establishing Superman as once again the *sole* survivor of the planet Krypton, and as being less powerful (and thereby theoretically more interesting). Clark Kent is, at last, his own man, a success on his own terms rather than just a disguise for Superman. Lois Lane is at last her own woman, and a very strong and positive female character, who can take or leave the Man of Steel. Superman's nemesis, Lex Luthor, is no longer the stereotypical evil scientist, but now the stereotypical evil businessman, meaning he gets away with murder while remaining an upstanding member of society. The stories in the Superman titles often interconnect.

Superboy is simpler fare, better suited to younger readers (ages 6–12), and is based on the popular syndicated television series. Part of the Superman make-over established that he never was Superboy, but began his career as an adult. DC says never mind all that—*Superboy* exists outside of the Superman continuity. Simple, is it not?

311 **Teenage Mutant Ninja Turtles.** 1984. m. $1.75 each (no subs.). Mirage Studios, P.O. Box 417, Haydenville, MA 01039. Illus. Adv. [*Aud:* Ages 12–18.]

This has to be one of the greatest success stories of all time—Kevin Eastman and Peter Laird, two struggling artists, as a lark, create a parody of several themes common in the comics of the early 1980s. Running with the idea, they self-publish an enormously successful first issue, and it grows into a multimillion-dollar industry, including toys, cartoons, cereal, and a major motion picture. At the center of it all are four radioactively evolved warrior reptiles, Donatello, Leonardo, Michaelangelo (*sic*), and Raphael. Only the first issue of *TMNT* was a parody, with the following issues taking a grittier tone. The title was not, and still is not, aimed at children, and appears in black and white on an irregular basis, though a monthly schedule is planned.

312   **Teenage Mutant Ninja Turtles Adventures.** 1988. 8/yr. $8. Archie Comic Publns., Inc., 325 Fayette Ave., Mamaroneck, NY 10543. Illus. Adv. [*Aud*: Ages 6–12.]

TMNT Adventures is based not on the original "Turtle" series, but on the animated TV series designed for children. Lots of mindless violence and mayhem, but it is all so silly that few complain.

313   **The Uncanny X-Men.** 1963. **The New Mutants.** 1983. **Classic X-Men.** 1986. **X-Factor.** 1986. **Excalibur.** 1988. All m. $12 (each). Marvel Comics, 387 Park Ave. S., New York, NY 10016. Illus. Adv. [*Aud*: Ages 13–18.]

These books are practically the core of Marvel Comics, for mutants are wildly popular with many Marvel fans. Mutants are individuals born with altered genetic schemes that provide some sort of nonhuman ability. Originally, the X-Men were a group of teenagers under the guidance of Professor Charles Xavier —himself a mutant of extraordinary mental abilities—who was constantly searching for mutants so he could teach them to control their abilities for the benefit of humanity. Original members are now the core of *X-Factor*, having been replaced by a newer group in their own title. As new mutants appear, their assimilation begins in the *New Mutants*. *Excalibur* is a branch of the group in Great Britain, and *Classic X-Men* is a reprint title, usually with new backup material. The threats are often cosmic or supernatural, and the characters (which include women, despite the sexist title) are very well defined. A major theme is the inability of humans to trust and accept mutants, so writers are free to explore persecution themes without fear of offending anyone. Except mutants.

314   **Walt Disney's Comics and Stories.** 1940. m. $18. Walt Disney Publns., Inc., 500 S. Buena Vista, Burbank, CA 91521. Illus. Adv. [*Aud*: Ages 5–13.]

After an absence from the comics scene, the Walt Disney folks licensed their characters to the small press publisher Gladstone, who experienced considerable success with a line of comics featuring Walt Disney characters, both reprint and critically acclaimed new material. Disney decided that they should be the sole beneficiary of that success, and decided to publish their own comics, which have recently hit the stands. Besides this one, there are titles devoted to Mickey Mouse, Donald Duck, and Uncle Scrooge; and new titles featuring Goofy, Roger Rabbit, and (based on their popularity as syndicated animated series) Duck Tales and Chip 'n Dale Rescue Rangers. There should be no one alive who is not familiar with the Disney characters (and the corporation wants their names if there are); likewise, everyone should know what to expect from these titles—fun for the whole family and all that. One great advantage to the comics format is that you can actually understand what the ducks are saying.

315   **Wolverine.** 1988. m. $12. Marvel Comics, 387 Park Ave. S., New York, NY 10016. Illus. Adv. [*Aud*: Ages 13–18.]

Logan, or Wolverine, is the most popular of Marvel's mutant characters. His main mutant power is his rapid and complete healing ability. He can be shot, stabbed—take almost any punishment—and the writers have no qualms about dishing it out regularly. Wolverine can dish it out, too. He is able to produce from the back of each hand three 12-inch claws of the unbreakable Marvel Universe metal Adamantium (which also supports his skeleton), capable of slicing through almost anything—or anyone. Yes, Wolverine is a killer, and his stories are among the most violent in mainstream comics. Still, he is presented as a sympathetic character who cannot always control his violent tendencies. A major theme is Logan's constant struggle to control the feral side of his nature and to assimilate himself into humanity, if not society. With the right writer, Wolverine is one of comics' most complex and intriguing characters.

316 Wonder Woman. 1987. m. $12. DC Comics, Inc., 666 Fifth Ave., New York, NY 10103. Illus. Adv. [*Aud*: Ages 10–18.]

Though Wonder Woman has been around since 1940, she is another of DC's characters who have recently been revamped. She is treated as a comparatively new arrival in the current DC Universe, and the stories often take a "stranger in a strange land" approach. Wonder Woman is Princess Diana of the Amazons—the mythological warrior women—come from the secluded Paradise Island to "man's world" to thwart the activities of Ares, the God of War, and to share with the world the hard-learned Amazonian wisdom regarding peace and justice. Her mentor is Professor Julia Kapatelis, an American classical Greek historian and a widow with a teenage daughter, Vanessa. Together the three women learn much about themselves, their societies, womanhood, and humanity. The title's chief attraction is its heart and soul, yet there is a generous amount of real action as well. Some students might appreciate the strong emphasis on Greek, Roman, and other mythologies and cultures.

•••••••••••••••••••••••••• **Publications about Comics** ••••••••••••••••••••••••

There are several publications about comics on the market, ranging from Marvel's blatantly commercial *Marvel Age* to the usually excellent *Comics Interview* (Rte. 1, P.O. Box 1241, Clayton, GA 30525). Fantagraphics Books (7563 Lake City Way N.E., Seattle, WA 98115) publishes *Amazing Heroes* and *Comics Journal*, the former the usual fanzine compendium of news and reviews, the latter often pretentious, trying too hard to be controversial. If a library could choose but one publication about comics, however, the best choice would be the *Comics Buyer's Guide* (Krause Publications, Inc., 700 E. State St., Iola, WI 54990—sample copy sent on request).

CBG is a trade paper/tabloid dedicated to "Serving the World of Comics Every Week." Each issue is devoted to news from the various publishers, including announcements of new series, changes in series, adaptations in other media, and so forth. It is also a trading post for collectors buying and selling, a source of reviews of comics and related publications, and a neutral forum for fans in general. In fact, the letters pages are often the most interesting aspect as various viewpoints are shared over such topics as literacy, censorship, the moral responsibilities of publishers and retailers, perceptions of comics readers by noncomics readers, and discussions of comics in general. The editors are Don and Maggie Thompson, who are well read not only in comics, and are intelligent, articulate, approachable advocates of literacy and comic books. They take rightful pride in producing weekly, and on time, the best source available for keeping up with the comics scene, and the voice of comic fandom. Largely through their efforts, *CBG* is often more interesting than the comics themselves.

■ **COMPUTERS**   [James J. Kopp]

See also: SCIENCE

The computer is a well-known technological teaching tool and is as familiar to most youngsters and teenagers as the telephone. Magazines selected here reflect this state in two ways. First, an effort is made to represent areas of computing of most interest to teachers and students alike. Second, there is a particular emphasis on microcomputers because of their widespread use in schools. Besides, there is a growing number of magazines of this type.

First choices   (1) *Personal Computing*; (2) *Compute!*; (3) *Family & Home Office Computing*; (4) *PC Magazine*.

Suitable for children   Ages 12–18: *Ahoy!*; *Analog Computing*; *Compute!*; *Family & Home Office Computing*; *InCider*; *Info*; *Nibble*; Rainbow.

317   **Ahoy!** 1984. m. $23. Michael R. Davila. Ion Intl., Inc., 45 W. 34th St., Suite 500, New York, NY 10001. Illus. Adv. Circ: 126,000. Vol. ends: Dec. [*Aud*: Ages 12–18.]

One of several computer magazines directed to the school or public library with a particular brand of computer. The text and illustrations follow the usual patterns of such titles. This magazine offers tips, advice, news, and other information for Commodore microcomputer users, in particular users of the C-64 and C-128. Recreational and educational aspects are emphasized, but programming tips and features are also included.

318   **Analog Computing.** 1982. m. $28. Clayton Walnum. L. F. P., Inc., 9171 Wilshire Blvd., Suite 300, Beverly Hills, CA 90210. Illus. Adv. Circ: 90,000. [*Aud*: Ages 12–18.]

Billed as the number one magazine for Atari computer owners, this magazine emphasizes that line of microcomputer products. Articles and reviews cover a broad range of topics with an emphasis on recreational applications. Several type-in programs are included in each issue, and some of the programs featured are also available on disk. (Subscription to the magazine *and* the disc service is $105 per year.)

319   **Byte: the small systems journal.** 1975. m. $23. Frederic S. Langa. McGraw-Hill, Inc., One Phoenix Mill Lane, Peterborough, NH 03458. Illus. Adv. Circ: 400,000. Vol. ends: Dec. Microform: UMI. Online: DIALOG, Mead Data Central. Reprint: UMI. [*Indexed*: ASTI, MI. *Bk. rev*: 5–7, 150 words, signed. *Aud*: Ages 14–18.]

Technical, massive, and not easy to read—still this remains the basic journal in the area for adults and for almost as many advanced teenagers. Its coverage is broad with an emphasis on microcomputers and their applications. Each issue contains critical reviews of hardware and software products. Features cover several aspects of microcomputing and several different systems are examined, making its scope generally broader than that of *PC Magazine* and other leading microcomputing magazines. Most articles are technically oriented and geared toward the experienced microcomputer user. However, some features will appeal to the less sophisticated user. The journal will be popular in high schools that include any aspect of computing in their curricula.

320   **Compute! the leading magazine of home, educational, and recreational computing.** 1979. m. $9.97. Peter Scisco. Compute! Publns., Inc., 324 W. Wendover Ave., Suite 200, P.O. Box 5406, Greensboro, NC 27408. Subs. to: P.O. Box 10955, Des Moines, IA 50347-0955. Adv. Circ: 225,000. Vol. ends: Dec. Microform: UMI. Reprint: UMI. [*Aud*: Ages 12–18.]

The subtitle tells it all, but the reader should understand that this magazine can be read by anyone of almost any age who is interested in computers. The emphasis is on home, educational, and recreational computing. Coverage is broad, with articles on a variety of topics, including games, word processing, computer security, and mail-order products. Reviews, announcements, and discussions of hardware and software products are also included. Several computer types are included in the discussions. Type-in programs used to be included in each issue but were recently dropped, partly because they appear in the machine-specific publications. This is one of the most popular of the general computing magazines, along with *Family & Home Office Computing*. It is a valuable addition to public libraries as well as to many school libraries.

321 **Desktop Press.** 1988. bi-m. $42. Dolf Calica. Desktop Press, One Wilshire Bldg., Suite 1210, 624 S. Grand Ave., Los Angeles, CA 90017. Illus. Adv. Sample. [*Aud:* Ages 14–18.]

A how-to-do-it journal, the 100 pages are filled with advertising, illustrations, and about a dozen articles. It is written for both beginners and partially advanced learners. The assumption is that the reader has some appreciation of computer jargon. Among topics covered in one issue are the mini-newspaper, sales letters, desktop software (more descriptive than evaluative, but it is all here), multicolor printing, and how to use a copier for printing. Sometimes it is hard to tell the ads from the copy. The lack of hard-hitting evaluation is a drawback. Still, so much basic information is packed into the pages that it is worth a try.

Another contender in this fast-growing field is *The Desktop Publishing Journal* (1988. bi-m. $13. Linda Hanson, 4027 C Rucker Ave., Suite 821, Everett, WA 98201). This is less advertising-oriented, more involved with product and software reviews.

322 **Family & Home Office Computing** (Formerly: *Family Computing*). 1983. m. $20. Claudia Cohl. Scholastic, Inc., 730 Broadway, New York, NY 10003. Illus. Adv. Circ: 400,000. Vol. ends: Dec. Microform: UMI. Reprint: B&H, UMI. [*Aud:* Ages 14–18.]

Family & Home Office Computing is one of the most popular general computing magazines. It initially was geared toward parents, but has features for young people. Articles are nontechnical, and when technical aspects or terms are introduced, they are often explained in understandable terms. Hardware and software reviews are included in each issue; and the "Software Guide" is very handy for software related to business and productivity, education and creativity, and entertainment. The annual "Buyer's Guide to Computers" is a helpful feature for individuals interested in determining what microcomputers are available and the features of each. A monthly section called "The Programmer" includes instructions and programs for a variety of applications from productivity programs to fun and games. Several versions of the programs are provided for different computer systems. This magazine is recommended for public libraries and may be a popular item in many school libraries as well.

323 **InCider.** 1983. m. $28. Dan Muse. IDG Communications/Peterborough, Inc., 80 Elm St., Peterborough, NH 03458. Illus. Adv. Circ: 105,000. Vol. ends: Dec. Microform: UMI. [*Indexed:* CIJE. *Aud:* Ages 12–18.]

This magazine is for the Apple II user. Useful features are "Tutorials" on software, "Hints/Techniques," and product reviews and announcements. Educational and recreational programs are included in the discussions in each issue, and graphics and professional and productivity applications are also highlighted. Novices and sophisticated users (of all ages) will find useful items in this magazine.

324 **Info.** 1983. bi-m. $20. Benn Dunnington. Info Publns., Inc., 123 N. Linn St., Suite 2A, Iowa City, IA 52240-2135. Illus. Adv. Circ: 120,000. [*Aud*: Ages 12–18.]

Another of the product-specific computer magazines that can be read by younger people and teenagers. It is for Commodore and Commodore Atari users and is billed as "the first personal computer magazine produced entirely with personal computers." Much of the magazine is devoted to hardware and software reviews for C-64, C-128, and Amiga computers, including a section on public domain software. Features and departments include "Magazine Index," which gives brief information on items in related computing magazines, and "User Group Forum," which gives information and ideas on user groups. This magazine is geared toward the hobbyist and will be popular in junior high school, high school, and public libraries with a community of Commodore users.

325 **MacUser.** 1985. m. $27. Steven Bobker. Ziff-Davis Publg. Co., One Park Ave., New York, NY 10016. Illus. Adv. Circ: 145,000. Vol. ends: Dec. [*Aud*: Ages 12–18.]

As with other Ziff-Davis publications, this is an independent journal not affiliated in any way with the vendor whose product is the primary focus of the publication—in this case Apple Computer, Inc. *MacUser* is geared toward the experienced Macintosh user and offers a wide assortment of articles and other features on the use of this product in a variety of settings. Special reports are included in some issues for such topics as desktop publishing and desktop engineering. Many of the columns and features will be useful to Macintosh aficionados. Especially valuable are the "Tip Sheet" section, which gives hints, tips, and shortcuts on uses of the Mac, and "MiniFinders," which provides brief reviews of software for the Mac. This is an excellent magazine for collections supporting Mac users.

326 **Macworld.** 1984. m. $30. Jerry Borrell. PCW Communications, Inc., 501 Second St., San Francisco, CA 94107. Illus. Adv. Circ: 150,000. Vol. ends: Dec. [*Aud*: Ages 12–18.]

Like *MacUser*, this publication is dedicated to articles and features on the Apple Macintosh line of microcomputers and has no affiliation with Apple Computer, Inc. Each issue contains several feature articles on topics related to hardware, software, and other products. Reviews are included for software and hardware and "How To" sections discuss a variety of applications. The "Best Sellers" section lists leading sellers of software and hardware for the Macintosh. Macintosh users will find something of value in each issue of this magazine. For libraries serving Macintosh users.

327 **Nibble.** 1980. m. $27. Mike Harvey. Mindcraft Publg. Corp., 52 Domino Dr., Concord, MA 01742. Adv. Circ: 75,000. [*Aud*: Ages 12–18.]

Another of the Apple computer titles, this is suitable for older children and high school students. Much attention is given to the Apple, but articles and features discuss broader implications of the computer and its use, particularly by laypersons.

328 **PC Magazine: the independent guide to IBM-standard personal computing** (Formerly: *PC*). 1982. 22/yr. $40. Bill Machrone. Ziff-Davis Publg. Co., One Park Ave., New York, NY 10016. Subs. to: P.O. Box 2445, Boulder, CO 80322. Adv. Circ: 448,456. [*Aud*: Ages 14–18.]

One of the most popular of the computing magazines, this is a good choice for most young adults, and should be in a majority of school and public libraries. As the subtitle indicates, the primary focus is on IBM-standard personal computing.

However, the coverage has become broader, and *PC Magazine* has now assumed for itself, in many respects, the mark of the "industry standard." One indication of its excellence is the "*PC Magazine* Editor's Choice" symbol, which appears on advertising in several publications for products receiving outstanding reviews in this magazine. Each issue has a cover story on a topic of interest (e.g., desktop publishing, LANs), and the "First Looks" section gives critical reviews of new products. Other features include "clinics" on such topics as spreadsheets and connectivity; "PC Tutor" and "PC Advisor" are helpful as well. The editorials and essays are thought provoking and often entertaining, and the "After Hours" section at the end of each issue is informative and amusing.

329 **Personal Computing: the personal systems magazine** (Formerly: *Personal Computing Plus*). 1976. m. $18. Fred Abatemarco. VNU Business Publns., Inc., 10 Holland Dr., Hasbrouck Heights, NJ 07604. Illus. Adv. Circ: 550,000. Vol. ends: Dec. Microform: UMI. Reprint: UMI. [*Indexed:* CIJE. *Aud:* Ages 14–18.]

If one general computer magazine must be selected in school and public libraries, this is that magazine. It is easy to read, and the illustrations and approach are such that it is well within the grasp of the average young adult. This magazine includes a broad array of articles and features related to hardware and software with the emphasis on microcomputer applications. There is a balance between technical articles and items for the nonspecialist. Helpful features include buyers' guides to such products as word processing packages, accelerator boards, and other software and hardware products. Also useful are product listings and reviews and the "Answers" section.

330 **Publish! the how-to magazine of desktop publishing** (Formerly: *Desktop Publishing*). 1986. m. $39.90. Susan Gubernat. PCW Communications, Inc., 501 Second St., San Francisco, CA 94107. Subs. to: P.O. Box 51966, Boulder, CO 80321. Illus. Adv. Index. Circ: 39,000. Vol. ends: Dec. [*Aud:* Ages 14–18.]

A. J. Liebling's famous dictum "Freedom of the press belongs to those who own one" is the title-page banner of this *PC World* spawn. The editors take the amateur-as-printer seriously and set out in each issue to interpret and help readers apply traditional principles of typography and graphic design in the microcomputer context. Each issue contains four or five tutorial articles and an in-depth hardware or software product review; a regular column reviews typefaces available for laser printers. Humor is often used to illustrate or explain, but examples of good newsletters, tabloids, brochures, technical documents, and manuals qualify for serious prizes in an annual design contest. School and public library collections supporting microcomputer use should consider this title.

331 **Rainbow: the Color Computer monthly magazine.** 1981. m. $31. Lawrence C. Falk. Falsoft, Inc., Falsoft Bldg., 9509 U.S. Hwy. 42, P.O. Box 385, Prospect, KY 40059. Illus. Adv. Index. Circ: 80,000. Vol. ends: No. 12. [*Aud:* Ages 12–18.]

While this journal is primarily limited to one type of computer, much of the material is suitable for younger readers as well as senior high school students. As its subtitle indicates, this is for users of the Tandy Color Computer (frequently referred to as the "CoCo"), and has something for the beginner ("Novices Niche") as well as for the experienced user. Product reviews are included in each issue, as are several other useful departments and columns. Some issues are devoted to special topics, such as the music issue, which includes articles on how to play, write, and hear music on the CoCo. Each issue contains several type-in programs for a variety of applications. These programs are also available on tape or on disk as a separate service from the publisher. This is the premier magazine for the Tandy Color Computer.

■ **CONSUMER EDUCATION**   [Mary K. Prokop]

Most of the emphasis in the magazines chosen for this section is on evaluation of specific products. While adults are more likely to be concerned with such titles, younger people are interested too, if only because consumer education is often part of their schoolwork. In addition, many of the magazines cover broader issues, from economics and business to the politics of the consumer.

First choices   (1) *Consumer Reports*; (2) *Zillions*; (3) *Changing Times*.
Suitable for children   Ages 8–14: *Zillions*. Ages 12–18: *Consumer Reports*.

332   **Changing Times: the Kiplinger magazine.** 1974. m. $18. Theodore J. Miller. Kiplinger Washington Editors, Inc., 1729 H St. N.W., Washington, DC 20006. Illus. Adv. Circ: 1,500,000. Vol. ends: Dec. Microform: B&H, MIM, UMI. Online: DIALOG. [*Indexed*: AbrRG, MI, PAIS, RG. *Aud*: Ages 14–18.]

Written for the adult with a high school education, this can be appreciated by almost any teenager. The articles are topical, illustrated, and easy to follow. The editorial matter ranges from economics and taxes to personal finance and nutrition and health. There is also information on travel and leisure pursuits, making this an appealing magazine for middle-income to upscale consumers seeking advice on getting the most for their money. Articles are typically in-depth, and are signed by both author and researcher. Few public or school libraries should be without *Changing Times*.

333   **Consumer Information Catalog** (Formerly: *Consumer Information*). 1971. q. Free. Sara B. Niccum. Consumer Information Center, P.O. Box 100, Pueblo, CO 81002. Illus. Circ: 14,000,000. Sample. [*Aud*: Ages 14–18.]

This is a government publication that is probably of more interest to teachers and librarians than to students, although the latter will find material here for papers and personal use. Each issue lists over 200 publications appropriate for all ages that are available from 44 participating federal agencies. Topics include child care, health, food, careers, housing, money management, federal benefits, and small business. Items are ordered centrally and are either free or very inexpensive. The catalog is not available to individuals, but nonprofit organizations able to distribute 25 copies of each issue may receive it regularly. Public and school library patrons snap them up in no time, and materials listed are often excellent for the vertical file.

334   **Consumer Reports.** 1936. m. $18. Irwin Landau. Consumers Union of the United States, Inc., 256 Washington St., Mt. Vernon, NY 10553. Illus. Index. Circ: 3,000,000. Vol. ends: Dec. Microform: UMI. Online: DIALOG. [*Indexed*: AbrRG, PAIS, RG. *Aud*: Ages 12–18.]

Consumer Reports is probably the most widely asked-for magazine of its type; even people who request other "titles" usually have this one in mind. Brand-name ratings and handy charts make comparison shopping convenient and probably account for the popularity of this title over other reliable magazines that offer more general consumer advice and fewer quick reference lists of brand names and model numbers. Self-indexing is also a plus. The major complaint voiced by library patrons is that major items (large appliances, central HVAC units, etc.) are not evaluated often enough, but the amount of research necessary for publication of most articles is no doubt staggering and time consuming. The April issue on cars is in itself worth the subscription price. Students often find useful information in back issues for science reports. Schools may order this title for 50 cents per copy, if 20 copies of an issue are purchased. The subcription includes the *Annual Buying Guide*. Certainly no public library can afford to be without *Consumer Reports*.

335 **Consumers Digest: best buys, best prices, best reports, for people who demand value.** 1959. bi-m. $16. John Manos. Consumers Digest, Inc., 5705 N. Lincoln Ave., Chicago, IL 60659. Illus. Adv. Index. Circ: 850,000. Vol. ends: Nov. Microform: UMI. [*Indexed*: MI. *Aud*: Ages 14–18.]

This complements *Consumer Reports* and is of more value to public than to school libraries. It is, however, likely to be of interest to numerous young adults. Articles on general consumer topics are included, but most of each issue is now devoted to specific product evaluations. An index to back issues is printed occasionally, but patrons would find it helpful if each issue had a current index, or if *Consumers Digest* were included in *Readers' Guide*.

336 **Consumers' Research Magazine: analyzing products, services and consumer issues.** 1927. m. $18. John M. Merline. Consumers' Research, Inc., 800 Maryland Ave. N.E., Washington, DC 20002. Illus. Index. Circ: 30,000. Vol. ends: Dec. Microform: B&H, UMI. [*Indexed*: MI, RG. *Aud*: Ages 14–18.]

Not so much a buying guide as a source of educational information on consumer issues, this magazine will not be used in the same way as similarly titled publications. It offers advice on how to evaluate services and types of products rather than comparisons of specific brand names, and contains timely information on legislation. A helpful feature of the *Consumers' Research* self-index is the use of boldface type for long, detailed articles. The subscription includes the *Handbook of Buying* issue. Libraries offering comprehensive coverage of consumer topics should own this title.

337 **Food News for Consumers.** 1980. q. $5. Mary Ann Parmley. U.S. Dept. of Agriculture, Rm. 1160 S., Washington, DC 20250. Illus. Circ: 6,000. Vol. ends: Winter. [*Aud*: Ages 14–18.]

Food safety is the focus of this visually appealing government document, published by the Food Safety & Inspection Service of the U.S. Department of Agriculture. Public library patrons and students with school assignments on food and nutrition would be well served by having such publications as this one displayed prominently in browsing areas, since it is not well known, nor is it indexed widely. Articles are signed, and information is certainly reliable. Toll-free hotline numbers are often given and sources of further information listed. The "Children's Page" is of interest to teachers and librarians working with young people. *Food News for Consumers* is a bargain and deserves wide readership.

338 **Nutrition Action Healthletter** (Formerly: *Nutrition Action*). 1974. 10/yr. $20. Steven B. Schmidt. Center for Science in the Public Interest, 1501 16th St. N.W., Washington, DC 20036. Illus. Circ: 80,000. [*Aud*: Ages 14–18.]

A good, consumer-oriented, 16-page newsletter full of useful information on nutrition, diet, and health. Each issue contains a three- to five-page feature article. The feature article of one issue discussed the pros and cons of using drugs or changes in diet to lower cholesterol. The "Health and Science" section of that issue covered the controversy over peanut butter and cholesterol levels.

Zillions. *See under* CHILDREN/GENERAL MAGAZINES.

■ **CRAFT AND RECREATIONAL PROJECTS**

[Craft: Linda Seckelson. Recreational Projects: Cheryl M. LaGuardia]

There is much confusion over the term *craft*, but as applied in this section it is art that is made to serve a practical purpose and is prized for the quality of workmanship. Recreational projects border on craft, but are much broader in definition. Many of the recreational magazines feature detailed instruction and pattern guides, which may not be found in the more popular craft titles. All libraries, public and school, should have a fair sampling of titles in this area.

First choices   (1) *American Craft*; (2) *Popular Mechanics*; (3) *Popular Science*; (4) *Ceramics Monthly*.

Suitable for children   Ages 5–13: *Pack-O-Fun*. Ages 10–18: *Popular Mechanics*; *Popular Science*. Ages 12–18: *Crafts 'n Things*; *Workbench*.

339   **American Craft** (Formerly: *Craft Horizons*). 1941. bi-m. $40. Lois Moran. Amer. Craft Council, 40 W. 53rd St., New York, NY 10019. Illus. Adv. Circ: 35,000. Vol. ends: Dec/Jan. Microform: UMI. [*Indexed*: ArtI, MI, RG. *Bk. rev*: 1–5, length varies, signed. *Aud*: Ages 14–18.]

If only one craft magazine is to be available in the school or public library, this is the choice. The premier journalistic advocate of post–World War II American fine craft, this substantial publication covers far more than its title indicates. It does not limit itself to craft produced in the United States, or to contemporary work. *American Craft* surveys and analyzes aesthetic, technical, and historical developments and trends among practicing craftspeople of the highest caliber. Issues include studies of individual artists, reviews of major exhibitions, historical surveys of specific craft genres and techniques, and overviews of major collections. This handsome and highly professional publication is the voice of the American Craft Council.

340   **Ceramic Arts and Crafts.** 1955. m. $17.40. Bill Thompson. Scott Advertising and Publg. Co, 30595 W. 8 Mile Rd., Livonia, MI 48152. Illus. Adv. Circ: 53,000. [*Aud*: Ages 14–18.]

A nuts-and-bolts "how-to" ceramics magazine with detailed instructions for featured projects spotlighting ceramic techniques. The many advertisements, trade announcements, technique updates, and full-color illustrations offer broad appeal to beginning and advanced enthusiasts.

341   **Ceramics Monthly.** 1953. m. (exc. July/Aug.). $18. William C. Hunt. Professional Publns., Inc., 1609 Northwest Blvd., Columbus, OH 43212. Illus. Adv. Index. Circ: 37,975. Vol. ends: Dec. Microform: B&H, UMI. [*Indexed*: Acs, ArtI, MI. *Bk. rev*: 0–4, length varies. *Aud*: Ages 14–18.]

Any young adult involved with pots and their making will turn here first. This is a comprehensive resource for the professional potter and serious hobbyist. It covers all aspects of ceramics. Each issue contains a balanced representation of technical information and historical treatment. Specific artists' work is featured and discussed with useful photographs, descriptions of production methods, and glaze recipes. The scope is not limited to American artists/potteries, but is international. There are extensive listings of ceramics-related events: exhibitions, workshops, seminars, symposia, conferences. These are also international in coverage. The April number features a detailed listing of summer ceramics programs. *Ceramics Monthly* is an invaluable resource for information on supplies and suppliers of ceramics materials and ceramics-related equipment as well.

342   Craft International. 1980. q. $16. Rose Slivka. World Crafts Foundation, 247 Centre St., New York, NY 10013. Illus. Adv. Circ: 7,000. [*Indexed:* ArtI. *Bk. rev:* 4, 350 words, signed. *Aud:* Ages 14–18.]

Newsprint in tabloid format, *Craft International* provides in-depth coverage of, primarily, folk and traditional crafts. The focus is worldwide, as the title indicates, and the emphasis is on aesthetic and ethnographic aspects of indigenous crafts and folklife. In addition to the several substantial articles in each issue, there are excellent reviews of exhibitions.

343   Crafts 'n Things (Incorporating *Creative Crafts and Miniatures*). 1975. 8/yr. $9.95. Nancy Tosh. Clapper Publg. Co., Inc., 14 Main St., Park Ridge, IL 60068. Illus. Adv. Index. Circ: 320,000. [*Bk. rev:* Occasional. *Aud:* Ages 12–18.]

Features: This is a standard how-to-do-it approach to crafts and related areas. It is quite suitable for older children because of the clear instructions, which stress the ease of the work. There is a cross section of several simple-to-do craft projects in each issue, including patterns and easy-to-follow instructions. This is for beginners, or for readers shopping for suppliers (heavy on advertisements). The emphasis on ads makes it less than ideal, although the ads can be informative for those seeking hard-to-find supplies. The editorial copy, however, is objective and high in quality.

344   Family Handyman: the do-it-yourself home improvement magazine (Incorporating *Home Garden*). 1951. 10/yr. $12.97. Gary Havens. Home Service Publns., Inc., 7900 International Dr., Suite 950, Minneapolis, MN 55425. Illus. Adv. Index. Circ: 1,300,000. Microform: UMI. Reprint: UMI. [*Indexed:* MI, RG. *Bk. rev:* Occasional. *Aud:* Ages 14–18.]

A basic magazine for any student who wants to carry shop into the home. The instructions are clear, and this is about as good a magazine of its type as one can purchase for either school or public library collections. It covers the gamut of home repair, maintenance, and improvement areas from basement to roof, inside and out. Instruction in lawn care, car maintenance, and general decorating is also provided. Instructions are sometimes detailed, sometimes summarized, depending on the complexity of the project. A generous number of home improvement quick tips that are easily applicable are offered.

345   Fine Woodworking. 1975. bi-m. $22. Dick Burrows. Taunton Press, Inc., 63 S. Main St., P.O. Box 355, Newtown, CT 06470. Illus. Adv. Index. Circ: 275,000. Vol. ends: Nov/Dec. [*Indexed:* ArtI. *Bk. rev:* 3, 450 words, signed. *Aud:* Ages 14–18.]

This is an advanced magazine for senior high school students with a serious interest in the subject. Most of the 15 or so articles in each issue concern techniques and equipment, though there is an occasional piece about the work and designs of current or historically important artists. Helpful diagrams and illustrations accompany the articles. Questions and answers, book reviews, and events listings are all of interest to the serious woodworker, as are the many supply-and-equipment advertisements.

346   Home Mechanix (Formerly: *Mechanix Illustrated*; incorporating *Electronics Illustrated*). 1928. m. $13.94. Michael Morris. Times-Mirror Magazines, 2 Park Ave., New York, NY 10016. Illus. Adv. Circ: 1,332,775. Reprint: UMI. [*Indexed*: MI, RG. *Bk. rev*: Occasional. *Aud*: Ages 14–18.]

A slightly slicker presentation of material than *Popular Mechanics*, with 10 to 15 feature articles on home and auto projects in each issue. Instructions are copiously illustrated but brief, and advertising is about par for magazines in this section. The "Worth Writing For/To" article footnotes provide contacts with materials suppliers.

347   Lapidary Journal. 1947. m. $20. Merle Berk. Lapidary Journal, Inc., 3564 Kettner Blvd., San Diego, CA 92101. Illus. Adv. Circ: 39,000. Vol. ends: Mar. [*Indexed*: MI. *Bk. rev*: 1–2, 200–400 words. *Aud*: Ages 14–18.]

"For gem cutters, collectors, jewelers," *Lapidary Journal* addresses all phases of gemology and lapidary techniques. Use of gems in jewelry making is a primary focus. Mining and rock-hunting expeditions are also treated. A particularly extensive calendar tracks events such as trade shows, as well as national and local gem, mineral, and rock society meetings. The large number of gemological equipment and suppliers listings and ads is especially valuable to the interested reader.

348   The Leather Craftsman (Formerly: *Make It with Leather: craftsman*). 1956. bi-m. $15. Nancy Sawyer. Craftsman Publg., P.O. Box 1749, Burleson, TX 76028. Illus. Adv. Index. Circ: 10,000. Microform: UMI. [*Bk. rev*: 2–4, 200–300 words. *Aud*: Ages 14–18.]

Aimed at the serious leather crafter, but with some material for beginners also. Detailed instructions with accompanying illustrations and the "Pattern Pull-Out Section" for a leather craft appear in each issue. This journal includes an interesting mix of project guides, discussion articles, and news items. For the enthusiast.

349   McCall's Needlework & Crafts. 1935. 6/yr. $11.97. Rosemary Maceiras. ABC Consumer Magazines, Inc., 825 Seventh Ave., New York, NY 10019-6001. Illus. Adv. Index. Circ: 600,112. [*Bk. rev*: 5–8, 125–200 words. *Aud*: Ages 14–18.]

A showcase for needlework with some home-craft projects and recipes added, this publication will instruct and motivate beginners. Directions are simple and complete, while the layout is very attractive. Accent is on designs and projects rather than on fitting in as much advertising as possible, and the diehard non-crafter will have difficulty passing by the next opportunity to pick up knitting needles and yarn and plunge in.

350   The Old-House Journal. 1973. bi-m. $21. Patricia Poore. The Old-House Journal Corp., 435 Ninth St., Brooklyn, NY 11215. Illus. Adv. Circ: 78,000. [*Aud*: Ages 14–18.]

The library that subscribes to the *Family Handyman* will wish to consider this related title. It, too, is for the advanced student who is interested in the restoration and maintenance of homes built before 1939. It includes articles on renovation, restoration, preservation, and repair techniques, histories, and product information and evaluation. The advertisements provide a valuable current-awareness service for products used in renovation and restoration work.

Pack-O-Fun. *See under* CHILDREN/GAMES AND HOBBIES.

351   **Popular Mechanics.** 1902. m. $15.94. Joe Oldham. Hearst Magazines, 224 W. 57th St., New York, NY 10019. Illus. Adv. Circ: 1,650,000. [*Indexed*: MI, RG. *Aud*: Ages 10–18.]

Very few children or young adults will not recognize this most popular of the recreational projects magazines. It should be in all school and public libraries. For the mechanic, do-it-yourselfer, handyperson, *PM* gives news updates, background, theory, instructions, and illustrations for learning and applying the mechanics of home projects, cars, boats, cycles, workshops, home labs, and electronics. Article coverage ranges from two paragraphs on the latest developments in energy sources to five-page discussions of drill bits. Directions are extremely clear and illustrations are excellent.

352   **Popular Science: the what's new magazine** (Formerly: *Popular Science Monthly*). 1872. m. $13.94. C. P. Gilmore. Times Mirror Magazines, Inc., 2 Park Ave., New York, NY 10016. Illus. Adv. Index. Circ: 2,000,000. Microform: UMI. Online: DIALOG. [*Indexed*: MI, RG. *Bk. rev*: Occasional. *Aud*: Ages 10–18.]

Along with *Popular Mechanics*, this is a magazine familiar to most younger readers and their parents. It is as basic as its competitor and a welcome addition to any library. Fairly complex projects are described and well illustrated. Theory and "how-tos" are defined in regular sections on science and technology, space and aviation, computers and electronics, cars, recreation, and home-focused areas. Project descriptions are clear but are slightly more esoteric than those in *Popular Mechanics*, and cover the physical sciences more often than do other publications in this section.

353   **Shuttle, Spindle & Dyepot.** 1969. q. $25 (Membership). Judy Robbins. Handweavers Guild of America, 120 Mountain Ave., Bloomfield, CT 06002. Illus. Adv. Index. Circ: 18,500. Vol. ends: Fall. Microform: UMI. Reprint: UMI. [*Indexed*: ArtI. *Bk. rev*: 3–4, signed. *Aud*: Ages 14–18.]

Here is the best magazine in its field, at least for the young adult with a serious interest in the subject. The magazine provides practical information on weaving and sewing handwoven fabrics. The emphasis is on wearable textiles, though recent issues have included pieces on baskets and paper. Weaving techniques and traditions of other countries and cultures are discussed. Detailed patterns, instructions, diagrams, and color photographs complement the text. Departments include a calendar of events and book reviews, and a section called "Test & Report" that conveys consumer-type information on supplies, equipment, computer software, and so forth. *Shuttle, Spindle & Dyepot* is a "hands-on" magazine for serious practitioners of weaving and spinning.

354   **Studio Potter.** 1972. s-a. $20. Gerry Williams. Studio Potter, P.O. Box 70, Goffstown, NH 03045. Illus. Index. Circ: 8,000. Vol. ends: June. [*Indexed*: ArtI. *Aud*: Ages 14–18.]

Each semiannual issue of *Studio Potter* focuses on a theme that is treated in an in-depth, substantive manner. Examples include "The Human Form in Clay," "Health and the Potter," electric kilns, "Glaze: Color and Light," and drawing as surface design. Artists are frequent contributors to the textual as well as photographic content of the articles. International and historical perspectives are included when appropriate. For example, issues on glazes and drawing treat these subjects from many angles. Articles often include lists of references, resources for further information, and/or glossaries of terms discussed. Potters by region are also explored, with biographical and descriptive text about individual ceramists and their work.

355   **Threads Magazine.** 1985. bi-m. $22. Betsy Levine. Taunton Press, Inc., 63 S. Main St., Newtown, CT 06470. Illus. Adv. Index. Circ: 100,000. Vol. ends: Nov/Dec. [*Bk. rev*: 2–4, 300–350 words. *Aud*: Ages 14–18.]

Suitable for both the beginner and the advanced student, this is an unusual and rewarding magazine that offers information in a "hands-on" manner through projects, patterns, and instructions. Each issue includes 10 to 12 articles on sewing, knitting, quilting, fashion designing, lace-making, and other subjects. Technical know-how is emphasized; needlework traditions of other countries and periods are occasionally touched on as a basis for adapting those motifs and/or techniques to other projects. Regular departments include a calendar, book reviews, and a section on locating supplies of a particular kind or in a specific place.

356   **Workbasket: and home arts magazine.** 1935. 10/yr. $8. Roma Jean Rice. Modern Handcraft, Inc., 4251 Pennsylvania Ave., Kansas City, MO 64111. Illus. Adv. Circ: 1,784,529. Microform: UMI. Online: DIALOG. [*Indexed*: MI. *Bk. rev*: Occasional. *Aud*: Ages 14–18.]

Ten to 15 projects in crocheting, knitting, tatting, quilting, and general crafting are presented in each issue with detailed instructions and illustrations for each. Recipes and simple sewing projects are included, as well as gardening, homemaking, and fashion tips. An eclectic combination of craft interests and advertising.

357   **Workbench.** 1946. bi-m. $8. Jay W. Hedden. Modern Handcraft, Inc., 4251 Pennsylvania Ave., Kansas City, MO 64111. Illus. Adv. Index. Circ: 896,830. Microform: UMI. Online: DIALOG. [*Indexed*: MI, RG. *Bk. rev*: 1–2, 200–300 words. *Aud*: Ages 12–18.]

This is by way of the ideal shop magazine and it is found often in schools and in many public libraries. Projects are clearly explained and illustrated and can be done by older children as well as young adults. *Workbench* provides easy-to-follow instructions and easy- (and fun) to-read articles on how to build (and where to buy the parts for) everything from the napkin holder on your kitchen table to the addition on the house. Informative and well organized.

■ DISABILITIES   [Samuel T. Huang]

See also: HEALTH AND MEDICINE; PROFESSIONAL EDUCATION AND LIBRARY JOURNALS/EDUCATION BY SUBJECT AREAS/DISABILITIES

Publications found here cover all aspects of disabilities with particular attention to the needs of young adults. Most of the titles are edited to be read for pleasure and differ in no way from general magazines other than that they may be in large print or have editorial bias toward the problems of the disabled. For additional information and magazines in this area, the following sources will be useful: *Magazines in Special Media* (Washington, D.C.: The Library of Congress, 1985); *Physical Disability: An Annotated Literature Guide* (New York: Marcel Dekker, Inc., 1984).

First choices   (1) *Dialogue*; (2) *Lifeprints*; (3) *Kaleidoscope*.

358 **Dialogue: the magazine for the visually impaired.** 1961. q. $15. Nolan Crabb. Dialogue, The Information Service for the Visually Impaired, 3100 Oak Park Ave., Berwyn, IL 60402. Adv. Circ: 50,000. Vol. ends: Winter. [*Aud*: Ages 14–18.]

This quarterly publication is published by the Dialogue, a national information service for people with sight loss. It is produced in recorded disc, braille, and large-print editions. Every issue contains interviews with successful blind people, reports of recent legislation, notes on new products and services, home and gardening hints, recipes, and information about vocational, recreational, and travel opportunities. Stories, articles, and poems by blind authors are also included.

359 **Disability Rag.** 1980. bi-m. $12. Mary Johnson. Advocado Press, Inc., P.O. Box 145, Louisville, KY 40201. Adv. Circ: 2,700. Sample. Vol. ends: Nov/Dec. Online: CompuServe. [*Indexed*: API. *Bk. rev*: 3, 200 words, signed. *Aud*: Ages 14–18.]

Disability Rag contains articles that deal with disability rights and the struggle for those rights; the necessity for public education about the kinds of help disabled individuals need; current events in disability legislation; problems with existing programs for the disabled; personal experience; self-help, inspiration, and self-encouragement; assertiveness; and mainstreaming. Although it appears to be directed at the disabled, this periodical would be of benefit to anyone interested in learning the viewpoints of the disabled themselves.

360 **Easy-to-Read Puzzles: large type for happy solving.** 1986. bi-m. $11.70. Anne Keffer. CBS Magazines, Popular Magazine Group, 1515 Broadway, New York, NY 10036. Illus. Circ: 47,008. Vol. ends: Sept/Oct. [*Aud*: Ages 14–18.]

This magazine, set in 18-point type, contains 33 crossword puzzles suitable for teenagers and young adults with low vision. The visual clarity is very good, and this title would be a welcome addition to a school or public library's collection for the target audience.

361 **Kaleidoscope: international magazine of literature, fine arts, and disabilities.** 1979. s-a. $11 (Individuals, $9). Darshan Perusek. Kaleidoscope Press, United Cerebral Palsy and Services for the Handicapped, 326 Locust St., Akron, OH 44302. Illus. Circ: 2,000. Sample. Vol. ends: Winter/Spring. [*Bk. rev*: 1, 1,000 words, signed. *Aud*: Ages 14–18.]

This publication contains lively, energetic, well-crafted fiction, poetry, and visual arts related to disabilities. It also includes critical essays, photo essays, book reviews, personal-experience narratives, and interviews. There is no bias as to style, but the editors are adamantly hostile to the sentimental and the trite, and responsive to originality of thought and innovative treatment of subjects. A short biographical sketch is given for each contributor, and there are brief articles on overcoming disabilities. A welcome publication for school and public libraries.

362 **Lifeprints.** 1983. 5/yr. $15. Carol M. McCarl. Blindskills, Inc., P.O. Box 5181, Salem, OR 97304. Circ: 400. Sample. Vol. ends: May/June. [*Bk. rev*: 2, 400 words, signed. *Aud*: Ages 14–18.]

This "recorded, braille and large print magazine" is geared primarily toward teenagers and young adults and the situations they encounter as students, dates, neighbors, and parents, as well as visually impaired members of society. The publication, set in 18-point type, deals with such diverse topics as clothes, school, careers, and sports. It includes profiles of successful professionals with visual handicaps. Among the writers are both social workers and teenagers giving personal advice. Many articles close with an invitation to the reader to contact the author for further information. The print is very legible. This is a worthwhile journal for its target audience.

363   Light. 1929. a. Free. Roy Belosic. Braille Inst. of America, Inc., 741 N. Vermont Ave., Los Angeles, CA 90029-3594. Illus. Circ: 66,000. Sample. [*Aud*: Ages 14–18.]

This magazine, the voice of a nonprofit group dedicated to assisting the blind, is published in September of each year. It reports on the organization's activities, particularly in terms of counseling, education, and job opportunities.

364   Mainstream: magazine of the able-disabled. 1975. m. (exc. Jan. & June). $14.98. Cyndi Jones. Exploding Myths, Inc., 2973 Beech St., San Diego, CA 92102. Illus. Adv. Index. Circ: 13,000. Sample. Vol. ends: Dec. [*Aud*: Ages 14–18.]

Mainstream contains news on legislation, current events, classified advertisements, and new products and technology for the disabled. Articles of interest to people with disabilities are also included. The objective of this publication is summed up in the subtitle, the emphasis being on what one can do.

365   Scrapbook Pages. 1984. bi-m. $15. Jane Cook. Thistledown Pages, P.O. Box 5583, Arlington, VA 22205. Illus. Vol. ends: Feb/Mar. [*Aud*: Ages 14–18.]

A recommended tabloid of six pages measuring $10\frac{1}{2}'' \times 14\frac{1}{2}''$ with at most two featured articles covering topics of current interest viewed in their historical perspective. These are well researched and well written and compare favorably with those in regular-print journals. The reader is frequently invited at the end of a piece to write to the editor for further information. A regular column called "Memories from Momma's Kitchen" reminisces about culinary customs from the past and a two-page insert provides step-by-step instructions for making handcrafts for children.

366   Teen Time. 6/yr. $6.75. Concordia Publg. House, 3558 Jefferson Ave., St. Louis, MO 63118. [*Aud*: Ages 14–18.]

This is typical of several religiously oriented magazines available for the blind or near blind. It comes in two editions: one braille and the other in large print. The content is varied, but as the organization explains: "All magazines produced by the Lutheran Ministry for the Blind are based on Christian religious teachings." Interested librarians/teenagers/teachers should contact the publisher for more information and for sample copies. Note, too, that Concordia publishes several other braille editions that may be of interest.

367   Young and Alive. 1954. m. Free. R. J. Kaiser. Christian Record Services, 4444 S. 52nd St., Lincoln, NE 68516. Circ: 19,000. Sample. [*Aud*: Ages 14–18.]

Another of a series of Christian magazines published for the blind and near blind, this is for the latter. The 24- to 36-point type stories and articles are primarily for teenagers and each 70-page issue has eight to ten entries. These range from biographical sketches and fiction to games. There is a section for pen pals, too. The writing style is good and the Christian support is not all that evident except in one or two features. The librarian should send for a listing of other free publications, from talking magazines to full-vision books—braille on one page and print and pictures on the other.

■ ENVIRONMENT, CONSERVATION, AND OUTDOOR RECREATION   [Phoebe F. Phillips]

See also: FISHING AND HUNTING; SPORTS

The problems with the environment are too well known to belabor here, but there is a need for children and young people to learn the value of green earth and its many species of inhabitants—as well as the current dangers. Knowledge is the key to the solution of these problems, and these magazines offer such knowledge. While most are edited for adults, the titles selected here are more than suitable for the young adult. Not only is the text easy to follow, but most of the magazines feature numerous, informative illustrations.

First choices   (1) *National Wildlife*; (2) *Conservationist*; (3) *Wilderness*; (4) *Sierra*.

Suitable for children   Ages 6–14: *Owl; Ranger Rick*. Ages 10–18: *International Wildlife; National Wildlife*. Ages 12–18: *Adirondack Life; Conservationist; National Parks; Sierra; Wilderness*.

368   **Adirondack Life.** 1970. bi-m. $15. Jeffrey Kelly. Adirondack Council, Church St., P.O. Box D-2, Elizabethtown, NY 12932. Illus. Adv. Circ: 48,000. Sample. [*Bk. rev*: Notes. *Aud*: Ages 12–18.]

Junior high and high school readers will enjoy this local title, which has information for people throughout the nation who are involved with conservation and outdoor sports and recreation. Articles are usually illustrated and concentrate on the sport of the season—skiing in winter and backpacking in summer. Particularly useful are the calendar of events and the recreational facilities directory.

369   **American Forests: the magazine of forests, soil, water, wildlife, and outdoor recreation.** 1895. bi-m. $24. Bill Rooney. Amer. Forestry Assn., 1516 P St. N.W., Washington, DC 20005. Illus. Adv. Circ: 25,000. Microform: UMI. [*Indexed*: MI. *Bk. rev*: 1–3, 150–500 words. *Aud*: Ages 14–18.]

The stated objective of the magazine is "to maintain and improve the health and value of trees and forests." Illustrations are both color and black and white with some quite good full-page color photos. A feature entitled "Twigs" consists of short paragraphs for "up-to-date news in the world of trees, forests, and forestry." This provides a good source of information at a glance for those who want to keep up with environmental and recreational issues such as recreation facilities for the handicapped. Generally, *American Forests* provides a good addition to the library at a reasonable price.

370   **Backpacker.** 1973. bi-m. $18. John Delves. Rodale Press, Inc., 33 E. Minor St., Emmaus, PA 18908. Illus. Adv. Circ: 175,000. Vol. ends: Nov. Microform: B&H, UMI. Online: DIALOG. Reprint: UMI. [*Indexed*: Acs, MI. *Aud*: Ages 14–18.]

Backpacker readers will find information about hiking, backpacking, climbing, and other outdoor sports such as skiing, rafting, and canoeing. Most issues contain articles about wildlife and the environment, recent events relating to various sports, getting started in a sport, and biographical articles or interviews. Also found are descriptions of geographical areas complete with details about planning trips and information about equipment and outdoor clothing, including product tests. This is a magazine that has something to offer active participants in an acitivity as well as those with a casual interest.

371   Buzzworm: the environmental journal. 1988. q. $12. Joseph Daniel. Buzzworm, 1818 16th St., Boulder, CO 80302. Illus. Adv. [*Aud*: Ages 14–18.]

Take a massive number of photographs, many in color, add six to ten easy-to-read articles, concentrate on the American environment, and you have what the editor terms "the first truly independent consumer magazine reporting on environmental conservation." The interest is with the individual and hands-on efforts to save the countryside. Authors and photographers are experts, yet know how to appeal to laypersons with factual, objective reporting. The public policy on environment, as well as lack of same, is of particular concern. One may not always agree with a solution, but few will argue with the pressing need to save our animals and waters from commercial takeovers. An impressive new and popular general environmental magazine, this can be recommended for any general library collection. Note, too, the low subscription price.

372   Camping Magazine. 1926. 7/yr. Membership (Nonmembers, $17.50). Christine O'Connor Brokaw. Amer. Camping Assn., Bradford Woods, 5000 SR 67 N, Martinsville, IN 46151-7902. Illus. Adv. Index. Circ: 8,000. Vol. ends: June. Microform: UMI. [*Indexed*: MI, RG. *Aud*: Ages 14–18.]

Issues are generally about 60 pages in length with black-and-white and color illustrations. This is the official journal of the American Camping Association (ACA) and is directed toward camp administrators and staff of professionally run camps. It includes such topics as computers and camps, camp maintenance, and camp counselors. ACA membership includes a subscription to this magazine. The cost is reasonable enough so that those with an interest in the field can subscribe without becoming members of the organization.

373   The Conservationist. 1946. bi-m. $10 ($3.50 to primary and secondary schools). John J. Dupont. New York State Dept. of Environmental Conservation, 50 Wolf Rd., Rm. 505, Albany, NY 12233. Illus. Circ: 180,000. Sample. Vol. ends: May/June. Microform: B&H, UMI. [*Indexed*: CIJE, RG. *Bk. rev*: 1–3, 350 words. *Aud*: Ages 12–18.]

This remains one of the best, basic magazines in the field. While the publication of a single state, the coverage is broader than that state alone. Most topics of interest to younger readers and young adults are covered. The black-and-white photos are good. Note, too, the low cost. Recommended for all school and public library collections.

374   Earth First: the radical environmental journal. 1980. 8/yr. $20. John Davis. Earth First, P.O. Box 5871, Tucson, AZ 85703. Illus. Adv. Circ: 15,000. [*Aud*: Ages 14–18.]

The tabloid format of this short (approximately 35 pages per issue) journal does not detract from the carefully written articles giving background information on legislation affecting the environment as well as information on new crises in the environment. The illustrations are black-and-white photographs. Articles are factual and take a stance, primarily expressing concern over the need to protect wildlife species from political mismanagement through improper supervision and from developers who disrupt their habitats. The paper presents in-depth studies of the issues rather than brief news notes. It deals primarily with issues of concern to the inhabitants of the United States.

International Wildlife. *See under* CHILDREN/ENVIRONMENT, CONSERVATION, AND OUTDOOR RECREATION.

375 **National Parks: the magazine of the National Parks & Conservation Association** (Formerly: *National Parks & Conservation Magazine: the environment journal*). 1919. bi-m. Membership (Libraries, $25). Michele Strutin. Natl. Parks, 1915 31st St. N.W., Washington, DC 20007. Illus. Adv. Index. Circ: 50,000. Microform: B&H, UMI. [*Indexed*: RG. *Aud*: Ages 12–18.]

This is a basic title for most school and public libraries, and although it is written for adults, the photographs and the easy-to-follow text make it an ideal choice for readers 12 years old and up. Each issue contains approximately 46 pages. Brief content notes explain general issues discussed in each article. Interest extends beyond the national parks and monuments to all aspects of the environment. Updates on legislative action that affects the environment are included and an annual index helps the reader find information in each volume. The reasonable price makes it a bargain. Single copies can be purchased at $2.50.

National Wildlife. *See under* CHILDREN/ENVIRONMENT, CONSERVATION, AND OUTDOOR RECREATION.

376 **Not Man Apart.** 1970. bi-m. $18. Ken Maize. Friends of the Earth, 530 Seventh St. N.W., Washington, DC 20003. Illus. Adv. Circ: 20,000. [*Indexed*: API. *Bk. rev*: Various number and length. *Aud*: Ages 14–18.]

Tabloid format makes this a lesser *Sierra* with similar attitudes and insights, but more emphasis on the technical aspects of safeguarding the environment. It offers alternative sources of energy and approaches to using the environment not found in the more popular magazine. The modest cost makes it a good investment for most libraries wanting to keep some titles on the environment.

377 **Outdoor Canada.** 1972. q. $25.95. Teddi Brown. Outdoor Canada Magazine, Ltd., 801 York Mills Rd., Toronto, Ont. M3B 1X7, Canada. Illus. Adv. Circ: 148,000. Vol. ends: Dec/Jan. Microform: MIM. [*Indexed*: CanI. *Aud*: Ages 14–18.]

An informative magazine for those who fish, hike, or canoe. The well-illustrated articles make even the armchair traveler yearn for a trip to Yoho or the Queen Charlotte Islands. When national parks are discussed, a useful section on how to get there is always appended to the article. Sections discuss how to choose equipment and how to use and care for it. Wild edibles are covered for those who like to live off the land. Recommended for public libraries and school libraries with an interest in wildlife conservation.

378 **Outside.** 1976. m. $18. Lawrence J. Burke. Mariah Publns. Corp., 1165 N. Clark St., Chicago, IL 60610. Illus. Adv. Circ: 300,000. Vol. ends: Dec. Microform: B&H, UMI. Reprint: UMI. [*Indexed*: Acs. *Bk. rev*: 2–4, 200–400 words, signed. *Aud*: Ages 14–18.]

Articles about a wide variety of outdoor sports, including camping, hiking, kayaking, running, bicycling, skiing, and climbing, appear in *Outside*. The reader will find equipment reviews, profiles of participants in various sports, a calendar of events, and an expedition services directory. There are also articles about environmental issues and natural history. Aimed at a wide audience, this is a magazine that can be read and enjoyed by people who are only armchair enthusiasts of outdoor sports.

Owl Magazine. *See under* CHILDREN/ENVIRONMENT, CONSERVATION, AND OUTDOOR RECREATION.

Ranger Rick. *See under* CHILDREN/ENVIRONMENT, CONSERVATION, AND OUTDOOR RECREATION.

379   **Sierra: the Sierra Club bulletin.** 1893. bi-m. Membership $33 (Nonmembers, $15). John F. King. Sierra Club, 730 Polk St., San Francisco, CA 94109. Illus. Adv. Index. Circ: 180,000. Vol. ends: Dec. Microform: B&H, UMI. [*Indexed*: RG. *Bk. rev*: 8, 150–500 words, signed. *Aud*: Ages 12–18.]

The interesting anecdotal section titled "Afield" adds spice to this publication with its short pieces on interesting tidbits like Ben & Jerry's Homemade Ice Cream starting a hog farm to feed their milk solid wastes to pigs rather than overtaxing the Waterbury sewage-treatment plant. Generally, this is not a publication that is squeamish about taking sides. Articles often involve political and social issues and their impact on the environment, but also present information on camping and hiking. Colorful photography and illustrations make it a good browsing item acquisition for any library.

380   **Wilderness** (Formerly: *The Living Wilderness*). 1935. q. $30. T. H. Watkins. Wilderness Soc., 1400 Eye St. N.W., Washington, DC 20005. Illus. Adv. Index. Circ: 30,000. Vol. ends: Summer. Microform: MIM, UMI. [*Indexed*: GSI, MI, RG. *Bk. rev*: 7, 100–500 words, signed. *Aud*: Ages 12–18.]

A helpful description of each article is included with the title in the table of contents. Color illustrations and photographs as well as those in black and white are well done. With just 60 pages to each issue, this is easily browsed for specific articles of interest. After *National Wildlife*, this is one of the best general conservation magazines for teenagers. It presents environmental issues as they are related to society. With conservationist viewpoints and an interest in developing government support for conservation interests, the magazine takes a definite stance.

■ EUROPE

[Judith K. Ohles]

See also: FOREIGN LANGUAGE; NEWS AND OPINION; USSR AND EASTERN EUROPE

Western European magazines reflect wide diversity. One can find periodicals on virtually any subject. Here, however, the focus is on two types of magazines: the first of assistance to the student in a foreign-language program, and the second helping the young adult to broaden a personal view of the world. The majority of titles are in German, French, or Italian, although some of the general newsmagazines more than cover the rest of the continent. Almost all presume at least one year of study of the particular language, and many at least two years. Most titles, then, are not for the beginner. On the other hand, there are several English-language magazines covering England and Europe that are suitable for the general collection and require no particular language skills.

First choices   (1) *Champs-Elysées*;   (2) *Stern Magazin*;   (3) *Paris Match*;   (4) *Oggi*.

381   **Britannia: keeping in touch with the British way of life.** 1983. m. $22.95. Terry Fletcher. U.S. Britannia, 117 Queen St. E., Toronto, Ont. M5C 1S2, Canada. Illus. Adv. Circ: 30,000. Sample. Vol. ends: Dec. [*Aud*: Ages 14–18.]

Teenagers will enjoy this rather fluffy view of England, and while it may lack depth it is long on entertainment. In 48 pages, *Britannia* offers six major articles and several brief sections and articles. It includes all sorts of news, some of which borders on gossip. The magazine contains many photographs and illustrations. Although it sometimes looks too busy, it provides readers with current information about Great Britain. Regular features include the following: "Great

Britons," which often includes photographs and news items about British royalty; a news section of two parts, "News Digest" and "What the Papers Say: A Compilation of Current Headlines from British Newspapers"; and "Nosh an' Slosh," which offers various recipes.

382 **Champs-Elysées.** 1984. 14/yr. $118. Wes Green. Champs-Elysées, P.O. Box 158067, Nashville, TN 37215. [*Aud:* Ages 14–18.]

An effective way for a young adult to learn French: through a cassette that gives the listener an accurate view of French life. It is essentially a practical lesson in spoken French, but delivered in a sparkling, entertaining fashion. The "magazine" is in two parts. A cassette consists of about 45 minutes of news and notes on travel, cooking, entertainment, current affairs, and sports. Most of the items are interlaced with popular French songs. The second part is a printed version of the cassette material. This is in French with a vocabulary of basic words and idiomatic expressions. While there are seven issues a semester, a full subscription consists of 14 cassettes sent over the school year. Supervised by experienced American teachers, this is an effort that should have wide appeal.

The publisher issues a similar service in Spanish, *Puerta de Sol.* The biweekly cassette is produced in Madrid and the 45-minute program follows much the same format as its corresponding work in French. A third (and again similar) service is *Schau ins Land*, at the same price, but this time in German.

383 **Esprit.** 1932. m. $45. Paul Thibaud. Esprit, 19, rue Jacob, 75006 Paris, France. Adv. Index. Circ: 14,000. Vol. ends: Dec. [*Bk. rev:* 10–12, 300–500 words, signed. *Aud:* Ages 14–18.]

Two years of high school French study is an absolute necessity to be able to read this journal unless the student is exceptional. Issues average 120 to 160 pages, but a special issue can contain up to 320 pages. One such special issue covered the new age of sports. This is a general literary review covering politics, society, and culture. Current French and worldwide issues are tackled. For example, one issue featured articles on Irangate, China, and Christianity and Marxism. Although this is not a religious title, articles often criticize the Catholic Church.

384 **Europa.** 1981. q. $40 (Individuals, $30). Karz/Segil, 320 W. 105th St., New York, NY 10025. Illus. Adv. Sample. [*Indexed:* PAIS. *Aud:* Ages 14–18.]

Subtitled "a quarterly magazine of European politics and culture," this appears to take an objective position on various current issues. Contributors range from teachers to writers to political figures, and coverage from literature and economics to politics and personalities. The writing style is suitable for young adults, but the price is high for a slim 64 or so pages.

385 **Europe Review.** 1985. a. $64. Richard Green. World of Information, 21 Gold St., Safron Walden, Essex CB10 1EJ, England. Illus. Index. [*Aud:* Ages 14–18.]

A yearbook, this is another version of the better known *Europa.* It differs from both, not only in its lower price, but in considerably more emphasis on statistical data that is quite current. There are the usual summaries of national sources of pride, from government to industry, but the primary strength is the emphasis on key statistical facts. Each entry follows a standard pattern—there are numerous essays, tables, and charts. Most sections are signed by contributors. All of the guide is easy to follow, and it is as suitable for the teenager as the expert. The same publisher offers similar approaches to Latin America, Africa, and so forth. Here the focus is on some 37 European countries, from the smallest to the USSR.

386 **L'Express.** 1953. w. $96. Yann de l'Ecotais. Groupe Express S.A., 61, ave. Hoche, 75008 Paris, France. Illus. Adv. Circ: 600,000. [*Bk. rev*: 2–3, 200 words, signed. *Aud*: Ages 14–18.]

A good title for relative beginners in French, *L'Express* is a weekly newsmagazine of France. Each issue covers recent developments in France and the world. Colorful photographs and pleasing layouts make this magazine enjoyable and easy to read. Regular sections include science, a portrait of a newsworthy individual, and business, the arts, and current books. Very similar to *Time* and *Newsweek*, it is suitable for those with a high school knowledge of French. Recommended for both school and public libraries.

387 **Forum.** 1978. q. Free. Nicole Rontchevsky. Directory of Press and Information, Council of Europe, 67006 Strasbourg Cedex, France. Illus. Circ: 100,000. [*Bk. rev*: 1–3, 300 words, signed. *Aud*: Ages 14–18.]

A government publication, this is in four languages, including English. The advantage is that the school can order the English- and a foreign-language edition so the student can check one against the other. "The official publication of the Council of Europe," *Forum* is a newsy magazine devoted to current events. Each 30-plus-page issue covers various topics, such as human rights, politics, culture, universities, and democracy. One issue included a special section on Europe's relationship with Latin America, and contained brief articles on sports, women, and science. A pleasing layout and many photographs make this very enjoyable to read or browse through. A list of recent Council of Europe publications is included. *Forum* is published in English, French, German, and Italian.

388 **Le Français dans le Monde.** 1961. 8/yr. $58 (Individuals, $47). Jacques Pecheur. Hachette Edicef, 26, rue de Fosses Saint-Jacques, 75005 Paris, France. Adv. Circ: 15,000. [*Aud*: Ages 14–18.]

This is for the young adult with at least one year and preferably two years of French. In approximately 80 pages, brief articles covering every aspect of French life and culture are included. This attractive magazine is generously illustrated and includes a "Fiches Practiques" for practice in French. A delightful title for high school or public libraries.

389 **The German Tribune: a weekly review of the German press.** 1962. w. $19. Friedrich Reinecke Verlag GmbH, Hartwicusstr., 3-4, D-2000 Hamburg 76, Fed. Rep. of Germany. Illus. Adv. Circ: 56,400. Sample. [*Aud*: Ages 14–18.]

One to two years of German study is required to read the German-language edition of this magazine. A 16-page tabloid-sized title, it covers current events in Germany. Sections such as industry, business, environment, modern living, the arts, and media are included. Articles are actually full length or condensed versions of articles from the German press. Editions are available in English, French, Italian, Portuguese, and Spanish. A good title for keeping abreast of contemporary Germany.

390 **The Illustrated London News.** 1842. m. $43. Henry Porter. Illustrated London News & Sketch, Ltd., 20 Upper Ground, London SE1 9PF, England. Illus. Adv. Index. Circ:

65,916. Sample. Microform: MIM. [*Indexed*: BoRvI. *Bk. rev*: 2–3, essays, signed. *Aud*: Ages 14–18.]

A lively and colorful magazine, *The Illustrated London News* features four to seven articles on various topics. The material is popularly written and covers typical tourist information. Regular features include restaurant reviews, food and wine, and theater and book reviews. Useful to the tourist or those living in London is "The Capital List: A Discerning Guide to Events in the City." This five-page section covers all theater, film, music, art, and other current cultural events in London.

391   **Italian Journal: a quarterly digest of Italian affairs.** 1987. q. $24.95. Victor Tesoro. Italian Academy Foundation, Inc., 278 Clinton Ave., Dobbs Ferry, NY 10522. Adv. Index. Circ: 25,000. [*Bk. rev*: 2–3, 300–500 words, signed. *Aud*: Ages 14–18.]

Published by the Italian Academy Foundation, the *Italian Journal* seeks to provide information about current Italian politics, society, and culture. One of its primary purposes is "to present a more balanced picture of Italy" than do some other publications about Italy. A diverse group of contibutors, from Italian professors to businesspeople associated with Italy, produce articles on equally diverse topics. Each issue also includes reviews of best-sellers in Italy. Recommended for both school libraries and public libraries with school patrons interested in Italian life and culture. All articles are in English.

392   **The Mediterranean.** 1985. s-a. $10. Alexander Damian. Orion Publg. House, 1472 Broadway, No. 319, New York, NY 10036. Illus. Adv. Sample. [*Aud*: Ages 14–18.]

An ambitious effort, this embraces archaeology, politics, history, and just about anything and everything dealing with the Mediterranean in times past and times present. The tone is semipopular, and the numerous charts, photographs, and a few colored illustrations are directed to the informed layperson, not the expert.

393   **Oggi.** 1945. w. $61. P. Occhipinti. Rizzoli-Corriere della Sera, Via A. Rizzoli 2, 20132 Milan, Italy. [*Aud*: Ages 14–18.]

A popular Italian-language magazine that is within the grasp of the first-year Italian student. Similar in format to *Paris Match*, but on a lower grade of paper and with less appealing photographs, this is the picture magazine of Italy. There are masses of advertisements in the 120–150 pages, and these are laced with the usual type of stories from news about sports and movie stars to television figures and events (usually sensational) in the news. The appeal is to the mass audience, and it more than succeeds in this endeavor. Quite easy to read and amusing to thumb through, *Oggi* is a basic magazine wherever there is a large Italian audience.

394   **Panorama.** 1962. w. $70. Carlo Rognoni. Arnoldo Mondadori Editore, Casella Postale 1772, 20090 Segrate, Milan, Italy. Illus. Adv. Circ: 346,000. Sample. [*Aud*: Ages 14–18.]

A magazine for first- to second-year Italian-language students, this may be a bit more difficult than its numerous cousins. A leading newsmagazine in Italy, *Panorama* resembles *Time* and *Newsweek*, but is a much larger publication (240–250 pages). Brief articles cover current events, business, Italian affairs, culture, science, and so forth. As in its American counterparts, most articles include a generous sprinkling of photographs.

395 **Paris Match.** 1949. w. $72. Bernard Bonnamour. Publns. Filipacchi, 63-65 Champs Elysees, 75008 Paris, France. Illus. Adv. Circ: 828,000. [*Aud*: Ages 14–18.]

Ideal for first- or second-year French students, because if the reader cannot grasp every word of the text, the pictures carry the story along. *Paris Match* resembles a cross between *People Magazine* and such newsmagazines as *Time*, *Newsweek*, and *Panorama*. It includes several brief articles about newsworthy people or celebrities. Each issue has a longer cover story about one newsmaker, such as Lady Diana or the French actress Isabelle Adjani. Several color photographs accompany each article. Brief articles about recent happenings in France and items of cultural interest are also included. A well-known French publication, *Paris Match* is a lively, enjoyable magazine that appeals to a diverse audience.

396 **Point.** 1972. w. $145. Claude Imbert. SEBDO, 140, rue de Rennes, 75006 Paris, France. Illus. Adv. Circ: 335,000. [*Aud*: Ages 14–18.]

Only the student with about two years of French will make much sense out of this title. A colorful weekly newsmagazine, *Point* resembles *Time, Newsweek,* and *Der Spiegel.* It includes typical sections—France, the world, society, the economy—and brief news items on science, film, and books. An attractive feature is a nine-page guide that lists activities in Paris and all of France, from television, film, and theater to fashion and tourism. Several photographs, some in color, as well as illustrations, charts, and tables, are included. A must for any library with an interest in contemporary France.

397 **Scala International.** 1961. bi-m. $14. Werner Wirthle. Frankfurter Societaets-Druckerei GmbH, Postfach 100801, Frankenallee 71-81, D-6000 Frankfurt 1, Fed. Rep. of Germany. Illus. Adv. Circ: 340,000. [*Aud*: Ages 14–18.]

One can buy both English and German editions and then students can measure their progress in mastering the German langauge (it comes in Spanish as well). *Scala International* is a picture magazine of current German and world events. More independent than other German newsmagazines, it is also more sophisticated. Its 60 or so pages feature typical sections on people, cultural life, and business.

398 **Scandinavian Review.** 1913. q. $15. Patricia McFate. Amer. Scandinavian Foundation, 725 Park Ave., New York, NY 10021. Illus. Adv. Index. Circ: 5,000. Sample. Vol. ends: Dec. Microform: UMI. Reprint: UMI. [*Indexed*: PAIS, SocSc. *Bk. rev*: 5, 450 words, signed. *Aud*: Ages 14–18.]

Published by the American Scandinavian Foundation, *Scandinavian Review* covers a variety of topics concerning the Scandinavian countries—Denmark, Finland, Iceland, Norway, and Sweden. Brief articles cover politics, trade, cultural identity, the arts, history, intellectual life, and sports. Many are accompanied by illustrations and photographs. Issues range from 90 to 170 pages and resemble an expanded version of *The Saturday Review.* All articles are in English.

399 **Der Spiegel.** 1947. w. $230. Rudolf Augstein. German Language Publns., Inc., 560 Sylvan Ave., Englewood Cliffs, NJ 07632. Illus. Adv. Circ: 1,100,000. Sample. Vol. ends: Dec. [*Bk. rev*: 1–3, 200 words, signed. *Aud*: Ages 14–18.]

No one with less than one year of German-language study will feel even mildly comfortable with this title. *Stern* is a better choice for most school libraries. The primary newsmagazine of Germany, *Der Spiegel* resembles *Time* and *Newsweek*, but issues average nearly 300 pages, almost three times the size of its American counterparts. Written by liberal journalists, it covers the current events of Germany and the world. It also hosts sections similar to other newsmagazines, such as sports, the arts, personalities, trends, best-sellers, and so forth. Coverage of both international and domestic news is fair and objective. Articles are accompanied by pictures, usually in black and white. A large part of the magazine is devoted to advertisements.

400 Stern Magazin. 1948. w. $106. Heiner Bremer, Michael Juergs, and Klaus Liedtke. Gruner & Jahr AG & Co., Postfach 30 20 40, 2000 Hamburg 36, Fed. Rep. of Germany. Illus. Adv. Circ: 1,465,000. Microform: UMI. Reprint: UMI. [*Aud:* Ages 14–18.]

Thanks to the abundant use of photographs and a writing style that is not difficult, this is a good choice for students with a year or more of German. Germany's primary picture magazine, a combination of *Life* and *Time* or *Newsweek*, it is directed to the German middle classes and reflects their values in its editorial material. Coverage is primarily of the week's past events in Germany, although it does include the rest of Europe and the remainder of the world from time to time. With the addition of the word *magazin* to its title in the 1980s, the magazine has made a concerted effort to be something more than an oversized *People*. There is now more editorial matter than in the past, but it remains a highly popular approach to people and activities. Americans, too, are struck by the nudity, which the Germans treat much as we do violence—casually and as part of the passing scene. The nudity may be offensive in some situations and the librarian would do well to check out a few sample copies, or view the magazine in another library, before ordering for schools. Public libraries need not be so cautious.

■ FAN MAGAZINES   [Sue Kopp]

See also: GENERAL INTEREST; MUSIC AND DANCE

A "fan magazine" is an illustrated publication devoted to gossip and anecdotal articles about the lives, loves, and careers of movie and television stars, as well as other entertainers. "Fanzines" are not included, because they tend to devote themselves to one particular celebrity.

In general, fan magazines tend to be low-budget publications; most of them are printed on newsprint, and often they will include glossy color pinups. Those targeting the teenage sector may also include wallet-sized pictures. They all have the important "Letters to the Editor" section.

The teenage group is by far the most prolific in titles if the teenage and music fan magazines are combined. A magazine may publish the addresses of the current musical stars (or try to sell you its book of addresses), link pen pals, have contests and/or giveaways, and include record and video reviews. Most advertising is in-house, and in general these titles appeal to the 10–16 year age group.

The soap opera magazines follow the daytime stars. They seldom rely on current plots as a feature, although they may list who is who by show, and who is new. There is little variation among the magazines; the general format depends on interviews with the stars and candid photographs.

Musicians are often featured in general fan publications, but there are many magazines devoted to particular types of music stars, such as country, hard rock, or black performers. There is rarely a racial or musical mixture in the magazines. Pinups are also quite popular.

First choices (1) *Super Teen*; (2) *Country Music*; (3) *Star Hits*; (4) *Daytime TV*.

Suitable for children Ages 10–18: *Big Bopper*. Ages 11–15: *Splice*; *Super Teen*; *Teen Beat*; *Teen Generation*; *Tiger Beat*. Ages 12–18: *16 Magazine*; *Wow*.

401 **The Big Bopper.** 1987. m. $19.95. Julie Laufer. Laufer Publg. Co., 3500 W. Olive Ave., Suite 850, Burbank, CA 91505. Illus. Adv. [*Aud*: Ages 10–18.]

The Big Bopper and *Bop*, both by Laufer and self-declared sister publications, are very similar, often covering the same stars in the same month. *The Big Bopper* contains approximately 20 pages more per issue than *Bop*, including more glossy color pinup pages. They are both printed on newsprint. Both magazines include a wide range of features, including star interviews, questions and answers, contests, star addresses, pen pals, trivia, quotes, and gossip. For five dollars a year more, *The Big Bopper* is probably worth it, but be aware that it is also relatively new and therefore not strongly established. One or the other of these sister publications is recommended for young adult library sections after *Super Teen*.

402 **Black Beat.** m. $19. Steve Ivory. Sterling's Magazines, Inc., 355 Lexington Ave., New York, NY 10017. Illus. Adv. [*Aud*: Ages 14–18.]

Although *Black Beat* is not exclusively music oriented, 9 of the 12 featured performers are rock stars. Also found in this newsprint magazine are penpals, short record reviews, "Gossip Beat," a color centerfold pinup, and "Catch Our Rising Star," a column in which new talent is highlighted. The features are fairly substantial for a fan magazine, and this is recommended for a general, predominately black audience.

403 **Circus.** 1969. m. $22. Gerald Rothberg. Circus Enterprises, 3 W. 18th St., New York, NY 10011. Illus. Adv. Circ: 281,000. Sample. Microform: UMI. [*Indexed*: Acs. *Aud*: Ages 14–18.]

The emphasis of this entertainment magazine is rock and its focus is on personalities in the business. A group or individual receives main coverage in each issue and is presented in a lengthy article with extensive color and some black-and-white photography. Extending beyond the typical fanzine, this title also contains rock tour schedules, lyrics, music, and bestselling album lists. Of particular interest is the "Music Gear" department, which provides test results and guides for purchasing guitars and other musical instruments. Loyal rock fans for which this title is intended should find it quite comprehensive and satisfactory.

404 **Country Music.** 1972. bi-m. $13.98. Helen Barnard. Silver Eagle Pubs., 342 Madison Ave., Suite 2118, New York, NY 10173. Illus. Adv. Circ: 350,000. [*Indexed*: Acs, MI. *Aud*: Ages 14–18.]

Country Music is celebrating nearly 20 years of publication. It is a well-written, glossy, full-color magazine that is well established and well received. Approximately five stars are featured per issue with a "People" section that spreads the latest word on a variety of celebrities, plus a question-and-answer column featuring a star. There is also a substantial signed record review section that gives in-depth reviews. If your library includes country music fans, this magazine is highly recommended.

405   **Country Song Roundup.** 1947. m. $25. William T. Anderson. Charlton Publns., Inc., 1 Division St., Derby, CT 06418. Illus. Adv. Circ: 127,627. [*Aud*: Ages 14–18.]

This black-and-white newsprint publication would appeal to country and western music fans. The photographs are a bit fuzzy, but the drawing card for this magazine is the space devoted to song lyrics, complete with song index. This publication relies more on the typical fan-magazine format than does *Country Music*, as it includes short biographical bits on singers and groups, short record reviews, questions and answers, trivia, and the "Country Classified" section. If your patrons are "into" country, this magazine would complement *Country Music* nicely.

406   **Daytime TV.** 1967. m. $19. Anne Marie Allocca. Sterling's Magazines, Inc., 355 Lexington Ave., New York, NY 10017. Illus. Adv. Circ: 250,000. [*Aud*: Ages 14–18.]

Soap opera fan magazines are amazingly similar, but of those reviewed, *Daytime TV* is the one that stands out. Its editorial staff varies the format with "50 Fabulous Facts" about a celebrity, picks its "Star of the Month," and features "Plotline Hotline." Printed on newsprint, the photographs are both candid and posed. Besides the typical fan features such as birthdays of the stars and a gossip column, it also includes "Roll Call," in which the casts from each soap are listed. One other feature worth mentioning is that this publication shows a sense of humor that is not as evident in the others within this category.

407   **Dream Guys.** 1986. 9/yr. $2.95/copy. Grace Catalano. Dream Guys, Inc., 250 W. Fifth St., Suite 2012, New York, NY 10019. Illus. Circ: 170,000. Sample. Vol. ends: Dec. [*Aud*: Ages 14–18.]

A teen fanzine, this title would probably be appreciated by girls more than by boys, for the scope of its celebrity coverage is "guys." Like others, it covers the gamut of the entertainment industry—music, film, television—focusing mostly on younger male stars. An added attraction is a centerfold larger than the typical double-page size. Each issue offers a 21″ × 32″ two-sided color pinup of the featured idol.

408   **Metal Mania.** bi-m. $3/issue. P. Vitucci. Tempo Publg. Co., Inc., 475 Park Ave. S., Suite 2201, New York, NY 10016. Illus. Adv. [*Aud*: Ages 14–18.]

For aficionados of spandex, leather, and sweat printed on glossy paper with full color, this is the magazine. *Metal Mania* is a better choice than *Rock Scene* in that the photographs are not as posed. A section reviewing demos sent in by fledgling groups is interesting, as are the record and video reviews. Hard rock music is graphic, and so is the language that the members of the groups use while being interviewed.

Que Pasa? *See under* Latin America, Latino (U.S.).

409   **Right On!** 1971. m. $17.99. Cindy Horner. Sterling's Magazines, Inc., 355 Lexington Ave., New York, NY 10017. Illus. Adv. Circ: 300,000. [*Aud*: Ages 14–18.]

Targeting older teens to young adults, *Right On!* is a good general fan magazine. Its particular interest is the black performer. Included in the format are featured performers, pen pals, short biographies on celebrities, full-color glossy pinups, and the latest scoop on the stars. Professional and attractive, this is recommended for libraries with black patrons.

410 **Rock & Soul** (Formerly: *Rock and Soul Songs; Rock and Roll Songs*). 1956. m. $20. John Shelton Ivany. Charlton Publns., Inc., 1 Division St., Derby, CT 06418. Illus. Adv. Circ: 75,000. [*Aud*: Ages 14–18.]

This magazine deserves consideration. Printed on glossy paper but predominately black and white, approximately eight black performers are featured per issue. It covers a variety of music types. Also included are reader polls, short celebrity biographies, candid photographs, "hotline" gossip, and its drawing card—song lyrics. *Rock & Soul* is recommended for libraries with patrons interested in the black music world.

411 **Rock Scene.** 1973. m. Richard Robinson. Tempo Publg. Co., Inc. 475 Park Ave. S., Suite 2201, New York, NY 10016. Illus. Adv. [*Aud*: Ages 14–18.]

Rock Scene is a glossy, full-color publication that shows off colorful spandex costumes to advantage. Even the black-and-white photographs are worthy of the effort put into the clothes. Approximately seven groups/individuals are highlighted in an issue. A number of pinups are included as well as interviews. The photographs are all posed, which detracts somewhat from the appeal. One caution: There is very strong language and imagery.

412 **16 Magazine.** 1957. m. $18.95. Randi Reisfeld and Hedy End. 16 Magazine, 157 W. 57th St., Suite 1001-1003, New York, NY 10019. Illus. Adv. Circ: 400,000. Sample. Vol. ends: May. [*Aud*: Ages 12–18.]

This fanzine has been in production for over three decades and is still popular with teens, as its circulation attests. The entertainment world is well covered in 82 pages, as personalities of appeal to teens in television, film, and music are presented in color and black-and-white photographs, and also portraye din brief narrative and longer "exclusive interviews." A distinguishing featur eof this title is a column of recommended books, which appears irregularly.

413 **Soap Opera Digest.** 1975. bi-w. $32. Meredith Brown. Murdoch Magazines, 755 Second Ave., New York, NY 10017. Illus. Adv. Circ: 991,435. Sample. [*Aud*: Ages 14–18.]

By now there are several titles that explain the ins and outs of the romances, including numerous newspaper columns. Still, this is the original of the species and it remains one of the best. The synopses of plots—the heart of such publications—are well written and usually accurate. A nod is given to the evening programs that rapidly are continuing the efforts of the folks in the afternoon. The profiles of the actors and directors and even writers are pretty much what one expects from a public relations firm. It is all soap, fun, and spoof, but it serves the highly desirable purpose of getting many people who do not read to try print.

414 **Soap Opera Stars.** 1953. bi-m. $10. David M. Goodspeed. Sterling's Magazines, Inc., 355 Lexington Ave., New York, NY 10017. Illus. Adv. [*Aud*: Ages 14–18.]

This is a typical soap opera fan magazine. It is certainly what soap fans like to read, and it is acceptable for a public library. It contains a who's who column, fan club addresses, viewer's ballot for favorite soaps and stars, as well as gossip, interviews, and question-and-answer articles.

415   **Soap Opera Update.** 1988. 26/yr. $52. Allison J. Waldman. Soap Opera Update, 158 Linwood Plaza, Fort Lee, NJ 07024. Illus. Adv. Circ: 300,000. Sample. [*Aud*: Ages 14–18.]

A rival to the long-lived *Soap Opera Digest*, with more suds and bubbles. This is a 65-page glossy package of colorful advertisements and massive numbers of technicolor shots of the people who populate the daytime/evening romances. As in its rival, a major section is given over to the latest soap opera plots. There are games, a regular called "soap du jour," and news about fan clubs. The writing style, in lockstep with the stories and features, is the stuff of publicity releases and dreams. While formats differ, the two magazines are close cousins with millions of friends. It is great reading for anyone who agrees with the editor that "we have some terribly desperate women out there in soap land."

416   **Splice.** 1986. bi-m. $12.75. Bob W. Woods. Ira Friedman, Inc., 10 Columbus Circle, New York, NY 10019. Illus. Adv. Circ: 200,000. Sample. Vol. ends: Dec/Jan. [*Aud*: Ages 11–15.]

A distinctive aspect of this fanzine is its physical format. Contrasted with others, which contain both newsprint and glossy pages, this magazine's pages are completely glossy. For the most part, portraits and candid photographs of celebrities in the entertainment field are in color; very very few, if any, are in black and white. The attractive layout and sophisticated style make it a most desirable title.

417   **Star Guide.** a. $9.95 (plus $1.95 postage). Terry Robinson. Axiom Information Resources, P.O. Box 8015, Ann Arbor, MI 48107. Circ: 8,000. Sample. [*Aud*: Ages 14–18.]

This handy paperback book lists the personal addresses of virtually any famous person a fan could want. It is divided nicely into five sections: movie and television stars, famous musicians and recording stars, sports stars, politicians and royalty, and "Other Famous People" (artists, astronauts, authors, etc.). This book is easy to read and use. It would be an asset to public libraries, from the smallest to the largest. The annual updating characteristic of this title is an advantage over other monographs of this type that are revised only every few years.

418   **Star Hits.** 1983. m. $21.95. Susan Freeman. Pilot Communications, Inc., 831 Federal Rd., P.O. Box 804, Brookfield, CT 06804. Illus. Adv. Circ: 165,000. [*Aud*: Ages 14–18.]

Star Hits follows a traditional fan-magazine style complete with birthdays of the month, fan club addresses, a celebrity personal file, and the "This Is Your Life" column on a star, as well as featured performers, questions and answers, and trivia quizzes. Two outstanding features of this magazine are the glossy paper with full color and the song lyrics (approximately six per issue). The emphasis is not hard rock. This publication has potential for a public library.

419   **Super Teen.** 1977. m. $19. Sharon Gintzeer. Sterling's Magazines, Inc., 355 Lexington Ave., New York, NY 10017. Illus. Adv. [*Aud*: Ages 11–15.]

As with some of the other Sterling publications, *Super Teen* gives the extra touches that make a magazine stand out. All teen fan magazines have a variety of features, but this one has them all: advice column, questions and answers, interviews, featured performers, stars' addresses, pen pals, dating tips, beauty column, give-aways and contests, color pinups, and even wallet-size picture cards. This magazine is highly recommended for all public (and possibly) school libraries.

420   **Teen Bag.** 1977. bi-m. $9. Lillian Smith. Lopez Publns., Inc., 111 E. 35th St., New York, NY 10016. Illus. Adv. Circ: 125,000. [*Aud*: Ages 14–18.]

Several glossy pages of color photographs interspersed with newsprint pages place the format a step above that of an all-newsprint fanzine; the targeted audience is the middle teens. There is emphasis on television idols, with a few representatives from other entertainment fields. Speculation, gossip, interviews, news items, and contests appear in a series of undistinguished articles. Far from a good magazine, but *Teen Bag* has an attractive format and an older clientele than *Tiger Beat*. Buy it if you must.

421   **Teen Beat.** 1976. m. $19.95. Sheila Steinbach. Macfadden Holdings, Inc., 233 Park Ave. S., New York, NY 10003. Illus. Adv. Circ: 186,923. [*Aud*: Ages 11–13.]

Judging from the letters to the editor, *Teen Beat* appeals predominantly to the female 11–13 age group. This newsprint publication provides readers with color pinups, horoscopes, puzzles, star addresses, advice, surveys, and a movie guide. Many teen stars are featured, but very little is said about any of them.

422   **Teen Generation** (Formerly: *Today's Generation; Canadian High News*). 1940. bi-m. $8. Stoney McCart and Donna Douglas. Teen Generation, Inc., 202 Cleveland St., Toronto, Ont. M4S 2W6, Canada. Illus. Adv. Circ: 163,000. Sample. [*Indexed*: CMI. *Aud*: Ages 11–18.]

A supplemental title for young teen magazine collections is this Canadian import that features short articles (rarely more than two pages each) on a variety of topics relevant to young adults. A major topic like Canadian politics might take up most of the nonfiction space allocated for that month but generally the pages are divided into three or four contemporary topics like martial arts, shyness, and drunk driving. Four careers are highlighted in each issue, as are recipes and fashion ideas. Standard columns (news, advice, media) fill in the rest. Although the slant is Canadian, this is a good addition to large young adult collections in junior high schools and public libraries.

423   **Teen Machine.** m. $19. Marie Therese Morreale. Sterling's Magazines, Inc., 355 Lexington Ave., New York, NY 10017. Illus. Adv. [*Aud*: Ages 14–18.]

Another version of the teen fanzine, this title offers no major departure from the established format of newsprint, color pinups, interviews, contests, feature stories, and gossip about entertainment personalities of interest to teens. The subjects are both male and female teen celebrities.

424   **Tiger Beat.** 1965. m. $17.99. Diane Umansky. D. S. Magazines, Inc., 1086 Teaneck Rd., Teaneck, NJ 07666. Illus. Adv. [*Bk. rev*: 3, 75 words. *Aud*: Ages 11–15.]

Tiger Beat is another teen fan magazine that can be readily recommended for public libraries. It is fairly substantial in content, including the usual featured performers, contests, give-aways, fan addresses, celebrity birthdays, and quotes, as well as trivia, color pinups, and advice. A standout in this publication is the section featuring male stars giving dating tips to their male audience. Also, it is the only fan magazine reviewed that carried an ad from the National Wildlife Federation reminding readers to take responsibility for their environment.

425   **Tutti Fruitti.** 9/yr. $18. Lisa Lillien. Jimmijack Publg. Co., 807 Vivian Court, Baldwin, NY 11510. Illus. [*Aud*: Ages 14–18.]

The four general headings in this fanzine are "Cool/Contests"; "Extra Special Features," which includes a variety of scoops and interviews; "Sizzling Pin-Ups," including about six; and "Exclusively Tutti Fruitti," a potpourri of advice, more gossip, pen pals, and trivia. It clearly has the variety of content that would appeal to the typical teen fanzine reader.

426   **Wow.** 1976. m. $17.95. Philip Johnson. Pilot Communications, 831 Federal Rd., P.O. Box 804, Brookfield, CT 06804. Illus. Adv. Circ: 150,000. [*Aud*: Ages 12–18.]

This publication stands out from others in that it is printed on a heavier newsprint, and there is greater care taken with graphic layout. Borders, background designs, large, clear print, and varying shades of gray are used to please the eye. The featured celebrities and movie reviews are fairly substantial for this genre. Innovative regular departments include "The World According to . . .," spotlighting a celebrity; "Menu Match-Up," where fans are to match the stars with their favorite foods; and "New Faces," promoting newcomers on the scene. The magazine also includes pen pals, advice, horoscopes, pinups, trivia, and—it is a little more unusual in this category—song lyrics and soap opera star updates. Because of its graphics and perspective, this is another prime choice for public libraries.

■ **FICTION**

See also: Literature

There are few magazines as popular in schools and public libraries serving young people as science fiction and fiction. All libraries should have a liberal representation of these titles. The important task is to select titles that are within both the reading abilities of the students and their emotional, experiential level. In this situation it is fairly safe to rely on science fiction and mystery for the less sophisticated readers, although both, to be sure, can stretch the mind and the reading capacities of some students.

The general short story magazine tends to be edited for adults. Here one presupposes the younger reader has a better-than-average grasp of style and content.

First choices   (1) *Analog Science Fiction/Science Fact*; (2) *Starlog*; (3) *Fiction (New York)*; (4) *Alfred Hitchcock's Mystery Magazine*.

Suitable for children   Ages 9–12: *Short Story International. Seedling Series. Ages 13–17: Analog Science Fiction/Science Fact*; Student Series: Short Story International.

427   **Alfred Hitchcock's Mystery Magazine.** 1956. 14/yr. $19.50. Cathleen Jordan. Davis Publns., 380 Lexington Ave., New York, NY 10017. Illus. Adv. Circ: 208,000. Vol. ends: Dec. Microform: UMI. [*Bk. rev*: 2–7, 40–100 words, signed. *Aud*: Ages 14–18.]

A lively collection of mystery stories, this publication has successfully capitalized on the late director Alfred Hitchcock's fame and reputation. Although Hitchcock never had any editorial connection with the magazine, his influence is evident in the tone of some of the stories, which, like his endeavors on screen, have plot twists and offbeat conclusions. Each issue contains eight to ten short mystery stories and a "mystery classic," a previously published story. The writing style and the general plots are well within the understanding of the average teenage reader. Issues also include "Booked & Printed," an essay on the works of a particular mystery author, followed by reviews of current mystery books; and "Murder by Direction," a review of a recent or upcoming television or motion picture production. This is a good mystery periodical, though overshadowed by *Ellery Queen's Mystery Magazine*. *Hitchcock* is a good second mystery magazine for a high school or public library collection.

428   **Amazing Science Fiction Stories.** 1926. bi-m. $9. Patrick Lucien Price. TSR, Inc., P.O. Box 110, Lake Geneva, WI 53147. Illus. Adv. Circ: 13,000. Sample. Vol. ends: Mar. [*Aud*: Ages 14–18.]

This is one of the more suitable science fiction magazines for teenagers. Each issue of *Amazing* features six to ten stories, interviews, essays on SF topics, poetry, art, editorials, and letters. This magazine appears regularly and includes fiction by both established writers and newcomers, some of whose works are nominated for science fiction awards. *Amazing* is one of the few widely available sources for science fiction poetry. The nonfiction materials are interesting and provocative, and foster informed responses from the readers. *Amazing*, which offers a slightly different mix of content than other SF magazines, is a good support title for active SF collections.

429   **Analog Science Fiction/Science Fact.** 1930. 14/yr. $33.95. Stanley Schmidt. Davis Publns., 380 Lexington Ave., New York, NY 10017. Illus. Adv. Circ: 97,000. Sample. Vol. ends: Dec. Microform: UMI. [*Bk. rev*: 8–12, 100–500 words, signed. *Aud*: Ages 14–18.]

One of the best science fiction choices for young adults, this is a first choice in school and public libraries. *Analog* continues to be one of the leading science fiction magazines, presenting literate, thoughtful SF, somewhat more technologically oriented than the offerings of other SF magazines. Each issue features five to eight fiction offerings, ranging from short stories to novel-length serials. In addition, issues generally feature one or two nonfiction pieces, frequently on technical topics and almost always interesting. Pointed, thought-provoking editorials lead off each issue. The book review column contains sound evaluations of current offerings.

430   **Canadian Fiction Magazine.** 1971. q. $30. Geoffrey Hancock. Canadian Fiction Magazine, P.O. Box 946, Sta. F, Toronto, Ont. M4Y 2N9, Canada. Illus. Adv. Circ: 2,000. Microform: UMI. [*Indexed*: CMI, CanI. *Aud*: Ages 14–18.]

Here the fiction is more sophisticated than in many such magazines and it is best for high school seniors or mature young people. Each issue of this publication features from 10 to 20 works of contemporary fiction by writers in Canada and Canadians in other countries. An issue may also include interviews, essays, photographs, and graphics. Of special note are thematic issues whose contents represent special areas.

431   **Ellery Queen's Mystery Magazine.** 1941. 14/yr. $27.97. Eleanor Sullivan. Davis Publns., 380 Lexington Ave., New York, NY 10017. Illus. Adv. Circ: 230,000. Vol. ends: Dec. Microform: UMI. [*Aud*: Ages 14–18.]

The school or public library that subscribes to Hitchcock's version will want this as well, at least if there is a demand for this type of fiction. Mystery magazines come and go, but Ellery Queen's hardy publication always seems to be with us. It has justly been called the world's leading mystery magazine. Each issue contains 10 to 12 stories, all original except for an occasional reprinted work. The authors are the best, including many famous names and some good newcomers. Each issue also has a book review column. One minor blemish on this otherwise fine periodical is the occasional inclusion of short poems of doubtful worth, written on mystery themes. This periodical is well written and well edited.

432   **Extrapolation.** 1959. q. $15. Donald M. Hassler. Kent State Univ. Press, Journals Dept., Kent, OH 44242. Illus. Adv. Index. Circ: 981. Sample. Vol. ends: Dec. Microform: Greenwood, UMI. Reprint: JAI. [*Bk. rev*: 3–12, 50–300 words, signed. *Aud*: Ages 14–18.]

Extrapolation is the oldest academic publication devoted to science fiction and fantasy. While written for college students and graduates, it will appeal to many senior high school readers. As such it is recommended for some school and public libraries. In each issue, it offers a broad range of coverage, including eight to ten critical articles, bibliographies, and articles on teaching SF. The annual "Year's Scholarship" returned to *Extrapolation* in 1985, further increasing the utility of the journal.

433   **Fiction (New York).** 1972. irreg. $20/3 issues. Mark Jay Mirsky. Fiction (New York), Dept. of English, City College of New York, New York, NY 10031. Illus. Circ: 5,000. Microform: UMI. [*Aud*: Ages 14–18.]

One of the leading fiction magazines, this is very much for adults, but will have appeal for senior high school students with a good background in English. It is not always easy going in either style or subject matter, but it is well worth the effort. This well-known publication is an outstanding medium for the works of highly talented authors. Its distinctive appeal is its inclusion of new short fiction by major contemporary American writers. Issues may also present some previously published pieces, book excerpts, and translations. The 15 to 20 writers included in each issue may range from bestselling novelists to first-timers. Skillful writing is to be expected in this magazine.

434   **Isaac Asimov's Science Fiction Magazine.** 1976. 14/yr. $33.95. Gardner Dozois. Davis Publns., 380 Lexington Ave., New York, NY 10017. Subs. to: P.O. Box 1933, Marion, OH 43305. Illus. Adv. Index. Circ: 81,000. Sample. Vol. ends: Dec. Microform: UMI. [*Bk. rev*: 6–15, 50–100 words, signed. *Aud*: Ages 14–18.]

Asimov's continues to maintain a position as one of the top SF magazines, ranking with *Analog* and *Magazine of Fantasy and Science Fiction* in quality. Each digest-sized issue features six to eight quality fiction pieces, an editorial by Asimov, columns on books and gaming, nonfiction essays, a convention listing, and a letter column.

435   **Locus: the newspaper of the science fiction field.** 1968. m. $28. Charles N. Brown. Locus Publns., P.O. Box 13305, Oakland, CA 94661. Illus. Adv. Index. Circ: 7,600. Sample. Vol. ends: Dec. Microform: UMI. [*Bk. rev*: 5–15, 100–500 words, signed. *Aud*: Ages 14–18.]

Locus is the premier source of news available for the SF and fantasy fields. In the course of a year, it provides an amazing array of information, including feature articles, news stories, photographs, obituaries, surveys, awards (including the "Locus Awards"), market reports, book announcements, convention listings, convention reports, lists of books published, classified and display advertising, media notes, book reviews, and other information.

436   **Magazine of Fantasy and Science Fiction.** 1949. m. $21. Edward L. Ferman. Mercury Press, P.O. Box 56, Cornwall, CT 06753. Illus. Adv. Circ: 61,500. Sample. Vol.

ends: June & Dec. Microform: UMI. [*Indexed*: BoRvI. *Bk. rev*: 2–10, 200–1,000 words, signed. *Aud*: Ages 14–18.]

The *Magazine of Fantasy and Science Fiction* continues to maintain its reputation as one of the highest quality fiction magazines in the field. Each issue offers six to ten original and readable stories, a review column, a film column, and Isaac Asimov's monthly science column. Asimov's column continues to explore an amazing breadth of scientific material in interesting, readable, and accurate articles. *MF&SF* is a core journal for any library with an active SF clientele.

437 Modern Short Stories. 1988. bi-m. $9.95. Glenn Steckler. Clagg Publns., Inc., Bldg. A, Suite 101-C, 4828 Alpine Pl., Las Vegas, NV 89017. [*Aud*: Ages 14–18.]

A pocket-sized 130-page collection of about a dozen original short stories, this offers conservative fiction. What the stories lack in psychological overtones and insight, they make up for in action, predictable love scenes, and a great stress on friendship. One could think of worse launching platforms. The writers are semiprofessional, although all have a natural knack and there is no hint of the amateur about. It is the kind of magazine that anyone who breezes through *Reader's Digest* or longs for the fiction of the *Saturday Evening Post* will enjoy. Recommended for general collections.

438 Short Story International: SSI. 1977. bi-m. $22. Sylvia Tankel. Intl. Cultural Exchange, 6 Sheffield Rd., Great Neck, NY 10021. Illus. Circ: 75,000. [*Aud*: Ages 13–15.]

This periodical publishes previously printed short stories by contemporary authors from around the world. Other than translation into English if necessary, the stories are not abridged or revised. Entertaining and well written, the stories help to further the publisher's goal of encouraging better understanding among peoples. Set in varying locales, the stories impart a flavor of different countries and cultures, yet show a human universality of experience and character, thus introducing readers to works from societies that they would otherwise not have encountered.

Short Story International: Seedling Series. *See under* CHILDREN/LANGUAGE ARTS.

439 Starlog. 1976. m. $27.49. David McDonnel. Starlog Group, Inc., 475 Park Ave. S., New York, NY 10016. Illus. Adv. Circ: 350,000. Sample. [*Aud*: Ages 14–18.]

Each 70- to 76-page issue features articles and interviews on the SF movie and television scene. It also includes news notes, TV episode guides, and articles on special effects in the media. *Starlog* should appeal to the younger SF/motion picture viewer, but contains a surprising amount of detail and fact in its coverage. It is valuable for both general and SF research collections.

440 Stories. 1982. q. $18. Amy R. Kaufman. Stories, 14 Beacon St., Boston, MA 02108. Adv. Circ: 3,000. [*Aud*: Ages 14–18.]

A superior fiction magazine for adults, this may puzzle all but the most sophisticated teenagers. It is a fine choice for advanced schools, but is not the best for average students. "*Stories* is a source of exciting work by prominent international authors and by authors of great promise," according to the promotional copy. Indeed, stories printed in this magazine have won several literary awards and have appeared in anthologies elsewhere. The works in this publication, including some translations and previously published pieces, are excellent and deserve consideration.

441   **Story.** 1989. q. $17. Lois Rosenthal. F&W Publns., 1507 Dana Ave., Cincinnati, OH 45207. Illus. Adv. [*Aud*: Ages 14–18.]

The 130 pages offer both established writers and new voices, for example, Norman Mailer, Robert Olmstead, Rick Bass, Elizabeth Graves, Fred Chappell, and a half dozen more. Each author is introduced by a paragraph or two, a helpful feature. It is difficult to find any particular style or focus for the dozen yarns. The author is allowed, even encouraged, to go his or her own way, and style, content, and imagination seem to be all. The subject matter, by so many skilled writers, is sure to appeal to almost any teenager who still takes time to read short stories, whether in *The New Yorker* or any of the newsstand women's or men's magazines. In a word, there is something of quality here for everyone's taste.

442   **Story Quarterly.** 1975. 2/yr. $14 (Individuals, $12). Anne Brashler and Diane Williams. Story Quarterly, Inc., P.O. Box 1416, Northbrook, IL 60065. Adv. Circ: 1,500. [*Aud*: Ages 14–18.]

The fiction here is suitable for most junior and senior high school students. A self-described "independent magazine of the short story," this publication presents a selection not only of short stories, but also occasional essays and interviews. The writers range from the previously published and prolific to some first-timers.

443   **Student Series: Short Story International.** 1981. q. $16. Sylvia Tankel. Intl. Cultural Exchange, 6 Sheffield Rd., Great Neck, NY 11021. Circ: 24,000. Sample. Vol. ends: Dec. [*Aud*: Ages 13–17.]

In efforts to preserve the integrity of the short story as a staple in magazine publishing, the editors of this title seek to present a collection of short stories of international and national settings by contemporary authors. That task is well accomplished. Each issue contains 10 or 11 unabridged (except for necessary translation) stories of sound literary quality. The editors also succeed at a second purpose, which is "to promote better understanding among people worldwide though literature." Global relations are certainly promoted as a typical issue contains entries from Australia, Canada, England, Norway, Sierra Leone, Tanzania, the United States, Vietnam, and Wales. The publication itself has received recognition from the United Nations for its contribution to international understanding through the short story. The stories are quite interesting and should provide enlightening reading experiences for teens.

Other levels in the series are *Seedling* (grades four to seven) and *Short Story International* (advanced placement high school).

444   **Weird Tales.** 1923. q. $18. George H. Scithers, Darrell Schweitzer, and John Betancourt. Terminus Publg. Co., P.O. Box 13418, Philadelphia, PA 19101-3418. Illus. Adv. Sample. [*Bk. rev*: 10–25, 150–500 words, signed. *Aud*: Ages 14–18.]

Weird Tales has had a long history as a popular and well-received fantasy and weird fiction magazine. This incarnation of *Weird Tales* is edited by a group of highly qualified editors who have re-created *Weird Tales* very accurately. The editors intend to maintain the character of the magazine, but to offer mostly new fiction and articles. The fiction is well written and interesting, and the nonfiction features and book reviews are added bonuses. The current popular literature support of both fantasy and horror indicates a significant potential readership; librarians would be well advised to try *Weird Tales* for a year or two.

■ **FILMS**   [William M. Gargan]

See also: TELEVISION, VIDEO, AND RADIO

Films are a part of the lives of teenagers and an important addition to almost any library collection, if only in videocassette form. A knowledge of both current and historical films is helpful for younger readers and, what is more interesting, of great concern to those same readers. The titles gathered here represent those that are likely to be of value to the young adult. They are adult magazines. A few are not easy to read, but they challenge the young person to look at film in a way different from the usual. As such they are of value to both school and public library collections.

First choices   (1) *Film Comment*; (2) *Film Quarterly*; (3) *Films in Review*; (4) Sight and Sound.

445   **American Film: the magazine of the film and television arts** (Formerly: *AFI News*). 1975. 10/yr. Membership $20. Peter Biskind. Amer. Film Inst., M.D. Publns., Inc., 3 E. 54th St., New York, NY 10022. Subs. to: Amer. Film Inst., P.O. Box 966, Farmingdale, NY 11737. Illus. Circ: 135,000. Sample. Vol. ends: Sept. Microform: UMI. Reprint: UMI. [*Indexed*: MI. *Bk. rev*: 1–3, 1,200 words, signed. *Aud*: Ages 14–18.]

Young adults seeking an intelligent magazine on film can do no better than this title. At the same time it offers a fairly exhaustive view of both Hollywood and video flicks. A joint venture of the American Film Institute and the AMS Foundation for the Arts, Sciences, and Humanities, this publication presents clear, interesting articles on American film and television with an eye toward Hollywood. It provides excellent coverage of current films and popular film personalities. More and more space is being devoted to television. "Dialog on Film," a regular feature, presents, in an interview or seminar format, a lively discussion on various aspects of film with well-known critics or filmmakers. Additional departments provide news, editorial matter, and columns on television and video. Numerous photos and illustrations are included.

446   **Animation Magazine.** 1987. q. $15. Terry Thoren. VSD Publns., Inc., 6750 Centinela Ave., Suite 300, Los Angeles, CA 90230. Illus. Adv. Circ: 25,000. Sample. [*Aud*: Ages 14–18.]

Back in the 1960s the editor attended film school at the University of Southern California. There he discovered the topic of his 52-page magazine. Directed to both the professional animator and the fan, the numerous articles and features cover the field in considerable depth. "New age tv cartoons," the return of Daffy Duck, Ralph Bakshi's magic, information on how an animated film is made, all are here in the short, well-written pieces by men and women who understand the finer points of the art. There are few magazines of this scope, and even fewer filled with so much intelligent enthusiasm.

447   **Black Film Review.** 1985. q. $20 (Individuals, $10). David Nicholson. Black Film Review, 110 S St. N.W., Washington, DC 20001. Illus. Adv. Circ: 1,000. Vol. ends: Fall. [*Aud*: Ages 14–18.]

A "forum for critical thought concerning the images of Blacks in American film." Begun as a two-page photocopied newsletter, this attractive, glossy publication now contains in each issue 20 pages of critical essays, professional articles, interviews, notes on film festivals, and signed film reviews. Coverage includes black independent filmmakers, Hollywood as it affects black images, African film, and film from the African Diaspora and the third world.

448 **Cine Cubano.** 1961. m. $12.32. Gloria Villazon Hernandez. Cine Cubano, Calle 23, No. 1155, Havana, Cuba. Illus. Index. Circ: 25,000. [*Aud*: Ages 14–18.]

Native Spanish-speaking teenagers will enjoy this title, as well as profit from the content. Others with at least one year of Spanish-language study will find it of value too. This Spanish-language magazine has provided outstanding coverage of Latin American cinema for over 25 years. The average 100-page issue is loaded with articles on Latin American, Soviet, and third-world films. Topics in issues examined ranged from a survey of Soviet film in Cuba to an article on the last photographs of Marilyn Monroe. Although there is an evident political bias present, most articles are intelligent and informative. They are accompanied by numerous photographs and illustrations. This is an interesting title that should be available in most public and school libraries serving Spanish-speaking communities.

449 **Cineaste.** 1967. q. $21 (Individuals, $13). Cineaste Pubs., Inc., 200 Park Ave. S., New York, NY 10003. Illus. Adv. Index. Circ: 7,000. Sample. Vol. ends: Fall. Microform: UMI. [*Indexed*: API. *Bk. rev*: 6, 500–1,500 words, signed. *Aud*: Ages 14–18.]

For the young person with a serious interest in film and filmmaking, this is a required item. Subtitled "America's Leading Magazine of the Art and Politics of the Cinema," this journal delivers what it promises. Its 50 to 60 pages are packed with politically oriented material on both American and foreign films. On the whole, the articles are clear, straightforward, and rational. The emphasis is intellectual rather than emotional. Each issue contains three or more interviews with noted individuals in the film world as well as five to ten full-length film reviews. Separate sections are devoted to independent filmmakers and film festivals.

450 **Cinemacabre** (Formerly: *Black Oracle*). 1979. irreg. $10/3 issues. George Stover. Cinemacabre, P.O. Box 1005, Baltimore, MD 21285. Illus. Adv. Circ: 3,000. [*Aud*: Ages 14–18.]

Subtitled "an appreciation of the fantastic," this $5\frac{1}{2}" \times 8\frac{1}{2}"$ glossy magazine embraces all aspects of the genre. Each 64-page issue is crammed full of well-written articles about fantastic film, video, and television. Articles are informational and analytical rather than prescriptive. Interviews with the directors and actors are regularly included, as well as several detailed film reviews. Reviews are signed, three to four pages in length, and fairly timely. Numerous photos, a few in color, accompany most articles.

451 **Film Comment.** 1962. bi-m. $14.95. Richard T. Jameson. Film Soc. of Lincoln Center, 140 W. 65th St., New York, NY 10023. Illus. Adv. Index. Circ: 35,000. Sample. Vol. ends: Nov/Dec. Microform: UMI. Reprint: ISI, UMI. [*Indexed*: HumI, RG. *Bk. rev*: 2–3, 1,500 words, signed. *Aud*: Ages 14–18.]

This is not easy reading, and it is not meant for the person who flips through *Photoplay*. It is for the relatively serious young adult who is involved with film as an art form. At the same time the unique style, enhanced by numerous photos and pleasing layouts, makes it appealing to even those without a dedicated interest in film. The articles are informative and serious without being pedantic. An excellent general-interest film magazine containing original, well-written articles and reviews by such prominent critics as Richard Corliss, Elie Wiesel, and Donald Spoto. Features in issues examined included a survey of recent films about hookers, interviews with Robert Redford and Cher, and a tribute to John Huston. Although the emphasis is on American movies, foreign films receive good coverage. Television and independent film are given some attention.

452   **Film Culture.** 1955. q. $20. Jonas Mekas. Film Culture, c/o Film Art Fund, Inc., 32-43 Second Ave., New York, NY 10003. Illus. Adv. Index. Circ: 4,500. Sample. Microform: UMI. Reprint: UMI. [*Indexed*: ArtI. *Aud*: Ages 14–18.]

This 150- to 300-page journal is one of the few publications to give serious consideration to experimental and avant-garde films. Articles include lectures, interviews with filmmakers, and news of film festivals, as well as insightful essays and critiques. Publication is very irregular; double and even triple issues often appear as part of the four-issue subscription price. There is, as editor Jonas Mekas points out, "no regular financial backing." A new issue is published only after enough money is collected to pay the printer for the previous issue. Yet issue after issue does eventually appear, and they are well worth the wait. Any high school library with a serious interest in film will want this magazine.

453   **Film Quarterly** (Formerly: *Quarterly of Film, Radio, and Television*). 1945. q. $28 (Individuals, $14). Ernest Callenbach. Univ. of California Press, Berkeley, CA 94720. Illus. Adv. Index. Circ: 4,000. Sample. Vol. ends: Summer. Microform: UMI. Reprint: UMI. [*Indexed*: ArtI, HumI. *Bk. rev*: Various number and length, signed. *Aud*: Ages 14–18.]

Begun in 1945 as the *Hollywood Quarterly*, this journal focused on the social and cultural aspects of film and radio. In 1958, after a series of changes, it assumed its current title. Since then, it has become more international in scope and has grown in reputation. Each issue contains five or six features on various aspects of film. The writing is authoratative and scholarly, yet free of jargon or specialized language. This approach makes it of interest to young as well as academic audiences. The detailed film reviews in each issue are more informative than most, although they will be more useful as critical studies than as viewing guides, since they are seldom timely. The book reviews are equally comprehensive and should prove a boon for the film bibliographer. The "Annual Book Roundup" in the summer issue provides a comprehensive survey of English-language film books published during the past year.

454   **Films in Review.** 1950. 10/yr. $18. Robin Little. Natl. Board of Review of Motion Pictures, Inc., P.O. Box 589, New York, NY 10021. Illus. Adv. Index. Circ: 8,600. Sample. Vol. ends: Dec. Microform: UMI. Reprint: UMI. [*Indexed*: ArtI. *Bk. rev*: 3–7, 150–1,000 words, signed. *Aud*: Ages 14–18.]

This $5\frac{1}{2}'' \times 7\frac{1}{2}''$ magazine should be of interest to all film buffs. The average 60-page issue contains about five articles and ten signed film reviews. Articles deal with all aspects of filmmaking; reports on film festivals are frequently included. Articles focus on famous as well as lesser known figures, newer as well as older stars. Interviews are occasionally featured. Useful filmographies follow each biographical piece. Signed film reviews tend to provide critical analysis rather than summary information. Separate departments cover film music, television, and video.

455   Photoplay: movies and video (Formerly: *Photoplay Movie and Video Monthly; Photoplay Film and TV Scene*). 1950. m. $25.80. Ken Ferguson. Argus Specialist Publns., Ltd., 1 Golden Sq., London W1R 3AB, England. Illus. Adv. Circ: 51,771. [*Bk. rev: 2–3, 500 words. Aud: Ages 14–18.*]

This is the epitome of the popular film magazine, and, as such, it may be welcome in many school and public libraries. At the same time, it does not match the higher quality of the other titles in this section. The typical 62-page issue contains several feature articles, news and editorial matter, and 300- to 500-word reviews of current films. The emphasis is on Hollywood and on commercially successful films. Articles tend to focus on popular screen personalities such as Michael Douglas, Tom Berenger, Faye Dunaway, and Farah Fawcett, although essays on the making of particular films such as *Empire of the Sun* and *RoboCop* are also featured. Similar coverage is provided for video and television. Each issue contains numerous black-and-white, and some color, illustrations. The eye-catching covers might be especially effective on a browsing rack.

456   Sight and Sound: the international film quarterly. 1932. q. $14. Penelope Houston. British Film Inst., 21 Stephen St., London W1P 1PL, England. Subs. to: Eastern News Distributors, Inc., 1671 E. 16th St., Suite 176, Brooklyn, NY 11229. Illus. Adv. Index. Circ: 30,000. Sample. Vol. ends: Autumn. Microform: MIM, W. [*Indexed: ArtI. Bk. rev: 3–4, 500–1,500 words, signed. Aud: Ages 14–18.*]

This attractive, scholarly journal provides excellent, well-balanced coverage of the international film scene. Each issue contains news as well as critiques: An article on Hollywood studios and the relaxation of antitrust legislation may be found side by side with a retrospective piece on *From Here to Eternity*. Interviews with producers, directors, and cinematographers are sometimes featured. The film reviews are first-rate. There is some coverage of television and video. All articles are well written, often by well-known critics. A basic acquisition.

■ **FISHING AND HUNTING**   [Roland C. Person]

See also: Environment, Conservation, and Outdoor Recreation; Sports

Every school and public library should have the basic titles listed here. There are numerous magazines in this area, but titles included here are limited to those likely to be of interest to young adults and some older children. Some of the best magazines have yet to find a general index, but this should not prevent the librarian from subscribing. Many provide valuable information in related areas.

The thorny issue of gun control and firearm regulation receives a good deal of attention. There is increasing evidence of women in the pages of these magazines, both as participants in hunting, fishing, and shooting activities and as authors and editors.

First choices   (1) *Field & Stream*; (2) *Outdoor Life*; (3) *Sports Afield*; (4) *Fishing Facts*.

Suitable for children   Ages 10–18: *Fishing Facts*. Ages 12–18: *Field & Stream*; *Outdoor Life*.

457 **Archery World: all-season bowhunter action.** 1952. 9/yr. $20. Tim Dehn. Winter
Sports Publg., Inc., 319 Barry Ave. S., Suite 101, Wayzata, MN 55391. Illus. Adv. Circ:
165,000. Sample. Vol. ends: Dec. Microform: UMI. [*Aud*: Ages 14–18.]

A useful magazine for both the archery class in high school and the casual
reader. As the subtitle indicates, the emphasis is on hunting. Each issue has three
parts: "In the Field Features" recounts hunting experiences; "Special Features"
includes how-to articles and an interview with a noted archer; and "Departments" covers technical issues, questions and answers, new products, industry
news, and more.

458 **Bow and Arrow Hunting: the world's leading archery magazine.** 1963. 7/yr.
$18. Jack Lewis. Gallant/Charger Publns., Inc., 34249 Camino Capistrano, Capistrano
Beach, CA 92624. Illus. Adv. Circ: 110,000. Vol. ends: June. [*Aud*: Ages 14–18.]

After *Archery World*, this is a good second choice. This magazine concentrates on hunting, but continues to test equipment, although it is not overly
technical. Nine feature articles include many first-person accounts, while the
departments cover bowhunting, technical talk, deer, and tackle. The big game
range from antelope to mountain lions, and there is much expert advice on
hunting techniques. This title compares favorably with *Bowhunter*, although the
latter may be a bit broader in appeal. Take a look at both.

459 **Bowhunter: the magazine for the hunting archer.** 1971. 8/yr. $20. M.R. James.
Cowles Magazines, Inc., 2245 Kohn Rd., P.O. Box 8200, Harrisburgh, PA 17015-8200.
Illus. Adv. Circ: 170,000. Sample. Vol. ends: Aug/Sept. [*Aud*: Ages 14–18.]

Unlike the other two archery magazines, this is of more interest to the adult
and the hunter than to the amateur or the high school student. Still, it is a good
third. This is a big, well-illustrated magazine with many articles, most of them
written in the first person. Topics include hunting all kinds of North American
big game, personalities in the field, notes on equipment, and Professional
Bowhunters Society news. Competition archery is not covered. Recently, this
title went from bimonthly publication to eight issues per year, adding "Deer
Hunting Annual" and "Whitetail Bowhunter" as regular issues.

460 **Field & Stream.** 1895. m. $15.94. Duncan Barnes. Times Mirror Magazines, Inc., 2 Park
Ave., New York, NY 10016. Illus. Adv. Circ: 2,000,000. Sample. Vol. ends: Apr.
Microform: B&H, MIM, UMI. Reprint: UMI. [*Indexed*: MI, RG. *Aud*: Ages 12–18.]

If only one hunting and outdoor magazine is found in the school or public
library, this is that magazine. It has appeal for younger children as well as
teenagers, and a good deal of the copy is within the reach of the 12-year-old. For
many years the premier hunting and fishing magazine and the largest in circulation (the two closest are *Outdoor Life* and *Sports Afield*), this excellent publication is published by the same company as *Outdoor Life*. Zane Grey's *Riders of
the Purple Sage* was serialized here; authors ranging from Robert Ruark to Jean
Shepherd have appeared; A. J. McClane, Corey Ford, and Ed Zern have been
synonymous with the title. In addition to its broad coverage of hunting, fishing,
and related outdoor activities, this magazine continues to have a strong voice on
conservation, outdoor education, and legislation affecting outdoor sports. Quality
fiction and humor are also characteristics of this magazine. The articles, which
have considerable literary as well as historical emphasis, are frequently international in scope. More recently, five regional inserts have been added to provide
special coverage of hot spots by area and regional news items. Unlike most titles
in this section, it has long been indexed—a big plus for library use.

461 **Fishing Facts: the magazine for today's freshwater fisherman** (Formerly: *Fishing News*). 1963. m. $19.97. George Pazik. Northwest Publg. Co., Inc., U.S. Highways 41-45, P.O. Box 609, Menomonee Falls, WI 53051. Illus. Adv. Circ: 152,000. Sample. Vol. ends: Dec. [*Aud*: Ages 10–18.]

Published in both northern and southern editions. A typical issue of this magazine duplicates four of the seven articles and all of the departments, even the letters. Half of the articles are by staff editors. It is nontechnical and, as a staff member says, aimed at the "average freshwater angler who is interested in improving his or her skills and increasing their enjoyment of the sport." Articles emphasize "how to" rather than "where to." Strong emphasis on conservation/education, good illustrations, great quantities of ads (but no saltwater or fly-fishing articles).

462 **Fur-Fish-Game: Harding's magazine.** 1925. m. $11. Mitch Cox. A.R. Harding Publg. Co., 2878 E. Main St., Columbus, OH 43209. Illus. Adv. Circ: 145,000. Sample. Vol. ends: Dec. [*Aud*: Ages 14–18.]

"Down to earth" its readers call it, and that is an apt description. Articles have a strong appeal for fellow outdoors people without the snobbishness of some magazines. In addition to a wide range of hunting and fishing articles, there is a strong emphasis on conservation and, unlike other general magazines, there is a considerable coverage of trapping. The appeal is to practitioners—novices as well as veterans, some of whom may fish, hunt, or trap for a living—rather than to the trophy hunter. The low price, the outdoor ethic, and the appeal to the "ordinary outdoors person" make this a good choice for many libraries, particularly those in rural areas.

463 **In-Fisherman: the journal of freshwater fishing.** 1975. bi-m. $16.95. Doug Stange. In-Fisherman, Inc., P.O. Box 959, 651 Edgewood Dr., Hwy. 371 N., Brainerd, MN 56401-0999. Illus. Adv. Circ: 300,000. Vol. ends: Dec. [*Indexed*: Acs. *Aud*: Ages 14–18.]

Early issues of this publication were modeled after scientific journals and published as a series of study reports with no advertising, but this situation has changed dramatically over the years. The magazine has expanded into the largest of the fishing titles (in pages per issue devoted to fishing). It is big—150 pages or more with many articles and nine seasonal features; others on news, issues, and a regular one called "For Kids of All Ages." It is lavishly illustrated with superior graphics and impressive color photography.

464 **Outdoor Life.** 1898. m. $13.94. Clare Conley. Times Mirror Magazines, Inc., 2 Park Ave., New York, NY 10016. Illus. Adv. Circ: 1,500,000. Sample. Vol. ends: Dec. Microform: B&H, UMI. Online: DIALOG. Reprint: UMI. [*Indexed*: MI, RG. *Aud*: Ages 12–18.]

The second-choice title for high school and public libraries in this area, this is among the best of the magazines in the field. Much of it may be suitable, too, for younger readers. *Outdoor Life* emphasizes hunting and fishing with articles about personal experiences in the field. Other articles and columns are concerned with conservation, boating, dogs, new products, bowhunting, guns and shooting, and cooking. As one of the few magazines in this section to have been indexed for a long time (see also *Field & Stream*, above in this section), it has to be among first choices for libraries. There now are regional editions for local interest and, since 1984, it has included some fiction.

465   **Petersen's Hunting.** 1973. m. $16.94. Craig Boddington. Petersen Publg. Co., 8490 Sunset Blvd., Los Angeles, CA 90069. Illus. Adv. Circ: 300,000. Sample. Vol. ends: Dec. Microform: UMI. [*Aud*: Ages 14–18.]

Wide ranging in subjects categorized as big game, small game, upland game, waterfowl, exotic (e.g., safaris), and general, this fine magazine also offers a range in audience appeal from beginner to expert. Departments include blackpowder, bowhunting, gun dogs, handloading, and even vehicles for hunting. All this, plus historical articles and a conservation emphasis, make this title a good choice for any library.

466   **Sports Afield.** 1887. m. $13.97. Tom Paugh. Hearst Corp., 250 W. 55th St., New York, NY 10019. Illus. Adv. Circ: 535,000. Sample. Vol. ends: Dec. Microform: B&H, UMI. [*Indexed*: Acs, MI. *Aud*: Ages 14–18.]

The oldest of the big three general outdoor magazines (with *Field & Stream* and *Outdoor Life*), its quality and range of coverage and its illustrations equal or surpass those of the other two. Columns and features go beyond hunting and fishing to include camping, canoeing, nature, gun-engraver biographies, historical pieces, international articles, and consumer interests. The editors stress the entire outdoors experience with articles on art, Indians, cooking, weather, and wildlife organizations; this sets it somewhat apart from most hunting and fishing magazines.

■ **FOREIGN LANGUAGE**

See also: EUROPE

There are two types of foreign-language publications. The first, and most prevalent in the United States, is the classroom publication, which can be used by beginning language students of any age. Most of these are published by Scholastic. The second is the children's or young adult publication for the reader who is a native to the country or region where the language is spoken. Again, most of these are suitable for students of the language.

First choices   None. Select as needed.

467   **Amigo.** 1973. bi-m. $4.25. Germain Cantin. Service Mond-Ami, 3333, rue Sherbrooke Est, Montreal, Que. H1W 1C5, Canada. Illus. [*Aud*: Ages 9–12.]

Published by the French counterpart of the Holy Childhood Association, this is a witty, well-illustrated Catholic classroom publication that offers games, puzzles, geography, history, and just about anything else likely to be in the curriculum for students from age 9 to 12. There are colorful, imaginative illustrations on each of the 16 pages. The worldview is appreciative of differences among people, and particularly children, without being patronizing. While edited for French-speaking children, it is an excellent introduction to French for Canadians and Americans who are at least one or two semesters into their study. Usually there is a one- or two-page essay with some religious message, but aside from that there is no emphasis on the Catholic Church as such.

468 **Amisol.** 1973. bi-m. $4. Germain Cantin. Service Mond-Ami, 3333, rue Sherbrooke Est, Montreal, Que. H1W 1C5, Canada. Illus. [*Aud*: Ages 6–9.]

This is a 16-page version of *Amigo* for French-speaking students from 6 to 9 years of age. It may be used by beginning French students as well. It follows the same pattern, and is equally as good, as *Amigo*, above.

469 **Bonjour.** 1960. w. $54. Nicole Bruyr. Editions de la Presse Europeenne, B.P. 54, B-3281 Averbode, Belgium. Illus. Sample. [*Aud*: Ages 6–8.]

Each 16-page issue is a mass of colorful, often full- or half-page pictures accompanied by an extremely simple text in French. Subject matter ranges from brushing teeth to the manners of a hippo in a restaurant. (The latter closely resembles disgruntled boys and girls.) A centerfold offers an imaginative drawing of an animal in action and often dressed in clothing familiar to young readers. The games, puzzles, cartoons, and so forth, make this a much above average addition to the French-language collection or for non-French students studying the language. Material is objective and there is no sign of advertising, politics, or religion.

The same publisher offers similar magazines for other age groups: *Doremi* (ages 3–6); *Dauphin* (ages 8–10); and *Tremplin* (ages 10–18). Frequency is the same, although the price varies from a low of $36 to a high of $57. Samples are available.

Coulicou. *See* **Chickadee Magazine** *under* CHILDREN/GENERAL MAGAZINES.

Hibou. *See* **Owl** *under* CHILDREN/ENVIRONMENT, CONSERVATION, AND OUTDOOR RECREATION.

470 **Video Presse.** 1971. m. $20. Editions Paulines, 3965 Boul. Henri-Bourassa Est, Montreal, P.Q. H1H 1L1, Canada. Illus. Circ: 40,000. [*Indexed*: CanI. *Aud*: Ages 12–18.]

A general French-language magazine, published in Montreal. The heavily illustrated 64 pages are directed primarily to French-speaking junior high and high school students. It seems particularly suited for the latter group, both in ideas and difficulty of reading matter. (As with almost all foreign-language magazines for young people, it could be used nicely in language classes as well.) About a dozen well-written articles cover the month's primary news events, personalities, and cultural activities. There are the usual puzzles, games, features, fiction, and so forth. The graphics are outstanding. Another useful feature is the appeal to the readers (who respond) to give their opinions on current issues. There are no advertisements. One may question the comic-strip approach to the classics (e.g., in the issue examined, Homer's *Odyssey* is re-created in ten pages), but on the whole it is a much better than average magazine for the general reader.

•••••••••••••••••••• **Scholastic Classroom Publications** ••••••••••••••••••••

All of the following are Scholastic publications (730 Broadway, New York, NY 10003) and are employed in the classroom for first-year, second-year, and so forth, language study. They are usually eight pages in length and have pictures, stories, word games, and, most important, the vocabulary of the language for the grade level the paper reaches. Teacher editions are available for each of the papers.

All follow a set 12-page or so pattern: There are articles of cultural and historical interest, teenage interviews, and the usual assortment of games, puzzles, illustrations, and so forth, in French, Spanish, or German with necessary vocabulary and guidance. All can be used for developing both reading and speaking skills.

There are six issues of each a year at $4.95 per year.

French
Level 1:. Bonjour
Level 2: Ça va
Level 3: Chez nous
German
Level 1: Das Rad
Level 2: Schuss
Level 3: Der Roller
Spanish
Level 1: Que tal
Level 2: El Sol
Level 3: Hoy Dia

■ **FREE MAGAZINES**   [Doris Cruger Dale]

The majority of free magazines are available from companies and organizations. In their publications these institutions present their own points of view and biases. In many instances, the magazines they publish also present very valuable information, although in some cases the information is very technical. The best of the magazines are beautifully illustrated and can be very useful to patrons of libraries. Some free publications are available from government bodies.

All of the titles are available free of charge if a request is made on letterhead. Some are available only to special groups of people; this information is noted in the annotations. Some of these titles are available in microform or in reprints, and many of them are indexed. However, none of them is online as yet.

First choices   None. Select as needed.

471   **Aramco World.** 6/yr. Free. Robert Arndt. Aramco World, P.O. Box 3725, Escondido, CA 92025-0925. Illus. Vol. ends: Dec. [*Aud*: Ages 14–18.]

Distributed without charge to readers with an interest in Aramco; the oil industry; or the history, culture, geography, and economy of the Middle East. Individual issues may feature topics of interest or articles about the culture of inhabitants of the United States whose ancestors came from the Middle East. Seldom, if ever, will there be an article specifically on Aramco or the petroleum industry. It informs with well-written articles and is devoid of political opinion. The credentials of the author are stated. Color illustrations and full-sized photographs are interspersed throughout each issue. Obvious care is given to the format and layout of a magazine designed to enhance the image of its corporate sponsor.

146

472   Canada Reports/Reportage Canada. Free. Irenka Farmilo and Mary Anne Dehler. External Communications Div., Dept. of External Affairs, Ottawa, Ont. K1A OG2, Canada. Illus. Sample. [*Aud*: Ages 14–18.]

General articles about art, sports, politics, and science in Canada, along with excellent color illustrations, make this a valuable magazine for all readers interested in Canada. The French edition would be useful for high school students of French.

473   Canada Today/d'Aujourd'hui (Formerly: *Canada Today*). 1973. q. Free. Judith Webster. Canadian Embassy, Rm. 300, 1771 N St. N.W., Washington, DC 20036-9484. Illus. Sample. [*Aud*: Ages 14–18.]

Covers commerce and development in and history of Canada along with excellent color illustrations. The journal is more technical than *Canada Reports*, but it is still useful for those interested in the Canadian scene. Although the title indicates that the magazine might be bilingual, it is written in English only.

474   Exxon USA. 1962. irreg. Free. Dow S. Matthews. Exxon USA, P.O. Box 2780, Houston, TX 77252-2180. Illus. [*Aud*: Ages 14–18.]

Exxon USA gets the message across by use of subtlety. In most articles, if the company is mentioned at all, it is with a carefully placed statement. For example, the Ridley sea turtle is an endangered species. Summer interns working with the National Marine Fisheries Service in a program designed to ensure the survival of the turtles are partly supported by grants from companies such as Exxon. The well-written and colorfully illustrated feature articles cannot help but attract the eye of a literate public. This publication, though issued irregularly, has educational and informational value.

475   Mobil Today. 1988. $1.95. J. E. Anderson. Mobil Oil Corp., 3225 Gallows Rd., Fairfax, VA 22037. Illus. Adv. [*Aud*: Ages 14–18.]

The column on the masthead states that the magazine is sent as a courtesy by "your supplier of Mobil products." It is assumed that the price listed on the cover is per issue and that the publication will be marketed commercially. It is also stated that "*Mobil Today* explores how science, technology and industry are reshaping today's world of work." Topics include the advantages of vacationing in a RV camper, aerodynamic cars, dry-land farmers preparing for planting in the northern states, and so forth. As a publication distributed without charge to Mobil suppliers and users of their services, the articles were interesting and offered some variety.

476   New Books: publications for sale by the Government Printing Office. Free. Supt. of Doc., Mail Stop: SSOM, Washington, DC 20402-9373. Sample. [*Aud*: Ages 14–18.]

A catalog of government publications issued by the U.S. government, each issue lists publications placed on sale during the previous two or three months. Publications are arranged by broad topics such as agriculture, business and labor, consumerism, education, health, military, science, and transportation. No annotations are given. Each title is listed only once. Order forms are included.

477   Newsweek on Health. 1987. q. Free. Anne E. Young. Newsweek, 445 Madison Ave., New York, NY 10022. Illus. Adv. Sample. [*Aud*: Ages 14–18.]

Job stress, microwave magic, multiple sclerosis, adult vaccines, AIDS fears, breast cancer, and women and love are but a few of the short reports found in this excellent freebie. As the editor points out, the reprint "follows the latest developments and trends in health, fitness, behavior, nutrition and medical care." The 38 pages are in the *Newsweek* format, and all of the articles have previously been published in that newsmagazine. Everything from the fine illustrations to the snappy, readable copy is easy to follow. It is also reliable and, while the magazine primarily is a vehicle to advertise *Newsweek* and those who supply doctors, it is equally meant for the layperson. The publisher notes that it is delivered "free to doctors and dentists for patients to read while waiting in their reception area." It is a great bargain.

478   Population Briefing Paper. Free. Judith Hinds. Population Crisis Committee, 1120 19th St. N.W., Suite 550, Washington, DC 20036. Illus. Sample. [*Aud*: Ages 14–18.]

These briefing papers cover issues of national and international importance in the population field and are prepared by the Population Crisis Committee. The series has been upgraded and is now published on glossy paper with colorful graphics.

479   Sky. 1962. Free. M. Lidle de Leon. Halsey Publg. Co., 12955 Biscayne Blvd., North Miami, FL 33181. Illus. Adv. [*Aud*: Ages 14–18.]

This Delta Airlines in-flight magazine is distributed aboard all Delta flights. As expected, there are articles about the attractions of cities served by the airline and suggested tours abroad. Feature articles cover a variety of subjects, however. The articles are aimed at the trendy, the educated, and the affluent, and some are useful for students. Essentially devoid of social or political commentary and with color illustrations, this light or semi-serious reading can help the traveler pass the time. Advertisements are frequently for expensive consumer items, which constitute a substantial percentage of each issue. *Sky* is basically similar to the in-flight publications of the other major domestic airlines.

480   Worksaver. 1977. 4/yr. Free. Rudy Schnasse. Melroe Co., P.O. Box 6019, Fargo, ND 58108. Illus. [*Aud*: Ages 14–18.]

Worksaver is distributed by Melroe Bobcat dealers as a complementary publication throughout the United States, Canada, and Australia. In this publication, one finds articles on the archaeology of the Northwest, particularly North Dakota, and the culture and traditions of Native Americans in that area. Interspersed with articles about local industry and farming are reports on the technological and engineering advances of the Melroe Company and the Bobcat loader. *Worksaver* also includes articles of general interest.

■ GAMES   [Amy L. Paster]

Games magazines cover all interests and may be found in the traditional form or as part of a computer program. Most of the emphasis is on role-playing games such as Dungeons and Dragons, but old-fashioned approaches from checkers to Go are also included. While all of the magazines are well within the understanding of the young adult, a few are beyond children under 12 years of age.

First choices (1) *Games*; (2) *Computer Gaming World*.
Suitable for children Ages 8–18: *Dragon*; *Frisbee Disc World*. Ages 10–18: *Computer Entertainer*; *Games*.

481 **The ACF Bulletin.** 1952. bi-m. $15. Charles C. Walker. Amer. Checker Federation, P.O. Box 365, Petal, MS 39465. Circ: 1,000. [*Aud*: Ages 14–18.]

The bulletin records official actions of the ACF, and reports news on the state, district, national, and foreign levels. It also reports the results of official ACF tournaments and affiliated tournaments and publishes the annotated games of the national tournaments. This is for the serious young checker player.

482 **American Go Journal.** 1948. q. Membership $20. Roy J. Laird. Amer. Go Assn., P.O. Box 397, Old Chelsea Sta., New York, NY 10113. Illus. Adv. Circ: 13,000. [*Bk. rev*: 300 words, signed. *Aud*: Ages 14–18.]

"Go is an ancient board game which takes simple elements and combines them with simple rules and generates subtleties which have enthralled players for millennia." This publication offers instruction, commentary, news, and articles of general interest about the game. The journal is suitable for all levels of players. The *American Go Newsletter* is a supplement and is designed to be a timely vehicle for tournament announcements, news, and club notices. The newsletter is included in the price of membership.

483 **Bridge World.** 1929. m. $30. Edgar Kaplan and Jeff Rubins. Bridge World Magazine, Inc., 39 W. 94th St., New York, NY 10025. Illus. Adv. Circ: 12,000. [*Aud*: Ages 14–18.]

This is a basic title in the field. The articles are short and tend to be rather technical, demanding that the reader have a good knowledge of the game. This title will have wide appeal for the dedicated player and might be the best bet for library acquisitions.

484 **Chess Life** (Formerly: *Chess Life and Review*). 1933. m. $25. Julie Anne Desch. U.S. Chess Federation, 186 Rte. 9W, New Windsor, NY 12550. Illus. Circ: 55,000. Vol. ends: Dec. Microform: UMI. [*Bk. rev*: 2–3, 250 words, signed. *Aud*: Ages 14–18.]

The primary mission of the U.S. Chess Federation is to provide news of international, national, and local significance to members. Its second mission is to print articles, notes, and features on how to improve one's game. This title is particularly useful for its close analyses of master games and excellent interviews.

485 **Computer Entertainer: the newsletter** (Formerly: *Video Game Update and Computer Entertainer*). 1982. m. $35. Celeste Dolan. Computer Entertainer, 14614 Raymer St., Van Nuys, CA 91405. Illus. Index. Circ: 10,000. [*Aud*: Ages 10–18.]

If one game computer magazine is ideal for both public and school libraries, this is it. The appeal is to almost all age groups. The longest running newsletter or magazine in the United States on gaming, it is in a newsletter format and packed with reviews of new games. It also lists the availability of the games. The philosophy of the newsletter is "to provide the reader with honest evaluations of products on the market." The reviews are grouped by system, that is, Apple, Atari, Commodore. The January issue carries a review index for the previous year that is very useful.

486   **Computer Gaming World.** 1981. m. $24. Johnny Wilson. Golden Empire Publns., 515 S. Harbor Blvd. No. B, Anaheim, CA 92005-4520. Illus. Adv. Index. Circ: 30,000. [*Aud*: Ages 14–18.]

While this is not suitable for younger readers, it is ideal for the older high school student and, not incidentally, for parents. It offers a detailed review of the latest games. Sections included are new games, with ratings by the readers; reviews of games (including name, type, system, number of players, author, price, publisher); and game strategies. An annual index is included and back issues are available.

With the growing popularity of the home computer, there has been an increase in the number of publications dealing with home computer games. Some of the titles libraries may wish to include are:

Computer Games. 1984. bi-m. $15. Carnegie Publg. Corp., 888 Seventh Ave., New York, NY 10106. Illus. Adv.

Video Games. 1982. bi-m. $30. Roger Sharpe. Pumpkin, Inc., 350 Fifth Ave., New York, NY 10188. Adv. Circ: 100,000.

487   **Different Worlds: journal of adventure gaming.** 1979. q. $15. Tadashi Ehara. Different Worlds Publns., 2814 19th St., San Francisco, CA 94110. Illus. Adv. Circ: 5,000. [*Bk. rev*: 5, 150 words, signed. *Aud*: Ages 14–18.]

This publication covers the entire spectrum of adventure gaming. Features include a calendar of conventions, signed game reviews, signed book reviews, and a section on new games in print. Articles and news items help to round this out. Serious reports are designed to help the adventure gamer make informed purchases. The journal is chock-full of professional graphics and illustrations, making this very enjoyable for all those interested in the hobby of adventure gaming.

Dragon. *See under* CHILDREN/GAMES AND HOBBIES.

488   **Enigma.** 1883. m. Membership $10. Judith Bagai. National Puzzlers' League, P.O. Box 9747, North Hollywood, CA 91609. Circ: 300. [*Aud*: Ages 14–18.]

This is the official publication of the National Puzzlers' League, originally known as the Eastern Puzzlers' League. Each issue contains a variety of puzzles —some standard and some more involved, answers to the previous month's puzzles, solvers' performance records, and favorite-puzzle votes. Also included is news about puzzling and puzzlers. This publication carries a variety of puzzles different from the ones normally seen.

Frisbee Disc World. *See under* CHILDREN/GAMES AND HOBBIES.

489   **Games.** 1977. bi-m. $11.97. R. Wayne Schmittberger. PSC Games Ltd. Partnership, 810 Seventh Ave., New York, NY 10019. Illus. Adv. Circ: 700,000. [*Aud*: Ages 10–18.]

With a circulation larger than that of many general magazines, this is the basic title in the area, and one that should be found in most school and public library collections. Features include contests, an events calendar, and short articles. Puzzle types include intellectual, photo identification, and crossword. Much of the material is to be worked out in the magazine itself—a drawback for libraries attempting to keep "clean" copies. *Games* is also published in deluxe and special editions.

490 **New in Chess.** 1984. s-a. $58. J. H. Timman. Chess Combination, Inc., P.O. Box 2423, Noble Sta., Bridgeport, CT 06608. Illus. Sample. Vol. ends: Apr. [*Aud*: Ages 14–18.]

The "new" sets this title apart from the other standard chess magazines in that it is one of the latest and, more important, one of the most international in scope. Over 5,000 selected games per year are included, with all major players and tournaments reported in the algebraic notations that are understood by chess players. Both good and bad moves are noted.

491 **Northwest Chess.** 1947. m. $12.50. Ralph Dubisch. Washington Chess Federation, P.O. Box 84746, Seattle, WA 98124-6046. Illus. Circ: 1,300. [*Bk. rev*: 1–2, 500 words, signed. *Aud*: Ages 14–18.]

This may be the most readable chess magazine in the United States. It is in no way provincial and will be of interest to any chess fan. This offset, 40-page newsprint journal is filled with chess materials, including fiction, artwork, and interviews.

■ **GENERAL INTEREST** [Margaret McKinley]

See also: CHILDREN/GENERAL MAGAZINES; FAN MAGAZINES

In one sense most of the magazines found in the Children's section and the Young Adult section are general. The difference is that the magazines here are primarily for adults, but suitable for young adults and some children. Many of the titles are well known and are found in homes and on newsstands. A few are more subject-specific than others, but placed here for their general appeal.

First choices More first choices are listed than normal because of the nature of the magazines. (1) *The Atlantic*; (2) *Current Biography*; (3) *Harper's Magazine*; (4) *Mother Jones*; (5) *National Geographic*; (6) *The New Yorker*; (7) *Smithsonian*; (8) *Mad*.

Suitable for children Ages 8–18: *National Geographic*. Ages 10–18: *Current Consumer & Lifestudies*; *Foxfire*; *Mad*. Ages 12–18: *Calliope*; *Current Biography*; *Life*; *Video Presse*.

492 **Alaska: the magazine of life on the last frontier** (Formerly: *Alaska Sportsman*). 1935. m. $24. Ron Dalby. Alaska Publg. Properties, Inc., 808 E St., Suite 200, Anchorage, AK 99501. Illus. Adv. Circ: 235,000. Vol. ends: Dec. [*Indexed*: Acs, MI. *Bk. rev*: 4, 100 words. *Aud*: Ages 14–18.]

There are numerous regional magazines, but this is one of the few that has wide national appeal and will be enjoyed by many teenagers. This is designed to make one want to move to Alaska. Each issue presents Alaska as a beautiful place to be, in words and fantastic pictures. The table of contents has a map of the state with references to articles in that issue that deal with a particular part of the state. The articles cover topics from hunting gold to good fishing places, as well as interesting places to visit.

493 **American Scholar.** 1932. q. $19. Joseph Epstein. United Chapters of Phi Beta Kappa, 1811 Q St. N.W., Washington, DC 20009. Illus. Adv. Index. Circ: 28,500. Vol. ends: Fall.

Microform: B&H, UMI. [*Indexed*: HumI, PAIS, RG. *Bk. rev*: 5–9, essays, signed. *Aud*: Ages 14–18.]

Senior high school students, or younger children with advanced reading skills, will profit from each and every issue. As ideas and style are much more sophisticated than average, it is not for the student who may be having reading problems or has only an average grasp of current affairs. Having celebrated American intellectual and artistic life for over half a century, *American Scholar* continues to thrive. It publishes the most distinguished American writers and academicians and features contemporary American poetry. Aristides' (actually editor Epstein's) column "Life and Letters" brings sociological observation and literature together with seamless skill. *American Scholar*'s gracefully written essays should be required reading for students in hot pursuit of the future, to be read and reread slowly and leisurely.

494   The Atlantic. 1857. m. $11.95. William Whitworth. Atlantic Monthly Co., 745 Boylston St., Boston, MA 02116. Subs. to: P.O. Box 2547, Boulder, CO 80322. Illus. Adv. Circ: 457,343. Vol. ends: June & Dec. Microform: B&H, UMI. [*Indexed*: AbrRG, RG. *Bk. rev*: 2–3, 500 words, signed. *Aud*: Ages 14–18.]

Along with its almost identical twin *Harper's Magazine*, this is found in most school and public libraries. It is not, however, the favored reading of many young adults. Like *Harper's*, it requires advanced reading skills and a degree of sophistication lacking in many adults. Each issue of *The Atlantic* includes two to four analyses of various aspects of American society or foreign affairs—some on the lighter side, others about more significant public issues. There are also three to four columns of reports and commentary. Poetry, humor, and fiction appear in each issue; and leisure activities, art, fashion, and health are explored in a number of columns. The writing is excellent, and topics are original. There is sure to be something in each issue of *The Atlantic* that will appeal to thoughtful readers.

495   Bulletin of the Atomic Scientists (Formerly: *Science and Public Affairs Bulletin of the Atomic Scientists*). 1945. m. (exc. Feb. & Aug.). $30 (Individuals, $24.50). Len Ackland. Educational Foundation for Nuclear Science, Inc., 6042 S. Kimbark, Chicago, IL 60637. Illus. Adv. Index. Circ: 25,000. Vol. ends: Dec. Microform: B&H, UMI. Reprint: UMI. [*Indexed*: BoRv, RG. *Bk. rev*: 5, 1,200 words, signed. *Aud*: Ages 14–18.]

In spite of its forbidding title, this is a magazine for the informed and inquiring younger reader. Although the dominant theme of many issues is the control of nuclear power or major weapons, many articles comment on other technological, scientific, or political matters of national or international concern. While contributors are experts in their fields, the writing is clear and free of scientific jargon. The editors are vitally concerned with the roles and responsibilities of scientists as informed citizens of the modern world. This is an influential and often-quoted publication. Highly recommended for inclusion in the collections of school and large public libraries.

496   Celebrity Focus. 1987. m. $18. Selig Adler. Globe Communications, 441 Lexington Ave., New York, NY 10017. Illus. Adv. Sample. [*Aud*: Ages 14–18.]

Where *People Weekly* leaves off, these 70 pages of color and black-and-white illustrations take over. The focus is on the folks who make up the media. Most of the sparkling prose seems to come hot out of a public relations office. This means lots of sobs, many laughs, and a thoughtful consideration of what life is all about, with or without a million or so each year. You would have to be a prude to hate this kind of thing and a masochist to read it cover to cover. It is bad taste to the point of good-natured humor. Teenagers and adults with a weakness for popular culture will love it.

Classical Calliope. *See* **Calliope** *under* CHILDREN/HISTORY.

497   **Contemporary Newsmakers: a biographical guide to people in the news in business, education ... and other fields.** 1985. q. $66. Peter M. Gareffa. Gale Research Co., Book Tower, Detroit, MI 48226. Illus. Index. [*Aud*: Ages 14–18.]

This is a guide to people in the news in any field one might ever care to mention, and most of them are mentioned in its subtitle. Its emphasis is on people involved in current news stories and on those whose biographies are not found in standard reference sources. *Contemporary Newsmakers* tries to avoid duplicating biographies in *Current Biography*. There are about 50 biographies in each issue. Longer biographies may have up to 4,000 words. Each biography begins with career highlights and includes at least one photo. Discographies or bibliographies of writings may also be included. There are also brief 750- to 1,000-word sketches of people who have appeared very recently in the news as well as obituaries. Information is obtained directly from the subjects where possible. This is a reference tool but it is also fun to read. The writing is vivid, and the subjects lead challenging and exciting lives. *Contemporary Newsmakers* would be a useful tool in most high school and public libraries.

498   **Courier** (Formerly: *UNESCO Courier*). 1948. m. $17. Edouard Glissant. UNESCO, Place de Fontenoy, 75700, Paris, France. Illus. Adv. Circ: 37,000. Vol. ends: Dec. Microform: B&H, MF, UMI. Online: DIALOG. [*Indexed*: MI, RG. *Aud*: Ages 14–18.]

A reminder to all of the importance of the United Nations in general and UNESCO in particular, this is a popular, often consulted magazine. Its primary use may be for papers and talks, but it can be read for pleasure, too. *Courier* presents cross-cultural views of education, art, living conditions, natural resources, history, and politics, frequently emphasizing third-world nations. Many issues have themes such as "The Photographic Memory," "The Circus," and "Man and Animals." Articles are well researched and written in an uncomplicated, direct fashion. This is an especially useful periodical for high school students. *Courier* offers its readers ample opportunity to learn about our earth and the diversity of its peoples and their cultures. Published in 34 languages and quarterly in braille in French, English, Spanish, and Korean, *Courier* should certainly be found in all public and school libraries.

499   **Current Biography.** 1940. m. (exc. Dec.). $48. Charles Moritz. H.W.Wilson Co., 950 University Ave., Bronx, NY 10452. Illus. Index. [*Indexed*: MI. *Aud*: Ages 12–18.]

The standard source of objective biographical material for older children and young adults, *Current Biography* features articles about newsworthy individuals in politics, the sciences, the arts, labor, and industry. Monthly issues are cumulated each year into one alphabet and then revised and printed in *Current Biography Yearbook*. Each year's index cumulates until there is a decennial index. The 2,000- to 3,000-word biographies may be devastatingly ruthless in their objective reportage but they are highly readable. Biographies are accompanied by small black-and-white photos. *Current Biography* also has obituaries with thumbnail sketches of the subjects. There is a cumulative index for 1940 to 1985.

500 **Current Consumer & Lifestudies: the practical guide to real life issues** (Formerly: *Current Consumer; Current Lifestudies*). 1976. 9/yr. $5.25. Carole Gomberg Rubenstein. General Learning Corp., 60 Revere Dr., Northbrook, IL 60062-1563. Illus. Circ: 350,000. Sample. Vol. ends: May. Microform: UMI. Reprint: UMI. [*Aud*: Ages 10–18.]

The audience for this publication is young people in classroom settings, but the format and topics covered are far from the all-too-often dull textbook fare. Clothes, skin care, friendship, and social issues are the subjects of signed articles ranging from one or two pages to eight or ten. Sources of additional information are listed. Classes in health, social studies, and home economics would find this a useful tool. The subcription price is per student, with a minimum of 15 subscriptions required to one address.

501 **Esquire.** 1933. m. $17.94. Philip Moffitt. Esquire Assocs., 1790 Broadway, New York, NY 10019. Subs. to: P.O. Box 11362, Des Moines, IA 50350. Illus. Adv. Circ: 700,500. Vol. ends: Dec. Microform: B&H, UMI. Reprint: UMI. [*Indexed*: MI, RG. *Aud*: Ages 14–18.]

Young male adults enjoy this standard title dedicated to the interests of the American man. There is much material (particularly the fiction) of interest to young women as well. In each issue there is information about contemporary life-styles, sports, finances, entertainment, men's fashions, and, surprisingly, ethics. A short story written for sophisticated readers usually appears, as well as celebrity profiles. *Esquire* is superbly written and edited, and many high school and public library periodical collections should certainly include it.

502 **Exploring.** 1971. q. $1.50/issue. Walter Babson. Boy Scouts of America, P.O. Box 152079, Irving, TX 75015-2079. Illus. Circ: 385,000. Sample. Vol. ends: Sept. [*Aud*: Ages 14–18.]

The Explorers (senior) division of the Boy Scouts of America is the intended audience for this title. In its brief length of 24 pages it covers sports, record reviews, careers, outdoor activity, and scouting news. A primary feature article may focus on any topic of general interest. Black-and-white photographs are highlighted with red and blue on the newsprint pages. The magazine is general enough in scope to have appeal for both male and female teens not involved in scouting.

503 **Firehouse.** 1976. m. $21. Janet Kimmerly. PTN Publg. Co., 210 Crossways Park Dr., Woodbury, NY 11797. Illus. Adv. Vol. ends: Dec. [*Aud*: Ages 14–18.]

This magazine is for and by fire fighters. The editors encourage participation from the readers by requesting letters, photographs, fire descriptions, friendly competition, and clips of recent incidents. The articles, often based on these contributions, are interesting and informative, discussing fire-fighting services and techniques as well as related topics. An impressive section is the "Haz Mat Guide Cards," which are quick reference pages on hazardous materials—their physical properties, names, formulas, and treatment.

504 **Folklife Annual.** 1985. a. $19. Alan Jabbour and James Hardin. Amer. Folklife Center, Library of Congress, Washington, DC 20540. Illus. [*Aud*: Ages 14–18.]

The American Folklife Center at the Library of Congress was established in 1976 by the American Folklife Preservation Act (P.L. 94-201). This hardcover publication of the center is a first-rate production with excellent typography, layout, and photography. The editors intend to promote the documentation of American folklore and folklife by having *Folklife Annual* serve as a national forum for the discussion of ideas relating to the shared traditions, values, and activities of American folk culture. Articles have also dealt with geographical areas outside the United States such as Canada, Peru, Finland, and the Caribbean.

505   **Foxfire.** 1967. q. $9. B. Eliot Wigginton. Foxfire Fund, P.O. Box B, Raburn Gap, GA 30568. Illus. Sample. Vol. ends: Winter. Microform: UMI. [*Indexed*: Acs. *Aud*: Ages 10–18.]

Produced by students of Raburn Gap County High School, Georgia, this magazine is a vehicle for the presentation of Appalachian culture. Student writers offer a variety of interviews with residents of the area who with intriguing candor share aspects of mountain life-style. Remedies, oral tradition, and the most interesting descriptions of processes such as curing beef and craftsmanship (such as making a gourd banjo) are regular features. Each issue is replete with black-and-white photographs of personalities and local scenes. Photos and diagrams complement the demonstration articles, which provide clear and simple step-by-step instructions. Also included are in-depth studies about contemporary issues affecting the region.

506   **Free Spirit.** 1987. bi-m. $10. Judy Galbraith and Pamela Espeland. Free Spirit Publg., 123 N. Third St., Minneapolis, MN 55401. Illus. Circ: 3,000. Sample. [*Aud*: Ages 14–18.]

Subtitled "news and views on growing up," this offers reasonably sound advice to teenagers about everything from dealing with parents and friends to passing a typical high school test. The features cover almost every interest of the average young person. There is the usual question-and-answer section as well as correspondence and contributions from readers. The material is well written and seems objective. This is a good general magazine for many collections. Send for a sample and see if it is for your library.

507   **The Futurist: a journal of forecasts, trends, and ideas about the future.** 1967. bi-m. $30 (Individuals, $25). Edward Cornish. World Future Soc., 4916 St. Elmo Ave., Bethesda, MD 20814. Illus. Adv. Index. Circ: 30,000. Vol. ends: Dec. Microform: UMI. [*Indexed*: MI, RG, SocSc. *Aud*: Ages 14–18.]

As the title suggests, this will have particular appeal to teenagers with an eye on what is likely to happen in their world. Some of it is a bit simplistic, but it is at least easy to follow and to read. The highly illustrated magazine is published by a society that seeks to provide information about trends in areas ranging from education to economics to religion. In addition to feature articles, every 60-page issue includes news notes.

508   **Greece and Rome.** 1931. s-a. $35. Ian McAuslan and P. Walcot. Classical Assn., Oxford Univ. Press, Pinkhill House, Southfield Rd., Eynsham, Oxford OX8 1SS, England. Illus. Adv. Circ: 1,600. Vol. ends: Oct. Microform: UMI. [*Indexed*: BritHum, HumI. *Bk. rev*: 4, 400 words, signed. *Aud*: Ages 14–18.]

Articles range from brief notes to 15 pages. They are well documented, but not overly technical. Most articles are literary critical discussions of classical texts, with a scattering of historical articles. In addition to the book reviews, there are excellent bibliographic essays on recent work in particular fields and the special sections "School Books" and "Reprints." The books in these sections are coded for academic level of interest. More for college and university libraries in America, but could be useful to high schools with programs in the classics.

509   **Harper's Magazine.** 1850. m. Lewis H. Lapham. Harper's Magazine Foundation, 666 Broadway, New York, NY 10012. Illus. Adv. Circ: 150,000. Vol. ends: June & Dec. Microform: UMI. Reprint: UMI. [*Indexed*: BoRv, BoRvI, MI, RG. *Aud*: Ages 14–18.]

Like *The Atlantic*, this should be found in most high schools, but it is not easy to read and is not for the average student (see comments for *The Atlantic*). *Harper's* essays on literature and contemporary society, its political commentary, and its fiction are written with verve and great style. Lewis Lapham's monthly column, "The Easy Chair," cajoles readers into bending their minds in unaccustomed ways to view American politics and life-styles. A major portion of each issue is devoted to "Readings," which are miscellaneous unexpected excerpts from books, periodicals, newspapers, speeches, unpublished memoranda, and press releases. They enlighten and amuse.

510   **Harrowsmith.** 1976. bi-m. $24. Mike Webster. Telemedia Publg., Inc., 7 Queen Victoria Rd., Camden East, Ont. K0K 1J0, Canada. Illus. Adv. Index. Circ: 155,000. Sample. Microform: UMI. Reprint: UMI. [*Indexed*: Acs, CanI. *Aud*: Ages 14–18.]

Bits and pieces of this will appeal to any young adult who has an interest in the environment and weekend farming. It is a bit rich for many of that age, but some of the articles will have appeal. Readers should be prepared to learn more than they ever wanted to know about gardening, plants, cooking, home-building skills, and other homely topics. The information provided approaches reference-work quality in some instances. Listings of specialized businesses, services, and mail-order houses could be particularly useful. Articles on conservation often present new facts and ideas not often found in other general-interest publications. There are profiles of unusual people engaged in some extraordinarily interesting activities. The photography and artwork are also outstanding.

511   **Horizon: the magazine of the arts.** 1958. m. (exc. Jan/Feb., July/Aug.). $21.95. Gray D. Boone. Horizon Pubs., Inc., Drawer 30, Tuscaloosa, AL 35402. Subs. to: Alice Howard, P.O. Box 96014, Washington, DC 20090-6014. Illus. Adv. Circ: 65,000. Vol. ends: Dec. Microform: B&H, UMI. Reprint: UMI. [*Indexed*: RG. *Aud*: Ages 14–18.]

Horizon is a splendid magazine, delighting the eye and mind with uncommon photography and writing. Each issue has five to seven feature articles on art, filmmaking, writing, theater, dance, museums, or other aspects of the best of American life. There are frequent reports of arts activities in specific U.S. cities. *Horizon* would be a worthwhile addition to public, as well as high school, collections.

512   **Interview.** 1969. m. $20. Shelley Wanger. Interview, Brant Publns., 980 Madison Ave., New York, NY 10021. Illus. Adv. Circ: 137,000. Microform: B&H, UMI. Reprint: UMI. [*Indexed*: Acs, MI. *Aud*: Ages 14–18.]

This is for the upbeat teen who has a certain degree of wisdom about art, night life, and the glitz side of society—particularly in and around New York and Los Angeles. Each issue features balanced and responsible interviews with well-known figures in the performing or visual arts, politics, sports, fashion, business, philanthropy, journalism, or literature. Introductory remarks of the interviewer are followed by questions and answers. Portraits of the interviewees emerge through their own words. There are also briefer interviews and biographical sketches of current personalities in the news. Travel articles are extravagant and beautiful. *Interview* is a far better buy for the money than *People Weekly*.

513 Journal of Irreproducible Results. 1955. bi-m. $14.90 (Individuals, $8.90). Alexander Kohn. George H. Scherr/Chem Orbital, P.O. Box 234, Chicago Heights, IL 60411. Illus. Adv. Circ: 20,000. Sample. Vol. ends: No. 6. [*Aud*: Ages 14–18.]

This is for the student wise in the ways of research, or with a suspicion that things (even in textbooks) are not quite what they seem. Using satire as its sword, *JIR* cuts a swath of humor through major scientific disciplines. *JIR* offers 20 or so articles in each issue on topics in medicine, dentistry, computer science, economics, education, law, management, political science, and zoology. Inside its glossy covers, one finds such typical articles as "Artificial Stupidity—An Introduction," or "Triple-Blind Study: The Subject Does Not Know What He Is Getting, the Nurse Doesn't Know What She Is Giving, and the Investigator Doesn't Know What He Is Doing."

514 Journal of Popular Culture. 1967. q. $25. Ray B. Browne. Popular Press, Bowling Green State Univ., Bowling Green, OH 43402. Illus. Adv. Circ: 2,500. Refereed. Vol. ends: Spring. Microform: Kraus, MIM, UMI. [*Bk. rev*: 3–12, length varies, signed. *Aud*: Ages 14–18.]

Every imaginable aspect of popular culture from rock music in the movies to comic magazines is covered in the 10 to 15 articles and occasional special issues of this journal. Although scholarly, the writing can be appreciated by many teenagers with an interest in the subjects covered.

515 Keynoter. 1950. 7/yr. $4. Tamara Burley. Key Club Intl., 3636 Woodview Trace, Indianapolis, IN 46268. Illus. Circ: 125,000. Sample. Vol. ends: May. [*Aud*: Ages 14–18.]

A 16-page publication of Key Club International, the youth-affiliate organization of Kiwanis International, this title is intended for the membership. Aside from reports of club activity, issues contain featured nonfiction articles on a variety of topics: pets, international careers, summer academic opportunities, behavior-habits, group dynamics. It is clear from the magazine's tone that service is promoted as the articles also imply or suggest how readers can make contributions to their communities. This could provide inspirational reading for teens inclined to make those kinds of commitments.

516 Life. 1978. m. (2 issues in Aug.). $32.50. James R. Gaines. Time, Inc., Time & Life Bldg., 1221 Ave. of the Americas, New York, NY 10020-1393. Illus. Adv. Circ: 1,736,797. Vol. ends: Dec. Microform: B&H, MCA. Online: DIALOG, Mead Data Central, VU/TEXT. [*Indexed*: AbrRG, Acs, MI. *Aud*: Ages 12–18.]

This is a middlebrow to lowbrow magazine by the same group that publishes *People Weekly*. Be that as it may, the reliance on photographs (many of which are truly excellent) gives it a place in high school and some junior high libraries. It is ideal for young people with reading problems. Some of the articles are designed to amuse and others to educate or instruct. *Life*'s writing is excellent, and the photography is breathtaking. It is unquestionably superior to the plebeian *People Weekly*. Teachers will find many of the photographs appropriate for clipping files or classroom display. *Life* would be a decorative and worthwhile addition to collections in public and some school libraries.

517 Mad. 1952. 8/yr. $11.75. Nick Meglin and John Ficarra. E. C. Publns., Inc., 485 Madison Ave., New York, NY 10022. Illus. Circ: 2,000,000. [*Aud*: Ages 10–18.]

From its "Marginal Thinking Department" to its back cover "Mad Fold-In," *Mad* has provided more laughs over the years than any other magazine ever published, with the possible exceptions of *National Enquirer* or *Time*. The difference is that *Mad* does not pretend to be anything other than fiction. (Some may even find more truth in *Mad*.) Every issue contains a satirical piece on the latest movie or television rage. *Mad* also offers tongue-in-cheek practical advice on everything from making it in the business world to everyday uses for well-trained porcupines. Two million loyal readers cannot be wrong! Far and away the most popular humor magazine in the Western world, *Mad* could prove to be the single most highly circulated item on any library's periodical shelf.

518   **Mother Jones.** 1976. m. (exc. Feb/Mar., July/Aug.). $30. Douglas Foster. Foundation for Natl. Progress, 1663 Mission St., Second Fl., San Francisco, CA 94103. Illus. Adv. Circ: 170,000. Vol. ends: Dec. Microform: UMI. Reprint: UMI. [*Indexed*: Acs, MI, PAIS, RG. *Bk. rev*: 3, 100–400 words, signed. *Aud*: Ages 14–18.]

This is an ideal magazine for young people with liberal ideals and notions of how to change America and the world. It is not, however, for the young conservative, or for the person who may have some reading problems. *Mother Jones* is named for Mary Harris Jones, a socialist and union organizer, and one of the great orators of her day. The editors of *Mother Jones* follow her example, supporting social and political reform, and priding themselves on their investigative reporting. Each issue includes three or four feature articles on a wide variety of topics such as the struggles of a primitive man in Mexico, a profile of a U.S. senator, an eyewitness account of Filipino politics, and a chronology of the development of a popular movie. Several column editors comment on contemporary life and politics in the United States and abroad.

National Geographic. *See under* GEOGRAPHY.

519   **National Lampoon: the bimonthly humor magazine.** 1970. bi-m. $15.95. Larry Sloman. NL Communications, Inc., 155 Ave. of the Americas, New York, NY 10013. Illus. Adv. Circ: 650,000. Microform: B&H. [*Aud*: Ages 14–18.]

If *Mad* is suitable for younger readers, this more advanced satire is for the advanced high school student. Despite its reputation for being cruel and victimizing at times, particularly in the areas of religion and sex, *NL* still occupies an important place among the few humor magazines aimed at a general audience. While one might think that religion and sex would provide continually fertile ground for fresh satire, apparently it has not provided enough subject matter over the years for *National Lampoon*, which recently switched from monthly to bimonthly publication. Advertising seems to be limited to condoms, X-rated movies, rolling papers, and MTV-related stuff.

520   **New York** (Formerly: *New York Magazine*). 1968. w. $37. Edward Kosner. News America Publg. Co., 755 Second Ave., New York, NY 10017-5998. Illus. Adv. Circ: 477,000. Vol. ends: Dec. Microform: B&H, UMI. Reprint: UMI. [*Indexed*: MI, RG. *Bk. rev*: 0–2, 1,000 words, signed. *Aud*: Ages 14–18.]

New York is only one of many periodicals bearing the name of a large city in the United States. Unlike many others, however, *New York* articles will have an appeal beyond the local audience. It reports on politics, personalities, social issues, and leisure activities. There are a number of columns devoted to politics, business, fashion, the arts, and bargains. *New York*'s writing is graceful and witty. Its illustrations and photography are excellent. The *New York* "Competition" is a favorite of those who love the twists and turns that the English language can take. There are entertainment listings that encompass New York City and surrounding areas, including movies, theaters, music, dance, art, and restaurants, as well as radio and television guides.

521   The New Yorker. 1925. w. $32. Robert Gottlieb. New Yorker Magazine, 25 W. 43rd St., New York, NY 10036. Subs. to: P.O. Box 56447, Boulder, CO 80322. Illus. Adv. Circ: 506,000. Microform: B&H, UMI. Reprint: UMI. [*Indexed*: BoRv, BoRvI, RG. *Bk. rev*: 0–9, 100–3,000 words, signed. *Aud*: Ages 14–18.]

While this rightfully claims to be America's best general magazine, among high school students it is only for the advanced. It presupposes that the reader is not only abreast of the general news, but has an appreciation for cultural personalities and events. The writing style presupposes at least a college degree and certainly familiarity with literature. Each issue includes fiction, poetry, commentaries on current political events, and reports on significant social problems. "Goings On about Town" lists and reviews, in one or two succinct sentences, visual and performing arts events, exhibitions at museums and libraries, sports, and movies. In addition, there are extended theater, music, film, dance, and record reviews and occasional commentaries on sports or fashions. *The New Yorker's* reputation has been built on its incomparable prose and poetry and has continued under the new, controversial editor. This weekly represents the finest in American periodical publishing and publishes the best American writers.

522   Omni. 1978. m. $24. Patrice Adcroft. Omni Publns. Intl., Ltd., 1965 Broadway, New York, NY 10023. Illus. Adv. Circ: 860,990. Microform: B&H, UMI. Reprint: UMI. [*Indexed*: MI. *Aud*: Ages 14–18.]

Libraries that subscribe to *The Futurist, Parabola,* and so forth, will include *Omni*—possibly first of the group. It has wide appeal for younger readers. Strong on graphics and slick in makeup, *Omni* cannot claim to probe deeply into scientific developments and research. It nevertheless offers a lively overview of some of the more spectacular occurrences as well as current issues in the world of science by writers who know their trade. There is a definitely futuristic outlook, and the contents even include science fiction tales. *Omni* strives to make all of science enjoyable and succeeds. Recommended for libraries that encourage science browsers.

523   Parabola: the magazine of myth and tradition. 1976. q. $18. Rob Baker. Soc. for the Study of Myth and Tradition, 656 Broadway, New York, NY 10012. Illus. Adv. Index. Circ: 16,000. Vol. ends: Winter. Microform: UMI. [*Indexed*: BoRvI. *Bk. rev*: 5–8, 600–1,200 words, signed. *Aud*: Ages 14–18.]

This may not be easy going for the average teenager, but the subject matter may prompt careful reading. It is of wide appeal to new-age groups. Each issue of *Parabola* has a single theme—repetition and renewal, addiction, forgiveness, the knight and the hermit—and brings together myth, folklore, religion, and the arts in ancient and contemporary cultures. There are myths told by surviving natives of ancient cultures as well as poetry, interviews, and fiction. Black-and-white photography or artwork skillfully complements the text of every article. In "Epicycles," legends and myths are reprinted from other sources. There are also record and theater reviews and exhibition announcements.

524   People Weekly (Formerly: *People*). 1974. w. (combined year-end issue). $75.06. Landon Y. Jones, Jr. Time, Inc., Time & Life Bldg., 1221 Ave. of the Americas, New York, NY

10020-1393. Illus. Adv. Circ: 2,900,000. Vol. ends: June & Dec. Microform: B&H, UMI. Online: VU/TEXT. [*Indexed*: MI, RG. *Aud*: Ages 14–18.]

This may not be the type of magazine parents would prefer their children to read, but both parents and teenagers make up its audience. It has the distinct advantage of presenting material in a lively yet easy to follow style. It requires only a basic command of reading skills. As its title suggests, articles and photographs of well-known personalities, performers, artists, writers, politicians, and others with broad popular appeal dominate each issue of *People Weekly*. There are also profiles of ordinary people and instant-fame folks. There are reviews of television movies, theater films, and records. This periodical emphasizes the positive aspects of its subjects' life-styles and practices responsible journalism. With rare exceptions, it avoids social, political, and religious controversies. *People Weekly* will be heavily used in any library that houses it, and readers will demand it.

525 **Psychology Today.** 1967. m. $15.99. Wray Herbert. Amer. Health Partners, 80 Fifth Ave., New York, NY 10011. Illus. Adv. Index. Circ: 884,224. Vol. ends: Dec. Microform: MIM, OMI. Online: DIALOG. [*Indexed*: MI, RG, SocSc. *Bk. rev*: 2–5, 75–400 words, signed. *Aud*: Ages 14–18.]

Despite its popular style, this is not easy reading for teenagers. It does presuppose a better-than-average education, and a real interest in motivational matters in its attempts to present the findings of psychology to the public in an understandable way. Topics include all aspects of psychology, with some leaning toward social psychology. Subjects of recent articles include aggression, nuclear war, AIDS, sex differences, and interpersonal relations. One of very few psychology magazines written for a popular audience.

526 **The Reader's Digest.** 1922. m. $17.93. Kenneth O. Gilmore. Reader's Digest Assn., Pleasantville, NY 10570. Illus. Adv. Index. Circ: 17,890,000. Vol. ends: Dec. Microform: B&H, UMI. Reprint: UMI. [*Indexed*: AbrRg, MI, RG. *Aud*: Ages 14–18.]

One of America's most simplistic popular magazines, this is found in almost all libraries. It should be, if only because it is so popular and the reading matter requires so little skill. *The Reader's Digest* is published in 16 languages in addition to large-type, braille, and talking books editions. Junior editions are popular in elementary and secondary schools. What other American magazine approaches this diversity in language and format? *The Reader's Digest* has successfully marketed middle-American conservatism for many years. Its heartwarming articles and anecdotes never embarrass or offend its readers. This is the only magazine that many people read, and it will be demanded by users in school and public libraries. Librarians should be prepared to supply it.

527 **Saturday Evening Post.** 1971. m. (exc. Jan/Feb., May/June, July/Aug.). $12.97. Cory SerVaas. Benjamin Franklin Literary & Medical Soc., 1100 Waterway Blvd., Indianapolis, IN 46202. Subs. to: P.O. Box 10675, Des Moines, IA 50336. Illus. Adv. Circ: 602,730. Vol. ends: Dec. Microform: B&H, UMI. Online: DIALOG. Reprint: UMI. [*Indexed*: AbrRG, MI, RG. *Aud*: Ages 14–18.]

The *Post* favors conservative, high-fiber life-styles, profiles Americans with spotless reputations, and includes traditional fiction. It promotes healthful living through instruction and examples. Authors of the *Post*'s feature articles write of the Middle America familiar to its readers. Published by a medical society, it offers articles and columns on medicine and assorted ailments. The *Post* does have a loyal readership and, for that reason, ought to have a place in general collections.

528   **Smithsonian.** 1970. m. $20. Don Moser. Smithsonian Assocs., 900 Jefferson Dr., Washington, DC 20560. Subs. to: P.O. Box 55593, Boulder, CO 80322-5593. Illus. Adv. Index. Circ: 2,241,000. Microform: UMI. [*Indexed*: MI, RG. *Bk. rev*: 4, 500 words, signed. *Aud*: Ages 14–18.]

Suitable as much for young adults as for adults, this is a marvelous magazine and a first choice in many libraries. *Smithsonian* has an interest in everything that would interest the Smithsonian Institution itself, a mind-boggling array of subjects. Virtually any topic under the sun has a chance of appearing in this magazine, including, in recent issues, trolleys, snakes, Nashville shrines, superdomes, and electronic light painting. The list could go on till sundown. There are about ten substantial articles in each issue, written for the intelligent layperson, containing a wealth of information.

529   **Southern Living.** 1966. m. $21.95. Gary E. McCalla. Southern Living, Inc., 820 Shades Creek Pkwy., Birmingham, AL 35209. Illus. Adv. Circ: 2,275,000. Sample. Microform: UMI. Reprint: UMI. [*Indexed*: BoRv, MI, RG. *Aud*: Ages 14–18.]

Southern Living should be considered a popular general-interest title. Each issue features articles on aspects of living in the southern states, ranging from architecture to politics. Much attention is given to the good life in articles and columns on gardening, cooking, the home, and travel. The format is as attractive as the writing is professional. While it is a bit conservative, *Southern Living* will have broad appeal, not only for southerners but also for readers in other parts of the country.

530   **Sunset: the magazine of western living** (Formerly: *Pacific Monthly*). 1898. m. $16 western states ($20 other states). William R. Marken. Land Publg. Co., Menlo Park, CA 94025. Subs. to: 80 Willow Rd., Menlo Park, CA 94025. Illus. Adv. Circ: 1,408,000. Vol. ends: Dec. Microform: B&H, UMI. Online: DIALOG. Reprint: UMI. [*Indexed*: MI, RG. *Aud*: Ages 14–18.]

Sunset has set standards for westerners in the culinary arts, home design and improvement, landscape design, travel and entertainment, crafts, and conservation. Of particular interest are brief articles describing home improvement or crafts projects designed and completed by westerners. Original recipes utilizing western or ethnic foods, many contributed by readers, are standard features in each issue. There are short feature articles describing little-known points of interest in the West. With four regional editions, *Sunset* is one of the best values going for magazine dollars. Only *Sunset*'s gardening sections might not always be applicable for eastern climates.

531   **TV Guide.** 1953. w. $37.44. David Sendler and Roger Youmen. Triangle Publns., 100 Matsonfont Rd., Radnor, PA 19088. Subs. to: P.O. Box 400, Radnor, PA 19088. Illus. Adv. Index. Circ: 17,165,000. Microform: Pub. [*Indexed*: Acs, MI. *Aud*: Ages 14–18.]

As this is found in almost every American home, libraries with tight budgets might relegate it to the bottom of the list. On the other hand, it is well produced and popular. The writing style is easy to follow and the magazine reports on matters of interest to most high school students. The publishers produce a surprisingly good, pocket-size magazine with regional listings for various areas in the country. The national section of the magazine has five or so entertaining and well-written articles in each issue, reporting on the medium of television, its performers, creators, critics, and technology. A 25-year index covering 1953 to 1977 and supplements covering 1978 to 1986 have also been published by Triangle Publications.

532   Vanity Fair. 1983. m. $24. Tina Brown. Conde Nast Publns., Conde Nast Bldg., 350 Madison Ave., New York, NY 10017. Subs. to: P.O. Box 5229, Boulder, CO 80322. Illus. Adv. Circ: 400,000. Vol. ends: Dec. [*Bk. rev*: 1, 1,500 words, signed. *Aud*: Ages 14–18.]

This is a jazzed-up version of *Esquire* and *People Weekly*, but with a wider audience in mind. Both men and women will enjoy the contents, which can be read by those in the last two years of high school without undue effort. Feature articles frequently report on the activities of well-known personalities. This is done with more style, sensitivity, and detail than in *People Weekly*. Other features delve into stories behind the headlines. Various columns cover cars, wines, theater, movies, architecture, and Europe. *Vanity Fair* is very elegant, very eastern seaboard–oriented, beautifully written, with superb photographs. It will be thoroughly read and enjoyed in libraries.

Video Presse. *See under* FOREIGN LANGUAGE.

533   Wilson Quarterly. 1976. 5/yr. $19. Joy Tolson. Woodrow Wilson Intl. Center for Scholars, 370 L'Enfant Promenade S.W., Suite 704, Washington, DC 20024-2518. Subs. to: P.O. Box 56161, Boulder, CO 80322-6161. Index. Circ: 110,000. Sample. Vol. ends: Nov. Microform: UMI. [*Indexed*: PAIS. *Bk. rev*: 11–16, 150–1,500 words, signed. *Aud*: Ages 14–18.]

Not an easy magazine for most teenagers, but a challenge that should be found in better libraries. Covering a wide variety of topics, the *Wilson Quarterly* devotes about 35 pages in each issue to impartial summaries of articles from current scholarly periodicals and recent research reports. In addition, every issue features two major themes of contemporary interest and includes three or four articles on each topic. Librarians will be particularly interested in two "Background Books" columns, which comment briefly on important books relevant to the issue's themes. There are also several essays on topics as diverse as language, evolution, pirates, and women. Articles are written by specialists for the intelligent and educated young adult and layperson.

534   Yankee. 1935. m. $19.95. Judson D. Hale, Sr. Yankee Publg., Inc., Dublin, NH 03444. Adv. Circ: 1,001,649. Vol. ends: Dec. Microform: B&H, UMI. Reprint: UMI. [*Indexed*: Acs. *Bk. rev*: 1, 500–1,000 words, signed. *Aud*: Ages 14–18.]

Celebrates New England in well-written articles, fiction, art, and poetry. There is even a monthly centerfold of a typical New England scene. The calendar of events covers happenings in New Hampshire, Rhode Island, Connecticut, Maine, Massachusetts, and Vermont. This almanac-size magazine is great fun and great reading.

■ **GEOGRAPHY**   [Douglas A. DeLong]

Geography is a multifaceted discipline that concerns itself with humankind's place in the environment as well as the environment itself. Geography also includes the representation of the earth's features through the medium of cartography. It is a subject that seems to be underestimated in too many schools. Witness recurrent studies showing that up to 50 percent of American high school graduates have difficulty locating Canada and Mexico. Be that as it may, the titles annotated here are both instructive and entertaining. All are ideal for class, and most are equally suited for reading at home.

First choices (1) *National Geographic*; (2) *Canadian Geographic*.

Suitable for children Ages 8–18: *National Geographic*; *National Geographic World*. Ages 12–18: *Focus*.

535 Alaska Geographic. 1972. q. $39. Penny Rennick. Alaska Geographic Soc., P.O. Box 93370, Anchorage, AK 99509. Illus. Circ: 20,000. Sample. Vol. ends: Dec. [*Bk. rev*: 3–6, 250 words, signed. *Aud*: Ages 14–18.]

Young people who do not live in Alaska will enjoy this outstanding regional magazine, which draws on the dreams and the love of adventure in almost any young adult. The focus is on Alaska and the Northwest Territories of Canada, and each issue is devoted to one topic. Photographs are used to excellent advantage. While some issues are mostly pictures, others combine photographs, including period pictures for historical topics, with well-written text. Individual issues are available and are sold under the topic title.

536 Canadian Geographic (Formerly: *Canadian Geographic Journal*). 1930. 6/yr. $26.75. Ross W. Smith. Royal Canadian Geographical Soc., 39 McArthur Ave., Vanier, Ont. K1L 8L7, Canada. Illus. Adv. Index. Circ: 153,000. Sample. Vol. ends: No. 6. Microform: MML, Pub. [*Indexed*: CMI, CanI, SocSc. *Bk. rev*: 10–12, 350–500 words, signed. *Aud*: Ages 14–18.]

Any young person who enjoys *National Geographic* will welcome this addition to the library. The aim of the Royal Canadian Geographical Society is to make Canada better known to Canadians and to the world, and to increase the awareness of the significance of geography in Canadian life, well-being, culture, and development. Geography is seen in its broadest sense, and this truly excellent journal with its informative articles and good photography surveys people and places, resources and environment, wildlife and wilderness, heritage, and evolution in the context of the beauty of Canada.

537 Discovery: the magazine of American travel. 1961. q. $8. Scott Powers. Hill & Knowlton, Inc., One Illinois Center, 111 E. Wacker Dr., Suite 1700, Chicago, IL 60601. Illus. Adv. Circ: 1,500,000. Microform: UMI. [*Aud*: Ages 12–18.]

This publication of the Allstate Motor Club offers four feature articles describing travel locations (in the United States) and providing a plan for visiting each area. "On the Go" guides the reader to regional seasonal events. The illustratios are good. An inexpensive, easy-to-read magazine, this is about the only travel title that is acceptable for younger children. (Others are good, particularly for pictures, but the subject matter is too involved for younger readers.)

538 The Explorers Journal. 1921. q. $20. Harry S. Evans. Explorers Club, 46 E. 70th St., New York, NY 10021. Illus. Adv. Index. Circ: 4,000. Vol. ends: Dec. Microform: UMI. [*Bk. rev*: 10–11, 100–400 words, signed. *Aud*: Ages 14–18.]

The Explorers Journal seems to defy ready categorization. A few articles are of the "adventure-in-the-wilds" type, but many emphasize anthropological, archaeological, geological, or historical research done on expeditions to sites all over the globe. All are written for the layperson. This is a publication that will appeal to many young adults.

Focus. *See under* CHILDREN/GEOGRAPHY AND TRAVEL.

539 **National Geographic** (Formerly: *National Geographic Magazine*). 1888. m. $19.50.
 Wilbur E. Garrett. Natl. Geographic Soc., 17 and M Sts. N.W., Washington, DC 20036.
Illus. Adv. Index. Circ: 10,750,000. Vol. ends: June & Dec. Microform: UMI. Reprint:
UMI. [*Indexed*: CMG, RG. *Aud*: Ages 8–18.]

There are few magazines with as much appeal for almost all age groups, and
the pictures alone make it suitable for children from age eight up. (Actually, even
younger readers may enjoy thumbing through the pages.) A remarkably healthy
and vigorous centenarian, the *Geographic* gives full value for its subscription
dollar. Its faithful readers (350,000 have subscribed for 30 years) are never
disappointed. *Geographic* authors, experts in their fields, share reports of excur-
sions into industrial, primitive, and scientific corners of the world in addition to
documenting everyday life in the United States. There are glimpses of the
distant past and the remote future. Conservation of natural resources and important social and political issues are frequent subjects of major articles. *Geographic*
articles are accurate and detailed. The photography is legendary. Separate maps,
valuable resources in themselves, are frequently inserted in issues. *Geographic*
entertains and informs in equal parts. There is something for every reader, from
the third grader struggling with the names of foreign cities to the scientist
struggling with a rapidly changing world. All libraries should subscribe.

540 **National Geographic Research: a scientific journal.** 1968. q. $40. Harm J. de Blij.
Natl. Geographic Soc., 1145 17th St. N.W., Washington, DC 20036. Illus. Circ: 6,000.
Refereed. Vol. ends: Fall. [*Aud*: Ages 14–18.]

This scholarly scientific journal has many of the attributes of the popular
National Geographic magazine, such as striking color photographs, excellent
maps, and a generally attractive appearance, but its range is broader, including
such sciences as anthropology, geology, paleontology, and zoology. In addition to
geography, the emphasis is on original findings based on field work. Some of the
articles report on research funded by grants from the society. About seven major
articles and shorter research reports appear in each issue. The Spring issue lists all
research grants awarded by the society during the preceding calendar year. For
general collections with a strong scientific bent.

National Geographic World. *See under* CHILDREN/GEOGRAPHY AND TRAVEL.

■ **HEALTH AND MEDICINE**   [Robin Braun and Linda L. Simmons]

Titles found in this section primarily help the young person to keep healthy. They
advise on what steps to take to maintain good health throughout life. A few discuss
medical problems, but even these are closely tied to the message of good health for all.
The choices are based on broad appeal with a nod, also, to career information in the
health sciences. All of the magazines are within the reading range of the average young
adult. None is suitable for the younger child, although note in the Children's section that
one publisher puts out a popular group of magazines devoted to questions of health.

First choices   (1) *Hippocrates*; (2) *Prevention*; (3) *American Health*.

Suitable for children   None are listed. See under Children/Health for titles.

541   **Alateen Talk.** 1965. bi-m. $2. AFG, Inc., P.O. Box 862, Midtown Sta., New York, NY 10018. Illus. Sample. [*Aud*: Ages 14–18.]

Sexual, physical, and mental abuse often occur in alcoholic families. It is to young people in such families that this four-page newsletter is addressed. The sponsoring organization is a group that reaches out to help the abused individual through personal contact, meetings, and the like. While written for the young person, each newsletter has comments from adult sponsors and news of conventions. Al-Anon also issues numerous pamphlets and booklets that may be of help to young people. The advice seems sound, objective, and without any particular religious or political bias. The editor states: "Al-Anon is an established resource for families of alcoholics, provides information and help for the family whether or not the alcoholic seeks help, or even recognizes the existence of a drinking problem."

542   **American Fitness** (Formerly: *Aerobics & Fitness Journal*). 1983. 9/yr. $27. Peg Jordan. Aerobics and Fitness Assn. of America, 15250 Ventura Blvd., Suite 310, Sherman Oaks, CA 91403. Illus. Adv. Circ: 30,000. Vol. ends: Dec/Jan. [*Aud*: Ages 14–18.]

American Fitness offers "upbeat, timely articles by outstanding writers, exploring in depth all aspects of fitness, exercise and recreation." This magazine investigates myths, highlights controversies, and generally motivates readers to enjoy a fit and vital life. Columns and departments include news, medicine and science information, exercise trends, research, a calendar of events, product reviews, opinions, and so forth.

543   **American Health: fitness of body and mind.** 1982. 10/yr. $15. Joel Gurin. Reader's Digest Assn., Inc., Pleasantville, NY 10570. Illus. Adv. Circ: 1,000,000. Vol. ends: Dec. [*Indexed*: RG. *Aud*: Ages 14–18.]

Directed primarily to young women, *American Health* presents "news-to-use" about medicine, mind and body, nutrition, fitness, walking, teeth, skin, scent, hair, clothing, pets, and so forth. This "upbeat" magazine catches the reader's attention with titles such as "Kids, Catfish and Cholesterol," "The Dark Truth about Tanning Salons," and "Danger to Dieters: The Yo-Yo Trap." The popular health information included is easy to read, with an abundance of illustrations and an overabundance of advertisements. Issues have focused on health-related concerns of celebrities such as Robert Redford and Paul Newman.

544   **FDA Consumer.** 1967. 10/yr. $10. William M. Rados. Food and Drug Admin. Subs. to: Supt. of Docs., U.S. Govt. Printing Office, Washington, DC 20402-9371. Illus. Circ: 16,000. Vol. ends: Dec/Jan. Microform: B&H, UMI. Reprint: UMI. [*Indexed*: MI, RG. *Aud*: Ages 14–18.]

A government publication that is useful for high school research papers, this should be found in most school and public libraries. The staff of the Food and Drug Administration (FDA) informs consumers about the safety of health-related products and services through this 40- to 50-page publication. A few feature articles (for example, "Artificial Fingernails: Apply with Caution," "An Order of Fries—Hold the Sulfites," and "Too Many Drinks Spiked with Urethane") reflect current FDA positions, while others focus on agency activities ("Benefit vs. Risk: How the FDA Approves New Drugs"). Striking black-and-white illustrations accompany many articles. Regular departments post product warnings, offer FDA and *Federal Register* news releases, and give reports from investigators. Presents a reliable report of government intervention efforts in the field of health.

545 **Hastings Center Report.** 1972. bi-m. $44 (Individuals, $42). Courtney S. Campbell. Hastings Center, 255 Elm Rd., Briarcliff Manor, NY 10510-9974. Index. Circ: 11,100. Sample. Refereed. Vol. ends: Dec. Microform: UMI. Reprint: UMI. [*Indexed:* GSI. *Bk. rev:* 2–3, essays, signed. *Aud:* Ages 14–18.]

This report offers scholarly consideration of ethical problems in the biomedical, behavioral, and social sciences. It focuses attention on a variety of controversial issues including organ transplants, death and dying, human-subject research, international bioethics, health care delivery and financing, and reproductive rights like surrogacy. A regular column, "Case Studies," poses real-life ethical dilemmas with commentaries. Issues contain special supplements, often half as long as the journal itself—for example, "AIDS: The Responsibilities of Health Professionals." A thoughtful journal to keep students sensitive to ethical issues.

546 **Health Letter.** 1985. m. $18. Sidney Wolfe. Public Citizen Health Research Group. Subs. to: Health Letter, Circulation Dept., 2000 P St. N.W., Washington, DC 20036. Adv. Circ: 35,000. Sample. Vol. ends: Dec. [*Aud:* Ages 14–18.]

Health Letter nicely complements *FDA Consumer* and is for the same audience. This 12-page newsletter is produced by the Public Citizen Health Research Group, founded in 1971 by Ralph Nader and Sidney Wolfe "to fight for the public's health, and to give consumers more control over decisions that affect their health." It treats six or so concerns per issue and features regular departments, for example, "Outrage of the Month" and "Medicare Update." Contributors pull no punches. An excellent source of critical information for consumers buying products and services in the health-care marketplace.

547 **Hippocrates: the magazine of health and medicine.** 1987. bi-m. $24. Eric Schrier. Hippocrates, Inc. Subs. to: P.O. Box 863, Boulder, CO 80322-6863. Illus. Adv. Vol. ends: Nov/Dec. [*Aud:* Ages 14–18.]

Thanks to its layout, easy-to-read articles, and up-to-date and accurate information, this is an ideal medical/health magazine for the average school or public library serving young adults. This stimulating addition to the field features lengthy articles on health issues drawn from all disciplines. "The Medicine Show" describes the television programs that supply many Americans with their medical information; "Guess What's Coming to Dinner" traces food poisoning in the average kitchen; and a special anniversary issue, "Choices of the Heart," follows ethical decisions being made by a mother, a doctor, a judge, and so on. Regular departments supply quick reading on food, drugs, mind, family, sports, vital statistics, and AIDS. Because of its creative choice of subjects, well-written articles, and colorful illustrations, *Hippocrates* is a sophisticated general health publication.

548 **Imprint.** 1968. 5/yr. Membership $15. Barbara Jo Nerone. Natl. Student Nurses' Assn., 555 W. 57th St., New York, NY 10019. Illus. Adv. Index. Circ: 35,000. Sample. Vol. ends: Dec/Jan. [*Aud:* Ages 14–18.]

Imprint is the journal of the National Student Nurses' Association and as such is the only journal directed specifically at the student nurse. Authors are student nurses, recent graduates, nursing school faculty, and practitioners. Most articles address career choices and nursing education. Clinical articles are rare. Sample topics include men in nursing, how to survive as a nontraditional nursing student, and the importance of assertive behavior. Recruitment ads are scattered lavishly throughout each issue. Appropriate for the high school library as a guidance tool.

549 **Journal of Drug Issues.** 1971. q. $60. Richard L. Rachin. School of Criminology, Florida State Univ. Subs. to: Journal of Drug Issues, P.O. Box 4021, Tallahassee, FL 32303. Illus. Adv. Index. Circ: 850. Sample. Refereed. Vol. ends: Fall. Microform: UMI. Reprint: UMI. [*Bk. rev*: Signed. *Aud*: Ages 14–18.]

The facts and only the facts about drugs are offered to the young reader. There is little or no moralizing, but the intent is to persuade through evidence. The *Journal of Drug Issues* focuses on policy issues—their social, legal, political, economic, historical, and medical aspects. Recent article titles include "Alcoholism and Gender: Patterns of Diagnosis and Response," "Is Smokeless Tobacco a Wolf in Sheep's Clothing?," and "The Influence of Literary and Philosophical Accounts on Drug Taking." Occasional issues are devoted to a single theme, for example, "On the Possibility of an Addiction-Free Mode of Being" or "Philosophies of Drug Giving and Drug Taking." Articles are well written, readable, and thought-provoking, making this title an excellent resource.

550 **Listen.** 1948. m. $14.95. Gary B. Swanson. Pacific Press Publg. Assn., 1350 Kings Rd., Nampa, ID 83651. Illus. Index. Circ: 100,000. Sample. Vol. ends: Dec. [*Aud*: Ages 14–18.]

The somewhat timely focus of this title makes it worthy of consideration. Its purpose is to provide "a vigorous, positive, educational approach to the problems arising out of the use of tobacco, alcohol and other drugs," with a secondary emphasis on other adolescent problems. A major monthly feature is a profile of a well-known personality. An advice column highlights a single problem in a thorough discussion. The magazine's orientation is balanced by several sections that depart from the purpose: "The Kitchen Sink" and "And So Forth" contain anecdotes and assorted trivia.

551 **Medical SelfCare.** 1976. bi-m. $15. Michael Castleman. Medical SelfCare, P.O. Box 701, Providence, RI 02901. Illus. Adv. Index. Circ: 100,000. Sample. Vol. ends: Nov/Dec. Microform: UMI. Reprint: Pub. [*Bk. rev*: 10, 80 words, signed. *Aud*: Ages 14–18.]

An important source of alternative medical information, *Medical SelfCare* encourages the student's participation in her or his own health care through the sharing of information. Regular columns reveal the magazine's emphasis: "Women's Health," "Children's Health," "People's Medical Journal," "Self-Medication," and "Home Black Bag." Young women are the target audience. Although the layout shows more polish than in former years, the content and article titles still reflect a concern for the "home-grown." Additional resources are listed in departments like "Self-Care Access." An excellent choice for libraries looking for alternative medicine titles.

552 **Medical World News: the newsmagazine of medicine.** 1960. s-m. $40. Don L. Gibbons. Miller Freeman Publns., 500 Howard St., San Francisco, CA 94105. Illus. Adv. Circ: 128,500. Sample. Vol. ends: No. 24. Microform: UMI. [*Aud*: Ages 14–18.]

Subtitled "the newsmagazine of medicine," this publication is packed with short, newsy items broadly classed under the headings clinical medicine and political/social. A regular section has also been added on AIDS. Lengthy, in-depth cover stories tackle larger problems. Written for health-care professionals, this is also an excellent source for consumers and for students seeking information on health-care costs, legislation, regulation, new therapies, technological innovations, and controversial aspects of medicine. A medical *Time* or *Newsweek* in style and coverage, but the advertisements can be distracting.

553 Monthly Vital Statistics Report. 1952. m. + annual supplement. Free. U.S. Natl. Center for Health Statistics, 3700 East-West Hwy., Hyattsville, MD 20782. Illus. Index. [*Aud*: Ages 14–18.]

The *Monthly Vital Statistics Report* reports provisional statistics that are later compiled into an annual summary. The report is concerned with births, deaths, marriages, and divorces. Schools having programs in demography, population studies, public health, and medicine will find the data useful. Since the report is available free of charge, public libraries could supplement the demographic information in their almanacs by subscribing.

554 Population Reports. 1973. 5/yr. Free. Ward Rinehart. Population Information Program, Johns Hopkins Univ., 624 N. Broadway, Baltimore, MD 21205. Illus. Circ: 110,000. Sample. Vol. ends: Nov. Reprint: Pub. [*Aud*: Ages 14–18.]

Despite the title, this is a basic work for those involved with the larger issues of health and medical care. The 30-page documents fit into 11 categories: oral contraceptives, intrauterine devices, female sterilization, male sterilization, law and policy, barrier methods, periodic abstinence, family planning programs, injectables and implants, issues in world health, and special topics. Each report is well written and well illustrated, and contains a substantial bibliography. Many of the reports are international in scope. Although only five reports are published each year, each offers an in-depth look at a carefully selected topic. Suitable for high school health classes.

555 Prevention. 1950. m. $14. Rodale Press, Inc., 33 E. Minor St., Emmaus, PA 18098. Illus. Adv. Circ: 2,850,000. Vol. ends: Dec. Microform: UMI. Reprint: UMI. [*Indexed*: MI, RG. *Aud*: Ages 14–18.]

This is probably the best known, most popular American health magazine. It is good reading, and particularly suitable for young adults. There may be some disagreement with the conclusions of the articles—particularly the advice on massive amounts of vitamin and mineral supplements—but the information tends to be accurate. Departments like "Walker's World" and "Active Vacations" as well as articles like "Think Yourself Healthy," "Nine Natural Prescriptions for Your Heart," and "Beating Stress with Autogenics" indicate the broader scope. Nutrition still holds an important place in the magazine's departments "Prevention Cuisine" and "High Nutrition." Most articles are brief, and some, but not all, are written by health-care professionals and include references.

556 Public Health Reports. 1878. bi-m. $9. Marian Priest Tebben. U.S. Public Health Service, 13 C-26 Parklawn Bldg., 5600 Fishers Lane, Rockville, MD 20857. Illus. Index. Circ: 4,000. Sample. Refereed. Vol. ends: Nov/Dec. Online: MEDIS. [*Aud*: Ages 14–18.]

Article subjects can range from the economic cost of senile dementia in the United States to the hearing sensitivity of farmers, to the establishment of an exposure level to tetrachloroethylene in ambient air in Vermont. Occasionally issues carry a special in-depth review of a particular subject. Each issue includes a two-page report from the U.S. National Center for Health Statistics, which documents some of its current research projects and selected findings and closes with a listing of new NCHS publications, including order information.

557 **Safety & Health** (Continuation of *National Safety and Health News*). 1919. m. $20.50 Members ($25.75 Nonmembers). Roy Fisher. Natl. Safety Council, 444 N. Michigan Ave., Chicago, IL 60611. Illus. Adv. Index. Circ: 50,000. Vol. ends: Dec. Microform: UMI. Reprint: UMI. [*Aud*: Ages 14–18.]

This trade journal informs the general public as well as the members of the National Safety Council of state-of-the-art events and safety products. Particularly noteworthy are the reviews of new safety standards and their availability. Although there are no book reviews, each issue has a fairly extensive listing of new books, pamphlets, and journals as well as publications available from the council. This popularly written journal would be most suitable for a public or a school library.

558 **Shape Magazine.** 1981. m. $20. Barbara S. Harris. Joe Weider Publns., 21100 Erwin St., Woodland Hills, CA 91367. Illus. Adv. Circ: 598,705. Vol. ends: Aug. [*Aud*: Ages 14–18.]

With an editorial advisory board of 27 respected medical and health-care professionals, this Joe Weider publication is chock-full of vital information on "mind and body fitness for women." An attractive, colorful, nicely formatted, and well-rounded magazine, *Shape Magazine* treats health, nutrition, weight control, beauty, fashion, travel, fitness, sports medicine, exercise, and other topics, supplemented by a variety of regular departments and columns. Strongly recommended for school and public libraries.

559 **Vegetarian Times.** 1974. m. $30 (Individuals, $25). Paul Obis, Jr. Vegetarian Life and Times, Inc. Subs. to: Vegetarian Times, P.O.Box 570, Oak Park, IL 60303. Illus. Adv. Circ: 100,000. Vol. ends: Dec. Microform: B&H. Reprint: UMI. [*Aud*: Ages 14–18.]

"The World's Leading Magazine for Vegetarians" presents nutritional information, recipes, health-care hints, and life-style profiles of other vegetarians. Regular departments include "Healthy by Choice" (a physician's column), "Well-Being" (for herbalists), and "VT Shopper" (new product information). Recipes include nutritional breakdowns for calories, protein, and so forth. Topics emphasized in the magazine in addition to vegetarianism are animal rights, environmental issues, and food policy.

560 **Winner.** 1957. 10/yr. $7.95. National Education, Inc., 6830 Laurel St. N.W., Washington, DC 20012. Illus. Circ: 24,000. [*Aud*: Ages 9–11.]

A sensible, easy-to-read 20-page publication, this gives data on drug abuse and what can be done by the individual reader to avoid the problem. Good games, puzzles, stories, and so forth. It is done without preaching and most of the material is presented in a lively fashion.

561 **World Health.** 1958. 10/yr. $17. John H. Bland. World Health Org., Ave. Appia, 1211 Geneva 27, Switzerland. Illus. Index. Circ: 160,000. Sample. Vol. ends: Dec. Microform: B&H. [*Aud*: Ages 14–18.]

World Health is an official publication of the World Health Organization and focuses on that organization's efforts "to bring about health for all by the year 2000." To appeal to the broadest possible audience, it is written in a popular style and is well illustrated. Articles vary from a discussion of plans to eradicate the guinea worm to a look at primary health care in maternal and child programs. Articles are short (two to three pages) and are written by field workers and program officials. The journal is most appropriate for high school and public libraries, whose users do not require the bibliographic documentation of academic and special library publications. The title is available in many foreign-language editions.

■ **HISTORY** [William F. Young]

History, like literature, is concerned with understanding and interpreting human motivation and behavior and the consequences of that behavior. There are numerous titles suitable for young adults. Many are high-circulation magazines. Others support a wide variety of local history efforts. A renewed interest in history—brought about as much by television shows such as the 11-hour drama-documentary on the Civil War as better teaching—gives these titles an important place in any library.

First choices   (1) *American Heritage*; (2) *History Today*; (3) *American West*.

Suitable for children   Ages 8–14: *Cobblestone*. Ages 10–18: *The Beaver*; *Early American Life*; *Roots*. Ages 12–18: *American Heritage*, *American History Illustrated*.

562   American Heritage. 1949. bi-m. $24. Byron Dobell. Amer. Heritage, Inc., 60 Fifth Ave., New York, NY 10114-0389. Illus. Adv. Index. Microform: B&H, MCA, MCE. [*Indexed*: AbrRG, MI, RG. *Aud*: Ages 12–18.]

Although limited to American history, this is by far the most popular of the history magazines for young adults, and even some children will enjoy the numerous illustrations. It is a first choice in school and public libraries. This deservedly successful and popular magazine focuses on all aspects of the American experience, whether monumental or somewhat trivial. The readable articles are of varying length. The numerous photographs and other illustrations result in a very handsome effect.

563   American History Illustrated: the adventures of the American past. 1966. 10/yr. $20. Ed Holm. Historical Times, Inc., 2245 Kohn Rd., P.O. Box 8200, Harrisburg, PA 17105-8200. Illus. Adv. Index. Circ: 135,000. Microform: UMI. Reprint: UMI. [*Indexed*: MI, RG. *Bk. rev*: 2–9, 200–300 words. *Aud*: Ages 12–18.]

Thanks to the easy style of writing and the illustrations, this magazine can be enjoyed by young adults and children alike. This highly successful and entertaining publication is based on the belief of its founder that "this country needed a magazine devoted to the popularization of American history." Short, well-written articles deal with all phases of the American experience, each colorfully illustrated. Articles on Hetty Green, inventor George Eastman, and World War I posters illustrate the eclectic nature of this interesting publication.

564   American Jewish History (Formerly: *American Jewish Historical Quarterly*). 1893. q. $20. Marc Lee Raphael. Amer. Jewish Historical Soc., 2 Thornton Rd., Waltham, MA 02154. Illus. Adv. Index. Circ: 3,800. Vol. ends: June. Reprint: ISI. [*Bk. rev*: 3–10, 1–2 1/2 pages, signed. *Aud*: Ages 14–18.]

This is typical of numerous historical magazines directed to a specific group or audience. Among the objectives of the society that publishes this quarterly is the "publication and popularization of material of every kind having reference to the settlement, history and life of Jews on the American continent." Frequently an entire issue, consisting of four to eight articles, will be devoted to a particular subject.

565 **The American Neptune: a quarterly journal of maritime history.** 1941. q. $32. Archibald R. Lewis. Peabody Museum of Salem, Massachusetts, 161 E. Essex St., East India Marine Hall, Salem, MA 01970. Illus. Adv. Index. Circ: 1,000. Vol. ends: Fall. Microform: UMI. [*Bk. rev*: 7–13, length varies, signed. *Aud*: Ages 14–18.]

Each issue of *Neptune* presents three to five articles, written by laypersons and historians, on naval and maritime history. An issue will sometimes focus on a specific chronology or theme as, for example, the colonial period in maritime history or the American Civil War. Ships, personalities, voyages, and incidents on the high seas are the ingredients that make this journal interesting reading. Occasional photographs and illustrations add to its general appeal. Each number also contains a relevant editorial and a note on recent acquisitions of the Peabody Museum of Salem.

566 **American West.** 1964. bi-m. $15. Sue Giles. American West Publg. Co., 7000 E. Tangue Verde Rd., Suite 30, Tucson, AZ 85715-5319. Illus. Adv. Circ: 125,000. Vol. ends: Nov. Microform: B&H, UMI. Reprint: B&H, UMI. [*Indexed*: RG. *Bk. rev*: 10–21, brief notes, signed. *Aud*: Ages 14–18.]

A colorful and glossy publication filled with photographs, illustrations, and, incidentally, an abundance of advertisements. This popular magazine is dedicated to the history and culture of America's far western states. In addition to the six articles per issue, special features include "Western Lore," "Western Art Notes," and "Western Snapshots," consisting of reader-supplied photographs that portray today's West as well as "bygone days." Recommended for its appeal to young people.

The Beaver. *See under* CHILDREN/HISTORY.

567 **Civil War Times Illustrated.** 1959. 10/yr. $20. John E. Stanchak. Historical Times, Inc., 2245 Kohn Rd., P.O. Box 8200, Harrisburg, PA 17105-8200. Illus. Adv. Index. Circ: 123,000. Reprint: UMI. [*Aud*: Ages 14–18.]

The apt self-description of this semi-popular title is "a magazine for persons interested in American History particularly in the Civil War period." All phases of the Civil War are examined, with some emphasis on military events and biography. The articles are skillfully written, but the numerous photographs and other illustrations are the key to this magazine's popular appeal. A selection particularly suited to the young person.

Cobblestone. *See under* CHILDREN/GENERAL MAGAZINES.

568 **Early American Life.** 1970. bi-m. $15. Frances Carnahan. Cowles Magazines, Inc., 2245 Kohn Rd., P.O. Box 8200, Harrisburg, PA 17105-8200. Illus. Adv. Index. Circ: 366,349. Microform: UMI. Reprint: UMI. [*Indexed*: MI. *Bk. rev*: Various number and length. *Aud*: Ages 10–18.]

Regular features include information about antiques and listings of forthcoming craft and antique exhibits. This handsome and colorful magazine would be an excellent and popular choice particularly for high school and public libraries. "Early American" means a focus on the colonial period to approximately the mid-nineteenth century. The articles are readable and interesting and deal with such matters as crafts, antiques, and historic sites, as well as historic events. Of particular interest here is an emphasis on the daily lives of people of the period and the restoration of homes, the latter displayed in attractive photographs.

569   **History Today.** 1951. m. $42. Gordon Marsden. History Today, c/o Expeditors of the Printed Word, 515 Madison Ave., New York, NY 10022. Illus. Adv. Index. Circ: 32,000. Vol. ends: Dec. Microform: UMI. Reprint: UMI. [*Indexed*: HumI, RG. *Bk. rev*: 8–18, length varies, signed. *Aud*: Ages 14–18.]

Somewhat the English equivalent of *American Heritage* and just as popular, this title has the distinct advantage of covering the history of much of the world and in such a way as to appeal to young adults. This handsomely illustrated and readable magazine features articles written by historians but aimed at the intelligent layperson. The major emphasis is on Britain but articles can be found on all places and time periods in the seven features that normally appear in each issue. Occasionally there are special issues devoted to the anniversary of a great historical event—for example, "1588, A New Look at the Armada" and "1688: Britain, the Netherlands and the Glorious Revolution." Some of the contents may be somewhat esoteric for the general reader. Nevertheless, intelligent suggestions for further reading and well-written book reviews are other aspects that make this monthly journal a good choice for many types of libraries.

570   **Illinois Historical Journal** (Formerly: *Journal of the Illinois State Historical Society*). 1908. q. $20 (Individuals, $25). Mary Ellen McElligott. Illinois State Historical Soc., Old State Capitol, Springfield, IL 62701. Illus. Index. Circ: 3,000. Microform: UMI. [*Bk. rev*: 3–13,600 words, signed. *Aud*: Ages 14–18.]

Numerous photographs and drawings illustrating the contents of this journal result in a pleasing effect. The contributors are mostly academics, and the subject focus centers not only on the state of Illinois but the entire Midwest. A significant number of the articles deal with the city of Chicago. An occasional feature is "Lincolniana," highlighting materials related to Abraham Lincoln owned by the Historical Society. The society also publishes *Illinois History: a magazine for young people*, which is free to all schools in Illinois and available for $3 a year out of state.

571   **Journal of the History of Ideas: a quarterly devoted to cultural and intellectual history.** 1940. q. $25 (Individuals, $15). Philip P. Wiener. Temple Univ., Philadelphia, PA 19122. Illus. Adv. Index. Circ: 3,700. Sample. Refereed. Vol. ends: Oct/Dec. Microform: MIM, UMI. Reprint: UMI. [*Indexed*: HumI. *Aud*: Ages 14–18.]

This is not easy reading, but it is suitable for above-average high school students. The aim of this journal is to encourage studies examining the "development and interrelations of several fields of historical study—the history of philosophy, of literature and the arts, of the natural and social sciences, of religion, and of political and social movements." Such work helps to draw the general systems and subsystems of intellectual progress out of the entanglements of disciplinary terminology by the application of the concepts of core cognition and core vocabulary. Seven or so articles may be accompanied by a review article. The general systematist will often find highly useful materials in this publication—for example, Peter Allen's article on Coleridge's *Church and State* and the idea of the intellectual establishment, and Laurent Sterm's "Hermeneutics and Intellectual History."

572   **Journal of the West: an illustrated quarterly devoted to Western history and culture.** 1962. q. $35 (Individuals, $25). Robin Hisham. Journal of the West, 1531 Yuma,

P.O. Box 1009, Manhattan, KS 66502-4228. Illus. Adv. Index. Circ: 4,250. Vol. ends: Oct. [*Indexed*: HumI. *Bk. rev*: 20–30, 250–500 words, signed. *Aud*: Ages 14–18.]

Written as much for the layperson as for the historian, the contents of this quarterly are well documented and, somewhat rare, equally well written. Each issue consists of approximately 100 pages with numerous black-and-white illustrations to support the dozen or so articles. A wide range of subject matter is considered, and from time to time a special issue is given over to a single topic as, for example, "Women in the West." This is a general-interest publication that should be considered by many public and school libraries.

573   **Old West.** 1964. q. $20. Jim Dullenty. Western Publg., 205 W. Seventh, Stillwater, OK 74075. Illus. Adv. Index. Circ: 96,850. Sample. Vol. ends: Summer. [*Bk. rev*: 4–5, 300–600 words, signed. *Aud*: Ages 14–18.]

Similar in format to *True West, Old West* is narrower in scope, with a distinct concentration on frontier history in the United States from 1830 to 1910. In addition to regular stories presenting original research on the history of the American West, *Old West* includes monthly columns on genealogy and western cooking and travel; book reviews; and notes on western events. Illustrations highlight most stories. Recommended as a solid addition to a high school or public library collection.

Roots. *See under* CHILDREN/HISTORY.

574   **True West.** 1953. m. $18. Jim Dullenty. Western Publg., 205 W. Seventh, Stillwater, OK 74075. Illus. Adv. Circ: 113,250. Sample. Vol. ends: Dec. [*Bk. rev*: 4–5, 300–600 words, signed. *Aud*: Ages 14–18.]

Attempts to provide a feeling of the Wild West by covering western history and culture from pre-Civil Way days to the present. This is easy reading, with good, authentic photographs and illustrations. The magazine includes factual accounts; reviews of nonfiction books; columns on western films and travel, family history, cooking, and miscellany; and a separate section of queries asking readers to share information. With its topical variety, it is likely to be of interest to a high school and general reading public.

■ **HOBBIES**

[*Antiques and Collections*: Gary Lenox. *Numismatics*: Margaret Norden. *Philately*: David R. Fuller]

See also: MODELS

It is difficult to isolate the various hobbies enjoyed by young people, but they primarily seem to be old-fashioned stamp and coin collecting. These are represented here, as are related areas from gardening to antiques. The subject-oriented hobby fan should turn to a subject-area section—for example, automobiles, home economics, and so on.

First choices   (1) *Scott Stamp Monthly*; (2) *Antiques & Collecting Hobbies*; (3) *Coins*; (4) *Organic Gardening*.

Suitable for children   Ages 10–18: *Coins*; *Doll Reader*; *Scott Stamp Monthly*; *Teddy Bear and Friends*.

575   **American Philatelist.** 1886. m. $24. Amer. Philatelic Soc., Inc. P.O. Box 8000, State College, PA 16801. Illus. Index. Circ: 56,500. Vol. ends: Dec. [*Bk. rev*: 10–12, 300 words. *Aud*: Ages 14–18.]

This is the official publication of the largest and oldest philatelic society in the United States. This publication consistently provides quality articles on all aspects of stamp collecting and postal history. Monthly columns cover many popular aspects of stamp collecting and provide a forum for members to exchange information and opinions. An informative question-and-answer section is very popular. A calendar of events and a regular philatelic book review section are standard features. As the official publication of the society, it offers all society news, activities, and items of interest to the members.

576   **Antique Automobile: dedicated to the history of the automobile.** 1935. 6/yr. $15. William H. Smith. Antique Automobile Club of America, Inc., 501 W. Governor Rd., P.O. Box 417, Hershey, PA 17033. Illus. Adv. Microform: UMI. [*Bk. rev*: 3–4, 500 words, signed. *Aud*: Ages 14–18.]

A useful guide for buffs seeking to learn the history of automobile models. Included in this publication are articles featuring specific cars or manufacturers, club activity news, automobile-meet lists, and advertisements for sale and exchange of cars and parts. It is an attractive house organ, nostalgically celebrating a bygone era of elegance, luxury, and innocence.

577   **Antiques & Collecting Hobbies: devoted to the preservation of the antique arts** (Formerly: *Hobbies*). 1931. m. $18.50. Frances L. Graham. Lightner Publg. Corp., 1006 S. Michigan Ave., Chicago, IL 60605. Illus. Adv. Circ: 16,000. Microform: UMI. [*Indexed*: BoRvI, MI, RG. *Aud*: Ages 14–18.]

As this covers all aspects of collecting, it may be of interest to some young adults with hobbies from postcards to toy soldiers. The "granddaddy" of magazines for collectors has a new name, which more accurately describes its mission. It features several departments that appear regularly: "Music Memorabilia," "Dolls," "Museum News," "Postcards," "Classics in China," "Numismatics," "Philately," "American Historical Glass," and "The Bookshelf," among others. Display and classified advertisements constitute about one-half of each issue. Although it now has many competitors, this is still a good general title for some school and all public libraries.

578   **Bank Note Reporter: your news and marketplace for all paper money.** 1973. m. $23.95. David C. Harper. Krause Publns., Inc., 700 E. State St., Iola, WI 54990. Illus. Adv. Circ: 5,000. Vol. ends: Dec. Microform: UMI. [*Aud*: Ages 14–18.]

This newspaper surveys paper money and bank notes throughout the world. It reports on the activities of the U.S. Bureau of Engraving and Printing, the American paper-money market, and foreign currency. Announcements of new issues and miscellaneous news, as well as offers of sale, fill the remaining pages. Several of the columns are contributed by authorities on numismatics. There are numerous black-and-white illustrations and photos.

579   **Canadian Philatelist.** 1950. bi-m. Membership $20. Jim Haskett. Royal Philatelic Soc. of Canada, P.O. Box 5320, Sta. F, Ottawa, Ont. K2C 3J1, Canada. Illus. Adv. Circ: 7,000. [*Bk. rev*: 10, 350 words. *Aud*: Ages 14–18.]

The official publication of the Royal Philatelic Society of Canada and an excellent publication for articles on the stamps and postal history of Canada. In addition to the philatelic articles, this publication provides information on the society, coming events, and local chapter meetings. The all-encompassing nature of this Canadian publication makes it one of the most important references in its field. The literature review section is excellent and alone is worth the cost of the membership.

580 **Coin Prices: complete market coverage for retail value of all U.S. coins.** 1967. bi-m. $14.95. Bob Wilhite. Krause Publns., Inc., 700 E. State St., Iola, WI 54990. Illus. Adv. Circ: 83,113. Sample. Vol. ends: Nov. Microform: MIM, PMC, UMI. [*Aud*: Ages 14–18.]

This guide concentrates on the various aspects of buying and selling coins, including grading, analyzing the coin market, and minting erors. Detailed charts indicate the current prices of coins in several grades of condition, as well as the prices of commemoratives, paper money, and auction sales. Since the journal is published on a timely 60-day schedule, this information is particularly useful. There are many coin illustrations, albeit on paper of poor quality. Subscriptions include a special annual in March on Canadian and Mexican coins and one in May on international coins.

581 **Coins: the complete magazine for coin collectors.** 1962. m. $17.50. Arlyn G. Sieber. Krause Publns., Inc., 700 E. State St., Iola, WI 54990. Illus. Adv. Circ: 56,834. Vol. ends: Dec. Microform: UMI. [*Aud*: Ages 10–18.]

The basic coin magazine for public and school libraries, this can be used by young adults as well as older children. Designed for both neophyte and veteran collectors, this journal emphasizes current American coinage. Each issue features several high-quality, signed articles on such topics as history, a new coin, or the coinage of a particular nation. Regular columns include coin finds, U.S. and world news, conventions and shows, tips on collecting, coin values, and letters to the editor. The commercial and classified advertisements and offers of sales, which are omnipresent in this field, fill the remaining pages. Most of *Coins* is printed on unsubstantial newsprint.

582 **Collectors News & The Antique Reporter.** 1960. m. $15.97. Linda Kruger. Collectors News Co., Grundy Center, IA 50638. Illus. Adv. Circ: 20,000. [*Bk. rev*: 10, 50 words. *Aud*: Ages 14–18.]

A monthly tabloid that calls itself "The 'Encyclopedia in Newsprint'—trusted by antiquers, collectors and dealers nationwide." In short articles, advertisements, calendars, and so on, it covers everything from collecting egg cups to Staffordshire pottery and old barber chairs, flea markets, and newer collector items. Not the first choice of this type of publication, this is of most interest to the private collector but may be considered by some school and public libraries.

583 **Collectors' Showcase: America's premiere pictorial magazine for collectors.** 1981. bi-m. $24. Donna C. Kaonis. Collectors' Showcase, 2909 Keats St., No. 1, San Diego, CA 92106. Illus. Adv. Circ: 28,000. [*Bk. rev*: 4, 50–100 words. *Aud*: Ages 14–18.]

One of the most attractive magazines for collectors, this includes features on everything (mostly old) that people collect—from children's sand pails to robots to Superman comics to sheet music. The emphasis is on toys (including dolls and teddy bears), advertising items, and memorabilia. It includes such departments as news, show and book reviews, auction reports, a collectors gallery and market-place, and others. This is a sheer delight for lovers of memorabilia, sentimentalists, and, of course, collectors, and the subtitle does not overstate this enjoyable magazine's quality. It should be considered for some school and all public libraries.

584   **Doll Reader.** 1972. 8/yr. $24.95. Carolyn B. Cook. Hobby House Press, Inc., 900 Frederick St., Cumberland, MD 21502. Illus. Adv. [*Aud*: Ages 10–18.]

While this is not a magazine for children or teenagers, it does have some attraction for both. The reason, aside from the topic focus, is the vast number of illustrations and the detail about dolls. Claiming to be "the ultimate authority," this 300-page magazine supplies information on everything having to do with dolls—collectible dolls, doll museums, doll designers, old dolls, patterns for doll clothes, doll cutouts, Moravian dolls, doll auctions, and lots more. Color photos and columns on doll prices, manufacturers, artists, shows/clubs, and so on make this an attractive and fascinating title on this popular collectible. Some of the dolls are "cute"; others are fantastic (literally), and the information here will be in demand in public libraries. For their furry counterparts see *Teddy Bear and Friends* (below in this section).

585   **Fine Gardening.** 1988. bi-m. $20. Roger Holmes. Taunton Press, 63 S. Main St., P.O. Box 355, Newtown, CT 06470-9989. Illus. Adv. [*Bk. rev*: 2–3, 300–500 words, signed. *Aud*: Ages 14–18.]

Gardening normally rates its own subject area, but it is under hobbies because it may be of interest to some teenagers. For them, this is an excellent choice. The most unusual feature of this publication is the fact that it combines high-quality production, perhaps the highest quality of any North American commercial gardening magazine, with articles written by readers rather than professional writers. The result is a magazine of exceptional appeal, definitely a fine addition to the gardener's library. The articles are well-written, practical pieces describing personal projects and accomplishments—reclaiming poor soil, creating a garden, building a pathway on a hillside, growing trilliums, gardening as archaeology in the Southwest, turning a suburban lot into a mini-botanical garden. The scope and climate coverage are wide.

586   **Flower & Garden: the home gardening magazine.** 1957. bi-m. $8. Rachel Snyder. Modern Handcraft, Inc., 4251 Pennsylvania Ave., Kansas City, MO 64111. Illus. Adv. Index. Circ: 639,158. Vol. ends: Dec. Microform: UMI. Reprint: UMI. [*Indexed*: MI. *Bk. rev*: 2, 100–150 words, signed. *Aud*: Ages 14–18.]

Aimed at a broad, popular market, this magazine has a circulation of over half a million. The emphasis is on the amateur gardener, especially the beginner. All aspects of gardening are treated—indoor and outdoor growing, flowers, vegetables, fruits, trees, shrubs, tools, lawns, building projects, and more. "Gardening with Your Regional Editor," appearing in each issue, gives specific advice for eight fairly narrowly defined climatic regions of the United States. Other regular features include "Notes for New Gardeners," "Easy-Does-It Ideas," and a calendar of events. Well written and illustrated, this may be the gardening magazine with greatest appeal to the average young gardener.

587   **Linn's Stamp News.** 1928. w. $28. Michael Laurence. Amos Press, Inc., P.O. Box 29, Sidney, OH 45365. Illus. Adv. Circ: 75,000. [*Bk. rev*: Occasional. *Aud*: Ages 14–18.]

By far the most widely read stamp weekly in the world. Extensive coverage of philatelic news from around the world and comprehensive coverage of U.S. postal materials are included weekly. Regular features are columns on such subject areas as airmail, British Commonwealth stamps, German stamps, postal history, postmarks, and stamp market tips. Educational features include the weekly columns "Philatelic Gems," "Who's Who on U.S. Stamps," "Collector's Workshop," and "Collecting Made Easy." Geographic listings by state are made of stamp shows, exhibits, and auctions. There is an extensive classified section at the back of each edition for buying, selling, and/or exchanging just about any type of philatelic item imaginable.

588 **National Gardening: the gardener's newsmagazine** (Formerly: *Gardens for All*). 1977. m. Membership $18. Kit Anderson. Natl. Gardening Assn., 180 Flynn Ave., Burlington, VT 05401. Illus. Adv. Index. Circ: 225,000. Vol. ends: Dec. [*Aud*: Ages 10–18.]

An unusual feature of this standard gardening magazine is an effort to appeal to young people and even children. Neither audience is given major attention, but at least youth gardening (one of the major interests of the sponsoring organization) appears occasionally as do articles about gardening with or by children. Thorough, well-illustrated, practical articles deal largely with edible plant culture, mostly vegetables, and, to a lesser extent, with herbs and fruits, although flowers do appear on its pages as well. Culture, varieties, pests, and tools are all apt to be discussed here. This is an attractive magazine full of useful advice and a flock of unusual and highly useful regular features including "Letters," "Help!," "Recipe Search," "Seed Swap," "Tips," and "Sources."

589 **Numismatist: for collectors of coins, medals, tokens and paper money.** 1888. m. Nonmembers, $28. Barbara Gregory. Amer. Numismatics Assn., 818 N. Cascade Ave., Colorado Springs, CO 80903-3279. Illus. Adv. Index. Circ: 32,000. Sample. Vol. ends: Dec. [*Aud*: Ages 14–18.]

The official publication of the American Numismatics Association (ANA) is worldwide in scope. Each monthly includes a few features on topics of interest to collectors. Issues have focused on U.S. commemoratives, Indian coins, and the coins of Sherlock Holmes. There are also regular columns of miscellaneous notes and news items, tax information, and suggestions for hobbyists. The ANA column chronicles conventions, new library acquisitions, museum news, and Certification Service Information. At least half of this journal is devoted to advertisements.

590 **Organic Gardening** (Formerly: *Rodale's Organic Gardening*). 1942. m. $20. Rodale Press, Inc., 23 E. Minor St., Emmaus, PA 18098. Illus. Adv. Circ: 1,333,836. Microform: UMI. Reprint: UMI. [*Indexed*: MI, RG. *Aud*: Ages 14–18.]

Organic Gardening resembles in size (8½″ × 11″), layout, and format (glossy paper, color photographs) other standard gardening magazines, but the message is gardening without chemicals. Down-to-earth how-to articles remain its strong point. Vegetables predominate, but flowers, lawns, and tools are also dealt with. Numerous good monthly departments are filled with succinct information. Regional calendars provide data on planting and local events.

591 **Scott Stamp Monthly.** 1920. m. $18. Richard L. Sine. Scott Publg. Co., P.O. Box 828, Sidney, OH 45365. Illus. Adv. Circ: 23,500. [*Aud*: Ages 10–18.]

This is the stamp magazine for all age groups and it should be in most school and public libraries. It updates the *Scott Standard Postage Catalogues* and provides the reader with several general-interest articles in addition to the country-by-country update of new postage stamp issues. A particularly useful feature is a topical index to new stamp issues by subject areas, such as agriculture, birds, Christmas, and medicine. The regular feature "To Err Is Divine" points out errors in the design of particular stamps, as opposed to printing mistakes. Another feature, "Report," includes changes in the stamp market, new discoveries, and editorials on stamps and stamp-related subjects.

592 **Stamps.** 1932. w. $19.80. Daniel R. Milliman. H. L. Lindquist Publns., 85 Canisteo St., Hornell, NY 14843. Illus. Adv. Index. Circ: 23,800. Microform: UMI. [*Bk. rev*: Occasional. *Aud*: Ages 14–18.]

A nicely written and widely circulated magazine on stamp collecting for all ages. Several general-interest articles are featured each week. Departments include not only information on new issues and events, but educational and interesting columns such as "U.S. Classics," "Identify the Stamp" (quiz), and "Speaking of Stamps, Etc." by the respected philatelic writer Herman Herst, Jr.

593 **Teddy Bear and Friends.** 1983. bi-m. $17.95. Carolyn B. Cook. Hobby House Press, Inc., 900 Frederick St., Cumberland, MD 21502. Illus. Adv. Circ: 60,000. [*Aud*: Ages 10–18.]

This claims to be the ultimate authority on teddy bears. It not only covers teddy bears in their original and recent incarnations, but it also covers panda bears, polar bears, and other cuddly friends like lions, horses, and the like. Color photographs illustrate the articles and advertisements on collectible, old, and museum-quality bears, a department on bear making and dressing, articles on the history of bears, books about bears, Australian bears, and so on. Bears, like dolls, are both toys and collectibles, a thriving business, and perennially popular, so this attractive magazine will be in demand in public libraries beside its counterpart, *Doll Reader*.

■ **HOME ECONOMICS**   [Cheryl M. LaGuardia and Judith Yankielun Lind]

The home economics section is composed of a group of living and home magazines that appeal to all age groups. If most are edited for adults, there is still material in them for the interested teenager. Typically, the titles provide ideas and practical advice. They cover price ranges from the most expensive taste to the budget variety. Assistance is provided for those with more savvy than savings, and for individuals who need to be more knowlegeable in working with interior decorators.

First choices   (1) *Teen Times*; (2) *Better Homes and Gardens*; (3) *Choices*.
Suitable for children   Ages 12–18: *Choices*.

594 **Americana.** 1973. bi-m. $13.95. Sandra J. Wilmot. Americana Magazine, Inc., 27 W. 38th St., New York, NY 10018. Illus. Adv. Circ: 400,000. Vol. ends: Jan/Feb. Microform: UMI. [*Indexed*: MI, RG. *Aud*: Ages 14–18.]

Teenagers who look at home economics in the broadest of terms will be right at home with this title. Focused on American tradition, this magazine highlights museums, collectibles, and crafts. Readers can make vacation plans or do some armchair traveling to locations where bygone days are brought to life. Articles inform about conservation and renovation. Suggestions are offered for decorating with antiques or realistic reproductions. Seasonal interests are blended with historic topics in articles combining tradition, food, entertaining, and decorating suggestions.

595   **Better Homes and Gardens: the magazine for American families.** 1922. m. $14.
David Jordan. Meredith Corp., 1716 Locust St., Des Moines, IA 50336. Illus. Adv. Circ:
8,060,065. Vol. ends: No. 12. Microform: UMI. [*Indexed*: MI, RG. *Aud*: Ages 14–18.]

Each issue of *Better Homes and Gardens* is filled with ideas that will inspire,
amuse, delight, and educate its readers. In this popular magazine geared to the
middle class, articles and features speak to concerns of the family unit. Here
there is something for everyone—from craft and hobby directions to information
on health, finances, furnishings, yard work, and travel. All of the suggestions
offer ways to make life simpler, more colorful, and increasingly more meaningful. Typically, the numerous recipes are easy to make yet elegant to serve.
Holidays enliven the issues with attention to foods and activities around the
home. A wide variety of topics are covered in articles that take for granted that
the world revolves around one's home. For information or entertainment, this
magazine is for all libraries.

Better Homes and Gardens publishes several titles focusing on particular
aspects of the home and of being a homeowner.

The annuals at $2.95 each include: *Better Homes and Gardens Country
Crafts*; *Country Kitchen Ideas*; *Holiday Cooking*; *Holiday Crafts*; *Low Cal
Recipes*.

The semi-annuals at $2.95 each include: *Better Homes and Gardens Bed-
room & Bath Ideas*; *Ideas & Outdoor Living*; *Do-It-Yourself Home Improvements & Repairs*.

There are two bi-monthly topical issues: *Better Homes and Gardens Wood*
($18) and *Better Homes and Gardens Traditional Homes* ($14.97).

596   **Choices: the magazine for personal development and practical living skills**
(Supersedes *Co-Ed*). 1956. 10/yr. $4.95. Maura Christopher. Scholastic, Inc., 730 Broad-
way, New York, NY 10003. Adv. Index. Circ: 249,552. Microform: B&H, UMI. [*Indexed*:
CMG, MI. *Aud*: Ages 12–18.]

Written for teenagers, *Choices* addresses some of their areas of concern:
personal hygiene, dating, food, family crises, teen pregnancy, money management, and communication skills, to name a few. It deals directly with some issues
other teen-oriented magazines do not touch (e.g., sex, child abuse, death) in a
nonpreaching, first-person style. Recommended for secondary school and public
libraries.

597   **Country Journal** (Formerly: *Blair and Ketchum's Country Journal*). 1974. m. $16.95.
Francis W. Finn. Historical Times, Inc., P.O. Box 8200, 2245 Kohn Rd., Harrisburg, PA
17105-8200. Illus. Adv. Circ: 325,000. Vol. ends: No. 12. Microform: UMI. [*Indexed*: MI,
RG. *Aud*: Ages 14–18.]

Teenagers who are in the country or want to live in the country will be
delighted with this by-now famous hymn to the great out-of-doors—as long as
there is a house about. *Country Journal* gives practical and authoritative information to those who either live in or dream of living in the country. Typically,
the readers are those who choose to be self-sufficient and live in close proximity
with nature. There is a particular concern with the environment. Regular features discusss growing and harvesting, the use of land, and items essential to life
in the country. Full of advice for those who coexist with nature.

598   **Family Economics Review** (Supersedes *Wartime Family Living*; *Rural Family Living*). 1957. q. $5 (Foreign, $6.26). Joan Courtless. Agriculture Research Service, Family
Economics Research Group, U.S. Dept. of Agriculture, 6505 Belcrest Rd., Rm. 439-A,

Hyattsville, MD 20782. Circ: 5,000. Microform: MIM, UMI. Reprint: UMI. [*Indexed*: PAIS. *Aud*: Ages 14–18.]

Published by the U.S. Department of Agriculture, this title offers useful information on government publications and programs. Articles discuss practical financial concerns as well as broader fiscal issues challenging the American family. The consumer-prices, food, and child-raising cost features should be of special interest. Recommended for school and public libraries.

599   The Family Handyman: the do-it-yourself home improvement magazine (Incorporating *Home Garden*). 1951. 10/yr. $11.97. Gary Havens. Home Service Publns., 7900 International Dr., Suite 950, Minneapolis, MN 55425. Illus. Adv. Circ: 1,300,000. Vol. ends: Dec. Microform: UMI. [*Indexed*: MI, RG. *Aud*: Ages 14–18.]

Those with an active interest in home improvements and remodeling will enjoy this publication. Major editorial categories include remodeling, repair and maintenance, energy efficiency, home furnishing and decorating, and yard and garden care. Regular features deal with woodworking, auto maintenance, new products, and housing. The graphic emphasis is on step-by-step photographs and illustrations as well as detailed plans and diagrams.

600   Gourmet. 1941. m. $18. Jane Montant. Conde Nast Publns., Inc., 350 Madison Ave., New York, NY 10017. Illus. Adv. Index. Circ: 797,893. Vol. ends: Dec. Microform: UMI. [*Indexed*: MI, RG. *Aud*: Ages 14–18.]

This is the oldest of all the cooking magazines and probably the best known. Each issue contains lengthy and interesting articles that give a personal view of travel, food, and wine, as well as 80 to 100 recipes. Regular features cover restaurants around the world and wine. Recipes can be a challenge for novices (and sometimes for experts!). Since *Gourmet* includes so much more than just recipes—the best of food and travel, enhanced by elegant photography—it should be considered by public and school libraries.

601   House and Garden: the magazine of creative living. 1901. m. $36. Nancy Novogrod. Conde Nast Publns., Inc., 350 Madison Ave., New York, NY 10017. Illus. Adv. Circ: 591,694. Vol. ends: No. 12. Microform: UMI. [*Indexed*: MI, RG. *Aud*: Ages 14–18.]

This is not for your average teenager, but it may be familiar to the young adult because it is around the house, and certainly it is seen on the newsstand. It is widely indexed and frequently referred to in home economics articles. The targeted audience is well-educated, sophisticated, middle-aged persons who purchase art in galleries and probably have household help to care for their fine furnishings. *House Beautiful* is geared toward a younger audience and acts as a guide to home furnishings and antiques. *House and Garden* assumes that the photographs of extremely expensive interior decorator-designed homes are all one needs to achieve one's dream decor. From architect-designed homes to penthouses and traditional homes, *House and Garden* reveals what interior designers are doing these days. What this magazine lacks in text, it makes up for in the quality and good taste of its photographs. For the targeted audience as well as browsers and dreamers, this title is a classic in school and public libraries.

602   House Beautiful. 1896. m. $15.97. JoAnn R. Barwick. Hearst Corp., 1700 Broadway, New York, NY 10019. Illus. Adv. Circ: 825,000. Vol. ends: No. 12. Microform: UMI. [*Indexed*: Acs, MI. *Aud*: Ages 14–18.]

One of the best known and most popular of the home magazines, *House Beautiful* is written for the upwardly mobile, young, middle-income couple.

Design schemes utilize different periods and styles, ranging from the austere to the sumptuous. While this type of periodical tends to emphasize illustrations rather than articles, short entertaining features can also be found. Mostly, it is a magazine for readers seeking decorating inspiration from the photographic home tours and interviews with homeowners who have put creative energy and enthusiasm into decorating their homes.

603 **Teen Times.** 1945. q. (during school year). Deb Olcott Taylor. Future Homemakers of America, 1910 Association Dr., Reston, VA 22091. Illus. Adv. Circ: 315,000. Sample. Vol. ends: Mar/Apr. [*Aud*: Ages 14–18.]

Although published primarily for its membership, this eight-page magazine of the Future Homemakers of America should appeal to nonmembers as well. In brief format and clear, precise style, it contains news of chapter activities and association affairs as well as articles of general interest to teens.

■ **HORSES** [Ellen B. Wells]

Many horse magazines specialize in breeds or activities, with a growing emphasis on the economics of horse breeding, training, and competition. Annual special issues often feature such topics as breeding, showing, health, and youth activities. Advertising and reviews routinely include video publications, which are mostly "how-to's" on riding, training, and showing. Nearly all of the publications have color, at least in the advertising. Those with heavy advertising include indexes to the advertisers in each issue. Several journals now provide annual indexes to articles, often published at the beginning of the new year or volume.

First choices   (1) *Horseman*; (2) *Western Horseman*.
Suitable for children   Ages 10–18: *Horse & Rider*; *Horseman*.

604 **The Chronicle of the Horse.** 1937. w. $35. John Strassburger, P.O. Box 46, Middleburg, VA 22117. Illus. Adv. Index. Circ: 22,100. Sample. [*Aud*: Ages 14–18.]

Although a considerable portion of the contents is devoted to show results, this newsy weekly continues to report and inform on sport horse activities. Features include shows, competition in dressage, combined training, polo, fox hunting, and racing. The *Chronicle* remains the official publication of nine American equestrian organizations. A major information source on horses.

605 **Equus.** 1977. m. $22.50. Ami Shinitzky. Fleet Street Corp., Quince Orchard Rd., Gaithersburg, MD 20878. Illus. Adv. Index. Circ: 108,000. [*Aud*: Ages 14–18.]

Perhaps the best general periodical on the horse published in the United States, concentrating on equine health and fitness. Articles examine and explain equine anatomy, physiology, and performance from biological and behavioral points of view. A helpful glossary accompanies each issue. Articles on riding and horse breeds appear as well, but no styles of riding or particular horse breeds are favored.

606 **Horse and Horseman.** 1973. m. $14. Jack Lewis. Gallant/Charger Pubs., P.O. Box HH, 34249 Camino Capistrano, Capistrano Beach, CA 92624. Illus. Adv. Circ: 82,827. [*Aud*: Ages 14–18.]

Aimed at young competitors and beginning horse owners and breeders, this journal is heavy on well-illustrated how-to articles. It focuses on problems in riding style, training horses, and showing both English and western, perhaps slanted more toward the western style. Occasional special issues feature different breeds, horse health concerns, or new products.

607   Horse & Rider. 1968. m. $17. Sue Copeland. Rich Publns., 941 Calle Negocio, San Clemente, CA 92672. Illus. Adv. Circ: 130,000. [*Aud*: Ages 10–18.]

This is a standard horse magazine found in many elementary and secondary school libraries as well as in public libraries. The focus is on western style and the horse owner who enters numerous competitions. Obviously, the text (if not the illustrations) can be a bit difficult for younger readers, but there is enough here to fascinate anyone who is in love with horses and riding. The best features for younger readers: tips on training, riding skills, and so forth.

608   Horse Illustrated. 1976. m. $21.99. Linda Lewis. Fancy Publns., P.O. Box 6050, Mission Viejo, CA 92690-9983. Illus. Adv. Index. Circ: 40,000. [*Aud*: Ages 14–18.]

Heavily illustrated, but with more substantial articles than in earlier years, this magazine includes information on horse physiology and behavior and how they apply to training and riding. Features include a veterinary column and product announcements.

609   Horse World USA (Formerly: *Eastern Horse World*). 1978. m. $18. Diana DeRosa. Garri Publns. Assocs., P.O. Box 249, Huntington Station, NY 11746. Illus. Adv. Circ: 55,000. Sample. [*Aud*: Ages 14–18.]

From a regional publication, this journal has in recent years broadened its scope to cover national and international news in the horse industry. It remains a major calendar source for equestrian events including major races, shows, clinics, and conferences. Features include health, business, and industry news and information. Annual special issues include intercollegiate equitation, Saratoga, Washington International, youth, driving, breeding, and polo. An extra issue provides an annual calendar.

610   Horseman. 1956. m. $22. Kathy Kadash. Horseman Publg. Corp., 25025 I-45N., Suite 390, Spring, TX 77300. Illus. Adv. Circ: 127,000. [*Aud*: Ages 10–18.]

While illustrations in almost all of the horse magazines will attract younger children, this is one of the few they can read, at least in part. Evenly balanced coverage of western- and English-style riding is provided in well-written, adequately illustrated articles. Some emphasis on how to succeed in the horse industry and competition is also given. Features include a news column and new products coverage.

611   Performance Horseman. 1981. m. $24.95. Pamela Goold. Gum Tree Store Press, Gum Tree Corner, Unionville, PA 19375. Illus. Adv. Circ: 35,000. [*Aud*: Ages 14–18.]

A thoughtful publication for the serious western-style rider, primarily containing how-to articles, addressing the economics of breeding and the use of western horses. The pictorial clinic feature is useful and reflects current showing styles. About half the features and articles are also published in its companion magazine, *Practical Horseman*.

612   **Practical Horseman** (Formerly: *Pennsylvania Horseman*). 1973. m. $19.95. Pamela Goold. Gum Tree Store Press, Gum Tree Corner, Unionville, PA 19375. Illus. Adv. Circ: 57,000. [*Aud*: Ages 14–18.]

Aimed at helping serious English-style competitive horse owners with articles on specific problems or purposes, such as conditioning, training, nutrition and health, stable management, and show preparation. Pictorial clinics are a special feature in this magazine and are very well done. About half the articles in each issue are also published in the companion magazine, *Performance Horseman*, for western-style riders.

613   **Western Horseman.** 1936. m. $15. Pat Close. Western Horseman, Inc., 3850 N. Nevada Ave., P.O. Box 7980, Colorado Springs, CO 80933. Illus. Adv. Circ: 185,000. [*Indexed*: BioAg. *Aud*: Ages 14–18.]

One of the oldest continuously published horse magazines in the country, and one of the best. Many outstanding writers on horsemanship have contributed columns or articles through the decades since it was founded. Its emphasis is on the western stock horse—its breeds, training, uses, and history. Features include book reviews, merchandise and product announcements, and historical notes. An important annual special issue is the October breed issue.

■ **INDIANS OF NORTH AMERICA**   [Patricia Brauch]

There are numerous local magazines that focus on the interest of Native Americans, but all too few are of national interest. The result is a limited choice, particularly when narrowed for teenagers and children. Nevertheless, within that selective group are some outstanding titles that should be found in most school and public libraries. Current affairs, politics, law, the arts, literature, education, and health are among the areas covered. The emphasis is on publications that will enhance the reader's knowledge and understanding of this ethnic group.

First choices   (1) *Akwesasne Notes*; (2) *Winds of Change.*
Suitable for children   Ages 9–14: *Daybreak Star*. Ages 10–18: *Turtle Quarterly.*

614   **Akwesasne Notes: a journal for native and natural people.** 1968. 6/yr. $15. Douglas George. Mohawk Nation, P.O. Box 196, Rooseveltown, NY 13683-0196. Illus. Adv. Circ: 20,000. Vol. ends: Dec. Microform: UMI. Reprint: UMI. [*Indexed*: API. *Bk. rev*: 1, 400 words, signed. *Aud*: Ages 14–18.]

This is one of the best of the Indian-focused newspapers and quite suitable for most teens. It is the official publication of the Mohawk Nation at Akwesasne. While primarily concerned with indigenous people of North and South America, it is an advocate for native people everywhere. Areas covered are civil rights, ecology, education, and cultural and political news events. Of particular interest to teachers are the lists of resources, books, posters, and records.

615   **Daybreak.** 1987. q. $12. John Mohawk. Oren Lyons, P.O. Box 98, Highland, MD 20777-0098. Illus. Adv. Sample. Vol. ends: No. 4. [*Aud*: Ages 14–18.]

A tabloid published by Native Americans and dedicated to the Seventh Generation. A relative newcomer to the field, and a good one. Representative articles are on Indian rights, world peace, women, art, and the environment. Two regular features, "Earthwatch" and "Ecomyopia," are especially good. The layout and graphics are first rate.

Daybreak Star. *See under* CHILDREN/AMERICANS: BLACKS, INDIANS, LATINOS.

616 **Northeast Indian Quarterly** (Formerly: *Indian Studies; Northeast Indian*). 1986. q. $35 (Individuals, $12). Jose Barreiro. Cornell Univ., 400 Caldwell Hall, Ithaca, NY 14853. Illus. Vol. ends: No. 4. [*Indexed*: API. *Bk. rev*: 1, 200 words, signed. *Aud*: Ages 14–18.]

An interdisciplinary journal concerned with the past, present, and future of the Native American, it covers 100 communities in the northeastern United States and southeastern Canada. Its professional staff of writers consists of persons from the Cornell Department of Communication and various New York State Indian tribes. Its purpose is to fortify a sense of community among Native Americans and to bridge the cultural gap between native and nonnative peoples. A valuable resource for teaching about New York State tribal communities.

617 **Rencontre.** q. Free. Diane Bilodeau. Sagmai, 875 Grand-Allée Est, P.Q., G1R 4Y8, Canada. Illus. Index. Circ: 41,500. Sample. Vol. ends: June. [*Aud*: Ages 14–18.]

A colorful magazine (in English) for Quebec's Amerindian and Inuit populations, this covers social, political, economic, and cultural areas. It also has information on programs and organizations that may be of use to persons in these groups. Good articles on the health hazards from industrial pollution also appear. A special feature is a children's corner, and there is a section on new books and publications. *Rencontre* has a wide circulation. It is interesting to compare the points of view and programs in this magazine with those available in the United States.

618 **Tśa' Ászi' (The Yucca): a magazine of Navaho Culture.** 1973. s-a. $9. RAMAH Navaho School Board, Pine Hill School, Pine Hill, NM 87321. Illus. Circ: 1,200. Microform: CPC. [*Aud*: Ages 14–18.]

An artistic little magazine published by Navaho high school students with the assistance of an advisor. Its focus is on the literature, folklore, art, and culture of the Navaho people. Typical articles are Coyote tales, legends, "how-to" essays, and interviews with the aged. The work is of high quality, and the illustrations are beautiful.

Turtle Quarterly. *See under* CHILDREN/AMERICANS: BLACKS, INDIANS, LATINOS.

619 **Winds of Change: a magazine for American Indians.** 1986. q. $16. James R. Weidlein, Robert S. Hill, Jr., and Michael D. Avritt. Amer. Indian Science & Engineering Soc., 1085 14th St., Suite 1224, Boulder, CO 80302. Illus. Adv. Vol. ends: Winter. [*Bk. rev*: 2, 250–600 words, signed. *Aud*: Ages 14–18.]

A shiny magazine with a focus on careers and education for the American Indian in science and engineering. Typical articles are on choice of careers, technical training, and the job interview. Chosen by an advisory board, they are solid and well researched. A regular feature, "Into the Wind," lists educational opportunities, conferences, and position openings. An encouraging and upbeat magazine for minority students.

■ **JOURNALISM AND WRITING**   [Connie V. Dowell]

Journalism is a broad field. It blends with many others such as political science, communications, publishing, and information science. Nevertheless, in the typical school situation it is limited in a practical way to courses and school newspapers and magazines. This section is compiled with that in mind, as well as the needs of young writers. Most of the titles reflect the moral/ethical view of journalism and writing as well as the how-to-do-it aspects of the subject.

First choices   (1) *Quill and Scroll*; (2) *Columbia Journalism Review*; (3) *Prism*; (4) *Merlyn's Pen*.

Suitable for children   Ages 8–14: *Shoe Tree*. Ages 10–18: *Quill and Scroll*. Ages 11–15: *Prism*; *Teen Power*. Ages 12–15: *Merlyn's Pen*.

620   **Columbia Journalism Review.** 1961. bi-m. $18. Suzanne Braun Levine. Columbia Univ., Grad. School of Journalism. Subs. to: P.O. Box 1943, Marion, OH 43302. Illus. Adv. Index. Circ: 34,000. Microform: B&H, UMI. [*Indexed*: BoRvI, HumI, PAIS. *Bk. rev*: 4–7, length varies, signed. *Aud*: Ages 14–18.]

The leading critic of the American press and television, this is required in school and public libraries to alert students to the faults (as well as the delights) of the American press. Covering all aspects of print and broadcast media, the three to seven primary articles frequently include the international media, legal and ethical issues, investigative reports, current trends, and some personal accounts by journalists. The short-reports section features legal cases, censorship issues, profiles, and assorted news briefs. Along with the section of editorial comments, *CJR* awards "Laurels" to applaud ethical behavior of specific publications and broadcasters—as well as "Darts." The intelligence and integrity of the *Columbia Journalism Review* make it a delight to read.

621   **Content for Canadian Journalists.** 1970. bi-m. $15. Dick MacDonald. Friends of Content, Inc., Unit 135, 90 Edgewood Ave., Toronto, Ont., Canada. Illus. Adv. Circ: 3,000. [*Indexed*: CanI. *Bk. rev*: Various number and length, signed. *Aud*: Ages 14–18.]

This journalism review contains critical analyses of Canadian print and broadcast news media and examines issues touching the practice of journalism. This bimonthly publication offers news, opinion, and humor of interest to working journalists, writers, and editors. *Content* is an obvious first choice for Canadian high school libraries and recommended for all journalism collections.

622   **Editor & Publisher: the fourth estate.** 1884. w. $45. Robert Brown. Editor & Publisher Co., 11 W. 19th St., New York, NY 10011. Illus. Adv. Circ: 30,000. Sample. Vol. ends: Dec. Microform: B&H, MIM, UMI. Reprint: UMI. [*Indexed*: BusI. *Aud*: Ages 14–18.]

This journalists' trade magazine is a weekly report on all aspects of journalism. The three to four main articles on the newspaper business may cover advertising, printing, technology, marketing, layout and design, syndicated features, legal or ethical issues, and personality profiles. News items keep readers up to date on the American newspaper scene. While *E&P* is clearly designed for those in the newspaper business, it is extremely valuable to high school journalism students.

623   **Eye.** 1978. 8/yr. $10. YMCA of Delaware, 11th & Washington Sts., Wilmington, DE 19801. Illus. Adv. Circ: 20,000. [*Aud*: Ages 14–18.]

Produced by teenagers, for teenagers, *Eye* is Delaware's only statewide youth publication. Actually, it is a 20- or so page tabloid that offers news and opinion. One issue, for example, discusses the various arguments about abortion. (While a YMCA publication, there is no interference by the publisher with the contents, which represent points of view that may vary from those of the YMCA.) The seasons are duly hailed with features suitable for Christmas or the Fourth of July and there are numerous brief comments on everything from music and sex to politics and family life. Delaware is often a focus, but most of the magazine can be enjoyed by teenagers in almost any part of the country. Also, it serves as a fine example of student writing and editing.

624   MediaFile: the publication of Media Alliance (Formerly: *Media Alliance Newsletter; Media Alliance News*). 1980. bi-m. $25. Pam Pfiffner. Media Alliance, Bldg. D, Fort Mason, San Francisco, CA 91123. Illus. Adv. Circ: 7,000. Sample. Vol. ends: Dec. [*Indexed*: API. *Bk. rev*: Various number and length. *Aud*: Ages 14–18.]

   This bimonthly media review covers national issues with only slight focus on California. Occasionally, special issues address topical subjects such as a recent one on women in the media. The graphics and tabloid format are reminiscent of the better underground papers of the 1970s. Most of the copy is written by journalists with an occasional piece by a layperson.

625   Merlyn's Pen. 1985. q. $19.95. R. James Stahl. Merlyn's Pen, 98 Main St., East Greenwich, RI 02818. Illus. [*Aud*: Ages 12–18.]

   Primarily composed of the prize writing of students, this magazine includes short stories, poetry, essays, and all of the other forms associated with senior literary reviews. Much of the material is fiction and shows, often in a moving way, the heartfelt problems of teenagers. The magazine is carefully edited and there is an unusual effort to strive for quality.

626   Poets and Writers (Formerly: *Coda*). 1972. bi-m. $18. Daryln Brewer. Poets & Writers, Inc., 72 Spring St., New York, NY 10012. Illus. Adv. Circ: 11,000. Microform: UMI. Reprint: UMI. [*Aud*: Ages 14–18.]

   This valuable bimonthly guide for writers is jointly funded by the New York State Council on the Arts and the National Endowment for the Arts. The sections on national and state grants and awards are especially worthwhile. The articles feature practical advice for writers and interviews with as well as essays by authors on what it means to write. Suitable for both the writer and anyone interested in the literary world and any library from high school through public.

Prism. *See under* CHILDREN/LANGUAGE ARTS.

627   Quill and Scroll. 1926. bi-m. (during school year). $9. Richard P. Johns. Univ. of Iowa, School of Journalism and Mass Communication, Iowa City, IA 52242. Illus. Adv. Circ: 13,000. Sample. Vol. ends: Apr/May. Microform: UMI. [*Indexed*: CIJE. *Bk. rev*: 7–11, 150–200 words, signed. *Aud*: Ages 10–18.]

   Intended for its membership, this magazine is the official publication of the International Honorary Society of High School Journalists. Charters are most often affiliated with high schools that publish yearbooks, newspapers, or magazines, but membership is also open to students (through their respective schools) who write for town or city newspapers. Regular departments include book reviews (useful in collection development) and news of professional interest. Each issue also contains a feature article, for example, "The Ups and Downs of Information Graphics," and a profile of an individual who has made a contribution to the profession. This is a solid title about the career of journalism presented for the young adult.

Scholastic Scope. *See under* CLASSROOM PUBLICATIONS.

Scholastic Search. *See under* CLASSROOM PUBLICATIONS.

Scholastic Voice. *See under* CLASSROOM PUBLICATIONS.

Shoe Tree. *See under* CHILDREN/LANGUAGE ARTS.

628 **Teen Power.** 1966. w. $6.75. Scripture Press Publns., 1825 College Ave., Wheaton, IL 60187. Illus. [*Aud:* Ages 11–15.]

A Christian six-page, hand-sized paper, this prints two to three original stories, articles, essays, and so forth, from its target audience. The teenage entries run from 600 to 1,200 words. The emphasis is on the Christian life, but the editor warns: "Thou shall not use tacked-on morals, sermons, or terms such as unsaved or redeemed that won't be understood by non-Christians. This area is the biggest reason for instant rejection." The result is good, objective writing that has a Christian point of view, but not in any intemperate fashion. It can be enjoyed by all faiths—and not a few who may have no faith at all.

Note: The magazine comes in two editions. One is called *Teen Power*, for junior high students (ages 11–15), and the other (which is similar but not reviewed here) is called *Free Way*, for high school students.

629 **Washington Journalism Review** (Short title: *W JR*). 1977. m. $24. William Monroe. Washington Journalism Review Assocs., Inc., 2233 Wisconsin Ave. N.W., Washington, DC 20007. Illus. Adv. Circ: 32,000. Vol. ends: Dec. Microform: UMI. [*Indexed:* Acs, BoRvI. *Bk. rev:* 3–6, 300–500 words, signed. *Aud:* Ages 14–18.]

Washington Journalism Review is as much a monthly news and feature magazine on the media as a journalism review. While offering some international coverage, national coverage of the press is *W JR*'s strong suit, with only slight emphasis on Washington. Feature-length profiles of journalists and publications and articles on trends and ethics make this an excellent source for the student of journalism.

630 **The Writer: the oldest magazine for literary workers.** 1887. m. $30. Sylvia K. Burack. The Writer, Inc., 120 Boylston St., Boston, MA 02116. Adv. Index. Circ: 55,000. Vol. ends: Dec. Microform: B&H, UMI. [*Indexed:* MI, RG. *Aud:* Ages 14–18.]

This important how-to-write periodical's articles mainly involve fiction, with an emphasis on book writing. While *The Writer* does not publish book reviews, the "Writer's Library" features lists of selected works with short annotations. Prizes, contests, and conferences are announced and each month a different "special market" for writers is listed.

631 **Writer's Digest: your monthly guide to getting published.** 1920. m. $24. William Brohaugh. F&W Publns., 1507 Dana Ave., Cincinnati, OH 45207. Illus. Adv. Index. Circ: 214,000. Sample. Vol. ends: Dec. Microform: B&H, MIM, UMI. Reprint: UMI. [*Indexed:* Acs, MI. *Bk. rev:* Various number and length, signed. *Aud:* Ages 14–18.]

This monthly publication contains practical, instructional articles on specific types of writing for the free-lance market. Articles cover techniques of fiction and nonfiction, playwriting, photojournalism, cartooning, poetry, and writing for television and radio. Along with interviews with well-known writers, *WD* offers profiles of first novelists. Most issues include in-depth market features on major magazine categories and book publishing firms.

Writing. *See under* CLASSROOM PUBLICATIONS.

■ **LATIN AMERICA, LATINO (U.S.)** [Salvador Guerena]

With one or two exceptions, selections in this area are all adult magazines, both in Spanish and in English. Fortunately, many have appeal for young adults. This is particularly welcome in the Spanish-language section.

An effort has been made to include the more popular women's magazines as well as those covering current news topics and the interests of teenagers. Diversity is the rule rather than the exception and that is why the magazines listed here cover so many areas while, at the same time, staying within the reading capabilities of younger people. The area is of major importance for many school and public libraries if for no other reason than that Latinos make up the fastest-growing segment of the U.S. population.

First choices English: (1) *Américas*; (2) *The Americas Review*.

Spanish: (1) *Buenhogar*; (2) *Claudia*.

Suitable for children Ages 8–12: *Chispa*. Ages 12–18: *Claudia*; *Hombre de Mundo*.

•••••••••••••••••••••••••••••• **English Language** ••••••••••••••••••••••••••••••

632 **Américas.** 1949. 6/yr. $15. Catherine Healy. Org. of Amer. States, 1889 F. St. N.W., Washington, DC 20006. Illus. Circ: 100,000. [*Indexed*: AbrRG, HAPI, HumI, RG. *Bk. rev*: 1–2, 600–1,200 words, signed. *Aud*: Ages 14–18.]

Always a pleasure to look at, *Américas* is a beautifully illustrated magazine containing interesting, informative articles and news of the Americas. Published by the General Secretariat of the Organization of American States (OAS), this magazine is available in both English and Spanish editions. Typically, each issue contains eight feature articles concerning the people, the history, or the geography of some locality in the Americas or the Caribbean. The "Departments" section features news and articles on food, trends, the arts and books, as well as a section devoted to the OAS. An added feature is the inclusion of a new short story in each issue. A colorful, informative publication with general appeal, *Américas* would be a good addition to many school and public libraries.

633 **The Americas Review: a review of Hispanic literature and art of the USA** (Formerly: *Revista Chicano-Requeña*). 1972. q. $20 (Individuals, $15). Julian Olivares and Evangelina Vigil-Piñon. Arte Público Press, Univ. of Houston, University Park, Houston, TX 77004. Illus. Adv. Refereed. [*Indexed*: HAPI. *Bk. rev*: 2–6, 500–1,000 words, signed. *Aud*: Ages 14–18.]

A very attractive small-format but major literary review. *The Americas Review* has over the years been an important outlet for Chicano, Puerto Rican, and other Latino and Latina writers and artists. According to its editors, the journal "aims to express the increasingly artistic and sociopoetic consciousness of the poets, artists, writers and literary critics of our America." Indeed, many established, as well as up-and-coming, writers have appeared in its pages. This is a well-rounded and visually appealing periodical that is highly recommended for school and public libraries serving Latino communities.

634 **Aztlán: international journal of Chicano studies research.** 1970. s-a. $20 (Individuals, $25). Chicano Studies Research Center, Univ. of California–Los Angeles, 405

Hilgard Ave., Los Angeles, CA 90024. Circ: 1,500. Refereed. Microform: UMI. [*Indexed*: HAPI, SocSc. *Bk. rev*: 0–7, 350–1,000 words, signed. *Aud*: Ages 14–18.]

This is the preeminent scholarly journal in Chicano studies, involving research dealing with the Mexican American experience. *Aztlán* is an important forum for research and essays in the social sciences and the arts. Thematic issues often appear, such as one special issue on the Chicano experience in Texas. Among *Aztlán's* main weaknesses is that it appears irregularly and several years late, and usually in the form of combined issues. Nevertheless, *Aztlán* should find a place in all collections concerned with the Chicano and Mexican experience. It also has a broader application beyond those areas and may serve the interests of other Latino communities in the United States.

635 **Bilingual Review/Revista Bilingue.** 1974. 3/yr. $24 (Individuals, $18). Gary D. Keller. Bilingual Review-Press, Hispanic Research Center, Arizona State Univ., Tempe, AZ 85287. Adv. Circ: 2,000. Refereed. Vol. ends: Dec. Microform: UMI. [*Indexed*: CIJE, EdI, HAPI. *Bk. rev*: 2–5, 1,000–1,500 words, signed. *Aud*: Ages 14–18.]

Both teachers and advanced teenagers will benefit from reading this bilingual magazine. Published mainly in English, its articles on research and criticism are contributed by academics in this country and abroad. Sample titles include "Bilingual Education in the Ethnic Schools of Miami" and "The New Mexican Poetry of Leroy Quintana." The professional-announcements section informs on upcoming conferences, literary prizes, and special programs in the field of bilingualism or literature. As a literary outlet, the journal publishes selections of creative writing such as short stories, poems, and, occasionally, interviews with writers. Special thematic issues appear occasionally. The *Bilingual Review* is highly recommended for libraries supporting language studies, Hispanic literature, and Chicano studies.

Chispa. *See under* CHILDREN/SCIENCE.

636 **Intercambios Femeniles.** q. $25. Margaret Cerudo. Natl. Network of Hispanic Women, Suite 353, 12021 Wilshire Blvd., Los Angeles, CA 90025. Illus. Adv. [*Bk. rev*: 0–10, 25–50 words. *Aud*: Ages 14–18.]

This is an English-language magazine. Formerly issued as a newsletter, it has taken on a new look, since it now has an attractive magazine format. This is an unusual periodical in that it uniquely addresses the issues and concerns of professional Hispanic women. It helps fill the need for a national-level periodical that focuses on the special interests and needs of Hispanic women who are challenged, on the one side, by the demands of the two cultures, and on the other by what is still a male-dominated society. The articles are well written throughout, offering valuable insights into such things as the role of Hispanic women in the women's movement, employment prospects, and educational development, as well as perspectives on family, careers, and changing life-styles. It regularly features separate sections on information resources, health-related topics, and the arts and entertainment.

637 **Mexico Journal.** 1987. w. $60. Carlos Payan Velver. Mexico Journal, P.O. Box 59, Vista Grande Sta., Daly City, CA 94106. Illus. Adv. Sample. Vol. ends: No. 50. [*Bk. rev*: 1, 800–1,000 words, signed. *Aud*: Ages 14–18.]

For those who have an interest in Mexico and want to be regularly informed about it in English on a current basis, *Mexico Journal* may be just what one needs. The issues of greatest concern are political and economic in nature, and these subjects tend to be emphasized, it also offers an array of general news items, reports, and essays on Mexican society and culture. By and large, readers of *Mexico Journal* will receive more balanced and thorough views than they may be accustomed to because the objective of the American news media is to reach a broad readership, and they thus give more generalized accounts. This would be a welcome addition to any library.

638   **NACLA Report on the Americas.** 1967. bi-m. $35 (Individuals, $20). Martha Dogget. North Amer. Congress on Latin America, 151 W. 19th St., 9th Fl., New York, NY 10011. Illus. Adv. Circ: 11,000. Vol. ends: Dec. Microform: UMI. [*Indexed*: API, HAPI, PAIS. *Bk. rev*: 10–13, 40–60 words. *Aud*: Ages 14–18.]

This is a small-format, well-illustrated newsmagazine providing excellent in-depth coverage of important developments in Latin America. While its principal aim is to report on the political economies of the Americas, its scope has included a series of special reports on U.S. counter-insurgency strategy, religion, labor, and the media. Special attention has been given to regional hot spots in Central America and the Caribbean. *NACLA* is known for its careful research, readability, and timeliness, which make it one of the most popular magazines in its field. Highly recommended for school and public libraries.

639   **U.S.-Mexico Report.** 1982. m. $35. Patricia A. Sullivan and Maria Telles-McGeagh. Joint Border Research Inst. for Latin American Studies and the Consortium of U.S. Research Programs for Mexico, 1200 University Ave., New Mexico State Univ., P.O. Box 30001, Las Cruces, NM 88003-0001. Sample. Vol. ends: Dec. [*Aud*: Ages 14–18.]

This periodical reports on current events in Mexico, consisting of translations of news articles originally appearing in Spanish in well-known Mexican newspapers. Its emphasis is on the Mexican border region of the United States. Organized in a week-to-week fashion, the articles in each issue represent timely information. Each issue also prints excerpts from *Daily Report: Latin America*, which is issued by the Foreign Broadcast Information Service of the U.S. Department of Commerce. Such excerpts include the text of speeches by Mexican President Miguel de la Madrid. Recommended for high school and public libraries.

•••••••••••••••••••••••• **Latino/Spanish Language** ••••••••••••••••••••••••

640   **Buenhogar.** 1966. bi-w. $65. Editorial America, S.A., Vanidades Continental Bldg., 6355 N.W. 36th St., Virginia Gardens, FL 33166. Illus. Adv. Circ: 375,000. Sample. [*Aud*: Ages 14–18.]

Billing itself as the magazine for the young homemaker, *Buenhogar* is often compared with the English-language *Good Housekeeping*. Its popularity is underscored by its loyal following among women who are Spanish readers. A glossy, full-color magazine, it combines human-interest stories such as accounts of personalities who have overcome problems with articles on such topics as parenting. One of its more popular features is its star-studded personalities parade. Its hallmark, however, lies in its copious attention to domestic life, such as home decorating, handicrafts, table etiquette, and recipes for those quintessential dishes that always look too good to eat. Its pages are replete with beauty tips, photo spreads on the latest fashions, and, yes, horoscopes.

641 **Claudia.** 1965. m. $67. Hilda O'Farrill Avila de Compean. Editorial Mex-Ameris, S.A., Av. Morelos 16, 4 Piso, Mexico 1, D.F., Mexico. Illus. Adv. Circ: 102,577. Sample. [*Aud*: Ages 14–18.]

The focus of *Claudia* is on high fashion and beauty. In addition to its many articles of interest to women are interviews with such well-known film personalities as Maria Felix of Mexico and Ava Gardner. There are a variety of domestic-type topics such as gardening, home decorating, and cookery. Celebrities from the world of television are covered, and there are health-related articles too. Astrology fans will like the horoscopes, and for avid readers the short stories will be appealing.

642 **Cosmopolitan en español.** 1973. m. $19.50. Cristina Salaregui. Editorial America, S.A., Vanidades Continental Bldg., 6355 N.W. 36th St., Virginia Gardens, FL 33166. Illus. Adv. Circ: 32,454. Sample. Microform: UMI. [*Bk. rev*: Irreg. *Aud*: Ages 14–18.]

Cosmopolitan en español is similar to, but not identical with, its U.S. version. For one thing, it does not seem to be as provocative as its American counterpart, even though it is aimed at a similar audience. Much of its material is oriented toward self-improvement and the enhancement of man-woman relationships. As with the English version, it is profusely illustrated with splashy color and black-and-white photos, which are indispensable to its fashion and beauty segments. Smaller articles and notes abound, covering nutrition, health, horoscopes, cinema, and new recordings. *Cosmopolitan en español* has a very loyal readership and is a magazine that is bound to circulate.

643 **Cuadernos Americanos: nueva epoca.** 1942. bi-m. $35. Jesus Silva Herzog. Cuadernos Americanos, Apartado Postal 965, C.P. 06000, Mexico, D.F., Mexico. Illus. Adv. Index. Circ: 2,500. Refereed. [*Indexed*: HAPI. *Bk. rev*: 1–3, 500–1,000 words, signed. *Aud*: Ages 14–18.]

This remains one of the oldest and most highly respected journals from Latin America. In addition to a multidisciplinary section, each issue is now divided into two or three thematic sections that are supported by several research articles on the subject. Topics have included Cuban history, the role of the university in Latin American politics, and Latin American literary criticism. The works of illustrious personages are occasionally given special treatment. The emphasis is on Latin America, although Iberian interests, international relations, and U.S. current affairs are occasionally examined. The journal is published entirely in Spanish.

644 **Fem.** 1976. m. $60. Elena Urratia. Difusion Cultural Feminista, A.C., Av. Universidad 1855, Piso 4, Col. Oxtupulco, C.P. 04310, Mexico, D.F., Mexico. Illus. Adv. Circ: 15,000. Vol. ends: Dec. [*Bk. rev*: 1–2, 500–1,000 words, signed. *Aud*: Ages 14–18.]

An important alternative to traditional women's magazines such as *Buenhogar* and *Claudia*, *Fem* is a provocative and unique magazine that advances progressive issues in Mexico on behalf of Mexican women. It offers perspectives generally not published elsewhere. Often these are social and political concerns of interest outside of Mexico, such as domestic violence, health-care issues, and women in the student movement. It is also a rich source of creative and artistic expression, giving women's views on art and the cinema. Included are short stories and poetry selections. *Fem* regularly provides brief news and notes that deal with women—issues and events in Mexico, Latin America, and abroad.

Thematic special issues have been devoted to such subjects as AIDS and prostitution. This is a very readable and copiously illustrated, thought-provoking periodical that deserves to be included in public and school library collections serving the interests of Latinas.

645 **Geomundo.** 1977. m. $36. Pedro J. Romanach. Editorial America, S.A., Vanidades Continental Bldg., 6355 N.W. 36th St., Virginia Gardens, FL 33166. Illus. Adv. Index. Circ: 7,189. [*Aud*: Ages 14–18.]

Offering a panoramic sweep of world cultures, wildlife, and the natural world, *Geomundo* is very much like *National Geographic*. In a similar manner, its most attractive quality lies in its copious color photography, although sometimes the pictures lack the acuity and luster of its American counterpart. In content, it features about twice as many articles as *National Geographic* does, about ten per issue, and they are shorter in length. Unlike the other geographic magazine, *Américas*, the focus is not on Latin America, although an article or two on Latin American countries or peoples regularly appear in each issue. Each issue also gives a pictorial on one of the world's great art museums, such as the Louvre, the New York Museum of Modern Art, or the Museo del Prado in Madrid. This is a beautiful, popular periodical that is highly recommended for all basic Spanish-language collections in school and public libraries.

646 **Guantes: la primera revista de boxeo de America.** m. $17.50. Chon Romero. Hispano Amer. Publns., Inc., 10-39 44th Dr., Long Island City, NY 11101. Illus. Adv. Vol. ends: Dec. [*Aud*: Ages 14–18.]

A popular Spanish-language magazine in the world of boxing, *Guantes* is chock-full of stories, commentaries, and black-and-white photographs that will be of primary interest to young male aficionados of this sport. All its contributors are of Latin American origin, covering bouts in the United States as well as in South America. Each issue also lists the worldwide top ten fighters in each class, with their national affiliations. This is a suggested title for high school and public libraries, given the appeal this sport has among this particular clientele and its modest subscription price.

647 **Hispanic: the magazine of the contemporary Hispanic.** 1988. m. $18. Alfredo Estrada. Hispanic Publg. Corp., 111 Massachusetts Ave. N.W., Suite 200, Washington, DC 20001. Illus. Adv. Sample. [*Indexed*: MI. *Bk. rev*: 1–2, essays, signed. *Aud*: Ages 14–18.]

A biased fan comments, "We finally have a national voice." That may be stretching it a bit, although this 70-page commercial magazine compares favorably with such standards as *Nuestro* and *Caminos*. The interest is on personalities and the Hispanic success story rather than militancy, politics, or social issues. Colorfully illustrated articles explain how such celebrities as Raquel Welch, Lee Trevino, and Ruben Blades made it in the United States. The professionally written and edited copy is in English. There are usually three or four feature stories and numerous departments, including a useful survey of Hispanic activities in various states and communities. It is recommended for general high school and public library collections.

648 **Hola.** w. $195. Eduardo Sanchez Junco. Empresa Editora Hola, S.A., Apartado de Correo No. 14707, Madrid, Spain. Illus. Adv. Sample. [*Aud*: Ages 14–18.]

Published in Spain, this magazine is similar to *Life*, *People*, and the *National Enquirer*. World-famous personalities are featured, including Hollywood types as well as the likes of European royalties. These have included Princess Diana,

Kirk Douglas, Yasmin Khan, and Yoko Ono. Some of the personalities covered include people not given much exposure in the U.S. press. There are reports on news events representing happenings throughout the Latino world in both hemispheres and in Spain. This is a very popular periodical in public libraries serving the Spanish-speaking public.

649   Hombre de Mundo. 1976. m. $30. Alma Rosa Alcala. Editorial America, S.A., 6355 N.W. 36th St., Virginia Gardens, FL 33166. Illus. Adv. Circ: 80,000. Vol. ends: Dec. [*Aud*: Ages 14–18.]

A cosmopolitan Spanish-language periodical distributed in the United States, Mexico, South America, Japan, Spain, and Europe. The 12 to 20 articles per issue are divided into such areas as style, world news, business and finance, and current events. Articles are generally three to four pages in length, with color and black-and-white photographs accompanying them. Various subjects are covered, including politics, art, religion, sports, health, fashion, travel, and food. Also included are humorous cartoons, recipes, and interviews with international personalities. *Hombre de Mundo* has an appealing format, and although the ads are directed toward men, the magazine would appeal to both men and women entrepreneurs and anyone interested in current world events.

650   Kena. m. $40. Liliana Moreno G. Editorial Armonia, S.A., Magdalena 135, Col. del Valle, Mexico 12, D.F., Mexico. Illus. Adv. [*Aud*: Ages 14–18.]

Kena is a Spanish-language publication for the upscale woman who aspires to bring a touch of the "good life" to her housekeeping style. It is lavishly illustrated, but what distinguishes it most is the dedication of each issue to extensive coverage of one broad topic. Thus, one month's issue will deal with entertaining, another with handcrafts, home decorating, beauty, and so forth. Topics that seem to be repeated are Mexican cooking, Christmas preparation, and children's parties.

651   Que Pasa? 1988. bi-m. $11.99. Celeste R. Gomes. D. S. Magazines, 1086 Teaneck Rd., Teaneck, NJ 07666. Illus. Adv. [*Aud*: Ages 14–18.]

Typical in content but unique in its target audience, this mostly teen fanzine is billed by its publishers as "The Bilingual Teen Entertainment/Lifestyle Magazine." Its intended primary readership is Hispanic teenagers. Presenting the latest news about and interviews with Latin performers and entertainers, it is weakly supplemented with news on beauty, fitness, and dating. Sample articles highlight fashions of a Hispanic designer, and cover personalities in the entertainment world. Regular departments in addition to feature stories include a gossip column, "TV Talk," "Silver Screen Update," "Best Buys" (featuring a limited assortment of beauty and fitness products), "Pen Pals," and, of course, the color pinup centerfold. This magazine should be seriously considered for its distinctive focus as it adequately fills an ethnic void in teen fanzines. It is more attractive than most fanzines.

652   Ritmo. bi-w. $32. Teresita del N.J. Garcia. Editorial Intermex, S.A. de C.V. Subs. to: P.O. Box 10990, Des Moines, IA 50340-0990. Illus. Adv. [*Aud*: Ages 14–18.]

Ritmo is a Spanish-language periodical that mirrors the Mexican rock scene. Since rock is international in appeal, the artists and groups featured in the magazine are from all countries that produce major popular music recordings. Along with numerous interviews with rock stars, monthly features include audience polls of favorite songs and musicians; gossip and rumors about famous personalities; a rock star recounting his or her most vivid dream (illustrated by cartoons); the usual horoscope; articles about the recordings themselves, which include lyrics; and a feature on fashion and beauty. Colored photos seem to be reserved for pictures of the stars. The magazine can be enjoyed by all Latino young people of any ethnicity or nationality.

653   Saguaro. 1984. a. $13 (Individuals, $8). Ignacio Garcia. Mexican Amer. Studies and Research Center, Douglass Bldg., Univ. of Arizona, Tucson, AZ 85721. Refereed. Vol. ends: Fall. [*Aud*: Ages 14–18.]

A bilingual literary journal, *Saguaro* has emerged as a significant outlet for creative writing by established and lesser-known Chicano and Chicana writers. Its editors state that "its purpose is to provide a vehicle for publication of the best works in both English and Spanish by Chicano poets, writers and playwrights on themes related to the Chicano/Mexican experience." The selections of short stories and poetry are richly diverse. Among its top writers have been Abelondo Delgado, Alurista, Sandro Cesneros, Sergio Elizondo, and Carmen Tofolla.

654   Selecciones del Reader's Digest. 1940. m. $27. Audon Coria. Reader's Digest Latinoamerica, S.A., 2655 LeJeune Rd., Suite 301, Coral Gables, FL 33134-5823. Illus. Adv. Circ: 650,000. Sample. Vol. ends: Dec. [*Aud*: Ages 14–18.]

Practically a carbon copy of the English-language *Reader's Digest*, *Selecciones* has the same format, size, and scope as its American counterpart. In fact, all the articles come from previous issues of *Reader's Digest*, but translated into Spanish. The same goes for the sections on humor and vocabulary building. Some librarians may question the value of subscribing to *Selecciones* since neither its subject scope nor its contributors have a Latin American base. Moreover, some people call into question its consistently conservative stance. In response to this, once again, attention is called to the diversity that exists within the Spanish-speaking community. *Selecciones*, with its inspirational stories, self-improvement topics, and coverage of health and medicine appeals to the interests of many Spanish-speakers. *Selecciones* has the same loyal following that *Reader's Digest* does. As such, it merits a place in school and public library collections.

655   Temas. 1950. m. $15. Jose de la Vega. Temas Magazine, Inc., 1650 Broadway, New York, NY 10019. Illus. Adv. Circ: 114,000. [*Aud*: Ages 14–18.]

Temas is a Spanish-language magazine that has been published in New York for 41 years. Inevitably, it emphasizes the doings and concerns of the expatriate Hispanic community in that area, but it has great appeal for any Latino interested in serious music, art, drama, or other cultural events. The cultural thrust of the magazine is expressed in several regular features. "Musica y Teatro" gives reviews of the major dramas and musical reviews on the East Coast, but also gives coverage to lesser-known Latin productions in that area. "Cine" reviews foreign films, especially those in Spanish, as well as new U.S. productions. "Variedades" gives entertainment news from the perspective of one who is familiar with the local and international Hispanic scene.

656   Vanidades. 1961. s-m. $58.50. Editorial America, S.A., Vanidades Continental Bldg., 6355 N.W. 36th St., Virginia Gardens, FL 33166. Illus. Adv. Sample. [*Aud*: Ages 14–18.]

As a long-running women's interest magazine, *Vanidades* has been most effective at reaching its primary readership, which traditionally has consisted of upscale women. It remains one of the most successful and well-known Spanish-language periodicals in its genre. Like *Cosmopolitan en español*, it includes articles on love and marriage, beauty and fashion, and obligatory coverage of the rich and famous. The modern homemaker will find tempting recipes and home-decorating tips, but these are only touched on. In fact, variety is the hallmark of *Vanidades*, which gives it its broad appeal. The photo-vignettes on people and places pique the curious, while the advice on such things as nutrition, health, and freeway safety for women give it a more mundane but yet very practical value. Given the popularity of Spanish television soap operas, each issue includes one of Corin Tellado's romance novelettes, printed in its entirety. A thumbs-up for public libraries.

■ LITERATURE [Robert Hauptman]

See also: FICTION; JOURNALISM AND WRITING

There are no literature journals suitable for young adults, or, for that matter, laypersons. They are much too technical, much too burdened with jargon. Still, here and there are literary reviews that consider the best in prose and poetry for publication and have less interest in the arguments of the literature professors. It is with these we are concerned here. These titles offer the young adult excellent examples of the best in the arts, social commentary, politics, history, and many other areas in addition to literature. All, however, are edited for fairly sophisticated adults and so require an above-average interest in the subject.

First choices (1) *TriQuarterly*; (2) *The Paris Review*; (3) *American Poetry Review*.

657 **American Poetry Review.** 1972. bi-m. $11. Ed. bd. World Poetry, Inc., 1616 Walnut St., Rm. 405, Philadelphia, PA 19103. Illus. Adv. Circ: 24,000. Sample. Vol. ends: Nov/Dec. Microform: UMI. [*Aud*: Ages 14–18.]

Poets of any age will enjoy and profit from this magazine, which comes in a newspaper tabloid format. What makes this poetry journal unique is that the reviews are composed of the actual work of the poet, that is, usually four to five poems from a current volume are printed in full. This is accompanied by a photograph of the poet, and there may be an interview with or an article about the individual. On the whole, though, the reprinted poems speak for themselves and it is up to the reader (including the librarian) to determine whether the book is worthy of purchase. Needless to add, most of the poets represented here—and they include every major name in America, as well as numerous foreigners and some beginners—are worthy of consideration by libraries.

658 **Antaeus.** 1970. s-a. $20/4 issues. Daniel Halpern. The Ecco Press, 26 W. 17th St., New York, NY 10011. Illus. Adv. Index. Circ: 5,000. [*Aud*: Ages 14–18.]

This speaks to sophisticated young adults who have an interest in international literature. Each issue is by way of an education. The sixtieth handsome issue of *Antaeus* contains over 300 pages of outstanding belles lettres. There is fiction by the Nobel Laureate Ivo Andrić and Joyce Carol Oates. Twenty-one poets from the United Kingdom, including Hughes, Heaney, and Abse, contribute work. Additional material comes from Lorca, Milosz, Jammes, Cortazer (an interview), Moravia (an essay), and more. Another recent number concentrated on the art of journal writing and featured an outstanding array of writers.

659 **The Antioch Review.** 1941. q. $25 (Individuals, $18). Robert S. Fogarty. Antioch Review, Inc., P.O. Box 148, Yellow Springs, OH 45387. Adv. Index. Circ: 3,600. Vol. ends:

Fall. Microform: B&H, UMI. Reprint: AMS. [*Indexed*: HumI, PAIS, SocSc. *Bk. rev*: 1, 7 pages, signed. *Aud*: Ages 14–18.]

The somewhat more relaxed style and easier approach to the worries of the world make this, above all others listed here, a good choice for the average high school or public library collection. This is not to detract from what is an excellent review, but only to point out that this one is not as "difficult" as some. A typical issue contains eight stories by writers like Gordon Lish and William Van Wert and poems by contributors including Bin Ramke and Jon Silkin. Each number is rounded out by some 50 brief book comments (rather than reviews).

660 **Grand Street.** 1981. q. $24 (Individuals, $20). Ben Sonnenberg. Grand Street Publns., 50 Riverside Dr., New York, NY 10024. Illus. Adv. Circ: 4,000. Vol. ends: Summer. [*Aud*: Ages 14–18.]

Although much of the excellent contents may be overwhelming for the average teenager, this is a joy for the reader who is experimenting with new areas of interest. There is something here for everyone. *Grand Street* continues to publish 250-page issues filled with the work of outstanding authors. To one issue John Hollander and Gavin Ewart contribute poems and James Salter fiction. There are letters from Virgil Thomson to Gertrude Stein, and David Plante is caught up in the intricacies of Moscow (for 45 pages). Penelope Gilliatt discusses Polish film and Guy Davenport discourses. Finally, things are rounded out by a graphics portfolio.

661 **The Kenyon Review.** n.s. 1979. q. $18 (Individuals, $15). Philip D. Church and Galbraith M. Crump. Kenyon College. Subs. to: P.O. Box 1308L, Fort Lee, NJ 07024. Illus. Adv. Index. Circ: 4,000. Refereed. Vol. ends: Fall. Microform: UMI. [*Bk. rev*: 3–4, 1,700–3,500 words, signed. *Aud*: Ages 14–18.]

Each issue is an equal mix of poetry (Louis Simpson, Brian Swann), fiction (Jack Matthews, Joyce Carol Oates), and two to three essays, for example, an unusual, nicely illustrated piece on Brueghel's *Children's Games* or the iconoclastic Paul Feyerabend on Xenophones. One issue contains Richard Kostelanetz's lengthy composite interview with John Cage. Reviewers include such well-known figures as Dave Smith, Jay Parini, and Carolyn G. Heilbrun.

Literary Calvacade. *See under* CLASSROOM PUBLICATIONS.

662 **The Paris Review.** 1953. q. $20. George A. Plimpton. Paris Review, Inc., 45-39 171 Pl., Flushing, NY 11358. Illus. Adv. Index. Circ: 10,000. Vol. ends: Winter. Microform: UMI. [*Indexed*: HumI, SocSc. *Aud*: Ages 14–18.]

Along with *Antioch Review*, this is suitable for the average young adult. It should be found in most school and public libraries. For 35 years, *The Paris Review* has been pleasing readers with poetry, fiction, features, art, and interviews of the famous. A recent issue is a 400-page blockbuster with prose (Pound, Stein, Gordimer), art (Stella, Neel), and poetry (49 contributors, virtually all of whom are of the highest caliber, e.g., Ginsberg, Milosz, Snyder). Yet another issue is equally impressive with all of the usual features and a special emphasis on poetry, with contributions from 21 poets. A consistently superior journal that belongs in virtually all collections.

663   **Parnassus: poetry in review.** 1973. s-a. $27 (Individuals, $17). Herbert Leibowitz. Parnassus, 41 Union Sq. W., Rm 804, New York, NY 10024. Illus. Adv. Index. Circ: 2,500. [*Aud*: Ages 14–18.]

Add this to *American Poetry Review*, and the average school or public library will have virtually complete coverage of the current poetry world. It is ideal for interested teenagers. While this title is issued twice a year, it is not unusual to have one number for an entire year (e.g., Spring/Summer/Fall/Winter 1985 is close to 700 pages and is dedicated to a "celebration of women and poetry"). Less ambitious semi-annual issues tend to concentrate on current poetry publications and may be one-half to one-third the size of the aforementioned individual volume. The essays and examples of poetry touch base with major critics and poets in the United States. In one issue alone there is material from Heln Vendler, Richard Wilbur, and Seamus Heaney (Irish, of course, but much in America).

664   **Salmagundi: a quarterly of the humanities and social sciences.** 1965. q. $16 (Individuals, $12). Robert Boyers. Skidmore College, Saratoga Springs, NY 12866. Illus. Adv. Index. Circ: 5,000. [*Bk. rev*: 4–8, 4–21 pages, signed. *Aud*: Ages 14–18.]

While this review is written primarily for academics and college graduates, the contents and the involvement with current issues make it suitable for school and public library collections with a particular interest in social issues and literature. *Salmagundi*, like most reviews, publishes fiction and poetry (Richard Howard, Seamus Heaney), but it specializes in the intellectual essay, frequently grouped according to a specific theme. Somehow the editor manages to solicit material from outstanding thinkers and writers, for example, George Steiner, Conor Cruise O'Brien, and Jose Donoso. One recent issue concentrates on the Spanish Civil War; another circles around Milan Kundera; here are two enlightening interviews with the novelist and essays by Terry Eagleton, Calvin Bedient, and others. One of the finest intellectual literary reviews published in America.

665   **Translation: the journal of literary translation.** 1974. s-a. $15. Ed. bd. Translation Center, 307A Mathematics Bldg., Columbia Univ., New York, NY 10027. Adv. [*Aud*: Ages 14–18.]

This is the only literary review that concentrates exclusively on translated works, including poetry, fiction, and essays. Issues can approach 400 pages in length and in one such blockbuster there is a section of Argentinian writing with contributions from Borges, Cortazar, Sábato, and many others. This is augmented by material by Vargas Llosa, Böll, Cardenal, Yevtushenko, Alberti, ad infinitum. Another number contains many translations from the Turkish. The only cavil one might note is that all of this is not presented bilingually. The emphasis here is obviously on the translated artifact as literature. For medium and larger collections and wherever comparative literature and translation are taught. Recommended.

666   **TriQuarterly.** 1964. 3/yr. $26 (Individuals, $18). Reginald Gibbons. Northwestern Univ., 2020 Ridge Ave., Evanston, IL 60208. Illus. Adv. Index. Circ: 5,000. Microform: UMI. Reprint: Kraus. [*Indexed*: HumI. *Bk. rev*: 11, 300–1,100 words, signed. *Aud*: Ages 14–18.]

The appeal to younger readers here is the energy this review imparts to all literature. It is about as lively as MTV at its best, and a trifle more literate. A typical issue of *TriQuarterly* can run 250 pages and feature eight pieces of fiction (Marie Luise Kaschnitz), poetry (Odysseus Elytis), a section of Polish poems, and much else. Many issues, however, are not typical. Consider the incredible 500-page number devoted entirely to new writing, photography, and art from South Africa. There is such a plethora of material that one is awestruck in admiration: Njabulo S. Ndebele, Nadine Gordimer, Mazisi Kunene, Dennis Brutus, J. M. Coetzee (two interviews), plus a chronology, bibliography, glossary, and map. Handsome, informative, and influential, *TriQuarterly* is quite simply the best general literary review published in the United States. No collection should be without it.

■ MATHEMATICS   [Gregg Sapp]

See also: SCIENCE

The literature of mathematics is prolific and extremely broad. The journals are highly specialized and few are for either the school or the public library. At the same time there are a handful of more or less general mathematical magazines—this side of those edited specifically for teachers—that can be found in libraries serving young adults. It is with these that this section is involved.

First choices   (1) *Mathematics Magazine*; (2) *Journal of Recreational Mathematics*.

667   **Chance: new directions for statistics and computing.** 1988. q. $55. William Eddy and Stephen Fienberg. Springer-Verlag, 175 Fifth Ave., New York, NY 10010. Illus. Adv. [*Aud*: Ages 14–18.]

Even the less than interested teenager is likely to find a mathematical problem in this excellent magazine that will appeal. *Chance* is the closest thing there is to a general-interest magazine covering mathematical concepts. The focus on statistics is broadly interpreted; in the debut issue, the editors state: "*Chance* is the magazine that you want to pick up if you want to read about what's happening in the world of statistics—about interesting applications, and about the latest methodological advance—in a form that is technically correct but without the mathematical mumbo jumbo." The large, glossy, colorful format adds to the journal's appeal. There is even a "Lighter Side" column.

668   **Fibonacci Quarterly: a journal devoted to the study of integers with special properties.** 1963. q. $25. G. E. Burgum. Fibonacci Assn., Univ. of Santa Clara, Santa Clara, CA 95053. Index. Circ: 900. Sample. Refereed. Vol. ends: No. 4. Microform: UMI. [*Aud*: Ages 14–18.]

This journal, written for college teachers and students, features articles that aim to "develop enthusiasm for number sequences or exploration of number facts" and is suitable for bright teenagers. Typically, articles describe, explore, and apply novel relationships among numbers. Material is contributed by teachers, students, researchers, and mathematically inclined laypeople. Readers also propose problems and offer solutions at both elementary and advanced levels. This unique journal works well in the classroom, but has a broader appeal to any readers who delight in numbers.

669   **Journal of Recreational Mathematics.** 1968. q. $55 (Individuals, $12.50). Joseph S. Madachy. Baywood Publg. Co., Inc., 120 Marine St., Farmingdale, NY 11735. Illus. Index. Sample. Refereed. [*Indexed*: GSI. *Bk. rev*: 3–6, 300 words, signed. *Aud*: Ages 14–18.]

It is difficult to find a mathematics magazine with wide appeal, but this may just do the trick for school and public libraries. Mathematical games, puzzles, and sundry brainteasers provide readers with equal portions of insight and frustration. This journal has a fanatical following and is appropriate for any general library collection. Solutions to the problems require more creativity than mathematical erudition; contributors come from all walks of life. Through its intriguing presentation of mathematical novelties, this journal provides a perfect antidote for math phobics and can intrigue those who complain that math is dull or irrelevant.

670 **Mathematical Intelligencer.** 1978. q. $39. Sheldon Axler. Springer-Verlag, 175 Fifth Ave., New York, NY 10010. Illus. Adv. Index. Microform: UMI. Reprint: ISI. [*Indexed*: GSI, MathR. *Bk. rev*: 3–4, 1,000 words, signed. *Aud*: Ages 14–18.]

A popular, entertaining, and informative magazine that will work well in high school and public library collections. Material is published on issues related to every aspect of mathematics; the writing style is relaxed and expository. There are opinions, narratives, illustrations, and numerous regular columns, including "The Mathematical Tourist," which describes landmarks and famous places related to the history of mathematics. Belongs with the *Journal of Recreational Mathematics* in a basic collection.

671 **Mathematical Log.** 1957. 4/yr. $2. H. Don Allen. Mu Alpha Theta, 601 Elm St., Rm. 423, Norman, OK 73019. Illus. Circ: 25,000. Sample. Microform: Pub. [*Aud*: Ages 14–18.]

Mu Alpha Theta, the National High School and Junior College Mathematics Club, supplies a good bit of educational and diversional material in its slim news organ. In addition to notes on meetings and chapters, it publishes short essays and problems contributed by educators and members, as well as occasional reprints from other publications. Discussions of educational and employment opportunities for students are included. Free copies are circulated to chapters of the society.

672 **Mathematics Magazine.** 1926. bi-m. (Sept–June). $11 Members ($28 Nonmembers). Gerald Alexanderson. Mathematical Assn. of America, 1529 18th St. N.W., Washington, DC 20036. Adv. Index. Circ: 8,000. Refereed. Vol. ends: No. 5. Microform: UMI. Reprint: UMI. [*Indexed*: GSI. *Aud*: Ages 14–18.]

A stylish, readable publication, *Mathematics Magazine* is interesting to students. The writing is clear and entertaining; the editors advise authors to "say something new in an appealing way or say something old in a refreshing way, but say it intelligibly, presuming a minimum of technical vocabulary." In accomplishing this objective, the magazine frequently publishes articles that relate mathematics to common, everyday events—from flipping coins to shuffling cards. The articles on the history of mathematics are exceptional. The "Reviews" section summarizes recent mathematical articles that have been published in popular and technical journals. This magazine is appropriate for larger high school and public libraries.

■ **MILITARY** [Jane L. Kellough and Joni Gomez]

The military as a career, or as a temporary stop on the way to becoming an adult, is of appeal to many teenagers of both sexes. The magazines annotated here are for those readers, as well as some who may wish to go into the reserve or simply are interested in the military and its history. Several types of titles are included. All are suitable for the average public or school library—and particularly those serving a military community or one where interest in the subject is high.

First choices (1) *Soldiers*; (2) *Naval History*; (3) *Air Force Magazine*.
Suitable for children Ages 8–12: *G.I. Joe*

673 **Air Force Magazine** (Formerly: *Air Force and Space Digest*). 1942. m. $21. John T. Correll. Air Force Assn., 1501 Lee Hwy., Arlington, VA 22209-1198. Illus. Adv. Circ: 234,928. Microform: UMI. Reprint: UMI. [*Bk. rev*: 2, 300 words, signed. *Aud*: Ages 14–18.]

Even teenagers who are not at all interested in military life will enjoy this view of the air from the point of view of the pilots and the personnel who keep the planes airborne. The style is easy to follow and the illustrations and makeup are particularly appealing. The eight to ten articles range from management problems to history, from career information to the role of government agencies in the development of policy. Edited for the professional Air Force person, as well as the industry connected with the Air Force, the magazine concentrates on material of interest to both, for example, data on retirement, pay scales, prominent figures, production, snags in a particular aircraft, and so forth. There are often special issues and sections devoted to international matters, such as the makeup of the Chinese or Soviet forces. While a bit specialized, its coverage is such that it will appeal to many students.

674 **Army Reserve Magazine** (Formerly: *Army Reservist*). 1954. q. Free. James M. Kroesen. U.S. Army Reserve, Office of the Chief, Washington, DC 20310. Illus. Index. Circ: 600,000. Vol. ends: No. 4. Microform: MIM. [*Aud*: Ages 14–18.]

Directed toward Army Reserve personnel not on active duty, this title includes updates of statutes affecting reservists and information about military extension courses devoted to the bicentennial of the Constitution. One issue included a winning essay submitted to the Army Reserve National Essay Contest, in which the author envisioned himself as one of the statesmen who came to Philadelphia in 1787 as a delegate to the Constitutional Convention. The majority of articles are devoted to happenings of reserve units. Public and academic libraries should acquire this and its related title, *Citizen Airman*.

Citizen Airman: official magazine of the Air National Guard and Air Force Reserve (Formerly: *Air Reservists*). 1954. bi-m. $5. Anthony J. Epifano. Supt. of Docs., Washington, DC 20402. Illus. Circ: 400,000. Vol. ends: Dec (No. 6). Microform: MIM [*Aud*: 14–18.]

G.I. Joe. *See under* COMICS.

675 **Leatherneck: Marines magazine.** 1917. m. $10. William White. Marine Corps Assn., P.O. Box 1775, Quantico, VA 22134. Illus. Adv. Index. Circ: 75,000. Sample. Vol. ends: Dec. Microform: UMI. [*Bk. rev*: 2, 300–750 words, signed. *Aud*: Ages 14–18.]

Except for the inclusion of advertising and book reviews, *Leatherneck* follows a format similar to titles published by other branches of the U.S. military. All are intended primarily for active-duty personnel, especially those in the lower enlisted ranks. At the same time they have a given appeal to young adults who may be considering this or that service. They inform readers about pertinent developments and benefits and are designed to inspire pride in the service, with *Leatherneck* being the best example. The articles, averaging nine per issue, are amply illustrated but not documented. Each issue usually contains at least one essay with a historical emphasis on subjects such as Marine aviators in World War I and World War II. Present-day interests are not ignored, especially in pieces on select military installations or naval ships. Special features include cartoons, "Gyrene Gyngles," and rosters of retiring Marines.

Leatherneck and other service magazines have a useful purpose beyond serving active-duty personnel. They provide the public, especially young people who are considering military service, with an insider's view of the armed forces. Depending on the interests of the user population, high school and public libraries may wish to acquire *Leatherneck* in addition to the titles noted below.

Airman: official magazine of the U.S. Air Force. 1955. m. $29. A.L. Batezel. Air Force Service Information and News Center, Kelly Air Force Base, TX 78241. Subs. to: Supt. of Docs., Washington, DC 20402. Illus. [*Aud:* Ages 14–18.]

All Hands: magazine of the United States Navy. 1923. m. $13. W.W. Reid, Navy Internal Relations Activity, Rm. 1046, 1300 Wilson Blvd., Arlington, VA 22209. Subs. to: Supt. of Docs., Washington, DC 20402. Illus. Index. Sample. Vol. ends: Dec. Microform: UMI. [*Aud:* Ages 14–18.]

676   Naval History. 1987. q. $24. Paul Stilwell. U.S. Naval Inst., Annapolis, MD 21402. Illus. Index. Sample. [*Bk. rev:* Various number and length, signed. *Aud:* Ages 14–18.]

This is published by a private press, and is not a government publication. In fact, the press is well known for many best-sellers and has a fine reputation. This magazine is up to other productions of the publisher. It is well illustrated and accurate, and the four to five historical articles reflect the best in naval history. Contributors are both professional historians and those who took part in a naval engagement or development. The illustrations are quite striking and the whole is written for the layperson as well as the academic and the high school student who may have an interest in the navy. It is one of the few military journals that deserve a wider audience than just military personnel.

677   Soldiers (Formerly: *Army Digest*). 1946. m. $17. Donald P. Maple. Soldiers, Cameron Sta., Alexandria, VA 22304-5050. Subs. to: Supt. of Docs., Washington, DC 20402. Illus. Index. Circ: 215,000. Vol. ends: Dec. Microform: MIM, UMI. Reprint: UMI. [*Indexed:* PAIS. *Aud:* Ages 14–18.]

Action is the key, and this title has wide appeal in public and school libraries. The official publication of the U.S. Army, its purpose is to provde timely, factual information on policies, plans, operations, and technical developments of the Army and other information on topics of interest to active and nonactive personnel. *Soldiers* offers personal glimpses of happenings within units, a focus on people, and articles on topics in U.S. military history.

■ MODELS

[Frederick A. Schlipf]

See also: HOBBIES

The magazines in this section cover the whole spectrum of model building and appreciation. All are suitable for teenagers as well as children who are able to read or follow the instructions. (Parents can help, and that is why all of the magazines here are recommended for both age groups.)

Anyone involved with this subject is referred to the compiler's introduction to the section and subsections in the sixth edition of *Magazines for Libraries*, pp. 781–796, which provides extensive detail and background that will be of help to the enthusiast. Many more magazines are listed and annotated there.

First choices   Select as needed. No first choices.

Suitable for children   Ages 8–18: All titles, at least where a parent is willing to help the child with the reading matter and instructions in some of the more advanced works.

678   **FineScale Modeler.** 1982. 8/yr. $17.95. Bob Hayden. Kalmbach Publg. Co., 1027 N. Seventh St., Milwaukee, WI 53233. Illus. Adv. Index. Circ: 77,748. Sample. Vol. ends: Dec. [*Bk. rev*: 12–20, 50–200 words. *Aud*: Ages 14–18.]

FineScale Modeler is the most important magazine on the general construction of static models. Its primary concern is with plastic models, although it also deals with cast metal military miniatures. The basic types of models covered include military equipment, soldiers, dioramas, automobiles and other road vehicles, airplanes, and ships. Most of the articles are construction articles, combining specific projects with pointers on model-building techniques. Most plastic modelers do a great deal of kit modifying and combining ("kit bashing") to arrive at models of specific prototypes or of equipment for which no kits are available, and many of the construction articles in *FineScale Modeler* are concerned with this type of work.

679   **Flying Models** (Incorporates *Flying Aces* and *R/C Model Boating*). 1929. m. $21. Robin W. Hunt. Carstens Publns., P.O. Box 700, Newton, NJ 07860-0700. Illus. Adv. Circ: 30,000. Sample. Vol. ends: Dec. [*Aud*: Ages 14–18.]

Flying Models is the oldest of all U.S. flying model magazines and one of the oldest model-making magazines in the world. Although it is not as thick as some of the flying model magazines, it has more editorial material each month than some of them do. Along with *Model Aviation*, it still devotes space to traditional free-flight and control-line models. Contents include the usual columns, construction articles, product reviews, and meetings reports, but there is a substantial number of more general articles as well. *Flying Models* is the only flying model magazine that devotes a major section each month to articles on r/c model boats, and it should therefore be a good choice for libraries that wish to cover r/c model boats without subscribing to a specialized publication.

680   **Live Steam.** 1966. m. $27. Joe D. Rice. Live Steam, Inc., P.O. Box 629, Traverse City, MI 49684. Illus. Adv. Index. Circ: 12,500. Sample. Vol. ends: Dec. Microform: UMI. [*Bk. rev*: Occasional. *Aud*: Ages 14–18.]

Live Steam is the major U.S. magazine in its subject area. It includes articles on the construction of a variety of live-steam equipment, with primary emphasis placed on steam locomotives and stationary steam engines. It also includes articles on construction techniques, on specific types of fittings, on the activities of associations and hobbyists (including schedules of forthcoming meetings), and occasionally on prototype equipment. Most of the information is of a highly specialized, technical nature. Most articles are illustrated with large numbers of excellent technical drawings, and drawings for large pieces of equipment often appear as foldouts.

681   **Military Modelling.** 1970. m. $34. Ken Jones. Argus Specialist Publns., P.O. Box 35, Wolsey House, Wolsey Rd., Hemel Hempstead, Herts. HP2 4SS, England. Subs. to: Joseph J. Daileda, 4314 W. 238th St., Torrance, CA 90505. Illus. Adv. Index. Sample. Vol. ends: Dec. [*Bk. rev*: 5–7, 100–500 words, signed. *Aud*: Ages 14–18.]

Military Modelling is published by Argus Specialist Publications, a British firm that publishes about ten model-building magazines. This title covers the entire field, but places particular emphasis on prototype information on historic military uniforms, with excellent color paintings and extremely detailed text. It also includes articles on military history, military armor and vehicles, outstanding figures and dioramas by hobbyists, model techniques, new commercial products, and hobby shows, contests, and other activities. A fair amount of attention is paid to war gaming, but the main thrust of the magazine is prototype military costume and its reproduction in high-quality scale miniatures. Although the emphasis is on British uniforms, coverage is definitely worldwide.

682 **Model Airplane News.** 1929. m. $25. Rich Uravitch. Air Age, Inc., P.O. Box 428, Mount Morris, IL 61054. Illus. Adv. Circ: 110,000. Sample. Vol. ends: Dec. [*Aud*: Ages 14–18.]

Model Airplane News is the second oldest U.S. flying model magazine and one of the most popular. As in the other magazines in this area, much of the editorial content consists of construction articles and regular monthly features on various specialties. It places particular emphasis on new commercial products, with both announcements and detailed test reviews. Its special-theme issues on such topics as, for example, model helicopters are impressive. *Model Airplane News* has gone through numerous changes in recent years. It has dropped its coverage of free-flight and control-line models to concentrate on r/c, and it has been completely restyled, with much more elaborate graphics than the average model magazine.

683 **Model Aviation.** 1975. m. $13.50 (Schools, $9; Individuals, $18). Carl R. Wheeley. The Academy of Model Aeronautics, 1810 Samuel Morse Dr., Reston, VA 22090. Illus. Adv. Index. Circ: 120,000. Vol. ends: Dec. [*Aud*: Ages 14–18.]

Model Aviation is the official organ of the Academy of Model Aeronautics (AMA). With 132,000 members, the AMA is probably the largest association of model builders in the world—although its huge membership is due in part to provision of liability insurance for its members and to the political necessity of having a strong group to secure the necessary radio bandwidths. Compared with other flying model magazines, *Model Aviation* tends to be straightforward and businesslike and even more structured, with a large number of monthly columns providing virtually complete coverage of all the various specialized areas of flying models. It also includes monthly reports from national and regional officers, organizational business, and a calendar of forthcoming "sanctioned" events that can run up to 15 pages of fine print. It provides extensive coverage of contests and competitions.

684 **Model Railroader.** 1934. m. $25. Russell G. Larson. Kalmbach Publg. Co., 1027 N. Seventh St., Milwaukee, WI 53233. Illus. Adv. Index. Circ: 181,683. Sample. Vol. ends: Dec. [*Bk. rev*: 0–8, 100–400 words, signed. *Aud*: Ages 14–18.]

Model Railroader is the dominant magazine in model railroading, with a circulation nearly twice that of any other model railroad magazine. It covers virtually the entire spectrum of model railroad activities, including the construction of model locomotives, cars, and buildings; layout design, construction, and wiring; prototype information; and features on contests, meetings, outstanding individual models and layouts, and leading personalities and companies in the field. It also includes extensive schedules of forthcoming events, and its classified ad section is by far the largest in the model railroad field. Coverage in such areas as live steam and European model trains is very limited. Although some material aimed at beginners is included, many of *Model Railroader*'s articles tend to be of the state-of-the-art variety, and this sometimes puts off people who are looking for simple projects. Photographs are crisp and finely printed—many in color.

685   Nutshell News. 1970. m. $29. Sybil Harp. Kalmbach Publg. Co., 1027 N. Seventh St., Milwaukee, WI 53233. Illus. Adv. Index. Circ: 28,000. Sample. Vol. ends: Dec. [*Bk. rev:* 2–3, 100–300 words. *Aud:* Ages 14–18.]

The digest-sized *Nutshell News* is the leading magazine on dollhouse miniatures. It emphasizes the work of both professional miniaturists and individual hobbyists. The typical issue contains columns on new miniatures, new kits, collectible miniatures, and forthcoming shows, and about 15 articles more or less evenly divided among the work of commercial miniature makers, the work and collections of individual hobbyists, and construction projects. Articles on shows and exhibits are also included. *Nutshell News* is well edited with a sprightly writing style. The quality of the photographs is high, but the drawings that accompany construction articles are sometimes a little crude. Large numbers of ads for commercial miniaturists and miniature shops are included.

686   R/C Modeler. 1963. m. $24. Patricia Crews. R/C Modeler Corp., P.O. Box 487, Sierra Madre, CA 91024. Illus. Adv. Index. Circ: 203,000. Sample. Vol. ends: Dec. [*Bk. rev:* 3–5, 250–400 words, signed. *Aud:* Ages 14–18.]

With a circulation of 203,000, *R/C Modeler* is the most popular of all model airplane magazines, and it may be the most widely sold of all model-making magazines. It is about 75 percent thicker than any other flying model magazine because of the huge volume of advertising it carries. This advertising has made *R/C Modeler* the standard hobby source for commercial information, and some modelers refer to it as the "catalog." The general belief is that many hobbyists buy it specifically for its advertisements from manufacturers and for its multipage sales lists from mail-order houses. The editorial contents of *R/C Modeler* are fairly typical. About a dozen columns or standard features appear each month; the rest of the magazine consists primarily of construction articles, in-depth product reviews, reports on events, and a few general articles. Radio-control boats and cars are covered briefly.

687   Radio Control Car Action. 1985. m. $25. Chris Chianelli. Air Age, Inc., P.O. Box 427, Mount Morris, IL 61054. Illus. Adv. Circ: 193,000. Sample. Vol. ends: Dec. [*Aud:* Ages 14–18.]

Radio Control Car Action is a colorful publication with professional graphics. It has a commercial flavor, with a large number of ads and product reviews, and with references to commercial product sources in most articles. Its articles include kit reviews and evaluations, kit assembly and customizing, troubleshooting, installation of aftermarket parts, race results, and so forth.

688   Railroad Model Craftsman (Formerly: *Model Craftsman*). 1933. m. $23. William C. Schaumburg. Carstens Publns., P.O. Box 700, Newton, NJ 07860. Illus. Adv. Index. Circ: 95,000. Sample. Vol. ends: May. [*Bk. rev:* Occasional. *Aud:* Ages 14–18.]

Railroad Model Craftsman is *Model Railroader's* major competitor and an excellent magazine. It stands strongly in second place among U.S. general-purpose model railroad magazines. Like *Model Railroader*, it covers virtually all aspects of model railroading, including construction of model locomotives, railroad cars, and suitable trackside buildings; design, construction, and wiring of layouts; prototype detail; product and book reviews; and conventions, contests, and other hobby activities. Because of their very similar scope and intentions, it is hard to draw firm comparisons between the two magazines. *Craftsman*'s articles are sometimes a little more down-to-earth and suited to the skills of the ordinary modeler. It devotes a little less space to electronics.

689   Railway Modeller. 1949. m. £22.50. John Brewer. Peco Publns. and Publicity, Ltd., Beer Seaton, Devon EX12 3NA, England. Illus. Adv. Index. Circ: 71,762. Sample. Vol. ends: Dec. [*Bk. rev*: 0–7, 100–500 words. *Aud*: Ages 14–18.]

Railway Modeller is Britain's leading model railroad magazine. It is published by Peco, which is also a manufacturer of model railroad products, particularly track. Like *Model Railroader* and *Railroad Model Craftsman* in the United States, *Railway Modeller* covers a general range of model railroad subjects, but it places relatively less emphasis on operation and electrical systems and more on finished layouts. In large part this reflects the British tradition of model railroading, which tends to be one of elegant, uncluttered layouts with careful attention to accurate historical detail and large numbers of scratch-built structures.

690   Scale Auto Enthusiast. 1979. bi-m. $15. Gary Schmidt. Highland Productions, 5918 W. North Ave., Milwaukee, WI 53208. Illus. Adv. Circ: 35,000. Sample. Vol. ends: Mar/Apr. [*Aud*: Ages 14–18.]

Scale Auto Enthusiast is the leading American publication devoted to static models of automobiles. Most of its articles are concerned with scale modeling and include kit reviews and articles on kit construction, superdetailing, modification, and painting. Most of the concern is with injection-molded styrene kits, but articles and reviews also deal with low-volume production kits in metal and resin, and with aftermarket detailing and conversion parts. Other articles deal with prototype information, general construction methods, and contest results. Monthly columns cover new diecast models, model trucks, and model fire equipment. The magazine's classified ad section is large, with many listings from modelers seeking specific kits or kit parts. The quality of photographs, editing, drawings, and layout is generally high.

691   Ships in Scale. 1983. bi-m. $18. Scottie Dayton. Model Expo Publns., 353 Richard Mine Rd., Wharton, NJ 07885. Illus. Adv. Index. Circ: 17,000. Sample. [*Bk. rev*: 1–9, 150–600 words. *Aud*: Ages 14–18.]

Ships in Scale is concerned with the construction of large, historically accurate models of both sailing and steam-powered ships. It covers both kit assembly and scratch-building, and places the heaviest emphasis on sailing ships but also covers a variety of steam-powered military and commercial vessels. Articles include kit reviews, detailed kit assembly instructions, scratch-building projects, maritime history, shop techniques, methods of modeling special details, and so forth. Like other ship-building magazines, it tends to have long articles that continue for many issues, sometimes for more than two years. *Ships in Scale* is wide in scope, including articles on plastic kit construction and on radio control. It devotes much attention to the assembly and improvement of difficult kits, as opposed to straight scratch-building. This approach probably reflects the needs of the majority of modelers.

692   **Train Collectors Quarterly.** 1955. q. $12. Bruce D. Manson, Jr. Train Collectors Assn., P.O. Box 248, Strasburg, PA 17579. Illus. Adv. Circ: 20,000. Sample. Vol. ends: Oct. [*Bk. rev*: Occasional, signed. *Aud*: Ages 14–18.]

The *Train Collectors Quarterly* is the official journal of the Train Collectors Association (TCA) and the outstanding journal in its field. The TCA is the largest of the four major toy train collectors' associations in the United States and has about 19,500 members. Toy train collectors are primarily interested in mass-produced toys rather than hand-crafted scale models, and they try to collect them in the original condition in which they left the factory. Although many train collectors have operating layouts, their central interest is accumulating and preserving the toys themselves, and they shudder at the thought of modifying factory-built equipment in any way. Articles in the *Train Collectors Quarterly* reflect this kind of specific interest in toys. Most of the articles are detailed studies of the history, current operations, and products of companies such as Lionel, American Flyer, Ives, and Marx, with primary emphasis paced on U.S. firms. Other articles cover association activities and the layouts and collections of various members. Also of interest to collectors are:

Classic Toy Trains. 1987. q. $14.95. Dick Christianson, Kalmbach Publg. Co., 1027 N. Seventh St., Milwaukee, WI 53233. Illus. Adv. Circ: 40,000. Sample. Vol. ends: Winter. [*Aud*: Ages 14–18.]

Garden Railways. 1984. bi-m. $18. Marc Horovitz. Sidestreet Bannerworks, P.O. Box 61461, Denver, CO 80206. Illus. Adv. Vol. ends: Nov/Dec. [*Aud*: Ages 14–18.]

S Gaugian. 1962. bi-m. $22. Donald J. Heimburger. Heimburger House Publg. Co., 310 Lathrop Ave., River Forest, IL 605305. Illus. Adv. Circ: 3,200. Vol. ends: Nov/Dec. [*Bk. rev*: 8–10, 200–500 words. *Aud*: Ages 14–18.]

■ **MUSIC AND DANCE**   [Music: Honora Raphael and Frank Hoffman. Dance: Mary Augusta Rosenfeld]

See also: Fᴀɴ Mᴀɢᴀᴢɪɴᴇs

The two large areas of music and dance are treated here as one, although they are arranged in two units. Often inseparable, they are closely associated and interest in both is high among children and young adults. There are great numbers of music magazines, if not dance titles; choices have to be made as much in terms of audiences as in areas covered. A balance is attempted among the classical, the popular, and the advanced. Some titles are listed that assist the student (and the librarian and teacher) to select the best recordings.

First choices   Music: (1) *Rolling Stone*; (2) *Stereo Review*; (3) *Circus*; (4) *CD Review Digest*.
Dance: (1) *Dance Magazine*.

Suitable for children   Ages 6–14: *On Key*. Ages 8–18: *Blast*; *Circus*. Ages 10–18: *American Square Dance*; *Dance Magazine*; *Guitar Player*; *Rolling Stone*; *Song Hits*.

Music/Classical

693   **Computer Music Journal.** 1977. q. $68 (Individuals, $33). Stephen Pope. The MIT Press, Journals Dept., 55 Hayward St., Cambridge, MA 02142. Illus. Adv. Index. Circ:

3,725. Vol. ends: Winter. Microform: UMI. Reprint: UMI. [*Bk. rev*: 4, 1,000 words, signed. *Aud*: Ages 14–18.]

This title is for the teenager who is more involved with computers than music, or has an interest in both. Even those of us who fear (after reading contemporary theoretical writings about music) that musicology is becoming a dry branch of numerology will take heart from this publication, which is humanistic. Its editor and contributors are aware that the transfer of science to music is not a simple one. The editorials and articles reflect that awareness.

694   Flute Talk. 1981. 10/yr. $13. Kathleen Goll-Wilson. Instrumentalist Publg. Co., 200 Northfield Rd., Northfield, IL 60093. Illus. Adv. Circ: 13,000. Sample. [*Aud*: Ages 14–18.]

Very specialized, this polished 35-page magazine is intended for high school flutists. The color cover prominently features an accomplished flutist. Technical advice from judges and principal flutists appears periodically. Regular features include new music reviews, classifieds, concert schedules of flutists on tour, and musical scores for flutes.

695   Guitar Player: for professional and amateur guitarists. 1967. m. $23.95. Tom Wheeler. GPI Corp., 20085 Stevens Creek, Cupertino, CA 95014. Illus. Adv. Index. Circ: 162,800. Sample. Microform: UMI. Reprint: UMI. [*Indexed*: MI. *Bk. rev*: 4–6, 50 words, signed. *Aud*: Ages 10–18.]

This is among the more popular magazines found in school and public libraries. All aspects of the guitar are treated here: tips to improve playing technique, the evaluation of guitar hardware and related equipment, and biographies of notable practitioners. The journal's contributors and board of advisers read like a who's who of exponents of the instrument. As with its GPI stablemate, *Keyboard*, a basic grounding in music notation and the technical properties of sound equipment is presumed on the part of the reader.

696   Keyboard: for all keyboard players (Formerly: *Contemporary Keyboard*). 1975. m. $23.95. Dominic Milano. GPI Publns., 20085 Stevens Creek, Cupertino, CA 95014. Illus. Adv. Index. Circ: 64,350. Microform: UMI. Reprint: UMI. [*Bk. rev*: 1–2, 500 words, signed. *Aud*: Ages 14–18.]

This journal cuts across stylistic boundaries in focusing on outstanding proponents of the various keyboard instruments, including electronic synthesizers. Particular attention is given to matters of technique; performers at all levels will find the information provided here of value. Treatment and format (attractive layouts including an abundance of photos) mirror GPI's other mass circulation entry, *Guitar Player*.

697   Latin American Music Review/Revista música latino americana. 1980. s-a. $26 (Individuals, $16). Gerard Béhague. Univ. of Texas Press, Journals Dept., P.O. Box 7819, Austin, TX 78713. Illus. Adv. Circ: 450. Vol. ends: Fall/Winter. Microform: MIM, UMI. [*Bk. rev*: 3, 2,000 words, signed. *Aud*: Ages 14–18.]

This superlative magazine deserves to be widely read. It chronicles the legacy of musical inter-Americanism through its scholarly articles, short studies, reviews (of books, sound recordings, films), and news items, written in English, Spanish, and occasionally Portuguese. Its scope is interdisciplinary: anthropology, sociology, musicology, ethnomusicology, urban studies, and history. Articles appear on diverse topics, for example, childbirth rituals of the Arawakan Wakeúnai, the history of Tex-Mex working-class music, Brazil's art music, an entire issue honoring music scholar Gilbert Chase. Highly recommended for all medium- to large-size public and school libraries.

698   **Musical America: the journal of classical music** (Formerly: *High Fidelity/Musical America*; Incorporating *Opus*). 1898. bi-m. $26. Shirley Fleming. ABC Consumer Magazines, 825 Seventh Ave., New York, NY 10019. Subs. to: P.O. Box 10759, Des Moines, IA 50340. Illus. Adv. Circ: 20,000. Vol. ends: Jan. Microform: B&H, MIM, UMI. Reprint: UMI. [*Bk. rev*: 6, 230 words, signed. *Aud*: Ages 14–18.]

This is a basic title for most serious music collections and should be found in many school and public libraries. Coverage of live performances (opera and dance), articles about classical music personalities, dozens of classical sound recording reviews, features about music education in America, an "art and technology" column, and short, perceptive book reviews are found in each 96-page issue. It is glossy, but not bland, and the writing can be acerbic— although always concerned with boosting classical music in this country.

On Key. *See under* CHILDREN/MUSIC AND DANCE.

699   **Opera.** 1950. m. (plus mid-Oct. "Festival" issue). $55. Rodney Milnes. Opera, DSB, 14/16 The Broadway, Wickford, Essex SS11 7AA, England. Illus. Adv. Index. Circ: 15,000. Microform: UMI. Reprint: UMI. [*Indexed*: HumI. *Bk. rev*: 4, 700 words, signed. *Aud*: Ages 14–18.]

Among opera lovers of all ages this is considered the leading journal— followed, of course, by its American counterpart. It should be in all school and public libraries with an interest in music. Staggering in its critical coverage of worldwide operas, operettas, musicals, and vocal performances (even "fringe" and school productions), it also features scholarly and sprightly articles on a wide range of opera-related topics, some of them nonmusical—for example, suicide in opera and opera collectibles. Although half of its readership is American, and the journal does have a most welcome (especially for a British music journal) pro-American bias, understandably its emphasis is on matters English and European. Should an American librarian have to choose between *Opera* and *Opera News* (see below in this section), though, the latter is to be preferred.

700   **Opera News.** 1936. m. (May–Nov.). bi-w. (Dec.–Apr.). $30. Patrick J. Smith. Metropolitan Opera Guild, Inc., 1865 Broadway, New York, NY 10023. Illus. Adv. Circ: 120,000. Vol. ends: May. Microform: B&H, UMI. Reprint: UMI. [*Indexed*: BoRvI, HumI. *Bk. rev*: 2, 400 words, signed. *Aud*: Ages 14–18.]

The leading U.S. journal devoted to opera began and functioned for years as the voice of the Metropolitan Opera Guild, focusing on the weekly Metropolitan radio broadcasts. There is a complete story of the current opera with information on the lead singers, as well as background data on theater sets, lighting, and so on. While the emphasis is on the Met's productions, articles and features cover opera in other parts of the nation and the world. Allied arts are considered, too. Still, its real value for most high school students is the focus on the Saturday broadcasts of the world's operas.

701   **The Piano Quarterly.** 1952. q. $16. Robert Joseph Silverman. The Piano Quarterly, Inc., P.O. Box 815, Wilmington, VT 05363. Illus. Adv. Index. Circ: 13,000. Vol. ends: Winter. Microform: UMI. [*Bk. rev*: 1, 600 words, signed. *Aud*: Ages 14–18.]

A delightful, informative magazine for both professional and amateur pianists and teachers; a winning blend of authoritativeness and readability. One-third of each typically 65-page issue is new music reviews. The review system is unique—by semi-anonymous committee members who report on every possible aspect of the music, including pianistic demands, age suitability, musical quality, and comparison with other editions. The first page of each score reviewed is, furthermore, reprinted in reduced size. Articles, interviews (with jazz as well as classical performers), musical analyses, job listings, and (eloquent) obituaries fill out each issue. *PG* cannot be praised enough; school and medium- to large-size public libraries, pounce.

702 **The Strad.** 1890. m. $50. Eric Wen. Novello & Co., Ltd., Borough Green, Sevenoaks, Kent TN15 8DT, England. Illus. Adv. Circ: 9,500. Vol. ends: Apr. Microform: UMI. Reprint: UMI. [*Aud*: Ages 14–18.]

Any serious young person with an interest in string instruments will turn here first. Knowledgeable, impassioned writing characterizes this 100-year-old magazine, the most famous in the string world. Every library with a music collection should subscribe. In addition to lengthy interviews, reminiscences, and articles, pungent reviews and short but meticulously detailed evaluations of authoritative performing editions of music appear each month. Sound recordings and, lately, videos are also reviewed. The monthly list of orchestral vacancies (many of them in the United States) is important.

Music/Popular

703 **Billboard: the international newsweekly of music and home entertainment.** 1894. w. $178. Ken Schlager. Billboard Publns., Inc., One Astor Plaza, 1515 Broadway, New York, NY 10036. Illus. Adv. Circ: 45,490. Vol. ends: Dec. Microform: B&H, Kraus, UMI. Online: DIALOG. Reprint: UMI. [*Indexed*: BusI. *Aud*: Ages 14–18.]

Referred to as the *New York Times* of the music industry by record company executive Clive Davis. All aspects of the business are well served by this trade tabloid. Articles generally take the form of compact news updates on legal matters, commercial trends, new technologies, concert itineraries, and so forth; however, specific issues often focus on one particular topic (country music, the 12-inch single) or artist. The charts—an indispensable facet of the magazine—cover every commercially viable music genre (mainstream pop, country, black contemporary, jazz, inspirational, Latin, easy listening) and audiovisual format (video software, compact discs, videotape, laser discs). Media reviews function to hype industry products.

Blast. *See under* CHILDREN/MUSIC AND DANCE.

Circus. *See under* CHILDREN/MUSIC AND DANCE.

704 **Cymbiosis.** 1987. q. $39.98. Ric Levine. Cymbiosis, Inc., 6201 Sunset Blvd., Suite 80, Hollywood, CA 90028. Illus. Adv. Circ: 15,000. Sample. [*Aud*: Ages 14–18.]

Listening and reading are combined in a 60-minute music cassette and a printed 50-page magazine that focus on rock and jazz. Each of the six musicians and composers on the tape is given a two- to three-page illustrated article. In addition to interviews, there are reviews of recent recorded music, discussions of modern rock and jazz, and a regular column on a variety of musical subjects. Writers and those interviewed view music as a serious experience and art, not as a commercial rip-off. It is refreshing and original. The sound is excellent. An ideal purchase for any type of library.

705   Dirty Linen. 1989. 3/yr. $15. Paul Hartman. Dirty Linen, P.O. Box 66600, Baltimore, MD 21239. Illus. Adv. Circ: 1,500. [*Aud:* Ages 14–18.]

Who can reject a magazine called *Dirty Linen*? To turn thumbs down on 80 illustrated pages churning with information on "folk, folk rock and traditional music" is downright un-American. Inside one can find an interview with Jerry Donahue, who plays a mean electric guitar; "recalling the pleasures of Amnesia"; record reviews; personality sketches; news of concerts; and above all a wild sense of dedication matched only by good humor and intelligence. Coverage is international, although most interest is in American rockers. Albert F. Riess (known to his friends as Al) is a contributing editor and reference librarian at SUNY College, Buffalo.

706   Down Beat: for contemporary musicians. 1934. m. $21. John Ephland. Maher Publns., 180 W. Park Ave., Elmhurst, IL 60126. Illus. Adv. Index. Circ: 88,253. Vol. ends: Dec. Microform: UMI. Reprint: UMI. [*Indexed:* MI. *Aud:* Ages 14–18.]

This magazine has forged a successfully broad-based formula that merges a popular journalistic style with impeccable standards of research. While a background in music composition and notation is not necessary, the articles presume a basic knowledge of jazz history and musicians. All periods and styles of jazz are covered from ragtime and Dixieland to recent jazz-pop-rock fusions. A lengthy record review section (25–35, approximately 500–1,000 words) and a "blindfold" identification column featuring celebrity guests commenting on their peers' releases are included. A must acquisition for school and public libraries.

707   Faces Rocks. 1983. m. $21. Lorena Alexander. Faces Magazines, Inc., 63 Grand Ave., Suite 230, River Edge, NJ 07661. Illus. Adv. Circ: 100,000. Vol. ends: Feb. [*Aud:* Ages 14–18.]

A mass-market fanzine geared to the teen market. Despite various lightweight departments (e.g., "Pick A Pen Pal," in which fans' addresses are listed under their respective fave artists), the coverage tends to be more intelligent than that of its primary competitors. It exhibits a pronounced heavy-metal/hard rock bias punctuated by occasional thrash-rock (hard-core) features. The abundance of rich color photos within a glossy stock format enhances the magazine's appeal to youth. An exhaustive review section (records, 40–50, 250 words; video, 4, 50–300 words) includes a spotlighted artist retrospective in each issue.

708   Hit Parader. 1954. m. $29.50. Andy Secher. Charlton Publns., Inc., Charlton Bldg., Derby, CT 06418. Illus. Adv. Circ: 157,970. Vol. ends: Dec. [*Bk. rev:* Occasional. *Aud:* Ages 14–18.]

Until the late sixties, this magazine stood alone in providing an intelligent overview of rock music for teen consumption. In the eighties, it chose to concentrate its coverage on heavy-metal acts. The articles and interviews comprising the bulk of each issue remain highly informative; they avoid the flippancy and condescending tone typifying the contents of many publications in this field. Much valued for its age-old practice of including the lyrics to currently popular recordings.

Note: Devoted as it is to heavy metal, the magazine sometimes uses verbatim remarks from the stars that include four-letter words.

709   Living Blues: a journal of the black American blues tradition. 1970. bi-m. $18. Peter Lee. Center for the Study of Southern Culture, Univ. of Mississippi, University, MS

38677. Illus. Adv. Index. Circ: 6,000. Vol. ends: Nov/Dec. Microform: UMI. [*Bk. rev:* Occasional. *Aud:* Ages 14–18.]

Differing from the antiquarian emphasis of most publications devoted to the genre, *Living Blues* seeks to delineate the capacity of the blues for continued growth and development. Features—divided between contemporary profiles and retrospectives of seminal artists—are supplemented by news of blues societies, festivals, and concert itineraries as well as listings of recent acquisitions by the Center for the Study of Southern Culture. Record reviews are lengthy and authoritative (50–60, 300–1,200 words).

710   Musician (Formerly: *Musician, Player and Listener; Music America*). 1976. m. $21. Jock Baird. Amordian Press, Inc., P.O. Box 701, 33 Commercial St., Gloucester, MA 01930. Illus. Adv. Circ: 115,000. Microform: UMI. Reprint: UMI. [*Aud:* Ages 14–18.]

While geared to the aspiring musician, this journal avoids a reliance on confusing technical jargon and an exhaustive reservoir of knowledge in order to challenge its reader. The perceptive analysis of all popular music forms and electronic equipment is comparable to that in *Rolling Stone*, sans the counterculture posturing and various show business distractions. Additional pluses: authoritative record reviews (12–20, 100–600 words) and lavish layouts equalled only by the best mass-market fanzines.

711   Rock & Roll Disc. 1987. m. $24. Tom Graves. TAG Enterprises, P.O. Box 17601, Memphis, TN 38137. Illus. Adv. Sample. [*Aud:* Ages 14–18.]

Concentrating solely on CD recordings and rock-and-roll stars, this 25-page tabloid is the kind of magazine teens and not a few older music fans love. One issue offers a page-long review, "The Frank Sinatra Story in Music," followed by a rare interview with Mick Taylor. The "feature review" is "The Allman Brothers Dreams," followed by the 250- to 500-word reviews of individual recordings. There are from 40 to 60 of these, and they seem to cover all current CD releases. "Sounding off" features two critics with different viewpoints talking about individual new discs—each with a thumbs up or thumbs down rating. Other features touch on jazz, collecting CDs, and so forth. The reviews are as critical as they are descriptive, and ideal for the librarian who may be lost when MTV and rock and roll pierce the quiet of the library. Experts will enjoy the sometimes less than popular points of evaluation. While CDs are covered in standard popular music magazines, this one concentrates only on this form. A good buy where needed.

712   Rolling Stone. 1967. bi-w. (m. July & Dec.). $23.95. Jann S. Wenner. Straight Arrow Pubs., Inc., 745 Fifth Ave., New York, NY 10151. Illus. Adv. Circ: 1,058,027. Microform: B&H, MCA. [*Indexed:* BoRvI, MI. *Bk. rev:* Occasional, 1–2 pages, signed. *Aud:* Ages 10–18.]

This is by far the most popular and best known of the music magazines directed specifically to an audience that enjoys MTV and all its features. Here, though, the writing is superior and the contents are often as good as any found in newsmagazines of a wider scope. Features—also concerned with social, political, and popular culture topics—and reviews are generally lengthy and include insightful commentary, albeit with a pronounced left-of-center bias. The latter include recordings (6–12, 1–3 pages) and video and audiovisual hardware. In recent years the magazine has adopted an upscale look (flashy graphics, high-fashion ads, show-biz gossip) in order to retain its original readership, many of whom comprise the "yuppie" stratum of American society. The one truly required acquisition in the pop music sector for all libraries.

Song Hits. *See under* CHILDREN/MUSIC AND DANCE.

713 **Spin.** 1985. m. $20. Scott Cohen. Spin Publg., Inc., 6 W. 18th St., New York, NY 10011-4608. Illus. Adv. Circ: 150,000. Vol. ends: Mar. [*Aud*: Ages 14–18.]

Seeks to emulate the stylishness and intelligent coverage (of politics, society, and the arts as well as music) exemplified by *Rolling Stone.* It succeeds admirably with respect to the latter; the format, punctuated by lush illustrations and striking graphic design, is without peer in the popular music field. The text, however, excels only when addressing musical subjects; alternative styles such as new wave and avant-garde are particularly well covered.

Dance

714 **American Square Dance** (Formerly: *Square Dance*). 1945. m. $12. Stan Burdick and Cathie Burdick. Burdick Enterprises, P.O. Box 488, Huron, OH 44839. Illus. Adv. Index. Circ: 24,000. Vol. ends: Dec. Microform: UMI. [*Bk. rev*: 250 words, signed. *Aud*: Ages 10–18.]

Students will find much to learn about and enjoy in this small-format magazine. Each month the editors present short articles on all aspects of square and round dancing including new or revised steps, tips on calling, dance etiquette, and moral support. Taking a chatty, positive tone, they report nationwide news from clubs, classes, and special events, filling out close to 100 pages with photographs and drawings. In 50 years of growing interest in square dancing, this publication has continued to emphasize the social and community benefits while keeping up with current trends. A calendar of events, nationwide, is included in each issue.

715 **Ballet Review.** 1965. q. $38 (Individuals, $19). Francis Mason. Dance Research Foundation, Inc., 150 Claremont Ave., Suite 2C, New York, NY 10027. Illus. Circ: 3,100. Vol. ends: Winter. Microform: UMI. [*Bk. rev*: Occasional, signed. *Aud*: Ages 14–18.]

This journal has a clear, readable though scholarly tone and includes both photographs and drawings to support the opinions presented. Leading ballet historians and critics contribute six or seven long articles on dance history and choreography, biographical features on important dancers, and reports on company performances. The in-depth coverage given to a ballet company's work or to the development of a particular ballet is necessary to any student of either the history or performance of dance.

716 **Country Dance and Song** (Formerly: *Country Dancer*). 1968. a. Membership $25. David Sloane. Country Dance Soc., Inc., 17 New South St., Northampton, MA 01060-4012. Illus. Circ: 2,000. Sample. Microform: UMI. Reprint: UMI. [*Aud*: Ages 14–18.]

This is an excellent small-format annual that contains articles on the history and performance of country dancing and regional traditions. The research presents the history, steps, and music of each dance. Many communities are holding historic reenactments as part of cultural preservation, and this is the type of information that is difficult to find and will be used. Since the history and context of country dance in the United States and abroad are presented, *Country Dance and Song* is suitable for the public or school library collection on dance or regional culture. Essays are usually supported by drawings, diagrams, and photographs.

Dance Exercise Today. *See I D E A Today.*

717 **Dance in Canada.** 1973. q. $15 Can. (Individuals, $10 Can.). Michael Grabb. Dance in Canada Assn., 38 Charles St. E., Toronto, Ont. M4Y 1T1, Canada. Illus. Adv. Index. Circ: 3,000. Sample. Microform: MML. [*Indexed*: CanI. *Bk. rev*: 1–2, 500 words, signed. *Aud*: Ages 14–18.]

Billed as Canada's only national dance magazine. Features include interviews; reviews of performances, books, films, videos, and records; and current news about the Canadian dance community. This is a lively, professionally designed four-color publication that discusses all types of dance from ballet to tap dance and musicals, but the emphasis remains on current performance and choreography for Canadian companies. Review sections look at U.S. companies and European performances as well. This title is written now entirely in English. Regular features on health and nutrition for practicing dancers and news briefs benefit the dance community. Since Canadian companies are now performing frequently in the United States, large public and school libraries will want to make this journal available for dance audiences.

718 **Dance Magazine.** 1926. m. $24.95. Richard Philp. Dance Magazine, Inc., 33 W. 60th St., New York, NY 10023. Illus. Adv. Index. Circ: 50,000. Vol. ends: Dec. Microform: B&H, UMI. Reprint: UMI. [*Indexed*: BoRvI, HumI, RG. *Bk. rev*: 2–3, 250–500 words, signed. *Aud*: Ages 10–18.]

Dance Magazine is the one journal that any public or school library collection must include in order to provide information on current dance performance and education in the United States. As the oldest continuously published dance periodical in the country, it attracts leading dance writers from all over the world and is the first magazine consulted by professionals. Because of its painstaking coverage of ballet, modern, and Broadway styles throughout the country, it is required reading for the professional dancer and teacher. It is also the best general source for the dance viewer as a guide to good performance. In addition to that of Herbert Migdoll, the best-known dance photographer, as designer, the work of most major dance photographers is represented and future scholars will be able to analyze much from their work. Each issue carries a schools directory for the entire nation, a monthly performance calendar, and news and class notes.

719 **Dancing Times.** 1910. m. $25. Mary Clarke. The Dancing Times, Ltd., Clerkenwell House, 45-47 Clerkenwell Green, London EC1R 0BE, England. Illus. Adv. Circ: 12,000. [*Bk. rev*: 1–2, 250 words, signed. *Aud*: Ages 14–18.]

While the main interest of this journal is dance in Britain, as the oldest continuing periodical on dance, it has much to offer U.S. audiences. Britain is still a major center for dance performance with a growing audience for modern dance, which is becoming recognized in *Dancing Times*. The in-depth reviews of the Royal Ballet and Sadler's Wells continue along with notes from all the schools and competitions, awards news, and discussions of dance education. Features include sections on health, on dance on television, which is well established in Britain, and more international dance. While the design suffers somewhat from comparison with glossier American publications, there is much here for the high school student of dance history, theory, and criticism.

720   **I D E A Today** (Formerly: *Dance Exercise Today*). 1984. 10/yr. Membership $48. Patricia Ryan. Intl. Dance Exercise Assn., Inc., 6190 Cornerstone Court E., San Diego, CA 92121. Illus. Adv. Index. Circ: 17,000. Sample. [*Aud*: Ages 14–18.]

The 72 pages of extensive advertisements and numerous illustrations are directed to fitness instructors and business operators. The four to five articles (teen workouts, stress stoppers, etc.) cover exercise and instructional techniques. Regular features are concerned with diet, aerobic and strength conditioning, injuries, and related matters. Authors are experienced instructors and academics. All ages are considered, but primary emphasis is on the teenage-to-30 group. Popular rather than classical dance is stressed. Most important, the primary focus is on dance as exercise, not dance per se. A reliable, useful title for any public or school library with an interest in the area.

Recording Reviews

All of these reviews include material suitable for children as well as young adults and adults, so the audience designation is deleted in this part.

721   **American Record Guide** (Formerly: *American Music Lover*; *Listener's Record Guide*). 1935. bi-m. $26 (Individuals, $20.50). Donald R. Vroom. Record Guide Productions, 4412 Braddock St., Cincinnati, OH 45204. Illus. Adv. Circ: 6,000. [*Indexed*: Acs.]

The primary value of this review service is that it compares new recordings with older versions and makes no bones about saying which is best or better. The reviews are current and well written, and cover classical recordings. This has been a standard guide for many years and is one of the best review services available. It will be of great use not only to librarians, but to laypeople looking for sound advice.

722   **The CD Review Digest.** 1987. q. $35. Janet Grimes. Peri Press, Hemlock Ridge, P.O. Box 348, Voorheesville, NY 12186.

This is the basic guide to CD reviews, and follows much the same pattern as the more familiar *Book Review Digest*. The service is in two parts. The classical 150 or so pages is in a large format, as is the separate jazz and popular music 100-page entry. (One may subscribe to both, or to the classical for $25 and the jazz and popular for $10.) The recordings are listed alphabetically under the composer's name and for each record there usually are one to three excerpts from reviews. Normally this is enough to make a decision, but, of course, full bibliographical data are given for those who wish to read the full notice. Reviews are from over 30 basic journals. Highly recommended for any library of any size or type that has readers involved with CD recordings.

723   **Fanfare: the magazine for serious record collectors.** 1977. bi-m. $27. Joel Flegler. Fanfare, Inc., P.O. Box 720, Tenafly, NJ 07670. Illus. Adv. Circ: 20,000. [*Bk. rev*: 3, 600 words, signed.]

Hundreds of superb comparative reviews of new sound recordings in each hefty issue, written by reviewers who pay attention not only to the recordings' musical and sonic qualities, but also to the packaging and liner notes. This daunting amount (one issue has 24 J. S. Bach and 37 Mozart entries) of critical commentary is, actually, fun to read. The writing is somewhat cantankerous and irreverent ("I must admit to a desire to use this CD as a coaster"), but above all enthusiastic and informed. Classical music is the focus, but recorded jazz, pop, and film music are also reviewed intelligently. Articles, interviews, and a few book reviews round out each issue.

724 **Opus** (Formerly: *Schwann*). 1989. q. $20. Richard Blackham. Schwann, 535 Boylston St., Boston, MA 02116. Adv. Circ: 55,000. Vol. ends: Fall. Microform: UMI.

The "Books in Print" of the classical music industry, this has been published since the late 1940s under various names. Many still call it simply *Schwann*, after the publisher. Compact discs now make up the majority of entries, although there are listings for cassette tapes and LPs. The entries are arranged primarily under the name of the composer. The last 75-or-so pages are divided into sections: collections, musicals, new age, and CD-videos. The addresses and price schedules of record labels assist in making it a key ordering tool for individuals and libraries. One caveat: The catalog is not an entirely accurate gauge of what is available at either the wholesale or retail levels.

Artist, the annual issue, arranges the entries by pianists, singers, orchestras, and so on.

Spectrum is a quarterly from the same publisher at the same price, which covers popular music from rock to jazz in a similar fashion as *Opus*.

Schwann. *See* **Opus.**

725 **Stereo Review** (Formerly: *Hi Fi Stereo Review*). 1958. m. $11.97. Louise Boundas. Diamandis Communications, Inc., 1633 Broadway, New York, NY 10019. Illus. Adv. Index. Circ: 557,640. Microform: B&H, MIM, UMI. Online: DIALOG. [*Indexed*: MI, RG. *Aud*: Ages 14–18.]

This has the twofold advantage for the younger reader of offering authoritative advice on both recordings and equipment. Reviews are written so they are easy to follow and one has no doubt as to the stand of the reviewer. The audio and video equipment news and reviews—which comprise the bulk of the publication —features (artist and composer profiles, stock listings, timely topics such as the DAT controversy), and reviews of sound recordings will assist anyone in the selection process.

■ **NEWS AND OPINION**

See also: GENERAL INTEREST; NEWSPAPERS

There are more suitable young adult magazines in the area of news and opinion than in any other section this side of general interest. These are all adult titles, although so familiar to younger readers that they are considered basic to library collections. Many are found on newsstands and even in the home. They are first sources for term papers and talks as well as for general background information on the world. Here one finds all points of view from the conservative to the radical, although particular emphasis is on the middle-of-the-road magazines.

First choices (1) *Newsweek*; (2) *Time*; (3) *The Nation*; (4) *U.S. News and World Report*; (5) *The MacNeil/Lehrer Report*.

Suitable for children None of these really is suitable for children, although *Time* and *Newsweek* might be considered, if only because they are found in so many homes.

726 **The American Spectator.** 1924. m. $30. R. Emmett Tyrell, Jr. American Spectator, P.O. Box 10448, Arlington, VA 22210. Circ: 33,000. Microform: UMI. [*Indexed*: MI, PAIS. *Bk. rev*: 7–10, essays, signed. *Aud*: Ages 14–18.]

While liberals claim that the conservative voice is heard in all popular news-magazines, the true conservative normally is limited to a few titles such as this and *National Review*. Both offer the young person a good introduction to the faith. In fact, this tabloid is one of the most thoughtful and well written of conservative publications. Articles are written by intellectual conservatives who are well placed in government and the national media. Articles are more than simply critical of liberal persons and policies and often propose concrete alternatives to deal with difficult situations. It is distinguished by a particularly incisive and witty editorial style. Regular features include editorials, excellent book and film reviews, a review of current events in Washington, and "Current Wisdom" —a page of quotations culled from more liberal writers.

727 **Commentary: journal of significant thought and opinion on contemporary issues.** 1945. m. $36. Norman Podhoretz. Amer. Jewish Committee, 165 E. 56th St., New York, NY 10022. Adv. Index. Circ: 45,000. Sample. Microform: B&H, ISI, MIM, UMI. Reprint: UMI. [*Indexed*: HumI, PAIS, RG. *Bk. rev*: 5–8, 1,000–2,500 words, signed. *Aud*: Ages 14–18.]

The vitriolic side of the conservative argument is presented to young adults in this highly controversial magazine. This journal covers national and international cultural and political affairs from a moderate-to-conservative point of view. Published by the American Jewish Committee, *Commentary* aims "to enlighten and clarify public opinion on problems of Jewish concern, to fight bigotry, and protect human rights, and to promote Jewish cultural interest and creative achievement in America." The majority of articles, however, deal with issues and events of general political and cultural interest. The book reviews are excellent and *Commentary* frequently contains short fictional works as well as essays.

728 **Current: the new thinking from all sources on the frontier problems of today.** 1960. m. $35 (Individuals, $20). Jerome J. Hanus. Helen Dwight Reid Educational Foundation, 4000 Albermarle St. N.W., Washington, DC 20016. Illus. Index. Circ: 6,000. Sample. Vol. ends: Dec. Microform: UMI. [*Indexed*: CIJE, RG. *Aud*: Ages 14–18.]

This may be one of the dullest of the new magazines, but it seems to have made its way into *Readers' Guide*. The flat presentation probably is due to an effort to be objective. It reprints, without comment, reports from other magazines, plus some book, television, and radio reviews. The effort to be politically objective is evident by the balance, but there is more here than politics. It includes material from the sciences and the humanities as well. As a type of *Reader's Digest* it is a success, although much more intelligent and certainly more objective and honest.

729 **Editorial Research Reports.** 1923. w. $519. Marcus Rosenbaum. Congressional Quarterly, 141 22nd St. N.W., Washington, DC 20037. Index. Circ: 2,500. Vol. ends: Dec. Microform: B&H, MIM, UMI. [*Indexed*: PAIS. *Aud*: Ages 14–18.]

Students seeking background material for talks or written reports would do well to start here. These weekly reports are primarily a reference aid, and rarely found on the periodical rack. Still, the 5,000 to 6,000 summaries of activities (from politics and science to art and the social sciences) are the best of their kind. They are objective in that both sides of an argument are presented, and they end with up-do-date reading lists. Each number shows the content of issues over the past 15 months or so. There is an excellent annual index. As a type of expanded "facts on file" this can be recommended highly for almost all types and sizes of libraries.

730   **Human Events.** 1944. w. $35. Thomas S. Winter. Human Events, Inc., 422 First St. S.E., Washington, DC 20003. Illus. Adv. Index. Circ: 50,000. Vol. ends: Dec. Microform: UMI. Reprint: UMI. [*Indexed*: BoRvI. *Aud*: Ages 14–18.]

Another conservative voice for young people, this was at one time, and may be still, Ronald Reagan's favorite reading matter. "In reporting the news *Human Events* is objective; it aims for accurate presentation of the facts. But it is not impartial. It looks at events through eyes that favor limited constitutional government, local self-government, private enterprise and individual freedom." This monthly tabloid generally stays close to the self-descriptive quote above. *Human Events* includes features such as congressional roll call vote counts on bills of interest to conservatives and 500- to 1,000-word essays on current political and cultural events.

731   **The MacNeil/Lehrer Report.** 1979. q. $135. Microfilming Corp. of America, 200 Park Ave., New York, NY 10166. Vol. ends: Dec. [*Aud*: Ages 14–18.]

Few would deny, no matter what their political persuasion, that the best television news is given by MacNeil/Lehrer on public broadcasting. The magazine is certainly a departure point for any thoughtful student. The *Report* is a summary of the daily programs but, unfortunately, published only quarterly. At the same time, it represents some of the best journalism in the United States today, and libraries that can afford it should consider it. For the money one gets abstracts of each of the broadcasts, which appear five days a week on public television stations across the United States. It is cumulated annually and provision is made for the purchase of transcripts of individual programs.

732   **The Nation.** 1865. w. $40. Victor Navasky. Nation Assocs., Inc., 72 Fifth Ave., New York, NY 10011. Subs. to: P.O. Box 1953, Marion, OH 43305. Illus. Adv. Index. Circ: 85,000. Vol. ends: June/Dec. Microform: UMI. [*Indexed*: BoRvI, PAIS, RG. *Bk. rev*: 3–7, 1,400 words, signed. *Aud*: Ages 14–18.]

If only one liberal magazine is in the school or public library, *Nation* should be that title. Liberal to the Left: first, foremost, and always. That is the policy of the distinguished editor, who has given the journal new life with a series of investigative reports that often make headlines. The articles range from the Nicaraguan debate to abortion to Israel and the politics of Washington, D.C. It is partisan, yet witty and extremely intelligent. Some of the best stylists in journalism are regular columnists in the arts and entertainment sections, for example, Alexander Cockburn, Christopher Hitchens, Jefferson Morley, and Andrew Kopkind. The editorials are superior in both content and style. This is a required magazine for almost all types and sizes of libraries.

733   **National Review: a journal of fact and opinion.** 1955. fortn. $39. William F. Buckley. Natl. Review, Inc., 150 E. 35th St., New York, NY 10016. Illus. Adv. Index. Circ: 110,000. Sample. Microform: B&H, MIM, UMI. Online: DIALOG. Reprint: UMI. [*Indexed*: MI, RG. *Bk. rev*: 3–8, 1,000–2,000 words, signed. *Aud*: Ages 14–18.]

This is the premier conservative journal. William F. Buckley has created a magazine that serves as the model for all popular conservative publications. Each issue has one feature article and several shorter articles on topics of current political, social, and cultural interest. There are excellent reviews of books, films, records, art exhibits, and other cultural events, and monthly editorials by the waspish and witty Buckley. In addition to good layout and graphics, each issue includes cartoons and a crossword/acrostic type puzzle. The indispensable voice of American conservatism.

734 **New Leader: a biweekly of news and opinion.** 1927. bi-w. $28. Myron Kolatch. Amer. Labor Conference on Intl. Affairs, Inc., 275 Seventh Ave., New York, NY 10001. Illus. Adv. Index. Circ: 25,000. Vol. ends: Dec. Microform: UMI. [*Indexed*: PAIS, RG. *Bk. rev*: 3–4, 1,100 words, signed. *Aud*: Ages 14–18.]

A liberal voice, this is close to the traditional literary review in that there is considerable focus on literature and the arts as well as on politics and government. Actually the strength does lie in the "back of the book," where the bi-weekly critics show stronger style and wit than that found in the news section. At one time this was considered a basic title and while it remains a useful reference source, it is hardly exciting reading.

735 **The New Republic.** 1914. w. $56. Ed. bd. New Republic, Inc., 1220 19th St. N.W., Washington, DC 20036. Illus. Adv. Index. Circ: 95,000. Vol. ends: July & Dec. Microform: B&H, UMI. [*Indexed*: BoRv, RG. *Bk. rev*: 7, 700–2,000 words, signed. *Aud*: Ages 14–18.]

Under a relatively new ownership, the one-time voice of the Left is now much further to the Center and Right. If it was hard to tell it from its cousin *The Nation*, that is no longer true. Still, the reporting remains excellent and this title can be recommended to any thoughtful teenager. It has lively criticism not only of the current political and economic scene, but of films, books, and other media. Some of the writers are the best in the business, and since there is now a more balanced view of the passing scene, this can be recommended to readers of all political persuasions. Charles Krauthammer is a conservative regular, as is Martin Peretz and Morton Kondracke—all of whom frequently appear on television talk shows. The editor, Michael Kinsley, represents the liberal point of view, although his is more a middle-of-the-road approach than found in, say, *The Nation*. This journal is sure to irritate either the far Left or far Right and probably those in between. Still, there is enough common sense here to justify it as a basic title in any type or size library.

736 **The New Statesman and Society.** 1913. w. $90. Stuart Weir. Statesman and Nation Publg. Co., Foundation House, Perseverance, 38 Kingsland Rd., London E28DQ, England. Illus. Adv. Index. Circ: 39,874. Vol. ends: June & Dec. Microform: UMI. [*Bk. rev*: 8–15, 1,000 words, signed. *Aud*: Ages 14–18.]

Young readers can discover in this magazine what English liberals think about the United States and the world—and learn the delights of good writing style. As the voice of the liberal wing of the Labour party the weekly lost, as did the party, much of its following after 1980. Critics claim there was too much attention to radical ideas and not enough to content. This was particularly true of the first half, where the news appears, though not so much of the second half, with its excellent book, film, and theater reviews. These remain independent of the politics of the front part and some of the best anywhere. With the merger of the two magazines (*New Statesman* and *New Society*) in 1988, the book section, always a strong point in *New Society*, is even better. Fresh themes are now found in the news sections as well, and the magazine seems to enter the 1990s with a sparkling spirit.

737   **New York Times Biographical Service.** 1969. m. $110. Univ. Microfilms Intl., 300 N. Zeeb Rd., Ann Arbor, MI 48910. Index. [*Indexed*: MI. *Aud*: Ages 14–18.]

Here one finds all of the biographical material published as part of the daily and Sunday *New York Times*, that is, the profiles, full articles, and related material. Often the articles are illustrated. None of the copy is reedited, and as sometimes the monthly service is several months behind, the data may not be all that current. At the same time, the information tends to be relatively objective and accurate. As a single source of information about people in the news—both here and abroad—it is hard to beat. (One can find the same material by consulting the newspaper's indexes, but this is much more difficult and often produces extraneous information.)

738   **Newsweek.** 1933. w. $39. Richard M. Smith. Newsweek, Inc., 444 Madison Ave., New York, NY 10022. Illus. Adv. Index. Circ: 3,000,000. Vol. ends: June. Microform: B&H, MCA, UMI. [*Indexed*: MI, RG. *Bk. rev*: 2–5, 500–1,300 words, signed. *Aud*: Ages 14–18.]

The first choice for high school and public libraries serving teenagers, this is so well known as hardly to need an introduction here. The "catch" is that, like *Time*, it presupposes a college-educated audience, and may be a trifle difficult for some teens. This rival of *Time* is so much like the other that sometimes it is hard to tell them apart—even the covers often "cover" the same event or personality. *Newsweek* differs from and is preferred to *Time* because of the overall editorial policy. It is somewhat more liberal, and its social consciousness is visible. Also, the regular columnists offer a better balance than those in *Time*. Jane Bryant Quinn, for example, is an excellent financial adviser, particularly for the average reader. George Will, one of the more intelligent voices of conservative policy, alternates with Meg Greenfield as a commentator. The cultural critics are superior. If a reader wants this kind of summary of the week's news, *Newsweek* is a much better package than *Time*.

739   **Our Generation.** 1961. q. $25 (Individuals, $7.50). Ed. bd. Our Generation, 3981 blvd. Saint-Laurent, Montreal, P.Q. H2W 1Y5, Canada. Illus. Adv. Index. Circ: 8,500. Sample. Vol. ends: Summer. Microform: UMI. [*Indexed*: API, CanI. *Bk. rev*: 3–5, 2,200 words, signed. *Aud*: Ages 14–18.]

One of Canada's leading journals of dissent, this is an independent, liberal approach to politics and social issues. While essentially a socialist voice, it is a moderate one and is more involved with people than with any single position. While some of the material may appear a trifle idealistic, it is grounded in the day-to-day political realities of Canada. (From time to time other parts of the world are considered, such as Central America, but for the most part the focus is on Canadian interests.) The material is normally well documented, and there are short "think pieces" and features. The detailed book reviews offer good overviews of Canadian titles.

740   **The Progressive.** 1909. $50 (Individuals, $30). Erwin Knoll. The Progressive, Inc., 409 E. Main St., Madison, WI 53703. Illus. Adv. Index. Circ: 50,000. Sample. Vol. ends: Dec. Microform: B&H, UMI. [*Indexed*: API, PAIS, RG. *Bk. rev*: 7–9, 300–800 words, signed. *Aud*: Ages 14–18.]

One of America's oldest liberal political journals, this is truly progressive, but it no longer represents a given party or position. Rather, it is involved with a wide spectrum of issues. The primary focus is on civil rights, corruption in government, the arms race, and nuclear and environmental issues. There are numerous features and departments and brilliant cartoons. There are many "names" in each issue, from Nat Hentoff to some of the leading writers for the national newspapers and other magazines. *The Progressive* over the years has won numerous journalism awards, and is a substantial item in almost any library collection. Note, too, that it is indexed in *Readers' Guide* and has a much above average circulation for this type of journal.

741 **Public Citizen** (Incorporating *Congress Watcher*). 1976. bi-m. $20. Ana Radelai. Public Citizen Foundation, 2000 P St. N.W., Suite 610, Washington, DC 20036. Illus. Adv. Circ: 70,000. Sample. Vol. ends: Dec. [*Indexed*: API. *Aud*: Ages 14–18.]

Any young person looking for a hero may find one in Ralph Nader. This is his voice as well as the voice of the group he represents. The title describes the purpose, that is, to monitor major federal legislation and the action or inaction of the individual congresspeople. The 12- to 16-page newsletter is inexpensive and relatively objective, although the sponsor has a particular interest in consumer and tax issues. Close watch is kept on records and the budget, and this is one of the best places to turn for a fairly easy explanation of where the money goes.

742 **Public Interest.** 1965. q. $18. Irving Kristol and Nathan Glazer. Natl. Affairs, Inc., 1112 16th St. N.W., Suite 545, Washington, DC 20036. Circ: 11,000. Sample. Microform: UMI. Reprint: ISI, UMI. [*Indexed*: PAIS, SocSc. *Bk. rev*: 1–3, 1,500–3,000 words, signed. *Aud*: Ages 14–18.]

While this conservative journal is somewhat more pedestrian than its fellows, it does have a point of view that may interest young adults. Also, the editors are often quoted in the news. Featuring articles on domestic American culture and society, *Public Interest* is edited by Irving Kristol, the publisher of *National Interest*. These journals share a scholarly, moderately conservative orientation. Missing the wit and fire of publications like the *National Review*, *Public Interest* instead provides considered, in-depth treatment of issues not possible in more popular journals.

Scholastic Update. *See under* CLASSROOM PUBLICATIONS.

743 **Tikkun.** 1986. bi-m. $25. Inst. for Labor and Mental Health, 5100 Leona St., Oakland, CA 94619. Illus. Adv. Index. Sample. [*Aud*: Ages 14–18.]

Described as the liberal alternative to *Commentary*. The 124-page issues generally follow the format of the rival *Commentary*. There are some seven or eight articles, about one-third devoted to Jewish concerns, the others to wider interests from psychology and social theory to politics and the women's movement. Fiction and a dozen long and short reviews round out the number. The writing is hard hitting. Drawing from the meaning of the title (to mend, repair, and transform the world), the magazine also suggests how to solve current national and international problems.

744 **Time.** 1923. w. $58. Time, Inc., Rockefeller Center, 1271 Ave. of the Americas, New York, NY 10028-1393. Illus. Adv. Index. Circ: 4,469,000. Vol. ends: June. Microform: B&H, MIM, UMI. [*Indexed*: BibI, MI, RG. *Bk. rev*: 2–11, 200–800 words, signed. *Aud*: Ages 14–18.]

Time is too well known to require a descriptive annotation. Needless to say, it reports the past week's activities from the point of view of a conservative, middle-of-the-road American, and the "back part" (from business and sports to books and theater) is often better written and edited than the speculative news stories. The chief rivals are *Newsweek* and *U.S. News and World Report*.

Neither, as good as they are, comes close to *Time* in terms of overall circulation and advertisement pages. The question is how long all these will last given the development of specialized-viewpoint newsmagazines and, most important, 24-hour news on cable television. In the case of *Time*, it will be no great loss.

745 **U.S. News and World Report.** 1933. w. $41. Mortimer B. Zuckerman. U.S. News and World Report, Inc., 599 Lexington Ave, New York, NY 10022. Illus. Adv. Index. Circ: 2,375,000. Sample. Vol. ends: June. Microform: B&H, MCA, MIM, UMI. [*Indexed*: PAIS, RG. *Aud*: Ages 14–18.]

Over the past few years this weekly has rapidly caught up with *Time* and *Newsweek* as a newsmagazine. It is no longer a business journal. While the tone remains somewhat conservative, *U.S. News* is not above telling it straight, even to the point of departing from the editorial viewpoint. It has gained a reputation for extreme reliability and, in certain areas from economics to good living, an equal reputation for objectivity. The editor-at-large, David Gergen, is a frequent guest on the MacNeil-Lehrer television program, and a particularly astute commentator with a practical point of view. This shows in the magazine, which grounds itself in pragmatic stories such as the annual "America's Best Colleges." There are graphs and charts covering every element of life in the back part of each issue. While not strong on foreign affairs, the writers and editors are great observers of the Washington and national scene. An excellent choice for all libraries.

746 **U.S.A. Today.** 1915. m. $24.95. Stanley Lehrer. Soc. for the Advancement of Education, 99 W. Hawthorne Ave., Valley Stream, NY 11580. Illus. Adv. Index. Circ: 235,000. Sample. [*Indexed*: CIJE, RG. *Bk. rev*: 2–5, 300–500 words, signed. *Aud*: Ages 14–18.]

Not to be confused with the newspaper of the same name (1982 to date, daily), this is a monthly news journal with wide appeal because of its relatively objective approach to national and world activities. It follows the *Time/Newsweek/U.S. News and World Report* format (although it is not so obviously commercial) and puts considerable emphasis on education. That is understandable, as much of the material is written by teachers. The first half or so includes basic articles on the political and social scene, while the rest includes reviews of the arts, science, and so forth. It is widely indexed, but is not often found in libraries—possibly because it is a rare item on newsstands. It is a good, solid title making an earnest effort to educate rather than entertain readers.

747 **Vital Speeches of the Day.** 1934. bi-m. $30. Thomas F. Daly III. City News Publg. Co., P.O. Box 1247, Mt. Pleasant, SC 29464. Index. Circ: 18,000. Vol. ends: Oct. Microform: UMI. [*Indexed*: RG. *Aud*: Ages 14–18.]

Possibly known as much for its drab format as for its content, this is a standard item in many libraries—one suspects more because it is in *Readers' Guide* than because of outstanding quality. It reprints 8 to 12 speeches by public officials, which is to say anyone in public life, not just in government. It is relatively inexpensive, middle-of-the-road to conservative in its choices, and quite unexceptional.

748 **The Washington Monthly.** 1969. m. $33 (Individuals, $24). Charles Peters. The Washington Monthly Co., 1711 Connecticut Ave. N.W., Washington, DC 20009. Illus.

Adv. Circ: 30,000. Sample. Vol. ends: Feb. Microform: B&H, UMI. [*Indexed*: BoRv, PAIS, RG, SocSc. *Bk. rev*: 1, 1,800 words, signed. *Aud*: Ages 14–18.]

Welcome to the single best magazine of opinion and news in America today—at least if your point of view is liberal. This pocket-size journal is a nice mixture of the best features of a good journalism review and the hard-hitting liberal magazine that is deeply concerned with the country's political patterns. It will take on anyone and anything, but always with wit, style, and an ability to document each and every statement, no matter how outrageous it may seem to the establishment under attack. For this reason it is deeply loved by its readers. It is one of the few newsmagazines indexed in *Readers' Guide* that deserves that place.

749 **World Press Review: news and views from around the world** (Formerly: *Atlas: World Press Review; Atlas*). 1961. m. $24.95. R. Edward Jackson. The Stanley Foundation, 230 Park Ave., New York, NY 10169. Subs. to: P.O. Box 915, Farmingdale, NY 11737. Illus. Adv. Circ: 86,000. Vol. ends: Dec. Microform: B&H, UMI. Reprint: B&H, UMI. [*Indexed*: MI, PAIS, RG, SocSc. *Bk. rev*: 1–2, 1,000 words, signed. *Aud*: Ages 14–18.]

World Press Review reprints and excerpts feature stories from foreign newspapers and magazines, many of which are English-language publications. One cover story is reported from the viewpoint of various leading periodicals or newspapers. Additional features on politics, modern living, and business are reprinted from important publications such as *The London Observer* or *Veja* (from Sao Paulo). This is a useful publicaton for high school and public libraries since it reports foreign news more fully than many other U.S. periodicals and provides foreign perspectives on U.S. events not readily available elsewhere.

■ NEWSPAPERS   [Richard D. Irving]

See also: NEWS AND OPINION

Every school and public library will, at a minimum, subscribe to the local newspaper. In addition, many will include the leading state and/or regional paper. Beyond that almost as many libraries will wish to subscribe to the closest thing we have to a national newspaper, the *New York Times*. The somewhat diminished *Christian Science Monitor* is another good paper, as is the *Washington Post*. A few school libraries and the majority of public libraries will have a subscription to the *Wall Street Journal* as well. Few may be able to afford the "master" index to these, *Newspaper Index*, but the *New York Times Index* should be in larger libraries.

First choices   (1) Local and regional newspapers; (2) *New York Times*.

750 **The Afro-American: national edition.** 1892. w. $26. Penny Demps. Afro-American Co. of Baltimore, Inc., 628 N. Eutaw St., Baltimore, MD 21201. Illus. Adv. Circ: 6,000. Microform: UMI. [*Aud*: Ages 14–18.]

The *Afro-American* publishes several local editions as well as the weekly national issue. The national issue emphasizes national stories of particular interest to black Americans. It frequently provides coverage of stories that are either ignored or given minimal coverage by the national daily newspapers. The editorial page is moderate in tone and provides diverse points of view, although a black perspective clearly predominates.

751   **Atlanta Constitution.** 1868. d. $107.64. Bill Kovach. Atlanta Newspapers, 72 Marietta
St. N.W., Atlanta, GA 30303. Illus. Adv. Circ: 265,262 (d); 646,094 (S). Microform: UMI.
Online: DIALOG. [*Indexed*: Atlanta Constitution and Journal Index. *Aud*: Ages 14–18.]

Founded during reconstruction and brought into prominence by editor Ralph
McGill, the *Atlanta Constitution* has a reputation as a politically progressive
newspaper. In 1950 it merged with the *Atlanta Journal*, which is its evening
sister paper. They maintain separate editorial staffs although they publish joint
Saturday and Sunday editions and during the week many stories in the *Journal*
are taken directly from the *Constitution*. Neither the *Constitution*, "For 119
Years, the South's Standard Newspaper," nor the *Journal*, "Covers Dixie Like
the Dew," comes close to living up to its slogan. They are quality newspapers but
their reporting on the South as a region is spotty at best. They maintain a
Washington bureau and provide adequate coverage of national politics as well as
some reporting on Latin America.

752   **Christian Science Monitor.** 1908. d. (exc. Sat., Sun., & holidays). $144. Earl W. Foell
and Katherine W. Fanning. The Christian Science Publg. Soc., One Norway St., Boston,
MA 02115. Illus. Circ: 165,000. Microform: UMI. Online: BRS, DIALOG, Nexis. [*In-dexed*: Christian Science Monitor Index, National Newspaper Index. *Aud*: Ages 14–18.]

The *Christian Science Monitor* is a "hard news" national newspaper. It covers
but does not dwell on the frill subjects so prevalent in the other major daily
newspapers and its main rival, *USA Today*. It also does not provide the in-depth
coverage or analysis found in the *New York Times*, *Washington Post*, and so
forth. However, for those wanting their news straight up the *Monitor* provides
excellent concise coverage by a first-rate staff of reporters. Its coverage of
international affairs is particularly noteworthy; the editorial page is not. The
religious views of the publisher, the First Church of Christ, are kept out of the
news reporting. There is a weekly world edition.

753   **Manchester Guardian Weekly.** 1919. w. $58. John Perkins. Guardian Newspapers,
Ltd., 20 E. 53rd St., New York, NY 10022. Circ: 25,000. Microform: UMI. Online: Nexis.
[*Indexed*: Guardian Index. *Aud*: Ages 16–18.]

A concise weekly including selected articles from the *Guardian*, *Le Monde* (in
English), and the *Washington Post*, as well as original articles. The primary
focus is on international news. Cheaper than the daily, it offers an alternative for
libraries that do not require daily reporting of European affairs or the in-depth
coverage found in the *Sunday Times*.

754   **New York Times.** 1851. d. $185. Max Frankel. The New York Times Co., 229 W. 43rd
St., New York, NY 10036. Illus. Adv. Circ: 1,078,443 (d); 1,647,577 (S). Microform: UMI.
Online: BRS, DIALOG, Nexis. [*Indexed*: National Newspaper Index, New York Times.
Aud: Ages 16–18.]

The *New York Times* still sets the standard by which all other newspapers are
measured. Other newspapers may approach or surpass the *Times* in reporting a
specific subject area—for example, the *Wall Street Journal*'s coverage of finance
and the *Washington Post*'s reportage of the federal government—but no other
newspaper provides the consistently high-quality across-the-board journalism
and commentary found in the *Times*. With bureaus and correspondents
throughout the world, the *Times* comes as close as possible to living up to its
motto "All the News That's Fit to Print." In addition, the *Times* provides
outstanding reporting of peripheral news topics such as travel, art, leisure, and
technology, as well as the *New York Times Book Review*. The op-ed page reflects

a diversity of opinion represented by renowned commentators such as William Safire, Tom Wicker, and Anthony Lewis, as well as the influential opinion pieces of its own editorial staff writers. Frequently referred to as the "paper of record," because its news stories are often accompanied by the text of speeches and official documents (e.g., U.S. Supreme Court decisions), the *Times* is an excellent source for historical documents.

755   **New Youth Connections.** 1980. 8/yr. $10. Al Desetta. Youth Communication, 135 W. 20th St., New York, NY 10011. Illus. Adv. Index. Circ: 76,000. Sample. Vol. ends: June. [*Aud*: Ages 12–18.]

This newsmagazine is produced on newsprint and assumes characteristics of a newspaper in format. Written by and for New York youth, it is aggressive and refreshingly candid in its approach as it addresses subjects of concern in the area. For example, one issue on youth and crime contains articles on weapons in school, police brutality, and the legal rights of youth. Central issue themes are explored in depth and with a variety of perspectives by the teenage staff. These are balanced by assorted articles on teens and religion, preparing for the prom, and the qualities of a good teacher. Contests are a regular feature. Advertisements are mostly for services such as pregnancy tests and advisement, youth health, and general counseling. Employment opportunities are also presented in the classified ads. The appeal of this title is in its content, which focuses on matters familiar to New York City teens, but is potentially enlightening for others.

756   **Purple Cow.** 1976. m. (during school year). Free to area high schools ($5 others). Todd Daniel. Sigma Publns., 3424 Piedmont Rd. N.E., Suite 320, Altanta, GA 30305-1742. Illus. Adv. Circ: 40,000. Sample. Vol. ends: June. [*Aud*: Ages 12–18.]

Similar to *New Youth Connections* in purpose, this title is billed as a newspaper for teens by teens. It is exclusively distributed to high schools and public libraries in the Atlanta, Georgia, and Tampa–St. Petersburg, Florida, areas. Although the area high school scenes are specifically addressed, some articles of general concern have wider appeal. Features on drugs, music, buying the first car, national and international travel, and job hunting are brief and written in a straightforward manner. A popular feature is the "Messages" section, which contains short greetings between readers.

757   **USA Today: the nation's newspaper.** 1982. d. (exc. Sat. & Sun.). $130. John C. Quinn. Gannett Co., Inc., P.O. Box 500, Washington, DC 20044. Illus. Adv. Circ: 1,500,000. Microform: UMI. Online: DataTimes, DIALOG. [*Indexed*: USA Today Index. *Aud*: Ages 10–18.]

The nation's "fast news" newspaper must be doing something right. It has a circulation of 1.5 million and claims a daily readership of over 5.5 million. For frequent travelers it is the friendly recognizable paper found at every newsstand. The format of *USA Today* is particularly appealing to the reader desiring the news in brief. The color photography and graphics are eye-catching, and the concise reporting is nicely supplemented by the ample use of charts and graphs. The emphasis is on national news broken down into four sections, "News," "Money," "Sports," and "Life." Each section has a summary of the news events on the front page, a cover story, and a summary of the daily news highlights from each of the 50 states and the District of Columbia.

758   **Wall Street Journal.** 1889. weekdays (exc. holidays). $119. Robert L. Bartley. Dow Jones & Co., Inc., 200 Liberty St., New York, NY 10281. Illus. Adv. Circ: 1,965,000.

Microform: UMI. Online: BRS, DIALOG, Dow Jones News/Retrieval. [*Indexed*: National Newspaper Index, Wall Street Journal Index. *Aud*: Ages 16–18.]

Originally founded as a financial newspaper, the *Wall Street Journal* has gradually expanded into a comprehensive national newspaper with a greater circulation than either the *New York Times* or *USA Today*. Its greatest strength lies in its in-depth coverage of national and international finance and business. However, its coverage of politics and government is also first rate. It maintains 17 domestic and 16 foreign bureaus and has in excess of 500 staff reporters. The conservative tone of the excellent editorial page provides a nice counterbalance to the liberal stance found in the *New York Times* and *Washington Post*. It publishes a European and Asian edition as well as the *Asian Wall Street Journal Weekly*.

759 **Washington Post.** 1877. d. $119.60. Benjamin C. Bradlee. The Washington Post Co., 1150 15th St. N.W., Washington, DC 20071. Illus. Adv. Circ: 796,659 (d); 1,112,802 (S). Sample. Microform: UMI. Online: BRS, DIALOG, Nexis, VU/TEXT. [*Indexed*: National Newspaper Index, Washington Post Index. *Aud*: Ages 16–18.]

The nation's most authoritative newspaper for coverage of the federal government and national politics. The *Washington Post* will long be associated with its investigative reporting of "Watergate," for which Bob Woodward and Carl Bernstein won Pulitzers. It maintains a strong and deep stable of reporters, which allows for comprehensive coverage of politics and government. David Broder is generally regarded as the dean of political correspondents. The opinion page and Sunday "Outlook" section are excellent and influential. The *Post* maintains an extensive network of overseas bureaus, which allows for full coverage of international affairs. Its business reporting is more than adequate. The *Post* also publishes a weekly national edition consisting of selected articles from the daily paper.

■ **OCCUPATIONS AND CAREERS**   [Jacob Welle]

High school students thinking about careers can use the magazines annotated here to help find a first job or as source materials for reports and talks. All are suitable for the age group, and some are edited specifically for young adults.

First choices   (1) *Career World—Real World*; (2) *Occupational Outlook Quarterly*.

Suitable for children   Ages 12–18: *Career World—Real World*.

760 **Affirmative Action Register.** 1974. m. $15 (Free to qualified libraries, agencies, and organizations). Warren H. Green. Affirmative Action, Inc., 8356 Olive Blvd., St. Louis, MO 63132. Adv. Circ: 60,000. Sample. Vol. ends: Feb. & Aug. [*Aud*: Ages 14–18.]

Minority job hunters, even the youngest, have distinct problems. This magazine tells the reader where to find the jobs others talk about. It does so by presenting, from cover to cover, ads from equal-opportunity employers seeking quality personnel with academic degrees. All the necessary information is here: a description of the job, qualifications needed, beginning salary, and who to contact. A large percentage of the ads are for faculty and/or academic administrative positions, but people interested in other professions will find a number of attractive job offerings. If nothing else the advertisements point up the necessity of a college degree, particularly for minority applicants. For that reason it is a useful addition to many school and public libraries.

761   **Career Opportunities News** (Also called: *CNews*). 1983. 6/yr. $30. Robert Calvert, Jr. Garrett Park Press, Garrett Park, MD 20896. Illus. Index. Circ: 2,000. Sample. Vol. ends: May/June. [*Bk. rev*: 1–5, 75 words. *Aud*: Ages 14–18.]

The editors of this newsletter search over 150 magazines, government reports, and government surveys conducted by professional organizations to find out what jobs are currently available, where the best possibilities of landing a job are, what future job prospects will be developing, and the educational opportunities open to young people focusing on an occupation or a career. They present this information in the form of brief news items, which usually include the sources to contact or consult for additional information. Each issue usually includes a feature article on some career-related topic. About one third of each issue is concerned with education and job opportunities for women and members of minority groups. The attractive and inviting format of this newsletter will appeal not only to students but also to busy counselors, who will find it a handy means of keeping up with the latest trends and developments in both the trades and the professions.

762   **Career World—Real World** (Formerly: *Career World*). 1972. m. (during school year). $5.60 per student (minimum 15 subs. to one address). Joyce Lain Kennedy. General Learning Corp., 60 Revere Dr., Northbrook, IL 60062-1563. Illus. Index. Circ: 140,000. Sample. Vol. ends: May. Microform: UMI. Reprint: UMI. [*Indexed*: CMG. *Aud*: Ages 12–18.]

The simple objective of this magazine is to get junior and senior high school students to think seriously about and, perhaps, even decide on a life occupation or career. It does this by interviewing people working in a particular job and letting them state in their own words what the job is like, the education and training they needed to prepare for the job, how much they are earning, how difficult it is to land this type of job, and so on. There are also other articles and features that deal with various career-related topics or that answer the many questions students may have regarding occupations and careers and what they have to do to prepare for them. Many of the articles and interviews are followed by lists of sources the reader can contact for additional information. The magazine is intended as a classroom tool, which can be used as a basis for discussion. There is a special teacher's edition containing suggestions to promote this discussion. Although this magazine is intended for classroom use, any library frequented by teenagers should have it on the periodical shelves.

763   **Careers.** 1980. 3/yr. $2.25/issue. Lois Cantwell. E.M. Guild, Inc., 1001 Ave. of the Americas, New York, NY 10018. Illus. Adv. Circ: 600,000. Sample. Vol. ends: Spring. [*Aud*: Ages 14–18.]

With a focus on careers, targeting the teen population, this 40-page magazine contains several regular departments: "High-tech Tools," "Taste Sensations," "Banking on It," "Clothes Call," "Shape Up," and "Fast Tracks" (talk, tips, and trends). Feature stories have covered ethics, tips for entrepreneurial teens, screenwriting careers, part-time employment, and profiles of high achievers. A particularly useful section is "Career Watch," which provides descriptions of careers and their options. An added bonus is a comprehensive index of career profiles from previous editions. This title would be a worthwhile addition to any library collection serving high school seniors.

764 **For Seniors Only.** 1970. s-a. $1.50/issue. Darryl G. Elberg. Senior Publns., 339 N. Main St., New York, NY 10956. Adv. Circ: 350,000. Sample. Refereed. Vol. ends: Mar. [*Aud*: Ages 14–18.]

A useful magazine for high school seniors, this compact title of approximately 50 pages provides information on career options for graduating seniors through either academic pursuits or military service. Examples of article titles include "Facts to Know in Picking a College," "Opportunities in the Military," "Planning for College," "Specialized Career Training." Regional editions containing advertisements of schools, colleges, and universities, and the U.S. government are indexed. A reader service is available to facilitate obtaining additional information about the advertisers.

765 **Getting Jobs** (Formerly: *New Dimensions*). 1974. bi-m. Free to educators. Bobbi Ray Madry. MPC Educational Pubs., 3839 White Plains Rd., Bronx, NY 10467. Illus. Circ: 6,000. Vol. ends: No. 6. [*Aud*: Ages 14–18.]

A colorful four-page newsletter "designed to provide teachers and counselors with information relevant to getting and keeping jobs." Actually, only some of the articles are directed to counselors and placement officers and offer suggestions for running successful placement programs. The other articles are directed to students and other job seekers and offer them all kinds of practical advice they can follow in the process of looking for, applying for, and being successful in a job.

766 **Hispanic Times Magazine.** 1978. 5/yr. $30 (Free to college career offices). Gloria J. Davis. Hispanic Times Enterprises, P.O. Box 6368, Westlake Village, CA 91359. Illus. Adv. Circ: 35,000. Vol. ends: No. 5. [*Aud*: Ages 14–18.]

This title features articles about job preparation, job selection, interviewing, and so on. It also carries articles on many other topics, such as Indian and Hispanic affairs, bilingual education, literacy, the Peace Corps, and the armed forces, as well as regular columns on sports, health, travel, cooking, and other topics of interest to college students. It serves as the voice of the Mexican-American Engineering Society and gives special emphasis to engineering careers. Numerous ads from government and business appeal directly to members of minority groups. This is an attractive magazine that will be picked up and perused by students. Recommended for libraries serving minority groups.

767 **Occupational Outlook Quarterly.** 1957. q. $5. Melvin Fountain. U.S. Bureau of Labor Statistics. Subs. to: U.S. Govt. Printing Office, Washington, DC 20402. Illus. Index. Circ: 20,000. Sample. Vol. ends: Winter. Microform: UMI. Reprint: UMI. [*Indexed*: BusI, CIJE, PAIS. *Aud*: Ages 14–18.]

Like its parent publication, *Occupational Outlook Handbook*, this magazine describes various kinds of occupations (including some rather unusual ones) stating what they are like, salaries and advancement possibilities, the qualifications needed for them, and so on. There are also articles covering broader occupational areas such as the health-care industry, the retail trade, overseas jobs, business services, and others, and discussing job prospects in these areas. Besides jobs, there is also advice on job preparation and job searching, and many of the articles include lists of sources to contact for additional information. Every two years the "Job Outlook in Brief" lists some 200 jobs and gives a rundown on job openings and employment prospects in each. There is also a biennial report on the job outlook for college students—a general discussion of job prospects over the next decade and where the demand will be. The audience of this magazine is mainly high school and college graduates planning professional careers.

768 **Student Guide to the SAT.** 1989. s-m. $49. Ben Ephraim. Krell Software, Flowerfield Bldg. No. 7, St. James, NY 11780. Illus. Adv. [*Aud*: Ages 14–18.]

This 12-page newsletter, issued twice a month, is edited by a former professor at the University of California and SUNY. Each number concentrates on the two components of the SAT. Math and verbal aspects are studied in detail in a large-type, two-part format: typical SAT questions followed by the answers and a brief explanation of why each response is correct. Except for a few cheering words about SAT and how it is structured, that is about it. A good book on the subject may do just as well, but some students may prefer the snappy presentation and the editor's grasp of what many students need by the way of coaching. Send for a sample before ordering.

■ **PEACE**   [Grant Burns]

Some magazines are dedicated to helping attain peace in our rapidly changing world. It is with at least a few of these that this section is concerned. All are for adults. All, at the same time, are within the reading range of the average young adult. At least one or two should be in every school and public library, particularly as they approach peace issues from different directions with different emphases.

First choices   (1) *Nuclear Times*; (2) *Fellowship*.

769 **The Defense Monitor.** 1972. 10/yr. $25. Gene R. LaRocque. Center for Defense Information, 1500 Massachusetts Ave. N.W., Washington, DC 20005. Illus. Circ: 65,000. Sample. Vol. ends: Dec. [*Aud*: Ages 14–18.]

Young people anxious to discover the "establishment" viewpoint on peace will find this eight-page newsletter invaluable. It provides a forum for the views of the Center for Defense Information (CDF), which is directed by a group of retired U.S. military officers. Although it supports an "effective defense," CDI also opposes excessive expenditures for weapons and policies that increase the danger of nuclear war. Individual issues concentrate on specific topics, with detailed analyses (in unsigned articles) of pros and cons, and end with a statement of "conclusions" about the topic in question. Peace activists will find this a valuable source of critical articles on the weapons and, more significantly, the thinking with which they must contend.

770 **F.A.S. Public Interest Report.** 1947. 10/yr. $50 (Individuals, $25). Jeremy J. Stone. Federation of Amer. Scientists, 307 Massachusetts Ave. N.E., Washington, DC 20002. Illus. Circ: 7,000. Vol. ends: Dec. [*Aud*: Ages 14–18.]

Founded in 1945 as the Federation of Atomic Scientists, the Federation of American Scientists has since widened its peace interests from the atomic bomb to third-world development and human rights for scientists. In its 8 to 16 pages, this magazine contains articles on both nuclear and conventional arms control, Soviet policies, and such third-world topics as relations between North and South Korea. A useful and interesting addition to the peace collection.

771   Fellowship. 1934. 8/yr. $12. Virginia Baron. Fellowship of Reconciliation, 523 N. Broadway, Nyack, NY 10960. Illus. Adv. Circ: 12,500. Vol. ends: Dec. Microform: UMI. Reprint: UMI. [*Indexed*: PAIS. *Bk. rev*: 2–3, 350 words, signed. *Aud*: Ages 14–18.]

The Fellowship of Reconciliation describes itself as "an association of women and men who have joined together to explore the power of love and truth for resolving human conflict." Articles concern grass-roots action, although the tone is less aggressive than reflective and philosophical, often with religious underpinnings. The outlook is international. Authors include teachers, community leaders, peace activists, and others who have made a personal commitment to the struggle for peace.

772   The Nonviolent Activist. 1984. 8/yr. $25 (Individuals, $15). Ruth Benn. War Resisters League, 339 Lafayette St., New York, NY 10012. Illus. Adv. Circ: 20,000. [*Aud*: Ages 14–18.]

The War Resisters League is one of the oldest peace organizations in the United States. Like several other activist-oriented periodicals, this 16-page magazine traverses considerable territory, from discussions of past wars and their effects to ways to prevent future wars to such immediately personal issues as responses to crimes of violence. Most subscribers will be individual activists.

773   Nuclear Times. 1982. bi-m. $23 (Individuals, $21). Elliott Negin. Nuclear Times, Inc., 1601 Connecticut Ave. N.W., Washington, DC 20009. Illus. Adv. Circ: 50,000. Vol. ends: Nov/Dec. [*Indexed*: API. *Bk. rev*: 2–5, 200–1,000 words, signed. *Aud*: Ages 14–18.]

If a school or public library in the United States can bring itself to subscribe to only one magazine covering the peace movement in the United States, this should be the one. *Nuclear Times* treats the breadth and depth of this territory in a friendly, informative way. The attractive layout will appeal to casual readers; cover stories such as "Hollywood Peaceniks" and "War Toys or Peace Toys" show good editorial sense about how to reach the public at large rather than preach to the already committed activist. There is good, comprehensible coverage of both domestic and foreign issues from the peace activist's point of view. A calendar of peace actions, lectures, and workshops held around the United States is included. Close to being a mainstream newsmagazine of the antinuclear movement, it is highly recommended.

■ PETS   [Vicki F. Croft]

See also: HORSES

There are only a few general magazines on the specific subject of pets. Most of these are included here, particularly as the majority are suitable for young adults. One should note that general magazines frequently carry regular columns dealing with animal care and behavior and/or animal health topics. One of the best ways to locate these is by consulting a general index, such as *Readers' Guide to Periodical Literature* and the *Magazine Index*.

First choices   (1) *Animals*; (2) *Pets Magazine.*
Suitable for children   Ages 8–18: *Pets Magazine.* Ages 10–18: *Cat Fancy; Dog Fancy; Tropical Fish Hobbyist.*

774   **Animals** (Continuation of *Our Dumb Animals*). 1868. bi-m. Membership $15. Joni Praded. Massachusetts Soc. for the Prevention of Cruelty to Animals, 350 S. Huntington Ave., Boston, MA 02130. Illus. Adv. Circ: 75,000. Vol. ends: Nov/Dec. Microform: UMI. [*Bk. rev*: 2, 250–450 words, signed. *Aud*: Ages 14–18.]

Animals is an attractive, glossy magazine filled with beautiful photographs of animals as well as many interesting and informative articles. The magazine contains material on a wide variety of animal-related issues such as pet care, nutrition, and geriatric pets as well as numerous articles on wild animals and environmental issues. Regular features include a veterinarian's question-and-answer section, opinion columns, "Animals in Peril," and a news section that spotlights news items on animal-related issues.

775   **Bird Talk.** 1982. m. $18. Karyn New. Fancy Publns., P.O. Box 6050, Mission Viejo, CA 92620. Illus. Adv. Index. Circ: 250,000. Sample. Vol. ends: Dec. [*Bk. rev*: 1–3, 200–300 words, signed. *Aud*: Ages 14–18.]

Published by Fancy Publications, the publishers of *Cat Fancy* and *Dog Fancy*, *Bird Talk* is an attractive, colorful magazine whose primary focus centers around the practical and proper care and feeding of pet birds. Feature articles include information on medical problems, behavior, training and breeding, and individual breed profiles. *Bird Talk*'s practical and informative approach to pet-bird care would be especially useful to the relatively new bird owner.

776   **Cat Fancy: the magazine for responsible cat owners** (Continuation of *International Cat Fancy*). 1966. m. $18. Linda W. Lewis. Fancy Publns., Inc., P.O. Box 6050, Mission Viejo, CA 92690. Illus. Adv. Index. Circ: 230,000. Vol. ends: Dec. Microform: UMI. [*Bk. rev*: 1–3, 150–450 words, signed. *Aud*: Ages 10–18.]

Cat Fancy is a magazine that will appeal to cat lovers of all ages. Its well-written, informative articles deal with all aspects of cat and kitten health, care, physiology, nutrition, and behavior. Issues have contained articles on why and how cats purr, feline diabetes, multicat households, and grooming long-haired cats. Like *Dog Fancy*, this is a very attractive, glossy magazine containing numerous black-and-white as well as color photographs of cats. An annual index is invaluable for locating articles in past issues.

Children and Animals. *See* **Kind News** *under* CHILDREN/PETS.

777   **Dog Fancy.** 1970. m. $18. Linda W. Lewis. Fancy Publns., Inc., P.O. Box 6050, Mission Viejo, CA 92690. Illus. Adv. Index. Circ: 130,000. Vol. ends: Dec. Microform: UMI. [*Bk. rev*: 1–4, 100–350 words, signed. *Aud*: Ages 10–18.]

This is a magazine for the reader who is interested in current, well-written articles dealing with a wide variety of topics relating to dog and puppy care and health. Tips on grooming and training, advice on behavioral problems, current information on health and nutrition, and the latest product information are all included, together with human-interest stories. Issues have contained articles on internal parasites, search and rescue dogs, training dogs to avoid dangers, feeding the older dog, traveling with your dog, and making your dog streetwise, plus "stranger-than-fiction" dog stories. Many issues also contain a breed profile, which provides factual information on the featured breed. Regular monthly features focus on behavior problems, grooming, and health problems. A classified section and a directory of dog breeders are included in each issue. This is an attractive magazine, with many photographs—both black and white and color. An annual article index facilitates access to material in past issues.

778 **DVM Newsmagazine: the newsmagazine of veterinary medicine.** 1970. m. $24. Maureen Hrehocik. Edgell Communications, Inc., Corporate Offices, 7500 Old Oak Blvd., Cleveland, OH 44130. Illus. Adv. Circ: 33,383. Refereed. Vol. ends: Dec. Microform: UMI. [*Aud:* Ages 14–18.]

This is a very unusual, appealing publication. Its format is that of a large magazine; it has no table of contents; it is not indexed; and it is very flashy. Features include articles on educating pet owners, women in the profession, editorial round-table discussions with the profession's leaders, and new surgical techniques. The publication has lots of color, and is written on a level that would make it interesting and enjoyable for middle school on up.

779 **Freshwater and Marine Aquarium: the magazine dedicated to the tropical fish enthusiast.** 1978. m. $22. Donald W. Dewey. RIC Modeler Corp., 144 W. Sierra Madre Blvd., Sierra Madre, CA 91024. Illus. Adv. [*Bk. rev:* 1–2, 250–400 words. *Aud:* Ages 14–18.]

Written for aquarium hobbyists at all levels of experience, *Freshwater and Marine Aquarium* features detailed articles on many aspects of tropical, cold-water, and marine fish and invertebrate breeding and aquaculture. There is also considerable coverage of available aquarium products. Similar to *Tropical Fish Hobbyist* in coverage, attractive appearance, and the presence of numerous color photographs; *Freshwater and Marine Aquarium* differs from the former in that there is less emphasis on individual fish biology and breeding habits, but more on the practical day-to-day aspects of fish care and breeding. A choice between this magazine and *Tropical Fish Hobbyist* would depend in large part on the emphasis desired.

Pets Magazine. *See under* CHILDREN/PETS.

780 **Tropical Fish Hobbyist.** 1952. m. $18. Ray Hunziker. T.F.H. Publns., Inc., 211 W. Sylvania Ave., Neptune, NJ 07753. Illus. Adv. Index. Circ: 60,000. Vol. ends: No. 12. [*Aud:* Ages 10–18.]

Thanks to the topic, the illustrations, and the easy-to-follow text, this is as good a magazine for a ten-year-old as for an older teenager. The scope of *Tropical Fish Hobbyist* includes not only tropical fish but also the plants, amphibians, reptiles, and invertebrates available to and of potential interest to the aquarium hobbyist. Issues contain exotic tropical fish supplements, which can be easily inserted into the loose-leaf edition of *Exotic Tropical Fishes*. Probably the best known and oldest of the tropical fish magazines, *Tropical Fish Hobbyist* is recommended for the young hobbyist.

■ **PHOTOGRAPHY**   [James C. Anderson and David Horvath]

Interest in photography, at all levels, continues to expand. At the same time, publishers do not offer enough general magazines in the area—the demise of *Modern Photography* is a case in point. Beyond the how-to-do-it title for the young adult is the art magazine, which puts emphasis on photography as an art form. There are few satisfactory titles in this area. Note, too, that "electronic imaging" is important and includes both video- and still-imaging systems, which are of as much interest to teenagers as to adults.

First choices   (1) *Popular Photography;* (2) *Petersen's Photographic Magazine;*
(3) *American Photo.*

Suitable for children   Ages 12–18: *Popular Photography*.

781   **Afterimage.** 1972. 10/yr. $32. David Trend. Visual Studies Workshop, 31 Prince St., Rochester, NY 14607. Illus. Index. Circ: 4,000. Sample. Vol. ends: May. Microform: UMI. [*Bk. rev*: 3–5, 1,500 words, signed. *Aud*: Ages 14–18.]

An art-photography tabloid, not a practical how-to-do-it title, this should have appeal for many young adults. It does require an interest in art and above-average reading ability. It carries up-to-date listings of exhibitions, workshops, conferences, job openings, and grants, as well as advance notice of deadlines for submission of work to shows and grants agencies. In addition, extended articles on a broad range of historical, critical, and aesthetic issues are featured. These articles are often the work of some of the best contemporary scholars and critics. Reviews of books and journals are many and brief, with new publications noted in a "sources" column. There are also extensive, signed reviews of three to five books and of current exhibitions. A publication with a very broad appeal, and a must for schools with programs in photography.

782   **American Photo.** 1978. m. $17.90. David Schonauer. Diamandis Communications, Inc., 1515 Broadway, New York, NY 10036. Illus. Adv. Sample. [*Indexed*: MI. *Bk. rev*: 1–3, 500–750 words, signed. *Aud*: Ages 14–18.]

The young reader will find here a nice combination of the practical and the theoretical. This blend gives the title an added dimension for many school and public libraries. While its primary appeal is to the advanced amateur or the professional photographer, the magazine's coverage of art, history, photojournalism, fashion, advertising, and studio photography would make it useful to any reader whose interests in photography go beyond the nuts-and-bolts approach of other popular photography magazines. Although technique and hardware are covered to some extent, the magazine regularly features several well-written pieces that include profiles and portfolios of working photographers representing fine art, historical, commercial, and photojournalist perspectives.

783   **Aperture.** 1952. q. $36. Nan Richardson. Aperture Foundation, Inc., 20 E. 23rd St., New York, NY 10010. Illus. Adv. Circ: 1,300. Sample. Vol. ends: Nov. [*Bk. rev*: 1, 2,500 words, signed. *Aud*: Ages 14–18.]

One of the best American publications devoted to photography, *Aperture* proudly claims to be "the only publication that emphasizes photography as art." Here, as elsewhere, the distinction between art and other photographic uses (news, documentary, advertising) is blurred. The result is that this fine magazine should appeal to anyone with an interest in photography. It was founded as an important little magazine in the fifties, and fine reproduction has always been its hallmark. Many issues now include color. Text varies from simple poems accompanying reproductions to extended interpretive essays by an impressive and wide-ranging list of contributors.

784   **Darkroom Photography.** 1979. 8/yr. $22. Kimberly Torgerson. Melrose Publns., 9021 Melrose Ave., Suite 301, Los Angeles, CA 90069. Illus. Adv. Circ: 75,000. Sample. Vol. ends: Nov/Dec. (No. 8). [*Aud*: Ages 14–18.]

This is a practical/how-to-do-it approach for teenagers interested in photography. It includes materials selection, film developing, printing the pictures, and everything else involved in producing a finished photograph. The magazine's design and flavor are similar to *Petersen's*, to which it would make a good companion title. Regular features include darkroom equipment and materials tests and specifications as well as longer pieces on "masters of photography," featuring the work of photographers who are well known for their darkroom skills.

785   **Exposure.** 1963. q. Membership $50. David L. Jacobs. Soc. for Photographic Education, P.O. Box BBB, Albuquerque, NM 87196. Illus. Adv. Sample. Vol. ends: Winter. [*Bk. rev*: 1, 1,000–1,500 words, signed. *Aud*: Ages 14–18.]

This excellent journal of photographic criticism, interpretation, aesthetics, theory, and history was begun in 1963 as the organ of the teacher-members of the Society for Photographic Education. Each issue features well-printed black-and-white and color reproductions, which accompany articles covering a broad range of issues, topics, and photographers. The writing is always top-notch, and often discusses work or issues that are more avant-garde or experimental than what is found in more general-circulation art journals. Contents (and guest editors) vary, sometimes including news, reviews, reports from the society, and a list of job openings in addition to the feature articles. This journal is a must for libraries in institutions where photography is taught.

786   **Petersen's Photographic Magazine.** 1971. m. $13.94. Karen Geller-Shinn. Petersen Publg. Co., 8490 Sunset Blvd., Los Angeles, CA 90069. Illus. Adv. Index. Circ: 275,000. Vol. ends: Apr. Microform: UMI. Online: DIALOG. [*Indexed*: BoRvI, MI, RG. *Aud*: Ages 14–18.]

Along with *Popular Photography* (both found in the basic indexes), this is the single best photo magazine for the high school or public library. Page-for-page, *Petersen's Photographic Magazine* contains more useful information for the amateur than any of the other popular photographic magazines. It differs from *Popular Photography* in that many of its how-to articles are directed to the handyman or -woman who wants to actually build a darkroom or assemble a studio setup. The "Users Reports" section provides a series of short but very useful articles as a consumers' guide to photo products, materials, and equipment. It manages to include 20 to 25 articles and departments of varying content while still retaining a high degree of freshness and currency with surprisingly little repetition. The approach covers almost all aspects of photographic technique from the camera to the darkroom to display.

787   **Popular Photography.** 1937. m. $11.97. Jason Schneider. Diamandis Communications, Inc., 1515 Broadway, New York, NY 10036. Illus. Adv. Index. Circ: 750,000. Sample. Vol. ends: Dec. Microform: B&H, UMI. Online: DIALOG. [*Indexed*: RG. *Aud*: Ages 12–18.]

Popular Photography has recently passed its fiftieth publishing year and it is the number one photo magazine in the United States in circulation. One of the major American popular photography magazines devoted largely to the technique and equipment of photography rather than interpretation and critical evaluation, it continues to hold its readership with consistent quality layout and content. While edited for adults, there is little of the copy that cannot be understood by a young adult, and most of the material will interest any teenager involved with photography. The articles and departments are of interest to both amateurs and professionals and include pieces on film and video. In addition to regular features there are specialty columns on various topics such as large format, camera repair, and so forth. Books are covered in an occasional feature review.

788   **Untitled.** 1972. 3/yr. Membership $40. David Featherstone. The Friends of Photography, 250 Fourth St., 101 The Embarcadero, San Francisco, CA 94103. Illus. Circ: 13,000. Sample. [*Aud*: Ages 12–18.]

Since Friends of Photography members now also receive their excellent newsletter *Re:view*, this magazine is now called the *Untitled* series. It is still the same excellent publication. Each issue feaatures a single photographer or theme, and contains numerous superbly printed images. Each issue of *Untitled* is also available as a monograph, selling for $15–$20, which makes the membership price a real bargain.

■ **POLITICAL SCIENCE**   [Henry E. York]

As commonly understood, political science is the discipline in which government, politics, and the state are studied. In high schools there may or may not be a political science course, but related matters are considered in the history and social sciences curriculum. In fact, political science has become increasingly interdisciplinary as it draws on other social sciences. Most of the titles are for the specialist, but here and there are a few for the younger reader, although one should always be aware that these journals are edited for adults. Therefore, few this side of *Current History* will find their way into any but the more specialized, sophisticated collections.

First choices   (1) *Current History*; (2) *Common Cause*; (3) *Congressional Digest*.

789   **American-Arab Affairs.** 1982. q. $20. Anne Joyce. Amer. Arab Affairs Council, 1730 M St. N.W., Suite 11, Washington, DC 20036. Circ: 18,500. Vol. ends: Spring. Microform: UMI. [*Indexed*: BoRvI, PAIS. *Aud*: Ages 14–18.]

This learned journal deals with all topics of Arab-American relations, both past and present, with heavy emphasis on the latest news. Very helpful for quick reference are salient paragraphs of each article set off in large type every few pages to provide a kind of abstract of each section. Interviews with policymakers, both Arab and American, offer current perspectives. Suitable for advanced high school seniors.

790   **Common Cause** (Formerly: *Frontline; In Common*). 1980. bi-m. Membership $12. Deborah Baldwin. Common Cause Magazine, 2030 M St. N.W., Washington, DC 20036. Illus. Circ: 280,000. Sample. Vol. ends: Nov/Dec. [*Indexed*: PAIS, RG. *Aud*: Ages 14–18.]

Thanks to the objective style and the interest in the "common" individual, this appeals particularly to teenagers. Political issues covered by other news publications (nuclear power, Central America, federal spending) are dealt with in more depth here by well-informed writers generally espousing a particular point of view. The writing style is lively and the format very attractive. Readers are urged to take action on various issues, and are advised as to how this can be done. Citizens interested in Capitol Hill goings-on and in prominent politicians' positions on timely issues will appreciate having *Common Cause* to supplement other accounts of current events.

791   **Congressional Digest.** 1921. 10/yr. $24. John E. Shields. Congressional Corp., 3231 P St. N.W., Washington, DC 20007. Index. Vol. ends: Dec. Microform: Pub. [*Indexed*: Acs, PAIS, RG. *Aud*: Ages 14–18.]

A basic work for any student who is doing work in this area. Most of the material is easy to understand and cleverly presented. It is advertised as an independent monthly featuring controversies in Congress, pro and con, not an official organ, not controlled by any party, interest, class, or sect—and it is just that. Each issue is devoted to an analysis of one current issue facing Congress, with several short sections giving background, recent actions, and so forth. Pros and cons are then given by an equal number of "debaters" (four to six) who are involved with the problem. Valuable for presenting all sides of the topic. Recommended, as the issues are short (generally 30 pages), good for reference work, and easily read.

792 Current History: world affairs journal. 1914. 9/yr. $27. Carol L. Thompson. Current History, Inc., 4225 Main St., Philadelphia, PA 19127. Illus. Index. Circ: 26,000. Sample. Vol. ends: Dec. Microform: UMI. [*Indexed*: PAIS, RG. *Bk. rev*: 2–6, 100–150 words, signed. *Aud*: Ages 14–18.]

One of the few political science/history journals edited for laypersons and young adults, this is a first choice in high school and public libraries serving teenagers. It is an international affairs journal with a style and appeal about midway between the newsmagazine and the journal of scholarly commentary such as *Foreign Affairs*. Each issue is devoted to one area or country with about eight short articles covering varying topics. Issues have covered the Middle East, Eastern Europe, and South America. The authors are generally American academics, but the writing style is nontechnical, focusing on summarizing and commenting on the most important aspects of recent events. In addition to the articles there is the most useful "Month in Review" section giving country-by-country daily chronologies of important events.

793 Current World Leaders. 1957. 8/yr. Price varies. Intl. Academy, 2060 Alameda Padre Serra, Santa Barbara, CA 93103. Circ: 2,000. Microform: MIM. [*Indexed*: PAIS. *Aud*: Ages 14–18.]

This nicely augments such works as *Current Biography* and is an ideal reference work in many high school and public libraries. It is invaluable for up-to-date information that is normally found in an almanac or yearbook, current information on world officials, and a running commentary on major events that have taken place throughout the world. A normal issue consists of individual or group biographies of leaders arranged by country; documents; current names of individuals in cabinets, parliaments, and other official positions; and shorter items of interest. There are also a necrology and a calendar of forthcoming events. This is in the form of a pocketbook magazine, but it is really a basic reference aid.

794 Department of State Bulletin. 1939. m. $25. Phyllis A. Young. Supt. of Docs., U.S. Govt. Printing Office, Washington, DC 20402. Illus. Index. Circ: 10,000. Vol. ends: Dec. Microform: B&H, MCA, MIM, UMI. Online: DIALOG. [*Indexed*: MI, RG. *Aud*: Ages 14–18.]

Subtitled "The official monthly record of United States foreign policy," this title provides information on the work of the foreign service and developments in foreign policy. Addresses and speeches of the president, secretary of state, and other key leaders on foreign relations issues are often included. Recurring issues, such as arms control and human rights, will often have several articles devoted to them. Each issue features a country or area of the world. In addition, regular features include information on treaties, press releases, and a list of publications from the U.S. State Department.

795   Foreign Affairs. 1922. 5/yr. $28. William G. Hyland. Council on Foreign Relations, Inc., 58 E. 68th St., New York, NY 10021. Illus. Adv. Index. Circ: 90,000. Vol. ends: Summer. Microform: B&H, MIM, UMI, WH. [*Indexed*: PAIS, RG. *Bk. rev*: 80–90, 125–400 words, signed. *Aud*: Ages 14–18.]

As highly recommended as this journal is, it is not easy reading, and it is only for advanced students. Perhaps the best known journal of world affairs, this periodical reaches an audience that is both large and elite, including many diplomats, government officials, policy analysts, and scholars. The parent is the Council on Foreign Relations, a nonpartisan middle-of-the-road organization that seeks to influence the shaping of the U.S. foreign policy debate with articles that represent "a broad hospitality of divergent ideas" rather than "identifying with one school." Each issue contains 10 to 12 articles by scholars, government officials, or journalists dealing with foreign policy topics, usually with policy recommendations offered. This journal provides very comprehensive book review coverage for titles in international relations.

796   Foreign Policy. 1970. q. $25 (Individuals, $21). Charles W. Maynes. Carnegie Endowment for Intl. Peace, 11 Dupont Circle N.W., Washington, DC 20036. Illus. Adv. Index. Circ: 25,000. Sample. Microform: B&H, UMI. [*Indexed*: PAIS, RG. *Aud*: Ages 14–18.]

Similar in difficulty to *Foreign Affairs*, this too is only for advanced students. Published by the Carnegie Endowment for International Peace, this quarterly review of American foreign policy and international relations has become an important factor in influencing debate on current American foreign policy decisions. It is considered essential reading by many government officials, educators, and members of the press. A typical issue contains about a dozen articles written by academics, foreign service officers, or members of various research or special-interest groups. Each issue has a lively letters to the editor section with lengthy reactions to articles previously published and accompanying responses by the authors.

797   Journal of Interamerican Studies and World Affairs. 1959. q. $44 (Individuals, $22). Jaime Suchlicki. Journal of Interamerican Studies and World Affairs, P.O. Box 24-8134, Univ. of Miami, Coral Gables, FL 33124. Index. Sample. Vol. ends: Winter. Microform: UMI. Reprint: UMI. [*Bk. rev*: 4–5, 2–3 pages, signed. *Aud*: Ages 14–18.]

Another scholarly journal that, while primarily for college graduates, will find some use in high schools. The Institute of Interamerican Studies at the University of Miami publishes this journal of foreign affairs with a focus exclusively on inter-American relations. It will be of interest to scholars, policymakers, and the informed general public concerned about contemporary U.S.–Latin American relations, U.S. foreign policy toward Latin America, and political developments and relations among the Latin American nations. Each issue has five or six articles plus a short book review section that deals exclusively with titles concerning Latin America. The "Books Received" section provides a useful bibliography of recent publications, arranged by country.

798   Major Legislation of the Congress. irreg. $25. Supt. of Docs., U.S. Govt. Printing Office, Washington, DC 20402. [*Aud*: Ages 14–18.]

This research guide for adults has wide use in high schools. The subject matter often affords the basis for a good paper or talk. This Congressional Research Service publication generally appears five to six times per congressional session. It is arranged by broad subject areas such as "Agriculture and Food" and "Education." A summary of the major legislation for the current session is listed under each of these headings. As the year progresses and if the bills become laws, each public law is summarized.

799   **The Middle East.** 1974. m. $70. Roger Harby. IC Publns., P.O. Box 261, 69 Great Queen St., London WC2B 5BZ, England. Illus. Circ: 24,194. [*Aud*: Ages 14–18.]

As an illustrated newsmagazine patterned after *Time*, this features not only politics and economics, but also cultural affairs of the countries in the area. Interviews with prominent and not-so-prominent citizens help draw a multidimensional picture of a part of the world that used to appear strange to Westerners.

800   **National Journal: the weekly on politics and government.** 1969. w. $364 (Individuals, $589). Richard S. Frank. Natl. Journal, Inc., 1730 M St. N.W., Washington, DC 20036. Illus. Adv. Index. Circ: 5,000. Sample. Microform: UMI. Online: Mead Data Central. [*Indexed*: PAIS. *Aud*: Ages 14–18.]

A quite marvelous journal for keeping up with government. This illustrated weekly provides a comprehensive review of current events with in-depth news reports. Unlike mass-circulation newsmagazines, the focus is on events on Capitol Hill, with particular emphasis on such topics as regulatory agencies, foreign trade, and White House legislative strategy. The intended audience consists of policymakers, congressional staff members, lobbyists, and business and association leaders. The style is suitable for students who desire to have the latest "inside" information. In addition to 10 to 12 articles written by experienced political journalists or government officials, each issue contains several report sections. Though not inexpensive, *National Journal* is an excellent source of in-depth reporting on current American politics at the federal level.

801   **Near East Report.** 1957. w. $30. Eric Rozenman. Near East Report, 444 N. Capitol St. N.W., Washington, DC 20001. Circ: 50,000. Vol. ends: Dec. [*Aud*: Ages 14–18.]

This four-page newsletter is addressed to policymakers in Congress and the State Department. Its frankly pro-Israeli slant is not hidden. News from Israel and the difficult relations with the Arabs both inside and outside of the Jewish state are given in capsule form. Pro-Israeli statements by American politicians are featured, while attacks on that country are refuted.

802   **Policy Review.** 1977. q. $15. Adam Meyerson. Heritage Foundation, Inc., 214 Massachusetts Ave., Washington, DC 20002. Adv. Index. Circ: 10,000. [*Indexed*: SocSc. *Aud*: Ages 14–18.]

An admitted conservative view of American public policy, both domestic and foreign. This title is directed to members of the government and their staffs, to academics, business leaders, and the general public. It is not easy reading, but may have some appeal in high schools with special political science/government courses. Each issue contains about a dozen short articles that critique or comment on policy matters of current interest. This title is differentiated from others with a similar focus by its orientation. It clearly reveals the political ideology of its publisher, the Heritage Foundation, a conservative "think tank." Some articles deal specifically with political topics, such as "The Lessons of Afghanistan." Others, such as "Good News for the Fetus" and "America's Permanent Dependent Class," deal with politicized social issues. Useful as a conservative counterbalance to the many titles that present a balanced or liberal viewpoint.

■ **RELIGION**   [Wayne Maxson]

Somewhere around 3,000 religious periodical titles are published each year in the United States alone. This section contains a selection of religious titles that are judged to be especially useful to public and many school libraries. Titles that exist largely for denominational communication, even though many are interesting to others, have not been included. Here the emphasis is on the magazine with a coverage broad enough to appeal to a number of younger readers.

First choices   (1) *Christian Century*; (2) *Commonweal*; (3) *Jewish Spectator*; (4) *The Humanist*.

Suitable for children   Ages 4–9: *Story Friends*. Ages 6–12: *Pockets*; *Wee Wisdom*. Ages 8–15: *La Bande a Quenoeil*. Ages 10–18: *Keeping Posted*.

803   **America.** 1909. w. $28. George W. Hunt. America Press, Inc., 106 W. 56th St., New York, NY 10019. Illus. Adv. Index. Circ: 35,000. Microform: UMI. [*Indexed*: RG. *Bk. rev*: 3–5, 1,500 words, signed. *Aud*: Ages 14–18.]

One of the best general magazines for young Catholics, this is indexed in *Readers' Guide* and is often used for background material for papers and talks. This weekly magazine, edited by lay Roman Catholics, presents views on current issues—religious, social, cultural, or political—as well as poetry and meditation. There is a variety of opinion and topics, and not all authors are identifiably Catholic. Catholic interests are clearly at the forefront, but the topics are of wider interest in terms of religion and otherwise.

La Bande a Quenoeil. *See under* CHILDREN/RELIGION.

804   **Christian Century: an ecumenical weekly.** 1908. w. $28. James M. Wall. Christian Century Foundation, 407 E. Dearborn St., Chicago, IL 60605. Subs. to: 5615 W. Cernak Rd., Cicero, IL 60605. Illus. Adv. Index. Circ: 38,500. Microform: UMI. [*Indexed*: RG. *Bk. rev*: 4–5, 250–500 words, signed. *Aud*: Ages 14–18.]

This is a good general religious title. A moderate-to-liberal journal, it is conscious of other Christian as well as non-Christian religious views. Articles, covering general religious news, and editorial opinion are strong on ethical and social issues. They are written for the educated layperson and religious professional. The journal's counterpart from the Catholic tradition is *America*.

805   **Christianity Today.** 1956. bi-w. $21. Harold L. Myra. Christianity Today, 465 Gunderson Dr., Carol Stream, IL 60188. Subs. to: P.O. Box 1915, Marion, OH 45305. Illus. Adv. Circ: 185,000. Microform: UMI. [*Indexed*: RG. *Bk. rev*: 4–5, 250–500 words. *Aud*: Ages 14–18.]

Everyone from the conservative to the fundamentalist can find material of benefit in the pages of this popular magazine of evangelical Christian views. The format, with its photography and artwork, is appealing to all ages. Recent articles have included "AIDS in Africa," "The Cross and the Couch," and "Baseball and the Atonement." It shows a strong interest in teenagers, and the writing level is appropriate for that age group.

806   Commonweal. 1924. bi-w. $32. Margaret O'Brien Steinfels. Commonweal Foundation, 15 Dutch St., New York, NY 10038. Illus. Adv. Circ: 20,000. Microform: B&H, UMI. [*Indexed*: CathI, RG. *Bk. rev*: 8–10, 500–1,000 words, signed. *Aud*: Ages 14–18.]

A lively liberal Catholic magazine of current thought, this covers "Public Affairs, Religion, Literature and the Arts." Some recent articles have been on the changes in the USSR, the textbook controversy, pastoral letters, Father Curran, El Salvador, and the cinema. The viewpoint is decidedly liberal, and writers take the Roman Catholic Church to task when they feel it deserves it. The writing is exceptionally good.

807   The Humanist. 1941. bi-m. $18. Lloyd L. Morain. Amer. Humanist Assn., 7 Harwood Dr., P.O. Box 146, Amherst, NY 14225-0146. Illus. Adv. Circ: 12,133. Microform: UMI. [*Indexed*: HumI, PAIS, RG. *Bk. rev*: 3–6, 1,000 words, signed. *Aud*: Ages 14–18.]

This title serves as an objective and cool balance for the religious collection and should be found in all public and school libraries where such a balance is needed. This is among the oldest of the humanist journals in the United States, and probably the best known. *The Humanist* is flamboyant and zealous for humanism. It is strong on social issues, carrying articles, for example, on comparable worth, the criminal justice system, and the shortage of doctors.

808   Jewish Spectator. 1935. q. $12.50. Trude Weiss-Rosmarin. Jewish Spectator, P.O. Box 2016, Santa Monica, CA 90406. Illus. Adv. Microform: UMI. [*Aud*: Ages 14–18.]

This journal of Jewish opinion makes the claim to be Jewry's only nonorganizational, independent journal. It should not be thought of, however, as being limited to Jewish readers. It carries a broad range of topics, opinions, experiences, poetry, fiction, and humor by Jewish writers who cut across religious/cultural lines. The editorial section is exceptionally well written.

Keeping Posted. *See under* CHILDREN/RELIGION.

809   The Other Side. 1965. m. $19.75. Mark Olson. Jubilee, Inc., 300 W. Apsly St., Philadelphia, PA 19144. Illus. Adv. Circ: 14,500. [*Bk. rev*: 2–5, 300–1,500 words, signed. *Aud*: Ages 14–18.]

This Christian magazine is heavily committed to "justice rooted in discipleship," with a biblical vision. It is well written and illustrated and carries articles that may be considered controversial—homosexuals in the church, Central America, Native Americans—but not with a sensationalist approach, and on topics that should appeal to the religious social conscience. In addition, it offers meditations, fiction, and poetry.

Pockets. *See under* CHILDREN/RELIGION.

Story Friends. *See under* CHILDREN/RELIGION.

810   Teenage. 1982. 10/yr. $7. Joani Schultz. Group Publg., Inc., 2890 N. Monroe Ave., P.O. Box 481, Loveland, CO 80539. Illus. Sample. [*Aud*: Ages 14–18.]

This is a typical church-oriented magazine that is one of hundreds of such titles used primarily in a given church and often in the same way classroom magazines are employed in schools. Each has its own religious viewpoint. Subtitled "for Christian young people," this colorfully illustrated 16-page publication considers such situations as friendship between Christians and non-Christians, shoplifting by Christians, and the virtues of virginity. The sometimes less than

tolerant approach is not everyone's idea of Christianity, but it serves the funda-
mentalists well. In addition to religious articles there are games, puzzles, sports,
and entertainment. It is nicely put together with illustrations on every page.

811   U.S. Catholic. 1963. m. $15. Mark J. Brummel. Claretian Publns., 1205 W. Monroe St.,
Chicago, IL 60606. Illus. Adv. Circ: 75,852. Sample. Microform: UMI. [*Indexed*: CathI,
RG. *Aud*: Ages 14–18.]

This illustrated monthly, published by the Claretians, speaks to Catholics and
others about the issues they face in their everyday lives. Such topics as racism,
complicity in the sins of others, and the homeless have been featured. The
articles and stories are written for the general reader and assume familiarity with
the Catholic faith.

Wee Wisdom. *See under* CHILDREN/GENERAL MAGAZINES.

812   Youth [Year] 90. 1981. 10/yr. Free. Worldwide Church of God, 300 W. Green St.,
Pasadena, CA 91123. Illus. Circ: 500,000. Sample. [*Aud*: Ages 14–18.]

A conservative, Sunday-school-type magazine for teenagers, this is sponsored
by the group whose founder is fundamentalist Herbert W. Armstrong. It is free
because it has a message that it wishes to spread about the powers of unity,
prayer, and practical Bible-based readings. The 30 well-illustrated pages are
optimistic and upbeat. Almost anything can be overcome. A good deal of
emphasis is placed on problems of youth, from divorced parents to the headache
of term pepers and the dangers of gangs. In between are quite well written short
pieces on sports and nature. Particular interest is shown in sports.

813   Youth Update (Yup). 1980. m. $6. Carol Ann Munchel. St. Anthony Messenger Press,
Cincinnati, OH 45210. Illus. Circ: 63,000. Vol. ends: Dec. [*Aud*: Ages 12–18.]

A four-page newsletter publication for Roman Catholics of high school age
and more mature junior high schoolers. A typical issue features an essay (for
example, "Summer Blahs" or "Vatican II") plus questions for discussion submitted by members of a teenage advisory board. This crisply written and edited title
is a staple in religious classes and groups on a parish level. It applies the teaching
of the gospel to modern problems and situations.

■ SCIENCE   [Natalie Kupferberg]

This section includes both general science and subject science magazines that
can be read by young adults and should be found in most school and public library
collections. Particular emphasis is on the general science title, although here and there
are more technical, specialized works—as, for example, in physics, marine science, and
chemistry. A vast number of scientific journals are published but only a select few are
suitable for younger readers, or, for that matter, the interested layperson. These tend to
be free of technical jargon and make an effort to present material with clarity and
precision.

First choices   (1) *Natural History*; (2) *Science*; (3) *Scientific American*.

Suitable for children   Ages 3–5: *Your Big Backyard*. Ages 5–8: *Scienceland*.
Ages 7–15: *Dolphin Log*. Ages 8–14: *Animal Kingdom*;
Discover; *Faces*. Ages 10–18: *Sea Frontiers*. Ages 12–18:
Science News.

814   **Alternative Sources of Energy.** 1972. 10/yr. $58. Larry Stoiaken. Alternative Sources of Energy, 107 S. Central Ave., Milaca, MN 56353. Illus. Adv. Circ: 30,000. Sample. Vol. ends: Dec. Microform: UMI. [*Indexed*: ASTI. *Bk. rev*: Occasional. *Aud*: Ages 14–18.]

Considering the state of the world's energy sources, this is a basic title for many high school and public libraries. Most of the material is within the reading ability of juniors and seniors in high school. *Alternative Sources of Energy* has evolved from a magazine as much for the enthusiast as the practitioner to a glossy trade magazine for several sizable industries. The same alternatives are offered, though: biomass, wind, solar, and hydroelectric—almost the classical four elements of earth, air, fire, and water. There is as much attention paid to financing the licensing as there is to technological development, with emphasis on the management point of view, but the underlying themes of conservation and environmental benefits remain. As a plus, there are occasional book and film reviews. As a good, single source of commercial developments in a number of energy areas, this is a useful magazine.

Animal Kingdom. *See under* CHILDREN/SCIENCE.

815   **Contemporary Physics.** 1959. bi-m. $190. J. S. Dugdale. Taylor and Francis, 4 John St., London WC1N 2ET, England. Illus. Adv. Index. Sample. Vol. ends: Nov/Dec. [*Indexed*: GSI. *Bk. rev*: 30–100, 100–500 words, signed. *Aud*: Ages 14–18.]

This is not an introductory journal, but presupposes a background in physics. It is a fine magazine for the advanced student with a year or so of science training. The goal of *Contemporary Physics* is to publish articles that are of interest to and understandable by researchers who are not experts in a particular subfield of physics. *Contemporary Physics* concentrates on lengthy review articles rather than reports of original research. Each review is intended to include enough background material for a reader working in another subfield to comprehend the information being presented. This enables students and researchers to keep abreast of and gain insights into all areas of the discipline and also to allow scientists in other fields to gain an understanding of basic physics research. In addition to the invited review articles, some shorter and more speculative essay reviews are included, as well as many book reviews.

Discover. *See under* CHILDREN/SCIENCE.

Dolphin Log. *See under* CHILDREN/SCIENCE.

816   **Earth Science.** 1946. q. $10. C. Petrini. Geological Inst., 4220 King St., Alexandria, VA 22302. Illus. Index. Sample. Vol. ends: Winter (No. 4). Microform: B&H, MIM, UMI. [*Indexed*: GSI, RG. *Bk. rev*: 12–16, 100–250 words, signed. *Aud*: Ages 14–18.]

Although this is published by a scholarly organization, it offers a basic introduction to the subject for high school students. In fact, the audience is anyone with an interest in the earth sciences. Articles, book reviews, a calendar of events, some meetings announcements, geological events (such as earthquakes and volcanic eruptions), and other general items of interest are included. The scope is any field of geology or planetary science, but on a very basic level. This periodical subscribes to the idea that science is not just for scientists.

Faces. *See under* CHILDREN/SCIENCE.

817   **Impact of Science on Society.** 1950. q. $45. Howard J. Moore. Taylor & Francis/UNESCO, 242 Cherry St., Philadelphia, PA 19106-1906. Illus. Circ: 3,500. Vol. ends: No. 4. Microform: MIM, UMI. [*Indexed*: PAIS, SocSc. *Aud*: Ages 14–18.]

Focusing on the effect of science and technology on society worldwide, each issue contains approximately ten articles that are normally devoted to a single subject, such as new and renewable sources of energy. Because of the wide scope, the effort to make scientific topics understandable and relevant to the nonspecialist, and the importance of the topics, the magazine is recommended for almost all types and sizes of libraries. Published in English, French, Chinese, Russian, Arabic, Portuguese, and Korean.

818   **Mosaic.** 1970. q. $5. Warren Kornberg. Natl. Science Foundation, 1800 G St. N.W., Washington, DC 20402. Illus. Circ: 15,000. Sample. Vol. ends: No. 4. Microform: UMI. [*Aud*: Ages 14–18.]

Various aspects of recent scientific discoveries and work, quite suitable for older students, are treated in each quarterly issue. This periodical covers a broad scientific range and sometimes deals with generalized subjects, such as science education and the role of women and minorities. Articles are about 10 to 15 pages long and contain numerous photographs and illustrations. Comprehensive science collections will want this periodical, as will libraries that need to keep up to date with what the government is doing in the field of science.

819   **National Geographic Research: a scientific journal.** 1968. q. $40. Harm J. de Blij. Natl. Geographic Soc., 1145 17th St. N.W., Washington, DC 20036. Illus. Circ: 6,000. Refereed. Vol. ends: Fall. [*Aud*: Ages 14–18.]

This scholarly scientific journal has many of the attributes of the popular *National Geographic* magazine, such as striking color photographs, excellent maps, and a generally attractive appearance, but its range is broader, including such sciences as anthropology, geology, paleontology, and zoology. In addition to geography, the emphasis is on original findings based on field work. Some of the articles report on research funded by grants from the society. About seven major articles and shorter research reports appear in each issue. The Spring issue lists all research grants awarded by the society during the preceding calendar year. For libraries with a strong scientific bent.

820   **Natural History.** 1900. m. $20. Alan Ternes. Amer. Museum of Natural History, Central Park W. & 79th St., New York, NY 10024. Illus. Adv. Index. Circ: 501,173. Vol. ends: Dec. Microform: B&H, MIM, UMI. Online: DIALOG. Reprint: UMI. [*Indexed*: MI, RG. *Bk. rev*: 1, 1,000 words, signed. *Aud*: Ages 14–18.]

This is often a first choice for school and public libraries because it is about as well known as any of the popular science magazines, and the quality of the editorial work and the photographs make it a natural drawing card for almost any reader. This readily available publication contains authoritative articles on the biological, natural, and earth sciences as well as reports on cultural and physical anthropology. Each issue is packed with beautiful photographs. Events at the American Museum of Natural History are listed, and there is a regular column by the science writer Stephen Jay Gould. This periodical takes a popular approach to specialized subjects.

821   **Nature.** 1869. w. $250 (Individuals, $125). John Maddox. Macmillan Magazines, Ltd., 4 Little Essex St., London WC2R 3LF, England. Illus. Adv. Index. Circ: 35,192. Refereed.

Vol. ends: Dec. Microform: B&H, UMI. Online: BRS. Reprint: UMI. [*Bk. rev*: 6–10, 500–1,000 words, signed. *Aud*: Ages 14–18.]

Here is a scholarly, often quoted English science journal that is suitable for advanced high school students. "*Nature* is an international journal covering all the sciences." It contains review articles, original research reports, short reports of outstanding novel findings, commentary, and news and views. It often presents the first reports of breakthroughs in science. Other useful features include book reviews, reviews of new products, and an extensive classified section listing job openings.

822   New Scientist. 1956. w. $99. Michael Kenward. IPC Magazines, Ltd., Holborn Publg. Group, Commonwealth House, 1-19 New Oxford St., London WCIA, England. Illus. Adv. Index. Circ: 77,300. Vol. ends: Dec. Online: VU/TEXT. [*Indexed*: ASTI. *Bk. rev*: 7, 500 words, signed. *Aud*: Ages 14–18.]

This is an English-based popular science magazine that should have more readers in American high schools. Each issue of this excellent weekly magazine is packed with international news and with feature articles on such topics as the ozone layer, AIDS, near-death experiences, or the green revolution. There are also editorials, book reviews, and cartoons. Although the contents are readily understandable to the layperson, professional scientists will also want to read this for lively coverage of what is going on in all the sciences.

823   Northeast Sun (Continuation of *NESSA Newsletter* and *MASEA Solar News*). 1974. 5/yr. $150 (Individuals, $50). Peg Smeltz. Northeast Solar Energy Assn., 14 Green St., P.O. Box 541, Brattleboro, VT 05301. Illus. Adv. Circ: 1,300. Sample. Refereed. Vol. ends: No. 5. [*Bk. rev*: 2, 500 words, signed. *Aud*: Ages 14–18.]

The official magazine of the Northeast Solar Energy Association, this publication promotes solar (and other renewable) energy and its efficient application. Emphasis appears to be on residential housing applications, such as photovoltaic panels, passive collection/distribution of heat, and energy-efficient construction. Attention is also paid to other uses of solar energy, such as solar-powered vehicles. Issues contain three to four short articles, society news, briefs on energy (commercial and governmental) developments, and a meetings calendar. *Northeast Sun* is a good example of a regional energy-oriented magazine and is recommended for large libraries.

824   Oceans. 1969. bi-m. $19.65. Michael W. Robbins. Oceanic Soc. Subs. to: Oceans Magazine, P.O. Box 10167, Des Moines, IA 50340. Illus. Adv. Circ: 60,000. Vol. ends: No. 6. Microform: UMI. Reprint: UMI. [*Indexed*: RG. *Bk. rev*: 3, 1,000 words, signed. *Aud*: Ages 14–18.]

This is a popular science magazine for all public and school libraries. It concentrates on marine sciences, and its outstanding color photos and drawings encourage the reader "to discover the richness and excitement of the ocean world." Articles cover a broad range of subjects—sportfishing in the Virgin Islands, theories on the origin of the oceans, sea passages in the *Iliad* and *Odyssey*, U.S. Coast Guard rescue missions, ocean bioluminescence, animals and plants of the Galapagos. Regular features include ocean science news, ships, recreation, shipwrecks, naval affairs, and upcoming Oceanic Society–sponsored natural history expeditions worldwide.

825   **Orion: nature quarterly.** 1982. q. $14. George K. Russell. Myrin Inst., 136 E 64th St., New York, NY 10021. Illus. Circ: 10,000. [*Bk. rev*: 5, 500 words, signed. *Aud*: Ages 14–18.]

Saving the environment is a key point in almost every issue of this quarterly. With wide appeal for almost everyone, including teenagers. This beautiful magazine contains about six lengthy articles devoted to a single theme such as water, migration, or animal-human relationships. The photographs are imaginative. There are also book reviews and lists of recommended readings in natural history. This magazine deserves to be indexed in periodical indexes because of its broad coverage of nature and its strong point of view.

826   **Physics Today.** 1948. m. Membership (Nonmembers, $85). Gloria B. Lubkin. Amer. Inst. of Physics, 335 E. 45th St., New York, NY 10017. Illus. Adv. Index. Circ: 71,453. Vol. ends: Dec. Microform: Pub. Reprint: Pub. [*Indexed*: ASTI, GSI. *Bk. rev*: 5–10, 300–700 words, signed. *Aud*: Ages 14–18.]

A physics journal that is only for advanced students, and not for beginners, *Physics Today* is the official journal of the American Institute of Physics and its member societies. It is written for physicists in all branches of the field and avoids presentation of highly technical material. Most of the articles published cover such topics as reviews of research in any area of physics; the relationship between physics and industry, government, or education; the history of the discipline; and problems facing the profession. This journal is the standard publication for physicists at all levels. If a library is to purchase only one physics journal, it should be this one.

827   **Robotics World.** 1983. m. $32. Larry Anderson. Communications Channels, Inc., 6255 Barfield Rd., Atlanta, GA 30328. Illus. Adv. Circ: 22,700. Refereed. Vol. ends: Dec. Microform: UMI. [*Aud*: Ages 14–18.]

Robotics World is a trade magazine emphasizing robotics applications in industrial settings, with most on a large scale. Recent issues featured several articles on welding, as well as robot painters, assemblers, and materials handlers. Articles are written by practitioners or by the magazine staff and generally lack references. The popular approach makes it a useful magazine in many high school and public libraries.

828   **Rocks and Minerals.** 1926. bi-m. $35. Robert I. Gait. Heldref Publns., 4000 Albermarle St. N.W., Washington, DC 20016. Illus. Adv. Index. Circ: 3,900. Microform: UMI. Reprint: UMI. [*Aud*: Ages 14–18.]

Popularly written articles by geologists cover many aspects of the earth sciences, including collecting sites, regional geological events, mineral exhibits, and shows. The primary audience remains the amateur, the interested student, and the layperson, but the level of writing is technical and the focus is on geology and fossils. The authors are concerned with the activities of museums, serious collecting, and various types of exhibits, and are less involved with the individual collector and the how-to-do-it approach. At the same time the material is easy enough to follow and is illustrated. A first choice for high school collections, public libraries, and popular education about the earth sciences.

829   **Science.** 1880. w. $98 (Individuals, $65). Daniel Koshland. Amer. Assn. for the Advancement of Science, 1333 H St. N.W., Washington, DC 20005. Illus. Adv. Index. Circ:

160,000. Sample. Refereed. Vol. ends: Dec. Microform: B&H, MIM, UMI. Reprint: UMI. [*Indexed*: ASTI, RG. *Bk. rev*: 3–5, 300–500 words, signed. *Aud*: Ages 14–18.]

One of the basic science magazines for all public and school libraries, this is easy to read and can be enjoyed by almost any high school student. Each weekly issue contains "News and Comment," a section that deals with current events and findings; general articles that review new developments in one field that may be of interest to readers in other fields; research articles containing information on breakthroughs; and reports written by eminent specialists that present the results of original research projects. Booklists, checklists, and news briefs keep the reader abreast of activities in the whole spectrum of science. For a summary of each issue, readers can turn to "This Week in Science" at the front of each issue.

Science Challenge. *See* **Biology Bulletin Monthly** *under* CLASSROOM PUBLICATIONS.

830 **Science News: the weekly news magazine of current science.** 1921. w. $34.50. Joel Greenberg. Science Service, Inc., 1719 N St. N.W., Washington, DC 20036. Illus. Adv. Circ: 175,000. Vol. ends: Dec. Microform: B&H, MIM, UMI. Online: DIALOG. Reprint: UMI. [*Indexed*: CIJE, GSI, MI, RG. *Aud*: Ages 12–18.]

This publication covers the "top of the news" each week in all the sciences. The articles are short and easy to read, and the facts are always well documented. There is also one long article on a current issue such as radioactive waste or marihuana as medicine. Two other useful features are "Science on the Air," which lists television programs of scientific interest, and a brief description of new books. The semiannual index makes it easy to trace events of the past year. All libraries will want this short and to-the-point publication.

Science World. *See* **Scholastic Science World** *under* CLASSROOM PUBLICATIONS.

Scienceland. *See under* CHILDREN/SCIENCE.

831 **Scientific American.** 1845. m. $24. Jonathan Piel. Scientific American, Inc., 415 Madison Ave., New York, NY 10017. Illus. Adv. Index. Circ: 622,806. Refereed. Vol. ends: Dec. Microform: B&H, MIM, UMI. Online: DIALOG. [*Indexed*: ASTI, GSI, RG. *Bk. rev*: 4, 1,000 words, signed. *Aud*: Ages 14–18.]

The best known general scientific magazine in America, this is not easy reading. It presupposes some background in science and at least a college degree, but attentive high school students will find numerous articles and short pieces of interest within their reading ability. This long-established magazine offers a broad range of articles covering archaeology, astronomy, earth science, medicine, psychology, technology—anything remotely considered science. It keeps up with the times: A regular feature, "Computer Recreations," is aimed at serious computer users as well as hobbyists. The illustrations and diagrams, many in color, are both informative and decorative. The book reviews are just the right length.

832 **Sea Frontiers: a publication of the International Oceanographic Foundation, University of Miami.** 1954. bi-m. $18. Gilbert L. Voss. Intl. Oceanographic Foundation, 3979 Rickenbacker Causeway, Virginia Key, Miami, FL 33149. Illus. Circ: 30,000. Vol. ends: No. 6. Microform: B&H, UMI. Reprint: UMI. [*Indexed*: RG. *Bk. rev*: 5, 500 words, signed. *Aud*: Ages 10–18.]

Now published in a larger size, with numerous attractive color photographs of marine life, this journal has an appeal similar to that of *Oceans*. It serves as the vehicle of the International Oceanographic Foundation, whose purpose is "to encourage the extension of human knowledge by scientific study and exploration of the oceans in all their aspects, including the study of game fishes, food fishes, ocean currents, geology, chemistry and physics of the sea floor.'' Many of the contributors are associated with the University of Miami or NOAA, and respond to readers' questions in *Sea Secrets*, now included as part of *Sea Frontiers*. The magazine is suitable for high school students interested in marine life.

833 **Seascape.** 1987. m. $19. Rick Hogben. Seascape Publns., Ltd., 52-54 Southwark St., London SE1 1UJ, England. Illus. Adv. Index. [*Bk. rev*: 3–4, 250–300 words, signed. *Aud*: Ages 14–18.]

A publication that aims to encourage a greater awareness of and enthusiasm for the sea, ships, and shipping. A wide range of topics is covered—modern ship technology including commercial sail propulsion, contemporary and historical naval affairs, maritime history, passenger shipping, the sea, ship modeling, and maritime art and collecting. There are occasional contributed articles of opinion. Each issue includes a section of photographs and a statistical feature. A good choice for general collections.

834 **Technology Review.** 1899. 8/yr. $27. John I. Mattill. Massachusetts Inst. of Technology, Alumni Assn., Rm. 10-140, Cambridge, MA 02139. Illus. Adv. Index. Circ: 75,000. Vol. ends: Nov/Dec. Microform: UMI. Reprint: UMI. [*Indexed*: ASTI, PAIS. *Bk. rev*: 3–4, 500–800 words. *Aud*: Ages 14–18.]

Less technical in tone than one might expect from its MIT sponsorship, *Technology Review* is edited with the public in mind. New developments are covered extensively, with practical and industrial applications usually emphasized. The magazine offers a good overview of what is going on in the scientific and technical worlds, but with more depth than is offered by most other general scientific publications. Illustrations are lively as well as illuminating—adjectives that characterize the magazine as a whole. Someday, the editors might consider a more enticing name for their publication, which should be in high school libraries, as well as in public libraries with substantial collections.

835 **Underwater Naturalist: bulletin of the American Littoral Society.** 1962. q. $20 Members ($25 Nonmembers). D. W. Bennett. Amer. Littoral Soc., Sandy Hook, Highlands, NJ 07732. Illus. Circ: 5,000. Vol. ends: No. 4. Microform: UMI. Reprint: UMI. [*Bk. rev*: 4, 500 words. *Aud*: Ages 14–18.]

The American Littoral Society is devoted to environmental conservation, protection, and education. Its journal carries popularly written articles on topics related to coasts, oceans, estuaries, freshwater rivers, and lakes. Each issue carries a report of the member-conducted fish-tagging program and an attractive color cover photo.

Your Big Backyard. *See under* CHILDREN/SCIENCE.

■ SOCIOLOGY   [Henry Neil Mendelsohn]

Sociology is concerned with many things, but primarily with the problems and social issues of our society. Unfortunately, most of the magazines in sociology are for the expert and are not edited for the layperson or young adult. Included here are those few magazines that have wider appeal and may be of use to the student in a particular course, or in quest of personal information. Needless to add, the titles are only an extremely small number of those available in this expanding area.

First choices (1) *Society*; (2) *Ekistics*.

836 **Ekistics: problems and science of human settlements.** 1955. bi-m. $60. Panayis Psomopolous. Athens Technological Org., Athens Center of Ekistics, P.O. Box 3471, 10210 Athens, Greece. Illus. Index. Circ: 2,000. Vol. ends: Nov/Dec. Microform: UMI. [*Indexed*: SocSc. *Aud*: Ages 14–18.]

Ekistics is a science that incorporates aspects of economics, politics, technology, and aesthetics in the study of human settlements. Each issue of this impressive work contains 70 to 100 pages of text and illustrations. The journal provides an informative mix of research articles and field reports. There are 12 to 15 articles per issue, and each issue focuses on a specific topic. Recent examples include a special double issue in memory of Mary Jacqueline Tyrwhitt (a co-founder and first editor of the journal) and the geography of Mediterranean settlements—urban networks at the regional, national, and local scale. This is an excellent journal for the advanced high school student seeking a worldview of communities.

837 **Explorations in Ethnic Studies: the journal for the National Association for Ethnic Studies.** 1978. s-a. $35 (Individuals, $25). Gretchen M. Bataille. Natl. Assn. for Ethnic Studies, 1861 Rosemont Ave., Claremont, CA 91711. Circ: 300. Refereed. Vol. ends: July. Reprint: UMI. [*Aud*: Ages 14–18.]

A scholarly, multidisciplinary journal that serves as an international forum for the exchange of ideas in the area of ethnic studies. Each issue contains three articles followed by two to three challenging critiques. Articles have dealt with thought-provoking issues concerning Italian women, female power, ethnicity and aging, Puerto Ricans, black and white college students, and so forth. Included with membership, in addition to this journal, are a semi-annual newsletter, *The Ethnic Reporter*, and an annual review supplement called *Explorations in Sights and Sounds*, which is composed of extensive reviews of over 50 books and nonprint media related to ethnic studies. Highly recommended for high school and public libraries.

838 **Family Planning Perspectives** (Formerly: *Planned Parenthood*). 1969. bi-m. $26. Deirdre Wulf. Alan Guttmacher Inst., 111 Fifth Ave., New York, NY 10003. Illus. Adv. Index. Circ: 16,000. Vol. ends: No. 6. Microform: UMI. Reprint: UMI. [*Bk. rev*: 1, 1,500–2,000 words, signed. *Aud*: Ages 14–18.]

The focus of this journal is on planned parenthood. The articles are concerned with the use and types of contraception, the health-related complications of contraception, infant mortality, prenatal care, and all topics related to family planning. Articles have examined paying for maternity care, adolescent fathers and mothers, risks with birth-control pills, and the high rate of early delivery in blacks. In addition to the articles, the "Digest" section provides brief information on research results and news pertinent to the focus of the journal. Because of its useful health-related information, this journal is recommended for some high school and public libraries.

839 **Journal of Housing: the magazine of housing and community development issues.** 1944. bi-m. $24. Terence K. Cooper. Natl. Assn. of Housing and Redevelopment

Officials, 1320 18th St. N.W., Washington, DC 20036. Illus. Adv. Index. Circ: 12,000. Vol. ends: Nov/Dec. [*Indexed*: PAIS, SocSc. *Bk. rev*: Occasional. *Aud*: Ages 14–18.]

The emphasis of this journal is on the political aspects of housing and urban policy. *Journal of Housing* is closer to a newsletter in style and format than it is to a scholarly journal. The articles tend to be informational rather than analytical, and each issue of the publication includes several newsletter-like features (state reports, city reports, opinion and comment, people in the news). The May/June issues includes the annual buying guide, which began in 1985; a new annual feature is a computer update and list of vendors in the March/April issue. This is a very useful publication for city planners and is also suitable for select public and high school libraries.

840 Migration World (Formerly: *Migration Today*). 1973. bi-m. $25 (Individuals, $19). Lydio Tomasi. Center for Migration Studies, 209 Flagg Pl., Staten Island, NY 10304. Adv. Circ: 1,750. [*Indexed*: CIJE. *Aud*: Ages 14–18.]

The focus of this journal is on immigrants and refugees and the issues and events affecting them. Each issue includes reports and analyses of current developments in judicial decisions affecting immigrants, and news updates, editorials, news analyses, and book reviews. A special section features migrant health and problems faced by migrants in the United States and internationally. Articles are well written and address issues across a wide range of interests. Legal, medical, and other current information on immigration laws and relevant news on immigration make this particularly interesting reading for all immigrants and for those who work with them. A resources section lists the latest books, films, and research in the field. An excellent choice for high schools, to create an awareness in students of the various issues and events affecting immigrants.

841 Population Bulletin. 1945. q. Membership (Nonmembers, $50). Roberta Yared. Population Reference Bureau, Inc., 777 14th St. N.W., Washington, DC 20005. Illus. Index. Circ: 10,000. Vol. ends: Dec. Microform: UMI. [*Indexed*: PAIS, SocSc. *Aud*: Ages 14–18.]

Primarily a 40- to 48-page monograph on population. Each issue features one subject and author; the articles are supported by many charts and diagrams, added readings, and an extensive bibliography. The material is written for the layperson in easy-to-understand, nontechnical language and is an objective look at the world's population. From time to time, specialized bibliographies are published. (*Note*: Subscriptions include *Population Today*, a popular magazine on population; *World Data Sheets*; *United States Population Data Sheet*; *Interchange Newsletter*; and *Population Trends and Public Policy* reports.)

842 Social Problems. 1953. 5/yr. $60 (Individuals, $45). Joseph W. Schneider. Univ. of California Press, Journals Dept. 21203, Berkeley, CA 94720. Adv. Index. Circ: 5,200. Refereed. Microform: MIM, UMI. [*Indexed*: PAIS, SocSc. *Aud*: Ages 14–18.]

This is the official journal of the Society for the Study of Social Problems, an organization composed of problem- and policy-oriented sociologists. Half a dozen articles per issue cover a broad range of social problems and issues, for example, "Gangs and the Community," "Rape and Sexual Harassment," "Women's Work." Because of its broad coverage of social problems this title is recommended for large public as well as school libraries.

843 Society: social science and modern society (Formerly: *Trans-Action: social science and modern society*). 1962. bi-m. $50. Irving Louis Horowitz. Society, P.O. Box A,

Rutgers Univ., New Brunswick, NJ 08903. Circ: 15,000. Vol. ends: Oct. Microform: B&H, JAI, Kraus, MIM, UMI. [*Indexed*: SocSc. *Bk. rev*: 3–5. *Aud*: Ages 14–18.]

This is the only semi-popular sociology magazine, and it should be found in most high school and public libraries. While not quite a popular treatment of social science (as *Psychology Today* is a popular treatment of psychology), *Society* does attempt to present social science research, debate, and commentary to a wide audience. Its articles address topics of popular concern and those concerned with policy issues. Articles are often but not always grouped around broad topics, as in the theme issues "Surrogate Motherhood," "The American Census of 1990, "A Quarter Century of Social Science," "Communal Lives and Utopian Hopes," and "Progressive Ethics and Commercial Advertising." Regular fetures include "Social Science and Public Policy," "Culture and Society," "Photo Essays," "Books in Review," and a regular column entitled "Social Science and the Citizen." Many prominent authors contribute jargon-free articles to this widely circulated journal. Recommended for public and high school libraries.

■ SPORTS [Fred Batt]

See also: Boats; Environment, Conservation, and Outdoor Recreation; Fishing and Hunting

Sports dominate the daily activities of many young people and are a major part of our culture, providing subjects for hero worship as well as entertainment. Fitness remains a mania and this is reflected in the titles listed here. Those related to sports in general and to specific sports are, of course, included too. Almost any of the titles in the sixth edition of *Magazines for Libraries* would be suitable for school and public libraries serving young adults. Listed here are those magazines specifically edited for younger readers or, more likely, adult magazines well within the framework of the experience and needs of teenage readers. If the specific sport cannot be found, one should turn to the main volume.

First choices (1) *Sports Illustrated*; (2) *Sport*; (3) *Inside Sports*; (4) any title that meets the needs of a particular sport.

Suitable for children Ages 8–18: *Sports Illustrated for Kids*. Ages 10–18: *Info AAA*; *Inside Sports*; *International Gymnast Magazine*; *Skiing*; *Sports Illustrated*; *Swimming World and Junior Swimmer*; *World Tennis*; *YABA World*. Ages 12–18: *Amateur Baseball News*; *Football Digest*; *Soccer Digest*; *Surfer Magazine*.

844 **ATA Magazines/Martial Arts and Fitness.** 1983. q. $7. Milo Daily. ATA Publns., P.O. Box 240835, Memphis, TN 38124. Illus. Adv. Circ: 15,000. Vol. ends: Winter. Microform: UMI. [*Aud*: Ages 14–18.]

This is a specialized magazine that will appeal to many young readers. It is geared to fitness, both physical and mental, through the practice of the Songahm style of Taekwondo, aerobics, and strength training. Articles also treat nutrition and traditional Korean culture with respect to the potential interest of Taekwondo students. This is the world's largest centrally administered martial arts association magazine. Public library fare but also useful for school libraries where martial arts are taught.

845   **Amateur Baseball News.** 1958. 7/yr. $5. Amer. Amateur Baseball Congress. P.O. Box 467, 215 E. Green, Marshall, MI 49068. Illus. Adv. Circ: 10,000. Sample. [*Aud*: Ages 12–18.]

A tabloid that gives the amateur the latest on the leagues and events across the United States, and beyond. The writing style is well within the grasp of the younger reader and almost anyone interested in the sport. There are numerous features on how to improve the game, as well as some book and media reviews.

846   **American Hockey Magazine** (Formerly: *American Hockey & Arena*). 1972. 10/yr. $12. Mike Schroeder. Amateur Hockey Assn. of the United States, 2997 Broadmoor Valley Rd., Colorado Springs, CO 80906. Illus. Adv. Circ: 30,000. Vol. ends: Oct. [*Aud*: Ages 14–18.]

Any teenager involved in hockey will want to find this in the library. "America's only amateur hockey magazine," this publication offers departments and features treating junior hockey, collegiate hockey, refereeing, coaching, profiles, products, and so forth for amateur hockey participants and enthusiasts. It would be of interest to school libraries in places where hockey is played and public libraries in hockey-oriented communities.

847   **BMX Action.** 1976. m. $16.50. Wizard Publns., Inc., 3162 Kashiwa St., Torrance, CA 90505. Illus. Adv. Circ: 217,000. Vol. ends: Dec. [*Aud*: Ages 14–18.]

Foot-powered bikes can be glamorous for young people, and this magazine, where the action is on a bicycle and not on a powered machine, makes that point nicely. It is directed almost exclusively to high school students, and the focus is on safety, skill, and heroes of the sport. The illustrated articles are short, factual, and filled with the kind of data that fascinate the young. There are good bike tests, but the highlight of each issue is the photography.

848   **Baseball Digest: baseball's only monthly magazine.** 1941. m. $14.95. John Kuenster. Century Publg. Co., 990 Grove St., Evanston, IL 60201. Illus. Adv. Circ: 275,000. Vol. ends: Dec. Microform: UMI. [*Aud*: Ages 14–18.]

Teens with possible reading blocks or difficulties can turn to this for information on a subject they love, offered in a fairly easy to read fashion. For the major league baseball fan, this magazine provides a cross section of easy-to-read articles, some of which are reprints from newspapers, written by noted baseball writers and by individuals in the game. The emphasis is on profiles and aspects of players' careers, as well as on historical themes—for example, the monthly "The Game I'll Never Forget." Issues also include diverse and interesting statistics, rosters, articles concerned with managing perspectives, and even quizzes and puzzles. *Baseball Digest* will see plenty of action in school and public libraries.

849   **Basketball Digest.** 1973. 8/yr. $9.95. Michael K. Herbert. Century Publg. Co., 990 Grove St., Evanston, IL 60201. Illus. Adv. Circ: 132,000. Vol. ends: June. Microform: UMI. [*Aud*: Ages 14–18.]

Again, a magazine for both young people with reading problems and for the average fan—by the people who bring you *Baseball Digest*. This magazine offers lively features, departments, interviews, and statistics. See *Baseball Digest* (above in this section) and *Hockey Digest* (below in this section) for additional descriptions of magazines in this Century Publications set that also includes *Football Digest*, *Auto Racing Digest*, *Bowling Digest*, and *Soccer Digest*.

850   **Bicycling.** 1962. 10/yr. $15.97. James C. McCullagh. Rodale Press, 33 E. Minor St., Emmaus, PA 18098. Illus. Adv. Index. Circ: 247,900. Vol. ends: Dec. Microform: UMI. [*Indexed*: Acs, MI. *Aud*: Ages 14–18.]

While this is edited for the adult who turns to the bike more for exercise than for transportation, it will appeal to younger readers. Bicycling is a major form of exercise for millions of people as well as a relatively inexpensive form of transportation for many others. For some individuals, bicycling is a way of life. This beautifully produced magazine offers diverse information for the bicycling enthusiast, including equipment analyses, clothing ideas, cycling techniques, health-related items, medical perspectives, safety considerations, training ideas, and even fiction and humor. Excellent photograhy and writing make this a good choice for many libraries.

851   **Bowling Digest.** 1983. bi-m. $12. Michael K. Herbert. Century Publg. Co., 990 Grove St., Evanston, IL 60201. Illus. Adv. Circ: 118,000. Sample. [*Aud*: Ages 14–18.]

A current, easy-to-follow magazine that should be found in collections where bowling is of interest. This is concerned with the daily activities of the dedicated bowler, no matter what the age, sex, or background. Here one finds tips for both the beginner and the expert, analyses of equipment, sketches and interviews, personalities, material on current competitions, and many other excellent features. The format is lively and the illustrations are excellent. This magazine also includes information on televised tours and professional touring groups as well as the usual statistics and records.

852   **Flex.** 1983. m. $20. Joe Weider. Brute Enterprises, 21100 Erwin St., Woodland Hills, CA 91367. Illus. Adv. Circ: 75,000. Vol. ends: Dec. [*Aud*: Ages 14–18.]

Young bodybuilders could do no better than to start with this magazine. It is for them and other beginners. A Joe Weider bodybuilding magazine, for both men and women, this publication offers numerous exercises and workout routines that are easy to follow. Much of the material is illustrated. There is a good balance between sensible tips on nutrition and safety and health precautions. Although it takes dedication to read each issue, those who persist will find useful information. Also includes contest information, profiles, and many monthly departments.

853   **Football Digest: pro football's monthly magazine.** 1971. 10/yr. $12.95. Michael K. Herbert. Century Publg. Co., 990 Grove St., Evanston, IL 60201. Illus. Adv. Circ: 200,000. Vol. ends: Aug. Microform: UMI. [*Aud*: Ages 12–18.]

An easy-to-read magazine for football fans by the same people who publish the other sports digest magazines. This, as do *Baseball Digest* and its numerous cousins, offers lively features, departments, interviews, and statistics.

854   **Golf Digest.** 1971. m. $19.94. Jerry Tarde. Gold Digest/Tennis Inc., 5520 Park Ave., Trumbull, CT 06611. Illus. Adv. Circ: 1,300,000. Vol. ends: Dec. Microform: UMI. [*Bk. rev*: Occasional. *Aud*: Ages 14–18.]

Offering an adult view of golf, this presupposes leisure, money, and some experience. At the same time, because it is so popular and so widely read, it will appeal to many young adults. It is billed as the golf magazine with the largest circulation. Many golfers swear by *Golf Digest*; others prefer *Golf Magazine*; quite a few cannot survive a month without digesting both publications. Similarities abound: beautiful photography, profiles of professionals, excellent instructions, and wonderful writing. *Golf Digest* has something to offer golfers at all levels. Major tournament previews and analyses, equipment reviews, fashion, rules analyses, medical advice, and the like round out this golf publication, which is considered the best by many and worthy of a place on the shelves of most libraries.

855   **Golf Magazine.** 1959. m. $15.94. George Peper. Times-Mirror Magazines, Inc., 380 Madison Ave., New York, NY 10017. Illus. Adv. Index. Circ: 950,000. Vol. ends: Dec. Microform: UMI. Online: DIALOG. [*Indexed*: MI. *Aud*: Ages 14–18.]

This magazine can stand on its own with its impressive array of playing and teaching editors (directed by Arnold Palmer), wonderful instructional articles, profiles of professional golfers, analyses and lists of the greatest courses in the world, humorous articles, beautiful photography, PGA & LPGA tour statistics, equipment information, and many other regular features and specials. Even the advertisements are a joy for golf aficionados. The February issue is a yearbook. This publication should be found next to *Golf Digest* on library shelves. Both are worth the price.

856   **Handball.** 1950. bi-m. $22. Vern Roberts. U.S. Handball Assn., 930 N. Benton Ave., Tucson, AZ 85711. Illus. Adv. Circ: 10,000. Vol. ends: Dec. Microform: UMI. [*Aud*: Ages 14–18.]

Youngsters who want to improve their handball can turn to this magazine for help six times a year. It is an ideal choice. "The official voice of the United States Handball Association" offers features geared to the membership, health-related articles, instructional sections, and tournament results, ranging from juniors to professionals. Primarily of interest to the handball competitor and tournament player, this is potentially useful to some libraries.

857   **Hockey Digest: pro hockey's monthly magazine.** 1972. 8/yr. $9.95. Michael K. Herbert. Century Publg. Co., 990 Grove St., Evanston, IL 60201. Illus. Adv. Circ: 80,000. Vol. ends: June. Microform: UMI. [*Aud*: Ages 14–18.]

Similar to *Baseball Digest*, this publication treats current and past hockey players, hockey teams, and other aspects of professional hockey in its features and departments. As with the other Century Publishing Company publications, lively and informative features are included, such as products, statistics, quizzes, and the "Game I'll Never Forget." This publication is potential library fare in areas where hockey interest is high.

858   **Hockey News: the international hockey weekly.** 1947. 41/yr. $34.95. Bob McKenzie. Transcontinental Publg., Inc., 85 Scarsdale Rd., Suite 100, Toronto, Ont. M3B 2R2, Canada. Illus. Adv. Circ: 115,000. Microform: UMI. [*Aud*: Ages 14–18.]

A Canadian view of the world of hockey. Most of the emphasis is on the activities of the National Hockey League, but it also includes minor pro, juniors, colleges, and international hockey. This weekly tabloid carries detailed scores, statistics, player profiles, interviews, and numerous action photographs. While a basic requirement for many Canadian libraries, this may not be so necessary in American libraries.

Info AAA. *See under* CHILDREN/SPORTS.

859 **Inside Sports.** 1979. m. $18. Michael K. Herbert. Century Publg. Co., 990 Grove St., Evanston, Il 60201. Illus. Adv. Circ: 500,000. Vol. ends: Dec. Microform: UMI. [*Indexed*: Acs. *Aud*: Ages 10–18.]

This is a somewhat simpler approach to sports in general than that found in rival publications, but this title is almost as popular and is certainly among the first choices for high school and public libraries serving young people. It provides articles of interest to a wide readership of sports enthusiasts. Included are interviews with sports figures; in-depth profiles; many well-written features, columns, and departments (e.g., media, humor); good photography; and everything one would expect from an all-purpose sports magazine. Place on library shelves next to *Sports Illustrated* and *Sport*.

860 **International Gymnast Magazine.** 1956. m. $18. Dwight Normile. SundbySports, 225 Brooks, Oceanside, CA 92054. Illus. Adv. Circ: 30,000. Vol. ends: Dec. Microform: UMI. [*Aud*: Ages 10–18.]

"Serving the sport of gymnastics for over a quarter of a century" and considered the world's leading gymnastics magazine, this heavily illustrated publication offers detailed reports on competitions and events throughout the world. It is a vehicle to find out what is going on—training camps, research, information, training tips—and who the major personalities in the sport are, through profiles and interviews.

861 **Muscle & Fitness** (Formerly: *Joe Weider's Muscle*). 1938. m. $35. Joe Weider. Brute Enterprises, 21100 Erwin St., Woodland Hills, CA 91367. Illus. Adv. Circ: 570,000. [*Aud*: Ages 14–18.]

With the inscription "we take body building seriously because you do," this thick publication, filled with great photography, offers many features, regular departments written by experts, and detailed instructional contributions geared to the would-be bodybuilders of all levels, from beginning to advanced. This Joe Weider publication reflects the same approach as other Weider publications. Among the many regular departments are nutrition, sports medicine, physiology, kinesiology, profiles, product reviews, and so on. About three articles per issue are geared specifically toward women. Although similar to the many other bodybuilding magazines, this impressive publication is a cut above its competitors and may be popular in public and school libraries.

862 **National Racquetball** (Incorporates *AARA in Review*). 1973. m. $16. Helen Quinn. Florida Trade Publns., Inc., P.O. Box 6126, Clearwater, FL 34618. Illus. Adv. Circ: 45,000. Vol. ends: Dec. Microform: UMI. [*Aud*: Ages 14–18.]

National Racquetball is the only publication covering the sport of racquetball. Its coverage of both the professional and the amateur game is very complete. Schedules of events, national rankings, and a new product section are featured monthly. It provides instruction from top professional players and certified instructors and has a lively and graphically pleasing format. Each issue includes a number of features and instructionals and a center-spread photo of a top player. A "must" for racquetball players at any level.

863 **The Olympian.** 1975. 10/yr. Membership $19.88. Bob Condron. U.S. Olympic Committee, 1750 E. Boulder St., Colorado Springs, CO 80909. Illus. Vol. ends: May. [*Aud*: Ages 14–18.]

Statistics, facts, profiles, and analyses from the U.S. Olympic Society. This also includes an insider's view of competitions leading up to the Olympic Games,

research on nutrition, new methods of training, how coaching affects performance, and similar topics. Contains excellent photography. (*Note*: Membership in
the U.S. Olympic Society is the only way to receive this publication.)

864   **The Ring.** 1922. m. $18. Nigel Collins. Ring Publg. Corp., 130 W. 37th St., New York,
NY 10018. Illus. Adv. Circ: 200,000. Vol. ends: Feb. [*Aud*: Ages 14–18.]

   The best boxing magazine for interested young adults, this may be a second
choice in many libraries, but if the sport is of major interest it should be among
the first. With recent stability in editorship, this publication again lives up to its
reputation as "a magazine which a man may take home with him. He may leave
it on his table safe in the knowledge that it does not contain one line of matter . . .
which would be offensive." This is the only boxing magazine offering detailed
coverage of boxing on a worldwide basis, preliminary bouts as well as main
events. It also includes sectional and national rankings (*The Ring* has appropriately returned to ratings in the traditional eight divisions in an attempt to stem
the tide of weight and class proliferation), excellent stories by boxing experts,
and profiles and features of ring heroes past and present.

865   **Runner's World** (Formerly: *Rodale's Runner's World*). 1966. m. $19.95. Amby
Burfoot. Rodale Press, Inc., 33 E. Minor St., Emmaus, PA 18049. Illus. Adv. Circ: 425,000.
Vol. ends: Dec. Microform: UMI. [*Aud*: Ages 14–18.]

   Runner's World offers many features and excellent columns and departments
to cover health, fitness, racing reports, training, equipment profiles, nutrition,
and other aspects of running. For libraries serving both the serious runner and
the weekend jogger.

866   **Ski.** 1936. 8/yr. $11.94. Dick Needham. Times-Mirror Magazines, 380 Madison Ave.,
New York, NY 10017. Illus. Adv. Circ: 430,000. Vol. ends: Apr. Microform: UMI. [*Aud*:
Ages 14–18.]

   This is a fine choice for teenagers, but it does presuppose that the reader has
the time, money, and leisure to enjoy the sport—particularly the money. Billed
as "America's oldest ski publication," this top-notch magazine is stuffed with
marvelous features, information about resorts and travel, detailed equipment
analyses, competition information, and ski instruction. The photography is fantastic. Special regional sections add to the overall appeal and coverage. If the
library takes this magazine it will want *Skiing* as well; if a choice has to be made,
the latter is preferable because it is indexed in *Readers' Guide*.

867   **Skiing.** 1947. 7/yr. $9.98. Bill Grout. BS Magazines, 1515 Broadway, New York, NY
10036. Illus. Adv. Circ: 440,000. Sample. Vol. ends: Mar. Microform: B&H, UMI. Online:
DIALOG. [*Indexed*: MI, RG. *Aud*: Ages 10–18.]

   As with *Ski*, this magazine offers reports on competitions, travel and resort
information, instruction on how to ski better, equipment tips, and a variety of
special sections and regular columns. Termed "the magazine for the serious
skier," *Skiing* emphasizes instruction and should be on the shelves alongside *Ski*
as a vehicle for skiers to learn the wheres, hows, and whys of their sport.

868 **Skin Diver.** 1951. m. $19.94. Bill Gleason. Peterson Publg. Co., 8490 Sunset Blvd., Los Angeles, CA 90069. Illus. Adv. Index. Circ: 224,786. Vol. ends: Dec. Microform: UMI. Online: DIALOG. [*Indexed*: MI. *Aud*: Ages 14–18.]

The "foremost authority in its field" is attractive and filled with well-written articles and beautiful photography (even the advertisements). Worldwide coverage includes underwater recreation, ocean exploration, scientific research, commercial diving, technological advancements, and so on. Regular features include travel, scuba techniques, underwater photography, equipment, marine biology, conservation, and much else. Obviously, the skin divers' bible for information and activities.

869 **Soccer America.** 1971. 50/yr. $38.97. Lynn Berling-Manuel. Berling Communications, Inc., P.O. Box 23704, Oakland, CA 94623. Illus. Adv. Circ: 15,000. Vol. ends: June. Microform: UMI. [*Aud*: Ages 14–18.]

This weekly soccer magazine is devoted to American professional soccer, college soccer, and the international soccer scene. There is a weekly record of all professional games and selected international contests as well as occasional profiles of major soccer figures. This tabloid is recommended for libraries of all types in places where interest in soccer is high.

870 **Soccer Digest.** 1978. 6/yr. $9.95. Michael K. Herbert. Century Publg. Co., 990 Grove St., Evanston, IL 60201. Illus. Adv. Circ: 65,000. Vol. ends: Mar. Microform: UMI. [*Aud*: Ages 12–18.]

Another in the *Baseball Digest* family, this follows the format of the other cousins. There are lively features that are easy to read. Departments, interviews, and statistics complete the circle of information for young soccer fans.

871 **Sport.** 1946. m. $12. Neil Cohen. Sport Magazine Assocs., 119 W. 40th St., New York, NY 10018. Illus. Adv. Circ: 930,000. Vol. ends: Dec. Microform: B&H, UMI. Online: DIALOG. [*Indexed*: MI, RG. *Aud*: Ages 14–18.]

This and *Sports Illustrated* are favored in high school and public libraries serving younger readers. A magazine that looks into the hows and whys of sports, it hardly needs an introduction. "Beers with . . ." is a relaxed, casual conversation with intriguing sports figures. "Sport Talk" offers short, off-beat, information-filled pieces. "Sweat" tells how to incorporate and understand professional athletes' workouts. *Sport* excels at behind-the-scenes and strategy-oriented articles. It also features revealing personality profiles. Photo essays and illustrative photographs receive special emphasis and add to the magazine's distinctive style.

872 **The Sporting News.** 1886. 57/yr. $62.13. Tom Barnidge. Sporting News Publg. Co., 1212 N. Lindbergh Blvd., P.O. Box 56, St. Louis, MO 63132. Illus. Adv. Circ: 725,000. Vol. ends: Dec. Microform: UMI. [*Indexed*: MI. *Aud*: Ages 14–18.]

Excellent columns by Stan Isle, Art Spander, Joe Gergen, Mike Downey, Bob Verdi, and others, plus the most complete and comprehensive sports coverage available on a weekly basis, make this one of the major publications for sports fans. Detailed summaries, box scores, and statistics are published for football, baseball, basketball, and hockey at both college and professional levels. Other sports are treated, including articles for major activities and short summaries for other events. Major stories pop up in some issues. This is a fine publication that complements *Sports Illustrated* and is recommended for most libraries despite its newspaper format.

873 **Sports Illustrated.** 1954. 54/yr. $64.26. Mark Mulvoy. Time, Inc., Time & Life Bldg., New York, NY 10020. Illus. Adv. Index. Circ: 2,900,000. Sample. Vol. ends: Dec. Microform: MCA, UMI. Online: DIALOG. [*Indexed*: MI, RG. *Bk. rev*: 1, 1–2 columns, signed. *Aud*: Ages 10–18.]

Even though there is an edition of this magazine for younger children, this edition should be in any school library with readers ten years old and up—if only so they can enjoy the pictures. *Sports Illustrated* offers the best writing by the best authors, paired with wonderful photography and a pleasing format. Coverage includes every sport imaginable from unique angles mixed with traditional sports coverage. This makes for variety and interest for any array of readers. Articles on minor sports are mixed with articles on major college and professional sports. Controversy is not avoided, and personality profiles always seem to go one step beyond the traditional article or interview. The "For the Record" section provides a concise roundup of the previous week's activities in virtually all sports as well as a milepost section and "Faces in the Crowd," which highlights unusual amateur accomplishments. Because of the timeliness, readability, and overall excellence of this magazine, it belongs in virtually all school and public libraries.

874 **Sports 'N Spokes.** 1975. bi-m. $9. Cliff Crase. PVA Publns., 5201 N. 19th Ave., Suite 111, Phoenix, AZ 88015. Illus. Adv. Circ: 9,000. [*Aud*: Ages 14–18.]

Sports 'N Spokes is owned by the Paralyzed Veterans of America and is published as a service to active persons with disabilities who are interested in wheelchair sports and recreation. Articles include results and statistics in competitive sports, information on recreational opportunities, explanations of specialized equipment, "how-to" reports to enable the disabled reader to actively participate in sports and recreation, and calendars of national and international events. Readers are athletes and interested parties in the medical, recreational, educational, and therapeutical fields. Generally, this effort covers wheelchair competitive sports and recreation primarily for those with spinal cord injuries, spinal bifida, amputations, or certain congenital defects.

Sports Illustrated for Kids. *See under* CHILDREN/SPORTS.

875 **Surfer Magazine.** 1960. m. $18. Paul Holmes. Surfer Publg., Inc., 3046 Calle Avidor, San Juan Capistrano, CA 92675. Illus. Adv. Circ: 117,500. [*Aud*: Ages 12–18.]

This is primarily for board surfers but also covers other forms, plus travel, equipment, events, techniques, and personality profiles.

876 **Swimming World and Junior Swimmer.** 1960. m. $16. Robert Ingram. Sports Publns., Inc., P.O. Box 45497, Los Angeles, CA 90045. Illus. Adv. Index. Circ: 35,000. Sample. Vol. ends: Dec. Microform: UMI. [*Aud*: Ages 10–18.]

No matter what age the competitive swimmer, this is the magazine of choice. Published by a collective of swimming coaches' organizations and the national governing board for U.S. amateur swimming, this title contains articles on swimming and swimmers and also regular columns on diving and water polo. It is billed as the "national magazine for competitive aquatics," covering elementary through college ages. Records and times set at both national and international meets are reported and an annual special attraction is a camp listing that provides information on eligibility, costs, opportunities, and staff. Those interested in aquatic competition will find this a useful and informative title.

877 **Tennis.** 1965. m. $17.94. Alexander McNab. Golf Digest/Tennis, Inc., 5520 Park Ave., P.O. Box 395, Trumbull, CT 06611. Illus. Adv. Circ: 525,000. Vol. ends: Dec. Microform: UMI. [*Indexed*: MI. *Aud*: Ages 14–18.]

Recommended by the U.S. Professional Tennis Association and the U.S. Professional Tennis Registry, this attractive and comprehensive bible for tennis players includes marvelous in-depth features by and/or about major tennis personalities as well as tips and lessons. Articles about nutrition and tennis performance, psychology, commentary, fitness, tennis clothes, travel information, tournament guides, professional and college tournament results, rankings of players, well-written columns, and so on, add to the luster of *Tennis* as an important magazine for most libraries.

878 **Volleyball Monthly.** 1982. m. $16. Jon Hastings and Dennis Steers. Straight Down, Inc., P.O. Box 3137, San Luis Obispo, CA 93403. Illus. Adv. Circ: 40,000. Vol. ends: Oct. [*Aud*: Ages 14–18.]

This glossy magazine reports on NCAA, junior, and major league volleyball with a number of informative departments, tips, tournament information, scoreboards, fashion information, and features. Excellent photography.

879 **Water Skier.** 1951. m. $8. Duke Cullimore. Amer. Water Skier Assn., P.O. Box 191, Winter Haven, FL 33882. Illus. Adv. Index. Circ: 21,000. Sample. Vol. ends: Jan. [*Indexed*: MI. *Aud*: Ages 14–18.]

This official publication of the AWSA provides tournament schedules, results of competitions, and standings. Articles by association staff and members focus on education, skills improvement, water skiing personalities, safety instruction, and history. New product announcements and affiliated division news are regular features. Although the emphasis is on U.S. activities, some international events are also included.

Women's Sports & Fitness. *See under* WOMEN.

880 **World Tennis.** 1953. m. $15.94. Neil Amdur. Family Media, Inc., 3 Park Ave., New York, NY 10016. Illus. Adv. Circ: 378,452. Vol. ends: May. [*Indexed*: MI, RG. *Aud*: Ages 10–18.]

This magazine has much to offer for every level of tennis player, from the beginner to the professional. Useful information on equipment, nutrition, and fitness adds to the overall effectiveness. Wonderful instructional articles and columns are offered. Tournament results and statistics are well organized. Feature articles are timely. This beautifully produced and entertaining publication belongs in most libraries along with its competitor, *Tennis*

881 **YABA World** (Formerly: *Young Bowler*). 1964. 6/yr. $2.50. Paul Bertling. Young Amer. Bowling Alliance, 5301 S. 76th St., Greendale, WI 53129. Illus. Adv. Circ: 80,000. Vol. ends: Apr. [*Aud*: Ages 10–18.]

This takes in bowlers of almost all ages, and is suitable, at least in part, for children as well as teens. It is the official magazine for young and collegiate bowlers. Regular departments are "Nation's Top Ten Lists" and "Ask the Coach." This is the publication in which to find announcements of tournaments, bowling camps, and supplies. About 20 cleverly designed pages.

■ **TELEVISION, VIDEO, RADIO, AND ELECTRONICS**

[Liese Adams, Jerry Hostetler, and Lois M. Nase]

See also: FAN MAGAZINES; MUSIC AND DANCE

Of the hundreds of magazines in this book, these may be among the most popular among teenagers. Certainly the ones dealing with television and video have a massive audience, and to a lesser extent so do those concerned with radio and electronics. Every library should have the basic magazines in the collection.

First choices (1) *Video Review*; (2) *Channels*; (3) *Audio*.

882 **Amateur Radio** (Formerly: *73: amateur radio's technical journal*). 1960. m. $24.97. Larry Ledlow, Jr. WGE Publg. Co., P.O. Box 931, Farmingdale, NY 11737. Illus. Adv. Circ: 70,000. Sample. Microform: UMI. Reprint: UMI. [*Aud*: Ages 14–18.]

Of all the radio magazines for the young fan, this is by far the easiest to understand and is often preferred in school and public libraries. Not as technical as *QST*, this publication is for the amateur radio enthusiast. Features range from taking communication equipment on the road (via bicycle) to digital electronics. Articles are well illustrated with electrical diagrams. Each issue has a short index, and there is plenty of news. "Barter & Buy" and "Ham Help" are two of the very practical columns.

883 **Audio.** 1917. m. $19.94. Eugene Pitts. DCI, Hachette Publns., Inc., 1515 Broadway, New York, NY 10036. Illus. Adv. Index. Circ: 125,000. Sample. Vol. ends: Dec. Microform: UMI. Reprint: UMI. [*Indexed*: ASTI, MI. *Aud*: Ages 14–18.]

This is for the teenager with a professional interest in audio, where the best is what is wanted and much attention must be given to technical data. Featured articles range from technical topics such as sound contamination and equipment design to general-interest stories about musicians, record producers, or concerts. The "Equipment Profiles" section provides photographs, specifications, prices, and the opportunity to request additional literature. Products reviewed include loudspeakers, microphones, compact disc players, and turntables, among others. This title should be selected for most public and school libraries.

884 **Audio Video Review Digest.** 1989. 3/yr. $145. Susan L. Stetler. Gale Research, Book Tower, Detroit, MI 48226. [*Aud*: Ages 14–18.]

This is an AV version of *Book Review Digest*. Each issue has complete bibliographic information on more than 3,000 excerpted reviews. The reviews cover the latest cassettes (audio and music), videocassettes, films (but not feature films), filmstrips, and records. Arrangement is alphabetical by title. There are two major indexes: subject and media. The greatest amount of space is given over to the ubiquitous videocassette. Reviews from more than 600 periodicals are scanned.

885 **CQ: the radio amateur's journal.** 1945. m. $18. Alan M. Dorhoffer. CQ Publg., Inc., 76 N. Broadway, Hicksville, NY 11801. Illus. Adv. Circ: 101,000. [*Aud*: Ages 14–18.]

Among younger radio enthusiasts this is often a favorite, although it is rather technical. Contest news, contest announcements, technique tips, and reviews are monthly features. The frequent product reviews are signed and readable, and provide purchase recommendations. The numerous construction articles are practical, clearly written, and well illustrated, and will appeal to both beginner and experienced equipment builders. Personal computer owners will find regular articles adapting computer equipment to radio applications. Extensive advertising provides access to new-product information. This magazine is written by knowledgeable hams for hams, and articles published here are often referred to in rag-chewing sessions.

886   **Channels: the business of communications** (Formerly: *Channels of Communication*). 1981. 11/yr. $65. Merrill Brown. Channels, 19 W. 44th St., New York, NY 10036. Illus. Adv. Circ: 25,000. Sample. Vol. ends: Dec. (No. 11). Reprint: Pub. [*Indexed*: Acs, RG. *Bk. rev*: Occasional. *Aud*: Ages 14–18.]

Although this title is no longer aimed at high school students, some material is still of interest to younger people. The targeted audience is now professionals in the broadcasting and allied fields, network syndicators, local broadcasters, cable operators, and programmers. The magazine still has interesting articles on advertising, new technology, marketing, promotions, and media deals. It also provides statistics on the top videocassette rentals and sales, well illustrated by charts and graphs. The "Field Guide to the Electronic Media" is issued as the December issue. *Channels* is for larger collections.

887   **Electronics** (Formerly: *Electronics Week*). 1930. m. $32. Robert W. Henkel. VNU Business Publns., Inc., 10 Holland Dr., Hasbrouck Heights, NJ 07604. Illus. Adv. Circ: 149,000. Sample. Vol. ends: Dec. Microform: UMI. Online: DIALOG, Mead Data Central. Reprint: ISI, UMI. [*Indexed*: ASTI, MI. *Aud*: Ages 14–18.]

This is the magazine for the young person trying to keep up with both the technical side and the business side of electronics. The news coverage is international in scope, describing new products and pace-setting corporations. Reviews range from the CD-ROM and VCR to sophisticated high-cost medical and computer equipment. A semiconductors column covers the latest developments in this burgeoning field.

888   **Electronics & Wireless World** (Formerly: *Wireless World*). 1911. m. $116. Philip Darrington. Reed Business Publg., Ltd., Quadrant House, The Quadrant, Sutton, Surrey SM2 5AS, England. Illus. Adv. Circ: 45,051. Sample. Vol. ends: Dec. Microform: UMI. Reprint: ISI, UMI. [*Indexed*: ASTI. *Bk. rev*: 4–6, 50–150 words. *Aud*: Ages 14–18.]

This is a companion to *Electronics*, for the young adult. Recent articles focused on integrated circuits, industry standards, semiconductors, and ultrasonics. News items also cover market and industry trends and there is a substantial listing of job opportunities. A unique feature is the pioneers series, which looks at people who were leaders in electrical communication development.

889   **Emmy: the magazine of the Academy of Arts and Sciences.** 1979. bi-m. $18. Hank Rieger. Academy of Television Arts and Sciences, 3500 W. Olive Ave., No. 700, Burbank, CA 91505-4268. Illus. Adv. Circ: 12,000. Sample. Vol. ends: Nov/Dec. (No. 6). Microform: UMI. Reprint: UMI. [*Indexed*: Acs. *Bk. rev*: 1–3, 500–750 words, signed. *Aud*: Ages 14–18.]

Teenagers do not know this as a rule, but they will love it. News of the stars and just about everything else associated with the famous television award are noted here. The information contained in *Emmy* is not found elsewhere. The column "Innverviews" and other articles provide excellent biographical information on actors, directors, and other people in the business. The writing is well above the media hype and gossip-mongering that generally follow these well-known individuals. *Emmy*'s biographical pieces are usually several pages in length. The articles are well researched and written and deal with important issues that affect television, such as FCC regulations, or new advances, such as teletext. The likes of movie critic Leonard Malton have contributed book reviews. The visual appearance of the publication is terrific.

890   **Home Viewer.** 1981. m. $12. Bruce Apar. Home Viewer Publns., 11 N. Second St., Philadelphia, PA 19106. Illus. Adv. Sample. [*Aud:* Ages 14–18.]

Any viewer with a VCR will turn to this for help. The heart of the magazine is the "Home Viewer Guide." About 50 films are briefly described, with evaluative comments. In addition there is "the a to z guide to every new video title available this month," which lists over 100 titles with buying information and a one-line descriptor. In both sections the focus is on "family" material—there is litte or no X-rated material. A couple of general articles and other comments round out each issue, which includes numerous advertisements. The 60 or so pages are worth the price, at least as an alerting device.

891   **Popular Communications** (Incorporating *SCAN Magazine*). 1982. m. $18. Tom Kneitel. Popular Communications, Inc., 76 N. Broadway, Hicksville, NY 11801. Circ: 85,000. Vol. ends: Dec. [*Bk. rev:* 4, 250–350 words. *Aud:* Ages 14–18.]

Among the radio and communication magazines, this is one of the most complete. It covers the whole spectrum of amateur communication—radio, CB, ham, telephone, radioteletype, scanners, and shortwave broadcasting. Short articles discuss timely subjects and almost every issue features an account of radio history. Regular departments include "New Products" and the "Pirates of the Den" (the latter covers illegal radio transmissions logged by readers). Article titles range from "The ELF [extremely low frequency communication] Is Here" to "Secrets of Shortwave Espionage." Twice a year selected English-language broadcasts from all over the world are listed. Most subjects are not covered in depth since the scope is so wide. *Popular Communications* would be a good publication for medium-size or large school and public libraries.

892   **QST.** 1915. m. $25. Paul Rinaldo. Amer. Radio Relay League, 225 Main St., Newington, CT 06111. Illus. Adv. Index. Circ: 140,000. Sample. Vol. ends: Dec. Microform: UMI. Reprint: UMI. [*Indexed:* ASTI. *Aud:* Ages 14–18.]

Along with *CQ*, a favorite among younger fans. Technical articles cover topics such as amplifiers, antennas, transceivers, and computer programs. There is one major product review per issue, which includes the manufacturer's claimed specifications and results of tests by the American Radio Relay League. The news articles concentrate on league meetings, projects, and awards. *QST* contains many advertisements that provide mail-order opportunities to purchase equipment. This is a good title for libraries to consider.

893   **Radio-Electronics.** 1929. m. $15.97. Brian Fenton. Gernsback Publns., Inc., 500 Bi-County Blvd., Farmingdale, NY 11735. Illus. Adv. Index. Circ: 242,000. Sample. Microform: UMI. Reprint: UMI. [*Indexed:* ASTI, MI, SciAb. *Aud:* Ages 14–18.]

A fine magazine for the electronics hobbyist who is interested in building components and making informed purchases of new products. It is a title with a long history and is indexed in many standard sources. There are special columns on robot design, video components, and radios. A classified section and an advertising index provide nice avenues to find the needed parts or products. Highly recommended for the medium- to large-size school and public library.

894 **Super Television** (Formerly: *Home Satellite TV*). 1985. q. $10. Bob Wolenik. Miller Magazines, Inc., 2660 E. Main St., Ventura, CA 93003. Illus. Adv. Circ: 100,000. Sample. Vol. ends: Fall. [*Aud*: Ages 14–18.]

Readers who are in the market for television sets, video equipment, satellite dishes, and camcorders will be interested in this publication. Each issue contains a specific buyer's guide that not only rates equipment but provides pictures of what it looks like. These buying guides are better than other well-known consumer publications since they rate more than one model for most brands—for example, in the recent "Camcorder Buyer's Guide," six different Zenith models are rated. Helpful hints on maintenance, production techniques, and repair also are covered. Indexing services should pick up this title since it could provide an inexpensive way to answer many consumer questions in libraries.

895 **Video Choice.** 1988. m. $24.95. Deborah Navas. Connell Communications, Inc., 331 Jaffrey Rd., Peterborough, NH 03458. Illus. Adv. Sample. [*Aud*: Ages 14–18.]

Video Choice lives up to its proclamation as being "the leading review magazine for the video enthusiast." While it includes hardware and product reviews and some "how-to" articles, the emphasis is clearly on the video reviews, which are wide-ranging. These reviews tend toward the descriptive/evaluative rather than the critical, and include topics from blues music to weddings. Recommended for high school and public libraries.

896 **Video Magazine.** 1978. m. $12. Judith Sawyer. Reese Communications, 460 W. 34th St., New York, NY 10001. Illus. Adv. Circ: 340,000. Sample. Vol. ends: Mar. [*Aud*: Ages 14–18.]

This video magazine is popular among teens, running second to *Video Review*. Both have good feature articles, equipment evaluations, critical reviews, and "kidvid." Librarians should be aware of a 12-page tear-out insert with "adult" advertisements covering everything from amateur bedroom video to sadomasochistic materials. The publishers note that they sealed the section as "an accommodation to those readers who have no interest in such materials." The 8 to 12 major video reviews in each issue are well done and signed. The "Kidvid" section is the best of all the video magazines examined because it covers educational video in addition to mainstream entertainment releases. Feature articles will catch the interest of any VCR owner. However, for definitive product reviews *Video Review* is superior.

897 **Video Review.** 1980. m. $12. James B. Meigs. Viare Publg. Co., 902 Broadway, New York, NY 10010. Illus. Adv. Circ: 370,000. Sample. Online: NEWSNET. [*Aud*: Ages 14–18.]

First choice for teenagers who want real information on what is better and best in video. The video reviewers—Leonard Malton, Neal Gabler, Jeffrey Lyons—are well-known movie critics, mostly from their work in television. The critical reviews are well done, and timely. *VR*'s greatest oversight is their "kidvid" reviews. They are well done, but cover mostly mainstream videos, with very few educational ones. The product evaluations are terrific. Easy-to-read, comparative charts complement the text and several models of each brand are compared. Products in all price ranges are covered and new technology is always a hot topic.

898   **Worldradio** (Formerly: *World Radio News*). 1971. m. $12. Christine Wilson. Martin Publns., Inc., 2120 28th St., Sacramento, CA 95818. Circ: 24,000. Vol. ends: June. [*Bk. rev*: Occasional, 250–500 words. *Aud*: Ages 14–18.]

Amateur radio operators will appreciate this title, billed by the publishers as an "international conversation." Those who are visually impaired will especially enjoy it since *Worldradio* also is available on cassette for the miraculously low price of $3. Contributions from readers are encouraged. *Worldradio*'s goal is to be "a valuable resource of ideas and experience beneficial to amateur operators" in addition to publicizing the humanitarian uses of amateur radio. Each month, this 60-plus-page newsprint magazine has an incredible amount of practical information on subjects such as "invisible antennas," software, personal computer interference, and ham activities. Regular columns cover packet radio, handicapped hams, Federal Communications Commission information, low-power operation (QRP), radio teletype, and international news.

■ THEATER

[Gary J. Lenox]

In most collections, it is wise to have a balance of titles representing drama and history (the playscripts and playwrights, their criticism and literary import, and history of production); theater productions (current theater—professional and amateur, plus reviews and description); and technical theater ("backstage" elements). For example, a small high school or public library might want to consider *American Theatre*, *Theatre Journal*, and *Theatre Crafts*. Special types of theater, such as mime, puppet theater, and children's theater, should be represented as needs demand.

First choices   (1) *American Theatre*; (2) *Theatre Crafts*; (3) *Theatre Journal*.

Suitable for children   Ages 8–18: *Plays*.

899   **American Theatre.** 1984. 11/yr. $27. Jim O'Quinn. Theatre Communications Group, 355 Lexington Ave., New York, NY 10017. Illus. Adv. Circ: 14,000. [*Bk. rev*: 15–20, 50 words. *Aud*: Ages 14–18.]

A basic magazine for those serving high school students, this is perhaps the most important theater magazine in the United States. This may be surprising considering the fact that its focus is limited to the nonprofit professional theater in the United States, but it is true because all theater—Broadway, educational, community, and other—is beholden in very large part to what is happening in the professional regional theaters. Along with its lively style and current relevance an occasional playscript, photos of productions, columns, calendars, and much more, make this the priority theater title for all libraries.

900   **Drama: the quarterly theatre review.** 1919. q. $21 (Individuals, $17). Christopher Edwards. British Theatre Assn., Regent's College, Inner Circle, Regent's Park, London NW1 4NW, England. Illus. Adv. Microform: UMI. [*Indexed*: HumI. *Bk. rev*: 3–4, 500–1,000 words. *Aud*: Ages 14–18.]

Features six or seven articles on many aspects of contemporary British and European theater—for example, theater publishing, labor agreements, management, actors, playwrights, and current drama. Articles are both descriptive and evaluative. There are good illustrations, and each issue has book reviews. "In Performance" is a good source of information on productions throughout England (arranged by area of the country), in the United States, and by type of performance, for example, opera and radio. A sort of counterpart of *American*

Theatre, this publication should be a first choice for many public and school libraries.

901 **Plays.** 1941. 7/yr. $20. Sylvia K. Burack. Plays, Inc., 120 Boylston St., Boston, MA 02116. Circ: 23,000. Vol. ends: May. [*Indexed*: CMG. *Aud*: Ages 8–18.]

Each 64-page issue contains approximately eight to ten plays and a choral reading. The plays run from lower grade school level to high school level. Holiday and seasonal plays are featured, as well as adaptations of classics (*She Stoops to Conquer, Jane Eyre*) and modern pieces. Production notes are included. Subscribers may produce the plays royalty free, although videotaping is not permitted. A fair warning on production rights and guidelines exists on the inside cover. All the information for production is here—stage set, playing time, props, lighting, and sound. The writing is good, by and large. Several of the characters' names are a bit old-fashioned in some of the modern plays. The choral reading choices are particularly good. This is the only magazine published to encourage future thespians. Purchase is recommended for schools or libraries supporting an interest in drama.

902 **Theater** (Formerly: *Yale/Theater*). 1968. 3/yr. $21 (Individuals, $17). Joel Schechter. Yale School of Drama/Yale Repertory Theatre, 222 York St., New Haven, CT 06520. Illus. Adv. Index. Microform: UMI. [*Indexed*: HumI. *Aud*: Ages 14–18.]

The journal sponsor is well known as an adventuresome young people's theater company, giving this magazine special appeal for teenagers. Each issue focuses on a specific theme—for example, Peter Brook and Company—and includes one or two new plays. "The Back of the Book" section features discussions of the most important current theatrical events in American regional theater and around the globe. Once the only publication of its type, it remains very important as a companion to *American Theatre* and should be in most libraries.

903 **Theatre Crafts: the magazine for professionals in theatre, film, video and the performing arts.** 1967. 10/yr. $30. Patricia MacKay. Theatre Crafts Assocs., 135 Fifth Ave., New York, NY 10010-7193. Subs. to: P.O. Box 630, Holmes, PA 19043-0630. Illus. Adv. Circ: 27,500. Microform: B&H, UMI. [*Indexed*: EdI, MI, RG. *Aud*: Ages 14–18.]

An important magazine that is both practical and theoretical for anyone involved with technical theater. Articles are for the professional and/or amateur responsible for lighting, costumes, billboards, advertising, and other elements of production. It frequently includes articles on the work of noted costumers or set designers, new equipment for the theater including computers, and the staging of particular professional productions. There are columns on new products. A very good "tech theater" title, with ideas that can be used, copied, imitated, or improvised by all theater companies. It is a necessity in public and high school libraries.

904 **Theatre History Studies.** 1980. a. $10 (Individuals, $6). Ron Engle. Theatre History Studies, Dept. of Theatre Arts, Univ. of North Dakota, Grand Forks, ND 58202. Illus. Adv. Circ: 1,000. Refereed. [*Bk. rev*: 10–15, 500 words, signed. *Aud*: Ages 14–18.]

International in scope but with an emphasis on American, British, and Continental theater, this fine journal includes seven to nine articles dealing with everything from Filipino theater during the Japanese occupation to numerous articles on Shakespearean production to American children's theater. The many book reviews, the illustrations in articles, the "Theatre History Obscurities" column on museums with reproductions of items from their archives, and the format make this official journal of the Mid-America Theatre Conference an excellent addition for large public and some school libraries.

905   **Theatre Journal** (Formerly: *Educational Theatre Journal*). 1941. q. $39 (Individuals, $17). Sue-Ellen Case. Johns Hopkins Univ. Press, Journals Div., 701 W. 40th St., Suite 275, Baltimore, MD 21211. Illus. Microform: UMI. [*Indexed*: CIJE, EdI, HumI. *Bk. rev*: 12–15, 750–1,000 words. *Aud*: Ages 14–18.]

Among the best known of the various theater journals, this can be recommended to dedicated young adults for an overview of theater. (It obviously does double duty for teachers and directors.) It is famous for its book reviews; professional, international, and university/college theater reviews; and contains six or seven articles. Some issues focus on special topics—"Brecht," "Film/Theatre," "Theatre of Color." Scholarly articles are on areas of theater history and theatrical theory and criticism.

906   **Variety.** 1905. w. $100. Roger Watkins. Variety, Inc., 475 Park Ave. S., New York, NY 10016-6999. Illus. Adv. Circ: 31,477. Microform: MIM. [*Indexed*: BusI. *Aud*: Ages 14–18.]

Starry-eyed young adults who want the real story about entertainment and related areas should turn first to this official newspaper of show business, complete with its legendary headlines. The language is peculiar to the magazine and echoes the language used in the entertainment field. Sections on movies, radio, and television; music and records; and even vaudeville are included, along with news of the theater world. In addition to general news items of the stage, the "legitimate" section contains reviews of on- and off-Broadway shows and shows abroad, information on casting, the amount of money grossed each week by Broadway and road shows, and where touring shows are playing.

■ **TRAVEL**   [Judith Ann Harwood]

The adventure and lure of travel attract everyone, including and perhaps especially the teenager who longs to get away from school and the hometown, to see a bit of the world. Even those who do not make the actual trip, and travelers are fewer and fewer these days, can enjoy the delights of going through the magazines and dreaming of distant places. The catch is the tremendous amount of advertising in most of these titles, indicating that one must own Trump Tower in order to travel nicely. Still, the stories tend to dispel this notion. In addition, there is the obvious benefit of travel magazines to courses in geography and history. Even for those with reading difficulties, the numerous illustrations, often in color, make a vicarious trip or two possible and pleasant.

First choices   (1) *Travel-Holiday*; (2) *World Magazine*; (3) *Student Traveler*.
Suitable for children   Ages 12–18: *Discovery*.

Discovery. *See under* YOUNG ADULT/GEOGRAPHY.

907   **Ford Times.** 1908. m. $6. Arnold Hirsch. Ford Motor Co., P.O. Box 1899, Dearborn, MI 48121. Illus. Adv. Circ: 1,170,000. Sample. Vol. ends: Dec. [*Aud*: Ages 14–18.]

Whether the young people are driving or in the back of the car, this is a good companion for the trip. This long-lived magazine for traveling Americans has become such an institution that it is no longer free. Still, the modest subscription price puts it well within the means of all libraries and, thanks to the 12 to 15 well-written and equally well-illustrated articles, it is a great buy. The material is primarily of interest to those who travel, and concentrates on such things as national parks, regional outdoor interests, history along the road, and help with making vacation plans. There are recipes and bits of information on automobiles, although advertising is minimal.

908 **National Geographic Traveler.** 1984. q. $14.95. Joan Tapper. Natl. Geographic Soc., 17th and M Sts. N.W., Washington, DC 20036. Illus. Adv. Circ: 900,000. [*Aud*: Ages 14–18.]

An easy-to-follow travel magazine for teens, this can be recommended for almost all school and public libraries. Most of the material concerns the United States. Where travel goes abroad, it is only to places likely to be of interest to Americans. The six to ten articles are well written and, as might be expected, beautifully illustrated. Numerous features aid the person interested in travel, for example, one section gives the highlights of events throughout the world of the next three months. An added feature: Full data—such as cost, phone numbers, addresses—for places discussed are given in each article.

909 **Student Traveler.** 1989. bi-m. $9. Rebecca Richardson. Student Traveler, P.O. Box 23, Streamwood, IL 60107. Illus. Adv. Sample. [*Aud*: Ages 14–18.]

If you are sick of glamorized travel magazines that assume you have a fortune to spend on planes, trains, and hotels, the answer to your problem is here. Financial considerations are balanced with tips on how to get to Bangkok and back. The 30 pages cover travel and such things as where to study abroad, world entertainment, making money on travel articles, and scholarship news. According to the editor, "every issue is written and produced by students. We are striving to break from the standard travel magazine format." The struggle is won.

910 **Transitions Abroad: the magazine of overseas opportunities** (Formerly: *Transitions*). 1977. 5/yr. $15. Clayton A. Hubbs. Transitions Publg., 18 Hulst Rd., P.O. Box 344, Amherst, MA 01004. Illus. Adv. Circ: 8,000. [*Aud*: Ages 14–18.]

This title is a fully independent resource guide to living, learning, employment, and specialty travel abroad. Emphasis is on "practical, usable information in timely and informative articles and first-hand reports." Each issue has a focus such as the Mediterranean, the Americas and off-season and off-beat travel, and Asia. Disability travel receives notice. This is a valuable magazine for high school and public libraries.

911 **Travel & Leisure** (Formerly: *Travel & Camera*). 1971. m. $29. Pamela Fiori. Amer. Express Publg. Corp., 1120 Ave. of the Americas, New York, NY 10036. Illus. Adv. Circ: 1,100,000. Microform: B&H, UMI. [*Indexed*: Acs. *Aud*: Ages 14–18.]

This is not the best travel magazine for youngsters, but it is well enough known that it may be of interest to them. It is published for holders of American Express cards. The articles feature exotic destinations such as Kashmir, French Polynesia, Las Brisas, and the Amazon. Travel topics include weather, health, photography, shopping, money, and dining. The photographs are outstanding. The writing is clear and very readable. Each issue averages 200 pages.

912   **Travel-Holiday: the magazine that roams the globe.** 1901. m. $11. Scott Shane. Travel Magazine, Inc., Travel Bldg., 51 Atlantic Ave., Floral Park, NY 11001. Illus. Adv. Circ: 800,000. Microform: B&H, UMI. [*Indexed*: RG. *Aud*: Ages 14–18.]

Popular stories, good illustrations, and an easy-to-follow style make this a first-choice travel title for any library working with young adults. Eight to ten feature articles cover the globe from New England and Hawaii to Rumania and Australia. In each issue one department covers travel topics, including health, photography, campgrounds, shopping, and general travel advice. The "Northeastern Roundup" features locations from South Dakota and Iowa through Virginia and New England to northeast Europe. Each issue is about 120 pages.

913   **World Magazine.** 1987. m. $48. Christopher Long. Hyde Park Publns., London. Subs. to: 3370 Fairfield Ave., Bridgeport, CT 06605. Illus. Adv. Index. Sample. [*Bk. rev*: 300, signed. *Aud*: Ages 14–18.]

Discussing the role of his 130-page, brilliantly illustrated publication, the editor observes: "We knew that there was a great need for a magazine devoted to people, places, races, wildlife and environment . . . non-political and non-partisan." The authors of this English import are more concerned with what one sees (from the Falklands to British orchids) than how one arranges travel plans. The dozen carefully researched and well-written articles (which reflect what is found in the *Smithsonian*) literally cover the world from Greenwich to Moscow. Advertisements are few.

■ **USSR AND EASTERN EUROPE**   [Harold M. Leich and Gloria Jacobs]

See also: EUROPE

The changes ushered in by Mikhail Gorbachev's policies of *glasnost'* (openness) and *perestroika* (restructuring) have been nowhere more obvious than in the pages of the periodicals and newspapers published in the USSR. Once strictly adhering to the official party line, and making for quite dull, predictable reading, Soviet publications are now displaying signs of independence unthinkable only three or four years ago. Soviet newspapers and magazines are now filled with such items as letters to the editor expressing critical, unorthodox views on a wide range of subjects; criticism and comments about shortcomings in official social, economic, and political policies; and articles attempting to fill in numerous "blank spots" in the country's history.

First choices   (1) *Soviet Life*; (2) *Sputnik*; (3) *Culture and Life*.

Suitable for children   Ages 10–15: *Murzilka (Russian language)*. Ages 11–18: *Soviet Life*.

914   **Culture and Life.** 1957. m. $17. Ado Kukanov. Union of Soviet Societies for Friendship and Cultural Relations with Foreign Countries, 16/2 Gorky St., Moscow 9, USSR. Subs. to: Victor Kamkin, Inc., 12224 Parklawn Dr., Rockville, MD 20852. Illus. Index. Vol. ends: Dec. Microform: B&H. [*Aud*: Ages 14–18.]

The library that takes *Soviet Life* may find that this journal nicely augments that title, particularly for older readers. With its articles, usually illustrated, on the theater, opera, ballet, art, and music, as well as profiles of prominent artists and stories on personalities in the Soviet republics, it fits into most high school and many public library collections. Cultural relations with foreign countries are given extensive coverage, reflecting the publisher's philosophy of seeking rapprochement with other countries through the exchange of artists. The English-language version is recommended for school and public libraries as a good source on the general cultural scene in the USSR. In the Russian version (*Kul'tura i zhizn'*), this is a useful study aid for beginning or intermediate language students.

915 **Current Digest of the Soviet Press.** 1949. w. $130. Robert S. Ehlers. Current Digest of the Soviet Press, Inc., 1480 W. Lane Ave., Columbus, OH 43221. Index. Vol. ends: No. 52. Online: Nexis. [*Aud*: Ages 14–18.]

Some of this is not easy going for the younger reader, but it is the type of challenge that should be offered in today's world. This is the basic source in English of material from the Soviet press. Much of the *Current Digest* material is selected for translation from the USSR's two chief dailies, *Pravda* and *Izvestiia*. However, selections are also taken from some 60 other newspapers and journals. When articles have been abridged, it is so noted, and full bibliographic details are given for each translation for those who need to consult the original. The editors refrain from commenting on the translations, thus affording the American user an excellent cross section of Soviet opinion and journalism. This title is currently the best single source for following recent Soviet events in detail in English. Essential for public and for high school libraries with an interest in providing up-to-date coverage of Soviet affairs.

916 **Krokodil (Crocodile).** 1922. 36/yr. $41.50. M. G. Semenov. Krokodil, ul. Pravdy, 24 Moscow 125407, USSR. Illus. Circ: 5,000,000. [*Aud*: Ages 14–18.]

This is in Russian, but even a rudimentary knowledge of the language will make much of it easy to follow. A very popular Soviet satire magazine both in the USSR and in Russian-language classrooms, *Krokodil* will appeal to Russian readers at various levels of ability. It is a colorful, well-illustrated magazine with contents ranging from two-line jokes and cartoons to full-page works of fiction. The cartoons poke fun at the Soviet bureaucracy and negative aspects of Soviet life. *Krokodil*'s anti-Western slant has diminished and the articles written about the West now focus on Western stereotypes of Soviet life. The content is less political than in previous years.

917 **Moscow News.** 1956. w. $21. Gennady Gerasimov. Union of Soviet Societies for Friendship and Cultural Relations with Foreign Countries, 16/2 Gorky St., Moscow 9, USSR. Subs. to: Victor Kamkin, Inc., 12224 Parklawn Dr., Rockville, MD 20852. Illus. Microform: UMI. [*Aud*: Ages 14–18.]

Teenagers will find this a well-edited, fascinating, and generally objective paper. Previously considered an "odd ball" in Moscow, it is now highly acceptable and widely read. This tabloid newspaper (available also in a number of other languages) offers current news from the Soviet Union. While aimed primarily at readers in English-speaking countries rather than at a Soviet audience, in the past few years it has become one of the most interesting and daring publications in the USSR. It has been in the vanguard of the policies of "openness" and "restructuring" as promoted by Mikhail Gorbachev since 1985, and has broken new ground for a Soviet publication, publishing previously suppressed stories about the Stalin purges, famines in the 1920s and 1930s, shortcomings of past Soviet leaders, and so forth. Some issues include supplements comprising translations into English of recent official Soviet speeches and decrees. Highly recommended for all types of libraries as a useful, current, and inexpensive source of recent and official Soviet news in English.

918   **Murzilka.** 1924. m. $3. A. Mitiaev. Murzilka, ul. Sushevskaya 21, Moscow A-55, USSR. Illus. Circ: 5,600,000. Vol. ends: Dec. [*Aud*: Ages 10–18.]

A Russian-language title for students of the language and edited specifically for younger readers. A publication of the All Union Pioneer Organization, *Murzilka* is written for members of the Young Pioneers, ages 10 to 15. Each issue features poems, short stories, fairy tales, and novellas in installments. Favorite topics include Soviet holidays, fraternal countries' youth organizations, revolutionary heroes, and other patriotic themes. *Murzilka* can be incorporated into an instructional Russian curriculum, giving the students practice with colloquial Russian, while at the same time exposing them to Soviet magazines for adolescents.

919   **New Times: a Soviet weekly of world affairs.** 1943. q. $21. Ed. bd. New Times, Pushkin Sq., Moscow 103782, USSR. Subs. to: Victor Kamkin, Inc., 12224 Parklawn Dr., Rockville, MD 20852. Illus. Index. Microform: UMI. [*Indexed*: PAIS. *Aud*: Ages 14–18.]

While young readers will soon see this magazine follows the line of those holding power, it still is critical enough and well enough written to warrant consideration in school and public libraries. It is issued in editions in eight languages and intended for export from the USSR rather than for readers at home. The news articles, editorials, and political commentaries tend to focus on areas of contention between East and West (Central America, the Middle East, or Afghanistan, for example). Attention is also given to aspects of life in the West that are less than desirable—crime, unemployment, drug abuse, and so on. *New Times* is a valuable source for those looking for the Soviet point of view on virtually any current event or situation of world interest.

920   **Pravda Pulse.** 1985. bi-w. $64.20. Tim Sinnott. News Pulse, Inc., Drawer 4323, Fort Pierce, FL 33448. Illus. Sample. [*Aud*: Ages 14–18.]

The perfect newspaper for the young adult to read in order to keep up with what people are doing in Russia. Almost every American recognizes that *Izvestiia* and *Pravda* are the Soviet Union's two leading daily newspapers. The latter is the official voice of the Communist party, and is here in part translated into clear English. The daily is reduced to eight to ten standard-size pages every two weeks. (On heavier paper, it is somewhat analogous to *The Guardian Weekly*, which includes material from *The Guardian*, among other papers.) The first page features "National Briefs" and a story or two on the past two weeks' events. There are four pages about the USSR and single pages devoted to people, international events, and commentary. Photographs and cartoons are interspersed throughout. The selection seems to be expertly done, and one has a sense of Russian attitudes about a wide variety of topics, from politics to culture.

921   **Science in the USSR.** 1981. bi-m. $29. G. K. Skriabin. Nauka Publg. House, Maronovskii per, 26, Moscow 117049, USSR. Subs. to: Victor Kamkin, Inc., 12224 Parklawn Dr., Rockville, MD 20852. Illus. Index. Vol. ends: Nov/Dec. (No. 6). [*Aud*: Ages 14–18.]

Of recent origin, this is the Soviet counterpart to *Scientific American* and is one of the most appealing and well produced of all Soviet journals. Issued by the prestigious Soviet Academy of Sciences, the journal is geared to the educated layperson with an interest in the latest developments in the sciences. The writing style is not technical or overburdened with detail, nor is it condescending or dull. In a number of scientific disciplines, the Soviets are on the cutting edge of current research (mathematics, astronomy, and ophthalmology, to name a few), and *Science in the USSR* does an excellent job of presenting news of Soviet science and information on scientific institutions, policies, and personalities.

922   **Smena (The Rising Generation).** 1924. bi-w. $89. A. D. Gulubev. Smena, 14 Bumazhnyi proezd, Moscow 101457, USSR. Illus. Circ: 1,200,000. Vol. ends: Dec. [*Aud*: Ages 14–18.]

A Russian-language magazine that does require some skill to master, but can be enjoyed by advanced students. Edited for teenage Komsomol members, and published by the Central Committee of the Leninist Young Communist League, *Smena* is both entertaining and educational in much the same way *Murzilka* is for a slightly younger audience. Each 32-page issue contains short stories and articles on health, sports, patriotic themes, science, and the arts. The articles are always well illustrated. The last page is devoted to games (such as chess, checkers, and crossword puzzles). Compared with other Soviet magazines, this one is of average quality, but one of the few catering to teenagers.

923   **Soviet Life.** 1956. m. $15. Ed. bd. Soviet Life, 1706 18th St. N.W., Washington, DC 20009. Illus. Vol. ends: Dec. (No. 12). [*Aud*: Ages 11–18.]

Thanks to numerous illustrations and an elementary text, this can be looked at and read by older children as well as young adults. This general-interest magazine, richly illustrated with beautiful color photos and printed in a glossy, large format, is a first choice for libraries. Many subjects are covered, including history, politics, nature and the environment, sports, medicine, and the arts. Each issue of 65 pages also features letters to the editor, question/answer columns about the USSR, and coverage of "friendship" events between Soviets and Americans. The magazine is published by reciprocal agreement between the U.S. and Soviet governments (the magazine *Amerika*, in Russian, is distributed in the USSR as the counterpart of *Soviet Life*).

924   **Sputnik: digest of the Soviet press.** 1967. m. $20. Ed. bd. Novosti Press Agency, 4 Zubovsky Blvd., Moscow 103786, USSR. Subs. to: Victor Kamkin, Inc., 12224 Parklawn Dr., Rockville, MD 20852. Illus. Adv. Vol. ends: Dec. (No. 12). [*Aud*: Ages 14–18.]

Somewhat more sophisticated in its approach than *Soviet Life*, *Sputnik* is noted for the profusion and beauty of its illustrations and the wide variety of its subject matter. Articles are selected for condensation from a large range of Soviet magazines and newspapers, and are written by scientists, journalists, government and party officials, and personalities in sports and the arts. Photographic essays, memoirs, interviews, fashion features, and humor complement the more serious features on history, politics, and economics. Designed solely for export from the USSR, this digest offers interesting and well-presented information on the Soviet Union. Secondary school libraries as well as public libraries will find this title useful for broad general coverage of the contemporary Soviet Union. In its Russian-language edition (also titled *Sputnik*), this is a valuable supplementary source for beginning and intermediate students of Russian.

■ **WOMEN**   [Libby K. White and Bernice K. Lacks]

Many women's magazines, from the general to the feminist and special-interest, are suitable for young adults. In fact, several are directed specifically to the teenager. These magazines, in an effort to keep up with the needs and demands of the younger woman, have changed over the past decade or so. No longer do a few titles dominate the market. The image of the past, of the perfect woman—especially the physically perfect woman, who never existed—is discredited. Advertisers are changing their ways and targeting women as serious consumers of large-ticket items. Most general women's magazines are trying for a two-track approach. *Woman's Day* editor Ellen Levine opts for "mixing real life with home life." "Women have added to their interests, not subtracted from them," she suggests. Given the confusion and uncertainty, we can only hope to be spared the ever-recurring, querulous, and patronizing "What do woman want?" Better to ask in the 1990s, "Who can women be?"

First choices (1) *Mademoiselle*; (2) *Elle*; (3) *Essence*; (4) *Teen*.

925 **Black Elegance/BE.** 1986. 9/yr. $19.98. Sharyn J. Skeeter. Go-Stylish Publg., Inc., 475 Park Ave. S., New York, NY 10016. Illus. Adv. Circ: 150,000. [*Aud*: Ages 14–18.]

Here is a companion to *Essence* for the young black reader. Despite the upscale title and ambitions, *BE* will appeal to a somewhat younger and less affluent audience than the established *Essence*. *BE* is more specifically ethnic in focus yet does not press a political orientation. Beauty and fashion pages are pleasing and instructive. Standard women's magazine departments—health and fitness, nutrition, parenting—are represented. Black entertainment personalities are profiled. The "Arts and Entertainment" section offers brief reviews of musical recordings, television shows, and films featuring black contributors.

926 **Bride's.** 1934. 6/yr. $12. Barbara D. Tober. Conde Nast Publns., Inc., 350 Madison Ave., New York, NY 10017. Illus. Adv. Circ: 342,912. Sample. Vol. ends: Nov/Dec. Microform: B&H, UMI. Reprint: UMI. [*Aud*: Ages 14–18.]

This is one of those dream magazines that may or may not inspire, but it is much in demand among some of the younger set. Each issue is approximately 500 pages in length and carries many ads geared to the bride-to-be—wedding dresses, bridesmaid dresses, silver, china, travel. Departments include "Looking Ahead to Marriage"; "Fashion, Health, and Beauty"; "Planning Your Wedding"; "Your Home Together"; and "Travel." This is a sophisticated, up-scale publication and an ideal resource for future brides.

927 **Chatelaine.** 1928 (French ed.); 1960 (English ed.). m. $15 Can.; $30 U.S. Mildred Istona. MacLean Hunter, Ltd., 777 Bay St., Toronto, Ont. M54 1A7, Canada. Subs. to: P.O. Box 4541, Buffalo, NY 14240. Illus. Adv. Circ: 304,313 (French ed.); 1,089,496 (English ed.). Vol. ends: Dec. [*Indexed*: CMI, MI. *Bk. rev*: 4–6, 20–80 words, signed. *Aud*: Ages 14–18.]

Available in French and English, this is aimed at older teens and is a good choice for many public and school libraries. This sleek magazine celebrates Canadian identity. Its aim is to be a national publication, but regional and provincial history and events are regular subjects. *Chatelaine* has a breezy, open, "among friends" style well suited to older teens and young career and working women. Articles such as "Great Canadian Art under $2,500" and "Grading the Provinces on Women's Issues" represent Canadian concerns. Canadian and commonwealth women achievers are interviewed. Family life is important to the editors and readers. Fashion, beauty, health (a good section), food, decorating, and crafts have their places, but *Chatelaine* does not eschew controversy in its articles, its "Pro and Con" debate section, and its "Woman Poll." "Show-time," which reviews books, films, recordings, and television programs, is written with verve, wit, and expertise.

928   **Connexions: an international women's quarterly.** 1981. q. $24 (Individuals, $12). People's Translation Services, 4228 Telegraph Ave., Oakland, CA 94609. Illus. Adv. Circ: 3,000. [*Indexed*: API. *Aud*: Ages 14–18.]

Feminists and younger women simply interested in women writers will turn to this title. The intent of *Connexions* is to contribute to the building of an international women's movement by making women's writing from around the world available in the United States. Each issue is devoted to a single theme. Recent subjects include "The Politics of Health," "Visual Arts," "Crisis and Transition," and "Facets of Racism." Issues include original articles, interviews, personal narratives, creative work, and reprints and excerpts from feminist periodicals, news sources, books, and other publications. The quality of the translations is excellent. This is the single most important source for the study of women internationally, and contains the best expression of women's voices from around the world.

929   **Daughters of Sarah: the magazine of Christian feminists.** 1974. bi-m. $14.75. Reta Halteman Finger. Daughters of Sarah, P.O. Box 416790, Chicago, IL 60641. Illus. Circ: 3,600. Vol. ends: Nov/Dec. Microform: UMI. [*Bk. rev*: 7–10, 200–300 words, signed. *Aud*: Ages 14–18.]

The subtitle explains the viewpoint, and while this is hardly for the average teenager, it is a good choice for those dedicated to a Christian road to feminism. It defines its purpose in a bit of free verse, "Who We Are: We are Christians/We are also feminists/Some say we cannot be both/but for us/ Christianity and feminism are inseparable." In its articles and stories it is "working at integrating faith with feminism in three general areas: biblical-theological; historical; and socio-political." Issues are devoted to a single theme, for example, "Women and Mental Health," "Domestic and Sexual Violence," "Work, Family, and Self," and "Feminists Straight and Lesbian." *Daughters* is thoughtfully and deeply concerned with the implications of Christianity and the patriarchal tradition for the realities of everyday life.

930   **Elle** (Formerly: *Elle International*). 1985. m. $24. Catherine Ettlinger. Murdoch Magazines and Hachette Publns., Inc., 551 Fifth Ave., New York, NY 10176. Illus. Adv. Circ: 375,000. Vol. ends: Aug. [*Aud*: Ages 14–18.]

Striking in appearance and editorial matter, this is a favorite among many teenagers. It may originate in France, but it has universal appeal. Forget all those how-to-do-its in other women's magazines. The reader will be immersed in a blaze of bold color and innovative style. *Elle* is a trendspotter, beginning with its stunning covers. Models are young and beautiful with a touch of the exotic in appearance, makeup, and hair style. Ads for high-priced products have the look of art. In addition to visual appeal, *Elle* delivers on substance, revealing its French connection with articles like "You Should Have a French Lover" and "Why French Women Don't Get Fat." Articles on art and literature are regular features too. There is so much to like in *Elle* that it seems ungracious to point to negatives. However, it is difficult to locate page numbers. More than annoying is *Elle*'s inability to resist cuteness—"turning the other chic," "no has bean [lentils]", "Le write stuff" (graphology).

931   **Essence: the magazine for today's black woman.** 1970. m. $12. Stephanie Stokes Oliver. Essence Communications, Inc., 1500 Broadway, New York, NY 10036. Subs. to: P.O. Box 53400, Boulder, CO 80322-3400. Illus. Adv. Circ: 800,248. Vol. ends: Dec.

Microform: UMI. Reprint: UMI. [*Indexed*: BoRvI, INeg, MI, RG. *Bk. rev*: 2–3, 50–300 words, signed. *Aud*: Ages 14–18.]

This is by far the best known of the women/teenage black magazines, and it should be in all high school and many public libraries. *Essence* is about sophistication and high style. While deeply committed to black interests and causes, *Essence* has extended its appeal to a larger readership—and no wonder. Imaginative fashions in bold photo layouts, intelligent health, consumer, and career features, and a nifty travel column are compelling reasons. The magazine remains a showcase for products for the black community—Flori Roberts and Naomi Sims cosmetics, Dark and Lovely hair coloring, Brown Sugar pantyhose, and so forth. For its cover stories, *Essence* relies on celebrities, mostly show-business types, but the "About People" department introduces lesser-known significant black Americans. Articles that speak to black problems and opportunities are thoughtful works by writers of stature like Marion Wright Edelman and June Jordan. Profiles of figures in the political arena are uncritical and the subjects seem to be chosen to mirror *Essence's* decidedly left-of-center orientation. Of interest and value to the general reader are excerpts of current biographies of newsworthy black women.

932 **Fighting Woman News.** 1975. q. $15 (Individuals, $10). Valerie Eads. Fighting Woman News, P.O. Box 1459, Grand Central Sta., New York, NY 10163. Illus. Adv. Circ: 5,000. Vol. ends: Winter. [*Bk. rev*: 2–10, length varies. *Aud*: Ages 14–18.]

Teen readers will find this of value at two levels: It teaches the martial arts and, at the same time, shows the benefits of being an independent woman. This magazine publishes articles, fiction, poetry, and reviews of books, periodicals, and videos. A recent issue included a round-table discussion in which six women martial artists and self-defense teachers reviewed self-defense videos, and articles on training during pregnancy and rehabilitation after injuries. Few libraries subscribe, but this magazine would be appropriate wherever there is an interest in women's sports and training.

933 **Glamour** (Incorporating *Charm*). 1939. m. $15. Ruth Whitney. Conde Nast Publns., Inc., 350 Madison Ave., New York, NY 10015. Subs. to: P.O. Box 5203, Boulder, CO 80322. Illus. Circ: 2,300,807. Vol. ends: Dec. Microform: UMI. Reprint: UMI. [*Indexed*: Acs, MI, RG. *Bk. rev*: 3–4, 200–300 words, signed. *Aud*: Ages 14–18.]

The "how-to fashion magazine for young women" is for the reader on the brink, the reader whose life is about to take off in new directions. *Glamour* offers and evaluates the possibilities in an energetic, friendly spirit. Pieces like "Seven Basic Do's and Don'ts on the Job," "The Tensions and Torture of Being a First-time Home Owner," and the monthly "Your Pregnancy" column are typical. Health is a major concern when *Glamour* reports on beauty, fitness, and sex. Articles on sex avoid sensationalism, as does the "Sexual Ethics" department. Above all, *Glamour* women are nice though up-to-date. Fashion, travel, and entertainment wrap-ups are bright, and *Glamour* is no slouch when it comes to general-interest articles on current issues or personalities. There is an extensive education section with many ads for college and occupational training, especially in the retailing field.

934 **Good Housekeeping.** 1885. m. $15.97. John Mack Carter. Hearst Magazine Corp., 959 Eighth Ave., New York, NY 10019. Subs. to: P.O. Box 10055, Des Moines, IA 50350. Illus.

Adv. Circ: 5,203,000. Vol. ends: June/Dec. Microform: UMI. Reprint: UMI. [*Indexed*: AbrRg, MI, RG. *Aud*: Ages 14–18.]

This may not be the most sparkling title for the teenager, but it has a wide audience, if only because it is found in so many homes. Geared to the woman who is more or less settled, encyclopedic in its coverage, *Good Housekeeping* despite its honorable years has a lot of life in its pages. Columnists and contributors include big names: Elizabeth Post (etiquette), Heloise (household hints), Stephen Birmingham (travel), Joyce Brothers (sex, marriage, and family problems). As readers have come to expect, menus and recipes are something to stay home for. A section on microwave cookery and food appliances is a plus. "The Better Way" advises on money matters, lists booklists to send for, and includes an invaluable product-recalls update. There are beauty (monthly makeovers), fashion, and crafts sections. Often celebrity covers are tie-ins to profiles that stress *Good Hosekeeping*'s areas of interest: Elizabeth Taylor and dieting, Cheryll Ladd and exercising. General articles are investigative, based on nostalgia, or personal accounts—"Somebody Had to Stop Him" (a school social worker skewers her principal for his sexual trespasses). *Good Housekeeping* publishes short stories by established authors and excerpts new novels. One of the seven sisters.

935 **Harper's Bazaar** (Incorporates *Junior Bazaar*). 1867. m. $16.97. Anthony Mazzola. Heast Magazines Corp., 1700 Broadway, New York, NY 10019. Subs. to: P.O. Box 10081, Des Moines, IA 50350. Illus. Adv. Circ: 769,369. Vol. ends: Dec. Microform: UMI. Reprint: UMI. [*Indexed*: MI, RG. *Aud*: Ages 14–18.]

Glamour plus is the trademark and while few young women (or, for that matter, older women) can afford the styles, this magazine offers numerous suggestions on how to be sophisticated in dress and person. *Harper's Bazaar* exudes a unique mix of elegance and culture. The magazine is a joy to the eye; its beautiful pages invite leisurely reading. Status advertisers grace its pages, but ads are colorful rather than brash. In the fashion section photos and articles chronicle the "metropolitan style." New trends are marked. Models are often prominent and successful women caught in the course of their busy lives. Clothes are sometimes sexy, but never sleazy. Beauty and health topics are earnest business here. So is survival in the world of work. Leisure and enrichment reviews are an important part of the magazine. *Harper's Bazaar* is very good at introducing the reader to the best in books, music, film, and travel destinations, but it is the world of art that is this title's great passion. Coverage is extensive and expert. Profile subjects reflect the magazine's confident insider image. *Harper's Bazaar* presents designer trunk show collections at boutiques and up-scale restaurants throughout the United States.

936 **Lilith: the Jewish women's magazine.** 1976. q. $20 (Individuals, $14). Susan Weidman Schneider. Lilith Publns., Inc., 250 W. 57th St., Suite 2432, New York, NY 10107. Illus. Circ: 10,000. [*Bk. rev*: 0–4, 500–1,000 words, signed. *Aud*: Ages 14–18.]

This is a useful feminist magazine where there are young Jewish women about. It is recommended for many public and school libraries. *Lilith* is concerned with all of the issues of Jewish women's lives. It has stimulating, thought-provoking articles, creative writing, news items, and information about resources. A regular column, "Tsena Rena," lists events, publications (including video and music), groups, projects, and calls for materials. The table of contents is titled "The Prepared Table," which is a reference to the authoritative code of behavior according to Jewish law. The editors state, "As Jewish feminists continue to rediscover and rework tradition, custom and practice, a new egalitarian Prepared Table will emerge. We list here selections from this evolving Prepared Table." *Lilith* is very different in appearance and tone from *Daughters of Sarah*, but both periodicals are concerned with integrating feminism into religious beliefs and practices.

937   **Mademoiselle.** 1935. m. $15. Amy Levin Cooper. Conde Nast Publns., Inc., 350 Madison Ave., New York, NY 10017. Subs. to: P.O. Box 5204, Boulder, CO 80322. Illus. Adv. Circ: 1,297,938. Vol. ends: Dec. Microform: UMI. [*Indexed*: MI, RG. *Bk. rev*: 2, 500–1,500 words, signed. *Aud*: Ages 14–18.]

This is a fashion/beauty magazine for young women, for those college-bound, planning or involved in a career, or looking for a serious relationship. The *Mademoiselle* reader will be younger and a bit less venturesome than the woman who feels that *Glamour* is her magazine. As claimed, she will find *Mademoiselle* "a resource book of product information and trend-setting direction." The reader will experience a shock of recognition on encountering the dewy-eyed beauties lovingly photographed by Avedon and articles such as "Now You're Chic . . . Now You're Cheap . . . Do Not Cross That Fine Beauty Line" and "The ABC's of VCR Dating." Serious commentary appears in "Private Eye" by Barbara Grizzuti Harrison ("Fatal Attraction—Single Girl, Double Standard") and in features like "Women-bashing Comics: The Joke's on Us." Every issue includes a short story. *Mademoiselle* runs a fiction contest with prizes of money and the possibility of publication in the magazine.

938   **Marie Claire Bis (Marie Claire Encore).** 1980. s-a. $14 (U.S.). Catherine S. Lardeur. Marie Claire, 11 bis rue Bossy-d'Anglas, 75008 Paris, France. Illus. Adv. [*Aud*: Ages 14–18.]

Any young woman who wants to go to Paris will thoroughly enjoy this title. This special edition of the popular French monthly *Marie Claire* is published in Spring/Summer and Winter/Fall issues. It is truly a "movable feast"—a term used to describe Paris itself. There is some English text at the front, and facility in French is not really needed to become a devotee. Fashion, photographed against mostly French backgrounds, is "a question of atmosphere, a longing to be dressed practically, and pleasurably, a question of wit and one's personal style." In addition to highlighting the work of designers working in the Paris houses— many with new names—*Marie Claire Bis* is big on accessory ideas.

939   **McCalls.** 1876. m. $13.95. Elizabeth Sloan. McCall Publg. Co., 230 Park Ave., New York, NY 10169. Subs. to: P.O. Box 56093, Boulder, CO 80322. Illus. Adv. Circ: 6,312,403. Microform: UMI. [*Indexed*: MI, RG. *Aud*: Ages 14–18.]

Somewhat like *Good Housekeeping* in its overall approach, this may not be a first choice of teenagers but it is a good all-around magazine for libraries. Women in the news from British princesses to television stars to political wives and would-be officeholders appear in these pages. *McCalls* takes pride in providing assimilable information on the basics of fashion, beauty, health, fitness, psychology, and parenting. A special treat is "America Entertains" by Colette Rossant, a cookbook author who knows her field as a cultural subject. Rossant is only one of the prominent contributors. Socialite Charlotte Ford writes on etiquette. Psychologist Lee Salk advises on problems with children, and veterinarian Michael Fox offers the compassionate and useful "Pet Life" column. Lee Radziwill is the magazine's arbiter of taste. Lest any would-be reader mistakenly suppose *McCalls* a lightweight publication, publisher Lang confirms: "We make sure that there's an issue in every issue."

940 **Modern Bride.** 1949. bi-m. $18.98. Cele Goldsmith Lalli. Cahners Publg. Co., 475 Park Ave. S., New York, NY 10016. Illus. Adv. Circ: 389,500. Vol. ends: Nov/Dec. Microform: B&H, UMI. [*Indexed*: MI. *Aud*: Ages 14–18.]

Modern Bride is very similar to *Bride's*. Both have essentially the same content. Everything from planning and executing a wedding to the honeymoon and wedded life thereafter is included. Lots of ads for china, silver, and wedding dresses are featured, and each bimonthly issue is quite hefty, averaging around 600 pages. The only readily apparent difference between the two is the subscription price.

941 **New Directions for Women** (Formerly: *New Directions for Women in New Jersey*). 1972. bi-m. $16 (Individuals, $10). Phyllis Kriegel. New Directions for Women, 108 W. Palisade Ave., Englewood, NJ 07631. Illus. Adv. Index. Circ: 55,000. Vol. ends: Nov. Microform: UMI. [*Indexed*: API. *Bk. rev*: 5–10, 300–1,200 words, signed. *Aud*: Ages 14–18.]

This developed out of the women's movement in New Jersey, but is now much broader in appeal and will be of interest to many young readers. It covers news of importance and discusses controversial issues in a very forthright way. It regularly reports on health and health care, employment issues, media, national and international politics, legal matters, and women of color, older women, and women prisoners, plus good coverage of the arts. Typical articles are "Women against Racism," "Disabled and Sexual," and "Will Workfare Do the Job." In addition to the book reviews, the "Editors Book Shelf" has topical essays listing many new titles. *New Directions for Women* provides important documentation for social history.

942 **Radiance: the magazine for large women.** 1984. q. $10. Alice Ansfield. Radiance, P.O. Box 31703, Oakland, CA 94604. Illus. Adv. Circ: 10,000. Vol. ends: Fall. [*Aud*: Ages 14–18.]

Many teenagers are overweight, or think they are, and this magazine offers assurance that all is well. It aims "to support women *all* sizes of large, of all ethnic backgrounds, lifestyles, ages, and philosophies." Its pages are full of attractive, positive images of large women. Issues are devoted to themes such as "Children and Weight," "Women of Color," and "Sports for Any Body!" Articles and regular features point out the oppression of women that comes from American society's obsession with thinness. Articles such as Rayna Green's "A Woman on Her Own Terms" discuss other cultural influences on body image—in this case Native American culture. The "Health and Well Being" department has solid information about diet and exercise. Each issue's "Images" column features a designer who specializes in clothing for large women. National advertisements provide information on products and services. This is an attractive and affordable magazine that provides a necessary corrective to mistaken notions about body image. It should be in every high school and public library.

943 **Redbook.** 1903. m. $11.97. Annette Capone. Hearst Corp., 959 Eighth Ave., New York, NY 10019. Subs. to: P.O. Box 10702, Des Moines, IA 50347-0702. Circ: 4,100,000. Microform: UMI. [*Indexed*: MI, RG. *Aud*: Ages 14–18.]

Ease of reading and its many-faceted coverage of teen interests make it a useful addition in high school and public libraries. Although the requisite women's-interest sections are here, proportions have changed in recent years. Crafts, for example, have been downplayed while fashion coverage has been expanded. This title now welcomes nontraditional worlds of pop culture and café society and New Age vision to its pages. Movie and television stars are frequent subjects, often with tie-ins to stories of family relationships or spirituality ("The Goldie [Hawn] Nobody Knows but Me by Her Big Sister," "A Psychic Changed My Life" by Linda Evans—on channeling). *Redbook* pulls no punches on matters of sexuality. It is alternately clinical—"Sexual Prematurity: Is Your Child Growing Up Too Fast?"—and therapeutic—"Can America's Top Sex Experts Save Charles and Di's Marriage?" Each issue carries articles of advice of all sorts, medical reports ("Are You a Type C–Cancer Prone Personality"?), investigative reporting, true stories that may be straight or "heart tuggers" ("I Gave My Children Everything—but Love"). Contributing editors include Benjamin Spock of child-rearing fame and author Judith Viorst. Short stories are a regular feature.

944 **Sassy.** 1988. m. $14.98. Jane Pratt. Matilda Publns., Inc., One Times Sq., New York, NY 10036. Illus. Adv. [*Aud*: Ages 14–18.]

A fashion and beauty magazine with a name that appropriately reflects its tone. Compared with *YM* and *Seventeen*, it is stylistically much more direct and frank in its coverage of the teen scene. The regular contents contain four feature articles including fiction, celebrity profiles, fashion, beauty and health, and regulars such as reviews, a quiz, personal stories from readers, a buying guide, astrology, and so forth. Contemporary issues are also tackled: A featured story on racism is a revealing and candid discussion of the problem. This large-size title with creative photographic layouts provides some variety in this category of teen fashion magazines and predictably will be well received by its intended readership.

945 **Self.** 1979. m. $15. Valorie Griffith Weaver. Conde Nast Publns., 350 Madison Ave., New York, NY 10017. Subs. to: P.O. Box 5216, Boulder, CO 80322. Illus. Adv. Circ: 1,090,027. Vol. ends: Dec. Microform: UMI. Reprint: UMI. [*Aud*: Ages 14–18.]

Self has a commitment to good health and good looks; its approach is sensible and balanced, rather than manic. "All the News to Keep You Fit" is a regular roundup of briefs on body, health, and mind. In the belief that nutrition awareness is capturing America, *Self* has increased its coverage of food matters. Features on healthy eating, menus, and recipes are innovative and practical. Articles on work, money, family, and parenting are also good. There are often excerpts from recent books, usually dealing with man/woman relationships. *Self* can sometimes be cutesy and plain silly, notably in its "Man Scan" department, but it is overall a well-edited, serious effort.

946 **Seventeen.** 1944. m. $15.95. Sarah Crichton. Triangle Communications, P.O. Box 100, Radnor, PA 19088. Illus. Circ: 1,750,000. Vol. ends: Dec. Microform: UMI. Online: WILSONLINE. [*Indexed*: AbrRG, RG. *Aud*: Ages 14–18.]

A perennial favorite, this title is undoubtedly the most popular fashion and beauty magazine among female teenagers. Profuse advertisements and feature articles readily reflect its focus. Standard features are presentations in the "Beauty," "Fashion," "Fiction," "Articles," and "Decorating/Food" sections and columns containing reviews, interviews, advice, astrology, and discussions of social relations and sexuality ("Sex and Your Body"). Directed to the older teen, but its adolescently classy style and mature tone do not inhibit young teens, who find the fashion content quite appealing.

947 **Shape: mind and body fitness for women.** 1981. m. $20. Barbara Harris. Weider Publns., 21100 Erwin St., Woodland Hills, CA 91367. Illus. Adv. Circ: 556,783. Vol. ends: Aug. [*Aud*: Ages 14–18.]

Here is a sane approach to health, beauty, and curves. The goal of this journal is to make the reader understand that good health is the individual's own responsibility. *Shape* sees body image as an integral part of self-image. Psychological and personal development get as much attention as exercise and nutrition. Regular features include "Body of Betty" (Betty Weider), on health, dieting, beauty, and fashion. *Shape* has good advice on keeping to a diet while working or partying. Many serious, helpful medical articles are written by physicians. Product reviews include exercise videocassettes. Models are young and svelte. A recent Miss America was a *Shape* cover girl, but as an indication of the jittery state of women's magazinedom, an accompanying article included an apology for beauty pageants.

948 **Sing Heavenly Muse: women's poetry and prose.** 1977. s-a. $40 (Individuals, $21). Sue Ann Martinson. Sing Heavenly Muse, P.O. Box 13299, Minneapolis, MN 55414. Illus. Circ: 1,200. [*Aud*: Ages 14–18.]

One of the better literature magazines for younger women, this has a feminist tone but is not stringent. *Sing Heavenly Muse* publishes poetry, fiction, and "creative prose" (defined as "journal, creative essay, memoir"), and sponsors contests for poetry and fiction. Issues include artwork such as a selection of photographs from Bambi Peterson's "Mother's Messages" series and a set of photographs of Amy Cordova's quilts. "The journal is feminist in an open, generous sense [encouraging] women to range freely, honestly, and imaginatively over all subjects, philosophies, and styles." It seeks to encourage new writers, and welcomes men's work that is sensitive to women's consciousness. The 100 or so pages of *Sing Heavenly Muse* contain a good sampling of new writing by women.

949 **Teen.** 1957. m. $12.95. Petersen Publg. Co., 8490 Sunset Blvd., Los Angeles, CA 90069. Illus. Adv. Circ: 1,076,000. Sample. Online: DIALOG. [*Indexed*: Acs, BioI, MI, RG. *Aud*: Ages 14–18.]

One of the more widely read of the teenage magazines, this is primarily for the clothes-conscious girl of 13 to 18, with special emphasis on the early teens. There is little here that will inspire, but a lot that will help young girls find themselves in the middle-class world of fashion, good manners, cooking, and, yes, the workplace. A type of *Good Housekeeping* for the younger set, this does include serious, excellent advice on problems faced by readers, from sex to overeating, plus fiction, poetry, and the arts. While not up to the quality of *Seventeen*, it is close behind, and a welcome addition in most libraries—particularly as it is so well indexed.

950 **Teenage: the magazine for sophisticated young women.** 1981. bi-m. $9.95. Jeannie Ralston. Highwire, 928 Broadway, New York, NY 10010. Illus. Adv. Circ: 170,000. Sample. [*Bk. rev*: Various number and length. *Aud*: Ages 14–18.]

This is a bright, controversial publication edited for the young woman. While much of the material is suitable for college women, just as much is applicable to the high school student. There is attention given to national and international news, but most of the focus is on humor, satire, and matters guaranteed to be of interest to those who find other teenage magazines a bore. It is nicely illustrated and there are much-above-average reviews of everything from books to film and music. A sample definitely is in order because this is a magazine that deserves a much wider audience.

951 **Tradeswomen: a quarterly magazine for women in blue-collar work.** 1981. q. $25. Ed. bd. Tradeswoman, Inc., P.O. Box 40664, San Francisco, CA 94104. Illus. Adv. Circ: 2,000. Vol. ends: Fall. [*Indexed*: API. *Bk. rev*: 0–2, 500–1,000 words, signed. *Aud*: Ages 14–18.]

"Tradeswomen, Inc., is dedicated to securing a permanent place for women in the blue-collar workforce." It approaches this task through advocacy, peer support, and education. This magazine is the only national publication for women working in blue-collar jobs. *Tradeswomen* seeks contributions from its readers and publishes articles, interviews, photos, fiction, and poetry by and about women in a wide range of trades. A typical issue features articles concerned with safety on the job, psychological tools for survival, the pros and cons of working with other tradeswomen, and an interview with a self-employed worker. This is an important magazine for high school libraries because of the information it contains about blue-collar career options. It is also recommended for public libraries, especially those whose users include blue-collar workers.

952 **Vogue.** 1892. m. $28. Anna W. Wintour. Conde Nast Publns., Inc., 350 Madison Ave., New York, NY 10017. Illus. Adv. Circ: 1,200,000. Sample. Vol. ends: Dec. Microform: UMI. Reprint: UMI. [*Indexed*: MI, RG. *Bk. rev*: 2–3, 500–1,000 words, signed. *Aud*: Ages 14–18.]

One of the oldest, best-known fashion magazines in the world, *Vogue* has several international editions—Argentinian, Australian, Brazilian, British, French, German, and Italian. Long a standard-bearer in the fashion field, this magazine continues to be one of the best. While primarily a fashion publication, it also includes the following sections: "Beauty & Health," "People Are Talking About," "Living," "Travel," and "In Every Issue." Grace Mirabella, former editor-in-chief, states, "*Vogue* is a fashion magazine. While that's a key subject, the fact is we do many other things around that. Our attitude at *Vogue* since 1970 is [one] that follows smart women's interest in how they look, in health and image." This is a sophisticated, up-scale magazine.

953 **W.** 1971. bi-w. $30. Michael F. Coady. Fairchild Publns., Inc., 7 E. 12th St., New York, NY 10003. Illus. Adv. Circ: 175,000. Vol. ends: Dec. Microform: MIM. [*Indexed*: Acs. *Aud*: Ages 14–18.]

Every two weeks this tabloid suggests to young women the joys of the sophisticated/rich life. Few of the problems are mentioned. W offers the latest in trendy fashions and features fine homes, resorts, furniture, art, parties, beautiful people, food, and wine. W's readership median age is 47.6 years. Affluent women spend an average of $7,362 annually on fashion merchandise. Recommended if the young reader wants to see how the "other half" lives.

954 **Woman Today.** 1988. bi-m. $15. Rochelle Larkin. M & O Communications, Inc., P.O. Box 651, Murray Hill Sta., New York, NY 10156. Illus. Adv. Vol. ends: Nov. [*Bk. rev*: 1–2, 500–1,500 words, signed. *Aud*: Ages 14–18.]

This is one of the few solid, down-to-earth women's magazines with appeal for younger readers. Although it covers pretty much the same issues that other women's magazines do, it eschews the sensationalism of its competitors. Instead it relies on good research, professional editing, and competent writing. One hopes that is enough. Although many *Woman Today* articles are excerpted from other sources—usually recent books—these sources are highly credible and their authors are fully identified. The excerpts are well integrated into the magazine as a whole. Articles like "Artist Mother, Model Child," in which an illustrator explains how she balances career and family responsibilities, and a review essay on 1920s hedonist painter Tamara De Lempecka are delightfully different from what is usually served up in women's magazines.

955 **Women's Sports & Fitness** (Formerly: *Women's Sports*)). 1979. 10/yr. $12.95. Nancy K. Crowell. World Publns., Inc., P.O. Box 2456, Winter Park, FL 32790. Illus. Adv. Circ: 350,000. Microform: UMI. [*Indexed*: MI, RG. *Bk. rev*: 1, 1–2 columns. *Aud*: Ages 14–18.]

The membership publication of the Women's Sports Foundation, this magazine offers a variety of monthly departments (e.g., walking, sports medicine, cycling, aerobics, weight training, diet, water sports, and so on) and many useful features (e.g., training routines, endurance, energy, equipment, fashion, "how-to" sports tips, product testing, and profiles). Excellent photography.

956 **YM.** 1953. 10/yr. $14. Nancy Axelrod Comer. Grumer & Jahr Publg., 685 Third Ave., New York, NY 10164. Illus. Adv. Circ: 850,000. [*Aud*: Ages 14–18.]

Aimed at the teenage female audience, this title emphasizes fashion and beauty. An entertainment section contains profiles of teen stars and a music review. Poetry and fiction are featured in addition to frank discussions on topics of interest such as social problems, weight loss, and parental and peer relationships. Colorful and polished, this magazine should serve its target audience well.

■ CLASSROOM PUBLICATIONS ■

See also: CHILDREN/CLASSROOM PUBLICATIONS

See the explanatory note in the Children's section on classroom publications. For foreign-language classroom publications see Professional Education and Library Journals/Education by Subject Areas/Arts and Humanities—Foreign-Language Teaching.

First choices   None. Select as needed.

Suitable for children   Depending on the reading ability of the younger child, most of these may be suitable for junior high.

Addresses of primary publishers are (1) Scholastic, Inc., 730 Broadway, New York, NY 10003. (2) Curriculum Innovations, 3500 Western Ave., Highland Park, IL 60035.

957   **Art and Man.** 1970. 6/yr. $6.50. Janet Soderberg. Scholastic, Inc. Subs. to: P.O. Box 644, Lyndhurst, NJ 07071. Illus. Circ: 143,000. Vol. ends: May. Microform: UMI. [*Aud*: Ages 12–18.]

This superb magazine is prepared in cooperation with the National Gallery of Art in Washington, D.C. It takes a thematic approach and seeks to show the relationships among art, literature, and culture. Students are introduced to great artists from the Renaissance to the contemporary period, and aspiring artists are frequently featured. *Art and Man* is printed on glossy-coated paper with full-color reproductions. There is even a centerfold—"The Masterpiece of the Month." Although targeted for grades 7 to 12, it can be adapted for use by younger students.

958   **Biology Bulletin Monthly** (Formerly: *Science Challenge*). 1978. 9/yr. $39.95. Curriculum Innovations. Illus. [*Aud*: Ages 12–18.]

Here the reader interest is at the high school level, and the writers presuppose a passing interest in general science subjects. The well-illustrated articles cover events in the news and give useful background information on basic science problems. Energy and the environment are stressed, primarily because this magazine is the successor to *Current Energy & Ecology*.

Coed. *See* **Scholastic Choices.**

959   **Images of Excellence.** 1986. bi-m. $5. Robert Detjen. Images of Excellence, P.O. Box 1131, Boiling Springs, NC 28017. Illus. [*Aud*: Ages 12–18.]

Complete with a teacher's supplement, here is an 18-page classroom approach to biography. Each issue, filled with color and black-and-white illustrations, is devoted to a single person, and Florence Nightingale, Thomas Jefferson, Martin Luther King, Jr., Mother Teresa, and Raoul Wallenberg are typical subjects. Selection is based as much on appeal to young people as on the effort to furnish heroes and role models. The writing style is journalistic, yet never insulting or simple. The text often quotes from the person under study and offers objective notes dealing with chronology and the individual's role in history. The compilers have a healthy respect for their potential readers. Aside from praise for the individuals, the editorial matter is objective and indicates no particular bias. The organization is a bit haphazard. According to the editor, the magazine is produced by a nonprofit corporation and "a small group of volunteers, college faculty and high school and elementary school teachers."

960   **Literary Cavalcade.** 1948. 8/yr. $5.95. Katherine Robinson. Scholastic, Inc. Illus. Adv. Circ: 310,000. Vol. ends: May. Microform: UMI. [*Aud*: Ages 12–18.]

A contemporary literature magazine with high standards. It contains interviews, "how-to" articles, short stories, poetry, and plays. Famous authors such as Truman Capote, Saul Bellow, George Orwell, and John Steinbeck have been represented, along with student writers. Every issue lists the favorite books of a famous personality. The final issue of the year publishes the work of Scholastic award winners.

961   **Scholastic Choices** (Formerly: *Co-Ed*). 1978. 8/yr. $5.50. Scholastic, Inc. Adv. Sample. (CMG) [*Indexed*: CMG; *Aud*: Ages 12–18.]

A basic home-economics class paper with articles and stories written more for girls than for boys. All topics are considered that are apt to be part of the standard junior high or high school curriculum. It includes stories, puzzles, illustrations, and so forth. While the content is suitable for seniors, the reading level is much lower. The advertisements are for girls and the 50 to 60 pages are more like a junior version of a woman's magazine than anything else. Harmless, but hardly inspirational—particularly the fiction.

962 **Scholastic Science World.** 1970. 16/yr. $5.95. Scholastic, Inc. Illus. Adv. [*Indexed*: CMG. *Aud*: Ages 12–18.]

This title follows current developments in science—or at least those most likely to be seen on television or in the local newspaper. There is particular attention to the environment. Coverage is worldwide and the writing is good to excellent. The photographs and illustrations are equally good. The catch—as in so many Scholastic magazines—is that the advertising can be rather offensive.

963 **Scholastic Scope.** 1964. 20/yr. $5.95. Fran Claro. Scholastic, Inc. Illus. Adv. Circ: 1,046,000. Vol. ends: May. Microform: UMI. [*Aud*: Ages 12–18.]

A hi-lo language arts magazine, this publication offers a balanced program of reading for pleasure and improvement in vocabulary and comprehension. Competency-test help is given on a regular basis. Published in newsprint and in a large typeface, with a glossy-coated cover, and many features have film or television tie-ins.

964 **Scholastic Search.** 1972. 8/yr. $5.50. Scholastic, Inc. Illus. Adv. Circ: 223,000. [*Aud*: Ages 14–18.]

Written for high school social studies classes, this is a lively magazine with a nice touch—the reading level is for lower grades (about sixth to eighth). The advertising is not too obtrusive, and the illustrations are excellent. All topics of interest to social studies are considered, from history to politics.

965 **Scholastic Update** (Formerly: *Senior Scholastic*). 1920. 16/yr. $5.95. Eric Oatman. Scholastic, Inc. Illus. Adv. Circ: 211,000. Vol. ends: May. Microform: UMI. [*Indexed*: AbrRG, MI, RG. *Aud*: Ages 14–18.]

A perennial that continues to challenge the average and above-average student to read and think critically. Recently, single public affairs topics have been the focus of individual issues. These have included "Conflict and Change in Latin America," "The Free Press," and "The Drug Trade." A worthy supplement to social studies courses.

966 **Scholastic Voice.** 1946. 16/yr. $5.95. David Goddy. Scholastic, Inc. Illus. Adv. Circ: 275,000. [*Aud*: Ages 12–18.]

Here the benefits of learning and applying practical English are stressed. Both critical writing and reading skills are encouraged through excellent plays, short stories, humor, and so forth. The authors tend to be much above average. Advertising, unfortunately, does not help matters, but the illustrations and makeup are quite winning.

Science Challenge. *See* **Biology Bulletin Monthly.**

967 **Writing** (Formerly: *Current Media*). 1977. m. (Sept-May). $5.60. Allen Lenhoff. Field Publns., 245 Long Hill Rd., Middletown, CT 06457. Vol. ends: May. [*Aud*: Ages 12–18.]

Designed to supplement language arts classes for grades 7 to 12, this periodical on writing does a reasonably good job of combining explanation with examples and practice. Each issue examines one writing format (personality profiles, magazine articles, television scripts) in depth. An interview with a practitioner and a sample of his or her writing usually precede the how-to basics. Three shorter articles cover other aspects of writing: the use of language (slang, jargon), a spotlight on a writing career (editor, ghostwriter, sports reporter), and the discussion of a writing technique (selecting a voice, figures of speech), followed by practice exercises. An example of award-winning student writing is always included.

PROFESSIONAL EDUCATION AND LIBRARY JOURNALS

The titles listed here are for teachers and administrators as well as librarians, in public and school libraries.

This part is in three sections. The first is dedicated to general education, which has by far the greatest number of titles. The second section is a listing of the basic professional journals in subject fields. The third section covers library-oriented journals, including book and media reviews.

Audience levels, that is, the primary use of the title in preschool through high school *by* professionals, is indicated by age groups (and all are preceded by Pr/).

Preschool: Ages 3–6 (2 or 3 titles are for even younger children and are so indicated)
Elementary/middle school/junior high: Ages 6–14
High school: Ages 14–18

■■■■■■ EDUCATION—GENERAL ■■■■■■

[Sy Sargent]

First choices   Elementary/Junior High: (1) *Instructor*; (2) *Learning*.
Elementary through High School: (1) *American Educator*; (2) *Education Digest*; (3) *Phi Delta Kappan*; (4) *Theory into Practice*.

968   **American Educator.** 1977. q. $8. Elizabeth McPike. Amer. Federation of Teachers, 555 New Jersey Ave. N.W., Washington, DC 20001. Illus. Adv. Circ: 527,000. Vol. ends: Winter. [*Indexed*: CIJE, EdI, MI, RG. *Aud*: Pr/Ages 6–18.]

Although a publication of the American Federation of Teachers, *AE* carries little material that deals directly with the economic interests of teachers. Rather, it is a readable, generally commonsense magazine that divides its attention between current issues of education policy and practical classroom methods. The articles tend to be protective of teachers, particularly when their prerogatives confront those of administrators, but they also insist on the social and professional responsibilities of teachers. The magazine should be of interest to teachers, administrators, and perhaps students.

969   **The American School Board Journal.** 1891. m. $38. Gregg W. Downey. Natl. School Boards Assn., 1680 Duke St., Alexandria, VA 22314. Illus. Adv. Index. Circ: 45,000. Vol. ends: Dec. Microform: B&H, MIM. Reprint: UMI. [*Indexed*: CIJE, EdI. *Bk. rev*: 1, 500–1,000 words. *Aud*: Pr/Ages 6–18.]

Eleven or so short articles per issue deal with the financial, administrative, and educational aspects of running a school system, with most of the emphasis on the educational. There are also columns reviewing new products, providing information about recent legal and political developments, and giving advice on difficult policy questions. This is a readable magazine with useful material not only for school board members, but also for teachers, parents, and community leaders.

970   **The Black Scholar: journal of black studies and research.** 1969. 6/yr. $35 (Individuals, $25). Robert Chrisman. Black World Foundation, 485 65th St., Oakland, CA

94609. Illus. Adv. Index. Circ: 7,000. Sample. Vol. ends: Nov/Dec. Microform: B&H, MIM, UMI. Reprint: B&H, UMI. [*Indexed*: CIJE, INeg, PAIS. *Bk. rev*: 1–3, 500–1,200 words, signed. *Aud*: Pr/Ages 6–18.]

The Black Scholar's militant, informative articles appeal to the general public. The cover art, followed by a stinging introductory essay, sets the tone for each number's contents. Political, economic, and social issues relevant to blacks throughout the African diaspora are aired through articles, interviews, poetry, fiction, excerpts of speeches, documents, photographs, editorials, and book/film reviews. Two notable features are "Black Books Roundup" and "The Black Scholar Classified." The former is an annotated compilation of works dealing with Afro–third world questions; the latter is a listing of available academic positions.

971   Canadian Journal of Native Education (Formerly: *Indian Education*). 1973. 3/yr. $12. Robert Carney. Univ. of Alberta, Dept. of Educational Foundations, 5-109 Education N., Edmonton, Alta. T6G 2G5, Canada. Adv. Circ: 650. Refereed. Vol. ends: No. 3. [*Indexed*: CIJE, CanEdI. *Bk. rev*: 2–12, 200–500 words, signed. *Aud*: Pr/Ages 6–18.]

Concerned with the education of native peoples in North America, including the Inuit and Métis, with a focus on Canada. Scholarly articles and case studies cover all aspects of their education, both urban and rural, and comparisons are made with native education in other countries. School systems, inner-city schools, and art education are covered. In 1987, an agreement was reached to publish one issue each from three diverse universities—those of Alberta, British Columbia, and Saskatchewan. Recommended for all education libraries.

972   Childhood Education. 1924. 5/yr. $45 (Individuals, $36). Lucy Prete Martin. Assn. for Childhood Education Intl., 11141 Georgia Ave., Suite 200, Wheaton, MD 20902. Illus. Adv. Index. Circ: 14,000. Microform: UMI. [*Indexed*: CIJE, EdI. *Bk. rev*: 2, 100 words, signed. *Aud*: Pr/Ages 6–14.]

This journal is the voice of the Association for Childhood Education International (ACEI). It is written in a popular style suitable for parents as well as professionals involved in the education of children and young adults. The articles stress a practical approach, and the goal is to "stimulate thinking rather than advocate fixed practices," which the journal achieves admirably. Regular departments include book reviews of books for children as well as for professionals, reviews of films and pamphlets, summaries of current research in magazine articles and ERIC documents, software reviews, information from the field, and comments from readers. It is recommended that this magazine be considered for purchase by all libraries. It is essential.

973   Children Today (Formerly: *Children*). 1954. bi-m. $14. Carolyn Reece. Office of Human Development Services, Dept. of Health and Human Services, Rm. 356-G, 200 Independence Ave. S.W., Washington, DC 20201. Illus. Index. Circ: 18,000. Microform: MIM, UMI. Online: DIALOG. [*Indexed*: EdI, MI, RG. *Bk. rev*: 2–4, lengthy, signed. *Aud*: Pr/Ages 6–14.]

A well-rounded interdisciplinary journal for the professions serving children. Specialists contribute approximately seven popularly written articles per issue concerned with children, youth, and families as well as articles for the professional. Regular departments include news and reports from the field, book reviews, and a page of U.S. government publications that are related to children. The latter would be extremely useful in ordering free and inexpensive material.

974 Children's Environments Quarterly. 1983. q. $70 (Individuals, $30). Ed. bd. Lawrence Erlbaum Assocs., Inc., 365 Broadway, Hillsdale, NJ 07642. Illus. Circ: 500. [*Aud*: Pr/Ages 6–14.]

In some 70 illustrated pages, professors write about "the planning, design and management of children's environments." Three out of the four issues each year focus on a particular theme, for example, one issue examined is concerned with the home and its nine documented articles consider such matters as housing floor plans, noise in the nursery, and family day care. According to the CUNY editor, the journal "is produced in our program by a small active group of scholars and has gradually grown in circulation through word of mouth." It deserves much wider attention for three reasons: It is the only magazine of its type; it focuses on matters of concern to parents, teachers, and anyone involved with the development of children; and the articles deal with the practical and most offer sound suggestions on how to improve the environment. Additional readings and sources are cited, too. This is an unusual journal suitable for both specialized and general collections.

975 Children's House/Children's World (Formerly: *Children's World*). 1966. bi-m. $9.50. Kenneth Edelson. Children's House, Inc., P.O. Box 111, Caldwell, NJ 07006. Illus. Circ: 45,000. Sample. Refereed. Vol. ends: June. [*Bk. rev*: 8–30, 200–500 words. *Aud*: Pr/Ages 3–15.]

CH/CW publishes numerous articles dealing with the Montessori method of elementary education, as well as special education and dyslexia. It also publishes general-interest articles on education and children in the 3–15 age range. The articles are generally short and practical and should be of interest to parents as well as teachers. This is a good choice for elementary education libraries.

976 The Clearing House: for the contemporary educator in middle and secondary schools. 1925. 9/yr. $37. Nancy Lenihan Geltman. Heldref Publns., 4000 Albemarle St. N.W., Washington, DC 20016. Illus. Adv. Circ: 4,100. Refereed. Vol. ends: May. Microform: UMI. [*Indexed*: CIJE, EdI, MI. *Aud*: Pr/Ages 14–18.]

CH publishes short, informal articles on all aspects of middle and high school education. Some of the articles explain or advocate particular classroom methods. Some are opinion pieces dealing with controversial education topics: teacher education, textbook quality, challenging the gifted, and so forth. Most of the articles are readable and some are stimulating and the magazine has the virtue of publishing material with a wide range of points of view, but more force and originality would be welcome.

977 Connect: Teaching with Television. 1989. m. Free. Robert Moses. Crosby Vandeburth Group, 420 Boylston St., Boston, MA 02116. Illus. Adv. [*Aud*: Pr/Ages 6–18.]

Connect is a mildly useful, free guide for teachers. Educational offerings on television, drawn from programming from ABC to USA Network, are listed in 50 pages by month and by date under a dozen curriculum headings, with numerous subheads. For example, English/Language Arts lists "literary adaptations" beginning with "2001" on the Movie Channel and ending 40 entries later with AMC's "Wuthering Heights." Under each movie one finds a 15-word annotation and the date and times, given for the different time zones. There is no indication of age group for which the movie is suited—teachers really need professional help as to what is suitable for, say, a third grader or a high school senior. A plus is the material on background of major programs such as "Tale of Two Cities." A minus is the page or two dedicated to teachers who delight in television in the classroom. Unfortunately, much of the really first-rate material is available only through pay-television, and there is nothing said about the masses of commercials that accompany most of the films. Still, this is a handy listing of better television offerings, and it is free.

978 **Contemporary Education.** 1929. q. $25 (Individuals, $12). Russell L. Hamm. School of Education, Indiana State Univ., Terre Haute, IN 47809. Index. Circ: 3,800. Vol. ends: Summer. Microform: KTO, UMI. [*Indexed*: CIJE, EdI. *Bk. rev*: 5–6, 500–1,000 words, signed. *Aud*: Pr/Ages 6–18.]

CE publishes 8 to 12 short articles in each issue. Most are opinion pieces discussing various phases of K–12 education and teacher education, but research reports are included occasionally. *CE* takes interest in comparative education and in administrative and personnel issues such as censorship of school publications, teacher certification requirements, and burnout.

979 **Day Care and Early Education.** 1973. q. $49 (Individuals, $19). Randa Roen Nachbar. Human Sciences Press, Inc., 72 Fifth Ave., New York, NY 10011. Illus. Adv. Circ: 25,000. Sample. Vol. ends: Summer. Microform: UMI. Reprint: ISI, UMI. [*Indexed*: CIJE, EdI. *Bk. rev*: 1, 600–800 words. *Aud*: Pr/Ages 3–6.]

Early childhood educators and child-care professionals will find this an extremely useful journal. Articles provide curriculum ideas for teachers, information on how best to meet the needs of the parents as well as the children served, updates on current issues, and managerial advice to administrators. Throughout, there is a strong tone of advocacy and respect for young people.

980 **Early Education and Development.** 1989. q. $78.75 (Individuals, $42). Richard Abidin. Univ. of Virginia. Subs. to: Psychology Press, 39 Pearl St., Brandon, VT 05733. Illus. Adv. Sample. [*Aud*: Pr/Ages 1–8.]

"Early" in this title means from birth to age eight. Education and development is a wide net covering interests from preschool and day-care programs to staff competencies and program evaluations. The audience is not the early primary school teacher, but professors who teach the subject to teachers, as well as researchers and psychologists who give direction to the professors. The circuitous route is mapped by the editor, from the Curry School of Education at the University of Virginia. He presides over 2 associate editors and 27 editorial board officers, of whom only one apparently works in public schools. The five articles per issue are by dedicated professors and carry such titles as "Establishing the Integrity of the Independent Variable in Early Intervention Programs."

981 **Education and Society.** 1988. q. $18. Caren Keller Ness. Anti-Defamation League of B'nai B'rith, 823 United Nations Plaza, New York, NY 10017. Illus. Adv. Vol. ends: Winter. [*Bk. rev*: 18, 100–400 words. *Aud*: Pr/Ages 6–18.]

This magazine is committed to combating racial and cultural bigotry through education. Issues discuss such topics as the effect of popular culture on public education, the treatment of religion in schools, and the role of the private sector in promoting democratic education. A special insert section provides ideas and materials for classroom use in elementary, middle, and high schools. There are separate departments reviewing children's and adult books.

982 **The Education Digest.** 1935. 9/yr. $21. Alan H. Jones. Prakken Publns., Inc., 416 Longshore Dr., P.O. Box 8623, Ann Arbor, MI 48107. Adv. Index. Circ: 38,000. Sample.

Vol. ends: May. Microform: UMI. Reprint: UMI. [*Indexed*: EdI, MI, RG. *Bk. rev*: 4–5, 100–200 words. *Aud*: Pr/Ages 6–18.]

Each issue contains 16 to 18 abridged articles, most from education periodicals, a few from general-interest magazines like *New Republic* and *American Scholar*. The abridgments are fairly and skillfully done, preserving the tone as well as the main lines of thought. There is some coverage of all the main aspects of education, but most articles seem to deal with management problems and to take the perspective of K–12 administrators. Relatively few deal with specific problems of pedagogy, or focus on aspects of individual subject areas.

983 **Education Week: American education's newspaper of record.** 1981. 40/yr. $47.90. Ronald Wolk. Editorial Projects in Education, Inc., P.O. Box 6987, Syracuse, NY 13217. Illus. Adv. Index. Circ: 60,000. Vol. ends: June. Microform: UMI. [*Aud*: Pr/Ages 6–18.]

A tabloid weekly newspaper that provides general coverage of K–12 education in the United States. Superficially like the *Times Educational Supplement* s. *TCJ* seems to put more emphasis on traditional academic values,and on and the *Chronicle of Higher Education*, it makes little effort, as they do, to cover ideas and scholarship in depth. It reads much like an ordinary, good-quality newspaper in which all the articles happen to be about education. Political and economic developments in the relation between schools and society get the most attention, but human-interest articles about unusual accomplishments of teachers and students are also frequent. The classified ads section is an important job-market feature for principals and other administrators.

984 **The Educational Forum.** 1936. q. $12. Kaoru Yamamoto. Kappa Delta Pi, P.O. Box A, West Lafayette, IN 47906. Illus. Index. Circ: 48,000. Refereed. Vol. ends: Summer. Microform: B&H, MIM, UMI. Reprint: UMI. [*Indexed*: CIJE, EdI. *Bk. rev*: 2–5, 1,200–2,000 words, signed. *Aud*: Pr/Ages 6–18.]

EF publishes urbane essays on controversial issues of educational policy—secular humanism, school-parent relations, liberal versus vocational goals, and so forth. Compared with most general education journals, it is perhaps less preoccupied with social amelioration and more interested in preserving traditional values, though in a decidedly humane version. "On the Shoulders of Giants," a department that reprints selections from important educators from the past, is characteristic of the content. To balance things, another department, "Voices of the Young," publishes selections by elementary school students. *EF* is the organ of an education honor society.

985 **Educational Horizons.** 1921. q. $15 (Individuals, $12.50). Christine A. Swanson. Pi Lambda Theta, 4101 E. Third St., Bloomington, IN 47401. Illus. Adv. Circ: 18,000. Microform: UMI. Reprint: UMI. [*Indexed*: CIJE, EdI. *Bk. rev*: 2, 300–500 words, signed. *Aud*: Pr/Ages 6–18.]

The official publication of Pi Lambda Theta, an education honor society, *EH* is an unpretentious magazine that publishes short, nontechnical articles on both educational philosophy and the more immediate aspects of pedagogy. Most of the articles address real issues in a thoughtful, nonsimplistic way. "On Balance" is a special section in which teachers and researchers discuss issues in terms of their individual research or teaching experience. *EH* should be available to K–12 teachers, and it would be a good choice for public libraries that want to provide readable material on education to parents and other interested library users.

986 **Educational Leadership.** 1943. 8/yr. $24. Ronald S. Brandt. Assn. for Supervision and Curriculum Development, 125 N. West St., Alexandria, VA 22314-2798. Illus. Adv. Index. Circ: 80,000. Microform: UMI. Reprint: UMI. [*Indexed*: CIJE, EdI. *Bk. rev*: 0–15, 100–200 words, signed. *Aud*: Pr/Ages 6–18.]

Definitely a magazine rather than a journal, *EL* provides 13 to 18 short, readable articles in each issue. The focus is on practical problems of K–12 schools, seen from an administrator's viewpoint. Though straight research articles are not included, much of the content is explicitly based on research. Each issue contains a group of articles on a common theme. In addition to the articles, there are several regular departments that present short essays by working principals, short reports of research, and notices of useful books and other materials. For public libraries that are frequented by school board members, principals, administrators, and concerned parents.

987 **The Elementary School Journal.** 1900. 5/yr. $39 (Individuals, $25). Thomas L. Good. Univ. of Chicago Press, Journals Div., P.O. Box 37005, Chicago, IL 60637. Illus. Adv. Index. Circ: 6,000. Refereed. Vol. ends: May. Microform: C, JAI, UMI. [*Indexed*: CIJE, EdI. *Aud*: Pr/Ages 6–14.]

ESJ publishes mostly medium-to-long formal reports of research; occasionally pieces are devoted to theoretical analyses and to reviews of research on a particular topic. Most of the research articles report studies of teacher behavior and of the effectiveness of specific classroom materials and procedures. This is a quality journal, basic for libraries that serve programs in elementary education.

988 **The Executive Educator.** 1979. m. $45. Gregg W. Downey. Natl. School Boards Assn., 1680 Duke St., Alexandria, VA 22314. Illus. Adv. Circ: 16,000. Vol. ends: Dec. Microform: B&H, UMI. Reprint: UMI. [*Indexed*: CIJE. *Bk. rev*: 0–1, 700–1,800 words. *Aud*: Pr/Ages 6–18.]

Judging from the titles of some of the articles, one would definitely take *EE* to be the Rambo of education periodicals, but the bark turns out to be worse than the bite. *EE* does urge a vigorous, no-nonsense administrative style, but it also publishes articles encouraging programs to keep pregnant teenagers in school, and advising praise rather than punishment as a means of controlling rowdiness during assemblies. There is not much profundity here, but there is some sensible advice.

989 **Feminist Teacher.** 1984. 3/yr. $20 (Individuals, $12). Ed. bd. Feminist Teacher Editorial Collective, 442 Ballantine Hall, Indiana Univ., Bloomington, IN 47405. Illus. Circ: 400. [*Indexed*: API. *Bk. rev*: 0–1, 1,000 words, signed. *Aud*: Pr/Ages 6–18.]

Feminist Teacher is "committed to combatting sexism and other forms of oppression in the classroom." It seeks contributions from its readers of articles on the theory of teaching, on teaching strategies, and on personal experiences. It also asks readers to submit bibliographies and course syllabi. A unique feature is the "Network" column, which publishes lists of names of those who would like to contact feminist educators who share their interests. Readers are encouraged to write to anyone on the list in care of the journal. If the list is any indicator of readership, *Feminist Teacher* is reaching exactly the audience it seeks—"feminists who teach in a variety of disciplines and on all grade levels—preschool to graduate school." Another very helpful feature of this journals is the column "Teaching Resources." Issues seem to appear on an irregular schedule, but this is a minor problem. The journal belongs in every school library.

990 **The High School Journal.** 1917. bi-m. $17. Gerald Unks. Univ. of North Carolina Press, P.O. Box 2288, Chapel Hill, NC 27514. Index. Circ: 1,690. Refereed. Vol. ends: Aug/Sept. Microform: UMI. Reprint: UMI. [*Indexed*: CIJE, EdI. *Aud*: Pr/Ages 14–18.]

HSJ's stated policy is to publish articles dealing with "research, informed opinion and—occasionally—successful practice." Most of the articles deal with broad policy questions or with students viewed from a sociological or psychological perspective. Though administrators and policymakers seem to be the primary audience, many of the articles should be of interest to teachers. The articles are not excessively technical, but jargon is sometimes a problem. This is a useful but not essential journal for high schools.

991 **Independent School.** 1941. 3/yr. $17.50 (Member schools, $15; member teachers, $10). Blair McElroy. Natl. Assn. of Independent Schools, 18 Tremont St., Boston, MA 02108. Illus. Adv. Index. Circ: 8,750. Vol. ends: Spring. Microform: UMI. Reprint: UMI. [*Bk. rev*: 1–2, essay length, signed. *Aud*: Pr/Ages 6–18.]

Though its primary concern is with independent (i.e., private) schools, *IS* is an exceptionally well-done magazine in which most of the articles should be of interest to public school administrators and teachers, and even the general public. Most of the articles deal with the purposes and methods of education taken in a broad perspective; occasionally there are pieces on the demands and rewards of teaching as a profession. The views of the authors vary, but the overall attitude is moderately traditional, with an emphasis on social responsibility. The essay-length book reviews in this title are outstanding.

992 **Instructor.** 1891. 9/yr. $16. John Lent. Instructor, P.O. Box 3018, Southeastern, PA 19398. Illus. Adv. Index. Circ: 254,361. Vol. ends: May. [*Indexed*: CIJE, CMG, EdI, MI. *Bk. rev*: Occasional. *Aud*: Pr/Ages 6–14.]

Instructor is a profusely illustrated magazine that tries to brighten the existence of both elementary school teachers and their pupils. Each issue has several medium-length feature articles that suggest projects for the classroom, discuss broader teaching problems and approaches, and sometimes discuss outstanding programs that have worked for imaginative teachers. In addition to the articles, there is a large foldout poster in each issue, and numerous departments with a variety of news notes, games, novel science demonstrations, and notes about free and inexpensive materials for the classroom. Two especially useful and unusual departments are "Putting Research to Work," which discusses common classroom problems in terms of recent research; and "Mindwinders," which provides puzzles useful for the elementary school. Comparison with *Learning, Instructor*'s chief rival, is inevitable. *Learning* seems closer to the classroom; its visuals are a bit fresher. *Instructor* seems closer to the teacher's perspective; its verbal content is perhaps more thoughtful. Both are good, and they are different enough so that all elementary schools and many public libraries should have both.

993 **International Journal of Early Childhood.** 1969. 2/yr. $7 (Nonmembers, $10). Anne McKenna. World Org. for Early Childhood Education, c/o Margaret Devine, 81 Irving Pl., Apt. 16, New York, NY 10003. Index. Circ: 1,650. Microform: UMI. [*Indexed*: EdI, CIJE. *Bk. rev*: 8, 400 words, signed. *Aud*: Pr/Ages 6–14.]

The purpose of this journal is to "spread information about child psychology, preschool education, child health and nutrition, good toys and play materials, playgrounds and free areas with appropriate equipment for children, architecture of preschool institutions and of private homes, information to parents, and other items regarding surroundings, the treatment and care of children from birth to seven or eight years of age." The text is written in English, French, and Spanish, and throughout there is a warm tone toward children.

994   **Journal of American Indian Education.** 1961. 3/yr. $14. John W. Tippeconnic III. Center for Indian Education, College of Education, Arizona State Univ., Tempe, AZ 85287-1311. Illus. Index. Circ: 1,000. Vol. ends: May. Microform: JAI, KTO, UMI. Reprint: UMI. [*Indexed*: CIJE, EdI. *Aud*: Pr/Ages 6–18.]

A small but scholarly journal covering all aspects of the education of the North American Indian. The articles are chosen by an editorial advisory board of Native American educators and university professors. The emphasis is on experimental and historical research, as well as field study reports.

995   **Journal of Black Studies.** 1970. q. $72 (Individuals, $30). Molefi Kete Asante. Sage Publns., Inc., 2111 W. Hillcrest Dr., Newbury Park, CA 91320. Adv. Index. Circ: 3,500. Sample. Vol. ends: June. Microform: UMI. Reprint: UMI. [*Indexed*: CIJE, INeg, PAIS. *Bk. rev*: 2, 600–2,100 words, signed. *Aud*: Pr/Ages 6–18.]

The scholarly research reported in this journal analyzes problems afflicting blacks throughout the world. Although the approach is interdisciplinary, education and social/political science studies predominate. Literary topics occasionally receive attention. Articles are well organized. Abstracts, summaries, and conclusions permit scanning. Contributors tend to be academics who are experts in their fields.

996   **Journal of Child & Adolescent Psychotherapy.** 1984. q. $25 (Individuals, $12). Robert W. Wood. Rivendell Foundation, 5100 Poplar Ave., Suite 2820, Memphis, TN 28200. Vol. ends: Dec. [*Bk. rev*: 6–7, lengthy. *Aud*: Pr/Ages 6–14.]

For professionals in the field, this attractive journal features an "emphasis on articles and information of a practical nature having direct application to clinical treatment, diagnosis, or delivery of health care services." Each issue presents six articles on such topics as child abuse, therapy, and single-parent families. Features include abstracts of current literature in other journals (information on reprints is provided), information about grants, book reviews, computer software news, a calendar of upcoming events, and employment opportunities. This is a quality journal and a solid addition to the field of literature on this subject.

997   **The Journal of Experiential Education.** 1978. 3/yr. $18. Peggy Walker Stevens. Assn. for Experiential Education, P.O. Box 249-CU, Boulder, CO 80309. Illus. Circ: 1,000. [*Bk. rev*: 1, 400–600 words, signed. *Aud*: Pr/Ages 14–18.]

"Experiential education" means programs such as Outward Bound, which educate through outdoor experiences that involve controlled physical stress and risk. The journal publishes articles that generally accept the soundness of this approach and discuss its problems and special techniques. Some readers will be uncomfortable with the proselytizing tone, but it seems to be the only periodical that deals with a subject that gets little attention in other education periodicals. *JEE* is not an essential journal except perhaps for libraries that support experiential education programs, but it will be useful for high school and public libraries.

998   **Journal of Negro Education: a Howard University quarterly review of issues incident to the education of black people.** 1932. q. $20 (Individuals, $16). Faustine C. Jones-Wilson. Bureau of Educational Research, School of Education, Howard Univ., Washington, DC 20059. Adv. Index. Circ: 2,000. Refereed. Vol. ends: Fall. Microform:

MIM, UMI. Reprint: Kraus. [*Indexed*: CIJE, EdI. *Bk. rev*: 3, 500–1,000 words, signed. *Aud*: Pr/Ages 6–18.]

The focus of this journal is problems relating to the education of black people throughout the world. Its inaugural issue stated the threefold purpose that continues to define its present-day goals. Besides encouraging the exploration of issues and the gathering and publication of data in its field of interest, this quarterly analyzes proposed solutions as well as current practices in black education. Contributions, whether research reports or essays, are judged on their importance and reliability. Articles appearing in the special yearbook issues are usually by invitation only. They provide an in-depth investigation of some question concerning the instruction of blacks. Over the decades, renowned scholars have written on a variety of aspects of Afro-American or African life that transcended the journal's general scope. This quality scholarly publication remains one of a core of outstanding sources of information on the black experience.

999   **Journal of Rural and Small Schools.** 3/yr. $45 (Individuals, $25). Ginger Oppenheimer. Natl. Rural Development Inst., Miller Hall 359, Western Washington Univ., Bellingham, WA 98225. Illus. Adv. Vol. ends: Spring. [*Indexed*: CIJE. *Aud*: Pr/Ages 6–18.]

The official journal of the National Rural and Small Schools Consortium, *JRSS* is primarily devoted to publishing short research reports on various aspects of rural education. There are also broad discussions of rural education policies, and occasional articles on rural education in other countries and on the history of rural education. Each issue has six to nine articles. There are also departments with news items of interest to rural educators, and a section where job-seekers and prospective employers can advertise their qualifications and needs.

1000   **Learning: creative ideas and activities for teachers.** 1972. 9/yr. $18. Charlene
 Gaynor. Springhouse Corp., 1111 Bethlehem Pike, Springhouse, PA 19477. Subs. to: P.O. Box 2580, Boulder, CO 80322. Illus. Adv. Circ: 222,000. Vol. ends: May/June. Microform: UMI. [*Indexed*: CIJE, CMG, EdI, RG. *Bk. rev*: Occasional. *Aud*: Pr/Ages 6–14.]

Learning is a cheerful magazine publishing short, informal articles for elementary school teachers. While most of the material describes novel projects and approaches for the classroom, there are occasional articles discussing general problems and policies of elementary education, and also burnout and other problems of teachers. Some articles are staff written and some are by faculty of schools of education, but many are by practicing elementary school teachers. In addition to the articles, the magazine has several regular departments carrying various kinds of news items about the profession and new materials. The occasional humor and the quality illustrations, including a large poster and a foldout calendar in each issue, contribute to the pleasant impression the magazine makes.

1001   **Lollipops.** 1981. 5/yr. Jerry Aten. Good Apple, Inc., 1204 Buchanan St., P.O. Box 299, Carthage, IL 62321. Illus. Adv. Circ: 17,000. Sample. [*Aud*: Pr/Ages 6–14.]

A teacher's magazine, this stresses activities for preschool and the first two grades of elementary school. All subjects are covered from the arts to the social sciences, although the former are stressed if only because of the age and interests of the children with whom the educators are working. The advice is as practical as it is useful and will be of considerable assistance to both beginner and expert.

1002 **Middle School Journal.** 1980. q. $20. John H. Lounsbury. Natl. Middle School Assn. Subs. to: 4807 Evanswood Dr., Columbus, OH 43229. Illus. Adv. Index. Circ: 4,500. Vol. ends: July. Microform: UMI. Reprint: UMI. [*Indexed*: CIJE, EdI. *Bk. rev*: 3, 300–600 words, signed. *Aud*: Pr/Ages 6–18.]

Each issue of *MSJ* contains 10 to 12 short, usually quite specific articles on various aspects of planning for and teaching middle school classes. Most of the emphasis is on the middle school student, but academics get a great deal of attention and relations with parents and the community are dealt with occasionally. Virtually all of the articles are opinion pieces or informal essays based on personal experience rather than reports of formal research, but two occasional departments, "Out of Research—Into Practice" and "What Research Says," discuss the bearing of recent research on specific middle school problems. This is one of the best of the journals dealing with a particular segment of the K–12 range.

1003 **Momentum: journal of the National Catholic Educational Association.**1970. q. $18. Patricia Feistritzer. Natl. Catholic Educational Assn., Suite 100, 1077 30th St. N.W., Washington, DC 20007. Illus. Adv. Circ: 20,650. Vol. ends: Nov. Microform: UMI. [*Indexed*: CIJE, EdI. *Bk. rev*: 3–6, 400–800 words, signed. *Aud*: Pr/Ages 6–18.]

The central concern here is preserving Catholic education by making it relevant to the contemporary world. Though it speaks for Catholic education and takes most of its examples from Catholic schools, *Momentum* is a journal that should dispel some common assumptions about dogmatism and narrow moralizing in Catholic education. It shows a commitment to traditional culture with a Catholic flavor, but it also shows a serious concern with generous, humanistic values, and an openness to the means of realizing them. The articles deal more with what is to be taught and with general pedagogical approaches than they do with detailed classroom methodology, but teachers and students in schools of education, including non-Catholics, should find the content interesting and useful. It is of course a basic title for Catholic schools. It would also be a useful title for public libraries.

1004 **NASSP Bulletin: the journal for middle level and high school administrators.** 1917. 9/yr. $60. Thomas F. Koerner. Natl. Assn. of Secondary School Principals, 1904 Association Dr., Reston, VA 22091. Adv. Index. Circ: 38,000. Vol. ends: May. Microform: UMI. Reprint: UMI. [*Indexed*: CIJE, EdI. *Bk. rev*: 4–6, 100–500 words, signed. *Aud*: Pr/Ages 14–18.]

Each issue of the *NASSP Bulletin* has 15 to 20 short articles dealing with the professional concerns of secondary school administrators. In most issues, several articles focus on a common theme, such as discipline problems or the evaluation of administrators. There are occasional articles that provide insights and fresh approaches, but in too many pieces stereotyped language simply repeats stale ideas.

1005 **Peabody Journal of Education.** 1923. q. $40 (Individuals, $24; students, $15). Catherine Marshall. George Peabody College of Vanderbilt Univ., 113 Payne Hall, P.O. Box 41, Nashville, TX 37203. Index. Circ: 2,600. Refereed. Vol. ends: Summer. Microform: UMI. Reprint: UMI. [*Indexed*: CIJE, EdI. *Aud*: Pr/Ages 6–18.]

Each issue of *PJE*, planned and put together with the help of an expert guest editor, focuses on some broad central theme. The articles are theoretical discussions rather than research reports; the writing is generally literate and urbane.

The point of view of the articles varies, and *PJE* is not the consistently conservative major journal some would like to see on the American education scene.

1006 **Phi Delta Kappan.** 1915. 10/yr. $25 (Individuals, $20). Pauline B. Gough. Phi Delta Kappa, Inc., Eighth and Union, P.O. Box 789, Bloomington, IN 47402. Illus. Adv. Index. Circ: 145,000. Vol. ends: June. Microform: B&H, UMI. Reprint: UMI. [*Indexed*: CIJE, EdI, RG. *Bk. rev*: 2–3, 500–1,500 words, signed. *Aud*: Pr/Ages 6–18.]

Though published for teachers, *PDK* publishes short, semipopular articles that should also interest a general audience. K–12 education is dealt with from a variety of perspectives. Articles defending the prerogatives of teachers are balanced by others that challenge them. The magazine shows a consistent interest in the relationship between education and social problems. Most of the authors are faculty members at schools of education, but some are K–12 teachers or administrators. Occasionally there is an article by someone of major reputation (Terrel H. Bell, Mortimer J. Adler). In addition to the high-quality articles, *PDK* has useful columns of news items about education at the state, national, and international levels.

1007 **Pre-K Today.** 1986. 8/yr. $32. Jackie Carter. Scholastic, Inc., 730 Broadway, New York, NY 10002. Illus. Adv. [*Aud*: Pr/Ages 3–6.]

This glossy, very practical journal is geared toward preschool and child-care teachers and is filled with acitivity and lesson ideas. Its aim is to offer "practical, hands on, ready-to-go content rather than academically oriented articles," and it meets this goal admirably. Five to six articles per issue run the gamut from music and art, health and science, getting the most out of a field trip, information about families, and other areas of concern and interest to those who work with this age group. Departments include "Circle Time" (activity plans for this traditional quiet time); "Classroom Clinic," which focuses on such problems as crying or whining children, the shy child, a child trying to run off; and a column for directors dealing with budgets and other managerial concerns. This is an excellent resource, with a high-quality look and content to match. Highly recommended for professional preschool and day-care teachers and school and public libraries.

1008 **Preschool Perspectives.** 1984. 10/yr. $18. Pamela Tuchscherer, P.O. Box 7527, Bend, OR 97708. Illus. Index. Circ: 2,000. Sample. Vol. ends: May. [*Aud*: Pr/Ages 3–6.]

Targeted specifically for educators of young children three to six years old, this quality newsletter provides very practical, up-to-date information on child development, teaching strategies, and management in an easy-to-read format. Articles on music, art, and helping children to cope with separation have appeared, and new resources are featured in each issue. Preschool teachers will find this an invaluable aid. Public libraries serving early childhood education programs will want to call this publication to the attention of its intended audience.

1009 **Principal: serving elementary and middle school principals.** 1921. 5/yr. Membership $70 (Individuals, $110). Leon E. Greene. Natl. Assn. of Elementary School Principals, 1615 Duke St., Alexandria, VA 22314. Illus. Adv. Index. Circ: 23,000. Vol. ends: May. Microform: UMI. Reprint: UMI. [*Indexed*: CIJE, EdI. *Aud*: Pr/Ages 6–14.]

Readable, practical articles directed at the elementary and junior high school principals. Most of the articles deal with managing children and encouraging learning, but relationships with teachers and the working conditions of teachers and administrators also get attention. The ideas are not always original, but they are usually presented in terms of real-life examples. "It's the Law," a department that also appears in *NASSP Bulletin* under the title "A Legal Brief," provides useful summaries of the legal implications of such matters as corporal punishment and relations with noncustodial parents. Though the magazine is addressed to principals, much of it deals directly with classroom matters and should be useful to teachers.

1010 Review of Educational Research. 1931. q. $29 (Individuals, $23). Penelope L. Peterson. Amer. Educational Research Assn., 1230 17th St. N.W., Washington, DC 20036. Adv. Index. Circ: 16,000. Refereed. Vol. ends: Winter. Microform: B&H, MIM, UMI. Reprint: UMI. [*Indexed*: CIJE, EdI. *Aud*: Pr/Ages 14–18.]

RER publishes medium-to-long articles that summarize and integrate the results of research in relatively broad areas in education. There are occasional articles that focus on research methodology. The topics covered are important and timely, and the articles are generally well written in a scholarly way.

1011 Roeper Review: a journal on gifted children. 1978. q. $30 (Individuals, $22; students, $16). Karen Williams. Roeper City and Country School, P.O. Box 329, Bloomfield Hills, MI 48013. Illus. Adv. Refereed. Vol. ends: May. Microform: UMI. Reprint: UMI. [*Indexed*: CIJE, EdI. *Bk. rev*: 0–3, 200–800 words, signed. *Aud*: Pr/Ages 6–18.]

RR publishes research reports, policy discussions, and how-to articles dealing with the education of gifted children. Most issues contain one or more groups of articles focusing on a common theme (the gifted in middle school, the administrator in the school for the gifted). "Open Space" is a department for short comments by parents of gifted children. "The Student Corner" sometimes publishes short research reports by graduate students who work with gifted children, and sometimes poetry and short essays by gifted children. Most of the articles are by faculty members at education schools; the Roeper City and Country School is an established school for gifted children.

1012 T. H. E. Journal: technical horizons in education. 1973. 10/yr. $29 (Free to qualified educators). Sylvia Charp. Information Synergy, Inc., 2626 S. Pullman, Santa Ana, CA 92705. Illus. Adv. Circ: 62,000. Vol. ends: Nov. Microform: UMI. [*Bk. rev*: 10, 100–200 words. *Aud*: Pr/Ages 14–18.]

Ninety percent of *T. H. E.* is devoted to brief descriptions of new products in the field of educational technology. Each issue also contains two to three articles dealing with a particular theme, for example, in-service training or model programs. Sections on applications, technology updates, and optical disc technology and a directory of special education products are regular features. The annual source guide to high-technology products that covers hardware, software, telecommunications, furniture and accessories, CAD, and video listings is reason enough to subscribe to the journal (qualified educators receive it free). For school libraries.

1013 Teaching K-8: the professional magazine for teachers (Formerly: *Early Years; Early Years K–8*). 1971. 8/yr. $19.77. Allen Raymond. Early Years, Inc., 40 Richards Ave., Norwalk, CT 06854. Illus. Adv. Circ: 160,000. Vol. ends: May. Microform: UMI. Reprint: UMI. [*Indexed*: CMG, EdI. *Aud*: Pr/Ages 6–14.]

Along with the name change has come a shift in emphasis away from the prekindergarten and kindergarten years toward the upper elementary period. Thus, "Your Green Pages," an activity section for the K–4 classroom, has recently been joined by "Your Green Pages II," which provides for grades 5–8. In other words, *Teaching K–8* is now less like *Young Children* and more like *Learning and Instructor*. It does not have quite the gusto of the first of these, perhaps, or the maturity of the second, but it does have, in a likable format, a variety of features and ideas that should be of use to elementary school teachers, as well as to parents.

1014 TechTrends: for leaders in education & training (Formerly: *Instructional Innovator*). 1956. 6/yr. $24. Leslie Hayward. Assn. for Educational Communications and Technology, 1126 16th St. N.W., Washington, DC 20036. Illus. Adv. Index. Circ: 9,000. Vol. ends: Nov. Microform: UMI. Reprint: UMI. [*Indexed*: CIJE, EdI. *Aud*: Pr/Ages 6–18.]

Written by educational AV directors and professionals involved in all types of educational media, this official publication of the Association for Educational Communications and Technology generally includes five to six articles on such topics as microcomputers in education, professional development, teaching library skills, desktop publishing, and media in reading and writing programs. Professionals will find articles dealing with such topics as the longevity and depreciation of AV equipment and how to plan and implement a teleconference extremely helpful. Columns on new products, instructional resources, and copyright awareness are regular features. School media specialists will find this enjoyable reading as well as an invaluable resource for keeping up with the latest in educational technology. This journal belongs in every school library.

1015 Theory into Practice. 1962. q. $30 (Individuals, $15). Donald G. Lux. College of Education, Ohio State Univ., 174 Arps Hall, 1945 N. High St., Columbus, OH 43210. Illus. Adv. Index. Circ: 5,000. Vol. ends: Fall. Microform: MIM, UMI. [*Indexed*: CIJE, EdI. *Aud*: Pr/Ages 6–18.]

A journal primarily for K–12 teachers and students in teacher-preparation programs, this publishes articles that attempt to relate "education" as an academic discipline, a body of theory and knowledge, to the concrete problems of the classroom. Most education journals do that in some sense, of course; but here, at least in most articles, there is explicit reference to a definite aspect of theory on the one hand, and to concrete classroom situations on the other. In other words, it falls somewhere between *Elementary School Journal* and the educational psychology journals, and classroom-oriented magazines like *Learning* and *Teaching K–8*. Not quite a basic title, probably, it is one that both K–12 teachers and faculty and students should find useful and stimulating.

1016 Today's Catholic Teacher. 1967. 8/yr. $14.95. Ruth A. Matheny. Peter Li, Inc., 2451 E. River Rd., Dayton, OH 45439. Illus. Adv. Circ: 51,719. Vol. ends: May. Microform: UMI. Reprint: UMI. [*Aud*: Pr/Ages 6–18.]

Primarily for teachers in K–12 Catholic schools, *TCT* publishes short articles and a variety of departments that cover a broad range of topics: funding for Catholic schools, academic standards, moral issues, the problems of administering Catholic schools, and so on. A comparison with the competitor journal, *Momentum*, is inevitable. The latter has fewer but longer and probably more thoughtful articles; it seems to be somewhat more concerned with the Catholic response to the problems of the modern world, particularly social problems. *TCT* seems to put more emphasis on traditional academic values, and on the relationship between education and traditional Catholic symbols and rituals. Both are important for libraries in Catholic schools.

1017 **Totline.** 1979. bi-m. $15. Jean Warren. Warren Publg. House, P.O. Box 2255, Everett, WA 98203. Illus. Adv. Circ: 8,000. [*Aud*: Pr/Ages 3–6.]

Parents and teachers of preschool children will find this creative newsletter brimming with creative ideas. Activities are suggested on themes such as holidays, with appropriate stories, songs, poems, crafts, and sugarless snack ideas. Movement exercises and activities to develop the young child's concept of self are all part of the stress on creativity. A nice plus is that there is permission to copy up to three activities per issue, as long as proper credit is given to *Totline*. Public libraries with strong preschool programming collections will find this useful, as will preschools and day-care centers, and will want to feature it in parenting collections.

1018 **Urban Education.** 1966. q. $78 (Individuals, $30). Warren Button. Sage Publns., Inc., 2111 W. Hillcrest Dr., Newbury Park, CA 91320. Adv. Refereed. Vol. ends: Jan. Microform: UMI. [*Indexed*: CIJE, EdI. *Bk. rev*: 1, 1,000–4,000 words, signed. *Aud*: Pr/Ages 6–18.]

UE publishes both research and analytical articles dealing with the problems of urban K–12 schools. Many of the articles deal with social problems and take a generally sociological approach. Others discuss administrative problems, and some are historical.

1019 **The Urban Review: issues and ideas in public education.** 1966. q. $44 (Individuals, $22). David E. Kapel and William T. Pink. Agathon Press, Inc., 49 Sheridan Ave., Albany, NY 12210. Adv. Index. Refereed. Vol. ends: No. 4. Microform: UMI. Reprint: ISI, UMI. [*Indexed*: CIJE, EdI. *Aud*: Pr/Ages 6–18.]

UR publishes mostly scholarly, rather lengthy articles on various aspects of urban education, with the emphasis on sympathetic discussion of the problems of inner-city schools. Some articles are primarily research reports, and some are theoretical discussions. As compared with *Urban Education*, a similar title, *UR* seems to show a bit more concern with educational philosophy and less with sociology.

1020 **Young Children.** 1944. bi-m. $25. Ed. bd. Natl. Assn. for the Education of Younger Children, 1834 Connecticut Ave. N.W., Washington, DC 20009-5786. Illus. Adv. Index. Circ: 55,000. Vol. ends: Sept. Microform: UMI. Reprint: UMI. [*Indexed*: CIJE, EdI. *Bk. rev*: 1–8, 400–800 words, signed. *Aud*: Pr/Ages 6–14.]

YC very definitely takes the teacher's perspective in dealing with the education of young children—birth through age 8, according to the masthead. In tone and flavor, it is somewhere between the colorful, classroom-oriented magazines like *Teaching K–8* and *Learning* and an academic journal like the *Elementary School Journal*. The articles are relatively popular in tone and do not usually present formal research, or statistical analyses. They do discuss and analyze broad purposes and perspectives from a professional point of view. *YC* also carries some articles that discuss policy questions in terms of the relationship between teachers and supervisors. "Research in Review" is a useful section, appearing in most issues, that summarizes and comments on recent research relevant to some particular topic. In addition to a section of reviews of books for professionals, there is a column that provides brief notices of children's books. *YC* is a very desirable title for practicing elementary school teachers.

1021 **Youth Policy: the monthly report on national youth programs and issues.** 1978. m. $75. Youth Policy Inst., 1221 Massachusetts Ave. N.W., Washington, DC 20005. Illus. Sample. [*Aud*: Pr/Ages 6–18.]

The publisher is a nonprofit organization that "monitors over 250 federal programs, tracks legislations and congressional activity, and follows the actions of non-governmental groups as they are related to youth" and reports on them in a 60-page journal packed with records of ongoing activities. Each copy opens with "State of Youth," a revealing collection of statistics about the young. Then come primary articles by such writers as Lynn Curtis (head of the M. S. Eisenhower Foundation) and youth experts. All seem free of political bias and demonstrate an interest in improving our educational system and related matters, from housing to parks. Anything that has a bearing on youth is considered. The issues covered range from community development at the neighborhood level to specific proposals of the Public Spaces Project on Transportation, Community Security, Education and Creating Vital Downtowns. This type of information is of value to everyone, of course, but it is of particular interest to those concerned with youth. This is a first-rate magazine, which deserves much wider attention. True, the price is high, but it is well worth it. Highly recommended.

1022 **Zero to Three.** 1979. 5/yr. $18. Natl. Center for Clinical Infant Programs, 733 15th St. N.W., Suite 912, Washington, DC 20005. Illus. [*Aud*: Pr/Ages 1–3.]

As the title of this 30- to 40-page magazine makes clear, this is for the professional and the parent involved with children from birth to age three. The nonprofit-organization publisher explores the child's experience of the world at all levels from health and care to education and parental problems. Articles are authoritative, easy to read, and quite topical. There are sections devoted to new publications, conferences, training programs, and so forth.

EDUCATION—BY SUBJECT AREAS

Arts and Humanities

First choices General: (1) *Design for Arts in Education*; (2) *School Arts*.
Foreign-Language Teaching: (1) *The Modern Language Journal*.
Language Arts: (1) *English Journal*; (2) *The Reading Teacher*.
Music: (1) *American Music Teacher*.
Theater: (1) *Theatre Crafts*.

■ GENERAL

1023 **Art Education: the journal of the National Art Education Association.** 1948. bi-m. $55 (Membership, $16.50). Hilda Present Lewis. Natl. Art Education Assn., 1916 Association Dr., Reston, VA 22091. Illus. Adv. Index. Circ: 11,534. Refereed. Microform: UMI. [*Indexed*: CIJE, EdI. *Aud*: Pr/Ages 14–18.]

AE provides articles that discuss the teaching of art at all levels, but with particular emphasis on grades K–12. Each issue contains six to eight short to medium-length articles. The articles generally do not present formal or quantitative research; rather the emphasis is on theoretical discussions and on explanations of methods that have worked in the classroom. A useful section, "Instructional Resources," presents four good-quality reproductions of artworks and with each a short, systematic lesson plan for using it in the classroom. *AE* emphasizes teaching the appreciation of art rather than techniques for producing it. It differs from similar titles in putting more emphasis on specific classroom techniques.

1024   **Art to Zoo.** 1982. 3 or 4/yr. during school year. Free to schools. Betsy Eisendrath. Office of Elementary and Secondary Education, Smithsonian Institution, Washington, DC 20560. Illus. Sample. Vol. ends: Spring. [*Aud*: Pr/Ages 6–13.]

This brings news from the Smithsonian Institution to teachers of grades one through eight. The purpose is to help teachers use museums, parks, libraries, zoos, and many other resources within the community to open up learning opportunities for elementary and junior high school students. It is the philosophy of the Smithsonian Institution that objects have a tremendous power to educate, and that it is important for students to learn to use objects as research tools. All of the articles deal with methods of working with students and objects. Lesson plans are included. The inner two pages are both in English and Spanish and contain materials for projects. Once on the mailing list, a teacher receives four copies of each issue so that the magazine can be shared with other teachers. Highly recommended for elementary and junior high school teachers.

1025   **Arts and Activities: the nation's leading art education magazine.**1932. 10/yr. $20. Leven C. Leatherbury. Pubs. Development Corp. Subs. to: 591 Camino de la Reina, Suite 200, San Diego, CA 92108. Illus. Adv. Index. Circ: 22,000. Vol. ends: Jan. Microform: B&H, UMI. Reprint: UMI. [*Indexed*: EdI. *Bk. rev*: 6–8, 50–100 words, signed. *Aud*: Pr/Ages 6–18.]

In one of the most stimulating education magazines, photography, children's art, traditional high art, and industrial art are blended in a combination of pedagogical intelligence and aesthetic flair. Though K–12 art teachers are the primary audience, the magazine tries successfully to be useful to teachers who have had no formal art training. In addition to the articles, there are departments with short notes about new teaching techniques and materials. This is a basic title for elementary and secondary school libraries and for academic libraries that support programs in elementary education or art education. It would also be an excellent choice for public libraries, especially those with a good proportion of young parents among their users.

1026   **Children's Folklore Review.** 1978. 3/yr. $5. C. W. Sullivan III. Children's Folklore Review, English Dept., East Carolina Univ., Greenville, NC 27858. [*Aud*: Pr/Ages 6–14.]

This eight-page newsletter is primarily for adults who are involved with folklore for children, but each year a prize is given for the best student essay on a topic in the field. This is printed in the newsletter, and will be of some interest to high school students. On balance, though, this review is for the teacher who is involved in the subject from nursery stories to playground activities that foster folk stories.

1027   **Design for Arts in Education** (Formerly: *Design*). 1899. bi-m. $35 (Individuals, $20). Sheila Barrows. Heldref Publns., 4000 Albemarle St. N.W., Washington, DC 20016. Adv. Circ: 2,400. Vol. ends: July/Aug. Microform: UMI. Reprint: Pub. [*Indexed*: CIJE, RG. *Aud*: Pr/Ages 6–18.]

DAE is primarily concerned with art education as a problem of education policy. It does not exactly ignore questions of pedagogical method and aesthetic value, the topics that are central to *Arts and Activities* (see above in this subsection), but here the focus is on the general philosophy of art education, and on the question of how art fits into the overall curriculum. Though this perspective is, in a sense, rather specialized, *DAE* is commendably open to a full range of opinions, with cultural conservatives occupying as much space as liberals. Unlike other art periodicals, *DAE* covers music as well as the visual arts. A no-frills art magazine, *DAE* has six to eight articles of moderate length in each issue, no illustrations, and no special departments.

1028 **The History Teacher.** 1967. q. $28 (Individuals, $22; students, $15). Edward A. Gosselin. Soc. for History Education, Inc., Dept. of History, Univ. of California, Long Beach, 1250 Bellflower Blvd., Long Beach, CA 90840. Illus. Adv. Index. Circ: 2,500. Refereed. Vol. ends: Aug. Microform: UMI. Reprint: Pub. [*Indexed*: CIJE, EdI. *Bk. rev*: 12–15, 600–1,200 words, signed. *Aud*: Pr/Ages 6–18.]

HT publishes three kinds of articles: discussions of courses, curricula, and classroom techniques; analyses of important concepts and trends in historiography; and essay reviews of printed and nonprinted materials likely to be used in the classroom. About half the articles on pedagogy deal with secondary school, and about half with college. Most of the articles are by faculty members at colleges and universities, though there are occasional pieces by high school teachers, and by professionals from the National Park Service and other places outside the teaching profession. Particularly stimulating and commendably free from jargon are the frequent articles discussing the intellectual underpinning of written history. The review section is usually extensive and history teachers will probably appreciate the large, separate sections devoted to audiovisual materials and to textbooks. All in all, this is an exceptionally well done journal.

1029 **Journal of Geography.** 1902. bi-m. $48. Robert S. Bednarz. Natl. Council for Geographic Education, Western Illinois Univ., Macomb, IL 61455. Adv. Index. Circ: 3,200. Refereed. Vol. ends: Dec. Microform: UMI. [*Indexed*: CIJE, EdI. *Aud*: Pr/Ages 6–18.]

An educator's journal, aimed at teachers from elementary school through college. It emphasizes methods of teaching geography, suggesting techniques and audiovisual aids, but also contains some professional articles. Written by teachers in the field, the well-illustrated articles include footnotes and occasionally a bibliography. Sections are regularly found on remote sensing and classroom projects (including lesson plans); a preview of films available for teaching geography is included. Microcomputer software is reviewed in some issues. For larger school libraries.

1030 **The New Advocate.** 1988. q. $45 (Individuals, $27). Joel Taxel. Christopher Gordon Pubs., Inc., 480 Washington St., Norwood, MA 02062. Illus. Adv. Sample. [*Bk. rev*: 15–25, 150 words, signed. *Aud*: Pr/Ages 6–14.]

Here the purpose is to advocate, through five to eight well-written articles, the delights of a literature-based curriculum in elementary and junior high schools. (The editor is a professor in the Department of Language Education at the University of Georgia, and the authors are working grade school teachers, as well as education instructors.) Articles range from reading tests and story understanding to the mysteries of the child's creative process. It is usually jargon free and is aimed as much at the teacher and librarian as the parent. The 75 or so pages conclude with several dozen short critical reviews of children's books.

1031 **Religious Education.** 1906. q. $35. John Westerhoff III. Religious Education Assn., 409 Prospect St., New Haven, CT 06510. Adv. Index. Circ: 5,050. Microform: UMI. [*Indexed*: EdI. *Bk. rev*: 10, 700–900 words, signed. *Aud*: Pr/Ages 14–18.]

The subtitle of this journal is "platform for the free discussion of issues in the field of religion and their bearing on education." For the most part the journal lives up to that description. The sponsoring association is an interfaith one, and the articles appearing in the journal are written by religious educators, practicing or teaching. Religious education in both public schools and denominational settings is covered. Religious education collections should not be without it.

1032 **School Arts: the art magazine for teachers.** 1901. 9/yr. $18. David W. Baker and Gilbert S. Davis. Davis Publns., Inc., School Arts, 50 Portland St., Worcester, MA 06108. Illus. Adv. Index. Circ: 24,000. Vol. ends: May. Microform: B&H, UMI. [*Indexed*: CIJE, EdI, MI. *Aud*: Pr/Ages 6–18.]

SA uses a combination of short, enthusiastic articles and imaginative illustrations to encourage K–12 art teachers to do a livelier job of introducing children to art. Craft projects are emphasized; there is an implicit assumption that art instruction should be a blend of doing and guided observing. The "clip cards" section contains short lesson plans contributed by readers and printed on 3″ × 5″ cards for convenient filing. Though there is no separate book-review section, books useful for the art teacher are reviewed in brief notes, along with videocassettes and other materials, in the "Resource Center" department. In each issue, most of the articles develop some common subject—clay as a medium, art and exceptional students, and so forth. *SA* is a shade less appealing, particularly in its illustrations, than its main rival, *Arts and Activities* (see above in this subsection), but the content of its articles is likely to be just as useful in the classroom. Both magazines should be available to all present and prospective art teachers and elementary school teachers, and for that matter, to parents.

1033 **Teaching Political Science: politics in perspective.** 1973. q. $45 (Individuals, $25). Jerome J. Hanus. Heldref Publns., 4000 Albemarle St. N.W., Washington, DC 20016. Adv. Index. Circ: 600. Sample. Vol. ends: July. [*Bk. rev*: 2–4, length varies, signed. *Aud*: Pr/Ages 14–18.]

The focus of this journal is on topics broadly related to the teaching of political science in high schools and colleges. Many of the articles attempt to improve classroom teaching through reporting on or recommending specific approaches to subjects or discussing the development of programs at individual universities. Other articles discuss in more general terms the role of political science in education or examine questions of interest to both students and teachers. Some of the four or five articles, written by American university professors, have pragmatic value.

■ FOREIGN-LANGUAGE TEACHING

1034 **Bilingual Review/Revista Bilingue.** 1974. 3/yr. $24 (Individuals, $18). Gary D. Keller. Bilingual Review-Press, Hispanic Research Center, Arizona State Univ., Tempe, AZ 85287. Adv. Circ: 2,000. Refereed. Vol. ends: Dec. Microform: UMI. [*Indexed*: CIJE, EdI. *Bk. rev*: 2–5, 1,000–1,500 words, signed. *Aud*: Pr/Ages 6–18.]

Libraries count on *Bilingual Review*'s dual value of providing solid scholarship in the field of bilingualism in the United States and serving as a respected Hispanic literary journal. Published mainly in English, its articles on research and criticism are contributed by academics in this country and abroad. The professional announcements section informs on upcoming conferences, literary prizes, and special programs in the field of bilingualism or literature. As a literary outlet, the journal publishes selections of creative writing such as short stories, poems, and (occasionally) interviews with writers. Special thematic issues appear occasionally. *Bilingual Review* is highly recommended for libraries supporting language studies, Hispanic literature, and Chicano studies.

1035 **First Language.** 1980. 3/yr. $43 (Individuals, $27). Kevin Durkin and Sinclair Rogers. Science History Publns., Ltd., Alpha Academic, Halfpenny Furze, Mill Lane, Chalfont St. Giles, Buckinghamshire HP8 4NR, England. Adv. Index. Vol. ends: Oct. [*Bk. rev*: 7–8, 1–2 pages, signed. *Aud*: Pr/Ages 6–14.]

This title fills the gap between researchers and practitioners by contributing current findings and current problems in all areas of first-language development and acquisition. Special editorial remarks discuss problems in children's acquisition of the first language. The brief research overviews describe new products. Most of the articles are about children acquiring English as their first language. Specialized topics are discussed in special issues of the journal. Discussions are both highly scholarly and general. Recommended for elementary and junior high school teachers.

1036 **Foreign Language Annals.** 1967. bi-m. $40 (Individuals, $35). Vicki Galloway. Amer. Council on the Teaching of Foreign Languages, 579 Broadway, P.O. Box 408, Hastings-on-Hudson, NY 10706. Illus. Adv. Index. Circ: 9,000. Sample. Vol. ends: Dec. Microform: MIM, UMI. [*Indexed*: CIJE, EdI. *Aud*: Pr/Ages 14–18.]

This periodical serves teachers, administrators, and researchers, and is devoted to the development of all phases of the profession of foreign-language teaching. Articles are as short and useful as they are innovative and include successful teaching methods in educational research and experimentation. They do not cover the major linguistic theories, but are centered on methodology and language testing. The information is current. Regular features include educational research, classroom experiments, and teachers' surveys as used by teachers of foreign languages at the high school level.

1037 **The French Review.** 1927. bi-m. $25. Ronald W. Tobin. Amer. Assn. of Teachers of French, P.O. Box 149, Chapel Hill, NC 27514. Adv. Index. Circ: 13,000. Sample. Vol. ends: May. Microform: UMI. [*Indexed*: CIJE, EdI. *Aud*: Pr/Ages 14–18.]

This journal is devoted to the French language and French linguistics, and even to French-language teaching and literature. It is useful to non-French speakers because the articles are written in both English and French. This is the official journal of the American Association of Teachers of French, and it provides a total experience of learning French and the culture of France. The reviews are divided into "literary history and criticism, linguistics, creative works, textbooks, CAI software, methodology, film and civilization." An index is provided in the last issue of the volume. Because of the short reviews of new publications and various notes on new developments, high school libraries may find this basic source on teaching French very useful.

1038 **German Quarterly.** 1928. q. $22. Henry J. Schmidt. Amer. Assn. of Teachers of German, 523 Bldg., Suite 201, Rte. 38, Cherry Hill, NJ 08034. Adv. Index. Circ: 7,600.

Sample. Vol. ends: Fall. Microform: PMC, UMI. Reprint: UMI. [*Indexed*: EdI. *Bk. rev*: 30–35, 1–2 pages, signed. *Aud*: Pr/Ages 14–18.]

This periodical is supported in part by a grant from the German Department and the College of Humanities, Ohio State University. It is devoted to German literature and language. Besides the articles and book reviews, notes of interest are provided to teachers and scholars as an additional source of information. The book reviews are arranged by subject, such as literary theory and collections, linguistics, culture and social history, and so on. Manuscripts are accepted in German and English. Each issue consists of four or five scholarly articles covering German literature, language, linguistics, and culture. High school libraries may find this useful.

1039 Hispania: a journal devoted to the interests of the teaching of Spanish and Portuguese. 1917. q. $25. Theodore A. Sackett. Amer. Assn. of Teachers of Spanish and Portuguese, Inc., Univ. of Southern California, Dept. of Spanish and Portuguese, Los Angeles, CA 90089-0358. Illus. Adv. Index. Circ: 13,000. Sample. Vol. ends: Dec. Microform: UMI. Reprint: UMI. [*Indexed*: CIJE, EdI. *Bk. rev*: 20–30, 1–2 pages, signed. *Aud*: Pr/Ages 6–18.]

This publication offers critical articles on Spanish and Portuguese language and literature. It also includes bibliographies in Spanish and Portuguese or in the other languages of Latin American countries. Articles are accepted in the inter-disciplinary and comparative fields of teaching Spanish and Portuguese. A department on theoretical linguistics provides traditional approaches to methodology in teaching these languages, and articles are written in English, Spanish, and Portuguese in the section entitled "Articles on Language and Literature." Departments such as "The President's Corner," "The Hispanic and Luso-Brazilian World," "Chapter News," and "Official Announcements" disseminate current information on cultural, literary, and linguistics activities. Forthcoming articles are noted. This publication is the most important in offering standard, basic information to all levels of Spanish and Portuguese language teachers.

1040 Italica. 1924. q. $30. Robert J. Rodini. Italica, Dept. of French and Italian, 618 Van Hise Hall, Univ. of Wisconsin, Madison, WI 53706. Adv. Sample. Vol. ends: Winter. [*Indexed*: CIJE. *Bk. rev*: 7–10, 2–3 pages, signed. *Aud*: Pr/Ages 6–18.]

This periodical is an official journal of the American Association of Teachers of Italian, which is a constituent member of the National Federation of Modern Language Teachers Association. The purpose of the federation is to promote study of the Italian language in the United States and Canada. The articles cover Italian language, literature, grammar, linguistic analysis, and other such topics. Educative, step-by-step approaches to learning language and literature are provided. Most of the articles are written in Italian. Reviews are scholarly, and topics of forthcoming issues are discussed. Various announcements and brief notes on events are circulated to the teachers and scholars who are the readers of this periodical. This title can be used by teachers of Italian language at all levels.

1041 The Modern Language Journal. 1916. q. $30 (Individuals, $13). David P. Benseler. Univ. of Wisconsin Press, Journals Div., 114 N. Murray St., Madison, WI 53715. Illus. Adv. Index. Circ: 6,000. Vol. ends: Dec. Microform: MIM, PMC, UMI. Reprint: UMI. [*Indexed*: CIJE, EdI, HumI. *Aud*: Pr/Ages 6–18.]

This journal is published by the National Federation of Modern Language Teachers Association. It is basically "devoted to pedagogical research, and topics of professional interest to all language teachers" from elementary school to the graduate level. The articles cover teaching strategies, bilingualism, applied linguistics, innovative foreign-language programs, developments in curriculum, teaching materials, testing and evaluations, and so on. Language learning with audiovisual aids is emphasized. Experimental research in teaching foreign languages is often discussed. Articles with linguistic analyses and literary interests appear in this publication. The reviews are categorized according to the subject or language, such as pedagogy, French, German, linguistics, and so on. This basic journal may be extremely helpful to the teachers of foreign languages.

1042 NABE: journal of the National Association for Bilingual Education. 1975. 3/yr. $45 (Individuals, $30). Reynaldo F. Macias. USC Center for Multilingual, Multicultural Research, WPH 702, Los Angeles, CA 90089-0031. Adv. Refereed. [*Indexed*: CIJE, EdI. *Bk. rev*: 1–2, 500–1,000 words, signed. *Aud*: Pr/Ages 6–18.]

Bilingual education and its interdisciplinary relationships are the focus of this seminal scholarly journal. According to its editorial policy, it "serves as a forum for research, policy analyses, evaluation studies, and essays relating to bilingualism and schooling in the United States." Its scope encompasses instruction methodology in bilingual, English-as-a-second-language, and foreign-language teaching and offers a variety of perspectives. The journal serves as an important link between theory and practice, publishing articles that deal with applied issues in the field. The emphasis is on clear and accessible writing, so that the journal will be as readable to busy practitioners and policymakers as it is to academicians. A brief abstract precedes each article. Considering the increasing public awareness of the issues surrounding the education of minority language groups, this is a recommended selection not only for education and Hispanic studies collections in academic libraries, but also for medium-to-large public libraries seeking to provide focused information about minority language groups.

1043 TESOL Quarterly: a journal for teachers of English to speakers of other languages and of standard English as second dialect. 1967. q. $75 (Individuals, $42). Stephen J. Gaies. TESOL, 1118 22nd St. N.W., Washington, DC 20037. Illus. Adv. Circ: 10,000. Sample. Vol. ends: Dec. Microform: UMI. Reprint: UMI. [*Indexed*: HumI. *Bk. rev*: 2–3, 2–3 pages, signed. *Aud*: Pr/Ages 6–18.]

TESOL is an international organization concerned with teaching the English language through new approaches, new methods, and new techniques. Each issue offers seven or eight articles on how to speak proper English, the teaching of writing for academic purposes, proper pronunciation and grammar, English-language test performance, and experimental and communicative courses in English. Reviews include audiovisual materials. This is the basic title in the field of teaching English as a second language, and will be helpful to teachers.

1044 Yelmo: la revista del profesor de español. 1971. q. $20. Manuel Criado de Val. Yelmo, Apdo. 877, 28080 Madrid, Spain. Index. Circ: 3,000. Microform: UMI. [*Indexed*: CIJE. *Bk. rev*: 2–4, 1,000–2,000 words, signed. *Aud*: Pr/Ages 6–18.]

Presented entirely in Spanish, this journal is targeted for teachers of the Spanish language. Each issue contains documented articles dealing with the theory and methodology of instruction, as well as the linguistic development of the Spanish language and the evolution of Spanish dialects. Specialized topics are also covered, such as the humanistic approach to instruction, sociolinguistic themes, and the problems presented by translation. Most book reviews are reprinted from other sources, as is a regular section that features news articles from various publications concerning Spanish language and linguistics. Literature is discussed, but from the diachronic and didactic view of language. A reputable journal, it would be a good addition to library collections that support Spanish-language and linguistic instruction.

■ LANGUAGE ARTS

1045 **Black American Literature Forum.** 1967. q. $25 (Individuals, $17). Joe Weixlmann. Indiana State Univ., Parsons Hall, Terre Haute, IN 47809. Illus. Adv. Index. Circ: 1,100. Sample. Vol. ends: Dec. Microform: UMI. Reprint: UMI. [*Indexed*: BoRvI, HumI, INeg. *Bk. rev*: 3, 1,000–2,500 words, signed. *Aud*: Pr/Ages 14–18.]

Although primarily a literary journal, this official publication of the Modern Language Association's Division on Black American Literature and Culture also covers topics ranging from art, drama, film, and photography to more general matters relating to Afro-American life. Originally, the journal sought to call attention to the works of much-neglected black writers and to present methods for teaching minority literature. During the last several years, however, the latter focus has shifted in favor of scholarly criticism, creative writing (especially poetry), and excellent bibliographies. These features, along with interviews with leading artists, make *BALF* an outstanding platform for the discussion of black culture. Frequently, a theme unifies all or several articles in an issue. Recently, the physical format has been made more appealing. To summarize, *BALF* presents sensitive—and sometimes disturbing—insights in an attractive, well-edited, and stimulating package.

1046 **C:JET (Communication: Journalism Education Today).** 1967. q. $30. Molly J. Clemons. Journalism Education Assn., Inc., P.O. Box 99, Blue Springs, MO 64015. Illus. Adv. Index. Circ: 3,000. Microform: UMI. Online: BRS, DIALOG. [*Indexed*: CIJE. *Aud*: Pr/Ages 14–18.]

Contains articles written by and for secondary school journalism advisers and teachers. Each issue includes five to ten signed articles and several regular features less than 20 pages in length. Reprints of proceedings of national meetings, certification requirements, membership and organizational lists, and book and film reviews are included annually. Ambivalent about its own title (sometimes it is abbreviated; sometimes it is written out), this professional journal is required reading for its specialized audience.

1047 **Classical World** (Formerly: *The Classical Weekly*). 1907. bi-m. $18. Jerry Clack. Classical Assn. of the Atlantic States, Duquesne Univ., Pittsburgh, PA 15282. Adv. Circ: 2,700. Refereed. Vol. ends: Aug. Microform: MIM, UMI. [*Indexed*: BoRv, BoRvI. *Bk. rev*: 15–30, 300 words, signed. *Aud*: Pr/Ages 14–18.]

In addition to two to three brief, readable articles and briefer "Scholia," *CW* contains many departments useful to the high school Latin teacher. There is an annual survey of audiovisual material in the classics, along with bibliographies of textbooks and notes on current teaching practice. The frequent and very valuable bibliographic essays on recent scholarship on a particular subject or author will make this journal required for many libraries.

1048 **English Education: official journal of the Conference on English Education.** 1969. q. $12. Gordon M. Pradl and Mary K. Healy. Natl. Council of Teachers of English,

1111 Kenyon Rd., Urbana, IL 61801. Adv. Circ: 3,259. Vol. ends: Dec. Microform: UMI. Reprint: UMI. [*Indexed*: CIJE, EdI. *Aud*: Pr/Ages 14–18.]

EE is distinctive for the emphasis it puts on the basic purposes and assumptions of English teaching, rather than on specific methods or analyses of particular literary works. Essays by several major scholars are published but *EE* has also been receptive to straight-from-the-trenches pieces by young teachers. Given the importance of English studies and *EE*'s modest price, it certainly belongs in all academic libraries and should also be available to secondary school English teachers.

1049 English Journal. 1912. 8/yr. $40 (Individuals, $35). Ben F. Nelms. Natl. Council of Teachers of English, 1111 Kenyon Rd, Urbana, IL 61801. Illus. Adv. Index. Circ: 45,000. Vol. ends: Apr. Microform: UMI. Reprint: UMI. [*Indexed*: CIJE, EdI, RG. *Bk. rev*: Irregular. *Aud*: Pr/Ages 6–18.]

EJ provides balanced coverage of the various professional concerns of junior high and high school English teachers: the nature of appropriate training for the profession; the effectiveness of various classroom approaches to composition, literature, and critical thinking; the responsibility of the profession for sustaining the quality of language and culture. More than most education journals, *EJ* goes out of its way to obtain articles by practicing junior high and high school teachers. In addition to a section focusing on a controversial issue and one or two groups of theme-related articles, a typical issue has an *EJ* workshop section containing notes and short, practical articles, mostly by secondary school teachers. Though there is no regular book review section, essay reviews of groups of books frequently appear in the *EJ* workshop. A generally excellent magazine, *EJ* should be available to all prospective as well as present English teachers, and to their teachers.

1050 English Today: the international review of the English language. 1985. q. $50. Tom McArthur and David Crystal. Cambridge Univ. Press, 40 W. 20th St., New York, NY 10011. Illus. Adv. Circ: 4,100. Sample. Vol. ends: Oct. [*Bk. rev*: 4–5, length varies, signed. *Aud*: Pr/Ages 14–18.]

This unique magazine is for everyone concerned with or interested in the English language. *English Today* focuses on the uses and the users of the language throughout the world, on their unities and diversities, controversies, experiences of English and other languages in contact (and conflict), and many other aspects of the world's first truly global medium of communication. Interspersed throughout are a number of regular features including a crossword puzzle, book reviews, excerpts from new publications, news items, and a column on English-language usage. The journal tends to focus on British English and is written by well-qualified academicians. It is printed in readable dark type on bright, coated paper, with a sturdy, compact format. It should find a large audience among lexicographic, bibliophilic, and linguistic devotees of all ages as well as journalists. This journal would be of great use to high school teachers.

1051 Journal of the American Forensic Association. 1964. q. $25. Raymie E. McKerrow. Amer. Forensic Assn., Dept. of Speech Communication, Univ. of Maine, Orono, ME 04469. Adv. Circ: 1,500. Vol. ends: Spring. Microform: UMI. Online: BRS, DIALOG. Reprint: UMI. [*Indexed*: CIJE. *Bk. rev*: 3–5, 1,000 words, signed. *Aud*: Pr/Ages 14–18.]

This journal is devoted to increasing knowledge in all areas of communication theory and practice relevant to forensics in schools and colleges. It publishes pedagogical, theoretical, and critical studies of argumentation, persuasion, discussion, debate, parliamentary deliberation, and forensic activities. A regular issue contains five to six articles on the practice and theory of forensics and argumentation and its teaching. An abstract is given at the beginning of each article. Occasionally, information on debate tournaments is also included. Useful for forensic faculty and individuals with an interest in debating. Recommended for high school libraries.

1052 **Language Arts.** 1924. 8/yr. $40 (Personal membership, $35). David Dillon. Natl. Council of Teachers of English, 1111 Kenyon Rd., Urbana, IL 61801. Illus. Adv. Index. Circ: 18,000. Refereed. Vol. ends: Dec. Microform: UMI. Reprint: UMI. [*Indexed*: CIJE, EdI. *Bk. rev*: Occasional. *Aud*: Pr/Ages 6–14.]

LA is the National Council of Teachers of English journal for the elementary and junior high grades. It deals with composition skills and literature, but its real strength is in articles that go beyond offering techniques for making concepts interesting, and convey an understanding of how language and story are involved in children's acquiring a sense of themselves and their world. "Research Currents" is an impressive department in which the editors and guest authors dramatize the insights of major theorists like Suzanne Langer, Lev Vygotsky, and Jerome Bruner, and bring them to bear on the fundamentals of learning the use of language. *LA* goes out of its way to get contributions from elementary school teachers and school librarians; it also happens to be among the best-written, most thought-provoking journals in the education field. A basic title for elementary school and junior high school libraries.

1053 **Quill and Scroll.** 1926. bi-m. (during school year). $9. Richard P. Johns. Univ. of Iowa, School of Journalism and Mass Communication, Iowa City, IA 52242. Illus. Adv. Circ: 13,000. Sample. Vol. ends: Apr/May. Microform: UMI. [*Indexed*: CIJE. *Bk. rev*: 7–11, 150–200 words, signed. *Aud*: Pr/Ages 14–18.]

Intended for its membership, this magazine is the official publication of the International Honorary Society of High School Journalists. Charters are most often affiliated with high schools that publish yearbooks, newspapers, or magazines, but membership is also open to students through their respective schools who write for town or city newspapers. Regular departments include book reviews (useful in collection development) and news of professional interest. Each issue also contains a feature article and a profile of an individual who has made a contribution to the profession. This is a solid title about the career of journalism presented for the young adult.

1054 **The Reading Teacher: a journal of the International Reading Association.** 1947. 9/yr. $30. Janet Ramage Binkley. Intl. Reading Assn., 800 Barksdale Rd., P.O. Box 8139, Newark, DE 19714-8139. Illus. Adv. Index. Circ: 44,269. Refereed. Vol. ends: May. Microform: UMI. Reprint: UMI. [*Indexed*: CIJE, EdI. *Bk. rev*: 5–6, 700–1,200 words, signed. *Aud*: Pr/Ages 6–14.]

Each issue of *RT* contains 8 to 12 short, clearly written articles that focus on various practical aspects of the process of learning to read. Most articles are by faculty at schools of education, but K–6 teachers and administrators occasionally contribute, and a regular department, "The Classroom Reading Teacher," gives teachers a chance to share short "how-to" pieces. In addition to five or six reviews of professional books, most issues carry a review of a software item and an essay review commenting on a group of recent children's books. *RT* deals with reading instruction at the elementary level. A basic item for elementary school teachers and for libraries serving programs in elementary education, *RT* is also a good choice for public libraries, especially those that serve a large number of young parents.

1055 **Research in the Teaching of English.** 1967. q. $20 (Individuals, $15). Judith A. Langer and Arthur N. Applebee. Natl. Council of Teachers of English, 1111 Kenyon Rd., Urbana, IL 61801. Adv. Circ: 3,300. Vol. ends: Dec. Microform: UMI. Reprint: UMI. [*Indexed*: CIJE, EdI. *Aud*: Pr/Ages 14–18.]

The actual scope of *RTE* is narrower than its title implies. Rather than reporting research on the full range of subjects that English teachers deal with— linguistics, composition, and literature—it deals mainly with two somewhat overlapping areas: practical methods for improving the teaching of composition at all levels, and concepts and models that attempt to explain the fundamental processes by which language is learned and used. The research methods are generally quite sophisticated and tend to use concepts and methods borrowed from linguistics and cognitive psychology. On a day-to-day basis, English teachers are likely to find this less useful than *English Journal, Language Arts,* and the other NCTE periodicals, but its long-range impact is likely to be great, and it should certainly be available to all teachers of English teachers.

1056 **Scholastic Editor's Trends in Publications** (Formerly: *Scholastic Editor*). 1921. 7/yr. $18. Ron E. Rolnicki. Natl. Scholastic Press Assn. and Associated Collegiate Press, 620 Rarig Center, 330 21st Ave. S., Univ. of Minnesota, Minneapolis, MN 55455. Illus. Adv. Index. Circ: 2,000. Vol. ends: May. Microform: UMI. Reprint: UMI. [*Indexed*: CIJE. *Aud*: Pr/Ages 14–18.]

Geared for advisers and editors, this how-to magazine issued seven times a year focuses primarily on high school–level publications. The articles discuss how to put together newspapers, yearbooks, and magazines and promote the accomplishments of student journalists around the country.

1057 **Speaker and Gavel.** 1964. q. $5. Jack Kay. Delta Sigma Rho-Tau Kappa Alpha Forensic Honor Soc., c/o James Weaver, Dept. of Speech Communications, Iowa State Univ., Ames, IA 50011. Circ: 1,200. Vol. ends: Summer. Microform: UMI. Reprint: UMI. [*Bk. rev*: 3–5, 100 words. *Aud*: Pr/Ages 14–18.]

This journal deals exclusively with forensics and debating, offering brief articles, about three to five pages in length. Book reviews are occasionally included. It is not a scholarly journal but is designed to provide information for teachers and coaches of debate and forensics. Recommended for high school libraries.

1058 **Writing Instructor.** 1981. q. $16 (Individuals, $12). Freshman Writing Program, Univ. of Southern California, Los Angeles, CA 90089. Circ: 950. Sample. Refereed. Vol. ends: Summer. [*Bk. rev*: Number varies, 400–600 words, signed. *Aud*: Pr/Ages 14–18.]

Aimed at writing teachers in high schools, colleges, and universities. Authors in this quarterly emphasize practical applications frequently including exercises or handouts. The seven to ten articles on "pedagogy based on rhetorical or educational theory" focus on classroom management, the student as communicator or audience, or the instructor as communicator, facilitator, or audience. Reviews of textbooks or resource books for writing instructors are frequently treated like short articles and notes on other useful materials are also included. This excellent publication for writing instructors is highly recommended.

■ **MUSIC**

1059 **American Music Teacher: the official journal of Music Teachers National Association.** 1951. bi-m. $16. Robert J. Elias. Music Teachers Natl. Assn., Suite 2113, 441 Vine St., Cincinnati, OH 45202-2982. Illus. Adv. Circ: 23,000. Vol. ends: June/July. Microform: UMI. Reprint: UMI. [*Indexed*: EdI. *Bk. rev*: 9, 350 words, signed. *Aud*: Pr/Ages 14–18.]

Even though libraries and other institutions can subscribe without joining the Music Teachers National Association, individuals must belong to the association to receive this title. A typical 70-page issue will have five feature articles "pertaining to the art of music and the profession of music teaching"; books, music, and periodical reviews that are short but thorough; columns such as national, state, and local association news, studio tips, financial advice for educators, membership news, national certification and student chapter news, and information about student competitions and other programs. Readable and informative, practical and not scholarly, this should be considered for purchase. Recommended for high school and public libraries wherever music teachers and their students are found.

1060 **Clavier.** 1962. m. (exc. June & Aug.). $15. Barbara Kreader. The Instrumentalist Publg. Co., 200 Northfield Rd., Northfield, IL 60093. Illus. Adv. Index. Circ: 21,000. Vol. ends: Dec. [*Indexed*: Edi. *Bk. rev*: 1–2,600 words, signed. *Aud*: Pr/Ages 14–18.]

A slick, commercial offering (lots of ads) that should appeal to piano teachers and players. Most of the articles are short and a few are forgettable, but the majority of contributors are respected piano pedagogues. A typical issue has an interview with a pianist in the news, a musicological article, a pedagogical article, the complete score of a piano work with critical commentary, lots of marvelous capsule reviews of new music, a few book reviews, and reviews of films, videos, and software that would intrigue pianists.

1061 **Folksong in the Classroom.** 1980. q. $7. Tony Scott and Laurence Seidman. Folksong in the Classroom, 140 Hill Park Ave., Great Neck, NY 11021. Illus. Sample. [*Aud*: Pr/Ages 6–18.]

A small offset of 30 pages, this journal proves that quality need not be measured by a startling format. The two editors, who use folksongs in teaching, decided to contact other teachers for use of folk music and they came up with a novel publication. Each number is dedicated to a single topic. About a dozen songs are printed, complete with music and commentary that helps teachers— particularly although not exclusively those in the social sciences. There are bibliographies of books and records, "Follow-up Ideas for Your Students," and a helpful correspondence section. This nonprofit publication is "a work of love" and it offers stimulating ideas. As the editors say: "Folksongs can be used with all kinds of students. Also it is for all grade levels and subject areas." Who could ask for more, and for only $7?

1062 **The Instrumentalist.** 1946. m. $20. Elaine Guregian. The Instrumentalist Publg. Co., 200 Northfield Rd., Northfield, IL 60093. Illus. Adv. Circ: 20,000. Vol. ends: July. [*Indexed*: EdI. *Bk. rev*: 4, 450 words, signed. *Aud*: Pr/Ages 14–18.]

A chatty but sophisticated magazine for teachers and students of band and orchestra instruments, especially on the high school and college levels, without a footnote in sight—and that is not a criticism. It offers mostly educational articles and profiles of performers. Succinct, graded reviews of new music are provided, plus reviews reflecting the increase in jazz programs, computers, and instructional videotapes in schools.

1063 **Music Educators Journal.** 1914. m. (exc. June, July, & Aug.). $34. Maribeth Rose. Music Educators Natl. Conference, 1902 Association Dr., Reston, VA 22091. Illus. Adv. Circ: 60,000. Vol. ends: May. Microform: UMI. [*Indexed*: CIJE, EdI. *Bk. rev*: 6–10, 250–1,500 words, signed. *Aud*: Pr/Ages 6–18.]

This journal is geared to music educators spanning all levels and including adult education. The stylistic coverage is equally wide ranging, including most pop, jazz, and classical genres. The features tend to employ a show-and-tell approach (this program worked for me, try it yourself) rather than rigorous research methodologies. A widely read, and highly influential, publication.

1064 **Notes: quarterly journal of the Music Library Association.** 1942. q. $65 (Nonmembers, $60). Michael Ochs. Music Lib. Assn., Inc., P.O. Box 487, Canton, MA 02021. Illus. Adv. Index. Circ: 3,535. Vol. ends: June. Microform: UMI. Reprint: AMS. [*Indexed*: BoRv. *Bk. rev*: 9, 1,500 words, signed. *Aud*: Pr/Ages 14–18.]

If a music library had to subsist on just one journal, this would be it. One of the world's most respected sources of music bibliography, it is also a principal source of information on events and trends in music publishing and music librarianship. Articles about music archives, important recent acquisitions, and manuscripts and biobibliographic studies abound. Book and music reviews offer the same serious consideration whether the item is a scholarly edition of chansons or a Spike Jones discography. The index to music necrology, lists of recently published music publishers' catalogs, and critical commentary on new periodicals are a few of the indispensable regular features.

■ THEATER

1065 **Dramatics.** 1929. m. (Sept.–May). $15. Don Corathers. Intl. Thespian Soc., 3368 Central Pkwy., Cincinnati, OH 45225. Illus. Adv. Index. Circ: 34,000. Sample. Vol. ends: May. Microform: UMI. [*Indexed*: Acs. *Aud*: Pr/Ages 14–18.]

All black-and-white illustration except for the cover characterizes the physical format of this 50-page magazine, which is the official publication of the International Thespian Society, dedicated to secondary school theater. About five or six articles on such varied aspects of theater as directing, summer stock, Shakespearean drama, dialect, playwriting, and performance are contained in each issue. A script is featured in most issues and all contain an interview with a professional in the field. The profuse advertisements annnounce educational and performance opportunities, and calls for auditions. The February issue provides extensive coverage of summer training programs and summer stock opportunities.

1066 **Secondary School Theatre Journal.** 1962. 3/yr. $6. David Grote. Amer. Theatre Assn., Secondary School Theatre Assn., 1000 Vermont Ave. N.W., Washington, DC 20005. Illus. Adv. Circ: 900. Sample. Vol. ends: Fall. Microform: UMI. Reprint: UMI. [*Indexed*: CIJE. *Bk. rev*: 1, 500–700 words, signed. *Aud*: Pr/Ages 14–18.]

An unassuming but pleasant little magazine serving members of the Secondary School Theatre Association, who are mostly drama and theater arts teachers. Besides serving as a communications vehicle for association news and policy, it offers articles, usually submitted by association members, on practical teaching ideas and strategies, often highlighting innovative theater programs in sepcific schools across the country. Regular columns announce professional workshops or new teaching aids products and a chance to exchange ideas on solutions to common problems in the profession. Some of the articles might also appeal to students involved in school theater. This magazine could be useful in the library of a secondary school with an active theater department.

1067 **Studies in American Drama, 1945–Present.** 1986. a. $8. Philip C. Kolin and Colby H. Kullman. Humanities Div., Behrend College, Erie, PA 16563. Illus. Adv. Circ: 400. [*Aud*: Pr/Ages 14–18.]

"An annual journal that publishes scholarly articles on theatre history, dramatic influence, and technique as well as original interviews, theatre documents, and useful bibliographies. Each issue also carries [about eight lengthy] theatre reviews." Half a dozen articles, a couple of interviews, and reviews of American plays produced in New York, regional theaters, and around the globe round out this journal. It is particularly important for academic and university libraries in institutions producing newer American scripts and where contemporary literature is studied.

1068 **Theatre Crafts: the magazine for professionals in theatre, film, video, and the performing arts.** 1967. 10/yr. $30. Patricia MacKay. Theatre Crafts Assocs., 135 Fifth Ave., New York, NY 10010-7193. Subs. to: P.O. Box 630, Holmes, PA 19043-0630. Illus. Adv. Circ: 27,500. Microform: B&H, UMI. [*Indexed*: MI, RG. *Aud*: Pr/Ages 14–18.]

An important magazine that is both practical and theoretical for anyone involved with technical theater. Articles are for the professional and/or amateur responsible for lighting, costumes, billboards, advertising, and other elements of production. It frequently includes articles on the work of noted costumers or set designers, new equipment for the theater including computers, and the staging of particular professional productions. There are columns on new products. A very good "tech theater" title, with ideas that can be used, copied, imitated, or improvised by all theater companies. A necessity in public and high school libraries.

1069 **Theatre Journal** (Formerly: *Educational Theatre Journal*). 1941. q. $39 (Individuals, $17). Sue-Ellen Case. Johns Hopkins Univ. Press, Journals Div., 701 W. 40th St., Suite 275, Baltimore, MD 21211. Illus. Microform: UMI. [*Indexed*: CIJE, EdI, HumI. *Bk. rev*: 15, 750–1,000 words. *Aud*: Pr/Ages 14–18.]

Theatre Journal, now published in cooperation with the Association of Theatre in Higher Education, has not changed its editorial policy. It offers 15 or more book reviews; as many professional, international, and university/college theater reviews; and six or seven articles. Some issues focus on special topics. Scholarly articles are on areas of theater history and theatrical theory and criticism. This basic title should be in some public libraries for use by selection librarians and in theater and literature departments.

•••••••••••••••••••••••••••••••• **Sciences** ••••••••••••••••••••••••••••••••

First choices   General: (1) *Science and Children*; (2) *Science Teacher*.
Computers: (1) *Electronic Education*; (2) *Electronic Learning*.
Mathematics: (1) *Arithmetic Teacher*; (2) *Mathematics Teacher*.

■ GENERAL

1070 AIDS Education and Prevention. 1989. q. $60 (Individuals, $30). Francisco S. Sy. Guilford Publns., 72 Spring St., New York, NY 10012. Illus. Adv. [*Aud*: Pr/Ages 6–18.]

Education about AIDS crosses all grade levels, all social barriers, and all countries. It involves professionals who work with victims, their families, or the population at large. This 90-page interdisciplinary journal is for doctors, teachers, social workers, and anyone involved with explaining to adolescents or adults the dangers involved with this disease. Among the articles, commentaries, and features, typical topics include AIDS and women; fear of AIDS; a perspective on AIDS in Africa; and personal service workers as a critical link in the AIDS educational chain. The articles are well documented and objective, and address present problems. The consideration of everything from the latest medical reports to strategies and programs on education makes this a valuable weapon in the war against AIDS.

1071 American Biology Teacher. 1938. 8/yr. $38 (Membership, $32). Randy Moore. Natl. Assn. of Biology Teachers, 11250 Roger Bacon Dr., No. 19, Reston, VA 22090. Illus. Adv. Index. Circ: 9,400. Vol. ends: Nov/Dec. Microform: UMI. Reprint: UMI. [*Indexed*: EdI, GSI. *Bk. rev*: 3–9, 300–500 words, signed. *Aud*: Pr/Ages 12–18.]

Aimed at biology teachers in middle school and high school, and beginning undergraduate students. Articles are written by scientists and teachers, and those in each issue's "How-To-Do-It" section give suggestions on teaching methods and tools. Others describe natural history phenomena or current research. Book reviews are accompanied by signed reviews of audiovisual materials appropriate for classroom use. Other regular departmental features include "Research Reviews" (discussion of useful articles appearing in other journals), "Computer Center" (an article on computer applications or software reviews), "Biology Today" (discussing current biological topics of interest), "Labs" (about laboratory teaching techniques), and "Teacher-To-Teacher" (classroom issues). Basic for junior high and high school libraries.

1072 American Journal of Physics (Formerly: *American Physics Teacher*). 1933. m. $145 (Members, $65). Robert H. Romer. Amer. Inst. of Physics, 335 E. 45th St., New York, NY 10017. Illus. Adv. Index. Vol. ends: Dec. Microform: Pub. Reprint: Pub. [*Indexed*: ASTI, GSI. *Bk. rev*: 4–5, 400–800 words, signed. *Aud*: Pr/Ages 14–18.]

Unlike physics journals that are designed to present new experimental or theoretical work in the field, the *American Journal of Physics* intends to provide physics educators with new techniques and ideas in the teaching of physics. It is an official publication of the American Association of Physics Teachers and provides information for educators at all levels from secondary school through graduate work, although it concentrates primarily on undergraduate-level material. Each issue contains an editorial on physics education, several papers presenting new techniques or problems in physics teaching, some short notes and discussion papers, book reviews, and a set of problems that can be used in the classroom. Answers to the problem sets always appear in the next issue.

1073 BioScience (Formerly: *AIBS Bulletin*). 1950. m. $84 (Individuals, $39.50). Julie Ann Miller. Amer. Inst. of Biological Sciences, 730 11th St. N.W., Washington, DC

20001-4584. Illus. Adv. Refereed. Vol. ends: Dec. Microform: UMI. Reprint: UMI. [*Indexed*: CIJE. *Bk. rev*: 7–10. *Aud*: Pr/Ages 14–18.]

BioScience covers the entire range of current topics in biology. Included in each issue are several features and articles summarizing current research or policy issues, editorials, and news and announcements of interest to biologists. "The Biologist's Toolbox" includes descriptions and reviews of equipment and computer hardware and software. A section of observations and opinions in biology teaching has been introduced. This section, along with "The Biologist's Toolbox," "Roundtable," and "Viewpoint" sections, is unrefereed. Special book issues with additional reviews are published in the spring and fall.

1074 **Education in Chemistry.** 1964. bi-m. Royal Soc. of Chemistry, Burlington House, London W1V 0BN, England. Illus. Adv. Index. Vol. ends: Dec. Microform: UMI. Online: STN. Reprint: UMI. [*Indexed*: 6–8, 400–500 words, signed. *Aud*: Pr/Ages 14–18.]

Similar in scope to *Journal of Chemical Education*. Contributions include articles written primarily by high school and college teachers covering practical chemistry, experiments, and biographies. Included are sections on recent awards, new products, computer software, and meeting notices. An important source for high school collections.

1075 **Journal of Chemical Education.** 1924. m. $50 (Individuals, $25). J. J. Lagowski. Amer. Chemical Soc., Div. of Chemical Education, 1155 16th St. N.W., Washington, DC 20036. Illus. Adv. Index. Circ: 20,000. Sample. Refereed. Vol. ends: Dec. Microform: UMI. Online: STN. Reprint: UMI. [*Bk. rev*: 5–8, 200–300 words, signed. *Aud*: Pr/Ages 14–18.]

Articles are directed to teachers and high school students as well as chemists in university, government, private, and industrial laboratories. Areas such as laboratory experiments and demonstrations and problems in teaching, history, and safety are included. Reviews include state-of-the-art instrumentation and software.

1076 **Journal of Geological Education.** 1951. 5/yr. $28. James H. Shea. Natl. Assn. of Geology Teachers, 1041 New Hampshire St., Lawrence, KS 66044. Illus. Index. Microform: UMI. [*Indexed*: CIJE, EdI. *Bk. rev*: 12,500 words, signed. *Aud*: Pr/Ages 14–18.]

Published by the National Association of Geology Teachers, this journal presents articles that are pertinent to and informative for those who teach geology. Papers describing how to present topics in geology as well as geological topics of interest for classroom presentation are published. Along with association business news, items of interest to teachers, discussion of software available for classroom use, and book reviews—especially of textbooks—are included.

1077 **Journal of Research in Science Teaching.** 1963. 9/yr. $104. Russell H. Yeany. John Wiley & Sons, 605 Third Ave., New York, NY 10158. Adv. Index. Circ: 2,150. Sample. Vol. ends: Dec. Microform: Pub. Reprint: Pub. [*Indexed*: CIJE, EdI. *Aud*: Pr/Ages 14–18.]

The official journal of the National Association for Research in Science Teaching, *JRST* publishes three to seven articles in each issue. Most of the articles are reports and analyses of a narrowly and precisely defined topic, but occasionally there are articles that discuss science teaching from a broader perspective. The articles typically assume considerable knowledge of statistical methods and research procedures, and make sophisticated use of psychological theories such as Piaget's theory of developmentalism. Some attention is given to science teaching at all levels, but secondary school gets the most emphasis.

1078 **Naturescope.** 1984. 10/yr. $24. Judy Braus. Natl. Wildlife Federation, 1412 16th St. N.W., Washington, DC 20036. Illus. Sample. [*Aud*: Pr/Ages 6–14.]

Naturescope is for "teachers and others who work with young people in the field of environmental education." Each issue is devoted to one subject and is loaded with activities and experiments for children. This publication is well organized, with a variety of activities on different grade levels. It contains good black-and-white artwork. An absolute necessity for school libraries, and public libraries that support school curricula should also consider purchasing it. A wonderful publication.

1079 **Physics Teacher.** 1963. 9/yr. $50. Donald F. Kirwan. Amer. Assn. of Physics Teachers, 5112 Berwyn Rd., College Park, MD 20740. Illus. Adv. Index. Vol. ends: Dec. Microform: Pub, UMI. Reprint: Pub, UMI. [*Indexed*: CIJE, EdI, GSI. *Bk. rev*: 4–6, 100–300 words, signed. *Aud*: Pr/Ages 14–18.]

Physics Teacher is dedicated to strengthening introductory physics education at all levels. Whereas the *American Journal of Physics* (see above in this section) is aimed primarily at undergraduate-level physics instruction, *Physics Teacher* fulfills the same role for the secondary school teacher. Each issue contains several articles on broad topics in physics teaching along with several short notes promoting innovations and new ideas. Some issues are built around a theme that may inspire students to take more interest in physics, such as the physics of an amusement park or physics at the Olympics.

1080 **Science Activities.** 1969. q. $35. Marjorie King. Helen Dwight Reid Educational Foundation, Heldref Publns., 4000 Albermarle St. N.W., Washington, DC 20016. Illus. Adv. Index. Circ: 1,500. Refereed. Vol. ends: No. 4. Microform: UMI. [*Indexed*: CIJE, EdI. *Bk. rev*: 4–10, 200–500 words, signed. *Aud*: Pr/Ages 6–18.]

Science teachers who want ideas for teaching will find them here. Articles suggest sources of experiments, explorations, and projects for all levels of students. Also included are book reviews and information about classroom aids that give data on computer hardware and software. For all school libraries with science education programs.

1081 **Science and Children.** 1963. 8/yr. $42 (Individuals, $33). P. R. Marcuccio. Natl. Science Teachers Assn., 1742 Connecticut Ave. N.W., Washington, DC 20009. Illus. Adv. Index. Circ: 18,500. Vol. ends: May. Microform: UMI. Reprint: UMI. [*Indexed*: CIJE, EdI. *Bk. rev*: 8–12, 50–100 words, signed. *Aud*: Pr/Ages 6–14.]

This magazine is aimed at science teachers—preschool through junior high. Its emphasis is on the practical rather than the theoretical. Teachers can find ideas for science projects and experiments, reviews of new books, and AV and software information. There is also news of the National Science Teachers Association. Illustrations are plentiful and excellent. This belongs in teacher collections in all elementary and junior high schools.

1082 Science Education. 1916. 5/yr. $72. Leopold E. Klopfer. John Wiley & Sons, Inc., 605 Third Ave., New York, NY 10158. Adv. Index. Circ: 2,045. Refereed. Vol. ends: Oct. Microform: RP. Reprint: RP. [*Indexed*: CIJE, EdI. *Aud*: Pr/Ages 6–18.]

This scholarly publication is aimed at science educators, elementary school through college. It explores research on curriculum development, teacher training, and the philosophy of science education. Some case histories are based on experiences from abroad.

1083 Science Teacher. 1934. 9/yr. $43 (Individuals, $33). Juliana Texley. Natl. Science Teachers Assn., 1742 Connecticut Ave. N.W., Washington, DC 20009. Illus. Adv. Index. Circ: 26,013. Vol. ends: May. Microform: UMI. [*Indexed*: CIJE, EdI. *Bk. rev*: 5–10, 150–300 words, signed. *Aud*: Pr/Ages 14–18.]

Most of the contributors are high school science teachers, and they deal quite specifically with teaching techniques and problems. "Science Briefs" is a regular department containing news items that may be useful in the classroom. Books, software, and other teaching aids are reviewed, and the doings of the association are chronicled.

■ **COMPUTERS**

Classroom Computer Learning. *See Technology & Learning.*

1084 Computers & Education. 1976. q. $155. David F. Rogers and P. R. Smith. Pergamon Press, Inc., Maxwell House, Fairview Park, Elmsford, NY 10523. Illus. Index. Circ: 1,100. Vol. ends: No. 4. Microform: MIM, UMI. [*Indexed*: CIJE. *Bk. rev*: 1–2, 500 words, signed. *Aud*: Pr/Ages 6–18.]

This international journal presents a forum for discussion of the use of computers in all levels of education, from primary grades through graduate school. Each issue contains 10 to 12 papers on such topics as educational system development, simulation, computer-aided design, language instruction, and graphical applications. Also included are discussions on the methods of introducing computers on the campus, faculty-administration problems related to computing, and selection and maintenance of appropriate systems. Reviews and summaries of various software and hardware products can also be found in this journal. The first number of each volume contains selected proceedings from the previous year's Computer-Assisted Learning Symposium.

1085 Computers in the Schools: the interdisciplinary journal of practice, theory and applied research. 1984. q. $48 Libraries (Institutions, $36). D. Lamont Johnson. Haworth Press, Inc., 75 Griswold St., Binghamton, NY 13904. Illus. Adv. Circ: 450. Refereed. [*Indexed*: CIJE. *Aud*: Pr/Ages 6–18.]

This journal offers a wide range of scholarly papers and research notes on the theory and practice of the use of computers in education. Topics range from discussions of trends in software and hardware development to analysis of such applications as computer-assisted instruction, expert systems, and artificial intelligence. Papers on the role of computers in teaching such subjects as mathematics, science, reading, and language arts are included.

1086 Computing Teacher: journal of the International Council for Computers in Education. 1979. 9/yr. $29. David Moursund. Int. Council for Computers in Education,

Univ. of Oregon, 1787 Agate St., Eugene, OR 97403-9905. Illus. Adv. Index. Circ: 14,000. Refereed. Vol. ends: No. 9. [*Indexed*: CIJE. *Aud*: Pr/Ages 14–18.]

This journal emphasizes the instructional use of computers and covers such topics as teaching about computers, teaching with the use of computers, teacher education, and the impact of computers on curricula. Each issue contains five to seven papers on different aspects of these topics, and an occasional issue will be devoted to a special topic, such as telecommunications in the classroom. Software reviews and lists also are included, as is news of the International Council for Computers in Education.

1087 Electronic Education. 1981. 8/yr. $18. Don Wood. Electronic Communications, 1311 Executive Center Dr., Tallahassee, FL 32301. Illus. Adv. Circ: 76,000. Sample. [*Indexed*: CIJE, EdI. *Bk. rev*: Various number and length, signed. *Aud*: Pr/Ages 6–18.]

How does one use computers in school systems, specifically in the classroom (grades K–12) and in the administrative offices? Drawing on personal experience, technical know-how, and a good approach to what is/is not needed, the authors present authoritative, up-to-date information. Particularly useful are the numerous, current book reviews of literature in the field of computer education. *Note*: This is a controlled-circulation publication, and while there is a subscription price, the librarian should query the publisher—it might be obtained at no cost.

1088 Electronic Learning. 1981. 8/yr. $23.95. Jonathan Goodspeed. Scholastic, Inc. Subs. to: P.O. Box 2041, Mahopac, NY 10541. Illus. Adv. Index. Circ: 58,000. Vol. ends: May/June. Reprint: B&H, UMI. [*Indexed*: EdI. *Aud*: Pr/Ages 14–18.]

Essentially a newsmagazine that focuses on technical developments in computerized education. Each issue contains four to six short articles that discuss developments and problems with respect to broad trends. Several departments and columns provide brief news items and reviews of hardware and software. Though teachers interested in computer applications will find much of the material interesting, *EL* seems to be written and edited primarily for administrators. There is relatively little emphasis on pedagogical methods, or on computer applications in specific subject areas.

1089 The Good Apple Newspaper. 1972. 5/yr. $12. Gary Grimm and Don Mitchell. The Good Apple Newspaper, P.O. Box 299, Carthage, IL 62321. Illus. Sample. Vol. ends: June. [*Indexed*: CMG. *Aud*: Pr/Ages 6–14.]

A highly imaginative newspaper approach to ideas for teachers of grades 2 through 8. The editorial matter covers all subjects, with almost as many innovative approaches. It is designed for the teacher, not for the child. According to the publisher, each issue is crammed with "games, projects, contracts, task cards, posters and ready to use skill building activities." There is no reason to argue. Unlike related types of instructional material published by Scholastic or Xerox, this is far from conventional. It is an ideal paper for the teacher, and, incidentally, for the parent.

1090 Technology & Learning (Formerly: *Classroom Computer Learning; Classroom Computer News*). 1980. 8/yr. $24. Holly Brady. Peter Li, Inc., 2451 E. River Rd., Dayton, OH 45439. Illus. Adv. Circ: 80,000. Sample. Microform: UMI. [*Indexed*: CIJE, CMG. *Aud*: Pr/Ages 6–18.]

This journal can be used in any grade from kindergarten through the senior class in high school. There is easy-to-understand material for both the beginning teacher and the one with more experience. Articles cover a wide range of interests (and grade levels), with particular emphasis on how the computer can be used in a practical way to improve the educational process. There is useful advice on new software and hardware, and most of it is quite evaluative as well as descriptive. Little of interest to the individual working with a computer is left out. Recommended for all school libraries.

■ MATHEMATICS

1091　**Arithmetic Teacher.** 1954. m. (Sept.–May). $40 (Individuals, $35). Harry B. Tunis. Natl. Council of Teachers of Mathematics, 1906 Association Dr., Reston, VA 22091. Illus. Adv. Index. Circ: 32,000. Refereed. Vol. ends: May. Microform: MIM, UMI. Reprint: UMI. [*Indexed*: CIJE, EdI. *Bk. rev*: 5–10, 500–1,500 words, signed. *Aud*: Pr/Ages 6–14.]

Written for elementary school (grades K–8) mathematics teachers, this magazine emphasizes pedagogical methods and innovations. The editors and contributors come from eclectic professional backgrounds that include scholars, teachers, and administrators. The "Ideas" column is a favorite, in which contributors describe creative approaches to teaching mathematical concepts. Many of the published graphs, figures, and puzzles are useful for classroom instruction. The excellent review section covers books, documents, software, and educational materials. Essential for elementary school collections.

1092　**Journal for Research in Mathematics Education.** 1970. 5/yr. $17. Jeremy Kirkpatrick. Natl. Council of Teachers of Mathematics, 1906 Association Dr., Reston, VA 22091. Adv. Index. Circ: 4,400. Refereed. Vol. ends: No. 5. Microform: MIM, UMI. Reprint: UMI. [*Indexed*: CIJE, EdI. *Bk. rev*: 2–3, 800–1,200 words. *Aud*: Pr/Ages 6–18.]

The National Council of Teachers of Mathematics, the leading American Association of its kind, is "devoted to the interests of teachers of mathematics and mathematics education at all levels—preschool though adult." This journal emphasizes research and its implications over pedagogy and technique. Most articles are by university professors. There are four distinct types of materials: reports of research, research articles, brief notes, and brief commentaries. Additionally, issues often contain reviews, bibliographies, and conference announcements. Along with the council's other fine journals, *Arithmetic Teacher* and *Mathematics Teacher*, this is a solid title for education collections.

1093　**Mathematics and Computer Education** (Formerly: *MATYC Journal*). 1967. 3/yr. $40. George M. Miller. MATYC Journal, Inc., P.O. Box 158, Old Bethpage, NY 11804. Illus. Adv. Circ: 3,000. Refereed. Vol. ends: No. 3. Microform: UMI. Reprint: UMI. [*Indexed*: CIJE. *Bk. rev*: 6–10, 400–600 words, signed. *Aud*: Pr/Ages 14–18.]

The editors list three objectives for this journal: (1) to develop materials for the improvement of classroom effectiveness in the senior high schools and the first years of college, (2) to encourage higher academic standards, and (3) to evaluate and disseminate articles on mathematics and computer education. Articles describe mathematical concepts and suggest their practical classroom applications; the focus is on the means of assimilating, presenting, and using these concepts. There are also editorials, software and book reviews, and the "Problem Department," where readers propose solutions. With computers now commonly used in mathematics classes, this journal serves as an important vehicle for the exchange of new teaching innovations.

1094 **Mathematics Teacher.** 1908. m. (Sept.–May). $40. Ed. bd. Natl. Council of Teachers of Mathematics, 1906 Association Dr., Reston, VA 22091. Illus. Index. Circ: 39,000. Refereed. Vol. ends: May. Microform: UMI. [*Indexed*: CIJE, EdI. *Bk. rev*: 10–15, 400–600 words, signed. *Aud*: Pr/Ages 14–18.]

Designed to pick up where *Arithmetic Teacher*, the council's other publication, leaves off, this journal is read by mathematics teachers from high school to college-sophomore level. Articles discuss and summarize mathematical concepts, with classroom applications emphasized. There are also sections for commentaries, announcements, and courseware reviews. Widely read by high school teachers.

1095 **Mathematics Teaching.** 1956. q. $30. Tony Brown. Assn. of Teachers of Mathematics, Kings Chamber, Queen St., Derby DE1 3DA, England. Illus. Index. Circ: 6,000. Vol. ends: Dec. Microform: UMI. [*Indexed*: CIJE, EdI. *Aud*: Pr/Ages 6–18.]

The British Association of Teachers of Mathematics is the equivalent of America's National Council of Teachers of Mathematics. This journal is the most widely read of the association's publications. With a glossy, $8\frac{1}{2} \times 11''$ format, *Mathematics Teaching* is visually appealing and full of lively graphics. Most articles are written by teachers for teachers, addressing issues that are of concern and consequence to the teaching profession. In many cases, the journal exhibits a clear British focus. The "Work in Progress" column describes the association's activities and goals. This journal provides a vivacious forum for the discussion of teaching methods, problems, and concepts.

1096 **UMAP Journal: the journal of undergraduate mathematics and its applications.** 1980. q. $72 (Individuals, $42). Paul J. Campbell. Consortium for Mathematics and Its Applications, 60 Lowell St., Arlington, MA 02174. Illus. Adv. Index. Vol. ends: No. 4. [*Bk. rev*: 3–10, 250–1,500 words, signed. *Aud*: Pr/Ages 14–18.]

Sponsored by several organizations, including the Society for Industrial and Applied Mathematics and the National Council of Teachers of Mathematics, this attractive journal "acquaints readers with a wide variety of professional applications of the mathematical sciences and provides a forum for discussion of new directions in mathematical education." Generally, contributions come from professors writing at an undergraduate or advanced high school level. The "On Jargon" column prints lively mathematical editorials, surveys, and/or case studies.

•••••••••••••••••••••• **Physical Education and Sports** ••••••••••••••••••••••

First choices Physical Education: *Journal of Physical Education, Recreation and Dance.*
Sports: *Scholastic Coach.*

■ **PHYSICAL EDUCATION**

1097 **American Journal of Sports Medicine.** 1972. bi-m. $60 (Individuals, $50). Jack C. Hughston. Amer. Orthopaedic Soc. for Sports Medicine, 6262 Hamilton Rd., Columbus,

GA 31906. Illus. Adv. Circ: 10,672. Refereed. Vol. ends: Nov/Dec. Microform: Pub. [*Indexed*: EdI. *Aud*: Pr/Ages 14–18.]

This publication offers original articles addressed to orthopedic surgeons, team physicians, physical therapists, athletic directors, and team trainers. The primary focus is on the causes and effects of injury or disease resulting from or affected by athletic injury. A wide variety of team and individual sports are covered. Each issue contains approximately 18 to 20 original research articles written primarily by physicians, which are generally well illustrated and highly technical in nature. Sections at the end of the issues include extensive "Announcements."

1098 **Journal of Physical Education, Recreation and Dance.** 1896. 9/yr. $60. Frances Ferguson Rowan. Amer. Alliance for Health, Physical Education, Recreation and Dance, 1900 Association Dr., Reston, VA 22091. Illus. Adv. Index. Circ: 30,000. Sample. Refereed. Vol. ends: Dec. [*Indexed*: CIJE, EdI. *Bk. rev*: 2–5, 150–500 words. *Aud*: Pr/Ages 14–18.]

The professional journal for physical education instructors, recreation leaders, and dance teachers in the alliance. The purpose of this journal is to communicate research; articles are geared to health, leisure, and movement-related activities, and the contributions of these activities toward human well-being. News notes, announcements of upcoming workshops and conferences, inexpensive teaching aids, and instructional tips are useful features.

1099 **National Strength & Conditioning Association Journal.** 1979. bi-m. $39 Professional or collegiate coaches (High school coaches, $22; students of patron member, $20). Susan Cloidt. National Strength & Conditioning Association, 916 O St., P.O. Box 81410, Lincoln, NE 68501. Illus. Adv. Index. Circ: 12,000. Vol. ends: Jan. [*Aud*: Pr/Ages 14–18.]

The main education publication of the National Strength & Conditioning Association, this journal is dedicated to "optimum athletic performance through total conditioning" and is the link between the sports science research laboratory and the strength training facility. According to the editors, the articles attempt to bridge the gap between exercise physiology research and the athletic playing field by presenting research results along with practical applications, thereby aiding coaches in developing the most effective workout program for their athletes. Emphasis is on the basic components of conditioning, that is, speed, strength, power, muscular and cardiovascular endurance, flexibility, and agility. This quality magazine should be in libraries used by coaches.

1100 **The Physical Educator.** 1940. q. $15. David O. Matthews. The Physical Educator, 901 W. New York St., Indianapolis, IN 46223. Circ: 8,500. Refereed. Vol. ends: Winter. Microform: UMI. [*Indexed*: CIJE, EdI. *Aud*: Pr/Ages 6–18.]

The official publication of Phi Epsilon Kappa, a national professional fraternity for physical educators, this periodical offers a wide variety of articles of interest to the physical educator—many with applications to daily activities. Contributions vary from poetry to articles on specific physical education teaching approaches and concepts from elementary school through college.

1101 **The Physician and Sportsmedicine.** 1973. m. $41. Richard Strauss. McGraw-Hill Publg. Co., 4530 W. 77th St., Minneapolis, MN 55435. Illus. Adv. Index. Circ: 123,500.

Sample. Refereed. Vol. ends: Dec. Microform: UMI. [*Bk. rev*: 4, 100–200 words, signed. *Aud*: Pr/Ages 14–18.]

"Serving the practicing physician's professional and personal interests in the medical aspects of sports, exercise, and fitness," this publication's columns, brief reports, interviews, and research articles are also of interest to therapists, trainers, coaches, and students. Well-written, interesting articles and excellent illustrations make this one of the best titles in the field and accessible to those involved in a wide array of sports-related activities.

1102   **Research Quarterly for Exercise and Sport.** 1930. q. $50. Jerry R. Thomas. Amer. Alliance for Health, Physical Education, Recreation and Dance, 1900 Association Dr., Reston, VA 22091. Illus. Adv. Index. Circ: 30,000. Refereed. Vol. ends: Dec. Microform: UMI. [*Indexed*: CIJE, EdI. *Bk. rev*: 4, 600–1,200 words, signed. *Aud*: Pr/Ages 14–18.]

This scholarly journal is devoted to research in physical education exercise and sports. It includes articles and research notes, primarily of interest to the physical education researcher and teacher, but also potentially accessible to the student. Sections include biomechanics, exercise, epidemiology, growth and development, history and philosophy, measurement and evaluation, motor control and learning, pedagogy, physiology, psychology, sociology, and cultural anthropology. Emphasis is on the art and science of human movement contributing to knowledge and to the development of theory.

■ SPORTS

1103   **Athletic Training.** 1956. q. $28. Steve Yates. Natl. Athletic Trainers' Assn., Inc., 1001 E. Fourth St., Greenville, NC 27858. Illus. Adv. Circ: 11,500. Vol. ends: Winter. Microform: UMI. [*Bk. rev*: 2, 100–250 words, signed. *Aud*: Pr/Ages 14–18.]

This journal of the National Athletic Trainers' Association is concerned specifically with the progress of the athletic training profession. Articles consider the effects of anabolic steroids on female athletes, sports injuries, legal liability, ankle tape jobs, pool therapy, sports medicine centers, and many other related technical topics written by experts. Each issue includes a quiz, articles, and tips from the field of interest not only to athletic trainers, but also to individuals doing research from related fields. The "Potpourri" section, editorials, columns, lists of current publications, medical updates, new products, and other sections are well written and add to the overall usefulness of this publication.

1104   **Referee: the magazine of sports officiating.** 1976. m. $30. Barry Mano. Referee Enterprises, Inc., P.O. Box 161, Frankville, WI 53126. Illus. Adv. Index. Circ: 35,000. Sample. Vol. ends: Dec. [*Aud*: Pr/Ages 14–18.]

Although this magazine is geared toward a specialized audience of referees and individuals involved in sports officiating, the news sections, columns, features, interviews, and so on, are of potential interest to anyone who plays or watches the broad array of sports treated. Intriguing features include legal analyses, psychological approaches, and individual sections on various sports. An addition to any sports collection that gives one the opportunity to see sports from the other side, that is, from the point of view of the individual who has to control the proceedings.

1105   **Scholastic Coach** (Incorporating *Athletic Journal*). 1931. 10/yr. $15.95. Herman L. Masin. Scholastic, Inc., 730 Broadway, New York, NY 10003. Illus. Adv. Index. Circ:

42,500. Vol. ends: May. Microform: B&H, UMI. [*Indexed*: EdI. *Bk. rev*: 5–7, 30–50 words. *Aud*: Pr/Ages 14–18.]

Scholastic Coach is a nuts-and-bolts magazine for high school/college coaches, trainers, physical educators, and administrators. Written by coaches, trainers, and so forth, it covers the techniques of individual and team play, with heavy emphasis on organization, individual moves, plays, strategy, and conditioning. Every issue also contains pertinent material on weight training, athletic administration, sports medicine, and new equipment products, plus a special coaching humor page, perhaps the best editorial page in sports, and an in-depth interview with a famous coach. Sections include track, baseball, football, basketball, strength, administration, fitness/training, interviews, buyer's guide, women scene, and other departments. Excellent illustrations and bold, handsome layouts. A must for the coaching profession and libraries.

•••••••••••••••••••••••••••••• **Disabilities** ••••••••••••••••••••••••••••••

First choices   None. Select as needed.

1106   Academic Therapy. 1965. 5/yr. $25 (Individuals, $20). Betty Lou Kratoville. Academic Therapy Publns., Inc., 20 Commercial Blvd., Novato, CA 94947. Illus. Adv. Index. Circ: 6,500. Sample. Vol. ends: May. Microform: UMI. [*Indexed*: EdI. *Aud*: Pr/Ages 6–18.]

This interdisciplinary journal features a practical approach that would be most useful for special education teachers, classroom teachers with no special education background, and adults working with disabled youth. The approximately 15 articles per issue support the journal's intent to focus attention on "the inefficient learner, who, although intellectually capable, is unable to achieve academically by traditional educational methods." Throughout, there is a heavy emphasis on language arts and reading and an increased awareness of the importance of involving parents. Regular departments include information about materials and resources; software reviews are a new addition.

1107   Accent on Living. 1956. q. $6. Betty Garee. Cheever Publg., Inc., Gillum Rd. and High Dr., P.O. Box 700, Bloomington, IL 61702. Illus. Adv. Index. Circ: 19,500. Sample. Vol. ends: Winter. Microform: UMI. [*Bk. rev*: Various numbers, 100–300 words. *Aud*: Pr/Ages 14–18.]

Accent on Living is an informative magazine aimed at the disabled, especially those with orthopedic problems. Its primary emphasis is practical information about up-to-date special aids, equipment, and techniques that improve the quality of life for disabled persons. Cheever Publishing also offers Accent on Information (AOI), a computerized retrieval system containing information on activities of daily living for the disabled. Biannually Cheever also publishes the *Accent on Living Buyer's Guide*, which lists manufacturers and distributors of products for the disabled.

1108   Braille Book Review. 1932. bi-m. Free to qualified individuals. Ruth Nieland. Natl. Lib. Service for the Blind and Physically Handicapped, Lib. of Congress, Washington, DC 20542. Circ: 13,000. Sample. Vol. ends: Nov/Dec. [*Aud*: Pr/Ages 6–18.]

This publication from the National Library Service comes in both large print and braille. Set in 14-point type, it lists magazines and books available through a network of cooperating libraries. The titles are limited to the recent acquisitions of the national collection, and all entries are annotated. The annotations indicate occurrences of strong language and explicit descriptions of sex or violence. The review is arranged into four broad categories: "Books for Adults," "Books for Children," "Handcopied Braille—Other Agencies," and "Braille Magazines." The categories are further subdivided into "Press Braille," "Handcopied Braille," and "Fiction and Nonfiction." The author/title index is also subdivided into "Press Braille," "Handcopied Braille—NLS," and "Handcopied Braille—Other Agencies." Along with *Talking Book Topics*, it provides access to a wealth of material for the visually impaired.

1109 **Education and Training of the Mentally Retarded.** 1966. q. $20 (Nonmembers, $24). Stanley H. Zuckor. Council for Exceptional Children, 1920 Association Dr., Reston, VA 22091. Illus. Adv. Index. Circ: 7,500. Vol. ends: Dec. Microform: UMI. [*Indexed*: CIJE, EdI. *Aud*: Pr/Ages 6–18.]

Aimed at professionals working with the mentally retarded, this journal "focuses on the education and welfare of persons who are retarded. Major emphasis is on identification and assessment, educational programming, characteristics, training of instructional personnel, habilitation, prevention, community understanding and provisions, and legislation." Articles vary from the very practical to the more scholarly. Recommended only for larger academic libraries and for professionals in the field.

1110 **Education of the Handicapped: the independent biweekly news service on legislation, programs and funding for special education.** 1975. bi-w. $180. Maggie Hume. Capitol Publns., Inc., 1101 King St., P.O. Box 1453, Alexandria, VA 22313-2053. Index. Sample. [*Aud*: Pr/Ages 6–18.]

This loose-leaf-format newsletter covers the most current pertinent information about federal legislation, regulations, programs, and funding for educating children with disabilities. Information included in this biweekly publication is concise and to the point. Occasionally, the newsletter features "Document Retrieval Service," which includes reports, computer adaptations, and booklets. An order form for these documents is included.

1111 **Exceptional Children.** 1934. 6/yr. $30. James E. Yeseldyke. Council for Exceptional Children, 1920 Association Dr., Reston, VA 22091. Illus. Adv. Index. Circ: 53,000. Vol. ends: May. Microform: UMI. [*Indexed*: CIJE, EdI. *Bk. rev*: 5–7, 300 words, signed. *Aud*: Pr/Ages 6–18.]

This journal publishes articles on professional issues of concern to special educators as well as articles on the education and development of exceptional students. Specialists in the field contribute fairly technical articles on planning curriculum, current research and development, and suggestions for the classroom. Often an issue will relate to one theme. All articles are abstracted. Departments report on professional conferences and news, upcoming events, classified advertisements, professional opportunities, and video reviews.

1112 **Exceptional Parent: parenting your disabled child.** 1971. 8/yr. $24 (Individuals, $16). Maxwell J. Schleifer. Psy-Ed Corp., 605 Commonwealth Ave., Boston, MA 02215.

Illus. Adv. Circ: 35,000. Vol. ends: No. 8. Microform: UMI. Reprint: UMI. [*Indexed*: CIJE, EdI. *Aud*: Pr/Ages 6–18.]

Each issue of this journal for parents of learning-disabled or physically handicapped children is devoted to a particular theme—for example, technology, financial planning, and preparing the child for independent living. Each feature article begins with an indication of its relevance to all families. The "What's Happening" column presents new approaches and treatments. Rather than book reviews, this journal has 400- to 600-word excerpts from books concerned with exceptional children.

1113 **Handicapped American Report** (Formerly: *Handicapped Rights and Regulations*). 1980. bi-w. $190. Kimberly M. Scott. Business Pubs., Inc., 951 Pershing Dr., Silver Spring, MD 20910-4464. Sample. [*Aud*: Pr/Ages 6–18.]

A valuable publication on all issues affecting the disabled community. Brief articles provide information to keep readers abreast of current proposals, court decisions, legislation, programs, and grants that affect disabled Americans. The "News In Brief " section has one-paragraph news bulletins and notices. Although the price is high, this is a useful source for professionals involved with federal and state funding and legislation affecting employment or services.

1114 **Magazines in Special Media: subscription sources.** 1961. a. Free. Natl. Lib. Service for the Blind and Physically Handicapped, Lib. of Congress, Washington, DC 20542. Circ: 50,000. Sample. Vol. ends: Winter. [*Aud*: Pr/Ages 6–18.]

This reference circular, set in 14-point type, covers information about magazines in braille, cassette, disc, large type, and moon type. The information is provided by magazine producers. Section I is an alphabetical list of magazines with the following information: title, frequency, special medium, source, subscription price, and a brief description of the contents. The term "direct" or "loan" signifies that eligible patrons can get material on free subscription or from one of the cooperating libraries. Section II contains indexes by subject and type of material and includes a list of distributors as well as a bibliography.

1115 **The Musical Mainstream** (Formerly: *New Braille Musician; A Braille Musician*). 1942. q. Free to qualified personnel. Shirley P. Emanuel. Natl. Lib. Service for the Blind and Physically Handicapped, Music Section, Lib. of Congress, Washington, DC 20542. Circ: 3,200. Vol. ends: Oct. [*Aud*: Pr/Ages 6–18.]

This is one of five music periodicals (the others are *Braille Music Magazine, Contemporary Sound Track, Musical America*, and *Popular Music Lead Sheets*) available to U.S. residents and citizens who are eligible for the National Service for the Blind and Physically Handicapped program of free library service. Libraries can also receive *Musical Mainstream*. It is available in three formats/editions: large-print, braille, and 8 rpm flexible disc. Its contents include "reprints of articles from national magazines on classical music and music education, original articles on subjects relating to music for blind and physically handicapped individuals, bibliographies, and new acquisitions to the National Library Service for the Blind and Physically Handicapped music collection."

1116 **National Braille Association. Bulletin** (Formerly: *National Braille Club. Bulletin*)). 1949. q. $15. Aletha E. Calligan. Natl. Braille Assn., Inc., 1290 University Ave., Rochester,

NY 14607. Circ: 2,300. Vol. ends: No. 4. Online: BRS, DIALOG. [*Indexed*: CIJE. *Aud*: Pr/Ages 6–18.]

This publication is designed to inform and educate braille transcribers and narrators and teachers of the visually impaired. It contains regular departments, of which the most important is a series of columns called "Sharpen Your Skills," a thorough summary of technical advice to keep braille transcriber-readers up-to-date on the latest developments in their particular area of specialization. News and feature articles focus on modification of codes, availability of publications, tips to transcribers, and subjects of interest to members and to persons working in the field of services to the visually impaired. This publication is available in braille, print, and recorded tap formats. Recommended for libraries involved with the visually impaired.

1117 **Palaestra.** 1984. q. $24 (Individuals, $18). David P. Beaver. Challenge Publns., Ltd., P.O. Box 508, Macomb, IL 61455. Illus. Adv. Circ: 6,000–8,000. Sample. Refereed. Vol. ends: Summer. [*Aud*: Pr/Ages 6–18.]

Both the intent and the quality of this magazine make it a special publication. After analyzing numbers of self-serving (albeit useful and entertaining) publications, *Palaestra* is a breath of fresh air. This publication offers a well-balanced combination of features and was "born out of respect for the challenges, problems, and rewards experienced by disabled students and athletes and by those working with them." Articles deal primarily with the seven disability areas (amputee, blind, cerebral palsy, deaf, les autres, mentally handicapped, and spinally paralyzed). Editorial content includes technical how-to pieces, practical research, equipment and facility modification, and recreation and physical education activities for all individuals with disabilities. Special Olympics and other competitions for the disabled are reported. Public and school libraries should consider this title.

1118 **Talking Book Topics.** 1935. bi-m. Free to qualified individuals. Natl. Lib. Service for the Blind and Physically Handicapped. Lib. of Congress, Washington, DC 20542. Circ: 207,000. Sample. Vol. ends: Nov/Dec. [*Aud*: Pr/Ages 6–18.]

This bimonthly publication from the National Library Service to the Blind and Physically Handicapped (similar in format to *Braille Book Review*) is available in both large-print (14-point type) and flexible-disc editions. Included are all recent acquisitions to the service's recorded collection, and each entry is annotated. The listings are arranged under four categories: "Books for Adults," "Books for Children," "Foreign Language Books," and "Talking Book Magazines." Adult and children's books are further arranged by "Fiction," "Non-Fiction," "Disc," and "Cassette." Foreign-language books are subdivided by language. The author/title index also provides access by disc and cassette. Appropriate for libraries serving the elderly and other visually impaired users.

1119 **Teaching Exceptional Children.** 1968. q. Membership (Nonmembers, $20). Cynthia Warger. Council for Exceptional Children, 1920 Association Dr., Reston, VA 22091. Adv. Index. Circ: 52,000. Vol. ends: Summer. Microform: UMI. [*Indexed*: CIJE, EdI. *Aud*: Pr/Ages 6–18.]

This is the most practical of the publications produced by this organization. It is specifically designed for teachers of handicapped and gifted children, and the eight articles per issue are very useful. Information about the organization is included, and a column provides for the exchange of information. School and academic libraries with the appropriate clientele should purchase this journal.

[Library and Media: Barbara Via and Sally Bowdoin. Book Reviews: Paula A. Baxter]

First choices   General: (1) *Library Journal*; (2) *School Library Journal*; (3) *VOYA*; (4) *Emergency Librarian*; (5) *Wilson Library Bulletin*.
Book Reviews: (1) *Booklist*; (2) *Center for Children's Books. Bulletin*; (3) *School Library Journal*.
Media and Media Reviews: (1) *Media & Methods*; (2) *Parents' Choice*.

■ **GENERAL**

1120   American Libraries. 1907. m. (bi-m. July/Aug.). Membership (Nonmembers, $40). Amer. Lib. Assn., 50 E. Huron St., Chicago, IL 60611. Illus. Adv. Circ: 41,500. Microform: B&H, MIM, UMI. Online: DIALOG, WILSONLINE. [*Indexed*: CIJE, EdI, MI. *Aud*: Pr/Ages 6–18.]

The official journal of the American Library Association, this publication is unmatched for keeping readers abreast of the U.S. library scene. The magazine is colorful, the articles and regular features are readable, and the information provided is essential. Special features include the Reference and Adult Services Division Annual "Outstanding Reference Sources," special reports on library buildings and furniture, and detailed coverage of ALA conferences. Regular columns include a question-and-answer exchange and quick bibliographies on timely topics. This is an absolutely essential purchase for all U.S. libraries.

1121   Canadian Children's Literature. 1975. q. $16. Mary Rubio and Elizabeth Waterston. C C Press, P.O. Box 335, Guelph, Ont. N1H 6K5, Canada. Illus. Adv. Circ: 2,000. Sample. [*Indexed*: CanI. *Aud*: Pr/Ages 6–14.]

According to the stated editorial policy, this quarterly is devoted "to the literary analysis, criticism and review of books written for Canadian children." Each issue, thematic in approach, is an interesting, often scholarly, blend of literary analysis and book reviewing. A few articles are written in French, or in French and English, but the text is predominantly English. Black-and-white illustrations from material discussed and photographs appear occasionally. Contributors are authors, librarians, teachers of children's literature, and university professors.

1122   Canadian Library Journal. 1944. bi-m. $40 Can. Jackie Easby. Canadian Lib. Assn., 200 Elgin St., Suite 602, Ottawa, Ont. K2P 1L5, Canada. Illus. Adv. Circ: 6,000. Vol. ends: Dec. Online: DIALOG, WILSONLINE. [*Indexed*: CanI. *Bk. rev*: 10–15, 300–800 words, signed. *Aud*: Pr/Ages 6–18.]

The Canadian Library Association's official publication, this journal offers several well-written, descriptive articles in each issue. The topics covered are often of interest to U.S. librarians as well. The February issue includes the registration form and program details for the annual conference. The October issue covers the annual conference in depth. Reviews are provided of professional reading. A must for Canadian libraries.

1123 **Catholic Library World.** 1929. bi-m. Membership (Nonmembers, $35). Marianne C. Sailus. Catholic Lib. Assn., 461 Lancaster Ave., Haverford, PA 19041. Illus. Adv. Index. Vol. ends: June. Microform: UMI. [*Indexed*: CIJE. *Aud*: Pr/Ages 6–18.]

Broader in scope and potential audience than its title implies, the official publication of the Catholic Library Association (CLA) is one of the better of its type. It has a pleasing format and articles on library management that will appeal to school and public librarians. Of course, in fulfilling its mission as the organ of CLA, the journal's coverage of Catholic library activities and the Catholic press is rich and varied.

1124 **Children's Literature.** 1973. a. $10.95. Francelia Butler. Yale Univ. Press, 92A Yale Sta., New Haven, CT 06520. Illus. [*Bk. rev*: 6–8, 2–10 pages, signed. *Aud*: Pr/Ages 6–14.]

CL, sponsored by the MLA Division on Children's Literature and the Children's Literature Association, is a 200-page compilation of essays, comments, and reviews. It is meant for scholars rather than children or laypersons. Issues offer 9 to 11 articles, often by authors of note.

1125 **Emergency Librarian.** 1973. 5/yr. $40 prepaid (Billed, $45). Ken Haycock. Emergency Librarian. Subs. to: Dept., P.O. Box C34069, Dept. 284, Seattle, WA 98124-1069. Illus. Adv. Circ: 5,000. Vol. ends: May/June. Microform: UMI. Online: DIALOG, WILSONLINE. [*Indexed*: CMG, CanI. *Aud*: Pr/Ages 6–14.]

A top-notch publication from Canada aimed at teachers and librarians working with children and young adults. Each issue of 70 pages includes feature articles and reviews of professional reading, children's recordings, magazines for young people, and paperbacks for children and young adults. Included are departments—"Microcomputers" and "One Minute Management." This journal continues to provide stimulating articles and a refreshing open-mindedness toward children's and young adult librarianship.

1126 **The Horn Book Magazine: about books for children and young adults.** 1924. 6/yr. $36. Anita Silvey. Horn Book, Inc., 14 Beacon St., Boston, MA 02108. Illus. Adv. Index. Circ: 22,000. Sample. Vol. ends: Nov. Microform: B&H, MIM, UMI. [*Indexed*: BoRv, BoRvI, CMG, MI, MRD. *Aud*: Pr/Ages 6–14.]

Horn Book is one of the oldest, most reputable review journals for children's literature and educational materials. Every issue contains highly readable articles, ranging from profiles or interviews with prominent figures in the field to scholarly essays on literary manuscripts. Almost every issue contains an article on some aspect of juvenile education. However, the reviews are the "meat" of this magazine, covering new editions and reissues, suggested paperback purchases, books in Spanish, and even occasional recommendations for storytelling or exhibition-viewing purposes. The reviews contain concise, critical commentary, usually favorable in tone. The magazine can be quickly scanned through use of its indexes to advertisers and book reviews (by author and title). *Horn Book* is an authoritative tool for professionals who work with preschool to junior high school readers.

1127 **International Review of Children's Literature and Librarianship.** 1986. 3/yr. $65. Margaret Kinnell. Taylor Graham Publg., 500 Chesham House, 150 Regent St., London W1R 5FA, England. Vol. ends: Winter. [*Bk. rev*: 6–8, 500–800 words, signed. *Aud*: Pr/Ages 6–16.]

This is an attractively designed journal with a distinguished editorial board. There are usually four feature articles in each number, on topics such as a case study of library service for city children and a user survey of 13–16 year-olds in Nottinghamshire.

1128 **Journal of Youth Services in Libraries** (Formerly: *Top of the News*). 1987. q. Membership (Nonmembers, $30). Joni Bodart-Talbot. Amer. Lib. Assn., 50 E. Huron St., Chicago, IL 60611. Illus. Adv. Index. Circ: 9,500. Vol. ends: Summer. Microform: UMI. Online: DIALOG, WILSONLINE. [*Indexed*: CIJE. *Aud*: Pr/Ages 6–18.]

Sponsored by the Association for Library Service to Children and the Young Adult Services Division of the American Library Association, this publication provides news, eight to ten feature articles, regular columns like "Focus on Research" and "Focus on Technology," and reviews of professional reading. This is a solid journal providing coverage of diverse topics for youth library services.

1129 **Library Hi Tech.** 1983. q. $125. C. Edward Wall. Pierian Press, P.O. Box 1808, Ann Arbor, MI 48106. Illus. Adv. Circ: 10,200. Online: BRS, DIALOG, WILSONLINE. [*Indexed*: CIJE. *Aud*: Pr/Ages 6–18.]

This journal provides five to ten in-depth articles per issue on every facet of library technology. The articles are consistently well written, detailed, nicely illustrated, and understandable to the noncomputer specialist. Unfortunately its price makes it an unlikely candidate for libraries with limited budgets.

1130 **Library Journal.** 1876. s-m. (m. Jan., July, Aug., Dec.). $69. John N. Berry III. R. R. Bowker, Library Journal, P.O. Box 1977, Marion, OH 43302. Illus. Adv. Index. Vol. ends: Dec. Microform: UMI. Online: BRS, DIALOG, WILSONLINE. [*Indexed*: CIJE, EdI, MI. *Aud*: Pr/Ages 6–18.]

The leading library periodical in the United States. It is hard to imagine any library not subscribing to this journal. Each issue abounds with news, feature articles, columns on magazines and people, a calendar of events, and reviews, reviews, and more reviews. Special issues include the Spring and Fall Book Announcement Numbers and the Annual Buying Guide. No other library science journal can compare to this one for timeliness, coverage of the library world, and reviewing services, all in one neat package.

1131 **Public Libraries.** 1962. q. $12.50 Members (Nonmembers, $25). Kenneth Shearer. Amer. Lib. Assn., 50 E. Huron St., Chicago, IL 60611. Illus. Adv. Circ: 5,750. Microform: UMI. Online: DIALOG, WILSONLINE. Reprint: UMI. [*Indexed*: CIJE. *Bk. rev*: 3–5, 100–300 words, signed. *Aud*: Pr/Ages 6–18.]

Published by the American Library Association's Public Library Association (PLA), this journal provides a practical approach to issues facing public librarians. Feature articles lean toward the how-to-do-it or straight reporting type. Regular features include columns on planning and evaluation, services to children and young adults, research in action, and PLA news. Particularly useful is the "Public Laws/Public Libraries" column. This is a worthwhile, practice-oriented journal.

1132 **Rural Libraries.** 1980. s-a. $6. Rebekah Sheller. Center for the Study of Rural Librarianship, College of Lib. Science, Clarion Univ. of Pennsylvania, Clarion, PA 16214. Online: DIALOG, WILSONLINE. [*Aud*: Pr/Ages 6–18.]

This is an important publication devoted to an area of librarianship much neglected in the literature. Recent issues include articles on topics such as site selection for rural public libraries and a rural campaign against illiteracy. The format is plain and simple, but the contents of this journal provide a rich resource of information on rural libraries. Highly recommended for all libraries serving nonurban populations.

1133 School Librarian's Workshop. 1980. m. $40. Ruth Toor. Lib. Learning Resources, Inc., 61 Greenbriar Dr., P.O. Box 87, Berkeley Heights, NJ 07922. Circ: 7,500. [*Aud*: Pr/Ages 6–18.]

Practical advice is given to the school librarian on everything from selection of materials to dealing with common problems. The material is particularly useful because it is current and practical. It seems especially useful for librarians working with the lower grades, as well as for people who may not have a library degree.

1134 School Library Journal. 1954. m. (exc. June & July). Lillian N. Gerhardt. School Library Journal, P.O. Box 1978, Marion, OH 43302. Illus. Adv. Circ: 44,000. Vol. ends: Aug. Microform: UMI. Online: BRS, DIALOG, WILSONLINE. [*Indexed*: CIJE, CMG, EdI. *Aud*: Pr/Ages 6–18.]

This is the leading magazine for children's and young adult public librarians and school librarians. The articles are timely, well edited, and full of information. Besides the feature articles, the journal includes a calendar, news, notes on people, a checklist of inexpensive pamphlets, posters, and the like, and lots of reviews, concisely written and evaluative. The annual *SLJ* "Reference Books Roundup" is a very useful selection tool for locating the "best" reference books of the year. Besides reviews of books, *SLJ* provides reviews of micro software and audiovisuals. This is an absolutely essential purchase for all libraries serving children and/or young adults.

1135 School Library Media Quarterly. 1952. q. Membership (Nonmembers, $35). Marilyn W. Greenburg. Amer. Lib. Assn., 50 E. Huron St., Chicago, IL 60611. Circ: 7,400. Vol. ends: Summer. Microform: UMI. Online: BRS, DIALOG, WILSONLINE. [*Indexed*: CIJE. *Aud*: Pr/Ages 6–18.]

The official organ of the American Association of School Librarians features three or four articles per issue on practical topics like using micros as fiction finders and analytical articles on topics such as young people's critical thinking about imaginative works. Notable among the regular features are the readers' queries column, the idea exchange, and the reviews of resources—books, software, films, and so forth. Although this is not as essential as *School Library Journal*, it is a very worthwhile purchase for its intended audience.

1136 Sipapu. 1970. s-a. $8. Noel Peattie. Sipapu, Rte. 1, P.O. Box 216, Winters, CA 95694. Illus. Index. Circ: 400. Sample. [*Indexed*: API. *Bk. rev*: Various number and length. *Aud*: Pr/Ages 14–18.]

Sipapu is a "newsletter for librarians, collectors, and others interested in the alternative press," which, for Peattie, includes small, underground, third-world, dissent and peace, feminist, and anarchist presses. For two decades, the magazine has published the front-line literature of these movements; the editor's concern is peace in a nuclear-weapons world. Peattie's broader concerns have not changed: informing and educating readers about movements and publications outside the mainstream and challenging librarians, in particular, to expand their intellectual horizons. The bulk of each issue is devoted to an interview with an alternative pressperson, publication announcements, and reviews.

1137 **Story Art: a magazine for storytellers.** 1934. q. $5. Marylouise Reighart. Natl. Story League, 872 High St., No. 5710, Canal Fulton, OH 44614. Illus. Circ: 3,100. [*Aud*: Pr/Ages 6–14.]

This periodical is the official publication of the National Story League, an organization founded in 1903 "to encourage the appreciation of the good and beautiful in life and literature through the art of storytelling." Issues include wholesome and instructive stories and poems (some of seasonal relevance) written by league members and others. The stories are suitable for oral presentation to groups of children or adults. Also included are articles on storytelling techniques and news of league activities.

1138 **Video Librarian.** 1986. m. $35. Randy Pitman. Video Librarian, 2219 E. View Ave. N.E., Bremerton, WA 98310. Sample. [*Aud*: Pr/Ages 6–18.]

Produced by librarians, this small journal offers ten pages of practical advice for the librarian. While it is of particular value to the video/television specialist, it will be of equal worth to the generalist working in a small library. Among its features are video sources, references, information on turning video patrons into library patrons, LSCA grants for videocassettes, copyright law and video, and so forth. There are numerous, 200-word critical and descriptive reviews of video features.

1139 **VOYA: voice of youth advocates.** 1978. bi-m. $27. Dorothy M. Broderick. Scarecrow Press, Dept. VOYA, 52 Liberty St., P.O. Box 4167, Metuchen, NJ 08840. Illus. Adv. Index. Circ: 3,000. Vol. ends: Feb. Microform: UMI. Online: BRS, DiALOG, WILSONLINE. [*Indexed*: CIJE, ChildLitAb. *Bk. rev*: Various number, 100–200 words, signed. *Aud*: Pr/Ages 6–18.]

A very attractive journal devoted to library service to young adults, *VOYA* features four to five articles per issue on topics such as young adult creative writing contests and teen reading clubs. The bulk of each issue consists of reviews of materials for young adults. The reviews are concise and to the point. The feature articles are candid and often take on controversial issues. This is an excellent journal for YA librarians.

1140 **Wilson Library Bulletin.** 1914. m. (exc. July/Aug.). $38. H. W. Wilson Co., 950 University Ave., Bronx, NY 10452. Illus. Adv. Vol. ends: June. Microform: UMI. Online: BRS, DIALOG, WILSONLINE. [*Indexed*: CIJE, EdI. *Aud*: Pr/Ages 6–18.]

Other than *Library Journal*, the only other commercially published large-circulation magazine devoted to the library scene is *Wilson Library Bulletin*. Long noted for its beautiful covers, this publication becomes more attractive with every volume. The contents are also rich in color and design. Regular features include columns on publishing, Will Manley's public library commentary, dateline Washington, microcomputing, and such departments as news, calendar, marketplace, and reviews of books for children, young adults and adults, and library professionals. Reviews of films, sound recordings, and software are also included.

Feature articles are practical pieces, often dealing with public services and outreach. A basic purchase for most professional collections, especially in public libraries.

■ **BOOK REVIEWS**

Note: Many of the library periodicals carry book and media reviews as well—particularly *Library Journal*, *School Library Journal*, and *VOYA*.

See also the Book Review Section in the main listing for reviews of materials suitable for young adults and of general, popular books.

1141 **Adventures for Kids.** 1986. q. Free. Jody Fickes. Adventures for Kids, 3457 Telegraph Rd., Ventura, CA 93003. Illus. Adv. [*Aud*: Pr/Ages 4–14.]

This 16- to 20-page newsletter is the publication of a book dealer who offers the books reviewed for sale. The reviews are descriptive and evaluative and end with an indication of age suitability. Author, price, and title, but no other bibliographical information, are given. While this is not a reliable source of data for a large number of books, it is well written and the selection is carefully made, suggesting a few dozen titles that would be welcome in most libraries and homes. The editor is an experienced librarian who knows her audience. A nice bonus is that it is free.

1142 **The Book Report: the journal for junior and senior high school librarians.** 5/yr. $35. Carolyn Hamilton. Linworth Publg. Co., 5701 N. High St., Suite 1, Worthington, OH 43085. Illus. Adv. Circ: 10,000. Vol. ends: May. Online: WILSONLINE. [*Indexed*: BoRvI, CMG. *Aud*: Pr/Ages 6–18.]

This is a lively publication for anyone working with teenagers in a school or public library setting. The articles are practical in approach and often provide ideas for programs and promotion of library service to teens. The reviews are bountiful and often enhanced by copies of book cover illustrations. The reviews are honest and often take on controversial books.

1143 **Bookbird.** 1962. q. $18. Lucia Binder. Knud-Egil Hauberg-Tychsen, Mayerhofgasse 6, A-1040 Vienna, Austria. Illus. [*Aud*: Pr/Ages 6–14.]

This journal is issued by the International Board on Books for Young People (IBBY), an organization whose purpose is to promote greater understanding among the children of the world through children's literature. Approximately 45 countries contribute material to the journal through the associate editor named from each country. Each issue includes two major articles and several shorter pieces on some facet of children's literature: reviews of children's books of international interest from a number of countries, reviews of professional literature, news from IBBY national sections, and a calendar of events. The text is written in English, but a summary of the major articles is done in Spanish. This is a fascinating and unique publication, which should be of interest to anyone involved with children's literature.

1144 **Booklist.** 1905. 22/yr. $51. Paul Brawley. Amer. Lib. Assn., 50 E. Huron St., Chicago, IL 60611. Illus. Adv. Index. Circ: 37,000. Sample. Vol. ends: Aug. Microform: UMI. [*Indexed*: BoRvI. *Bk. rev*: 250, 150 words. *Aud*: Pr/Ages 6–18.]

Booklist's clear organizational format facilitates selective scanning. Only recommended titles are reviewed, allowing the reader a quick, high-quality overview of the best in new books. The "Upfront: Advance Reviews" feature presents those adult fiction and nonfiction works expected to be in high demand. Regular sections review new books for young adults and children and survey the latest films, videos, classroom filmstrips, and selected educational microcomputer software. There are also numerous selective bibliographic essay features that appear on a rotating basis. These bibliographies show real attention to the reading needs of ethnic groups and serve as excellent general collection acquisition lists. An inserted section, "Reference Books Bulletin," appearing in each issue, constitutes a separate publication with longer profiles of major reference works and more abbreviated entries on continuations, supplements, and serials. *Booklist* is an essential and increasingly valuable selection tool for public and school libraries.

1145 Books in Canada. 1971. 9/yr. $20 (Individuals, $15). Doris Cowan. Canadian Review of Books, Ltd., 366 Adelaide St., Suite 432, Toronto, Ont. M5A 3X9, Canada. Illus. Adv. Index. Circ: 20,000. Vol. ends: Nov. Microform: MMP. [*Indexed*: BoRvI, CanI. *Bk. rev*: 15–20, 500–1,000 words. *Aud*: Pr/Ages 14–18.]

This magazine is a "national review of books" and the publishing industry in Canada. *Books in Canada* possesses an attractive format. Features consist of one or two profiles or news stories, many of them recording accomplishments in a country that has had its share of literary setbacks and recoveries. Book reviews predominate, whether brief "Critical Notices" or the longer, thoughtful essays on notable titles, usually a balance of fiction and nonfiction. The magazine covers all types of publications, from first novels to the latest work by Tom Wolfe. Librarians looking for significant Canadian materials will appreciate the regular "Received Books" lists, in addition to the substantive reviews.

1146 Center for Children's Books. Bulletin. 1947. 11/yr. $24 (Individuals, $15). Betsy Hearne. Univ. of Chicago Press, 5801 S. Ellis Ave., Chicago, IL 60637. Adv. Index. Circ: 8,000. Sample. Vol. ends: July. Microform: UMI. Reprint: ISI, UMI. [*Indexed*: BoRvI, ChBkRvI. *Bk. rev*: 70, 50–100 words. *Aud*: Pr/Ages 6–14.]

As a children's book review service, this practical bulletin ranks along with *School Library Journal* for quality coverage. *CCBB* reviews about 70 fiction and nonfiction works in brief and primarily descriptive terms, reserving criticism for the designated rating that ranges from "recommended" to "unusual appeal." The bulletin is published for the Graduate Library School at the University of Chicago, and its quality is consistently satisfactory in the choice of titles for both school and leisure reading requirements. It gives complete bibliographic and price information for each work reviewed; every effort seems to be made to keep the contents current and informative for selection purposes.

1147 Children's Book News. 1978. q. Free. Peter Carver. Children's Book Centre, 229 College St. W., 5th Fl., Toronto, Ont. M5T 1R4, Canada. Illus. Circ: 40,000. [*Aud*: Pr/Ages 6–14.]

Descriptive book reviews make up half of each 20-or-so-page issue. The books are for grades one to nine, with more emphasis on the lower grades. Reviews are about 50 words each, with a picture of the book cover. They serve to alert rather than to discriminate, but are useful in that they are accurate and give reading-ability grade levels for each title. The other half of the publication brings news of Canadian children's publishers, authors, libraries, and so forth. Free, and extremely useful for elementary and junior high school teachers and librarians.

1148 Children's Book Review Service. 1972. 14/yr. $40. Ann Kalkhoff. Children's Book Review Service, 220 Berkeley Pl., No. 1D, Brooklyn, NY 11217. Circ: 400. Sample. [*Aud*: Pr/Ages 6–14.]

Resembling a smaller edition of *Kirkus*, this 12- to 20-page reviewing service covers briefly 60 to 80 books in each monthly issue. The 50- to 100-word annotations are both descriptive and critical. They are written and signed by librarians and teachers who are well versed in their subject. Full bibliographic information is given as well as the ages of readers to whom the books are directed. Most of the titles seem to be current and there is an understandable concentration on picture books, which are set off in each issue and usually occupy three to six pages. This is followed by a section for "younger readers" (ages 5–10, two to three pages); older readers (ages 10–14, four to five pages); and an author index. The January number lists the reviewers for the year. The service compares favorably with better known reviews, and is particularly strong in its excellent coverage of younger reader interests, including the picture books.

1149 **Curriculum Review.** 1960. bi-m. $35. Irene M. Goldman. Curriculum Advisory Service, 517 S. Jefferson St., Chicago, IL 60607. Adv. Index. Circ: 8,000. Sample. Vol. ends: Nov. Microform: UMI. Reprint: UMI. [*Indexed*: BoRvI, CIJE, EdI. *Bk. rev*: 60–100, 500 words, signed. *Aud*: Pr/Ages 5–18.]

The journal is a reviewing service for hard-to-find elementary and secondary school instructional materials, including both books and nonprint materials. Published by the Curriculum Advisory Service, the publication champions editorial objectivity to the exclusion of advertising and other subtle biases. The result is a fair-minded examination of theoretical and practical-application writings about curriculum development. Each issue usually begins with a set of two to five articles that thematically discuss a "hot" education topic. New technology is treated—for example, "Computer Center" addresses the growth of this medium in K–12 instruction. The reviews evaluate publications on the basis of educational veracity, organization, and methodology. The reviews are divided into four subject areas: language arts, mathematics, science, and social studies. The end sections contain ordering information, a review index, and a publisher address list. *CR* will be wanted by many educators and is an important tool for school library collections.

1150 **Freebies.** 1978. bi-m. $6.97. Gene Zannon. Freebies Publg. Co., P.O. Box 20283, Santa Barbara, CA 93120. Illus. Circ: 350,000. Sample. [*Aud*: Pr/Ages 6–18.]

Freebies features carefully screened free or inexpensive materials from manufacturers, retailers, associations, institutes, and government agencies that offer catalogs, newsletters, brochures, pamphlets, crafts, and a wide variety of miscellaneous products. The free materials are arranged in broad subject sections. There are freebies especially for teachers and children. Each offer is annotated and includes clear and straightforward ordering instructions. *Freebies* follows up on readers' complaints about the nonreceipt of items requested. It will appeal to readers of all ages.

1151 **Government Periodicals and Subscription Services: price list # . . .** q. Supt. of Docs., U.S. Govt. Printing Office, Washington, DC 20402. Vol. ends: Fall. Online: DIALOG. [*Aud*: Pr/Ages 14–18.]

This title is very useful for determining the availability and price of periodicals published by various agencies of the U.S. government. Issued quarterly as a price list, it contains information on serials published on both regular and irregular schedules. Further, it identifies new titles, discontinued publications, and title changes. In addition to general instructions for placing orders, which can be accomplished through the DIALORDER feature of DIALOG, each quarterly installment contains an agency index. This is followed by an alphabetical list of the titles currently available. Each periodical entry contains information on price and frequency and a brief annotation. The major disadvantage with this source is timeliness.

1152 **Kirkus Reviews.** 1933. s-m. $255. Ron de Paulo. Kirkus Service, Inc., 200 Park Ave. S., New York, NY 10003. Index. Circ: 5,000. Vol. ends: Dec 15. Microform: UMI. [*Indexed*: BoRvI. *Bk. rev*: 150–300 words. *Aud*: Pr/Ages 6–18.]

Kirkus Reviews has had a durable reputation for quality and convenience. This book-reviewing service is fairly well known to the general reader and is regularly consulted in many public libraries. The reviews, which often appear several months before the books' actual publication release, provide concise summaries of content. Reviews conclude with critical, "tell-it-like-it-is" judgments that enable the librarian or bookseller to anticipate public demand more clearly. The format is also useful; with a loose-leaf construction and neat divisions between adult and juvenile literature categories, material can be accessed quickly. The "Pointers" section preceding each review category contains highlighted summaries of the issue's featured titles and their significance as new publications. *Kirkus* is an effective, albeit expensive, acquisition tool that should be in most medium- to large-size school and public libraries.

1153 **The Kobrin Letter.** 1979. 7/yr. $12. Beverly Kobrin. The Kobrin Letter, 732 Greer Rd., Palo Alto, CA 94303. Illus. [*Aud*: Pr/Ages 7–15.]

A four-page newsletter, this reviews "children's books about real people, places and things." Essentially, this means nonfiction suitable for ages 7 to 15, although from time to time there is a book noted that would do well in a senior high school. About a dozen books are considered in each number. The 50-to 100-word reviews are primarily descriptive and almost always favorable. Hence, this is more an alerting service about books the editor and reviewers think worthwhile than anything else. It has a nice personal touch and often considers books not found in major reviewing services. A sample is $2.

1154 **Lector.** 1982. bi-m. $40. John Frank. Hispanic Information Exchange, P.O. Box 4273, Berkeley, CA 94704. Illus. Adv. Sample. Vol. ends: May/June. [*Bk. rev*: 100, 150–500 words, signed. *Aud*: Pr/Ages 6–18.]

A significant proportion of the population of the United States is Hispanic; *Lector* is a book review service for Spanish-language and bilingual Hispanic literature. It is published by a nonprofit organization dedicated to the promotion of literacy for Spanish speakers. The information provided in this magazine is invaluable. Issues have grown in size and substance. Feature articles, variously popular or scholarly in nature, explore minority publishing and bibliographical ventures. The reviews are a balance of adult and juvenile publications, including books and nonprint materials; the reviews themselves vary in length, but are always terse and judgmental. Emphasis is placed on reviewing fiction and nonfiction titles over textbooks or technical literature. These reviews are divided into *Library Journal*–type subject categories. Recommendation codes at the end of each review designate type of audience, collection, and (uncommon but helpful) binding information. *Lector* has a place in every library serving a Spanish-speaking readership.

1155 **The Lion and the Unicorn.** 1977. a. $7.95 (Individuals, $4). Geraldine de Luca and Roni Natov. Brooklyn College, Dept. of English, Brooklyn, NY 11210. Illus. Circ: 1,000. [*Aud*: Pr/Ages 6–14.]

Subtitled "A Critical Journal of Children's Literature." Each issue explores one theme or genre or one aspect of the field of children's literature. Issues have focused on comedy, fantasy, social issues, biography, and informational books, to list a few, and they include book reviews, critical pieces, and interviews. The articles are concise, analytical, and often critical, and should appeal to students and professionals interested in this subject.

1156 **Science Books and Films** (Variant title: *AAAS Science Books and Films*). 1965. 5/yr. $20. Kathleen S. Johnston. Amer. Assn. for the Advancement of Science, 1333 H St., Washington, DC 20005. Adv. Index. Circ: 4,000. Sample. Vol. ends: May. Microform: UMI. [*Indexed*: BoRvI. *Bk. rev*: 300, 200 words, signed. *Aud*: Pr/Ages 6–18.]

This review service assists in the selection of scientific and technical books and nonprint media. Titles are reviewed for designated readers in elementary school through college, and for general audiences. Trade books, textbooks (except those for grades K–12), 16mm films, video programs, and educational filmstrips are covered. The reviews are arranged by Dewey Decimal Classification and are rated by four evaluation definitions, from "highly recommended" to "not recommended." Levels of difficulty are also noted. Reviewers' comments are practical, highlighted appraisals of content and quality. Materials deficient in technical accuracy are soundly criticized. *Science Books and Films* readily serves curriculum and collection development needs for classroom and school libraries.

1157 **Signal: approaches to children's books.** 1970. 3/yr. $14.50. Nancy Chambers. Thimble Press, Lockwood Sta. Rd., South Woodchester, Glos. GL5 5EQ, England. Illus. Vol. ends: Sept. [*Aud*: Pr/Ages 6–14.]

Signal's aim is "to reflect the children's book world from many points of view, offering its contributors as much article space as they need to present their ideas fully." This British journal includes a collection of articles dealing with such subject areas as history or children's books, critical theory and practice, and educational practice and research as it relates to literature and reading, among others. Approaches in articles range from the practical to the scholarly, and most of the contributors are British authors, publishers, teachers, and other professionals concerned with children's literature.

1158 **Women's Review of Books.** 1983. m. $25 (Individuals, $14). Linda Gardiner. Women's Review, Inc., Wellesley College Center for Research on Women, Wellesley, MA 02181. Illus. Adv. Circ: 10,500. Sample. Vol. ends: Sept. Microform: UMI. [*Indexed*: API, BoRvI. *Bk. rev*: 15, 700–1,500 words, signed. *Aud*: Pr/Ages 14–18.]

Published as a monthly tabloid, this is a feminist book-reviewing service. Issues offer lengthy reviews that are critical and descriptive in nature. Reviewers are notable scholars and writers, who provide thoughtful commentary on new publications by and about women. *WRB*'s academic focus is often evident since nonfiction and biographies appear frequently. The literary reviews in this journal are stimulating explications in their own right; librarians and other readers interested in women's studies will find relevant works treated here that are frequently bypassed in the mainstream review literature.

■ **MEDIA AND MEDIA REVIEWS**

1159 **AV Guide: the learning media newsletter.** 1922. m. $15. Deborah A. Hegg. Scranton Gillette Communications, Inc., 380 Northwest Hwy., Des Plaines, IL 60016. Illus. Adv. Circ: 1,200. Sample. Vol. ends: Dec. Microform: UMI. [*Indexed*: CIJE, EdI. *Aud*: Pr/Ages 6–18.]

Providing practical information on products, services, and news concerning audiovisual equipment and computer software/hardware, this four-page newsletter is a handy tool for the educational professional who is interested in keeping abreast of, but not awash in, new tools and trends. Product announcements, which include purchasing information, are descriptive but not evaluative. Book announcements, calls for conference papers, awards, and descriptions of unique educational research projects are regularly included. Recommended for libraries serving educational program administrators.

1160 **Children's Video Report.** 1985. bi-m. $35. Martha Dewing. Great Mountain Productions, 145 W. 96th St., New York, NY 10025. Circ: 1,200. Sample. Vol. ends: Mar/Apr. (No. 6). Reprint: Pub. [*Aud*: Pr/Ages 6–14.]

Many video magazines have a column geared toward children's videos, but none are as comprehensive as *Children's Video Report*. The goal of the publishers is to aid children's librarians in the selection process, but the information would also be valuable to parents looking for good video materials for their children. Therefore *CVR* is a must for medium-size and large public libraries. The reviewers are experts in the fields of child development and media. This publication does not have or need the glitz of many of the video magazines. It is a simple, eight-page, black-and-white publication. The five to six major reviews are critical 250-plus-word essays, while reviews of new releases are two to three sentences long. *Parents' Choice*, which is more comprehensive, would probably be a better choice for a smaller library.

1161 **Educational Technology: the magazine for members of change in education.** 1961. m. $89. Lawrence Lipsitz. Educational Technology Publns., Inc., 720 Palisades Ave., Englewood Cliffs, NJ 07632. Illus. Adv. Index. Circ: 5,000. Vol. ends: Dec. Microform: UMI. [*Indexed*: CIJE, EdI. *Bk. rev*: 2–4, 200–400 words, signed. *Aud*: Pr/Ages 6–18.]

Each issue has six to ten short-to-moderate-length articles, mostly by faculty members of schools of education. Some articles report research, but most are analysis and opinion pieces intended to stimulate media specialists and supervisors to develop new approaches to the use of educational technology. Most articles deal with computers, but television and other types of technology receive some attention. The tone of most articles is informal, but the emphasis is on theory rather than detailed how-to material. Some articles discuss media applications at the college level, but the emphasis is on K–12. This is a basic item for libraries that support programs training media specialists; it should be available to all working media personnel.

1162 **Journal of Film and Video** (Formerly: *University Film Association. Journal; University Film Producers Association. Journal*). 1947. q. $12. Michael E. Selig. Div. of Mass Communication, Emerson College, 100 Beacon St., Boston, MA 02116. Illus. Index. Circ:

1,300. Sample. Refereed. Vol. ends: Fall. Microform: UMI. Reprint: UMI. [*Bk. rev*: 1–3, 1,500 words, signed. *Aud*: Pr/Ages 14–18.]

"Focuses on the problems and substance in teaching the fields of film production, history, theory, criticism, and aesthetics." The emphasis here is holistic, with a special interest in "articles which break down the traditional boundaries between film production and film study, between film and photography, between film and video." Reports on various conferences, a couple of detailed book reviews, and lists of books received are also included. Author indexes are provided in Number 4 (Fall) of each volume. Issues are frequently devoted to studies on particular themes such as Japanese cinema or community-access cable television.

1163 Landers Film Reviews: the information guide to 16mm films. 1956. q. $45. Bertha Landers. Landers Assocs., P.O. Box 27309, Escondido, CA 92027. Index. Circ: 3,600. Sample. Vol. ends: Summer. [*Aud*: Pr/Ages 6–18.]

An excellent guide to 16mm film. The average issue contains about 125 brief reviews describing the contents of each film. Technical qualities are commented on to a lesser extent. The film's subject, purpose, and intended audience are clearly stated. The "Source Directory" in the front of each issue lists addresses of distributors. The cumulative annual index has been discontinued, but each issue retains its own title and subject indexes. This is an especially important title for elementary and secondary schools, though public libraries dealing with 16mm films might also find it useful.

1164 Media & Methods: educational products, technologies & programs for schools & universities (Formerly: *Teacher's Guide to Media and Methods*). 1964. bi-m. (during school year). $29. Robin A. Larsen. Amer. Soc. of Educators, 1429 Walnut St., Philadelphia, PA 19102. Illus. Adv. Index. Circ: 40,000. Vol. ends: May/June. Microform: UMI. [*Indexed*: EdI. *Bk. rev*: 2–3, 150–200 words. *Aud*: Pr/Ages 6–18.]

Founded by educators concerned with burgeoning audiovisual technologies almost 30 years ago, this journal has covered not only technological developments but also the educators who have been at the forefront of the movement linking instructional technology with practical applications. Each issue has three to six articles dealing with such topics as interactive video, curriculum models, social views in the classroom, computers, automating small libraries, and case studies of successful media programs. Regular features cover budgeting and buying, product "premiers," media reviews, and library management. Two special features— the annual "Portfolio" which evaluates the year's best educational media, and the annual computer buyers guide—are just two reasons why *Media & Methods* has become a core journal for all school libraries and media centers.

1165 Media Spectrum. 1965. q. $12. Freda Richards and Marian S. West. Michigan Assn. for Media in Education, REMC 7, Ottowa Area Intermediate School District, 13565 Port Sheldon Rd., Holland, MI 49424. Illus. Adv. Index. Circ: 1,400. Sample. Vol. ends: No. 4. [*Bk. rev*: 1, 500 words, signed. *Aud*: Pr/Ages 6–18.]

Although the focus of this journal is on media programs in Michigan, this should not detract from its usefulness as a resource for innovative uses of media in elementary and high school libraries and audiovisual (AV) centers. Each issue is theme-oriented, dealing with such topics as emerging technologies and enlivening the "word" in media programs. Contributors are teachers and AV managers who have practical suggestions for the improvement of educational programs through the use of all types of media, including posters and realia as well as the more fashionable electronic tools.

1166 **Parents' Choice: a review of children's media** (Formerly: *It's the Parent's Choice*). 1978. q. $15. Diane Huss Green. Parents' Choice Foundation, 1191 Chestnut St., Newton, MA 02164. Circ: 20,000. Sample. Vol. ends: Dec. (No. 4). Reprint: Pub. [*Bk. rev*: 12, 75–100 words. *Aud*: Pr/Ages 6–18.]

The most important feature of *Parents' Choice* is the well-balanced reviews of children's media. Selection guidance is provided for parents and librarians on books, television programs, movies, videos, computer software, music, toys, and games. The movie reviews are not only written from the standpoint of what is educational, but they also look through the eyes of the children to see what is enjoyed. Annotated bibliographies provide an opportunity for further research. Articles are entertaining and often provide helpful hints on how to contribute informally to a child's education. The advisory board is composed of eminent professors, authors, poets, and publishers. *Parents' Choice* awards honor those materials in the formats covered on an annual basis.

1167 **Sightlines.** 1967. q. $20 (Individuals, $16). Judith Trojan. Amer. Film and Video Assn., 920 Barnsdale Rd., Suite 152, La Grange Park, IL 60525. Illus. Adv. Index. Circ: 3,000. Sample. Vol. ends: Summer. Microform: UMI. Reprint: UMI. [*Bk. rev*: Various number and length. *Aud*: Pr/Ages 6–18.]

Formed by the merger of the *EFLA* (Educational Film Library Association) *Bulletin*, *Filmlist*, and *Film Review Digest*, this publication is directed toward libraries, schools, colleges, and community organizations that utilize 16mm films. Issued under the auspices of the American Film and Video Assocation (formerly EFLA), it contains articles on film and video production, interviews with noted filmmakers, reports on festivals and awards, and AFVA news. Includes reviews, availability listings of new releases, and excellent filmographies.

Numbers refer to magazine entry numbers, unless preceded by "p." to indicate page number. Subjects are printed in small capital letters.

Titles are arranged alphabetically within suggested age groups as well as by grade levels under Children's Classroom Publications. These age and grade designations are to be used only as a guideline. Students' interests may vary a grade level or two above or below these suggested ranges. Also included here is a listing of Professional Journals, which follows the Young Adult Magazines list. All numbers refer to entry numbers, not page numbers.

**Children's Classroom
Publications: By Grade**

Grades 1–5

Grades 4–6

Grades 6–9

Young Adult Magazines

Ages 14–18